Alexandre Dumas

Marguerite De Valois

Alexandre Dumas

Marguerite De Valois

1st Edition | ISBN: 978-3-75237-931-0

Place of Publication: Frankfurt am Main, Germany

Year of Publication: 2020

Outlook Verlag GmbH, Germany.

MARGUERITE DE VALOIS.

CHAPTER I.

MONSIEUR DE GUISE'S LATIN.

On Monday, the 18th of August, 1572, there was a splendid festival at the Louvre.

The ordinarily gloomy windows of the ancient royal residence were brilliantly lighted, and the squares and streets adjacent, usually so solitary after Saint Germain l'Auxerrois had struck the hour of nine, were crowded with people, although it was past midnight.

The vast, threatening, eager, turbulent throng resembled, in the darkness, a black and tumbling sea, each billow of which makes a roaring breaker; this sea, flowing through the Rue des Fossés Saint Germain and the Rue de l'Astruce and covering the quay, surged against the base of the walls of the Louvre, and, in its refluent tide, against the Hôtel de Bourbon, which faced it on the other side.

In spite of the royal festival, and perhaps even because of the royal festival, there was something threatening in the appearance of the people, for no doubt was felt that this imposing ceremony which called them there as spectators, was only the prelude to another in which they would participate a week later as invited guests and amuse themselves with all their hearts.

The court was celebrating the marriage of Madame Marguerite de Valois, daughter of Henry II. and sister of King Charles IX., with Henry de Bourbon, King of Navarre. In truth, that very morning, on a stage erected at the entrance to Notre-Dame, the Cardinal de Bourbon had united the young couple with the usual ceremonial observed at the marriages of the royal daughters of France.

This marriage had astonished every one, and occasioned much surmise to certain persons who saw clearer than others. They found it difficult to understand the union of two parties who hated each other so thoroughly as did, at this moment, the Protestant party and the Catholic party; and they wondered how the young Prince de Condé could forgive the Duc d'Anjou, the King's brother, for the death of his father, assassinated at Jarnac by Montesquiou. They asked how the young Duc de Guise could pardon Admiral de Coligny for the death of his father, assassinated at Orléans by Poltrot de Méré.

Moreover, Jeanne de Navarre, the weak Antoine de Bourbon's courageous wife, who had conducted her son Henry to the royal marriage awaiting him, had died scarcely two months before, and singular reports had been spread abroad as to her sudden death. It was everywhere whispered, and in some places said aloud, that she had discovered some terrible secret; and that Catharine de Médicis, fearing its disclosure, had poisoned her with perfumed gloves, which had been made by a man named Réné, a Florentine deeply skilled in such matters. This report was the more widely spread and believed when, after this great queen's death, at her son's request, two celebrated physicians, one of whom was the famous Ambroise Paré, were instructed to open and examine the body, but not the skull. As Jeanne de Navarre had been poisoned by a perfume, only the brain could show any trace of the crime (the one part excluded from dissection). We say crime, for no one doubted that a crime had been committed.

This was not all. King Charles in particular had, with a persistency almost approaching obstinacy, urged this marriage, which not only reëstablished peace in his kingdom, but also attracted to Paris the principal Huguenots of France. As the two betrothed belonged one to the Catholic religion and the other to the reformed religion, they had been obliged to obtain a dispensation from Gregory XIII., who then filled the papal chair. The dispensation was slow in coming, and the delay had caused the late Queen of Navarre great uneasiness. She one day expressed to Charles IX. her fears lest the dispensation should not arrive; to which the King replied:

"Have no anxiety, my dear aunt. I honor you more than I do the Pope, and I love my sister more than I fear him. I am not a Huguenot, neither am I a blockhead; and if the Pope makes a fool of himself, I will myself take Margot by the hand, and have her married to your son in some Protestant meeting-house!"

This speech was soon spread from the Louvre through the city, and, while it greatly rejoiced the Huguenots, had given the Catholics something to think about; they asked one another, in a whisper, if the King was really betraying them or was only playing a comedy which some fine morning or evening might have an unexpected ending.

Charles IX.'s conduct toward Admiral de Coligny, who for five or six years had been so bitterly opposed to the King, appeared particularly inexplicable; after having put on his head a price of a hundred and fifty thousand golden crowns, the King now swore by him, called him his father, and declared openly that he should in future confide the conduct of the war to him alone. To such a pitch was this carried that Catharine de Médicis herself, who until then had controlled the young prince's actions, will, and even desires, seemed to be growing really uneasy, and not without reason; for, in a moment of confidence, Charles IX. had said to the admiral, in reference to the war in Flanders,

"My father, there is one other thing against which we must be on our guard —that is, that the queen, my mother, who likes to poke her nose everywhere, as you well know, shall learn nothing of this undertaking; we must keep it so quiet that she will not have a suspicion of it, or being such a mischief-maker as I know she is, she would spoil all."

Now, wise and experienced as he was, Coligny had not been able to keep such an absolute secret; and, though he had come to Paris with great suspicions, and albeit at his departure from Chatillon a peasant woman had thrown herself at his feet, crying, "Ah! sir, our good master, do not go to Paris, for if you do, you will die—you and all who are with you!"—these suspicions were gradually lulled in his heart, and so it was with Téligny, his son-in-law, to whom the King was especially kind and attentive, calling him his brother, as he called the admiral his father, and addressing him with the familiar "thou," as he did his best friends.

The Huguenots, excepting some few morose and suspicious spirits, were therefore completely reassured. The death of the Queen of Navarre passed as having been caused by pleurisy, and the spacious apartments of the Louvre were filled with all those gallant Protestants to whom the marriage of their young chief, Henry, promised an unexpected return of good fortune. Admiral Coligny, La Rochefoucault, the young Prince de Condé, Téligny,—in short, all the leaders of the party,—were triumphant when they saw so powerful at the Louvre and so welcome in Paris those whom, three months before, King Charles and Queen Catharine would have hanged on gibbets higher than those of assassins.

The Maréchal de Montmorency was the only one who was missing among all his brothers, for no promise could move him, no specious appearances deceive him, and he remained secluded in his château de l'Isle Adam, offering as his excuse for not appearing the grief which he still felt for his father, the Constable Anne de Montmorency, who had been killed at the battle of Saint Denis by a pistol-shot fired by Robert Stuart. But as this had taken place more than three years before, and as sensitiveness was a virtue little practised at that time, this unduly protracted mourning was interpreted just as people cared to interpret it.

However, everything seemed to show that the Maréchal de Montmorency was mistaken. The King, the Queen, the Duc d'Anjou, and the Duc d'Alençon did the honors of the royal festival with all courtesy and kindness.

The Duc d'Anjou received from the Huguenots themselves well-deserved compliments on the two battles of Jarnac and Montcontour, which he had gained before he was eighteen years of age, more precocious in that than either Cæsar or Alexander, to whom they compared him, of course placing the conquerors of Pharsalia and the Issus as inferior to the living prince. The Duc d'Alençon looked on, with his bland, false smile, while Queen Catharine, radiant with joy and overflowing with honeyed phrases, congratulated Prince Henry de Condé on his recent marriage with Marie de Clèves; even the Messieurs de Guise themselves smiled on the formidable enemies of their house, and the Duc de Mayenne discoursed with M. de Tavannes and the admiral on the impending war, which was now more than ever threatened against Philippe II.

In the midst of these groups a young man of about nineteen years of age was walking to and fro, his head a little on one side, his ear open to all that was said. He had a keen eye, black hair cut very close, thick eyebrows, a nose hooked like an eagle's, a sneering smile, and a growing mustache and beard. This young man, who by his reckless daring had first attracted attention at the battle of Arnay-le-Duc and was the recipient of numberless compliments, was the dearly beloved pupil of Coligny and the hero of the day. Three months before—that is to say, when his mother was still living—he was called the Prince de Béarn, now he was called the King of Navarre, afterwards he was known as Henry IV.

From time to time a swift and gloomy cloud passed over his brow; unquestionably it was at the thought that scarce had two months elapsed since his mother's death, and he, less than any one, doubted that she had been poisoned. But the cloud was transitory, and disappeared like a fleeting shadow, for they who spoke to him, they who congratulated him, they who elbowed him, were the very ones who had assassinated the brave Jeanne d'Albret.

Some paces distant from the King of Navarre, almost as pensive, almost as gloomy as the king pretended to be joyous and open-hearted, was the young Duc de Guise, conversing with Téligny. More fortunate than the Béarnais, at two-and-twenty he had almost attained the reputation of his father, François, the great Duc de Guise. He was an elegant gentleman, very tall, with a noble and haughty look, and gifted with that natural majesty which caused it to be said that in comparison with him other princes seemed to belong to the people. Young as he was, the Catholics looked up to him as the chief of their party, as the Huguenots saw theirs in Henry of Navarre, whose portrait we have just drawn. At first he had borne the title of Prince de Joinville, and at the siege of Orléans had fought his first battle under his father, who died in his arms, denouncing Admiral Coligny as his assassin. The young duke then, like Hannibal, took a solemn oath to avenge his father's death on the admiral and his family, and to pursue the foes to his religion without truce or respite, promising God to be his destroying angel on earth until the last heretic should be exterminated. So with deep astonishment the people saw this prince, usually so faithful to his word, offering his hand to those whom he had sworn to hold as his eternal enemies, and talking familiarly with the son-in-law of the man whose death he had promised to his dying father.

But as we have said, this was an evening of astonishments.

Indeed, an observer privileged to be present at this festival, endowed with the knowledge of the future which is fortunately hidden from men, and with that power of reading men's hearts which unfortunately belongs only to God, would have certainly enjoyed the strangest spectacle to be found in all the annals of the melancholy human comedy.

But this observer who was absent from the inner courts of the Louvre was to be found in the streets gazing with flashing eyes and breaking out into loud threats; this observer was the people, who, with its marvellous instinct made keener by hatred, watched from afar the shadows of its implacable enemies and translated the impressions they made with as great clearness as an inquisitive person can do before the windows of a hermetically sealed ball-room. The music intoxicates and governs the dancers, but the inquisitive person sees only the movement and laughs at the puppet jumping about without reason, because the inquisitive person hears no music.

The music that intoxicated the Huguenots was the voice of their pride.

The gleams which caught the eyes of the Parisians that midnight were the lightning flashes of their hatred illuminating the future.

And meantime everything was still festive within, and a murmur softer and more flattering than ever was at this moment pervading the Louvre, for the youthful bride, having laid aside her toilet of ceremony, her long mantle and flowing veil, had just returned to the ball-room, accompanied by the lovely Duchesse de Nevers, her most intimate friend, and led by her brother, Charles IX., who presented her to the principal guests.

The bride was the daughter of Henry II., was the pearl of the crown of France, was MARGUERITE DE VALOIS, whom in his familiar tenderness for her King Charles IX. always called "*ma sœur Margot*," "my sister Margot."

Assuredly never was any welcome, however flattering, more richly deserved than that which the new Queen of Navarre was at this moment receiving. Marguerite at this period was scarcely twenty, and she was already the object of all the poets' eulogies, some of whom compared her to Aurora, others to Cytherea; she was, in truth, a beauty without rival in that court in which Catharine de Médicis had assembled the loveliest women she could find, to make of them her sirens.

Marguerite had black hair and a brilliant complexion; a voluptuous eye, veiled by long lashes; delicate coral lips; a slender neck; a graceful, opulent figure, and concealed in a satin slipper a tiny foot. The French, who possessed her, were proud to see such a lovely flower flourishing in their soil, and foreigners who passed through France returned home dazzled with her beauty if they had but seen her, and amazed at her knowledge if they had discoursed with her; for Marguerite was not only the loveliest, she was also the most erudite woman of her time, and every one was quoting the remark of an Italian scholar who had been presented to her, and who, after having conversed with her for an hour in Italian, Spanish, Latin, and Greek, had gone away saying:

"To see the court without seeing Marguerite de Valois is to see neither France nor the court."

Thus addresses to King Charles IX. and the Queen of Navarre were not wanting. It is well known that the Huguenots were great hands at addresses. Many allusions to the past, many hints as to the future, were adroitly slipped into these harangues; but to all such allusions and speeches the King replied, with his pale lips and artificial smiles:

"In giving my sister Margot to Henry of Navarre, I give my sister to all the Protestants of the kingdom."

This phrase assured some and made others smile, for it had really a double sense: the one paternal, with which Charles IX. would not load his mind; the other insulting to the bride, to her husband, and also to him who said it, for it recalled some scandalous rumors with which the chroniclers of the court had already found means to smirch the nuptial robe of Marguerite de Valois.

However, M. de Guise was conversing, as we have said, with Téligny; but he did not pay to the conversation such sustained attention but that he turned away somewhat, from time to time, to cast a glance at the group of ladies, in the centre of whom glittered the Queen of Navarre. When the princess's eye thus met that of the young duke, a cloud seemed to over-spread that lovely brow, around which stars of diamonds formed a tremulous halo, and some agitating thought might be divined in her restless and impatient manner.

The Princess Claude, Marguerite's eldest sister, who had been for some years married to the Duc de Lorraine, had observed this uneasiness, and was going up to her to inquire the cause, when all stood aside at the approach of the queen mother, who came forward, leaning on the arm of the young Prince de Condé, and the princess was thus suddenly separated from her sister. There was a general movement, by which the Duc de Guise profited to approach Madame de Nevers, his sister-in-law, and Marguerite.

Madame de Lorraine, who had not lost sight of her sister, then remarked, instead of the cloud which she had before observed on her forehead, a burning blush come into her cheeks. The duke approached still nearer, and when he was within two steps of Marguerite, she appeared rather to feel than see his presence, and turned round, making a violent effort over herself in order to give her features an appearance of calmness and indifference. The duke, then respectfully bowing, murmured in a low tone,

"*Ipse attuli.*"

That meant: "I have brought it, or brought it myself."

Marguerite returned the young duke's bow, and as she straightened herself, replied, in the same tone,

"*Noctu pro more.*"

That meant: "To-night, as usual."

These soft words, absorbed by the enormous collar which the princess wore, as in the bell of a speaking-trumpet, were heard only by the person to whom they were addressed; but brief as had been the conference, it doubtless composed all the young couple had to say, for after this exchange of two words for three, they separated, Marguerite more thoughtful and the duke with his brow less clouded than when they met. This little scene took place without the person most interested appearing to remark it, for the King of Navarre had eyes but for one lady, and she had around her a suite almost as numerous as that which followed Marguerite de Valois. This was the beautiful Madame de Sauve.

Charlotte de Beaune Semblançay, granddaughter of the unfortunate Semblançay, and wife of Simon de Fizes, Baron de Sauve, was one of the ladies-in-waiting to Catharine de Médicis, and one of the most redoubtable auxiliaries of this queen, who poured forth to her enemies love-philtres when she dared not pour out Florentine poison. Delicately fair, and by turns sparkling with vivacity or languishing in melancholy, always ready for love and intrigue, the two great occupations which for fifty years employed the court of the three succeeding kings,—a woman in every acceptation of the word and in all the charm of the idea, from the blue eye languishing or flashing with fire to the small rebellious feet arched in their velvet slippers, Madame de Sauve had already for some months taken complete possession of every faculty of the King of Navarre, then beginning his career as a lover as well as a politician; thus it was that Marguerite de Valois, a magnificent and royal beauty, had not even excited admiration in her husband's heart; and what was more strange, and astonished all the world, even from a soul so full of darkness and mystery, Catharine de Médicis, while she prosecuted her project of union between her daughter and the King of Navarre, had not ceased to favor almost openly his amour with Madame de Sauve. But despite this powerful aid, and despite the easy manners of the age, the lovely Charlotte had hitherto resisted; and this resistance, unheard of, incredible, unprecedented, even more than the beauty and wit of her who resisted, had excited in the heart of the Béarnais a passion which, unable to satisfy itself, had destroyed in the young king's heart all timidity, pride, and even that carelessness, half philosophic, half indolent, which formed the basis of his character.

Madame de Sauve had been only a few minutes in the ballroom; from spite or grief she had at first resolved on not being present at her rival's triumph, and under the pretext of an indisposition had allowed her husband, who had been for five years secretary of state, to go alone to the Louvre; but when Catharine de Médicis saw the baron without his wife, she asked the cause that kept her dear Charlotte away, and when she found that the indisposition was but slight, she wrote a few words to her, which the lady hastened to obey. Henry, sad as he had at first been at her absence, had yet breathed more freely when he saw M. de Sauve enter alone; but just as he was about to pay some court to the charming creature whom he was condemned, if not to love, at least to treat as his wife, he unexpectedly saw Madame de Sauve arise from the farther end of the gallery. He remained stationary on the spot, his eyes fastened on the Circe who enthralled him as if by magic chains, and instead of proceeding towards his wife, by a movement of hesitation which betrayed more astonishment than alarm he advanced to meet Madame de Sauve.

The courtiers, seeing the King of Navarre, whose inflammable heart they knew, approach the beautiful Charlotte, had not the courage to prevent their meeting, but drew aside complaisantly; so that at the very moment when Marguerite de Valois and Monsieur de Guise exchanged the few words in Latin which we have noted above, Henry, having approached Madame de Sauve, began, in very intelligible French, although with somewhat of a Gascon accent, a conversation by no means so mysterious.

"Ah, *ma mie!*" he said, "you have, then, come at the very moment when they assured me that you were ill, and I had lost all hope of seeing you."

"Would your majesty perhaps wish me to believe that it had cost you something to lose this hope?" replied Madame de Sauve.

"By Heaven! I believe it!" replied the Béarnais; "know you not that you are my sun by day and my star by night? By my faith, I was in deepest darkness till you appeared and suddenly illumined all."

"Then, monseigneur, I serve you a very ill turn."

"What do you mean, *ma mie*?" inquired Henry.

"I mean that he who is master of the handsomest woman in France should only have one desire—that the light should disappear and give way to darkness, for happiness awaits you in the darkness."

"You know, cruel one, that my happiness is in the hands of one woman only, and that she laughs at poor Henry."

"Oh!" replied the baroness, "I believed, on the contrary, that it was this person who was the sport and jest of the King of Navarre." Henry was alarmed at this hostile attitude, and yet he bethought him that it betrayed jealous spite, and that jealous spite is only the mask of love.

"Indeed, dear Charlotte, you reproach me very unjustly, and I do not comprehend how so lovely a mouth can be so cruel. Do you suppose for a moment that it is I who give myself in marriage? No, *ventre saint gris*, it is not I!"

"It is I, perhaps," said the baroness, sharply,—if ever the voice of the woman who loves us and reproaches us for not loving her can seem sharp.

"With your lovely eyes have you not seen farther, baroness? No, no; Henry of Navarre is not marrying Marguerite de Valois."

"And who, pray, is?"

"Why, by Heaven! it is the reformed religion marrying the pope—that's all."

"No, no, I cannot be deceived by your jests. Monseigneur loves Madame Marguerite. And can I blame you? Heaven forbid! She is beautiful enough to be adored."

Henry reflected for a moment, and, as he reflected, a meaning smile curled the corner of his lips.

"Baroness," said he, "you seem to be seeking a quarrel with me, but you have no right to do so. What have you done to prevent me from marrying Madame Marguerite? Nothing. On the contrary, you have always driven me to despair."

"And well for me that I have, monseigneur," replied Madame de Sauve.

"How so?"

"Why, of course, because you are marrying another woman!"

"I marry her because you love me not."

"If I had loved you, sire, I must have died in an hour."

"In an hour? What do you mean? And of what death would you have died?"

"Of jealousy!—for in an hour the Queen of Navarre will send away her women, and your majesty your gentlemen."

"Is that really the thought that is uppermost in your mind, *ma mie*?"

"I did not say so. I only say, that if I loved you it would be uppermost in my mind most tormentingly."

"Very well," said Henry, at the height of joy on hearing this confession, the first which she had made to him, "suppose the King of Navarre should not send away his gentlemen this evening?"

"Sire," replied Madame de Sauve, looking at the king with astonishment for once unfeigned, "you say things impossible and incredible."

"What must I do to make you believe them?"

"Give me a proof—and that proof you cannot give me."

"Yes, baroness, yes! By Saint Henry, I will give it you!" exclaimed the king, gazing at the young woman with eyes hot with love.

"Oh, your majesty!" exclaimed the lovely Charlotte in an undertone and with downcast eyes, "I do not understand—No! no, it is impossible for you to turn your back on the happiness awaiting you."

"There are four Henrys in this room, my adorable!" replied the king, "Henry de France, Henry de Condé, Henry de Guise, but there is only one Henry of Navarre."

"Well?"

"Well; if this Henry of Navarre is with you all night"—

"All night!"

"Yes; will that be a certain proof to you that he is not with any other?"

"Ah! if you do that, sire," cried Madame Sauve.

"On the honor of a gentleman I will do it!"

Madame de Sauve raised her great eyes dewy with voluptuous promises and looked at the king, whose heart was filled with an intoxicating joy.

"And then," said Henry, "what will you say?"

"I will say," replied Charlotte, "that your majesty really loves me."

"*Ventre saint gris*! then you shall say it, baroness, for it is true."

"But how can you manage it?" murmured Madame de Sauve.

"Oh! by Heaven! baroness, have you not about you some waiting-woman, some girl whom you can trust?"

"Yes, Dariole is so devoted to me that she would let herself be cut in pieces for me; she is a real treasure."

"By Heaven! then say to her that I will make her fortune when I am King of France, as the astrologers prophesy."

Charlotte smiled, for even at this period the Gascon reputation of the Béarnais was already established with respect to his promises.

"Well, then, what do you want Dariole to do?"

"Little for her, a great deal for me. Your apartment is over mine?"

"Yes."

"Let her wait behind the door. I will knock gently three times; she will open the door, and you will have the proof that I have promised you."

Madame de Sauve kept silence for several seconds, and then, as if she had looked around her to observe if she were overheard, she fastened her gaze for a moment on the group clustering around the queen mother; brief as the moment was, it was sufficient for Catharine and her lady-in-waiting to exchange a look.

"Oh, if I were inclined," said Madame de Sauve, with a siren's accent that would have melted the wax in Ulysses' ears, "if I were inclined to make your majesty tell a falsehood"—

"*Ma mie*, try"—

"Ah, *ma foi*! I confess I am tempted to do so."

"Give in! Women are never so strong as after they are defeated."

"Sire, I hold you to your promise for Dariole when you shall be King of France."

Henry uttered an exclamation of joy.

At the precise moment when this cry escaped the lips of the Béarnais, the Queen of Navarre was replying to the Duc de Guise:

"*Noctu pro more*—to-night as usual."

Then Henry turned away from Madame de Sauve as happy as the Duc de Guise had been when he left Marguerite de Valois.

An hour after the double scene we have just related, King Charles and the queen mother retired to their apartments. Almost immediately the rooms began to empty; the galleries exhibited the bases of their marble columns. The admiral and the Prince de Condé were escorted home by four hundred Huguenot gentlemen through the middle of the crowd, which hooted as they passed. Then Henry de Guise, with the Lorraine gentlemen and the Catholics, left in their turn, greeted by cries of joy and plaudits of the people.

But Marguerite de Valois, Henry de Navarre, and Madame de Sauve lived in the Louvre.

CHAPTER II.

THE QUEEN OF NAVARRE'S BEDCHAMBER.

The Duc de Guise escorted his sister-in-law, the Duchess de Nevers, to her hôtel in the Rue du Chaume, facing the Rue de Brac, and after he had put her into the hands of her women, he went to his own apartment to change his dress, put on a night cloak, and armed himself with one of those short, keen poniards which are called "*foi de gentilhomme*," and were worn without swords; but as he took it off the table on which it lay, he perceived a small billet between the blade and the scabbard.

He opened it, and read as follows:

"*I hope M. de Guise will not return to the Louvre to-night; or if he does, that he will at least take the precaution to arm himself with a good coat of mail and a proved sword.*"

"Aha!" said the duke, addressing his valet, "this is a singular warning, Maître Robin. Now be kind enough to tell me who has been here during my absence."

"Only one person, monseigneur."

"Who?"

"Monsieur du Gast."

"Aha! In fact, methinks I recognize the handwriting. And you are sure that Du Gast came? You saw him?"

"More than that, monseigneur; I spoke with him."

"Very good; then I will follow his advice—my steel jacket and my sword."

The valet, accustomed to these changes of costume, brought both. The duke put on his jacket, which was made of rings of steel so fine that it was scarcely thicker than velvet; he then drew on over his coat of mail his small clothes and a doublet of gray and silver, his favorite colors, put on a pair of long boots which reached to the middle of his thighs, covered his head with a velvet toque unadorned with feathers or precious stones, threw over his shoulders a dark-colored cloak, hung a dagger by his side, handed his sword to a page, the only attendant he allowed to accompany him, and took the way to the Louvre.

As he went down the steps of the hôtel, the watchman of Saint Germain l'Auxerrois had just announced one o'clock in the morning.

Though the night was far gone and the streets at this time were very far from safe, no accident befell the adventurous prince on the way, and safe and sound he approached the colossal mass of the ancient Louvre, all the lights of which had been extinguished one after the other, so that it rose portentous in its silence and darkness.

In front of the royal château was a deep fosse, looking into which were the chambers of most of the princes who inhabited the palace. Marguerite's apartment was on the first floor. But this first floor, easily accessible but for the fosse, was, in consequence of the depth to which that was cut, thirty feet from the bottom of the wall, and consequently out of the reach of robbers or lovers; nevertheless the Duc de Guise approached it without hesitation.

At the same moment was heard the noise of a window which opened on the ground floor. This window was grated, but a hand appeared, lifted out one of the bars which had been loosened, and dropped from it a silken lace.

"Is that you, Gillonne?" said the duke, in a low voice.

"Yes, monseigneur," replied a woman's voice, in a still lower tone.

"And Marguerite?"

"Is waiting for you."

"'T is well."

Hereupon the duke made a signal to his page, who, opening his cloak, took out a small rope ladder. The prince fastened one end to the silk lace, and Gillonne, drawing it up, tied it securely. Then the prince, after having buckled his sword to his belt, ascended without accident. When he had entered, the bar was replaced and the window closed, while the page, having seen his master quietly enter the Louvre, to the windows of which he had accompanied him twenty times in the same way, laid himself down in his cloak on the grass of the fosse, beneath the shadow of the wall.

The night was extremely dark, and large drops of warm rain were falling from the heavy clouds charged with electric fluid.

The Duc de Guise followed his guide, who was no other than the daughter of Jacques de Matignon, maréchal of France. She was the especial confidante of Marguerite, who kept no secret from her; and it was said that among the number of mysteries entrusted to her incorruptible fidelity, there were some so terrible as to compel her to keep the rest.

There was no light left either in the low rooms or in the corridors, only from time to time a livid glare illuminated the dark apartments with a vivid flash, which as instantly disappeared.

The duke, still guided by his conductress, who held his hand, reached a staircase built in the thick wall, and opening by a secret and invisible door into the antechamber of Marguerite's apartment.

In this antechamber, which like all the other lower rooms was perfectly dark, Gillonne stopped.

"Have you brought what the queen requested?" she inquired, in a low voice.

"Yes," replied the Duc de Guise; "but I will give it only to her majesty in person."

"Come, then, and do not lose an instant!" said a voice from the darkness, which made the duke start, for he recognized it as Marguerite's.

At the same moment a curtain of violet velvet covered with golden fleurs-de-lis was raised, and the duke made out the form of the queen, who in her impatience had come to meet him.

"I am here, madame," he then said; and he passed the curtain, which fell behind him. So Marguerite de Valois herself now became the prince's guide, leading him into the room which, however, he knew already, while Gillonne, standing at the door, had raised her finger to her lips and reassured her royal mistress.

As if she understood the duke's jealous apprehensions, Marguerite led him to the bedchamber, and there paused.

"Well," she said, "are you satisfied, duke?"

"Satisfied, madame?" was the reply, "and with what?"

"Of the proof I give you," retorted Marguerite, with a slight tone of vexation in her voice, "that I belong to a man who, on the very night of his marriage, makes me of such small importance that he does not even come to thank me for the honor I have done him, not in selecting, but in accepting him for my husband."

"Oh! madame," said the duke, sorrowfully, "be assured he will come if you desire it."

"And do you say that, Henry?" cried Marguerite; "you, who better than any know the contrary of what you say? If I had that desire, should I have asked you to come to the Louvre?"

"You have asked me to come to the Louvre, Marguerite, because you are anxious to destroy every vestige of our past, and because that past lives not only in my memory, but in this silver casket which I bring to you."

"Henry, shall I say one thing to you?" replied Marguerite, gazing earnestly at the duke; "it is that you are more like a schoolboy than a prince. I deny that I have loved you! I desire to quench a flame which will die, perhaps, but the reflection of which will never die! For the loves of persons of my rank illumine and frequently devour the whole epoch contemporary with them. No, no, duke; you may keep the letters of your Marguerite, and the casket she has given you. She asks but one of these letters, and that only because it is as dangerous for you as for herself."

"It is all yours," said the duke. "Take the one that you wish to destroy."

Marguerite searched anxiously in the open casket, and with a tremulous hand took, one after the other, a dozen letters, only the addresses of which she examined, as if by merely glancing at these she could recall to her memory what the letters themselves contained; but after a close scrutiny she looked at the duke, pale and agitated.

"Sir," she said, "what I seek is not here. Can you have lost it, by any accident? for if it should fall into the hands of"—

"What letter do you seek, madame?"

"That in which I told you to marry without delay."

"As an excuse for your infidelity?"

Marguerite shrugged her shoulders.

"No; but to save your life. The one in which I told you that the king, seeing our love and my exertions to break off your proposed marriage with the Infanta of Portugal, had sent for his brother, the Bastard of Angoulême, and said to him, pointing to two swords, '*With this slay Henry de Guise this night, or with the other I will slay thee in the morning.*' Where is that letter?"

"Here," said the duke, drawing it from his breast.

Marguerite almost snatched it from his hands, opened it anxiously, assured herself that it was really the one she desired, uttered an exclamation of joy, and applying the lighted candle to it, the flames instantly consumed the paper; then, as if Marguerite feared that her imprudent words might be read in the very ashes, she trampled them under foot.

During all this the Duc de Guise had watched his mistress attentively.

"Well, Marguerite," he said, when she had finished, "are you satisfied now?"

"Yes, for now that you have wedded the Princesse de Porcian, my brother will forgive me your love; while he would never have pardoned me for revealing a secret such as that which in my weakness for you I had not the strength to conceal from you."

"True," replied De Guise, "then you loved me."

"And I love you still, Henry, as much—more than ever!"

"You"—

"I do; for never more than at this moment did I need a sincere and devoted friend. Queen, I have no throne; wife, I have no husband!"

The young prince shook his head sorrowfully.

"I tell you, I repeat to you, Henri, that my husband not only does not love me, but hates—despises me; indeed, it seems to me that your presence in the chamber in which he ought to be is proof of this hatred, this contempt."

"It is not yet late, Madame, and the King of Navarre requires time to dismiss his gentlemen; if he has not already come, he will come soon."

"And I tell you," cried Marguerite, with increasing vexation,—"I tell you that he will not come!"

"Madame!" exclaimed Gillonne, suddenly entering, "the King of Navarre is just leaving his apartments!"

"Oh, I knew he would come!" exclaimed the Duc de Guise.

"Henri," said Marguerite, in a quick tone, and seizing the duke's hand, —"Henri, you shall see if I am a woman of my word, and if I may be relied on. Henri, enter that closet."

"Madame, allow me to go while there is yet time, for reflect that the first mark of love you bestow on him, I shall quit the cabinet, and then woe to him!"

"Are you mad? Go in—go in, I say, and I will be responsible for all;" and she pushed the duke into the closet.

It was time. The door was scarcely closed behind the prince when the King of Navarre, escorted by two pages, who carried eight torches of yellow wax in two candelabra, appeared, smiling, on the threshold of the chamber. Marguerite concealed her trouble, and made a low bow.

"You are not yet in bed, Madame," observed the Béarnais, with his frank and joyous look. "Were you by chance waiting for me?"

"No, Monsieur," replied Marguerite; "for yesterday you repeated to me that our marriage was a political alliance, and that you would never thwart my wishes."

"Assuredly; but that is no reason why we should not confer a little together. Gillonne, close the door, and leave us."

Marguerite, who was sitting, then rose and extended her hand, as if to desire the pages to remain.

"Must I call your women?" inquired the king. "I will do so if such be your desire, although I confess that for what I have to say to you I should prefer our being alone;" and the King of Navarre advanced towards the closet.

"No!" exclaimed Marguerite, hastily going before him,—"no! there is no occasion for that; I am ready to hear you."

The Béarnais had learned what he desired to know; he threw a rapid and penetrating glance towards the cabinet, as if in spite of the thick curtain which hung before it, he would dive into its obscurity, and then, turning his looks to his lovely wife, pale with terror, he said with the utmost composure, "In that case, Madame, let us confer for a few moments."

"As your Majesty pleases," said the young wife, falling into, rather than sitting upon the seat which her husband pointed out to her.

The Béarnais placed himself beside her. "Madame," he continued, "whatever many persons may have said, I think our marriage is a good marriage. I stand well with you; you stand well with me."

"But—" said Marguerite, alarmed.

"Consequently, we ought," observed the King of Navarre, without seeming to notice Marguerite's hesitation, "to act towards each other like good allies, since we have to-day sworn alliance in the presence of God. Don't you think so?"

"Unquestionably, Monsieur."

"I know, Madame, how great your penetration is; I know how the ground at court is intersected with dangerous abysses. Now, I am young, and although I never injured any one, I have a great many enemies. In which camp, Madame, ought I to range her who bears my name, and who has vowed her affection to me at the foot of the altar?"

"Monsieur, could you think—"

"I think nothing, Madame; I hope, and I am anxious to know that my hope is well founded. It is quite certain that our marriage is merely a pretext or a snare."

Marguerite started, for perhaps the same thought had occurred to her own mind.

"Now, then, which of the two?" continued Henri de Navarre. "The king hates me; the Duc d'Anjou hates me; the Duc d'Alençon hates me; Catherine de Médicis hated my mother too much not to hate me."

"Oh, Monsieur, what are you saying?"

"The truth, madame," replied the king; "and in order that it may not be supposed that I am deceived as to Monsieur de Mouy's assassination and the poisoning of my mother, I wish that some one were here who could hear me."

"Oh, sire," replied Marguerite, with an air as calm and smiling as she could assume, "you know very well that there is no person here but you and myself."

"It is for that very reason that I thus give vent to my thoughts; this it is that emboldens me to declare that I am not deceived by the caresses showered on me by the House of France or the House of Lorraine."

"Sire, sire!" exclaimed Marguerite.

"Well, what is it, *ma mie*?" inquired Henry, smiling in his turn.

"Why, sire, such remarks are very dangerous."

"Not when we are alone," observed the king. "I was saying"—

Marguerite was evidently distressed; she desired to stop every word the king uttered, but he continued, with his apparent good nature:

"I was telling you that I was threatened on all sides: threatened by the King, threatened by the Duc d'Alençon, threatened by the Duc d'Anjou, threatened by the queen mother, threatened by the Duc de Guise, by the Duc de Mayenne, by the Cardinal de Lorraine—threatened, in fact, by every one. One feels that instinctively, as you know, madame. Well, against all these threats, which must soon become attacks, I can defend myself by your aid, for you are beloved by all the persons who detest me."

"I?" said Marguerite.

"Yes, you," replied Henry, with the utmost ease of manner; "yes, you are beloved by King Charles, you are beloved" (he laid strong emphasis on the word) "by the Duc d'Alençon, you are beloved by Queen Catharine, and you are beloved by the Duc de Guise."

"Sire!" murmured Marguerite.

"Yes; and what is there astonishing in the fact that every one loves you? All I have mentioned are your brothers or relatives. To love one's brothers and relatives is to live according to God's heart."

"But what, then," asked Marguerite, greatly overcome, "what do you mean?"

"What I have just said, that if you will be—I do not mean my love—but my ally, I can brave everything; while, on the other hand, if you become my enemy, I am lost."

"Oh, your enemy!—never, sir!" exclaimed Marguerite.

"And my love—never either?"

"Perhaps"—

"And my ally?"

"Most decidedly."

And Marguerite turned round and offered her hand to the king.

Henry took it, kissed it gallantly, and retaining it in his own, more from a desire of investigation than from any sentiment of tenderness, said:

"Very well, I believe you, madame, and accept the alliance. They married us without our knowing each other—without our loving each other; they married us without consulting us—us whom they united. We therefore owe nothing to each other as man and wife; you see that I even go beyond your wishes and confirm this evening what I said to you yesterday; but we ally ourselves freely and without any compulsion. We ally ourselves, as two loyal hearts who owe each other mutual protection should ally themselves; 't is as such you understand it?"

"Yes, sir," said Marguerite, endeavoring to withdraw her hand.

"Well, then," continued the Béarnais, with his eyes fastened on the door of the cabinet, "as the first proof of a frank alliance is the most perfect confidence, I will now relate to you, madame, in all its details, the plan I have

20

formed in order that we may victoriously meet and overcome all these enmities."

"Sire"—said Marguerite, in spite of herself turning her eyes toward the closet, whilst the Béarnais, seeing his trick succeed, laughed in his sleeve.

"This is what I mean to do," he continued, without appearing to remark his young wife's nervousness, "I intend"—

"Sire," said Marguerite, rising hastily, and seizing the king's arm, "allow me a little breath; my emotion—the heat—overpowers me."

And, in truth, Marguerite was as pale and trembling as if she was about to fall on the carpet.

Henry went straight to a window some distance off, and opened it. This window looked out on the river.

Marguerite followed him.

"Silence, sire,—silence, for your own sake!" she murmured.

"What, madame," said the Béarnais, with his peculiar smile, "did you not tell me we were alone?"

"Yes, sire; but did you not hear me say that by the aid of a tube introduced into the ceiling or the wall everything could be heard?"

"Well, madame, well," said the Béarnais, earnestly and in a low voice, "it is true you do not love me, but you are, at least, honorable."

"What do you mean, sire?"

"I mean that if you were capable of betraying me, you would have allowed me to go on, as I was betraying myself. You stopped me—I now know that some one is concealed here—that you are an unfaithful wife, but a faithful ally; and just now, I confess, I have more need of fidelity in politics than in love."

"Sire!" replied Marguerite, confused.

"Good, good; we will talk of this hereafter," said Henry, "when we know each other better."

Then, raising his voice—"Well," he continued, "do you breathe more freely now, madame?"

"Yes, sire,—yes!"

"Well, then," said the Béarnais, "I will no longer intrude on you. I owed you my respects, and some advances toward better acquaintance; deign, then, to accept them, as they are offered, with all my heart. Good-night, and happy slumbers!"

Marguerite raised her eyes, shining with gratitude, and offered her husband her hand.

"It is agreed," she said.

"Political alliance, frank and loyal?" asked Henry.

"Frank and loyal," was the reply.

And the Béarnais went toward the door, followed by Marguerite's look as if she were fascinated. Then, when the curtain had fallen between them and the bedchamber:

"Thanks, Marguerite," he said, in a quick low tone, "thanks! You are a true daughter of France. I leave you quite tranquil: lacking your love, your friendship will not fail me. I rely on you, as you, on your side, may rely on me. Adieu, madame."

And Henry kissed his wife's hand, and pressed it gently. Then with a quick step he returned to his own apartment, saying to himself, in a low voice, in the corridor:

"Who the devil is with her? Is it the King, or the Duc d'Anjou, or the Duc d'Alençon, or the Duc de Guise? is it a brother or a lover? is it both? I' faith, I am almost sorry now I asked the baroness for this rendezvous; but, as my word is pledged, and Dariole is waiting for me—no matter. Yet, *ventre saint gris*! this Margot, as my brother-in-law, King Charles, calls her, is an adorable creature."

And with a step which betrayed a slight hesitation, Henry of Navarre ascended the staircase which led to Madame de Sauve's apartments.

Marguerite had followed him with her eyes until he disappeared. Then she returned to her chamber, and found the duke at the door of the cabinet. The sight of him almost touched her with remorse.

The duke was grave, and his knitted brow bespoke bitter reflection.

"Marguerite is neutral to-day," he said; "in a week Marguerite will be hostile."

"Ah! you have been listening?" said Marguerite.

"What else could I do in the cabinet?"

"And did you find that I behaved otherwise than the Queen of Navarre should behave?"

"No; but differently from the way in which the mistress of the Duc de Guise should behave."

"Sir," replied the queen, "I may not love my husband, but no one has the right to require me to betray him. Tell me honestly: would you reveal the secrets of the Princesse de Porcian, your wife?"

"Come, come, madame," answered the duke, shaking his head, "this is very well; I see that you do not love me as in those days when you disclosed to me the plot of the King against me and my party."

"The King was strong and you were weak; Henry is weak and you are strong. You see I always play a consistent part."

"Only you pass from one camp to another."

"That was a right I acquired, sir, in saving your life."

"Good, madame; and as when lovers separate, they return all the gifts that have passed between them, I will save your life, in my turn, if ever the need arises, and we shall be quits."

And the duke bowed and left the room, nor did Marguerite attempt to retain him.

In the antechamber he found Gillonne, who guided him to the window on the ground floor, and in the fosse he found his page, with whom he returned to the Hôtel de Guise.

Marguerite, in a dreamy mood, went to the opened window.

"What a marriage night!" she murmured to herself; "the husband flees from me—the lover forsakes me!"

At that moment, coming from the Tour de Bois, and going up toward the Moulin de la Monnaie, on the other side of the fosse passed a student, his hand on his hip, and singing:

"SONG.

"Tell me why, O maiden fair,
When I burn to bite thy hair,
And to kiss thy rosy lips,
And to touch thy lovely breast,
Like a nun thou feign'st thee blest
In the cloister's sad eclipse?
"Who will win the precious prize

Of thy brow, thy mouth, thine eyes—
    Of thy bosom sweet—what lover?
Wilt thou all thy charms devote
To grim Pluton when the boat
    Charon rows shall take thee over?

"After thou hast sailed across,
Loveliest, then wilt find but loss—
All thy beauty will decay.
When I die and meet thee there
In the shades I'll never swear
    Thou wert once my mistress gay!

"Therefore, darling, while we live,

Change thy mind and tokens give—
Kisses from thy honey mouth!
Else when thou art like to die
Thou 'lt repent thy cruelty,
Filling all my life with drouth!"

Marguerite listened with a melancholy smile; then when the student's voice was lost in the distance, she shut the window, and called Gillonne to help her to prepare for bed.

———

CHAPTER III.

THE POET-KING.

The next day and those that followed were devoted to festivals, balls, and tournaments.

The same amalgamation continued to take place between the two parties. The caresses and compliments lavished were enough to turn the heads of the most bigoted Huguenots. Père Cotton was to be seen dining and carousing with the Baron de Courtaumer; the Duc de Guise went boating on the Seine with the Prince de Condé. King Charles seemed to have laid aside his usual melancholy, and could not get enough of the society of his new brother-in-law, Henry. Moreover, the queen mother was so gay, and so occupied with embroidery, ornaments, and plumes, that she could not sleep.

The Huguenots, to some degree contaminated by this new Capua, began to assume silken pourpoints, wear devices, and parade before certain balconies, as if they were Catholics.

On every side there was such a reaction in favor of the Protestants that it seemed as if the whole court was about to become Protestant; even the admiral, in spite of his experience, was deceived, and was so carried away that one evening he forgot for two whole hours to chew on his toothpick, which he always used from two o'clock, at which time he finished his dinner, until eight o'clock at night, when he sat down to supper.

The evening on which the admiral thus unaccountably deviated from his usual habit, King Charles IX. had invited Henry of Navarre and the Duc de Guise to sup with him. After the repast he took them into his chamber, and was busily explaining to them the ingenious mechanism of a wolf-trap he had invented, when, interrupting himself,—

"Isn't the admiral coming to-night?" he asked. "Who has seen him to-day and can tell me anything about him?"

"I have," said the King of Navarre; "and if your Majesty is anxious about his health, I can reassure you, for I saw him this morning at six, and this evening at seven o'clock."

"Aha!" replied the King, whose eyes were instantly fixed with a searching expression on his brother-in-law; "for a new-married man, Harry, you are very early."

"Yes, sire," answered the King of Navarre, "I wished to inquire of the admiral, who knows everything, whether some gentlemen I am expecting are on their way hither."

"More gentlemen! why, you had eight hundred on the day of your wedding, and fresh ones join you every day. You are surely not going to invade us?" said Charles IX., smiling.

The Duc de Guise frowned.

"Sire," returned the Béarnais, "a war with Flanders is spoken of, and I am collecting round me all those gentlemen of my country and its neighborhood whom I think can be useful to your Majesty."

The duke, calling to mind the pretended project Henry had mentioned to Marguerite the day of their marriage, listened still more attentively.

"Well, well," replied the King, with his sinister smile, "the more the better; let them all come, Henry. But who are these gentlemen?—brave ones, I trust."

"I know not, sire, if my gentlemen will ever equal those of your Majesty, or the Duc d'Anjou's, or the Duc de Guise's, but I know that they will do their best."

"Do you expect many?"

"Ten or a dozen more."

"What are their names?"

"Sire, their names escape me, and with the exception of one, whom Téligny recommended to me as a most accomplished gentleman, and whose name is De la Mole, I cannot tell."

"De la Mole!" exclaimed the King, who was deeply skilled in the science of genealogy; "is he not a Lerac de la Mole, a Provençal?"

"Exactly so, sire; you see I recruit even in Provence."

"And I," added the Duc de Guise, with a sarcastic smile, "go even further than his majesty the King of Navarre, for I seek even in Piedmont all the trusty Catholics I can find."

"Catholic or Huguenot," interrupted the King, "it little matters to me, so they are brave."

The King's face while he uttered these words, which thus united Catholics and Huguenots in his thoughts, bore such an expression of indifference that the duke himself was surprised.

"Your Majesty is occupied with the Flemings," said the admiral, to whom Charles had some days previously accorded the favor of entering without being announced, and who had overheard the King's last words.

"Ah! here is my father the admiral!" cried Charles, opening his arms. "We were speaking of war, of gentlemen, of brave men—and *he* comes. It is like the lodestone which attracts the iron. My brother-in-law of Navarre and my cousin of Guise are expecting reinforcements for your army. That was what we were talking about."

"And these reinforcements are on their way," said the admiral.

"Have you had news of them?" asked the Béarnais.

"Yes, my son, and particularly of M. de la Mole; he was at Orléans yesterday, and will be in Paris to-morrow or the day after."

"The devil! You must be a sorcerer, admiral," said the Duc de Guise, "to know what is taking place at thirty or forty leagues' distance. I should like to know for a certainty what happened or is happening before Orléans."

Coligny remained unmoved at this savage onslaught, which evidently alluded to the death of François de Guise, the duke's father, killed before Orléans by Poltrot de Méré, and not without a suspicion that the admiral had advised the crime.

"Sir," replied he, coldly and with dignity, "I am a sorcerer whenever I wish to know anything positively that concerns my own affairs or the King's. My courier arrived an hour ago from Orléans, having travelled, thanks to the post, thirty-two leagues in a day. As M. de la Mole has only his own horse, he rides but ten leagues a day, and will not arrive in Paris before the 24th. Here is all my magic."

"Bravo, my father, a clever answer!" cried Charles IX.; "teach these young men that wisdom as well as age has whitened your hair and beard; so now we will send them to talk of their tournaments and their love-affairs and you and I will stay and talk of our wars. Good councillors make good kings, my father. Leave us, gentlemen. I wish to talk with the admiral."

The two young men took their departure; the King of Navarre first, then the Duc de Guise; but outside the door they separated, after a formal salute.

Coligny followed them with his eyes, not without anxiety, for he never saw those two personified hatreds meet without a dread that some new lightning flash would leap forth. Charles IX. saw what was passing in his mind, and, going to him, laid his hand on his arm:

"Have no fear, my father; I am here to preserve peace and obedience. I am really a king, now that my mother is no longer queen, and she is no longer queen now that Coligny is my father."

"Oh, sire!" said the admiral, "Queen Catharine"—

"Is a marplot. Peace is impossible with her. These Italian Catholics are furious, and will hear of nothing but extermination; now, for my part, I not only wish to pacify, but I wish to put power into the hands of those that profess the reformed religion. The others are too dissolute, and scandalize me by their love affairs and their quarrels. Shall I speak frankly to you?" continued Charles, redoubling in energy. "I mistrust every one about me except my new friends. I suspect Tavannes's ambition. Vieilleville cares only for good wine, and would betray his king for a cask of Malvoisie; Montmorency thinks only of the chase, and spends all his time among his dogs and falcons; the Comte de Retz is a Spaniard; the De Guises are Lorraines. I think there are no true Frenchmen in France, except myself, my brother-in-law of Navarre, and you; but I am chained to the throne, and cannot command armies; it is as much as I can do to hunt at my ease at Saint Germain or Rambouillet. My brother-in-law of Navarre is too young and too inexperienced; besides, he seems to me exactly like his father Antoine, ruined by women. There is but you, my father, who can be called, at the same time, as brave as Cæsar and as wise as Plato; so that I scarcely know what to do— keep you near me, as my adviser, or send you to the army, as its general. If you act as my counsellor, who will command? If you command, who will be my counsellor?"

"Sire," said Coligny, "we must conquer first, and then take counsel after the victory."

"That is your advice—so be it; Monday you shall leave for Flanders, and I for Amboise."

"Your Majesty leaves Paris, then?"

"Yes; I am weary of this confusion, and of these fêtes. I am not a man of action; I am a dreamer. I was not born to be a king; I was born to be a poet. You shall form a council which shall govern while you are at war, and provided my mother is not in it, all will go well. I have already sent word to Ronsard to join me; and yonder, we two together, far from all tumult, far from the world, far from evil men, under our mighty trees on the banks of the river, with the murmur of brooks in our ears, will talk about divine things, the only compensation which there is in the world for the affairs of men. Wait! Hear these lines in which I invite him to join me; I wrote them this morning."

Coligny smiled. Charles IX. rubbed his hand over his brow, yellow and shining like ivory, and repeated in a kind of sing-song the following couplets:

> "Ronsard, I am full sure that if you see me not,
> Your great King's voice by you will shortly be forgot.
> But as a slight reminder—know I still persevere
> In making skill of poesy my sole endeavor.
> And that is why I send to you this warm appeal,
> To fill your mind with new, enthusiastic zeal.
>
> "No longer then amuse yourself with home distractions;
> Past is the time for gardening and its attractions.
> Come, follow with your King, who loves you most of all,
> For that the sweet strong verses from your lips do fall.
> And if Ardoise shall not behold you shortly present,
> A mighty quarrel will break out and prove unpleasant!"

"Bravo! sire, bravo!" cried Coligny, "I am better versed in matters of war than in matters of poetry, but it seems to me that those lines are equal to the best, even written by Ronsard, or Dorat, or even Michel de l'Hôpital, Chancellor of France."

"Ah! my father!" exclaimed Charles IX.; "would what you said were true! For the title of poet, you see, is what I am ambitious, above all things, to gain; and as I said a few days ago to my master in poetry:

> "'The art of making verse, if one were criticised,
> Should ever be above the art of reigning prized.
> The crowns that you and I upon our brows are wearing,

I as the King receive, as poet you are sharing.
Your lofty soul, enkindled by celestial beams,
Flames of itself, while mine with borrowed glory gleams.
If 'mid the gods I ask which has the better showing,
Ronsard is their delight: I, but their image glowing.
Your lyre, which ravishes with sounds so sweet and bold,
Subdues men's minds, while I their bodies only hold!
It makes you master, lifts you into lofty regions,
Where even the haughty tyrant ne'er dared claim allegiance.'"

"Sire," said Coligny, "I was well aware that your Majesty conversed with the Muses, but I did not know that you were their chief counsellor."

"After you, my father, after you. And in order that I may not be disturbed in my relations with them, I wish to put you at the head of everything. So listen: I must now go and reply to a new madrigal my dear and illustrious poet has sent me. I cannot, therefore, give you the documents necessary to make you acquainted with the question now debating between Philip II. and myself. There is, besides, a plan of the campaign drawn up by my ministers. I will find it all for you, and give it to you to-morrow."

"At what time, sire?"

"At ten o'clock; and if by chance I am busy making verses, or in my cabinet writing, well—you will come in just the same, and take all the papers which you will find on the table in this red portfolio. The color is remarkable, and you cannot mistake it. I am now going to write to Ronsard."

"Adieu, sire!"

"Adieu, my father!"

"Your hand?"

"What, my hand? In my arms, in my heart, there is your place! Come, my old soldier, come!"

And Charles IX., drawing Coligny toward him as he bowed, pressed his lips to his white hair.

The admiral left the room, wiping away a tear.

Charles IX. followed him with his eyes as long as he could see, and listened as long as he could catch a sound; then, when he could no longer hear or see anything, he bent his head over toward his shoulder, as his custom was, and slowly entered his armory.

This armory was the king's favorite apartment; there he took his fencing-lessons with Pompée, and his poetry lessons with Ronsard. He had gathered there a great collection of the most costly weapons he had been able to find. The walls were hung with axes, shields, spears, halberds, pistols, and muskets, and that day a famous armorer had brought him a magnificent arquebuse, on the barrel of which were inlaid in silver these four lines, composed by the royal poet himself:

"Pour maintenir la foy,
Je suis belle et fidèle.
Aux ennemis du Roi,
Je suis belle et cruelle."[1]

Charles, as we have said, entered this room, and after having shut the door by which he had entered, he raised the tapestry that masked a passage leading into a little chamber, where a woman kneeling before a *priedieu* was saying her prayers.

As this movement was executed noiselessly, and the footsteps of the king, deadened by the thick carpet, made no more noise than a phantom's, the kneeling woman heard no sound, and continued to pray. Charles stood for a moment pensively looking at her.

She was a woman of thirty-four or thirty-five years of age, whose vigorous beauty was set off by the costume of the peasants of Caux. She wore the high cap so much the fashion at the court of France during the time of Isabel of Bavaria, and her red bodice was embroidered with gold, like those of the *contadine* of Nettuno and Sora. The apartment which she had for nearly twenty years occupied was close to the King's bed-chamber and presented a singular mixture of elegance and rusticity. In equal measure the palace had encroached upon the cottage, and the cottage upon the palace, so that the room combined the simplicity of the peasant woman and the luxury of the court lady.

The *priedieu* on which she knelt was of oak, marvellously carved, covered with velvet and with gold fringes, while the Bible from which she was reading (for she was of the reformed religion) was very old and torn, like those found in the poorest cottages; now everything in the room was typified by the *priedieu* and the Bible.

"Eh, Madelon!" said the King.

The kneeling woman lifted her head smilingly at the well-known voice, and rising from her knees,—

"Ah! it is you, my son," said she.

"Yes, nurse; come here."

Charles IX. let fall the curtain, and sat down on the arm of an easy-chair. The nurse appeared.

"What do you want with me, Charlot?"

"Come near, and answer in a low tone."

The nurse approached him with a familiarity such as might come from that maternal affection felt by a woman for her nursling, but attributed by the pamphlets of the time to a source infinitely less pure.

"Here I am," said she; "speak!"

"Is the man I sent for come?"

"He has been here half an hour."

Charles rose, approached the window, looked to assure himself there were no eavesdroppers, went to the door and looked out there also, shook the dust from his trophies of arms, patted a large greyhound which followed him wherever he went, stopping when he stopped and moving when he moved,— then returning to his nurse:

"Very well, nurse, let him come in," said he.

The worthy woman disappeared by the same passage by which she had entered, while the king went and leaned against a table on which were scattered arms of every kind.

Scarcely had he done so when the portière was again lifted, and the person whom he expected entered.

He was a man of about forty, his eyes gray and false, his nose curved like the beak of a screech-owl, his cheek-bones prominent. His face tried to look respectful, but all that he could do was to wear a hypocritical smile on his lips blanched with fear.

Charles gently put his hand behind him, and grasped the butt of a pistol of a new construction, that was discharged, not by a match, as formerly, but by a flint brought in contact with a wheel of steel. He fixed his dull eyes steadily on the newcomer; meantime he whistled, with perfect precision and with remarkable sweetness, one of his favorite hunting-airs.

After a pause of some minutes, during which the expression of the stranger's face grew more and more discomposed,

"You are the person," said the King, "called François de Louvièrs

Maurevel?"

"Yes, sire."

"Captain of petardeers?"

"Yes, sire."

"I wanted to see you."

Maurevel made a low bow.

"You know," continued Charles, laying a stress on each word, "that I love all my subjects equally?"

"I know," stammered Maurevel, "that your Majesty is the father of your people."

"And that the Huguenots and Catholics are equally my children?"

Maurevel remained silent, but his agitation was manifest to the King's piercing eyes, although the person whom he was addressing was almost concealed in the darkness.

"Does this displease you," said the King, "you who have waged such a bitter war on the Huguenots?"

Maurevel fell on his knees.

"Sire," stammered he, "believe that"—

"I believe," continued Charles, looking more and more keenly at Maurevel, while his eyes, which at first had seemed like glass, now became almost fiery, "I believe that you had a great desire at Moncontour to kill the admiral, who has just left me; I believe you missed your aim, and that then you entered the army of my brother, the Duc d'Anjou; I believe that then you went for a second time over to the prince's and there took service in the company of M. de Mouy de Saint Phale"—

"Oh, sire!"

"A brave gentleman from Picardy"—

"Sire, sire!" cried Maurevel, "do not overwhelm me."

"He was a brave officer," continued Charles, whose features assumed an aspect of almost ferocious cruelty, "who received you as if you had been his son; fed you, lodged you, and clothed you."

Maurevel uttered a despairing sigh.

"You called him your father, I believe," continued the King, pitilessly, "and a tender friendship existed between you and the young De Mouy, his son."

Maurevel, still on his knees, bowed low, more and more crushed under the indignation of the King, who stood immovable, like a statue whose lips only are endowed with vitality.

"By the way," continued the King, "M. de Guise was to give you ten thousand crowns if you killed the admiral—was he not?"

The assassin in consternation struck his forehead against the floor.

"As regards your worthy father, the Sieur de Mouy, you were one day acting as his escort in a reconnaissance toward Chevreux. He dropped his whip and dismounted to pick it up. You were alone with him; you took a pistol from your holster, and while he was bending over, you shot him in the back; then seeing he was dead—for you killed him on the spot—you escaped on the horse he had given you. This is your history, I believe?"

And as Maurevel remained mute under this accusation, every circumstance of which was true, Charles IX. began to whistle again, with the same precision and melody, the same hunting-air.

"Now, then, murderer!" said he after a little, "do you know I have a great mind to have you hanged?"

"Oh, your Majesty!" cried Maurevel.

"Young De Mouy entreated me to do so only yesterday, and I scarcely knew what answer to make him, for his demand was perfectly just."

Maurevel clasped his hands.

"All the more just, because I am, as you say, the father of my people; and because, as I answered you, now that I am reconciled to the Huguenots, they are as much my children as the Catholics."

"Sire," said Maurevel, in despair, "my life is in your hands; do with it what you will."

"You are quite right, and I would not give a groat for it."

"But, sire," asked the assassin, "is there no means of redeeming my crime?"

"None that I know of; only if I were in your place—but thank God I am not"—

"Well, sire, if you were in my place?" murmured Maurevel, his eyes fixed on the King's lips.

"I think I could extricate myself," said the King.

Maurevel raised himself on one knee and one hand, fixing his eyes upon Charles to make certain that he was not jesting.

"I am very fond of young De Mouy," said the King; "but I am equally fond of my cousin De Guise; and if my cousin asked me to spare a man that the other wanted me to hang, I confess I should be embarrassed; but for policy as well as religion's sake I should comply with my cousin De Guise's request, for De Mouy, brave captain though he be, is but a petty personage compared with a prince of Lorraine."

During these words, Maurevel slowly rose, like a man whose life is saved.

"In your critical situation it would be a very important thing to gain my cousin De Guise's favor. So I am going to tell you what he said to me last night."

Maurevel drew nearer.

"'Imagine, sire,' said he to me, 'that every morning, at ten o'clock, my deadliest enemy passes down the Rue Saint Germain l'Auxerrois, on his return from the Louvre. I see him from a barred window in the room of my old preceptor, the Canon Pierre Piles, and I pray the devil to open the earth and swallow him in its abysses.' Now, Maître Maurevel," continued the King, "perhaps if you were the devil, or if for an instant you should take his place, that would perhaps please my cousin De Guise."

Maurevel's infernal smile came back to his lips, though they were still bloodless with terror, and he stammered out these words:

"But, sire, I cannot make the earth open."

"Yet you made it open wide enough for the worthy De Mouy, if I remember correctly. After this you will tell me how with a pistol—have you not that pistol still?"

"Forgive me, sire, I am a still better marksman with an arquebuse than a pistol," replied Maurevel, now quite reassured.

"Pistol or arquebuse makes no difference," said the King; "I am sure my cousin De Guise will not cavil over the choice of methods."

"But," said Maurevel, "I must have a weapon I can rely on, as, perhaps, I shall have to fire from a long distance."

"I have ten arquebuses in this room," replied Charles IX., "with which I can hit a crown-piece at a hundred and fifty paces—will you try one?"

"Most willingly, sire!" cried Maurevel, with the greatest joy, going in the direction of one which was standing in a corner of the room. It was the one which that day had been brought to the King.

"No, not that one," said the King, "not that one; I reserve that for myself. Some day I am going to have a grand hunt and then I hope to use it. Take any other you like."

Maurevel took one down from a trophy.

"And who is this enemy, sire?" asked the assassin.

"How should I know," replied Charles, withering the wretch with his contemptuous look.

"I must ask M. de Guise, then," faltered Maurevel.

The King shrugged his shoulders.

"Do not ask," said he; "for M. de Guise will not answer. Do people generally answer such questions? Those that do not wish to be hanged must guess them."

"But how shall I know him?"

"I tell you he passes the Canon's house every morning at ten o'clock."

"But many pass that house. Would your Majesty deign to give me any certain sign?"

"Oh, that is easy enough; to-morrow, for example, he will carry a red morocco portfolio under his arm."

"That is sufficient, sire."

"You still have the fast horse M. de Mouy gave you?"

"Sire, I have one of the fleetest of horses."

"Oh, I am not in the least anxious about you; only it is as well to let you know the monastery has a back door."

"Thanks, sire; pray Heaven for me!"

"Oh, a thousand devils! pray to Satan rather; for only by his aid can you escape a halter."

"Adieu, sire."

"Adieu! By the way, M. de Maurevel, remember that if you are heard of before ten to-morrow, or are *not* heard of afterward, there is a dungeon at the Louvre."

And Charles IX. calmly began to whistle, with more than usual precision, his favorite air.

CHAPTER IV.

THE EVENING OF THE 24TH OF AUGUST, 1572.

Our readers have not forgotten that in the previous chapter we mentioned a gentleman named De la Mole whom Henry of Navarre was anxiously expecting.

This young gentleman, as the admiral had announced, entered Paris by the gate of Saint Marcel the evening of the 24th of August, 1572; and bestowing a contemptuous glance on the numerous hostelries that displayed their picturesque signs on either side of him, he spurred his steaming horse on into the heart of the city, and after having crossed the Place Maubert, Le Petit Pont, the Pont Notre-Dame, and skirted the quays, he stopped at the end of the Rue de Bresec, which we have since corrupted into the Rue de l'Arbre Sec, and for the greater convenience of our readers we will call by its modern name.

The name pleased him, no doubt, for he entered the street, and finding on his left a large sheet-iron plate swinging, creaking on its hinges, with an accompaniment of little bells, he stopped and read these words, "*La Belle Étoile*," written on a scroll beneath the sign, which was a most attractive one for a famished traveller, as it represented a fowl roasting in the midst of a black sky, while a man in a red cloak held out his hands and his purse toward this new-fangled constellation.

"Here," said the gentleman to himself, "is an inn that promises well, and the landlord must be a most ingenious fellow. I have always heard that the Rue de l'Arbre Sec was near the Louvre; and, provided that the interior answers to the exterior, I shall be admirably lodged."

While the newcomer was thus indulging in this monologue another horseman who had entered the street at the other end, that is to say, by the Rue Saint-Honoré, stopped also to admire the sign of *La Belle Étoile*.

The gentleman whom we already know, at least by name, rode a white steed of Spanish lineage and wore a black doublet ornamented with jet; his cloak was of dark violet velvet; his boots were of black leather, and he had a sword and poniard with hilts of chased steel.

Now if we pass from his costume to his features we shall conclude that he was twenty-four or twenty-five years of age. His complexion was dark; his eyes were blue; he had a delicate mustache and brilliant teeth which seemed to light up his whole face when his exquisitely modelled lips parted in a sweet and melancholy smile.

The contrast between him and the second traveller was very striking. Beneath his cocked hat escaped a profusion of frizzled hair, red rather than brown; beneath this mop of hair sparkled a pair of gray eyes which at the slightest opposition grew so fierce that they seemed black; a fair complexion, thin lips, a tawny mustache, and admirable teeth completed the description of his face. Taken all in all, with his white skin, lofty stature, and broad shoulders, he was indeed a *beau cavalier* in the ordinary acceptation of the term, and during the last hour which he had employed in staring up at all the windows, under the pretext of looking for signs, he had attracted the general attention of women, while the men, though they may have felt inclined to laugh at his scanty cloak, his tight-fitting small-clothes, and his old-fashioned boots, checked their rising mirth with a most cordial *Dieu vous garde*, after they had more attentively studied his face, which every moment assumed a dozen different expressions, but never that good-natured one characteristic of a bewildered provincial.

He it was who first addressed the other gentleman who, as I have said, was gazing at the hostelry of *La Belle Étoile*.

"By Heaven! monsieur," said he, with that horrible mountain accent which would instantly distinguish a native of Piedmont among a hundred strangers, "we are close to the Louvre, are we not? At all events, I think your choice is the same as mine, and I am highly flattered by it."

"Monsieur," replied the other, with a Provençal accent which rivalled that of his companion, "I believe this inn is near the Louvre. However, I am still deliberating whether or not I shall have the honor of sharing your opinion. I am in a quandary."

"You have not yet decided, sir? Nevertheless, the house is attractive. But perhaps, after all, I have been won over to it by your presence. Yet you will grant that is a pretty painting?"

"Very! and it is for that very reason I mistrust it. Paris, I am told, is full of sharpers, and you may be just as well tricked by a sign as by anything else."

"By Heaven!" replied the Piedmontese, "I don't care a fig for their tricks; and if the host does not serve me a chicken as well roasted as the one on his sign, I will put him on the spit, nor will I let him off till I have done him to a turn. Come, let us go in."

"You have decided me," said the Provençal, laughing; "precede me, I beg."

"Oh, sir, on my soul I could not think of it, for I am only your most obedient servant, the Comte Annibal de Coconnas."

"And I, monsieur, but the Comte Joseph Hyacinthe Boniface de Lerac de la Mole, equally at your service."

"Since that is the case, let us go in together, arm in arm."

The result of this conciliatory proposition was that the two young men got off their horses, threw the bridles to the ostler, linked arms, adjusted their swords, and approached the door of the inn, where the landlord was standing. But contrary to the custom of men of his profession, the worthy proprietor seemed not to notice them, so busy was he talking with a tall, sallow man, wrapped in a drab-colored cloak like an owl buried in his feathers.

The two gentlemen were so near the landlord and his friend in the drab-colored cloak that Coconnas, indignant that he and his companion should be treated with such lack of consideration, touched the landlord's sleeve.

He appeared suddenly to perceive them, and dismissed his friend with an "*Au revoir!* come soon and let me know the hour appointed."

"Well, *monsieur le drole*," said Coconnas, "do not you see we have business with you?"

"I beg pardon, gentlemen," said the host; "I did not see you."

"Eh, by Heaven! then you ought to have seen us; and now that you do see us, say, 'Monsieur le Comte,' and not merely 'Monsieur,' if you please."

La Mole stood by, leaving Coconnas, who seemed to have undertaken the affair, to speak; but by the scowling on his face it was evident that he was ready to come to his assistance when the moment of action should present itself.

"Well, what is your pleasure, Monsieur le Comte?" asked the landlord, in a quiet tone.

"Ah, that's better; is it not?" said Coconnas, turning to La Mole, who nodded affirmatively. "Monsieur le Comte and myself, attracted by the sign of your establishment, wish to sup and sleep here to-night."

"Gentlemen," said the host, "I am very sorry, but I have only one chamber, and I am afraid that would not suit you."

"So much the better," said La Mole; "we will go and lodge somewhere else."

"By no means," said Coconnas, "I shall stay here; my horse is tired. I will have the room, since you will not."

"Ah! that is quite different," replied the host, with the same cool tone of impertinence. "If there is only one of you I cannot lodge you at all, then."

"By Heaven!" cried Coconnas, "here's a witty animal! Just now you could not lodge us because we were two, and now you have not room for one. You will not lodge us at all, then?"

"Since you take this high tone, gentlemen, I will answer you frankly."

"Answer, then; only answer quickly."

"Well, then, I should prefer not to have the honor of lodging you at all."

"For what reason?" asked Coconnas, growing white with rage.

"Because you have no servants, and for one master's room full, I should have two servants' rooms empty; so that, if I let you have the master's room, I run the risk of not letting the others."

"Monsieur de la Mole," said Coconnas, "do you not think we ought to massacre this fellow?"

"Decidedly," said La Mole, preparing himself, together with Coconnas, to lay his whip over the landlord's back.

But the landlord contented himself with retreating a step or two, despite this two-fold demonstration, which was not particularly reassuring, considering that the two gentlemen appeared so full of determination.

"It is easy to see," said he, in a tone of raillery, "that these gentlemen are just from the provinces. At Paris it is no longer the fashion to massacre innkeepers who refuse to let them rooms—only great men are massacred nowadays and not the common people; and if you make any disturbance, I will call my neighbors, and you shall be beaten yourselves, and that would be an indignity for two such gentlemen."

"Why! he is laughing at us," cried Coconnas, in a rage.

"Grégoire, my arquebuse," said the host, with the same voice with which he would have said, "Give these gentleman a chair."

"*Trippe del papa!*" cried Coconnas, drawing his sword; "warm up, Monsieur de la Mole."

"No, no; for while we warm up, our supper will get cold."

"What, you think"—cried Coconnas.

40

"That Monsieur de la Belle Étoile is right; only he does not know how to treat his guests, especially when they are gentlemen, for instead of brutally saying, 'Gentlemen, I do not want you,' it would have been better if he had said, 'Enter, gentlemen'—at the same time reserving to himself the right to charge in his bill, master's room, so much; servants' room, so much."

With these words, La Mole gently pushed by the landlord, who was just on the point of taking his arquebuse, and entered with Coconnas.

"Well," said Coconnas, "I am sorry to sheathe my sword before I have ascertained that it is as sharp as that rascal's larding-needle."

"Patience, my dear friend, patience," said La Mole. "All the inns in Paris are full of gentlemen come to attend the King of Navarre's marriage or attracted by the approaching war with Flanders; we should not find another lodging; besides, perhaps it is the custom at Paris to receive strangers in this manner."

"By Heaven! how patient you are, Monsieur de la Mole!" muttered Coconnas, curling his red mustache with rage and hurling the lightning of his eyes on the landlord. "But let the scoundrel take care; for if his cooking be bad, if his bed be hard, if his wine less than three years in bottle, and his waiter be not as pliant as a reed"—

"There! there! my dear gentleman!" said the landlord, whetting his knife on a strap, "you may make yourself easy; you are in the land of Cocagne."

Then in a low tone he added:

"These are some Huguenots; traitors have grown so insolent since the marriage of their Béarnais with Mademoiselle Margot!"

Then, with a smile that would have made his guests shudder had they seen it:

"How strange it would be if I were just to have two Huguenots come to my house, when"—

"Now, then," interrupted Coconnas, pointedly, "are we going to have any supper?"

"Yes, as soon as you please, monsieur," returned the landlord, softened, no doubt, by the last reflection.

"Well, then, the sooner the better," said Coconnas; and turning to La Mole:

"Pray, Monsieur le Comte, while they are putting our room in order, tell me, do you think Paris seems a gay city?"

"Faith! no," said La Mole. "All the faces I have seen looked scared or forbidding; perhaps the Parisians also are afraid of the storm; see how very black the sky is, and the air feels heavy."

"Tell me, count, are you not bound for the Louvre?"

"Yes! and you also, Monsieur de Coconnas."

"Well, let us go together."

"It is rather late to go out, is it not?" said La Mole.

"Early or late, I must go; my orders are peremptory—'Come instantly to Paris, and report to the Duc de Guise without delay.'"

At the Duc de Guise's name the landlord drew nearer.

"I think the rascal is listening to us," said Coconnas, who, as a true son of Piedmont, was very truculent, and could not forgive the proprietor of *La Belle Étoile* his rude reception of them.

"I am listening, gentlemen," replied he, taking off his cap; "but it is to serve you. I heard the great duke's name mentioned, and I came immediately. What can I do for you, gentlemen?"

"Aha! that name is magical, since it renders you so polite. Tell me, maître,— what's your name?"

"Maître la Hurière," replied the host, bowing.

"Well, Maître la Hurière, do you think my arm is lighter than the Duc de Guise's, who makes you so civil?"

"No, Monsieur le Comte, but it is not so long," replied La Hurière; "besides," he added, "I must tell you that the great Henry is the idol of us Parisians."

"Which Henry?" asked La Mole.

"It seems to me there is only one," replied the landlord.

"You are mistaken; there is another, whom I desire you do not speak ill of, and that is Henry of Navarre; and then there is Henry de Condé, who has his share of merit."

"I do not know them," said the landlord.

"But I do; and as I am on my way to the King of Navarre, I desire you not to speak slightingly of him before me."

The landlord replied by merely touching his cap, and continued to lavish his assiduities on Coconnas:

"So monsieur is going to see the great Duc de Guise? Monsieur is a very fortunate gentleman; he has come, no doubt, for"—

"What?" asked Coconnas.

"For the festivity," replied the host, with a singular smile.

"You should say for the festivities," replied Coconnas; "for Paris, I hear, runs riot with festivals; at least there is nothing talked about but balls, festivals, and orgies. Does not every one find plenty of amusement?"

"A moderate amount, but they will have more soon, I hope."

"But the marriage of his majesty the King of Navarre has brought a great many people to Paris, has it not?" said La Mole.

"A great many Huguenots—yes," replied La Hurière, but suddenly changing his tone:

"Pardon me, gentlemen," said he, "perhaps you are of that religion?"

"I," cried Coconnas, "I am as good a Catholic as the pope himself."

La Hurière looked at La Mole, but La Mole did not or would not comprehend him.

"If you do not know the King of Navarre, Maître La Hurière," said La Mole, "perhaps you know the admiral. I have heard he has some influence at court, and as I have letters for him, perhaps you will tell me where he lives, if his name does not take the skin off your lips."

"He *did* live in the Rue de Béthizy down here at the right," replied the landlord, with an inward satisfaction he could not conceal.

"He *did* live?" exclaimed La Mole. "Has he changed his residence?"

"Yes—from this world, perhaps."

"What do you mean?" cried both the gentlemen together, "the admiral removed from this world?"

"What, Monsieur de Coconnas," pursued the landlord, with a shrewd smile, "are you a friend of the Duc de Guise, and do not know *that*?"

"Know what?"

"That the day before yesterday, as the admiral was passing along the place Saint Germain l'Auxerrois before the house of the Canon Pierre Piles, he was fired at"—

"And killed?" said La Mole.

"No; he had his arm broken and two fingers taken off; but it is hoped the

43

balls were poisoned."

"How, wretch!" cried La Mole; "hoped?"

"Believed, I mean," said the landlord, winking at Coconnas; "do not take a word too seriously, it was a slip of the tongue."

And Maître La Hurière, turning his back on La Mole, poked out his tongue at Coconnas in the most insulting way, accompanying this action with a meaning wink.

"Really!" said Coconnas, joyfully.

"Really!" said La Mole, with sorrowful stupefaction.

"It is just as I have the honor of telling you, gentlemen," said the landlord.

"In that case," said La Mole, "I must go instantly to the Louvre. Shall I find the King of Navarre there?"

"Most likely, since he lives there."

"And I," said Coconnas, "must also go to the Louvre. Shall I find the Duc de Guise there?"

"Most likely; for only a moment ago I saw him pass with two hundred gentlemen."

"Come, then, Monsieur de Coconnas," said La Mole.

"I will follow you, sir," replied Coconnas.

"But your supper, gentlemen!" cried La Hurière.

"Ah," said La Mole, "I shall most likely sup with the King of Navarre."

"And I," said Coconnas, "with the Duc de Guise."

"And I," said the landlord, after having watched the two gentlemen on their way to the Louvre, "I will go and burnish my sallet, put a match to my arquebuse, and sharpen my partisan, for no one knows what may happen."

―――――

CHAPTER V.

OF THE LOUVRE IN PARTICULAR, AND OF VIRTUE IN

The two young men, directed by the first person they met, went down the Rue d'Averon, the Rue Saint Germain l'Auxerrois, and soon found themselves before the Louvre, the towers of which were beginning to be lost in the early shades of the gloaming.

"What is the matter with you?" asked Coconnas of La Mole, who, as they came in sight of the old château, stopped and gazed, not without awe, on the drawbridges, the narrow windows, and the pointed belfries, which suddenly rose before his vision.

"I scarcely know," said La Mole; "my heart beats strangely. I am not timid, but somehow this old palace seems so gloomy and terrible."

"Well, as for me, I don't know any reason for it," replied Coconnas, "but I feel in excellent spirits. My dress is somewhat disordered," he went on to say, glancing at his travelling costume, "but never mind, it looks as if I had been riding. Besides, my instructions commanded promptness and I shall be welcome because I shall have obeyed punctually."

The two young men continued their way, each under the influence of the feelings he had expressed.

There was a strong guard at the Louvre and the sentinels were doubled. Our two cavaliers were somewhat embarrassed, therefore, but Coconnas, who had noticed that the Duc de Guise's name acted like a talisman on the Parisians, approached a sentinel, and making use of the all-powerful name, asked if by means of it he might not be allowed to enter.

The name seemed to produce its ordinary effect upon the soldier; nevertheless he asked Coconnas if he had the countersign.

Coconnas was forced to confess he had not.

"Stand back, then," said the soldier.

At this moment a person who was talking with the officer of the guard and who had overheard Coconnas ask leave to enter, broke off his conversation and came to him.

"Vat do you vant with Monsieur dee Gouise?" asked he.

"I wish to see him," said Coconnas, smiling.

"Imbossible! the duke is mit the King."

"But I have a letter for him."

"Ah, you haf a ledder for him?"

"Yes, and I have come a long distance."

"Ah! you haf gome a long tistance?"

"I have come from Piedmont."

"Vell, vell! dat iss anodder ting. And vat iss your name?"

"The Comte Annibal de Coconnas."

"Goot! goot! kif me the ledder, Monsieur Annibal, kif it to me!"

"On my word," said La Mole to himself, "a very civil man. I hope I may find one like him to conduct me to the King of Navarre."

"But kif me the ledder," said the German gentleman, holding out his hand toward Coconnas, who hesitated.

"By Heaven!" replied the Piedmontese, distrustful like a half-Italian, "I scarcely know whether I ought, as I have not the honor of knowing you."

"I am Pesme; I'm addached to Monsir le Douque de Gouise."

"Pesme," murmured Coconnas; "I am not acquainted with that name."

"It is Monsieur de Besme, my dear sir," said the sentinel. "His pronunciation misled you, that is all; you may safely give him your letter, I'll answer for it."

"Ah! Monsieur de Besme!" cried Coconnas; "of course I know you! with the greatest pleasure. Here is the letter. Pardon my hesitation; but fidelity requires one to be careful."

"Goot, goot! dere iss no need of any egscuse," said Besme.

"Perhaps, sir," said La Mole, "you will be so kind as to the same for my letter that you have done for my friend?"

"And vat iss your name, monsir?"

"The Comte Lerac de la Mole."

"Gount Lerag dee la Mole?"

"Yes."

"I don't know de name."

"It is not strange that I have not the honor of being known to you, sir, for like the Comte de Coconnas I am only just arrived in Paris."

"Where do you gome from?"

"From Provence."

"Vit a ledder?"

"Yes."

"For Monsir dee Gouise?"

"No; for his majesty the King of Navarre."

"I do not pelong to de King of Navarre," said De Besme coldly, "and derefore I gannot dake your ledder."

And turning on his heel, he entered the Louvre, bidding Coconnas follow him.

La Mole was left alone.

At this moment a troop of cavaliers, about a hundred in number, came out from the Louvre by a gate alongside that of which Besme and Coconnas had entered.

"Aha!" said the sentinel to his comrade, "there are De Mouy and his Huguenots! See how joyous they all are! The King has probably promised them to put to death the assassin of the admiral; and as it was he who murdered De Mouy's father, the son will kill two birds with one stone."

"Excuse me, my good fellow," interrupted La Mole, "did you not say that officer is M. de Mouy?"

"Yes, sir."

"And that those with him are"—

"Are heretics—I said so."

"Thank you," said La Mole, affecting not to notice the scornful word *parpaillots*, employed by the sentinel. "That was all I wished to know;" and advancing to the chief of the cavaliers:

"Sir," said he, "I am told you are M. de Mouy."

"Yes, sir," returned the officer, courteously.

"Your name, well known among those of our faith, emboldens me to address you, sir, to ask a special favor."

"What may that be, sir,—but first whom have I the honor of addressing?"

"The Comte Lerac de la Mole."

The young men bowed to each other.

"What can I do for you, sir?" asked De Mouy.

"Sir, I am just arrived from Aix, and bring a letter from M. d'Auriac,

47

Governor of Provence. This letter is directed to the King of Navarre and contains important and pressing news. How can I give it to him? How can I enter the Louvre?"

"Nothing is easier than to enter the Louvre, sir," replied De Mouy; "but I fear the King of Navarre will be too busy to see you at this hour. However, if you please, I will take you to his apartments, and then you must manage for yourself."

"A thousand thanks!"

"Come, then," said De Mouy.

De Mouy dismounted, threw the reins to his lackey, stepped toward the wicket, passed the sentinel, conducted La Mole into the château, and, opening the door leading to the king's apartments:

"Enter, and inquire for yourself, sir," said he.

And saluting La Mole, he retired.

La Mole, left alone, looked round.

The ante-room was vacant. One of the inner doors was open. He advanced a few paces and found himself in a passage.

He knocked and spoke, but no one answered. The profoundest silence reigned in this part of the Louvre.

"What was told me about the stern etiquette of this place?" said he to himself. "One may come and go in this palace as if it were a public place."

Then he called again, but without obtaining any better result than before.

"Well, let us walk straight on," thought he, "I must meet some one," and he proceeded down the corridor, which grew darker and darker.

Suddenly the door opposite that by which he had entered opened, and two pages appeared, lighting a lady of noble bearing and exquisite beauty.

The glare of the torches fell full on La Mole, who stood motionless.

The lady stopped also.

"What do you want, sir?" said she, in a voice which fell upon his ears like exquisite music.

"Oh, madame," said La Mole, casting down his eyes, "pardon me; I have just parted from M. de Mouy, who was so good as to conduct me here, and I wish to see the King of Navarre."

"His majesty is not here, sir; he is with his brother-in-law. But, in his absence, could you not say to the queen"—

"Oh, yes, madame," returned La Mole, "if I could obtain audience of her."

"You have it already, sir."

"What?" cried La Mole.

"I am the Queen of Navarre."

La Mole made such a hasty movement of surprise and alarm that it caused the queen to smile.

"Speak, sir," said Marguerite, "but speak quickly, for the queen mother is waiting for me."

"Oh, madame, if the queen mother is waiting for you," said La Mole, "suffer me to leave you, for just now it would be impossible for me to speak to you. I am incapable of collecting my ideas. The sight of you has dazzled me. I no longer think, I can only admire."

Marguerite advanced graciously toward the handsome young man, who, without knowing it, was acting like a finished courtier.

"Recover yourself, sir," said she; "I will wait and they will wait for me."

"Pardon me, madame," said La Mole, "if I did not salute your majesty at first with all the respect which you have a right to expect from one of your humblest servants, but"—

"You took me for one of my ladies?" said Marguerite.

"No, madame; but for the shade of the beautiful Diane de Poitiers, who is said to haunt the Louvre."

"Come, sir," said Marguerite, "I see you will make your fortune at court; you said you had a letter for the king, it was not needed, but no matter! Where is it? I will give it to him—only make haste, I beg of you."

In a twinkling La Mole threw open his doublet, and drew from his breast a letter enveloped in silk.

Marguerite took the letter, and glanced at the writing.

"Are you not Monsieur de la Mole?" asked she.

"Yes, madame. Oh, *mon Dieu*! Can I hope my name is known to your majesty?"

"I have heard the king, my husband, and the Duc d'Alençon, my brother, speak of you. I know they expect you."

And in her corsage, glittering with embroidery and diamonds, she slipped the letter which had just come from the young man's doublet and was still warm from the vital heat of his body. La Mole eagerly watched Marguerite's every movement.

"Now, sir," said she, "descend to the gallery below, and wait until some one comes to you from the King of Navarre or the Duc d'Alençon. One of my pages will show you the way."

And Marguerite, as she said these words, went on her way. La Mole drew himself up close to the wall. But the passage was so narrow and the Queen of Navarre's farthingale was so voluminous that her silken gown brushed against the young man's clothes, while a penetrating perfume hovered where she passed.

La Mole trembled all over and, feeling that he was in danger of falling, he tried to find a support against the wall.

Marguerite disappeared like a vision.

"Are you coming, sir?" asked the page who was to conduct La Mole to the lower gallery.

"Oh, yes—yes!" cried La Mole, joyfully; for as the page led him the same way by which Marguerite had gone, he hoped that by making haste he might see her again.

And in truth, as he reached the top of the staircase, he perceived her below; and whether she heard his step or looked round by chance, Marguerite raised her head, and La Mole saw her a second time.

"Oh," said he, as he followed the page, "she is not a mortal—she is a goddess, and as Vergilius Maro says: '*Et vera incessu patuit dea.*'"

"Well?" asked the page.

"Here I am," replied La Mole, "excuse me, here I am."

The page, preceding La Mole, descended a story lower, opened one door, then another, and stopping,

"You are to wait here," said he.

La Mole entered the gallery, the door of which closed after him.

The gallery was vacant except for one gentleman, who was sauntering up and down, and seemed also waiting for some one.

The evening was by this time beginning to scatter monstrous shadows from the depths of the vaulted ceiling, and though the two gentlemen were not twenty paces apart, it was impossible for either to recognize the other's face.

La Mole drew nearer.

"By Heaven!" muttered he as soon as he was within a few feet of the other, "here is Monsieur le Comte de Coconnas again!"

At the sound of footsteps Coconnas had already turned, and was staring at La Mole with no less astonishment than the other showed.

"By Heaven!" cried he. "The devil take me but here is Monsieur de la Mole! What am I doing? Swearing in the King's palace? Well, never mind; it seems the King swears in a different way from mine, and even in churches. Here we are at last, then, in the Louvre!"

"Yes; I suppose Monsieur de Besme introducedyou?"

"Oh, he is a charming German. Who brought you in?"

"M. de Mouy—I told you the Huguenots had some interest at court. Have you seen Monsieur de Guise?"

"No, not yet. Have you obtained your audience with the King of Navarre?"

"No, but I soon shall. I was brought here and told to wait."

"Ah, you will see there is some great supper under way and we shall be placed side by side. What a strange chance! For two hours fortune has joined us! But what is the matter? You seem ill at ease."

"I?" exclaimed La Mole, shivering, for in truth he was still dazzled by the vision which had been vouchsafed him. "Oh, no, but the place in which we are brings into my mind a throng of reflections."

"Philosophical ones, I suppose. Just the same as it is with me. When you came in I was just going over in my mind all my tutor's recommendations. Monsieur le Comte, are you acquainted with Plutarch?"

"Certainly I am!" exclaimed La Mole, smiling, "he is one of my favorite authors."

"Very well," Coconnas went on gravely, "this great man does not seem to me so far wrong when he compares the gifts of nature to brilliant but ephemeral flowers, while he regards virtue as a balsamic plant of imperishable perfume and sovereign efficacy for the healing of wounds."

"Do you know Greek, Monsieur de Coconnas?" said La Mole, gazing keenly at his companion.

"No, I do not; but my tutor did, and he strongly advised me when I should be at court to talk about virtue. 'That looks well,' he said. So I assure you I am well fortified with it. By the way, are you hungry?"

"No."

"And yet you seemed anxious to taste the broiled fowl of *La Belle Étoile*. As for me, I am dying of starvation!"

"Well, Monsieur de Coconnas, here is a fine chance for you to make use of your arguments on virtue and to put your admiration for Plutarch to the proof, for that great writer says somewhere: 'It is good to accustom the soul to pain and the stomach to hunger'—'*Prepon esti tên men psvchên odunê, ton de gastéra semó askeïn.*'"

"Ah, indeed! So you know Greek?" exclaimed Coconnas in surprise.

"Faith, yes," replied La Mole, "my tutor taught me."

"By Heaven! count, your fortune is made if that is so; you will compose poetry with Charles IX. and you will talk Greek with Queen Marguerite!"

"Not to reckon that I can still talk Gascon with the King of Navarre!" added La Mole, laughing.

At this moment the door communicating with the King's apartment opened, a step was heard, and a shade was seen approaching in the darkness. This shade materialized into a body. This body belonged to Monsieur de Besme.

He scrutinized both gentlemen, so as to pick out the one he wanted, and then motioned Coconnas to follow him.

Coconnas waved his hand to La Mole.

De Besme conducted Coconnas to the end of the gallery, opened a door, and stood at the head of a staircase.

He looked cautiously round, then up and down.

"Monsir de Gogonnas," said he, "vere are you staying?"

"At *La Belle Étoile*, Rue de l'Arbre Sec."

"Goot, goot! dat is glose by. Go pack to your hodel gwick and to-nide"—

He looked around him again.

"Well, to-night?"

"Vell, gome here mit a vite gross in your hat. De bassvord is 'Gouise.' Hush! nod a vord."

"What time am I to come?"

"Ven you hear de dogsin."

"What's the dogsin?" asked Coconnas.

"Ja! de dogsin—pum! pum!"

"Oh! the tocsin!"

"Ja, vot elus tid I zay?"

"Good—I shall be here," said Coconnas.

And, saluting De Besme, he took his departure, asking himself:

"What the devil does he mean and why should the tocsin be rung? No matter! I persist in my opinion: Monsieur de Besme is a charming Tedesco— Why not wait for the Comte de la Mole? Ah faith, no! he will probably be invited to supper with the King of Navarre."

And Coconnas set forth for the Rue de l'Arbre Sec, where the sign of *La Belle Étoile* like a lodestone attracted him.

Meantime a gallery door which led to the King of Navarre's apartment opened, and a page approached Monsieur de la Mole.

"You are the Comte de la Mole?" said he.

"That is my name."

"Where do you lodge?"

"At *La Belle Étoile*, Rue de l'Arbre Sec."

"Good, that is close to the Louvre. Listen—his majesty the King of Navarre has desired me to inform you that he cannot at present receive you; perhaps he may send for you to-night; but if to-morrow morning you have received no word, come to the Louvre."

"But supposing the sentinel refuse me admission."

"True: the countersign is 'Navarre;' that word will open all doors to you."

"Thanks."

"Wait, my dear sir, I am ordered to escort you to the wicket gate for fear you should get lost in the Louvre."

"By the way, how about Coconnas?" said La Mole to himself as soon as he was fairly in the street. "Oh, he will remain to supper with the Duc de Guise."

But as soon as he entered Maître la Hurière's the first thing La Mole saw was Coconnas seated before a gigantic omelet.

"Oho!" cried Coconnas, laughing heartily, "I see you have no more dined with the King of Navarre than I have supped with the Duc de Guise."

"Faith, no."

"Are you hungry now?"

"I believe I am."

"In spite of Plutarch?"

"Count," said La Mole, laughing, "Plutarch says in another place: 'Let him that hath, share with him that hath not.' Are you willing for the love of Plutarch to share your omelet with me? Then while we eat we will converse on virtue!"

"Oh, faith, not on that subject," cried Coconnas. "It is all right when one is at the Louvre and there is danger of eavesdroppers and one's stomach is empty. Sit down and have something to eat with me."

"There, now I see that fate has decidedly made us inseparable. Are you going to sleep here?"

"I have not the least idea."

"Nor I either."

"At any rate, I know where I shall spend the night."

"Where?"

"Wherever you do: that is settled."

And both burst out laughing and then set to work to do honor to Maître la Hurière's omelet.

CHAPTER VI.

THE DEBT PAID.

Now if the reader is curious to know why Monsieur de la Mole was not received by the King of Navarre, why Monsieur de Coconnas was not permitted to see Monsieur de Guise, and lastly, why instead of eating pheasants, partridges, and venison at the Louvre, both supped at the hotel of the *Belle Étoile* on an omelet, he must kindly accompany us to the old palace of kings, and follow the queen, Marguerite of Navarre, whom La Mole had lost from sight at the entrance of the grand gallery.

While Marguerite was descending the staircase, the duke, Henry de Guise, whom she had not seen since the night of her marriage, was in the King's closet. To this staircase which Marguerite was descending there was an outlet. To the closet in which Monsieur de Guise was there was a door, and this door and this outlet both led to a corridor, which corridor led to the apartments of the queen mother, Catharine de Médicis.

Catharine de Médicis was alone, seated near a table, with her elbow leaning on a prayer-book half open, and her head leaning on a hand still remarkably beautiful,—by reason of the cosmetics with which she was supplied by the Florentine Réné, who united the double duty of perfumer and poisoner to the queen mother.

The widow of Henry II. was clothed in mourning, which she had not thrown off since her husband's death. At this period she was about fifty-two or fifty-three years of age, and owing to her stoutness and fair complexion she preserved much of her early beauty.

Her rooms, like her dress, paraded her widowhood. Everything in them bore the impress of bereavement: hangings, walls, and furniture were all in mourning. Only above a kind of dais covering a throne, where at that moment lay sleeping the little greyhound presented to the queen mother by her son-in-law, Henry of Navarre, and bearing the mythological name of Phœbe, was a painted rainbow surrounded by that Greek motto which King François I. had given her: "*Phôs pherei ê de kai a'íthzên;*" which may be translated:

"*He brings light and serenity.*"

Suddenly, and at a moment when the queen mother appeared deeply plunged in some thought which brought a half-hesitating smile to her carmen-painted lips, a man opened the door, raised the tapestry, and showed his pale face, saying:

"Everything is going badly."

Catharine raised her head and recognized the Duc de Guise.

"Why do you say 'Everything is going badly'?" she replied. "What do you mean, Henry?"

"I mean that the King is more than ever taken with the accursed Huguenots; and if we await his leave to execute the great enterprise, we shall wait a very long time, and perhaps forever."

"Tell me what has happened," said Catharine, still preserving the tranquillity of countenance habitual to her, yet to which, when occasion served, she could give such different expressions.

"Why, just now, for the twentieth time, I asked his Majesty whether he would still permit all those bravadoes which the gentlemen of the reformed religion indulge in, since their admiral was wounded."

"And what did my son reply?" asked Catharine.

"He replied, 'Monsieur le Duc, you must necessarily be suspected by the people as the author of the attempted assassination of my second father, the admiral; defend yourself from the imputation as best you may. As to me, I will defend myself properly, if I am insulted;' and then he turned away to feed his dogs."

"And you made no attempt to retain him?"

"Certainly I did; but he replied to me, in that tone which you so well know, and looking at me with the gaze peculiar to him, 'Monsieur le Duc, my dogs are hungry; and they are not men, whom I can keep waiting.' Whereupon I came straight to you."

"And you have done right," said the queen mother.

"But what is now to be done?"

"Try a last effort."

"And who will try it?"

"I will! Is the King alone?"

"No; M. de Tavannes is with him."

"Await me here; or, rather, follow me at a distance."

Catharine instantly rose and went to the chamber, where on Turkey carpets and velvet cushions were the King's favorite greyhounds. On perches ranged along the wall were two or three valuable falcons and a small shrike, with which Charles IX. amused himself in bringing down the little birds in the garden of the Louvre, and that of the Tuileries, which they had just begun building.

On her way the queen mother put on a pale and anguished expression, while down her cheeks rolled a last or rather a first tear.

She noiselessly approached Charles IX. as he was giving his dogs fragments of cakes cut into equal portions.

"My son," said the queen, with a trembling in her voice so cleverly affected that the King started.

"What is it, madame?" said Charles, turning round suddenly.

"My son," replied Catharine, "I would ask your leave to retire to one of your châteaux, no matter which, so that it be as distant as possible from Paris."

"And wherefore, madame?" inquired Charles IX., fixing on his mother that glassy eye which, on certain occasions, became so penetrating.

"Because every day I receive new insults from persons of the new faith; because to-day I hear that you have been threatened by the Protestants even in your own Louvre, and I do not desire to be present at such spectacles."

"But then, madame," replied Charles IX., with an expression full of conviction, "an attempt has been made to kill their admiral. An infamous murderer has already assassinated the brave M. de Mouy. *Mort de ma vie*, mother, there must be justice in a kingdom!"

"Oh, be easy on that head, my son," said Catharine; "they will not fail justice; for if you should refuse it, they will still have it in their own way: on M. de Guise to-day, on me to-morrow, and yourself later."

"Oh, madame!" said Charles, allowing a first accent of doubt to show in his voice, "do you think so?"

"Oh, my son," replied Catharine, giving way entirely to the violence of her thoughts, "do you not see that it is no longer a question of François de Guise's death or the admiral's, of the Protestant religion or the Catholic religion, but simply of the substitution of Antoine de Bourbon's son for the son of Henry the Second?"

"Come, come, mother, you are falling again into your usual exaggeration," said the King.

"What, then, have you in mind, my son?"

"To wait, mother,—to wait. All human wisdom is in this single word. The greatest, the strongest, the most skilful is he who knows how to wait."

"You may wait, then; I will not."

Catharine made a courtesy, and stepping towards the door, was about to return to her apartment.

Charles IX. stopped her.

"Well, then, really, what is best to be done, mother?" he asked, "for above all I am just, and I would have every one satisfied with me."

Catharine turned toward him.

"Come, count," she said to Tavannes, who was caressing the King's shrike, "tell the King your opinion as to what should be done."

"Will your Majesty permit me?" inquired the count.

"Speak, Tavannes!—speak."

"What does your Majesty do when, in the chase, the wounded boar turns on you?"

"By Heaven! monsieur, I wait for him, with firm foot," replied Charles, "and stab him in the throat with my boar-spear."

"Simply that he may not hurt you," remarked Catharine.

"And to amuse myself," said the King, with a sigh which indicated courage easily aroused even to ferocity; "but I should not amuse myself killing my subjects; for, after all, the Huguenots are my subjects, as well as the Catholics."

"Then, sire," said Catharine, "your subjects, the Huguenots, will do like the wild boar who escapes the spear thrust into his throat: they will bring down the throne."

"Nonsense! Do you really think so, madame?" said Charles IX., with an air which denoted that he did not place great faith in his mother's predictions.

"But have you not seen M. de Mouy and his party to-day?"

"Yes; I have seen them, for I have just left them. But what does he ask for that is not just? He has requested that his father's murderer and the admiral's assassin be put to death. Did we not punish M. de Montgommery for the death of my father and your husband, although that death was a simple accident?"

"Very well, sire," said Catharine, piqued, "let us say no more. Your majesty is under the protection of that God who gives you strength, wisdom, and confidence. But I, a poor woman whom God abandons, no doubt on account of my sins, fear and yield."

And having said this, Catharine again courteseyed and left the room, making a sign to the Duc de Guise, who had at that moment entered, to remain in her place, and try a last effort.

Charles IX. followed his mother with his eye, but this time did not recall her. He then began to caress his dogs, whistling a hunting-air.

He suddenly paused.

"My mother," said he, "is a royal spirit, and has scruples! Really, now, it is a cool proposal, to kill off some dozens of Huguenots because they come to demand justice! Is it not their right?"

"Some dozens!" murmured the Duc de Guise.

"Ah! are you here, sir?" said the King, pretending to see him for the first time. "Yes, some dozens. A tolerable waste of life! Ah! if any one came to me and said; 'Sire, you shall be rid of all your enemies at once, and to-morrow there shall not remain one to reproach you with the death of the others,' why, then, I do not say"—

"Well, sire?"

"Tavannes," said the King, "you will tire Margot; put her back on her perch. It is no reason, because she bears the name of my sister, the Queen of Navarre, that every one should caress her."

Tavannes put the hawk on her perch, and amused himself by curling and uncurling a greyhound's ears.

"But, sire, if any one should say to your Majesty: 'Sire, your Majesty shall be delivered from all your enemies to-morrow'?"

"And by the intercession of what saint would this miracle be wrought?"

"Sire, to-day is the 24th of August, and therefore it would be by the interposition of Saint Bartholomew."

"A worthy saint," replied the King, "who allowed himself to be skinned alive!"

"So much the better; the more he suffered, the more he ought to have felt a desire for vengeance on his executioners."

"And will you, my cousin," said the King, "will you, with your pretty little gold-hilted sword, slay ten thousand Huguenots between now and to-morrow? Ha! ha! ha! *mort de ma vie!* you are very amusing, Monsieur de Guise!"

And the King burst into a loud laugh, but a laugh so forced that the room echoed with its sinister sound.

"Sire, one word—and one only," continued the duke, shuddering in spite of himself at the sound of that laugh, which had nothing human in it,—"one signal, and all is ready. I have the Swiss and eleven hundred gentlemen; I have the light horse and the citizens; your Majesty has your guards, your friends, the Catholic nobility. We are twenty to one."

"Well, then, cousin, since you are so strong, why the devil do you come to fill my ears with all this? Act without me—act"—

And the King turned again to his dogs.

Then the portière was raised, and Catharine reappeared.

"All goes well," she said to the duke; "urge him, and he will yield."

And the portière fell on Catharine, without Charles IX. seeing, or at least appearing to see her.

"But yet," continued De Guise, "I must know if, in acting as I desire, I shall act agreeably to your Majesty's views."

"Really, cousin Henry, you put the knife to my throat! But I shall live. By Heaven! am I not the king?"

"No, not yet, sire; but, if you will, you shall be so to-morrow."

"Ah—what!" continued Charles, "you would kill the King of Navarre, the Prince de Condé—in my Louvre—ah!"

Then he added, in a voice scarcely audible,—"Without the walls, I do not say"—

"Sire," cried the duke, "they are going out this evening to join in a revel with your brother, the Duc d'Alençon."

"Tavannes," said the King, with well-affected impatience, "do not you see that you are teasing the dog? Here, Actéon,—come!"

And Charles IX. went out without waiting to hear more, and Tavannes and the Duc de Guise were left almost as uncertain as before.

Meantime another scene was passing in Catharine's apartment. After she had given the Duc de Guise her counsel to remain firm, she returned to her rooms, where she found assembled the persons who were usually present when she went to bed.

Her face was now as full of joy as it had been downcast when she set out. With her most agreeable manner she dismissed her women one by one and her courtiers, and there remained only Madame Marguerite, who, seated on a coffer near the open window, was looking at the sky, absorbed in thought.

Two or three times, when she thus found herself alone with her daughter, the queen mother opened her mouth to speak, but each time a gloomy thought withheld the words ready to escape her lips.

Suddenly the portière was raised, and Henry of Navarre appeared.

The little greyhound, which was asleep on the throne, leaped up and bounded towards him.

"You here, my son!" said Catharine, starting. "Do you sup in the Louvre to-night?"

"No, madame," replied Henry, "we are going into the city to-night, with Messieurs d'Alençon and De Condé. I almost expected to find them here paying their court to you."

Catharine smiled.

"Go, gentlemen, go—men are so fortunate in being able to go about as they please! Are they not, my daughter?"

"Yes," replied Marguerite, "liberty is so glorious, so sweet a thing."

"Does that imply that I restrict yours, madame?" inquired Henry, bowing to his wife.

"No, sire; I do not complain for myself, but for women in general."

"Are you going to see the admiral, my son?" asked Catharine.

"Yes, possibly."

"Go, that will set a good example, and to-morrow you will give me news of him."

"Then, madame, I will go, since you approve of this step."

"Oh," said Catharine, "my approval is nothing—But who goes there? Send him away, send him away."

Henry started to go to the door to carry out Catharine's order; but at the same instant the portière was raised and Madame de Sauve showed her blond head.

"Madame," said she, "it is Réné, the perfumer, whom your majesty sent for."

Catharine cast a glance as quick as lightning at Henry of Navarre.

The young prince turned slightly red and then fearfully pale. Indeed, the name of his mother's assassin had been spoken; he felt that his face betrayed his emotion, and he went and leaned against the bar of the window.

The little greyhound growled.

At the same moment two persons entered—the one announced, and the other having no need to be so.

The first was René, the perfumer, who approached Catharine with all the servile obsequiousness of Florentine servants. He held in his hand a box, which he opened, and all the compartments were seen filled with powders and flasks.

The second was Madame de Lorraine, Marguerite's eldest sister. She entered by a small secret door, which led from the King's closet, and, all pale and trembling, and hoping not to be observed by Catharine, who was examining, with Madame de Sauve, the contents of the box brought by René, seated herself beside Marguerite, near whom the King of Navarre was standing, with his hand on his brow, like one who tries to rouse himself from some sudden shock.

At this instant Catharine turned round.

"Daughter," she said to Marguerite, "you may retire to your room. My son, you may go and amuse yourself in the city."

Marguerite rose, and Henry turned half round.

Madame de Lorraine seized Marguerite's hand.

"Sister," she whispered, with great quickness, "in the name of the Duc de Guise, who now saves you, as you saved him, do not go from here—do not go to your apartments."

"Eh! what say you, Claude?" inquired Catharine, turning round.

"Nothing, mother."

"You were whispering to Marguerite."

"Simply to wish her good-night, and convey a greeting to her from the Duchesse de Nevers."

"And where is that fair duchess?"

"At her brother-in-law's, M. de Guise's."

Catharine looked suspiciously at the women and frowning:

"Come here, Claude," said the queen mother.

Claude obeyed, and the queen seized her hand.

"What did you say to her, indiscreet girl that you are?" she murmured, squeezing her daughter's wrist until she nearly shrieked with pain.

"Madame," said Henry to his wife, having lost nothing of the movements of the queen, Claude, or Marguerite,—"madame, will you allow me the honor of kissing your hand?"

Marguerite extended her trembling hand.

"What did she say to you?" whispered Henry, as he stooped to imprint a kiss on her hand.

"Not to go out. In the name of Heaven, do not you go out either!"

This was like a flash; but by its light, swift as it was, Henry at once detected a complete plot.

"This is not all," added Marguerite; "here is a letter, which a country gentleman brought."

"Monsieur de la Mole?"

"Yes."

"Thank you," he said, taking the letter and putting it under his doublet; and, passing in front of his bewildered wife, he placed his hand on the shoulder of the Florentine.

"Well, Maître Réné!" he said, "and how go commercial affairs?"

"Pretty well, monseigneur,—pretty well," replied the poisoner, with his perfidious smile.

"I should think so," said Henry, "with men who, like you, supply all the crowned heads at home and abroad."

"Except the King of Navarre," replied the Florentine, impudently.

"*Ventre saint gris*, Maître Réné," replied the king, "you are right; and yet my poor mother, who also bought of you, recommended you to me with her dying breath. Come to me to-morrow, Maître Réné, or day after to-morrow, and bring your best perfumes."

"That would not be a bad notion," said Catharine, smiling; "for it is said"—

"That I need some perfumery," interrupted Henry, laughing; "who told you that, mother? Was it Margot?"

"No, my son," replied Catharine, "it was Madame de Sauve."

At this moment the Duchesse de Lorraine, who in spite of all her efforts could no longer contain herself, burst into loud sobs.

Henry did not even turn toward her.

"Sister, what is the matter?" cried Marguerite, darting toward Claude.

"Nothing," said Catharine, passing between the two young women, "nothing; she has those nervous attacks, for which Mazille prescribes aromatic preparations."

And again, and with still more force than before, she pressed her eldest daughter's arm; then, turning toward the youngest:

"There, Margot," she said, "did you not hear me request you to retire to your room? If that is not sufficient, I command you."

"Excuse me, madame," replied Marguerite, trembling and pale; "I wish your majesty good-night."

"I hope your wishes may be heard. Good-night—good-night!"

Marguerite withdrew, staggering, and in vain seeking to meet her husband's eyes, but he did not even turn toward her.

There was a moment's silence, during which Catharine remained with her eyes fastened on the Duchess of Lorraine, who, without speaking, looked at her mother with clasped hands.

Henry's back was still turned, but he was watching the scene in a mirror, while seeming to curl his mustache with a pomade which Réné had just given to him.

"And you, Henry," said Catharine, "are you still intending to go out?"

"Yes, that's true," exclaimed the king. "Faith, I was forgetting that the Duc d'Alençon and the Prince de Condé are waiting for me! These are admirable perfumes; they quite overpower one, and destroy one's memory. Good evening, madame."

"Good evening! To-morrow you will perhaps bring me tidings of the admiral."

"Without fail—Well, Phœbe, what is it?"

"Phœbe!" said the queen mother, impatiently.

"Call her, madame," said the Béarnais, "for she will not allow me to go out."

The queen mother rose, took the little greyhound by the collar, and held her while Henry left the apartment, with his features as calm and smiling as if he did not feel in his heart that his life was in imminent peril.

Behind him the little dog, set free by Catharine de Médicis, rushed to try and overtake him, but the door was closed, and Phœbe could only put her long nose under the tapestry and give a long and mournful howl.

"Now, Charlotte," said Catharine to Madame de Sauve, "go and find

Messieurs de Guise and Tavannes, who are in my oratory, and return with them; then remain with the Duchess of Lorraine, who has the vapors."

CHAPTER VII.

THE NIGHT OF THE 24TH OF AUGUST, 1572.

When La Mole and Coconnas had finished their supper—and it was meagre enough, for the fowls of *La Belle Étoile* had their pin feathers singed only on the sign—Coconnas whirled his chair around on one leg, stretched out his feet, leaned one elbow on the table, and drinking a last glass of wine, said:

"Do you mean to go to bed instantly, Monsieur de la Mole?"

"*Ma foi!* I am very much inclined, for it is possible that I may be called up in the night."

"And I, too," said Coconnas; "but it appears to me that, under the circumstances, instead of going to bed and making those wait who are to come to us, we should do better to call for cards and play a game. They would then find us quite ready."

"I would willingly accept your proposal, sir, but I have very little money for play. I have scarce a hundred gold crowns in my valise, for my whole treasure. I rely on that with which to make my fortune!"

"A hundred gold crowns!" cried Coconnas, "and you complain? By Heaven! I have but six!"

"Why," replied La Mole, "I saw you draw from your pocket a purse which appeared not only full, but I should say bloated."

"Ah," said Coconnas, "that is to defray an old debt which I am compelled to pay to an old friend of my father, whom I suspect to be, like yourself, somewhat of a Huguenot. Yes, there are here a hundred rose nobles," he added, slapping his pocket, "but these hundred rose nobles belong to Maître Mercandon. My personal patrimony, as I tell you, is limited to six crowns."

"How, then, can you play?"

"Why, it is because of that I wished to play. Besides, an idea occurs to me."

"What is it?"

"We both came to Paris on the same errand."

"Yes."

"Each of us has a powerful protector."

"Yes."

"You rely on yours, as I rely on mine."

"Yes."

"Well, then, it occurred to me that we should play first for our money, and afterwards for the first favor which came to us, either from the court or from our mistress"—

"Really, a very ingenious idea," said La Mole, with a smile, "but I confess I am not such a gamester as to risk my whole life on a card or a turn of the dice; for the first favor which may come either to you or to me will, in all probability, involve our whole life."

"Well, let us drop out of account the first favor from the court and play for our mistress's first favor."

"I see only one objection to that," said La Mole.

"What objection?"

"I have no mistress!"

"Nor I either. But I expect to have one soon. Thank God! we are not cut out to want one long!"

"Undoubtedly, as you say, you will have your wish, Monsieur de Coconnas, but as I have not the same confidence in my love-star, I feel that it would be robbery, I to pit my fortune against yours. But, if you will, let us play until your six crowns be lost or doubled, and if lost, and you desire to continue the game, you are a gentleman, and your word is as good as gold."

"Well and good!" cried Coconnas, "that's the talk! You are right, sir, a gentleman's word is as good as gold, especially when he has credit at court. Thus, believe me, I did not risk too much when I proposed to play for the first favor we might receive."

"Doubtless, and you might lose it, but I could not gain it; for, as I am with the King of Navarre, I could not receive anything from the Duc de Guise."

"Ah, the heretic!" muttered the landlord as he was at work polishing up his old helmet, "I got on the right scent, did I?" And he stopped his work long

66

enough to cross himself piously.

"Well, then," continued Coconnas, shuffling the cards which the waiter had just brought him, "you are of the"—

"Of the what?"

"Of the new religion."

"I?"

"Yes, you."

"Well, say that I am," said La Mole, with a smile, "have you anything against us?"

"Oh! thank God, no! It is all the same to me. I hate Huguenotry with all my heart, but I do not hate the Huguenots; besides, they are in fashion just now."

"Yes," replied La Mole, smiling; "to wit, the shooting at the admiral with an arquebuse; but supposing we have a game of arquebusades."

"Anything you please," said Coconnas, "provided I get to playing, it is all the same to me."

"Well, let us play, then," said La Mole, picking up his cards and arranging them in his hand.

"Yes, play ahead and with all confidence, for even if I were to lose a hundred crowns of gold against yours I shall have the wherewithal to pay you to-morrow morning."

"Then your fortune will come while you are asleep."

"No; I am going to find it."

"Where? Tell me and I'll go with you."

"At the Louvre."

"Are you going back there to-night?"

"Yes; to-night I have a private audience with the great Duc de Guise."

As soon as Coconnas began to speak about going to seek his fortune at the Louvre, La Hurière stopped polishing his sallet and went and stood behind La Mole's chair, so that Coconnas alone could see him, and made signs to him, which the Piedmontese, absorbed in his game and the conversation, did not notice.

"Well, it is miraculous," remarked La Mole; "and you were right when you said that we were born under the same star. I have also an appointment at the

Louvre to-night, but not with the Duc de Guise; mine is with the King of Navarre."

"Have you a pass-word?"

"Yes."

"A rallying sign?"

"No."

"Well, I have one, and my pass-word is"—

As the Piedmontese was saying these words, La Hurière made such an expressive gesture that the indiscreet gentleman, who happened at that instant to raise his head, paused petrified more by the action than by the turn of the cards which had just caused him to lose three crowns.

La Mole looked around, but saw only his landlord standing behind him with folded arms and wearing on his head the sallet which he had seen him polishing the moment before.

"What is the matter, pray?" inquired La Mole of Coconnas.

Coconnas looked at the landlord and at his companion without answering, for he could make nothing out of Maître La Hurière's redoubled gestures.

La Hurière saw that he must go to his aid:

"It is only that I am very fond of cards myself," said he, speaking rapidly, "and I came closer to see the trick which made you gain, and the gentleman saw me with my war helmet on, and as I am only a poor bourgeois, it surprised him."

"You make a fine figure, indeed you do!" cried La Mole, with a burst of laughter.

"Oh, sir," replied La Hurière with admirably pretended good nature and a shrug of the shoulders expressive of his inferiority, "we poor fellows are not very valiant and our appearance is not elegant. It is all right for you fine gentlemen to wear glittering helmets and carry keen rapiers, and provided we mount guard strictly"—

"Aha!" said La Mole, taking his turn at shuffling the cards. "So you mount guard, do you?"

"*Eh, mon Dieu, oui, Monsieur le Comte!* I am sergeant in a company of citizen militia."

After having said this while La Mole was engaged in dealing the cards, La Hurière withdrew, putting his finger on his lips as a sign of discretion for

Coconnas, who was more amazed than ever.

This signal for caution was doubtless the reason that he lost almost as rapidly the second time as the first.

"Well," observed La Mole, "this makes exactly your six crowns. Will you have your revenge on your future fortune?"

"Willingly," replied Coconnas.

"But before you begin, did you not say you had an appointment with the Duc de Guise?"

Coconnas looked toward the kitchen, and saw the great eyes of La Hurière, who was repeating his warning.

"Yes," he replied, "but it is not yet time. But now let us talk a little about yourself, Monsieur de la Mole."

"We should do better, I think, by talking of the game, my dear Monsieur de Coconnas; for unless I am very much mistaken, I am in a fair way of gaining six more crowns."

"By Heaven! that is true! I always heard that the Huguenots had good luck at cards. Devil take me if I haven't a good mind to turn Huguenot!"

La Hurière's eyes sparkled like two coals; but Coconnas, absorbed in his game, did not notice them. "Do so, count, do so," said La Mole, "and though the way in which the change came about is odd, you will be well received among us."

Coconnas scratched his ear.

"If I were sure that your good luck came from that," he said, "I would; for I really do not stickle so overwhelmingly for the mass, and as the King does not think so much of it either"—

"Then it is such a beautiful religion," said La Mole; "so simple, so pure"—

"And, moreover, it is in fashion," said Coconnas; "and, moreover, it brings good luck at cards; for the devil take me if you do not hold all the aces, and yet I have watched you closely, and you play very fairly; you do not cheat; it must be the religion"—

"You owe me six crowns more," said La Mole, quietly.

"Ah, how you tempt me!" said Coconnas; "and if I am not satisfied with Monsieur de Guise to-night"—

"Well?"

"Well, to-morrow I will ask you to present me to the King of Navarre and, be assured, if once I become a Huguenot, I will out-Huguenot Luther, Calvin, Melanchthon, and all the reformers on earth!"

"Hush!" said La Mole, "you will get into a quarrel with our host."

"Ah, that is true," said Coconnas, looking toward the kitchen; "but—no, he is not listening; he is too much occupied at this moment."

"What is he doing, pray?" inquired La Mole, who could not see him from where he was.

"He is talking with—devil take me! it is he!"

"Who?"

"Why, that night-bird with whom he was discoursing when we arrived. The man in the yellow doublet and drab-colored cloak. By Heaven! how earnestly he talks. Say, Maître La Hurière, are you engaged in politics?"

But this time Maître La Hurière's answer was a gesture so energetic and imperious that in spite of his love for the picture card Coconnas got up and went to him.

"What is the matter with you?" asked La Mole.

"You wish wine, sir?" said La Hurière, seizing Coconnas' hand eagerly. "You shall have it. Grégoire, wine for these gentlemen!"

Then he whispered in his ear:

"Silence, if you value your life, silence! And get rid of your companion."

La Hurière was so pale, the sallow man so lugubrious, that Coconnas felt a shiver run over him, and turning to La Mole said:

"My dear sir, I must beg you to excuse me. I have lost fifty crowns in the turn of a hand. I am in bad luck to-night, and I fear I may get into difficulties."

"Well, sir, as you please," replied La Mole; "besides, I shall not be sorry to lie down for a time. Maître la Hurière!"

"Monsieur le Comte?"

"If any one comes for me from the King of Navarre, wake me; I shall be dressed, and consequently ready."

"So shall I," said Coconnas; "and that I may not keep his highness waiting, I will prepare the sign. Maître la Hurière, some white paper and scissors!"

"Grégoire!" cried La Hurière, "white paper to write a letter on and scissors to cut the envelope with."

"Ah!" said the Piedmontese to himself. "Something extraordinary is going on here!"

"Good-night, Monsieur de Coconnas," said La Mole; "and you, landlord, be so good as to light me to my room. Good luck, my friend!" and La Mole disappeared up the winding staircase, followed by La Hurière.

Then the mysterious man, taking Coconnas by the arm, said to him, speaking very rapidly:

"Sir, you have very nearly betrayed a secret on which depends the fate of a kingdom. God saw fit to have you close your mouth in time. One word more, and I should have brought you down with my arquebuse. Now we are alone, fortunately; listen!"

"But who are you that you address me with this tone of authority?"

"Did you ever hear talk of the Sire de Maurevel?"

"The assassin of the admiral?"

"And of Captain de Mouy."

"Yes."

"Well, I am the Sire de Maurevel."

"Oho!" said Coconnas.

"Now listen to me!"

"By Heaven! I assure you I will listen!"

"Hush!" said Maurevel, putting his finger on his mouth.

Coconnas listened.

At that moment he heard the landlord close the door of a chamber, then the door of a corridor, and bolt it. Then he rushed down the stairs to join the two speakers.

He offered a chair to Coconnas, a chair to Maurevel, and took one for himself.

"All is safe now, Monsieur de Maurevel," said he; "you may speak."

It was striking eleven o'clock at Saint Germain l'Auxerrois. Maurevel counted each of the hammer-strokes as they sounded clear and melancholy through the night, and when the last echo had died away in space he turned to Coconnas, who was greatly mystified at seeing the precautions taken by the two men. "Sir," he asked, "are you a good Catholic?"

"Why, I think I am," replied Coconnas.

"Sir," continued Maurevel, "are you devoted to the King?"

"Heart and soul! I even feel that you insult me, sir, in asking such a question."

"We will not quarrel over that; only you are going to follow us."

"Whither?"

"That is of little consequence—put yourself in our hands; your fortune, and perhaps your life, is at stake."

"I tell you, sir, that at midnight I have an appointment at the Louvre."

"That is where we are going."

"Monsieur de Guise is expecting me there."

"And us also."

"But I have a private pass-word," continued Coconnas, somewhat mortified at sharing with the Sire de Maurevel and Maître La Hurière the honor of his audience.

"So have we."

"But I have a sign of recognition."

Maurevel smiled.

Then he drew from beneath his doublet a handful of crosses in white stuff, gave one to La Hurière, one to Coconnas, and took another for himself. La Hurière fastened his to his helmet. Maurevel attached his to the side of his hat.

"Ah," said Coconnas, amazed, "the appointment and the rallying pass-word were for every one?"

"Yes, sir,—that is to say, for all good Catholics."

"Then there is a festival at the Louvre—some royal banquet, is there not?" said Coconnas; "and it is desired to exclude those hounds of Huguenots,—good, capital, excellent! They have been showing off too long."

"Yes, there is to be a festival at the Louvre—a royal banquet; and the Huguenots are invited; and moreover, they will be the heroes of the festival, and will pay for the banquet, and if you will be one of us, we will begin by going to invite their principal champion—their Gideon, as they call him."

"The admiral!" cried Coconnas.

"Yes, the old Gaspard, whom I missed, like a fool, though I aimed at him with the King's arquebuse."

"And this, my gentleman, is why I was polishing my sallet, sharpening my sword, and putting an edge on my knives," said La Hurière, in a harsh voice consonant with war.

At these words Coconnas shuddered and turned very pale, for he began to understand.

"What, really," he exclaimed, "this festival—this banquet is a—you are going"—

"You have been a long time guessing, sir," said Maurevel, "and it is easy to see that you are not so weary of these insolent heretics as we are."

"And you take on yourself," he said, "to go to the admiral's and to"—

Maurevel smiled, and drawing Coconnas to the window he said:

"Look there!—do you see, in the small square at the end of the street, behind the church, a troop drawn up noiselessly in the shadow?"

"Yes."

"The men forming that troop have, like Maître la Hurière, and myself, and yourself, a cross in their hats."

"Well?"

"Well, these men are a company of Swiss, from the smaller cantons, commanded by Toquenot,—you know the men from the smaller cantons are the King's cronies."

"Oho!" said Coconnas.

"Now look at that troop of horse passing along the Quay—do you recognize their leader?"

"How can I recognize him?" asked Coconnas, with a shudder; "I reached Paris only this evening."

"Well, then, he is the one with whom you have a rendezvous at the Louvre at midnight. See, he is going to wait for you!"

"The Duc de Guise?"

"Himself! His escorts are Marcel, the ex-provost of the tradesmen, and Jean Choron, the present provost. These two are going to summon their companies, and here, down this street comes the captain of the quarter. See what he will

73

do!"

"He knocks at each door; but what is there on the doors at which he knocks?"

"A white cross, young man, such as that which we have in our hats. In days gone by they let God bear the burden of distinguishing his own; now we have grown more civilized and we save him the bother."

"But at each house at which he knocks the door opens and from each house armed citizens come out."

"He will knock here in turn, and we shall in turn go out."

"What," said Coconnas, "every one called out to go and kill one old Huguenot? By Heaven! it is shameful! It is an affair of cut-throats, and not of soldiers."

"Young man," replied Maurevel, "if the old are objectionable to you, you may choose young ones—you will find plenty for all tastes. If you despise daggers, use your sword, for the Huguenots are not the men to allow their throats to be cut without defending themselves, and you know that Huguenots, young or old, are tough."

"But are they all going to be killed, then?" cried Coconnas.

"All!"

"By the King's order?"

"By order of the King and Monsieur de Guise."

"And when?"

"When you hear the bell of Saint Germain l'Auxerrois."

"Oh! so that was why that amiable German attached to the Duc de Guise— what is his name?"

"Monsieur de Besme."

"That is it. That is why Monsieur de Besme told me to hasten at the first sound of the tocsin."

"So then you have seen Monsieur de Besme?"

"I have seen him and spoken to him."

"Where?"

"At the Louvre. He admitted me, gave me the pass-word, gave me"—

"Look there!"

"By Heaven!—there he is himself."

"Would you speak with him?"

"Why, really, I should not object."

Maurevel carefully opened the window; Besme was passing at the moment with twenty soldiers.

"*Guise and Lorraine!*" said Maurevel.

Besme turned round, and perceiving that he himself was addressed, came under the window.

"Oh, is it you, Monsir de Maurefel?"

"Yes, 'tis I; what are you looking for?"

"I am looking for de hostelry of de *Belle Étoile*, to find a Monsir Gogonnas."

"Here I am, Monsieur de Besme," said the young man.

"Goot, goot; are you ready?"

"Yes—to do what?"

"Vatefer Monsieur de Maurefel may dell you, for he is a goot Gatolic."

"Do you hear?" inquired Maurevel.

"Yes," replied Coconnas, "but, Monsieur de Besme, where are you going?"

"I?" asked Monsieur de Besme, with a laugh.

"Yes, you."

"I am going to fire off a leedle wort at the admiral."

"Fire off two, if need be," said Maurevel, "and this time, if he gets up at the first, do not let him get up at the second."

"Haf no vear, Monsir de Maurefel, haf no vear, und meanvile get dis yoong mahn on de right drack."

"Don't worry about me: the Coconnas are regular bloodhounds, and I am a chip off the old block."[2]

"Atieu."

"Go on!"

"Unt you?"

"Begin the hunt; we shall be at the death."

De Besme went on, and Maurevel closed the window.

"Did you hear, young man?" said Maurevel; "if you have any private enemy, even if he is not altogether a Huguenot, you can put him on your list, and he will pass with the others."

Coconnas, more bewildered than ever with what he saw and heard, looked first at his landlord, who was assuming formidable attitudes, and then at Maurevel, who quietly drew a paper from his pocket.

"Here's my list," said he; "three hundred. Let each good Catholic do this night one-tenth part of the business I shall do, and to-morrow there will not remain one single heretic in the kingdom."

"Hush!" said La Hurière.

"What is it?" inquired Coconnas and Maurevel together.

They heard the first pulsation from the bell in Saint Germain l'Auxerrois.

"The signal!" exclaimed Maurevel. "The time is set forward! I was told it was appointed at midnight—so much the better. When it concerns the interest of God and the King, it is better for clocks to be fast than slow!"

In reality they heard the church bell mournfully tolling.

Then a shot was fired, and almost instantly the light of several torches blazed up like flashes of lightning in the Rue de l'Arbre Sec.

Coconnas passed his hand over his brow, which was damp with perspiration.

"It has begun!" cried Maurevel. "Now to work—away!"

"One moment, one moment!" said the landlord. "Before we begin, let us protect the camp, as we say in the army. I do not wish to have my wife and children's throats cut while I am out. There is a Huguenot here."

"Monsieur de la Mole!" said Coconnas, starting.

"Yes, the heretic has thrown himself into the wolf's throat."

"What!" said Coconnas, "would you attack your guest?"

"I gave an extra edge to my rapier for his special benefit."

"Oho!" said the Piedmontese, frowning.

"I never yet killed anything but my rabbits, ducks, and chickens," replied the worthy inn-keeper, "and I do not know very well how to go to work to kill a man; well, I will practise on him, and if I am clumsy, no one will be there to laugh at me."

"By Heaven! it is hard," said Coconnas. "Monsieur de la Mole is my companion; Monsieur de la Mole has supped with me; Monsieur de la Mole has played with me"—

"Yes; but Monsieur de la Mole is a heretic," said Maurevel. "Monsieur de la Mole is doomed; and if we do not kill him, others will."

"Not to say," added the host, "that he has won fifty crowns from you."

"True," said Coconnas; "but fairly, I am sure."

"Fairly or not, you must pay them, while, if I kill him, you are quits."

"Come, come!" cried Maurevel; "make haste, gentlemen, an arquebuse-shot, a rapier-thrust, a blow with a mallet, a stroke with any weapon you please; but get done with it if you wish to reach the admiral's in time to help Monsieur de Guise as we promised."

Coconnas sighed.

"I'll make haste!" cried La Hurière, "wait for me."

"By Heaven!" cried Coconnas, "he will put the poor fellow to great pain, and, perhaps, rob him. I must be present to finish him, if requisite, and to prevent any one from touching his money."

And impelled by this happy thought, Coconnas followed La Hurière upstairs, and soon overtook him, for according as the landlord went up, doubtless as the effect of reflection, he slackened his pace.

As he reached the door, Coconnas still following, many gunshots were discharged in the street. Instantly La Mole was heard to leap out of bed and the flooring creaked under his feet.

"*Diable!*" muttered La Hurière, somewhat disconcerted; "that has awakened him, I think."

"It looks like it," observed Coconnas.

"And he will defend himself."

"He is capable of it. Suppose, now, Maître la Hurière, he were to kill you; that would be droll!"

"Hum, hum!" responded the landlord, but knowing himself to be armed with a good arquebuse, he took courage and dashed the door in with a vigorous kick.

La Mole, without his hat, but dressed, was entrenched behind his bed, his sword between his teeth, and his pistols in his hands.

"Oho!" said Coconnas, his nostrils expanding as if he had been a wild beast smelling blood, "this grows interesting, Maître la Hurière. Forward!"

"Ah, you would assassinate me, it seems!" cried La Mole, with glaring eyes; "and it is you, wretch!"

Maître la Hurière's reply to this was to take aim at the young man with his arquebuse; but La Mole was on his guard, and as he fired, fell on his knees, and the ball flew over his head.

"Help!" cried La Mole; "help, Monsieur de Coconnas!"

"Help, Monsieur de Maurevel!—help!" cried La Hurière.

"*Mafoi!* Monsieur de la Mole," replied Coconnas, "all I can do in this affair is not to join the attack against you. It seems all the Huguenots are to be put to death to-night, in the King's name. Get out of it as well as you can."

"Ah, traitors! assassins!—is it so? Well, then, take this!" and La Mole, aiming in his turn, fired one of his pistols. La Hurière, who had kept his eye on him, dodged to one side; but Coconnas, not anticipating such a reply, stayed where he was, and the bullet grazed his shoulder.

"By Heaven!" he exclaimed, grinding his teeth; "I have it. Well, then, let it be we two, since you will have it so!"

And drawing his rapier, he rushed on La Mole.

Had he been alone La Mole would, doubtless, have awaited his attack; but Coconnas had La Hurière to aid him, who was reloading his gun, and Maurevel, who, responding to the innkeeper's invitation, was rushing up-stairs four steps at a time.

La Mole, therefore, dashed into a small closet, which he bolted inside.

"Ah, coward!" cried Coconnas, furious, and striking at the door with the pommel of his sword; "wait! wait! and I will make as many holes in your body as you have gained crowns of me to-night. I came up to prevent you from suffering! Oh, I came up to prevent you from being robbed and you pay me back by putting a bullet into my shoulder! Wait for me, coward, wait!"

While this was going on, Maître la Hurière came up and with one blow with the butt-end of his arquebuse smashed in the door.

Coconnas darted into the closet, but only bare walls met him. The closet was empty and the window was open.

"He must have jumped out," said the landlord, "and as we are on the fourth story, he is surely dead."

"Or he has escaped by the roof of the next house," said Coconnas, putting his leg on the window-sill and preparing to follow him over this narrow and slippery route; but Maurevel and La Hurière seized him and drew him back into the room.

"Are you mad?" they both exclaimed at once; "you will kill yourself!"

"Bah!" said Coconnas, "I am a mountaineer, and used to climbing glaciers; besides, when a man has once offended me, I would go up to heaven or descend to hell with him, by whatever route he pleases. Let me do as I wish."

"Well," said Maurevel, "he is either dead or a long way off by this time. Come with us; and if he escape you, you will find a thousand others to take his place."

"You are right," cried Coconnas. "Death to the Huguenots! I want revenge, and the sooner the better."

And the three rushed down the staircase, like an avalanche.

"To the admiral's!" shouted Maurevel.

"To the admiral's!" echoed La Hurière.

"To the admiral's, then, if it must be so!" cried Coconnas in his turn.

And all three, leaving the *Belle Étoile* in charge of Grégoire and the other waiters, hastened toward the admiral's hôtel in the Rue de Béthizy; a bright light and the report of fire-arms guided them in that direction.

"Ah, who comes here?" cried Coconnas. "A man without his doublet or scarf!"

"It is some one escaping," said Maurevel.

"Fire! fire!" said Coconnas; "you who have arquebuses."

"Faith, not I," replied Maurevel. "I keep my powder for better game."

"You, then, La Hurière!"

"Wait, wait!" said the innkeeper, taking aim.

"Oh, yes, wait," cried Coconnas, "and meantime he will escape."

And he rushed after the unhappy wretch, whom he soon overtook, as he was wounded; but at the moment when, in order that he might not strike him behind, he exclaimed, "Turn, will you! turn!" the report of an arquebuse was heard, a bullet whistled by Coconnas's ears, and the fugitive rolled over, like a hare in its swiftest flight struck by the shot of the sportsman.

A cry of triumph was heard behind Coconnas. The Piedmontese turned round and saw La Hurière brandishing his weapon.

"Ah," he exclaimed, "I have handselled this time at any rate."

"And only just missed making a hole quite through me."

"Be on your guard!—be on your guard!" cried La Hurière.

Coconnas sprung back. The wounded man had risen on his knee, and, eager for revenge, was just on the point of stabbing him with his poniard, when the landlord's warning put the Piedmontese on his guard.

"Ah, viper!" shouted Coconnas; and rushing at the wounded man, he thrust his sword through him three times up to the hilt.

"And now," cried he, leaving the Huguenot in the agonies of death, "to the admiral's!—to the admiral's!"

"Aha! my gentlemen," said Maurevel, "it seems to work."

"Faith! yes," replied Coconnas. "I do not know if it is the smell of gunpowder makes me drunk, or the sight of blood excites me, but by Heaven! I am thirsty for slaughter. It is like a battue of men. I have as yet only had battues of bears and wolves, and on my honor, a battue of men seems more amusing."

And the three went on their way.

CHAPTER VIII.

THE MASSACRE.

The hôtel occupied by the admiral, as we have said, was situated in the Rue de Béthizy. It was a great mansion at the rear of a court and had two wings giving on the street. A wall furnished with a large gate and two small grilled doors stretched from wing to wing.

When our three Guisards reached the end of the Rue de Béthizy, which is a continuation of the Rue des Fossés Saint Germain l'Auxerrois, they saw the hôtel surrounded by Swiss, by soldiers, and by armed citizens; every one had in his right hand either a sword or a pike or an arquebuse, and some held in their left hands torches, shedding over the scene a fitful and melancholy glare which, according as the throng moved, shifted along the street, climbed the walls; or spread over that living sea where every weapon cast its answering flash.

All around the hôtel and in the Rues Tirechappe, Étienne, and Bertin Poirée the terrible work was proceeding. Long shouts were heard, there was an incessant rattle of musketry, and from time to time some wretch, half naked, pale, and drenched in blood, leaped like a hunted stag into the circle of lugubrious light where a host of fiends seemed to be at work.

In an instant Coconnas, Maurevel, and La Hurière, accredited by their white crosses, and received with cries of welcome, were in the thickest of this struggling, panting mob. Doubtless they would not have been able to advance had not some of the throng recognized Maurevel and made way for him. Coconnas and La Hurière followed him closely and the three therefore contrived to get into the court-yard.

In the centre of this court-yard, the three doors of which had been burst open, a man, around whom the assassins formed a respectful circle, stood leaning on his drawn rapier, and eagerly looking up at a balcony about fifteen feet above him, and extending in front of the principal window of the hôtel.

This man stamped impatiently on the ground, and from time to time questioned those that were nearest to him.

"Nothing yet!" murmured he. "No one!—he must have been warned and has escaped. What do you think, Du Gast?"

"Impossible, monseigneur."

"Why? Did you not tell me that just before we arrived a man, bare-headed, a drawn sword in his hand, came running, as if pursued, knocked at the door, and was admitted?"

"Yes, monseigneur; but M. de Besme came up immediately, the gates were shattered, and the hôtel was surrounded."

"The man went in sure enough, but he has not gone out."

"Why," said Coconnas to La Hurière, "if my eyes do not deceive me, I see Monsieur de Guise."

"You do see him, sir. Yes; the great Henry de Guise is come in person to watch for the admiral and serve him as he served the duke's father. Every one has his day, and it is our turn now."

"Holà, Besme, holà!" cried the duke, in his powerful voice, "have you not finished yet?"

And he struck his sword so forcibly against the stones that sparks flew out.

At this instant shouts were heard in the hôtel—then several shots—then a great shuffling of feet and a clashing of swords, and then all was again silent.

The duke was about to rush into the house.

"Monseigneur, monseigneur!" said Du Gast, detaining him, "your dignity commands you to wait here."

"You are right, Du Gast. I must stay here; but I am dying with impatience and anxiety. If he were to escape me!"

Suddenly the noise of feet came nearer—the windows of the first floor were lighted up with what seemed the reflection of a conflagration.

The window, to which the duke's eyes had been so many times lifted, opened, or, rather, was shattered to pieces, and a man, his pale face and white neck stained with blood, appeared on the balcony.

"Ah! at last, Besme!" cried the duke; "speak! speak!"

"Louk! louk!" replied the German coldly, and stooping down he lifted up something which seemed like a heavy body.

"But where are the others?" asked the duke, impatiently, "where are the others?"

"De udders are vinishing de udders!"

"And what have you done?"

"Vait! You shall peholt! Shtant pack a liddle."

The duke fell back a step.

At that instant the object Besme was dragging toward him with such effort became visible.

It was the body of an old man.

He lifted it above the balcony, held it suspended an instant, and then flung it down at his master's feet.

The heavy thud, the billows of blood spurting from the body and spattering the pavement all around, filled even the duke himself with horror; but this feeling lasted only an instant, and curiosity caused every one to crowd forward, so that the glare of the torches flickered on the victim's body.

They could see a white beard, a venerable face, and limbs contracted by death.

"The admiral!" cried twenty voices, as instantaneously hushed.

"Yes, the admiral, here he is!" said the duke, approaching the corpse, and contemplating it with silent ecstasy.

"The admiral! the admiral!" repeated the witnesses of this terrible scene, crowding together and timidly approaching the old man, majestic even in death.

"Ah, at last, Gaspard!" said the Duke de Guise, triumphantly. "Murderer of my father! thus do I avenge him!"

And the duke dared to plant his foot on the breast of the Protestant hero.

But instantly the dying warrior opened his eyes, his bleeding and mutilated hand was clinched for the last time, and the admiral, though without stirring, said to the duke in a sepulchral voice:

"Henry de Guise, some day the assassin's foot shall be felt on your breast. I did not kill your father. A curse upon you."

The duke, pale, and trembling in spite of himself, felt a cold shudder come over him. He passed his hand across his brow, as if to dispel the fearful vision; when he dared again to glance at the admiral his eyes were closed, his hand unclinched, and a stream of black blood was flowing from the mouth which had just pronounced such terrible words.

The duke raised his sword with a gesture of desperate resolution.

"Vell, monsir, are you gondent?"

"Yes, my worthy friend, yes, for you have revenged"—

"The Dugue François, haf I not?"

"Our religion," replied Henry, in a solemn voice. "And now," he went on, addressing the Swiss, the soldiers, and citizens who filled the court and street, "to work, my friends, to work!"

"Good evening, M. de Besme," said Coconnas with a sort of admiration, approaching the German, who still stood on the balcony, calmly wiping his sword.

"So you settled him, did you?" cried La Hurière; "how did you manage it?"

"Oh, zimbly, zimbly; he haf heerd de gommotion, he haf oben de door unt I joost brick my rabier troo his potty. But I tink dey am gilling Téligny now. I hear his gries!"

At that instant, in fact, several shrieks, apparently uttered by a woman in distress, were heard; the windows of the long gallery which formed a wing of the hotel were lighted up with a red glare; two men were seen fleeing, pursued by a long line of assassins. An arquebuse-shot killed one; the other, finding an open window directly in his way, without stopping to look at the distance from the ground, sprang boldly into the courtyard below, heeding not the enemies who awaited him there.

"Kill! kill!" cried the assassins, seeing their prey about to escape them.

The fugitive picked up his sword, which as he stumbled had fallen from his hand, dashed headlong through the soldiers, upset three or four, ran one through the body, and amid the pistol-shots and curses of the soldiers, rendered furious because they had missed him, darted like lightning in front of Coconnas, who was waiting for him at the gate with his poniard in his hand.

"Touched!" cried the Piedmontese, piercing his arm with his keen, delicate blade.

"Coward!" replied the fugitive, striking his enemy in the face with the flat of his weapon, for want of room to thrust at him with its point.

"A thousand devils!" cried Coconnas; "it's Monsieur de la Mole!"

"Monsieur de la Mole!" reëchoed La Hurière and Maurevel.

"He is the one who warned the admiral!" cried several soldiers.

"Kill him—kill him!" was shouted on all sides.

Coconnas, La Hurière, and a dozen soldiers rushed in pursuit of La Mole, who, covered with blood, and having attained that state of exaltation which is the last resource of human strength, dashed through the streets, with no other guide than instinct. Behind him, the footsteps and shouts of his enemies spurred him on and seemed to give him wings. Occasionally a bullet would whistle by his ears and suddenly add new swiftness to his flight just as it was beginning to slacken. He no longer breathed; it was not breath, but a dull rattle, a hoarse panting, that came from his chest. Perspiration and blood wet his locks and ran together down his face.

His doublet soon became too oppressive for the beating of his heart and he tore it off. Soon his sword became too heavy for his hand and he flung it far away. Sometimes it seemed to him that the footsteps of his pursuers were farther off and that he was about to escape them; but in response to their shouts, other murderers who were along his path and nearer to him left off their bloody occupations and started in pursuit of him.

Suddenly he caught sight of the river flowing silently at his left; it seemed to him that he should feel, like a stag at bay, an ineffable pleasure in plunging into it, and only the supreme power of reason could restrain him.

On his right was the Louvre, dark and motionless, but full of strange and ominous sounds; soldiers on the drawbridge came and went, and helmets and cuirasses glittered in the moonlight. La Mole thought of the King of Navarre, as he had before thought of Coligny; they were his only protectors. He collected all his strength, and inwardly vowing to abjure his faith should he escape the massacre, by making a detour of a score or two of yards he misled the mob pursuing him, darted straight for the Louvre, leaped upon the drawbridge among the soldiers, received another poniard stab which grazed his side, and despite the cries of "Kill—kill!" which resounded on all sides, and the opposing weapons of the sentinels, darted like an arrow through the court, into the vestibule, mounted the staircase, then up two stories higher, recognized a door, and leaning against it, struck it violently with his hands and feet.

"Who is there?" asked a woman's voice.

"Oh, my God!" murmured La Mole; "they are coming, I hear them; 'tis I —'tis I!"

"Who are you?" said the voice.

La Mole recollected the pass-word.

"Navarre—Navarre!" cried he.

The door instantly opened. La Mole, without thanking, without even seeing Gillonne, dashed into the vestibule, then along a corridor, through two or three chambers, until at last he entered a room lighted by a lamp suspended from the ceiling.

Behind curtains of velvet with gold fleurs-de-lis, in a bed of carved oak, a lady, half naked, leaning on her arm, stared at him with eyes wide open with terror.

La Mole sprang toward her.

"Madame," cried he, "they are killing, they are butchering my brothers—they seek to kill me, to butcher me also! Ah! you are the queen—save me!"

And he threw himself at her feet, leaving on the carpet a large track of blood.

At the sight of a man pale, exhausted, and bleeding at her feet, the Queen of Navarre started up in terror, hid her face in her hands, and called for help.

"Madame," cried La Mole, endeavoring to rise, "in the name of Heaven do not call, for if you are heard I am lost! Assassins are in my track—they are rushing up the stairs behind me. I hear them—there they are! there they are!"

"Help!" cried the queen, beside herself, "help!"

"Ah!" said La Mole, despairingly, "you have killed me. To die by so sweet a voice, so fair a hand! I did not think it possible."

At the same time the door flew open, and a troop of men, their faces covered with blood and blackened with powder, their swords drawn, and their pikes and arquebuses levelled, rushed into the apartment.

Coconnas was at their head—his red hair bristling, his pale blue eyes extraordinarily dilated, his cheek cut open by La Mole's sword, which had ploughed its bloody furrow there. Thus disfigured, the Piedmontese was terrible to behold.

"By Heaven!" he cried, "there he is! there he is! Ah! this time we have him at last!"

La Mole looked round him for a weapon, but in vain; he glanced at the queen, and saw the deepest pity depicted in her face; then he felt that she alone could save him; he threw his arms round her.

Coconnas advanced, and with the point of his long rapier again wounded his enemy's shoulder, and the crimson drops of warm blood stained the white and perfumed sheets of Marguerite's couch.

Marguerite saw the blood flow; she felt the shudder that ran through La Mole's frame; she threw herself with him into the recess between the bed and the wall. It was time, for La Mole, whose strength was exhausted, was incapable of flight or resistance; he leaned his pallid head on Marguerite's shoulder, and his hand convulsively seized and tore the thin embroidered cambric which enveloped Marguerite's body in a billow of gauze.

"Oh, madame," murmured he, in a dying voice, "save me."

He could say no more. A mist like the darkness of death came over his eyes, his head sunk back, his arms fell at his side, his legs gave way, and he sank on the floor, bathed in his blood, and dragging the queen with him.

At this moment Coconnas, excited by the shouts, intoxicated by the sight of blood, and exasperated by the long chase, advanced toward the recess; in another instant his sword would have pierced La Mole's heart, and perhaps Marguerite's also.

At the sight of the bare steel, and even more moved at such brutal insolence, the daughter of kings drew herself up to her full stature and uttered such a shriek of terror, indignation, and rage that the Piedmontese stood petrified by an unknown feeling; and yet undoubtedly had this scene been prolonged and no other actor taken part in it, his feeling would have vanished like a morning snow under an April sun. But suddenly a secret door in the wall opened, and a pale young man of sixteen or seventeen, dressed in black and with his hair in disorder, rushed in.

"Wait, sister!" he cried; "here I am, here I am!"

"François! François!" cried Marguerite; "help! help!"

"The Duc d'Alençon!" murmured La Hurière, grounding his arquebuse.

"By Heaven! a son of France!" growled Coconnas, drawing back.

The duke glanced round him. He saw Marguerite, dishevelled, more lovely than ever, leaning against the wall, surrounded by men, fury in their eyes, sweat on their foreheads, and foam in their mouths.

"Wretches!" cried he.

"Save me, brother!" shrieked Marguerite. "They are going to kill me!"

A flame flashed across the duke's pallid face.

He was unarmed, but sustained, no doubt, by the consciousness of his rank, he advanced with clinched fists toward Coconnas and his companions, who retreated, terrified at the lightning darting from his eyes.

"Ha! and will you murder a son of France, too?" cried the duke. Then, as they recoiled,—"Ho, there! captain of the guard! Hang every one of these ruffians!"

More alarmed at the sight of this weaponless young man than he would have been at the aspect of a regiment of reiters or lansquenets, Coconnas had already reached the door. La Hurière was leaping downstairs like a deer, and the soldiers were jostling and pushing one another in the vestibule in their endeavors to escape, finding the door far too small for their great desire to be outside it. Meantime Marguerite had instinctively thrown the damask coverlid of her bed over La Mole, and withdrawn from him.

When the last murderer had departed the Duc d'Alençon came back:

"Sister," he cried, seeing Marguerite all dabbled with blood, "are you wounded?" And he sprang toward his sister with a solicitude which would have done credit to his affection if he had not been charged with harboring too deep an affection for a brother to entertain for a sister.

"No," said she; "I think not, or, if so, very slightly."

"But this blood," said the duke, running his trembling hands all over Marguerite's body. "Where does it come from?"

"I know not," replied she; "one of those wretches laid his hand on me, and perhaps he was wounded."

"What!" cried the duke, "he dared to touch my sister? Oh, if you had only pointed him out to me, if you had told me which one it was, if I knew where to find him"—

"Hush!" said Marguerite.

"And why?" asked François.

"Because if you were seen at this time of night in my room"—

"Can't a brother visit his sister, Marguerite?"

The queen gave the duke a look so keen and yet so threatening that the young man drew back.

"Yes, yes, Marguerite," said he, "you are right, I will go to my room; but you cannot remain alone this dreadful night. Shall I call Gillonne?"

"No, no! leave me, François—leave me. Go by the way you came!"

The young prince obeyed; and hardly had he disappeared when Marguerite, hearing a sigh from behind her bed, hurriedly bolted the door of the secret passage, and then hastening to the other entrance closed it in the same way, just as a troop of archers and soldiers like a hurricane dashed by in hot chase of some other Huguenot residents in the Louvre.

After glancing round to assure herself that she was really alone, she again went to the "ruelle" of her bed, lifted the damask covering which had concealed La Mole from the Duc d'Alençon, and drawing the apparently lifeless body, by great exertion, into the middle of the room, and finding that the victim still breathed, sat down, placed his head on her knees, and sprinkled his face with water.

Then as the water cleared away the mask of blood, dust, and gunpowder which had covered his face, Marguerite recognized the handsome cavalier who, full of life and hope, had three or four hours before come to ask her to look out for his interests with her protection and that of the King of Navarre; and had gone away, dazzled by her beauty, leaving her also impressed by his.

Marguerite uttered a cry of terror, for now what she felt for the wounded man was more than mere pity—it was interest. He was no longer a mere stranger: he was almost an acquaintance. By her care La Mole's fine features soon reappeared, free from stain, but pale and distorted by pain. A shudder ran through her whole frame as she tremblingly placed her hand on his heart. It was still beating. Then she took a smelling-bottle from the table, and applied it to his nostrils.

La Mole opened his eyes.

"Oh! *mon Dieu!*" murmured he; "where am I?"

"Saved!" said Marguerite. "Reassure yourself—you are saved."

La Mole turned his eyes on the queen, gazed earnestly for a moment, and murmured,

"Oh, how beautiful you are!"

Then as if the vision were too much for him, he closed his lids and drew a sigh.

Marguerite started. He had become still paler than before, if that were possible, and for an instant that sigh was his last.

"Oh, my God! my God!" she ejaculated, "have pity on him!"

At this moment a violent knocking was heard at the door. Marguerite half raised herself, still supporting La Mole.

"Who is there?" she cried.

"Madame, it is I—it is I," replied a woman's voice, "the Duchesse de Nevers."

"Henriette!" cried Marguerite. "There is no danger; it is a friend of mine! Do you hear, sir?"

La Mole with some effort got up on one knee.

"Try to support yourself while I go and open the door," said the queen.

La Mole rested his hand on the floor and succeeded in holding himself upright.

Marguerite took one step toward the door, but suddenly stopped, shivering with terror.

"Ah, you are not alone!" she said, hearing the clash of arms outside.

"No, I have twelve guards which my brother-in-law, Monsieur de Guise, assigned me."

"Monsieur de Guise!" murmured La Mole. "The assassin—the assassin!"

"Silence!" said Marguerite. "Not a word!"

And she looked round to see where she could conceal the wounded man.

"A sword! a dagger!" muttered La Mole.

"To defend yourself—useless! Did you not hear? There are twelve of them, and you are alone."

"Not to defend myself, but that I may not fall alive into their hands."

"No, no!" said Marguerite. "No, I will save you. Ah! this cabinet! Come! come."

La Mole made an effort, and, supported by Marguerite, dragged himself to the cabinet. Marguerite locked the door upon him, and hid the key in her alms-purse.

"Not a cry, not a groan, not a sigh," whispered she, through the panelling, "and you are saved."

Then hastily throwing a night-robe over her shoulders, she opened the door for her friend, who tenderly embraced her.

"Ah!" cried Madame Nevers, "then nothing has happened to you, madame!"

"No, nothing at all," replied Marguerite, wrapping the mantle still more closely round her to conceal the spots of blood on her peignoir.

"'Tis well. However, as Monsieur de Guise has given me twelve of his guards to escort me to his hôtel, and as I do not need such a large company, I am going to leave six with your majesty. Six of the duke's guards are worth a regiment of the King's to-night."

Marguerite dared not refuse; she placed the soldiers in the corridor, and embraced the duchess, who then returned to the Hôtel de Guise, where she resided in her husband's absence.

CHAPTER IX.

THE MURDERERS.

Coconnas had not fled, he had retreated; La Hurière had not fled, he had flown. The one had disappeared like a tiger, the other like a wolf.

The consequence was that La Hurière had already reached the Place Saint Germain l'Auxerrois when Coconnas was only just leaving the Louvre.

La Hurière, finding himself alone with his arquebuse, while around him men were running, bullets were whistling, and bodies were falling from windows, —some whole, others dismembered,—began to be afraid and was prudently thinking of returning to his tavern, but as he turned into the Rue de l'Arbre Sec from the Rue d'Averon he fell in with a troop of Swiss and light cavalry: it was the one commanded by Maurevel.

"Well," cried Maurevel, who had christened himself with the nickname of King's Killer, "have you finished so soon? Are you going back to your tavern, worthy landlord? And what the devil have you done with our Piedmontese gentleman? No misfortune has happened to him? That would be a shame, for he started out well."

"No, I think not," replied La Hurière; "I hope he will rejoin us!"

"Where have you been?"

"At the Louvre, and I must say we were very rudely treated there."

"By whom?"

"Monsieur le Duc d'Alençon. Isn't he interested in this affair?"

"Monseigneur le Duc d'Alençon is not interested in anything which does not concern himself personally. Propose to treat his two older brothers as Huguenots and he would be in it—provided only that the work should be done without compromising him. But won't you go with these worthy fellows, Maître La Hurière?"

"And where are they going?"

"Oh, *mon Dieu*! Rue Montorguen; there is a Huguenot minister there whom I know; he has a wife and six children. These heretics are enormous breeders; it will be interesting."

"And where are you going?"

"Oh, I have a little private business."

"Say, there! don't go off without me," said a voice which made Maurevel start, "you know all the good places and I want to have my share."

"Ah! it is our Piedmontese," said Maurevel.

"Yes, it is Monsieur de Coconnas," said La Hurière; "I thought you were following me."

"Hang it! you made off too swiftly for that; and besides I turned a little to one side so as to fling into the river a frightful child who was screaming, 'Down with the Papists! Long live the admiral!' Unfortunately, I believe the little rascal knew how to swim. These miserable heretics must be flung into the water like cats before their eyes are opened if they are to be drowned at all."

"Ah! you say you are just from the Louvre; so your Huguenot took refuge there, did he?" asked Maurevel.

"*Mon Dieu!* yes."

"I gave him a pistol-shot at the moment when he was picking up his sword in the admiral's court-yard, but I somehow or other missed him."

"Well, I did not miss him," added Coconnas; "I gave him such a thrust in the back that my sword was wet five inches up the blade. Besides, I saw him fall into the arms of Madame Marguerite, a pretty woman, by Heaven! yet I confess I should not be sorry to hear he was really dead; the vagabond is infernally spiteful, and capable of bearing me a grudge all his life. But didn't you say you were bound somewhere?"

"Why, do you mean to go with me?"

"I do not like standing still, by Heaven! I have killed only three or four as yet, and when I get cold my shoulder pains me. Forward! forward!"

"Captain," said Maurevel to the commander of the troop, "give me three men, and go and despatch your parson with the rest."

Three Swiss stepped forward and joined Maurevel. Nevertheless, the two companies proceeded side by side till they reached the top of the Rue Tirechappe; there the light horse and the Swiss took the Rue de la Tonnellerie, while Maurevel, Coconnas, La Hurière, and his three men were proceeding down the Rue Trousse Vache and entering the Rue Sainte Avoye. "Where the devil are you taking us?" asked Coconnas, who was beginning to be bored by this long march from which he could see no results.

"I am taking you on an expedition at once brilliant and useful. Next to the admiral, next to Téligny, next to the Huguenot princes, I could offer you nothing better. So have patience, our business calls us to the Rue du Chaume, and we shall be there in a second."

"Tell me," said Coconnas, "is not the Rue du Chaume near the Temple?"

"Yes, why?"

"Because an old creditor of our family lives there, one Lambert Mercandon, to whom my father wished me to hand over a hundred rose nobles I have in my pocket for that purpose."

"Well," replied Maurevel, "this is a good opportunity for paying it. This is the day for settling old accounts. Is your Mercandon a Huguenot?"

"Oho, I understand!" said Coconnas; "he must be"—

"Hush! here we are."

"What is that large hôtel, with its entrance in the street?"

"The Hôtel de Guise."

"Truly," returned Coconnas, "I should not have failed to come here, as I am under the patronage of the great Henry. But, by Heaven! all is so very quiet in this quarter, we scarcely hear any firing, and we might fancy ourselves in the country. The devil fetch me but every one is asleep!"

And indeed the Hôtel de Guise seemed as quiet as in ordinary times. All the windows were closed, and a solitary light was burning behind the blind of the principal window over the entrance which had attracted Coconnas's attention as soon as they entered the street.

Just beyond the Hôtel de Guise, in other words, at the corner of the Rue du Petit Chantier and the Rue des Quatre Fils, Maurevel halted.

93

"Here is the house of the man we want," said he.

"Of the man you want—that is to say"—observed La Hurière.

"Since you are with me we want him."

"What! that house which seems so sound asleep"—

"Exactly! La Hurière, now go and make practical use of the plausible face which heaven, by some blunder, gave you, and knock at that house. Hand your arquebuse to M. de Coconnas, who has been ogling it this last half hour. If you are admitted, you must ask to speak to Seigneur de Mouy."

"Aha!" exclaimed Coconnas, "now I understand—you also have a creditor in the quarter of the Temple, it would seem."

"Exactly so!" responded Maurevel. "You will go up to him pretending to be a Huguenot, and inform De Mouy of all that has taken place; he is brave, and will come down."

"And once down?" asked La Hurière.

"Once down, I will beg of him to cross swords with me."

"On my soul, 'tis a fine gentleman's," said Coconnas, "and I propose to do exactly the same thing with Lambert Mercandon; and if he is too old to respond, I will try it with one of his sons or nephews."

La Hurière, without making any reply, went and knocked at the door, and the sounds echoing in the silence of the night caused the doors of the Hôtel de Guise to open, and several heads to make their appearance from out them; it was evident that the hôtel was quiet after the manner of citadels, that is to say, because it was filled with soldiers.

The heads were almost instantly withdrawn, as doubtless an inkling of the matter in hand was divined.

"Does your Monsieur de Mouy live here?" inquired Coconnas, pointing to the house at which La Hurière was still knocking.

"No, but his mistress does."

"By Heaven! how gallant you are, to give him an occasion to draw sword in the presence of his lady-love! We shall be the judges of the field. However, I should like very well to fight myself—my shoulder burns."

"And your face," added Maurevel, "is considerably damaged."

Coconnas uttered a kind of growl.

"By Heaven!" he said, "I hope he is dead; if I thought not, I would return to the Louvre and finish him."

La Hurière still kept knocking.

Soon the window on the first floor opened, and a man appeared in the balcony, in a nightcap and drawers, and unarmed.

"Who's there?" cried he.

Maurevel made a sign to the Swiss, who retreated into a corner, whilst Coconnas stood close against the wall.

"Ah! Monsieur de Mouy!" said the innkeeper, in his blandest tones, "is that you?"

"Yes; what then?"

"It is he!" said Maurevel, with a thrill of joy.

"Why, sir," continued La Hurière, "do you not know what is going on? They are murdering the admiral, and massacring all of our religion. Hasten to their assistance; come!"

"Ah!" exclaimed De Mouy, "I feared something was plotted for this night. I ought not to have deserted my worthy comrades. I will come, my friend,—wait for me."

And without closing the window, through which a frightened woman could be heard uttering lamentations and tender entreaties, Monsieur de Mouy got his doublet, his mantle, and his weapons.

"He is coming down! He is coming down!" muttered Maurevel, pale with joy. "Attention, the rest of you!" he whispered to the Swiss.

Then taking the arquebuse from Coconnas he blew on the tinder to make sure that it was still alight.

"Here, La Hurière," he added, addressing the innkeeper, who had rejoined the main body of the company, "here, take your arquebuse!"

"By Heaven!" exclaimed Coconnas, "the moon is coming out of the clouds to witness this beautiful fight. I would give a great deal if Lambert Mercandon were here, to serve as Monsieur de Mouy's second."

"Wait, wait!" said Maurevel; "Monsieur de Mouy alone is equal to a dozen men, and it is likely that we six shall have enough to do to despatch him. Forward, my men!" continued Maurevel, making a sign to the Swiss to stand by the door, in order to strike De Mouy as he came forth.

"Oho!" said Coconnas, as he watched these arrangements; "it appears that this will not come off quite as I expected."

Already the noise made by De Mouy in withdrawing the bar was heard. The Swiss had left their hiding-place to arrange themselves near the door, Maurevel and La Hurière were going forward on tiptoe, and Coconnas with a dying gleam of gentlemanly feeling was standing where he was, when the young woman who had been for the moment utterly forgotten suddenly appeared on the balcony and uttered a terrible shriek at the sight of the Swiss, Maurevel, and La Hurière.

De Mouy, who had already half opened the door, paused.

"Come back! come back!" cried the young woman. "I see swords glitter, and the match of an arquebuse—there is treachery!"

"Oho!" said the young man; "let us see, then, what all this means."

And he closed the door, replaced the bar, and went upstairs again.

Maurevel's order of battle was changed as soon as he saw that De Mouy was not going to come out. The Swiss went and posted themselves at the other corner of the street, and La Hurière, with his arquebuse in his hand, waited till the enemy reappeared at the window.

He did not wait long. De Mouy came forward holding before him two pistols of such respectable length that La Hurière, who was already aiming, suddenly reflected that the Huguenot's bullets had no farther to fly in reaching the street from the balcony than his had in reaching the balcony.

"Assuredly," said he to himself, "I may kill this gentleman, but likewise this gentleman may kill me in the same way."

Now as Maître La Hurière, an innkeeper by profession, was only accidentally a soldier, this reflection determined him to retreat and seek shelter in the corner of the Rue de Braque, far enough away to cause him some difficulty in finding with a certain certainty, especially at night, the line which a bullet from his arquebuse would take in reaching De Mouy.

De Mouy cast a glance around him, and advanced cautiously like a man preparing to fight a duel; but seeing nothing, he exclaimed:

"Why, it appears, my worthy informant, that you have forgotten your arquebuse at my door! Here I am. What do you want with me?"

"Aha!" said Coconnas to himself; "he is certainly a brave fellow!"

"Well," continued De Mouy, "friends or enemies, whichever you are, do you not see I am waiting?"

La Hurière kept silence, Maurevel made no reply, and the three Swiss remained in covert.

Coconnas waited an instant; then, seeing that no one took part in the conversation begun by La Hurière and continued by De Mouy, he left his station, and advancing into the middle of the street, took off his hat and said:

"Sir, we are not here for an assassination, as you seem to suppose, but for a duel. I am here with one of your enemies, who was desirous of meeting you to end gallantly an old controversy. Eh, by Heaven! come forward, Monsieur de Maurevel, instead of turning your back. The gentleman accepts."

"Maurevel!" cried De Mouy; "Maurevel, the assassin of my father! Maurevel, the king's assassin! Ah, by Heaven! Yes, I accept."

And taking aim at Maurevel, who was about to knock at the Hôtel de Guise to request a reinforcement, he sent a bullet through his hat.

At the noise of the report and Maurevel's shouts, the guard which had escorted the Duchesse de Nevers came out, accompanied by three or four gentlemen, followed by their pages, and approached the house of young De Mouy's mistress.

A second pistol-shot, fired into the midst of the troop, killed the soldier next to Maurevel; after which De Mouy, finding himself weaponless, or at least with useless weapons, for his pistols had been fired and his adversaries were beyond the reach of his sword, took shelter behind the balcony gallery.

Meantime here and there windows began to be thrown open in the neighborhood, and according to the pacific or bellicose dispositions of their inhabitants, were barricaded or bristled with muskets and arquebuses.

"Help! my worthy Mercandon," shouted De Mouy, beckoning to an elderly man who, from a window which had just been thrown open in front of the Hôtel de Guise, was trying to make out the cause of the confusion.

"Is it you who call, Sire de Mouy?" cried the old man: "are they attacking you?"

"Me—you—all the Protestants; and wait—there is the proof!"

That moment De Mouy had seen La Hurière aim his arquebuse at him; it was fired; but the young man had time to stoop, and the ball broke a window above his head.

"Mercandon!" exclaimed Coconnas, who, in his delight at sight of this fray, had forgotten his creditor, but was reminded of him by De Mouy's apostrophe; "Mercandon, Rue du Chaume—that is it! Ah, he lives there! Good! Each of us will settle accounts with our man."

And, while the people from the Hôtel de Guise were breaking in the doors of De Mouy's house, and Maurevel, with a torch in his hand, was trying to set it on fire—while now that the doors were once broken, there was a fearful struggle with a single antagonist who at each rapier-thrust brought down his foe—Coconnas tried, by the help of a paving-stone, to break in Mercandon's door, and the latter, unmoved by this solitary effort, was doing his best with his arquebuse out of his window.

And now all this dark and deserted quarter was lighted up, as if by open day, —peopled like the interior of an ant-hive; for from the Hôtel de Montmorency six or eight Huguenot gentlemen, with their servants and friends, had just made a furious charge, and, supported by the firing from the windows, were beginning to repulse Maurevel's and the De Guises' force, who at length were driven back to the place whence they had come.

Coconnas, who had not yet succeeded in smashing Mercandon's door, though he was working at it with all his might, was caught in this sudden retreat. Placing his back to the wall, and grasping his sword firmly, he began not only to defend himself, but to attack his assailants, with cries so terrible that they were heard above all the uproar. He struck right and left, hitting friends and enemies, until a wide space was cleared around him. As his rapier made a hole in some breast, and the warm blood spurted over his hands and face, he, with dilated eye, expanded nostrils, and clinched teeth, regained the ground lost, and again approached the beleaguered house.

De Mouy, after a terrible combat in the staircase and hall, had finally come out of the burning house like a true hero. In the midst of all the struggle he had not ceased to cry, "Here, Maurevel!—Maurevel, where are you?" insulting him by the most opprobrious epithets.

He at length appeared in the street, supporting on one arm his mistress, half naked and nearly fainting, and holding a poniard between his teeth. His sword, flaming by the sweeping action he gave it, traced circles of white or red, according as the moon glittered on the blade or a flambeau glared on its blood-stained brightness.

Maurevel had fled. La Hurière, driven back by De Mouy as far as Coconnas, who did not recognize him, and received him at sword's point, was begging for mercy on both sides. At this moment Mercandon perceived him, and knew him, by his white scarf, to be one of the murderers. He fired. La Hurière shrieked, threw up his arms, dropped his arquebuse, and, after having vainly attempted to reach the wall, in order to support himself, fell with his face flat on the earth.

De Mouy took advantage of this circumstance, turned down the Rue de Paradis, and disappeared.

Such had been the resistance of the Huguenots that the De Guise party, quite repulsed, had retired into their hôtel, fearing to be besieged and taken in their own habitation.

Coconnas who, intoxicated with blood and tumult, had reached that degree of excitement when, with the men of the south more especially, courage changes into madness, had not seen or heard anything, and noticed only that there was not such a roar in his ears, and that his hands and face were a little dryer than they had been. Dropping the point of his sword, he saw near him a man lying face downward in a red stream, and around him burning houses.

It was a very short truce, for just as he was approaching this man, whom he recognized as La Hurière, the door of the house he had in vain tried to burst in, opened, and old Mercandon, followed by his son and two nephews, rushed upon him.

"Here he is! here he is!" cried they all, with one voice.

Coconnas was in the middle of the street, and fearing to be surrounded by these four men who assailed him at once, sprang backward with the agility of one of the chamois which he had so often hunted in his native mountains, and in an instant found himself with his back against the wall of the Hôtel de Guise. Once at ease as to not being surprised from behind he put himself in a posture of defence, and said, jestingly:

"Aha, father Mercandon, don't you know me?"

"Wretch!" cried the old Huguenot, "I know you well; you are engaged against me—me, your father's friend and companion."

"And his creditor, are you not?"

"Yes; his creditor, as you say."

"Well, then," said Coconnas, "I have come to settle our accounts."

"Seize him, bind him!" said Mercandon to the young men who accompanied him, and who at his bidding rushed toward the Piedmontese.

"One moment! one moment!" said Coconnas, laughing, "to seize a man you must have a writ, and you have forgotten to secure one from the provost."

And with these words he crossed his sword with the young man nearest to him and at the first blow cut his wrist.

The wounded man retreated with a howl.

"That will do for one!" said Coconnas.

At the same moment the window under which Coconnas had sought shelter opened noisily. He sprang to one side, fearing an attack from behind; but instead of an enemy he saw a woman; instead of the enemy's weapon he was prepared to encounter, a nosegay fell at his feet.

"Ah!" he said, "a woman!"

He saluted the lady with his sword, and stooped to pick up the bouquet.

"Be on your guard, brave Catholic!—be on your guard!" cried the lady.

Coconnas rose, but not before the second nephew's dagger had pierced his cloak, and wounded his other shoulder.

The lady uttered a piercing shriek.

Coconnas thanked her, assured her by a gesture, and then made a pass, which the nephew parried; but at the second thrust, his foot slipped in the blood, and Coconnas, springing at him like a tiger-cat, drove his sword through his breast.

"Good! good! brave cavalier!" exclaimed the lady of the Hôtel de Guise, "good! I will send you succor."

"Do not give yourself any trouble about that, madame," was Coconnas's reply; "rather look on to the end, if it interests you, and see how the Comte Annibal de Coconnas settles the Huguenots."

At this moment old Mercandon's son aimed a pistol at close range to Coconnas, and fired. The count fell on his knee. The lady at the window shrieked again; but Coconnas rose instantly; he had knelt only to avoid the bullet, which struck the wall about two feet beneath where the lady was standing.

Almost at the same moment a cry of rage issued from the window of Mercandon's house, and an old woman, who recognized Coconnas as a Catholic, from his white scarf and cross, hurled a flower-pot at him, which struck him above the knee.

"Capital!" said Coconnas; "one throws flowers at me and at the other, flower-pots; if this goes on, they'll be tearing houses down!"

"Thanks, mother, thanks!" said the young man.

"Go on, wife, go on," said old Mercandon; "but take care of yourself."

"Wait, Monsieur de Coconnas, wait!" said the young woman of the Hôtel de Guise, "I will have them shoot at the windows!"

"Ah! So it is a hell of women, is it?" said Coconnas. "Some of them for me and the others against me! By Heaven! let us put an end to this!"

The scene in fact was much changed and was evidently approaching its climax. Coconnas, who was wounded to be sure, but who had all the vigor of his four and twenty years, was used to arms, and angered rather than weakened by the three or four scratches he had received, now faced only Mercandon and his son: Mercandon, an aged man between sixty and seventy; his son, a youth of sixteen or eighteen, pale, fair-haired and slender, had flung down his pistol which had been discharged and was therefore useless, and was feebly brandishing a sword half as long as the Piedmontese's. The father, armed only with an unloaded arquebuse and a poniard, was calling for assistance. An old woman—the young man's mother—in the opposite window held in her hand a piece of marble which she was preparing to hurl.

Coconnas, excited on the one hand by threats, and on the other by encouragements, proud of his two-fold victory, intoxicated with powder and blood, lighted by the reflection of a burning house, elated by the idea that he was fighting under the eyes of a woman whose beauty was as superior as he was sure her rank was high,—Coconnas, like the last of the Horatii, felt his strength redouble, and seeing the young man falter, rushed on him and crossed his small weapon with his terrible and bloody rapier. Two strokes sufficed to drive it out of its owner's hands. Then Mercandon tried to drive Coconnas back, so that the projectiles thrown from the window might be sure to strike him, but Coconnas, to paralyze the double attack of the old man, who tried to stab him with his dagger, and the mother of the young man, who was endeavoring to break his skull with a stone she was ready to throw, seized his adversary by the body, presenting him to all the blows, like a shield, and well-nigh strangling him in his Herculean grasp.

"Help! help!" cried the young man; "he is crushing my chest—help! help!"

And his voice grew faint in a low and choking groan.

Then Mercandon ceased to attack, and began to entreat.

"Mercy, mercy! Monsieur de Coconnas, have mercy!—he is my only child!"

"He is my son, my son!" cried the mother; "the hope of our old age! Do not kill him, sir,—do not kill him!"

"Really," cried Coconnas, bursting into laughter, "not kill him! What, pray, did he mean to do to me, with his sword and pistol?"

"Sir," said Mercandon, clasping his hands, "I have at home your father's note of hand, I will give it back to you—I have ten thousand crowns of gold, I will give them to you—I have our family jewels, they shall be yours; but do not kill him—do not kill him!"

"And I have my love," said the lady in the Hôtel de Guise, in a low tone, "and I promise it you."

Coconnas reflected a moment, and said suddenly:

"Are you a Huguenot?"

"Yes, I am," murmured the youth.

"Then you must die!" replied Coconnas, frowning and putting to his adversary's breast his keen and glittering dagger.

"Die!" cried the old man; "my poor child die!"

And the mother's shriek resounded so pitifully and loud that for a moment it shook the Piedmontese's firm resolution.

"Oh, Madame la Duchesse!" cried the father, turning toward the lady at the Hôtel de Guise, "intercede for us, and every morning and evening you shall be remembered in our prayers."

"Then let him be a convert," said the lady.

"I am a Protestant," said the boy.

"Then die!" exclaimed Coconnas, lifting his dagger; "die! since you will not accept the life which those lovely lips offer to you."

Mercandon and his wife saw the blade of that deadly weapon gleam like lightning above the head of their son.

"My son Olivier," shrieked his mother, "abjure, abjure!"

"Abjure, my dear boy!" cried Mercandon, going on his knees to Coconnas; "do not leave us alone on the earth!"

"Abjure all together," said Coconnas; "for one *Credo*, three souls and one life."

"I am willing," said the youth.

"We are willing!" cried Mercandon and his wife.

"On your knees, then," said Coconnas, "and let your son repeat after me, word for word, the prayer I shall say."

The father obeyed first.

"I am ready," said the son, also kneeling.

Coconnas then began to repeat in Latin the words of the *Credo*. But whether from chance or calculation, young Olivier knelt close to where his sword had fallen. Scarcely did he see this weapon within his reach than, not ceasing to repeat the words which Coconnas dictated, he stretched out his hand to take it up. Coconnas watched the movement, although he pretended not to see it; but at the moment when the young man touched the handle of the sword with his fingers he rushed on him, knocked him over, exclaiming, "Ah, traitor!" and plunged his dagger into his throat.

The youth uttered one cry, raised himself convulsively on his knee, and fell dead.

"Ah, ruffian!" shrieked Mercandon, "you slay us to rob us of the hundred rose nobles you owe us."

"Faith! no," said Coconnas, "and the proof,"—and as he said these words he flung at the old man's feet the purse which his father had given him before his departure to pay his creditor,—"and the proof," he went on to say, "is this money which I give you!"

"And here's your death!" cried the old woman from the window.

"Take care, M. de Coconnas, take care!" called out the lady at the Hôtel de Guise.

But before Coconnas could turn his head to comply with this advice, or get out of the way of the threat, a heavy mass came hissing through the air, fell on the Piedmontese's hat, broke his sword, and prostrated him on the pavement; he was overcome, crushed, so that he did not hear the double cry of joy and distress which came from the right and left.

Mercandon instantly rushed, dagger in hand, on Coconnas, now bereft of his senses; but at this moment the door of the Hôtel de Guise opened, and the old man, seeing swords and partisans gleaming, fled, while the lady he had called "Madame la Duchesse," her beauty terrible in the light of the flames, dazzling with diamonds and other gems, leaned half out of the window, in order to direct the newcomers, pointing her arm toward Coconnas.

"There! there! in front of me—a gentleman in a red doublet. There!—that is he—yes, that is he."

CHAPTER X.

DEATH, MASS, OR THE BASTILLE.

Marguerite, as we have said, had shut the door and returned to her chamber.

But as she entered, panting, she saw Gillonne, who, terror-struck, was leaning against the door of the closet, staring at the traces of blood on the bed, the furniture, and the carpet.

"Ah! madame!" she cried when she saw the queen. "Oh! madame! tell me, is he dead?"

"Silence!" said Marguerite in that tone of voice which gives some indication of the importance of the command.

Gillonne was silent.

Marguerite then took from her purse a tiny gilded key, opened the closet door, and showed the young man to the servant. La Mole had succeeded in getting to his feet and making his way to the window. A small poniard, such as women at that time were in the habit of carrying, was at hand, and when he heard the door opening he had seized it.

"Fear nothing, sir," said Marguerite; "for, on my soul, you are in safety!"

La Mole sank on his knees.

"Oh, madame," he cried, "you are more than a queen—you are a goddess!"

"Do not agitate yourself, sir," said Marguerite, "your blood is still flowing. Oh, look, Gillonne, how pale he is—let us see where you are wounded."

"Madame," said La Mole, trying to fix on certain parts of his body the pain which pervaded his whole frame, "I think I have a dagger-thrust in my shoulder, another in my chest,—the other wounds are not worth bothering about."

"We will see," said Marguerite. "Gillonne, bring me my balsam casket."

Gillonne obeyed, and returned holding in one hand a casket, and in the other a silver-gilt ewer and some fine Holland linen.

"Help me to lift him, Gillonne," said Queen Marguerite; "for in attempting to get up the poor gentleman has lost all his strength."

"But, madame," said La Mole, "I am wholly confused. Indeed, I cannot allow"—

"But, sir, you will let us do for you, I think," said Marguerite. "When we may save you, it would be a crime to let you die."

"Oh!" cried La Mole, "I would rather die than see you, the queen, stain your hands with blood as unworthy as mine. Oh, never, never!"

And he drew back respectfully.

"Your blood, sir," replied Gillonne, with a smile, "has already stained her majesty's bed and chamber."

Marguerite folded her mantle over her cambric peignoir, all bespattered with small red spots. This movement, so expressive of feminine modesty, caused La Mole to remember that he had held in his arms and pressed to his heart this beautiful, beloved queen, and at the recollection a fugitive glow of color came into his pallid cheeks.

"Madame," stammered La Mole, "can you not leave me to the care of the surgeon?"

"Of a Catholic surgeon, perhaps," said the queen, with an expression which La Mole understood and which made him shudder. "Do you not know," continued the queen in a voice and with a smile of incomparable sweetness, "that we daughters of France are trained to know the qualities of herbs and to make balsams? for our duty as women and as queens has always been to soften pain. Therefore we are equal to the best surgeons in the world; so our flatterers say! Has not my reputation in this regard come to your ears? Come, Gillonne, let us to work!"

La Mole again endeavored to resist; he repeated that he would rather die than occasion the queen labor which, though begun in pity, might end in disgust; but this exertion completely exhausted his strength, and falling back, he fainted a second time.

Marguerite, then seizing the poniard which he had dropped, quickly cut the lace of his doublet; while Gillonne, with another blade, ripped open the sleeves.

Next Gillonne, with a cloth dipped in fresh water, stanched the blood which escaped from his shoulder and breast, and Marguerite, with a silver needle with a round point, probed the wounds with all the delicacy and skill that Maître Ambroise Paré could have displayed in such a case.

"A dangerous but not mortal wound, *acerrimum humeri vulnus, non autem lethale*," murmured the lovely and learned lady-surgeon; "hand me the salve, Gillonne, and get the lint ready."

Meantime Gillonne, to whom the queen had just given this new order, had already dried and perfumed the young man's chest and arms, which were like an antique model, as well as his shoulders, which fell gracefully back; his neck shaded by thick, curling locks, and which seemed rather to belong to a statue of Parian marble than the mangled frame of a dying man.

"Poor young man!" whispered Gillonne, looking not so much at her work as at the object of it.

"Is he not handsome?" said Marguerite, with royal frankness.

"Yes, madame; but it seems to me that instead of leaving him lying there on the floor, we should lift him on this couch against which he is leaning."

"Yes," said Marguerite, "you are right."

And the two women, bending over, uniting their strength, raised La Mole, and laid him on a kind of great sofa in front of the window, which they opened in order to give them fresh air.

This movement aroused La Mole, who drew a long sigh, and opening his eyes, began to experience that indescribable sensation of well-being which comes to a wounded man when on his return to consciousness he finds coolness instead of burning heat, and the perfumes of balsams instead of the nauseating odor of blood.

He muttered some disconnected words, to which Marguerite replied with a smile, placing her finger on her lips.

At this moment several raps on the door were heard.

"Some one knocks at the secret passage," said Marguerite.

"Who can be coming, madame?" asked Gillonne, in a panic.

"I will go and see who it is," said Marguerite; "remain here, and do not leave him for a single instant."

Marguerite went into the chamber, and closing the closet door, opened that of the passage which led to the King's and queen mother's apartments.

"Madame de Sauve!" she exclaimed, suddenly drawing back with an expression which resembled hatred, if not terror, so true it is that a woman never forgives another for taking from her even a man whom she does not love,—"Madame de Sauve!"

"Yes, your majesty!" she replied, clasping her hands.

"You here, madame?" exclaimed Marguerite, more and more surprised, while at the same time her voice grew more and more imperative.

Charlotte fell on her knees.

"Madame," she said, "pardon me! I know how guilty I am toward you; but if you knew—the fault is not wholly mine; an express command of the queen mother"—

"Rise!" said Marguerite, "and as I do not suppose you have come with the intention of justifying yourself to me, tell me why you have come at all."

"I have come, madame," said Charlotte, still on her knees, and with a look of wild alarm, "I came to ask you if he were not here?"

"Here! who?—of whom are you speaking, madame? for I really do not understand."

"Of the king!"

"Of the king? What, do you follow him to my apartments? You know very well that he never comes here."

"Ah, madame!" continued the Baronne de Sauve, without replying to these attacks, or even seeming to comprehend them, "ah, would to Heaven he were here!"

"And why so?"

"Eh, *mon Dieu*! madame, because they are murdering the Huguenots, and the King of Navarre is the chief of the Huguenots."

"Oh!" cried Marguerite, seizing Madame de Sauve by the hand, and compelling her to rise; "ah! I had forgotten; besides, I did not think a king could run the same dangers as other men."

"More, madame,—a thousand times more!" cried Charlotte.

"In fact, Madame de Lorraine had warned me; I had begged him not to leave the Louvre. Has he done so?"

"No, no, madame, he is in the Louvre; but if he is not here"—

"He is not here!"

"Oh!" cried Madame de Sauve, with an outburst of agony, "then he is a dead man, for the queen mother has sworn his destruction!"

"His destruction! ah," said Marguerite, "you terrify me—impossible!"

"Madame," replied Madame de Sauve, with that energy which passion alone can give, "I tell you that no one knows where the King of Navarre is."

"And where is the queen mother?"

"The queen mother sent me to find Monsieur de Guise and Monsieur de Tavannes, who were in her oratory, and then dismissed me. Then—pardon me, madame—I went to my room and waited as usual."

"For my husband, I suppose."

"He did not come, madame. Then I sought for him everywhere and asked every one for him. One soldier told me he thought he had seen him in the midst of the guards who accompanied him, with his sword drawn in his hand,

107

some time before the massacre began, and the massacre has begun an hour ago."

"Thanks, madame," said Marguerite; "and although perhaps the sentiment which impels you is an additional offence toward me,—yet, again, I thank you!"

"Oh, forgive me, madame!" she said, "and I will return to my apartments stronger for your pardon, for I dare not follow you, even at a distance."

Marguerite extended her hand to her.

"I will go to Queen Catharine," she said. "Return to your room. The King of Navarre is under my protection; I have promised him my alliance and I will be faithful to my promise."

"But suppose you cannot obtain access to the queen mother, madame?"

"Then I will go to my brother Charles, and I will speak to him."

"Go, madame, go," said Charlotte, leaving Marguerite room to pass, "and may God guide your majesty!"

Marguerite darted down the corridor, but when she reached the end of it she turned to make sure that Madame de Sauve was not lingering behind. Madame de Sauve was following her.

The Queen of Navarre saw her go upstairs to her own apartment, and then she herself went toward the queen's chamber.

All was changed here. Instead of the crowd of eager courtiers, who usually opened their ranks before the queen and respectfully saluted her, Marguerite met only guards with red partisans and garments stained with blood, or gentlemen in torn cloaks,—their faces blackened with powder, bearing orders and despatches,—some going in, others going out, and all this movement back and forth made a great and terrible confusion in the galleries.

Marguerite, however, went boldly on until she reached the queen mother's antechamber. But this room was guarded by a double file of soldiers, who allowed only those who had a certain countersign to enter. Marguerite in vain tried to pass this living barrier; several times she saw the door open and shut, and each time she saw Catharine, her youth restored by action, as alert as if she were only twenty years of age, writing, receiving letters, opening them, addressing a word to one, a smile to another; and those on whom she smiled most graciously were those who were the most covered with dust and blood.

Amid this vast tumult which reigned in the Louvre and filled it with frightful clamors, could be heard the rattling of musketry more and more insistently repeated.

"I shall never get to her," said Marguerite to herself after she had made three ineffectual attempts to pass the halberdiers. "Rather than waste my time here, I must go and find my brother."

At this moment M. de Guise passed; he had just informed the queen of the murder of the admiral, and was returning to the butchery.

"Oh, Henry!" cried Marguerite, "where is the King of Navarre?"

The duke looked at her with a smile of astonishment, bowed, and without any reply passed out with his guards.

Marguerite ran to a captain who was on the point of leaving the Louvre and was engaged in having his men's arquebuses loaded.

"The King of Navarre!" she exclaimed; "sir, where is the King of Navarre?"

"I do not know, madame," replied the captain, "I do not belong to his majesty's guards."

"Ah, my dear Réné," said the queen, recognizing Catharine's perfumer, "is that you?—you have just left my mother. Do you know what has become of my husband?"

"His majesty the King of Navarre is no friend of mine, madame, you ought to remember that. It is even said," he added, with a contraction of his features more like a grimace than a smile, "it is even said that he ventures to accuse me of having been the accomplice, with Madame Catharine, in poisoning his mother."

"No, no!" cried Marguerite, "my good Réné, do not believe that!"

"Oh, it is of little consequence, madame!" said the perfumer; "neither the King of Navarre nor his party is any longer to be feared!"

And he turned his back on Marguerite.

"Ah, Monsieur de Tavannes!" cried Marguerite, "one word, I beseech you!"

Tavannes, who was going by, stopped.

"Where is Henry of Navarre?"

"Faith," he replied, in a loud voice, "I believe he is somewhere in the city with the Messieurs d'Alençon and de Condé."

And then he added, in a tone so low that the queen alone could hear:

"Your majesty, if you would see him,—to be in whose place I would give my life,—go to the king's armory."

"Thanks, Tavannes, thanks!" said Marguerite, who, of all that Tavannes had said, had heard only the chief direction; "thank you, I will go there."

And she went on her way, murmuring:

"Oh, after all I promised him—after the way in which he behaved to me when that ingrate, Henry de Guise, was concealed in the closet—I cannot let him perish!"

And she knocked at the door of the King's apartments; but they were encompassed within by two companies of guards.

"No one is admitted to the King," said the officer, coming forward.

"But I"—said Marguerite.

"The order is general."

"I, the Queen of Navarre!—I, his sister!"

"My orders admit of no exception, madame; I pray you to pardon me."

And the officer closed the door.

"Oh, he is lost!" exclaimed Marguerite, alarmed at the sight of all those sinister faces, which even if they did not breathe vengeance, expressed sternness of purpose. "Yes, yes! I comprehend all. I have been used as a bait. I am the snare which has entrapped the Huguenots; but I will enter, if I am killed in the attempt!"

And Marguerite ran like a mad creature through the corridors and galleries, when suddenly, as she passed by a small door, she heard a sweet song, almost melancholy, so monotonous it was. It was a Calvinistic psalm, sung by a trembling voice in the next room.

"My brother the king's nurse—the good Madelon—she is there!" exclaimed Marguerite. "God of the Christians, aid me now!"

And, full of hope, Marguerite knocked at the little door.

Soon after the counsel which Marguerite had conveyed to him, after his conversation with Réné, and after leaving the queen mother's chamber, in spite of the efforts of the poor little Phœbe,—who like a good genius tried to detain him,—Henry of Navarre had met several Catholic gentlemen, who, under a pretext of doing him honor, had escorted him to his apartments, where a score of Huguenots awaited him, who had rallied round the young prince, and, having once rallied, would not leave him—so strongly, for some hours, had the presentiment of that fatal night weighed on the Louvre. They had remained there, without any one attempting to disturb them. At last, at the first stroke of the bell of Saint-Germain l'Auxerrois, which resounded through all hearts like a funeral knell, Tavannes entered, and, in the midst of a death-like silence, announced that King Charles IX. desired to speak to Henry.

It was useless to attempt resistance, and no one thought of it. They heard the ceilings, galleries, and corridors creaking beneath the feet of the assembled soldiers, who were in the court-yards, as well as in the apartments, to the number of two thousand. Henry, after having taken leave of his friends, whom he was never again to see, followed Tavannes, who led him to a small gallery next the King's apartments, where he left him alone, unarmed, and a prey to mistrust.

The King of Navarre counted here alone, minute by minute, two mortal hours; listening, with increasing alarm, to the sound of the tocsin and the discharge of fire-arms; seeing through a small window, by the light of the flames and flambeaux, the refugees and their assassins pass; understanding nothing of these shrieks of murder, these cries of distress,—not even suspecting, in spite of his knowledge of Charles IX., the queen mother, and the Duc de Guise, the horrible drama at this moment enacting.

Henry had not physical courage, but he had better than that—he had moral fortitude. Though he feared danger, yet he smiled at it and faced it; but it was danger in the field of battle—danger in the open air—danger in the eyes of all, and attended by the noisy harmony of trumpets and the loud and vibrating beat of drums; but now he was weaponless, alone, locked in, shut up in a semi-darkness where he could scarcely see the enemy that might glide toward him, and the weapon that might be raised to strike him.

These two hours were, perhaps, the most agonizing of his life.

In the hottest of the tumult, and as Henry was beginning to understand that, in all probability, this was some organized massacre, a captain came to him, and conducted the prince along a corridor to the King's rooms. As they approached, the door opened and closed behind them as if by magic. The captain then led Henry to the King, who was in his armory.

When they entered, the King was seated in a great arm-chair, his two hands placed on the two arms of the seat, and his head falling on his chest. At the noise made by their entrance Charles looked up, and Henry observed the perspiration dropping from his brow like large beads.

"Good evening, Harry," said the young King, roughly. "La Chastre, leave us."

The captain obeyed.

A gloomy silence ensued. Henry looked around him with uneasiness, and saw that he was alone with the King.

Charles IX. suddenly arose.

"*Par la mordieu!*" said he, passing his hands through his light brown hair, and wiping his brow at the same time, "you are glad to be with me, are you not, Harry?"

"Certainly, sire," replied the King of Navarre, "I am always happy to be with your Majesty."

"Happier than if you were down there, eh?" continued Charles, following his own thoughts rather than replying to Henry's compliment.

"I do not understand, sire," replied Henry.

"Look out, then, and you will soon understand."

And with a quick movement Charles stepped or rather sprang to the window, and drawing with him his brother-in-law, who became more and more terror-stricken, he pointed to him the horrible outlines of the assassins, who, on the deck of a boat, were cutting the throats or drowning the victims brought them at every moment.

"In the name of Heaven," cried Henry; "what is going on to-night?"

"To-night, sir," replied Charles IX., "they are ridding me of all the Huguenots. Look yonder, over the Hôtel de Bourbon, at the smoke and flames: they are the smoke and flames of the admiral's house, which is on fire. Do you see that body, which these good Catholics are drawing on a torn mattress? It is the corpse of the admiral's son-in-law—the carcass of your friend, Téligny."

"What means this?" cried the King of Navarre, seeking vainly by his side for the hilt of his dagger, and trembling equally with shame and anger; for he felt that he was at the same time laughed at and threatened.

"It means," cried Charles IX., becoming suddenly furious, and turning frightfully pale, "it means that I will no longer have any Huguenots about me. Do you hear me, Henry?—Am I King? Am I master?"

"But, your Majesty"—

"My Majesty kills and massacres at this moment all that is not Catholic; it is my pleasure. Are you a Catholic?" exclaimed Charles, whose anger was rising higher and higher, like an awful tide.

"Sire," replied Henry, "do you remember your own words, 'What matters the religion of those who serve me well'?"

"Ha! ha! ha!" cried Charles, bursting into a ferocious laugh; "you ask me if I remember my words, Henry! '*Verba volant*,' as my sister Margot says; and had not all those"—and he pointed to the city with his finger—"served me well, also? Were they not brave in battle, wise in council, deeply devoted? They were all useful subjects—but they were Huguenots, and I want none but Catholics."

Henry remained silent.

"Do you understand me now, Harry?" asked Charles.

"I understand, sire."

"Well?"

"Well, sire, I do not see why the King of Navarre should not do what so many gentlemen and poor folk have done. For if they all die, poor unfortunates, it is because the same terms have been proposed to them which your Majesty proposes to me, and they have refused, as I refuse."

Charles seized the young prince's arm, and fixed on him a look the vacancy of which suddenly changed into a fierce and savage scowl.

"What!" he said, "do you believe that I have taken the trouble to offer the mass to those whose throats we are cutting yonder?"

"Sire," said Henry, disengaging his arm, "will you not die in the religion of your fathers?"

"Yes, *par la mordieu*! and you?"

"Well, sire, I will do the same!" replied Henry.

Charles uttered a roar of rage and, with trembling hand, seized his arquebuse, which lay on the table.

Henry, who stood leaning against the tapestry, with the perspiration on his brow, and nevertheless, owing to his presence of mind, calm to all appearance, followed every movement of the terrible king with the greedy stupefaction of a bird fascinated by a serpent.

Charles cocked his arquebuse, and stamping with blind rage cried, as he dazzled Henry's eyes with the polished barrel of the deadly gun:

"Will you accept the mass?"

Henry remained mute.

Charles IX. shook the vaults of the Louvre with the most terrible oath that ever issued from the lips of man, and grew even more livid than before.

"Death, mass, or the Bastille!" he cried, taking aim at the King of Navarre.

"Oh, sire!" exclaimed Henry, "will you kill me—me, your brother?"

Henry thus, by his incomparable cleverness, which was one of the strongest faculties of his organization, evaded the answer which Charles IX. expected, for undoubtedly had his reply been in the negative Henry had been a dead man.

As immediately after the climax of rage, reaction begins, Charles IX. did not repeat the question he had addressed to the Prince of Navarre; and after a moment's hesitation, during which he uttered a hoarse kind of growl, he went back to the open window, and aimed at a man who was running along the quay in front.

"I must kill some one!" cried Charles IX., ghastly as a corpse, his eyes suffused with blood; and firing as he spoke, he struck the man who was running.

Henry uttered a groan.

Then, animated by a frightful ardor, Charles loaded and fired his arquebuse without cessation, uttering cries of joy every time his aim was successful.

"It is all over with me!" said the King of Navarre to himself; "when he sees no one else to kill, he will kill me!"

"Well," said a voice behind the princes, suddenly, "is it done?"

It was Catharine de Médicis, who had entered unobserved just as the King was firing his last shot.

"No, thousand thunders of hell!" said the King, throwing his arquebuse across the room. "No, the obstinate blockhead—he will not consent!"

Catharine made no reply. She turned her eyes slowly where Henry stood as motionless as one of the figures of the tapestry against which he was leaning. She then gave a glance at the King, which seemed to say:

"Then why he is alive?"

"He is alive, he is alive!" murmured Charles IX., who perfectly understood the glance, and replied to it without hesitation,—"he is alive—because he is my relative."

Catharine smiled.

Henry saw the smile, and realized that his struggle was to be with Catharine.

"Madame," he said to her, "the whole thing comes from you, I see very well, and my brother-in-law Charles is not to blame. You laid the plan for drawing me into a snare. You made your daughter the bait which was to destroy us all. You separated me from my wife that she might not see me killed before her eyes"—

"Yes, but that shall not be!" cried another voice, breathless and impassioned, which Henry instantly recognized and which made Charles start with surprise and Catharine with rage.

"Marguerite!" exclaimed Henry.

"Margot!" said Charles IX.

"My daughter!" muttered Catharine.

"Sire," said Marguerite to Henry, "your last words were an accusation against me, and you were both right and wrong,—right, for I am the means by which they attempted to destroy you; wrong, for I did not know that you were going to your destruction. I, sire, owe my own life to chance—to my mother's forgetfulness, perhaps; but as soon as I learned your danger I remembered my duty, and a wife's duty is to share her husband's fortunes. If you are exiled, sire, I will follow you into exile; if you are put into prison I will be your fellow-captive; if they kill you, I will also die."

And she offered her husband her hand, which he eagerly seized, if not with love, at least with gratitude.

"Oh, my poor Margot!" said Charles, "you had much better bid him become a Catholic!"

"Sire," replied Marguerite, with that lofty dignity which was so natural to her, "for your own sake do not ask any prince of your house to commit a cowardly act."

Catharine darted a significant glance at Charles.

"Brother," cried Marguerite, who equally well with Charles IX. understood Catharine's ominous pantomime, "my brother, remember! you made him my husband!"

Charles IX., at bay between Catharine's commanding eyes and Marguerite's supplicating look, as if between the two opposing principles of good and evil, stood for an instant undecided; at last Ormazd won the day.

"In truth," said he, whispering in Catharine's ear, "Margot is right, and Harry is my brother-in-law."

"Yes," replied Catharine in a similar whisper in her son's ear, "yes—but supposing he were not?"

CHAPTER XI.

THE HAWTHORN OF THE CEMETERY OF THE INNOCENTS.

As soon as Marguerite reached her own apartments she tried in vain to divine the words which Catharine de Médicis had whispered to Charles IX., and which had cut short the terrible council of life and death which was taking place.

She spent a part of the morning in attending to La Mole, and the rest in trying to guess the enigma, which her mind could not discover.

The King of Navarre remained a prisoner in the Louvre, the persecution of the Huguenots went on hotter than ever. The terrible night was followed by a day of massacre still more horrible. No longer the bells rang the tocsin, but *Te Deums*, and the echoes of these joyous notes, resounding amid fire and slaughter, were perhaps even more lugubrious in sunlight than had been the last night's knell sounding in darkness. This was not all. A strange thing had happened: a hawthorn-tree, which had blossomed in the spring, and which, as usual, had lost its odorous flowers in the month of June, had blossomed again during the night, and the Catholics, who saw a miracle in this event, spread the report of the miracle far and wide, thus making God their accomplice; and with cross and banners they marched in a procession to the Cemetery of the Innocents, where this hawthorn-tree was blooming.

This method of acquiescence which Heaven seemed to show in the massacres redoubled the ardor of the assassins, and while every street, every square, every alley-way of the city continued to present a scene of desolation, the Louvre had become the common tomb for all Protestants who had been shut up there when the signal was given. The King of Navarre, the Prince de Condé, and La Mole were the only survivors.

Assured as to La Mole, whose wounds, as she had declared the evening before, were severe but not dangerous, Marguerite's mind was now occupied with one single idea: that was to save her husband's life, which was still threatened. No doubt the first sentiment which actuated the wife was one of generous pity for a man for whom, as the Béarnais himself had said, she had sworn, if not love, at least alliance; but there was, beside, another sentiment not so pure, which had penetrated the queen's heart.

Marguerite was ambitious, and had foreseen almost the certainty of royalty in her marriage with Henry de Bourbon. Navarre, though beset on one side by the kings of France and on the other by the kings of Spain, who strip by strip had absorbed half of its territory, might become a real kingdom with the French Huguenots for subjects, if only Henry de Bourbon should fulfil the hopes which the courage shown by him on the infrequent occasions vouchsafed him of drawing his sword had aroused.

Marguerite, with her keen, lofty intellect, foresaw and reckoned on all this. So if she lost Henry she lost not only a husband, but a throne.

As she was absorbed in these reflections she heard some one knocking at the door of the secret corridor. She started, for only three persons came by that door,—the King, the queen mother, and the Duc d'Alençon. She opened the closet door, made a gesture of silence to Gillonne and La Mole, and then went to let her visitor in.

It was the Duc d'Alençon.

The young prince had not been seen since the night before. For a moment, Marguerite had conceived the idea of asking his intercession for the King of Navarre, but a terrible idea restrained her. The marriage had taken place against his wishes. François detested Henry, and had evinced his neutrality toward the Béarnais only because he was convinced that Henry and his wife had remained strangers to each other. A mark of interest shown by Marguerite in her husband might thrust one of the three threatening poniards into his heart instead of turning it aside. Marguerite, therefore, on perceiving the young prince, shuddered more than she had shuddered at seeing the King or even the queen mother. Nevertheless no one could have told by his appearance that anything unusual was taking place either in the city or at the Louvre. He was dressed with his usual elegance. His clothes and linen breathed of those perfumes which Charles IX. despised, but of which the Duc d'Anjou and he made continual use.

A practised eye like Marguerite's, however, could detect the fact that in spite of his rather unusual pallor and in spite of a slight trembling in his hands— delicate hands, as carefully treated as a lady's—he felt a deep sense of joy in the bottom of his heart. His entrance was in no wise different from usual. He went to his sister to kiss her, but Marguerite, instead of offering him her cheek, as she would have done had it been King Charles or the Duc d'Anjou, made a courtesy and allowed him to kiss her forehead.

The Duc d'Alençon sighed and touched his bloodless lips to her brow.

Then taking a seat he began to tell his sister the sanguinary news of the night, the admiral's lingering and terrible death, Téligny's instantaneous death caused by a bullet. He took his time and emphasized all the bloody details of that night, with that love of blood characteristic of himself and his two brothers; Marguerite allowed him to tell his story.

"You did not come to tell me this only, brother?" she then asked.

The Duc d'Alençon smiled.

"You have something else to say to me?"

"No," replied the duke; "I am waiting."

"Waiting! for what?"

"Have you not told me, dearest Marguerite," said the duke, drawing his armchair close up to his sister's, "that your marriage with the King of Navarre was contracted against your wishes?"

"Yes, no doubt. I did not know the Prince of Béarn when he was proposed to me as a husband."

"And after you came to know him, did you not tell me that you felt no love for him?"

"I told you so; it is true."

"Was it not your opinion that this marriage would make you unhappy?"

"My dear François," said Marguerite, "when a marriage is not the height of happiness it is almost always the depth of wretchedness."

"Well, then, my dear Marguerite, as I said to you,—I am waiting."

"But what are you waiting for?"

"For you to display your joy!"

"What have I to be joyful for?"

"The unexpected chance which offers itself for you to resume your liberty."

"My liberty?" replied Marguerite, who was determined to compel the prince to express his whole thought.

"Yes; your liberty! You will now be separated from the King of Navarre."

"Separated!" said Marguerite, fastening her eyes on the young prince.

The Duc d'Alençon tried to endure his sister's look, but his eyes soon avoided hers with embarrassment.

"Separated!" repeated Marguerite; "let us talk this over, brother, for I should like to understand all you mean, and how you propose to separate us."

"Why," murmured the duke, "Henry is a Huguenot."

"No doubt; but he made no secret of his religion, and that was known when we were married."

"Yes; but since your marriage, sister," asked the duke, involuntarily allowing a ray of joy to shine upon his face, "what has Henry been doing?"

"Why, you know better than any one, François, for he has spent his days almost constantly in your society, either hunting or playing mall or tennis."

"Yes, his days, no doubt," replied the duke; "his days—but his nights?"

Marguerite was silent; it was now her turn to cast down her eyes.

"His nights," persisted the Duc d'Alençon, "his nights?"

"Well?" inquired Marguerite, feeling that it was requisite that she should say something in reply.

"Well, he has been spending them with Madame de Sauve!"

"How do you know that?" exclaimed Marguerite.

"I know it because I have an interest in knowing it," replied the young prince, growing pale and picking the embroidery of his sleeves.

Marguerite began to understand what Catharine had whispered to Charles, but pretended to remain in ignorance.

"Why do you tell me this, brother?" she replied, with a well-affected air of melancholy; "was it to remind me that no one here loves me or takes my part, neither those whom nature gave me as protectors nor the man whom the Church gave me as my husband?"

"You are unjust," said the Duc d'Alençon, drawing his armchair still nearer to his sister, "I love you and protect you!"

"Brother," said Marguerite, looking at him sharply, "have you anything to say to me from the queen mother?"

"I! you mistake, sister. I swear to you—what can make you think that?"

119

"What can make me think that?—why, because you are breaking off the intimacy that binds you to my husband, because you are abandoning the cause of the King of Navarre."

"The cause of the King of Navarre!" replied the Duc d'Alençon, wholly at his wits' end.

"Yes, certainly. Now look here, François; let us speak frankly. You have come to an agreement a score of times; you cannot raise yourself or even hold your own except by mutual help. This alliance"—

"Has now become impossible, sister," interrupted the Duc d'Alençon.

"And why so?"

"Because the King has designs on your husband! Pardon me, when I said *your husband*, I erred; I meant Henry of Navarre. Our mother has seen through the whole thing. I entered into an alliance with the Huguenots because I believed the Huguenots were in favor; but now they are killing the Huguenots, and in another week there will not remain fifty in the whole kingdom. I gave my hand to the King of Navarre because he was—your husband; but now he is not your husband. What can you say to that—you who are not only the loveliest woman in France, but have the clearest head in the kingdom?"

"Why, I have this to say," replied Marguerite, "I know our brother Charles; I saw him yesterday in one of those fits of frenzy, every one of which shortens his life ten years. I have to say that unfortunately these attacks are very frequent, and that thus, in all probability, our brother Charles has not very long to live; and, finally, I have to say that the King of Poland has just died, and the question of electing a prince of the house of France in his stead is much discussed; and when circumstances are thus, it is not the moment to abandon allies who, in the moment of struggle, might support us with the strength of a nation and the power of a kingdom."

"And you!" exclaimed the duke, "do you not act much more treasonably to me in preferring a foreigner to your own brother?"

"Explain yourself, François! In what have I acted treasonably to you?"

"You yesterday begged the life of the King of Navarre from King Charles."

"Well?" said Marguerite, with pretended innocence.

The duke rose hastily, paced round the chamber twice or thrice with a bewildered air, then came back and took Marguerite's hand.

It was cold and unresponsive.

"Good-by, sister!" he said at last. "You will not understand me; do not, therefore, complain of whatever misfortunes may happen to you."

Marguerite grew pale, but remained motionless in her place. She saw the Duc d'Alençon go away, without making any attempt to detain him; but he had scarcely more than disappeared down the corridor when he returned.

"Listen, Marguerite," he said, "I had forgotten to tell you one thing; that is, that by this time to-morrow the King of Navarre will be dead."

Marguerite uttered a cry, for the idea that she was the instrument of assassination caused in her a terror she could not subdue.

"And you will not prevent his death?" she said; "you will not save your best and most faithful ally?"

"Since yesterday the King of Navarre is no longer my ally."

"Who is, pray?"

"Monsieur de Guise. By destroying the Huguenots, Monsieur de Guise has become the king of the Catholics."

"And does a son of Henry II. recognize a duke of Lorraine as his king?"

"You are in a bad frame of mind, Marguerite, and you do not understand anything."

"I confess that I try in vain to read your thoughts."

"Sister, you are of as good a house as the Princesse de Porcian; De Guise is no more immortal than the King of Navarre. Now, then, Marguerite, suppose three things, three possibilities: first, suppose monsieur is chosen King of Poland; the second, that you loved me as I love you; well, I am King of France, and you are—queen of the Catholics."

Marguerite hid her face in her hands, overwhelmed at the depth of the views of this youth, whom no one at court thought possessed of even common understanding.

"But," she asked after a moment's silence, "I hope you are not jealous of Monsieur le Duc de Guise as you were of the King of Navarre!"

"What is done is done," said the Duc d'Alençon, in a muffled voice, "and if I had to be jealous of the Duc de Guise, well, then, I was!"

"There is only one thing that can prevent this capital plan from succeeding, brother."

"And what is that?"

"That I no longer love the Duc de Guise."

"And whom, pray, do you love?"

"No one."

The Duc d'Alençon looked at Marguerite with the astonishment of a man who takes his turn in failing to understand, and left the room, pressing his icy hand on his forehead, which ached to bursting.

Marguerite remained alone and thoughtful; the situation was beginning to take a clear and definite shape before her eyes; the King had permitted Saint Bartholomew's, Queen Catharine and the Duc de Guise had put it into execution. The Duc de Guise and the Duc d'Alençon were about to join partnership so as to get the greatest possible advantage. The death of the King of Navarre would be a natural result of this great catastrophe. With the King of Navarre out of the way, his kingdom would be seized upon, Marguerite would be left a throneless, impotent widow with no other prospect before her than a nunnery, where she would not even have the sad consolation of weeping for a consort who had never been her husband.

She was still in the same position when Queen Catharine sent to ask if she would not like to go with her and the whole court on a pious visitation to the hawthorn of the Cemetery of the Innocents. Marguerite's first impulse was to refuse to take part in this cavalcade. But the thought that this excursion might possibly give her a chance to learn something new about the King of Navarre's fate decided her to go. So she sent word that if they would have a palfrey ready for her she would willingly go with their majesties.

Five minutes later a page came to ask if she was ready to go down, for the procession was preparing to start.

Marguerite warned Gillonne by a gesture to look after the wounded man and so went downstairs.

The King, the queen mother, Tavannes, and the principal Catholics were already mounted. Marguerite cast a rapid glance over the group, which was composed of about a score of persons; the King of Navarre was not of the party.

Madame de Sauve was there. Marguerite exchanged a glance with her, and was convinced that her husband's mistress had something to tell her.

They rode down the Rue de l'Astruce and entered into the Rue Saint Honoré. As the populace caught sight of the King, Queen Catharine, and the principal Catholics they flocked together and followed the procession like a rising tide, and shouts rent the air.

"Vive le Roi!"

"Vive la Messe."

"Death to the Huguenots!"

These acclamations were accompanied by the waving of ensanguined swords and smoking arquebuses, which showed the part each had taken in the awful work just accomplished.

When they reached the top of the Rue des Prouvelles they met some men who were dragging a headless carcass. It was the admiral's. The men were going to hang it by the feet at Montfaucon.

They entered the Cemetery des Saints Innocents by the gate facing the Rue des Chaps, now known as the Rue des Déchargeurs; the clergy, notified in advance of the visit of the King and the queen mother, were waiting for their majesties to make them speeches.

Madame de Sauve took advantage of a moment when Catharine was listening to one of the discourses to approach the Queen of Navarre, and beg leave to kiss her hand. Marguerite extended her arm toward her, and Madame de Sauve, as she kissed the queen's hand, slipped a tiny roll of paper up her sleeve.

Madame de Sauve drew back quickly and with clever dissimulation; yet Catharine perceived it, and turned round just as the maid of honor was kissing Marguerite's hand.

The two women saw her glance, which penetrated them like a flash of lightning, but both remained unmoved; only Madame de Sauve left Marguerite and resumed her place near Catharine.

When Catharine had finished replying to the address which had just been made to her she smiled and beckoned the Queen of Navarre to go to her.

"Eh, my daughter," said the queen mother, in her Italian patois, "so you are on intimate terms with Madame de Sauve, are you?"

Marguerite smiled in turn, and gave to her lovely countenance the bitterest expression she could, and replied:

"Yes, mother; the serpent came to bite my hand!"

"Aha!" replied Catharine, with a smile; "you are jealous, I think!"

"You are mistaken, madame," replied Marguerite; "I am no more jealous of the King of Navarre than the King of Navarre is in love with me, but I know how to distinguish my friends from my enemies. I like those that like me, and detest those that hate me. Otherwise, madame, should I be your daughter?"

Catharine smiled so as to make Marguerite understand that if she had had any suspicion it had vanished.

Moreover, at that instant the arrival of other pilgrims attracted the attention of the august throng.

The Duc de Guise came with a troop of gentlemen all warm still from recent carnage. They escorted a richly decorated litter, which stopped in front of the King.

"The Duchesse de Nevers!" cried Charles IX., "Ah! let that lovely robust Catholic come and receive our compliments. Why, they tell me, cousin, that from your own window you have been hunting Huguenots, and that you killed one with a stone."

The Duchesse de Nevers blushed exceedingly red.

"Sire," she said in a low tone, and kneeling before the King, "on the contrary, it was a wounded Catholic whom I had the good fortune to rescue."

"Good—good, my cousin! there are two ways of serving me: one is by exterminating my enemies, the other is by rescuing my friends. One does what one can, and I am certain that if you could have done more you would!"

While this was going on, the populace, seeing the harmony existing between the house of Lorraine and Charles IX., shouted exultantly:

"*Vive le Roi!*"

"*Vive le Duc de Guise!*"

"*Vive la Messe!*"

"Do you return to the Louvre with us, Henriette?" inquired the queen mother of the lovely duchess.

Marguerite touched her friend on the elbow, and she, understanding the sign, replied:

"No, madame, unless your majesty desire it; for I have business in the city with her majesty the Queen of Navarre."

"And what are you going to do together?" inquired Catharine.

"To see some very rare and curious Greek books found at an old Protestant pastor's, and which have been taken to the Tower of Saint Jacques la Boucherie," replied Marguerite.

"You would do much better to see the last Huguenots flung into the Seine from the top of the Pont des Meuniers," said Charles IX.; "that is the place for all good Frenchmen."

"We will go, if it be your Majesty's desire," replied the Duchesse de Nevers.

Catharine cast a look of distrust on the two young women. Marguerite, on the watch, remarked it, and turning round uneasily, looked about her.

This assumed or real anxiety did not escape Catharine.

"What are you looking for?"

"I am seeking—I do not see"—she replied.

"Whom are you seeking? Who is it you fail to see?"

"La Sauve," said Marguerite; "can she have returned to the Louvre?"

"Did I not say you were jealous?" said Catharine, in her daughter's ear. "Oh, *bestia*! Come, come, Henriette," she added, shrugging her shoulders, "begone, and take the Queen of Navarre with you."

Marguerite pretended to be still looking about her; then, turning to her friend, she said in a whisper:

"Take me away quickly; I have something of the greatest importance to say to you."

The duchess courtesied to the King and queen mother, and then, bowing low before the Queen of Navarre:

"Will your majesty deign to come into my litter?"

"Willingly, only you will have to take me back to the Louvre."

"My litter, like my servants and myself, are at your majesty's orders."

Queen Marguerite entered the litter, while Catharine and her gentlemen returned to the Louvre just as they had come. But during the route it was observed that the queen mother kept talking to the King, pointing several times to Madame de Sauve, and at each time the King laughed—as Charles IX. laughed; that is, with a laugh more sinister than a threat.

As soon as Marguerite felt the litter in motion, and had no longer to fear Catharine's searching eyes, she quickly drew from her sleeve Madame de Sauve's note and read as follows:

"*I have received orders to send to-night to the King of Navarre two keys; one is that of the room in which he is shut up, and the other is the key of my chamber; when once he has reached my apartment, I am enjoined to keep him there until six o'clock in the morning.*

"*Let your majesty reflect—let your majesty decide. Let your majesty esteem my life as nothing.*"

"There is now no doubt," murmured Marguerite, "and the poor woman is the tool of which they wish to make use to destroy us all. But we will see if the Queen Margot, as my brother Charles calls me, is so easily to be made a nun of."

"Tell me, whom is the letter from?" asked the Duchesse de Nevers.

"Ah, duchess, I have so many things to say to you!" replied Marguerite, tearing the note into a thousand bits.

CHAPTER XII.

MUTUAL CONFIDENCES.

"And, first, where are we going?" asked Marguerite; "not to the Pont des Meuniers, I suppose,—I have seen enough slaughter since yesterday, my poor Henriette."

"I have taken the liberty to conduct your majesty"—

"First and foremost, my majesty requests you to forget my majesty—you were taking me"—

"To the Hôtel de Guise, unless you decide otherwise."

"No, no, let us go there, Henriette; the Duc de Guise is not there, your husband is not there."

"Oh, no," cried the duchess, her bright emerald eyes sparkling with joy; "no, neither my husband, nor my brother-in-law, nor any one else. I am free—free as air, free as a bird,—free, my queen! Do you understand the happiness there is in that word? I go, I come, I command. Ah, poor queen, you are not free—and so you sigh."

"You go, you come, you command. Is that all? Is that all the use of liberty? You are happy with only freedom as an excuse!"

"Your majesty promised to tell me a secret."

"Again 'your majesty'! I shall be angry soon, Henriette. Have you forgotten our agreement?"

"No; your respectful servant in public—in private, your madcap confidante, is it not so, madame? Is it not so, Marguerite?"

"Yes, yes," said the queen, smiling.

"No family rivalry, no treachery in love; everything fair, open, and aboveboard! An offensive and defensive alliance, for the sole purpose of finding and, if we can, catching on the fly, that ephemeral thing called happiness."

"Just so, duchess. Let us again seal the compact with a kiss."

And the two beautiful women, the one so pale, so full of melancholy, the other so roseate, so fair, so animated, joined their lips as they had united their thoughts.

"Tell me, what is there new?" asked the duchess, giving Marguerite an eager, inquisitive look.

"Isn't everything new since day before yesterday?"

"Oh, I am speaking of love, not of politics. When we are as old as dame Catharine we will take part in politics; but we are only twenty, my pretty queen, and so let us talk about something else. Let me see! can it be that you are really married?"

"To whom?" asked Marguerite, laughing.

"Ah! you reassure me, truly!"

"Well, Henriette, that which reassures you, alarms me. Duchess, I must be married."

"When?"

"To-morrow."

"Oh, poor little friend! and is it necessary?"

"Absolutely."

"*Mordi*! as an acquaintance of mine says, this is very sad."

"And so you know some one who says *mordi*?" asked Marguerite, with a smile.

"Yes."

"And who is this some one?"

"You keep asking me questions when I am talking to you. Finish and I will begin."

"In two words, it is this: The King of Navarre is in love, and not with me; I am not in love, but I do not want him, yet we must both of us change, or seem to change, between now and to-morrow."

"Well, then, you change, and be very sure he will do the same."

"That is quite impossible, for I am less than ever inclined to change."

"Only with respect to your husband, I hope."

"Henriette, I have a scruple."

"A scruple! about what?"

"A religious one. Do you make any difference between Huguenots and Catholics?"

"In politics?"

"Yes."

"Of course."

"And in love?"

"My dear girl, we women are such heathens that we admit every kind of sect, and recognize many gods."

"In one, eh?"

"Yes," replied the duchess, her eyes sparkling; "he who is called *Eros*, *Cupido*, *Amor*. He who has a quiver on his back, wings on his shoulders, and a fillet over his eyes. *Mordi, vive la dévotion!*"

"You have a peculiar method of praying; you throw stones on the heads of Huguenots."

"Let us do our duty and let people talk. Ah, Marguerite! how the finest ideas, the noblest actions, are spoilt in passing through the mouths of the vulgar!"

"The vulgar!—why, it was my brother Charles who congratulated you on your exploits, wasn't it?"

"Your brother Charles is a mighty hunter blowing the horn all day, and that makes him very thin. I reject his compliments; besides, I gave him his answer —didn't you hear what I said?"

"No; you spoke so low."

"So much the better. I shall have more news to tell you. Now, then, finish your story, Marguerite."

"I was going to say—to say"—

"Well?"

"I was going to say," continued the queen, laughing, "if the stone my brother spoke of be a fact, I should resist."

"Ah!" cried Henriette, "so you have chosen a Huguenot, have you? Well, to reassure your conscience, I promise you that I will choose one myself on the first opportunity."

"Ah, so you have chosen a Catholic, have you?"

"*Mordi*!" replied the duchess.

"I see, I see."

"And what is this Huguenot of yours?"

"I did not choose him. The young man is nothing and probably never will be anything to me."

"But what sort is he? You can tell me that; you know how curious I am about these matters."

"A poor young fellow, beautiful as Benvenuto Cellini's Nisus,—and he came and took refuge in my room."

"Oho!—of course without any suggestion on your part?"

"Poor fellow! Do not laugh so, Henriette; at this very moment he is between life and death."

"He is ill, is he?"

"He is grievously wounded."

"A wounded Huguenot is very disagreeable, especially in these times; and what have you done with this wounded Huguenot, who is not and never will be anything to you?"

"He is in my closet; I am concealing him and I want to save him."

"He is handsome! he is young! he is wounded. You hide him in your closet; you want to save him. This Huguenot of yours will be very ungrateful if he is not too grateful."

"I am afraid he is already—much more so than I could wish."

"And this poor young man interests you?"

"From motives of humanity—that's all."

"Ah, humanity! my poor queen, that is the very virtue that is the ruin of all

129

of us women."

"Yes; and you understand: as the King, the Duc d'Alençon, my mother, even my husband, may at any moment enter my room"—

"You want me to hide your little Huguenot as long as he is ill, on condition I send him back to you when he is cured?"

"Scoffer!" said Marguerite, "no! I do not lay my plans so far in advance; but if you could conceal the poor fellow,—if you could preserve the life I have saved,—I confess I should be most grateful. You are free at the Hôtel de Guise; you have neither brother-in-law nor husband to spy on you or constrain you; besides, behind your room there is a closet like mine into which no one is entitled to enter; so lend me your closet for my Huguenot, and when he is cured open the cage and let the bird fly away."

"There is only one difficulty, my dear queen: the cage is already occupied."

"What, have *you* also saved somebody?"

"That is exactly what I answered your brother with."

"Ah, I understand! that's why you spoke so low that I could not hear you."

"Listen, Marguerite: it is an admirable story—is no less poetical and
romantic than yours. After I had left you six of my guards, I returned with the rest to the Hôtel de Guise, and I was watching them pillage and burn a house separated from my brother's palace only by the Rue des Quatre Fils, when I heard the voices of men swearing and of women crying. I went out on the balcony and the first thing I saw was a sword flashing so brilliantly that it seemed to light up the whole scene. I was filled with admiration for this fiery sword. I am fond of fine things, you know! Then naturally enough I tried to distinguish the arm wielding it and then the body to which the arm belonged. Amid sword-thrusts and shouts I at last made out the man and I saw—a hero, an Ajax Telamon. I heard a voice—the voice of a Stentor. My enthusiasm awoke—I stood there panting, trembling at every blow aimed at him, at every thrust he parried! That was a quarter hour of emotion such as I had never before experienced, my queen; and never believed was possible to experience. So there I was panting, holding my breath, trembling, and voiceless, when all of a sudden my hero disappeared."

"How?"

"Struck down by a stone an old woman threw at him. Then, like Cyrus, I found my voice, and screamed, 'Help! help!' my guards went out, lifted him up, and bore him to the room which you want for your *protégé*."

"Alas, my dear Henriette, I can better understand this story because it is so nearly my own."

"With this difference, queen, that as I am serving my King and my religion, I have no reason to send Monsieur Annibal de Coconnas away."

"His name is Annibal de Coconnas!" said Marguerite, laughing.

"A terrible name, is it not? Well, he who bears it is worthy of it. What a champion he is, by Heaven! and how he made the blood flow! Put on your mask, my queen, for we are now at the palace."

"Why put on my mask?"

"Because I wish to show you my hero."

"Is he handsome?"

"He seemed magnificent to me during the conflict. To be sure, it was at night and he was lighted up by the flames. This morning by daylight I confess he seemed to me to have lost a little."

"So then my *protégé* is rejected at the Hôtel de Guise. I am sorry for it, for that is the last place where they would look for a Huguenot."

"Oh, no, your Huguenot shall come; I will have him brought this evening: one shall sleep in the right-hand corner of the closet and the other in the left."

"But when they recognize each other as Protestant and Catholic they will fight."

"Oh, there is no danger. Monsieur de Coconnas has had a cut down the face that prevents him from seeing very well; your Huguenot is wounded in the chest so that he can't move; and, besides, you have only to tell him to be silent on the subject of religion, and all will go well."

"So be it."

"It's a bargain; and now let us go in."

"Thanks," said Marguerite, pressing her friend's hand.

"Here, madame," said the duchess, "you are again 'your majesty;' suffer me, then, to do the honors of the Hôtel de Guise fittingly for the Queen of Navarre."

And the duchess, alighting from the litter, almost knelt on the ground in helping Marguerite to step down; then pointing to the palace door guarded by two sentinels, arquebuse in hand, she followed the queen at a respectful distance, and this humble attitude she maintained as long as she was in sight.

As soon as she reached her room, the duchess closed the door, and, calling to her waiting-woman, a thorough Sicilian, said to her in Italian,

"Mica, how is Monsieur le Comte?"

"Better and better," replied she.

"What is he doing?"

"At this moment, madame, he is taking some refreshment."

"It is always a good sign," said Marguerite, "when the appetite returns."

"Ah, that is true. I forgot you were a pupil of Ambroise Paré. Leave us, Mica."

"Why do you send her away?"

"That she may be on the watch."

Mica left the room.

"Now," said the duchess, "will you go in to see him, or shall I send for him here?"

"Neither the one nor the other. I wish to see him without his seeing me."

"What matters it? You have your mask."

"He may recognize me by my hair, my hands, a jewel."

"How cautious she is since she has been married, my pretty queen!"

Marguerite smiled.

"Well," continued the duchess, "I see only one way."

"What is that?"

"To look through the keyhole."

"Very well! take me to the door."

The duchess took Marguerite by the hand and led her to a door covered with tapestry; then bending one knee, she applied her eye to the keyhole.

"'Tis all right; he is sitting at table, with his face turned toward us; come!"

The queen took her friend's place, and looked through the keyhole; Coconnas, as the duchess had said, was sitting at a well-served table, and, despite his wounds, was doing ample justice to the good things before him.

"Ah, great heavens!" cried Marguerite, starting back.

"What is the matter?" asked the duchess in amazement.

"Impossible!—no!—yes!—on my soul, 'tis the very man!"

"Who?"

"Hush," said Marguerite, getting to her feet and seizing the duchess's hand; "'tis the man who pursued my Huguenot into my room, and stabbed him in my arms! Oh, Henriette, how fortunate he did not see me!"

"Well, then, you have seen him fighting; was he not handsome?"

"I do not know," said Marguerite, "for I was looking at the man he was pursuing."

"What is his name?"

"You will not mention it before the count?"

"No, I give you my promise!"

"Lerac de la Mole."

"And what do you think of him now?"

"Of Monsieur de la Mole?"

"No, of Monsieur de Coconnas?"

"Faith!" said Marguerite, "I confess I think"—

She stopped.

"Come, come," said the duchess, "I see you are angry with him for having wounded your Huguenot."

"Why, so far," said Marguerite, laughing, "my Huguenot owes him nothing; the slash he gave him under his eye"—

"They are quits, then, and we can reconcile them. Send me your wounded man."

"Not now—by and by."

"When?"

"When you have found yours another room."

"Which?"

Marguerite looked meaningly at her friend, who, after a moment's silence, laughed.

"So be it," said the duchess; "alliance firmer than ever."

"Friendship ever sincere!"

"And the word, in case we need each other?"

"The triple name of your triple god, '*Eros, Cupido, Amor.*'"

And the two princesses separated after one more kiss, and pressing each other's hand for the twentieth time.

––––––

CHAPTER XIII.

HOW THERE ARE KEYS WHICH OPEN DOORS THEY ARE NOT MEANT FOR.

The Queen of Navarre on her return to the Louvre found Gillonne in great excitement. Madame de Sauve had been there in her absence. She had brought a key sent her by the queen mother. It was the key of the room in which Henry was confined. It was evident that the queen mother for some purpose of her own wished the Béarnais to spend that night in Madame de Sauve's apartment.

Marguerite took the key and turned it over and over; she made Gillonne repeat Madame de Sauve's every word, weighed them, letter by letter, in her mind, and at length thought she detected Catharine's plan.

She took pen and ink, and wrote:

"Instead of going to Madame de Sauve to-night, come to the Queen of Navarre."

"MARGUERITE."

She rolled up the paper, put it in the hollow of the key, and ordered Gillonne to slip the key under the king's door as soon as it was dark.

This first duty having been attended to, Marguerite thought of the wounded man, closed all the doors, entered the closet, and, to her great surprise, found La Mole dressed in all his clothes, torn and blood-stained as they were.

On seeing her he strove to rise, but, still dizzy, could not stand, and fell back upon the sofa which had served for his bed.

"What is the matter, sir?" asked Marguerite; "and why do you thus disobey your physician's orders? I recommended you rest, and instead of following my advice you do just the contrary."

"Oh, madame," said Gillonne, "it is not my fault; I have entreated Monsieur le Comte not to commit this folly, but he declares that nothing shall keep him any longer at the Louvre."

"Leave the Louvre!" said Marguerite, gazing with astonishment at the young man, who cast down his eyes. "Why, it is impossible—you cannot walk; you are pale and weak; your knees tremble. Only a few hours ago the wound in your shoulder was still bleeding."

"Madame," said the young man, "as earnestly as I thanked your majesty for having given me shelter, as earnestly do I pray you now to suffer me to depart."

"I scarcely know what to call such a resolution," said Marguerite; "it is worse than ingratitude."

"Oh," cried La Mole, clasping his hands, "think me not ungrateful; my gratitude will cease only with my life."

"It will not last long, then," said Marguerite, moved at these words, the sincerity of which it was impossible to doubt; "for your wounds will open, and you will die from loss of blood, or you will be recognized for a Huguenot and killed ere you have gone fifty yards in the street."

"Nevertheless I must leave the Louvre," murmured La Mole.

"Must," returned Marguerite, fixing her serene, inscrutable eyes upon him; then turning rather pale she added, "ah, yes; forgive me, sir, I understand; doubtless there is some one outside the Louvre who is anxiously waiting for you. You are right, Monsieur de la Mole; it is natural, and I understand it.

Why didn't you say so at first? or rather, why didn't I think of it myself? It is duty in the exercise of hospitality to protect one's guest's affections as well as to cure his wounds, and to care for the spirit just as one cares for the body."

"Alas, madame," said La Mole, "you are laboring under a strange mistake. I am well nigh alone in the world, and altogether so in Paris, where no one knows me. My assassin is the first man I have spoken to in this city; your majesty the first woman who has spoken to me."

"Then," said Marguerite, "why would you go?"

"Because," replied La Mole, "last night you got no rest, and to-night"—

Marguerite blushed.

"Gillonne," said she, "it is already evening and time to deliver that key."

Gillonne smiled, and left the room.

"But," continued Marguerite, "if you are alone in Paris, without friends, what will you do?"

"Madame, I soon shall have friends enough, for while I was pursued I thought of my mother, who was a Catholic; methought I saw her with a cross in her hand gliding before me toward the Louvre, and I vowed that if God should save my life I would embrace my mother's religion. Madame, God did more than save my life, he sent me one of his angels to make me love life."

"But you cannot walk; before you have gone a hundred steps you will faint away."

"Madame, I have made the experiment in the closet, I walk slowly and painfully, it is true; but let me get as far as the Place du Louvre; once outside, let befall what will."

Marguerite leaned her head on her hand and sank into deep thought.

"And the King of Navarre," said she, significantly, "you no longer speak of him? In changing your religion, have you also changed your desire to enter his service?"

"Madame," replied La Mole, growing pale, "you have just hit upon the actual reason of my departure. I know that the King of Navarre is exposed to the greatest danger, and that all your majesty's influence as a daughter of France will barely suffice to save his life."

"What do you mean, sir," exclaimed Marguerite, "and what danger do you refer to?"

"Madame," replied La Mole, with some hesitation, "one can hear everything from the closet where I am."

"'Tis true," said Marguerite to herself; "Monsieur de Guise told me so before."

"Well," added she, aloud, "what did you hear?"

"In the first place, the conversation between your majesty and your brother."

"With François?" said Marguerite, changing color.

"Yes, madame, with the Duc d'Alençon; and then after you went out I heard what Gillonne and Madame de Sauve said."

"And these two conversations"—

"Yes, madame; married scarcely a week, you love your husband; your husband will come, in his turn, in the same way that the Duc d'Alençon and Madame de Sauve came. He will confide his secrets to you. Well, then, I must not overhear them; I should be indiscreet—I cannot—I must not—I will not be!"

By the tone in which La Mole uttered these last words, by the anxiety expressed in his voice, by the embarrassment shown in his eyes, Marguerite was enlightened as by a sudden revelation.

"Aha!" said she, "so you have heard everything that has been said in this room?"

"Yes, madame."

These words were uttered in a sigh.

"And you wish to depart to-night, this evening, to avoid hearing any more?"

"This moment, if it please your majesty to allow me to go."

"Poor fellow!" said Marguerite, with a strange accent of tender pity.

Astonished by such a gentle reply when he was expecting a rather forcible outburst, La Mole timidly raised his head; his eyes met Marguerite's and were riveted as by a magnetic power on their clear and limpid depths.

"So then you feel you cannot keep a secret, Monsieur de la Mole?" said Marguerite in a soft voice as she stood leaning on the back of her chair, half hidden in the shadow of a thick tapestry and enjoying the felicity of easily reading his frank and open soul while remaining impenetrable herself.

"Madame," said La Mole, "I have a miserable disposition: I distrust myself, and the happiness of another gives me pain."

"Whose happiness?" asked Marguerite, smiling. "Ah, yes—the King of

137

Navarre's! Poor Henry!"

"You see," cried La Mole, passionately, "he is happy."

"Happy?"

"Yes, for your majesty is sorry for him."

Marguerite crumpled up the silk of her purse and smoothed out the golden fringe.

"So then you decline to see the King of Navarre?" said she; "you have made up your mind; you are decided?"

"I fear I should be troublesome to his majesty just at the present time."

"But the Duc d'Alençon, my brother?"

"Oh, no, madame!" cried La Mole, "the Duc d'Alençon even still less than the King of Navarre."

"Why so?" asked Marguerite, so stirred that her voice trembled as she spoke.

"Because, although I am already too bad a Huguenot to be a faithful servant of the King of Navarre, I am not a sufficiently good Catholic to be friends with the Duc d'Alençon and Monsieur de Guise."

This time Marguerite cast down her eyes, for she felt the very depths of her heart stirred by what he said, and yet she could not have told whether his reply was meant to give her joy or pain.

At this moment Gillonne came back. Marguerite asked her a question with a glance; Gillonne's answer, also conveyed by her eyes, was in the affirmative. She had succeeded in getting the key to the King of Navarre.

Marguerite turned her eyes toward La Mole, who stood before her, his head drooping on his breast, pale, like one suffering alike in mind and in body.

"Monsieur de la Mole is proud," said she, "and I hesitate to make him a proposition he will doubtless reject."

La Mole rose, took one step toward Marguerite, and was about to bow low before her to signify that he was at her service; but an intense, keen, burning pang forced the tears from his eyes, and conscious that he was in danger of falling, he clutched a piece of tapestry and clung to it.

"Don't you see, sir," cried Marguerite, springing to him and supporting him in her arms, "don't you see that you still need me?"

A scarcely perceptible movement passed over La Mole's lips.

"Oh, yes!" he whispered, "like the air I breathe, like the light I see!"

At this moment three knocks were heard at Marguerite's door.

"Do you hear, madame?" cried Gillonne, alarmed.

"Already!" exclaimed Marguerite.

"Shall I open?"

"Wait! perhaps it is the King of Navarre."

"Oh, madame!" cried La Mole, recalled to himself by these words, which the queen had spoken in such a low tone that she hoped Gillonne only had heard them, "on my knees I entreat you, let me depart. Yes, dead or alive! madame, have pity on me! Oh! you do not answer. I will tell you all, and then you will drive me away, I hope."

"Be silent," said Marguerite, who found an indescribable charm in the young man's reproaches; "be silent."

"Madame," replied La Mole, who did not find that anger he expected in the voice of the queen, "madame, I tell you again, everything is audible in this closet. Oh, do not make me perish by tortures more cruel than the executioner could inflict"—

"Silence! silence!" said Marguerite.

"Oh, madame, you are merciless! you will not hear me, you will not understand me. Know, then, that I love you"—

"Silence! I tell you," interrupted Marguerite, placing on his mouth her warm, perfumed hand, which he seized between both of his and pressed eagerly to his lips.

"But"—he whispered.

"Be silent, child—who is this rebel that refuses to obey his queen?"

Then darting out of the closet, she shut the door and stood leaning against the wall pressing her trembling hand to her heart, as if to control it.

"Open, Gillonne."

Gillonne left the room, and an instant after, the fine, intellectual, but rather anxious countenance of the King of Navarre appeared behind the tapestry.

"You have sent for me, madame?"

"Yes, sire. Your majesty received my letter?"

"And not without some surprise, I confess," said Henry, looking round with distrust, which, however, almost instantly vanished from his mind.

"And not without some apprehension," added Marguerite.

"I confess it, madame! But still, surrounded as I am by deadly enemies, by friends still more dangerous, perhaps, than my open foes, I recollected that one evening I had seen a noble generosity shining in your eyes—'twas the night of our marriage; that one other evening I had seen the star of courage beaming in them—'twas yesterday, the day fixed for my death."

"Well, sire?" said Marguerite, smiling, while Henry seemed striving to read her heart.

"Well, madame," returned the king, "thinking of these things, I said to myself, as I read your letter bidding me come: 'Without friends, for he is a disarmed prisoner, the King of Navarre has but one means of dying nobly, of dying a death that will be recorded in history. It is to die betrayed by his wife; and I am come'"—

"Sire," replied Marguerite, "you will change your tone when you learn that all this is the work of a woman who loves you—and whom you love."

Henry started back at these words, and his keen gray eyes under their black lashes were fixed on the queen with curiosity.

"Oh, reassure yourself, sire," said the queen, smiling; "I am not that person."

"But, madame," said Henry, "you sent me this key, and this is your writing."

"It is my writing, I confess; the letter came from me, but the key is a different matter. Let it satisfy you to know that it has passed through the hands of four women before it reached you."

"Of four women?" exclaimed Henry in astonishment.

"Yes," said Marguerite; "Queen Catharine's, Madame de Sauve's, Gillonne's, and mine."

Henry pondered over this enigma.

"Now let us talk reasonably, sire," said Marguerite, "and above all let us speak frankly. Common report has it that your majesty has consented to abjure. Is it true?"

"That report is mistaken; I have not yet consented."

"But your mind is made up?"

"That is to say, I am deliberating. When one is twenty and almost a king, *ventre saint gris*! there are many things well worth a mass."

"And among other things life, for instance!"

Henry could not repress a fleeting smile.

"You do not tell me your whole thought," said Marguerite.

"I have reservations for my allies, madame; and you know we are but allies as yet; if indeed you were both my ally—and"—

"And your wife, sire?"

"Faith! yes, and my wife"—

"What then?"

"Why, then, it might be different, and I perhaps might resolve to remain King of the Huguenots, as they call me. But as it is, I must be content to live."

Marguerite looked at Henry in such a peculiar manner that it would have awakened suspicion in a less acute mind than his.

"And are you quite sure of succeeding even in that?" she asked.

"Why, almost; but you know, in this world nothing is certain."

"It is true," replied Marguerite, "your majesty shows such moderation and professes such disinterestedness, that after having renounced your crown, after having renounced your religion, you will probably renounce your alliance with a daughter of France; at least this is hoped for."

These words bore a significance which sent a thrill through Henry's whole frame; but instantaneously repressing the emotion, he said:

"Deign to recollect, madame, that at this moment I am not my own master; I shall therefore do what the King of France orders me. If I were consulted the least in the world on this question, affecting as it does my throne, my honor, and my life, rather than build my future on this forced marriage of ours, I should prefer to enter a monastery or turn gamekeeper."

This calm resignation, this renunciation of the world, alarmed Marguerite. She thought perhaps this rupture of the marriage had been agreed upon by Charles IX., Catharine, and the King of Navarre. Why should she not be taken as a dupe or a victim? Because she was sister of the one and daughter of the other? Experience had taught her that this relationship gave her no ground on which to build her security.

So ambition was gnawing at this young woman's, or rather this young queen's heart, and she was too far above vulgar frailties to be drawn into any selfish meanness; in the case of every woman, however mediocre she may be, when she loves her love has none of these petty trials, for true love is also an ambition.

"Your majesty," said Marguerite, with a sort of mocking disdain, "has no confidence in the star that shines over the head of every king!"

"Ah," said Henry, "I vainly look for mine now, I cannot see it; 'tis hidden by the storm which now threatens me!"

"And suppose a woman's breath were to dispel this tempest, and make the star reappear, brilliant as ever?"

"'Twere difficult."

"Do you deny the existence of this woman?"

"No, I deny her power."

"You mean her will?"

"I said her power, and I repeat, her power. A woman is powerful only when love and interest are combined within her in equal degrees; if either sentiment predominates, she is, like Achilles, vulnerable; now as to this woman, if I mistake not, I cannot rely on her love."

Marguerite made no reply.

"Listen," said Henry; "at the last stroke of the bell of Saint Germain l'Auxerrois you must have thought of regaining your liberty, sacrificed for the purpose of destroying my followers. My concern was to save my life: that was the most essential thing. We lose Navarre, indeed; but what is that compared with your being enabled to speak aloud in your room, which you dared not do when you had some one listening to you in yonder closet?"

Deeply absorbed as she was in her thoughts, Marguerite could not refrain from smiling. The king rose and prepared to seek his own apartment, for it was some time after eleven, and every one at the Louvre was, or seemed to be, asleep.

Henry took three steps toward the door, then suddenly stopped as if for the first time recollecting the motive of his visit to the queen.

"By the way, madame," said he, "had you not something to communicate to me? or did you desire to give me an opportunity of thanking you for the reprieve which your brave presence in the King's armory brought me? In truth it was just in time, madame; I cannot deny it, you appeared like a goddess of antiquity, in the nick of time to save my life."

"Unfortunate man!" cried Marguerite, in a muffled voice, and seizing her husband's arm, "do you not see that nothing is saved, neither your liberty, your crown, nor your life? Infatuated madman! Poor madman! Did you, then, see nothing in my letter but a rendezvous? Did you believe that Marguerite, indignant at your coldness, desired reparation?"

"I confess, madame," said Henry in astonishment, "I confess"—

Marguerite shrugged her shoulders with an expression impossible to describe.

At this instant a strange sound was heard, like a sharp insistent scratching at the secret door.

Marguerite led the king toward the little door.

"Listen," said she.

"The queen mother is leaving her room," said a trembling voice outside, which Henry instantly recognized as Madame de Sauve's.

"Where is she going?" asked Marguerite.

"She is coming to your majesty."

And then the rustling of a silk gown, growing fainter, showed that Madame de Sauve was hastening rapidly away.

"Oho!" exclaimed Henry.

"I was sure of this," said Marguerite.

"And I," replied Henry, "feared it, and this is the proof of it."

And half opening his black velvet doublet, he showed the queen that he had beneath it a shirt of mail, and a long Milan poniard, which instantly glittered in his hand like a viper in the sun.

"As if you needed weapon and cuirass here!" cried Marguerite. "Quick, quick, sire! conceal that dagger; 'tis the queen mother, indeed, but the queen mother only."

"Yet"—

"Silence!—I hear her."

And putting her mouth close to Henry's ear, she whispered something which the young king heard with attention mingled with astonishment. Then he hid himself behind the curtains of the bed.

Meantime, with the quickness of a panther, Marguerite sprang to the closet, where La Mole was waiting in a fever of excitement, opened the door, found the young man, and pressing his hand in the darkness—"Silence," said she, approaching her lips so near that he felt her warm and balmy breath; "silence!"

Then returning to her chamber, she tore off her head-dress, cut the laces of her dress with her poniard, and sprang into bed.

It was time—the key turned in the lock. Catharine had a key for every door in the Louvre.

"Who is there?" cried Marguerite, as Catharine placed on guard at the door the four gentlemen by whom she was attended.

And, as if frightened by this sudden intrusion into her chamber, Marguerite sprang out from behind the curtains of her bed in a white dressing-gown, and then recognizing Catharine, came to kiss her hand with such well-feigned surprise that the wily Florentine herself could not help being deceived by it.

CHAPTER XIV.

THE SECOND MARRIAGE NIGHT.

The queen mother cast a marvellously rapid glance around her. The velvet slippers at the foot of the bed, Marguerite's clothes scattered over the chairs, the way she rubbed her eyes as if to drive away her sleepiness, all convinced Catharine that she had awakened her daughter.

Then she smiled as a woman does when she has succeeded in her plans, and drawing up an easy chair, she said:

"Let us sit down, Marguerite, and talk."

"Madame, I am listening."

"It is time," said Catharine, slowly shutting her eyes in the characteristic way of people who weigh each word or who deeply dissimulate, "it is time, my daughter, that you should know how ardently your brother and myself desire to see you happy."

This exordium for one who knew Catharine was alarming.

"What can she be about to say?" thought Marguerite.

"To be sure," continued La Florentine, "in giving you in marriage we fulfilled one of those acts of policy frequently required by important interests of those who govern; but I must confess, my poor child, that we had no expectation that the indifference manifested by the King of Navarre for one so young, so lovely, and so fascinating as yourself would be so obstinate."

Marguerite arose, and folding her robe de chambre around her, courtesied with ceremonious respect to her mother.

"I have heard to-night only," continued Catharine, "otherwise I should have paid you an earlier visit, that your husband is far from showing you those attentions you have a right to claim, not merely as a beautiful woman, but as a princess of France."

Marguerite sighed, and Catharine, encouraged by this mute approval, proceeded.

"In fact, that the King of Navarre is openly cohabiting one of my maids of honor who is scandalously smitten with him, that he scorns the love of the woman graciously given to him, is an insult to which we poor powerful ones of the earth cannot apply a remedy, and yet the meanest gentleman in our kingdom would avenge it by calling out his son-in-law or having his son do so."

Marguerite dropped her head.

"For some time, my daughter," Catharine went on to say, "I have seen by your reddened eyes, by your bitter sallies against La Sauve, that in spite of your efforts your heart must show external signs of its bleeding wound."

Marguerite trembled: a slight movement had shaken the curtains; but fortunately Catharine did not notice it.

"This wound," said she with affectionate sweetness redoubled, "this wound, my daughter, a mother's hand must cure. Those who with the intention of securing your happiness have brought about your marriage, and who in their anxiety about you notice that every night Henry of Navarre goes to the wrong rooms; those who cannot allow a kinglet like him to insult a woman of such beauty, of such high rank, and so worthy, by scorning your person and neglecting his chances of posterity; those who see that at the first favorable wind, this wild and insolent madcap will turn against our family and expel you from his house—I say have not they the right to secure your interests by entirely dividing them from his, so that your future may be better suited to yourself and your rank?"

"And yet, madame," replied Marguerite, "in spite of these observations so replete with maternal love, and filling me with joy and pride, I am bold enough to affirm to your majesty that the King of Navarre is my husband."

Catharine started with rage, and drawing closer to Marguerite she said:

"He, your husband? Is it sufficient to make you husband and wife that the Church has pronounced its blessing upon you? And is the marriage consecration only in the words of the priest? He, your husband? Ah, my daughter! if you were Madame de Sauve you might give me this reply. But wholly contrary of what we expected of him since you granted Henry of Navarre the honor of calling you his wife, he has given all your rights to another woman, and at this very instant even," said Catharine, raising her voice,—"this key opens the door of Madame de Sauve's apartment—come with me and you will see"—

"Oh, not so loud, madame, not so loud, I beseech you!" said Marguerite, "for not only are you mistaken, but"—

"Well?"

"Well, you will awaken my husband!"

As she said these words Marguerite arose with a perfectly voluptuous grace, her white dress fluttering loosely around her, while the large open sleeves displayed her bare and faultlessly modelled arm and truly royal hand, and taking a rose-colored taper she held it near the bed, and drawing back the curtain, and smiling significantly at her mother, pointed to the haughty profile, the black locks, and the parted lips of the King of Navarre, who, as he lay upon the disordered bed, seemed buried in profound repose.

Pale, with haggard eyes, her body thrown back as if an abyss had opened at her feet, Catharine uttered not a cry, but a hoarse bellow.

"You see, madame," said Marguerite, "you were misinformed."

Catharine looked first at Marguerite, then at Henry. In her active mind she combined Marguerite's smile with the picture of that pale and dewy brow, those eyes circled by dark-colored rings, and she bit her thin lips in silent fury.

Marguerite allowed her mother for a moment to contemplate this picture, which affected her like the head of Medusa. Then she dropped the curtain and stepping on her tip-toes she came back to Catharine and sat down:

"You were saying, madame?"—

The Florentine for several seconds tried to fathom the young woman's naïveté; but as if her keen glance had become blunted on Marguerite's calmness, she exclaimed, "Nothing," and hastily left the room.

As soon as the sound of her departing footsteps had died away down the long corridor, the bed-curtains opened a second time, and Henry, with sparkling eyes, trembling hand, and panting breath, came out and knelt at

Marguerite's feet; he was dressed only in his short-clothes and his coat of mail, so that Marguerite, seeing him in such an odd rig, could not help laughing even while she was warmly shaking hands with him.

"Ah, madame! ah, Marguerite!" he cried, "how shall I ever repay you?"

And he covered her hand with kisses which gradually strayed higher up along her arm.

"Sire," said she, gently retreating, "can you forget that a poor woman to whom you owe your life is mourning and suffering on your account? Madame de Sauve," added she, in a lower tone, "has forgotten her jealousy in sending you to me; and to that sacrifice she may probably have to add her life, for you know better than any one how terrible is my mother's anger!"

Henry shuddered; and, rising, started to leave the room.

"Upon second thoughts," said Marguerite, with admirable coquetry, "I have thought it all over and I see no cause for alarm. The key was given to you without any directions, and it will be supposed that you granted me the preference for to-night."

"And so I do, Marguerite! Consent but to forget"—

"Not so loud, sire, not so loud!" replied the queen, employing the same words she had a few minutes before used to her mother; "any one in the adjoining closet can hear you. And as I am not yet quite free, I will ask you to speak in a lower tone."

"Oho!" said Henry, half smiling, half gloomily, "that's true! I was forgetting that I am probably not the one destined to play the end of this interesting scene! This closet"—

"Let me beg of your majesty to enter there," said Marguerite; "for I am desirous of having the honor of presenting to you a worthy gentleman, wounded during the massacre while making his way to the Louvre to apprise your majesty of the danger with which you were threatened."

The queen went toward the door, and Henry followed her. She opened it, and the king was thunderstruck at beholding a man in this cabinet, fated to reveal such continued surprises.

But La Mole was still more surprised at thus unexpectedly finding himself in the presence of Henry of Navarre. The result was that the king cast an ironical glance on Marguerite, who bore it without flinching.

"Sire," said she, "I am in dread lest this gentleman may be murdered even here, in my very chamber; he is devoted to your majesty's service, and for that reason I commend him to your royal protection."

147

"Sire," continued the young man, "I am the Comte Lerac de la Mole, whom your majesty was expecting; I was recommended to you by that poor Monsieur de Téligny, who was killed by my side."

"Aha!" replied Henry; "you are right, sir. The queen gave me his letter; but have you not also a letter from the governor of Languedoc?"

"Yes, sire, and I was recommended to deliver it to your majesty as soon as I arrived."

"Why did you not do so?"

"Sire, I hastened to the Louvre last evening, but your majesty was too much occupied to give me audience."

"True!" answered the king; "but I should think you might have sent the letter to me?"

"I had orders from Monsieur d'Auriac to give it to no one else but your majesty, since it contained, he said, information so important that he feared to entrust it to any ordinary messenger."

"The contents are, indeed, of a serious nature," said the king, when he had received and read the letter; "advising my instant withdrawal from the court of France, and retirement to Béarn. M. d'Auriac, although a Catholic, was always a stanch friend of mine; and it is possible that, acting as governor of a province, he got scent of what was in the wind here. *Ventre saint gris*! monsieur! why was not this letter given to me three days ago, instead of now?"

"Because, as I before assured your majesty, that using all the speed and diligence in my power, it was wholly impossible to arrive before yesterday."

"That is very unfortunate, very unfortunate," murmured the king; "we should then have been in security, either at Rochelle or in some broad plain surrounded by two or three thousand trusty horsemen."

"Sire, what is done is done," said Marguerite, in a low voice, "and instead of wasting your time complaining over the past you must do the best possible with the future."

"If you were in my place, madame," replied Henry, with his questioning look, "you would still have hope, would you?"

"Certainly I should; I should consider myself as playing a game of three points, of which I had lost only the first."

"Ah, madame," whispered Henry, "if I dared but hope that you would go partners with me in the game"—

"If I had intended to side with your adversaries," replied Marguerite, "I should scarcely have delayed so long."

"True!" replied Henry, "and I am ungrateful; and as you say, the past may still be repaired."

"Alas! sire," said La Mole, "I wish your majesty every kind of good fortune; but now the admiral is no more."

Over Henry's face passed that sly, peasant-like smile, which was not understood at court until after he became King of France.

"But, madame," said the king, attentively observing La Mole, "this gentleman cannot remain here without causing you considerable inconvenience, and being himself subject to very unpleasant surprises. What will you do with him?"

"Could we not remove him from the Louvre?" asked Marguerite, "for I entirely agree with you!"

"It will be difficult."

"Then could not Monsieur de la Mole find accommodation in your majesty's apartments?"

"Alas, madame! you speak as if I were still King of the Huguenots, and had subjects to command. You are aware that I am half converted to the Catholic faith and have no people at all."

Any one but Marguerite would have promptly answered: "He is a Catholic."

But the queen wished Henry himself to ask her to do the very thing she was desirous of effecting; while La Mole, perceiving his protectress's caution and not knowing where to set foot on the slippery ground of such a dangerous court as that of France, remained perfectly silent.

"But what is this the governor says in his letter?" said Henry, again casting his eyes over the missive he held in his hand. "He states that your mother was a Catholic, and from that circumstance originates the interest he felt in you."

"And what were you telling me, Monsieur le Comte," said Marguerite, "respecting a vow you had formed to change your religion? I confess my recollection on the subject is somewhat confused. Have the goodness to assist me, M. de la Mole. Did not your conversation refer to something of the nature the king appears to desire?"

"Alas! madame, what I did say was so coldly received by your majesty that I did not dare"—

"Simply because it in no way concerned me," answered Marguerite. "But

149

explain yourself to the king—explain!"

"Well, what was the vow?" asked the king.

"Sire," said La Mole, "when pursued by assassins, myself unarmed, and almost expiring from my two wounds, I fancied I beheld my mother's spirit holding a cross in her hands and guiding me to the Louvre. Then I vowed that if my life were preserved I would adopt the religion of my mother, who had been permitted to leave her grave to direct me to a place of safety during that horrible night. Heaven conducted me here, sire. I find myself here under the protection of a princess of France and of the King of Navarre; my life was miraculously saved, therefore I must fulfil my vow. I am ready to become a Catholic."

Henry frowned. Sceptic that he was, he could well understand a change of religion from motives of interest, but he distrusted abjuration through faith.

"The king does not want to take charge of my *protégé*," thought Marguerite.

La Mole still remained mute and awkward between the two opposing wills. He felt, without being able to define why, that he was in a ridiculous position. Marguerite's womanly tact came to his relief.

"Sire," said she, "we forget that the poor wounded gentleman has need of repose. I myself am half asleep. Ah, see!"

La Mole did indeed turn pale; but it was at Marguerite's last words, which he had interpreted according to his own ideas.

"Well, madame," answered Henry, "nothing can be simpler. Can we not leave Monsieur de la Mole to take his repose."

The young man fixed a supplicating look on Marguerite, and, in spite of the presence of the two majesties, sunk upon a chair, overcome with fatigue and pain.

Marguerite understood all the love in his look, all the despair in his weakness.

"Sire," said she, "your majesty is bound to confer on this young man, who imperilled his life for his king, since he received his wounds while coming hither to inform you of the admiral's death and Téligny's,—your majesty is bound, I repeat, to confer on him an honor for which he will be grateful all his life long."

"What is it, madame?" asked Henry. "Command me, I am ready."

"Monsieur de la Mole must sleep to-night at your majesty's feet, while you, sire, can sleep on this couch. With the permission of my august spouse," added Marguerite, smiling, "I will summon Gillonne and return to bed, for I assure you I am not the least wearied of us three."

Henry had shrewd sense and a quick perception of things; friends and enemies subsequently found fault with him for possessing too much of both. He fully admitted that she who thus banished him from the nuptial bed was well justified in so doing by the indifference he had himself manifested toward her; and then, too, she had just repaid this indifference by saving his life; he therefore allowed no self-love to dictate his answer.

"Madame," said he, "if Monsieur de la Mole were able to come to my quarters I would give him my own bed."

"Yes," replied Marguerite, "but your quarters just at the present time would not be safe for either of you, and prudence dictates that your majesty should remain here until morning."

Then without awaiting the king's reply she summoned Gillonne, and bade her prepare the necessary cushions for the king, and to arrange a bed at the king's feet for La Mole, who appeared so happy and contented with the honor that one would have sworn he no longer felt his wounds.

Then Marguerite, courtesing low to the king, passed into her chamber, the door of which was well furnished with bolts, and threw herself on the bed.

"One thing is certain," said Marguerite to herself, "to-morrow Monsieur de la Mole must have a protector at the Louvre; and he who, to-night, sees and hears nothing, may change his mind to-morrow."

Then she called Gillonne, who was waiting to receive her last orders.

Gillonne came to her.

"Gillonne," said she in a whisper, "you must contrive to bring my brother the Duc d'Alençon here to-morrow morning before eight o'clock."

It was just striking two at the Louvre.

La Mole for a few moments talked on political subjects with the king, who gradually grew drowsy and was soon snoring.

La Mole might have slept as well as the king, but Marguerite was not asleep; she kept turning from side to side in her bed, and the noise she made disturbed the young man's ideas and sleep.

"He is very young," murmured Marguerite in her wakeful mood, "he is very timid; perhaps—but we must see—perhaps it will be ridiculous. Yet he has handsome eyes—and a good figure, and he is very charming; but if he should not turn out to be brave!—He ran away!—He is renouncing his faith! It is too bad—the dream began well. However, let things take their course and entrust them to that madcap Henriette's triple god."

And toward daybreak Marguerite fell asleep, murmuring:

"*Eros, Cupido, Amor.*"

———

CHAPTER XV.

WHAT WOMAN WILLS, GOD WILLS.

Marguerite was not mistaken: the wrath distilled in the depths of Catharine's heart at sight of this comedy, the intrigue of which she followed without being in any way able to change its denouement, required a victim. So instead of going directly to her own room the queen mother proceeded to that of her lady in waiting.

Madame de Sauve was in expectation of two visits—one she hoped to receive from Henry, and the other she feared was in store for her from the queen mother. As she lay in her bed only partially undressed, while Dariole kept watch in the antechamber, she heard a key turn in the lock, and then slowly approaching footsteps which would have seemed heavy if they had not been deadened by thick rugs. She did not recognize Henry's light, eager step; she suspected that Dariole was prevented from coming to warn her, and so leaning on her elbow she waited with eye and ear alert. The portière was lifted and the trembling young woman saw Catharine de Médicis appear.

Catharine seemed calm; but Madame de Sauve, accustomed for two years to study her, well knew what dark designs, and possibly cruel vengeance, might be concealed beneath that apparent calm.

At sight of Catharine, Madame de Sauve was about to spring from her bed, but Catharine signed to her to stay where she was; and poor Charlotte was fixed to the spot, inwardly endeavoring to collect all the forces of her soul to endure the storm which was silently gathering.

"Did you convey the key to the King of Navarre?" inquired Catharine, without the tone of her voice betraying any change; and yet as she spoke her lips grew paler and paler.

"I did, madame," answered Charlotte, in a voice which she vainly tried to make as firm and assured as Catherine's was.

"And have you seen him?"

"Who?" asked Madame de Sauve.

"The King of Navarre."

"No, madame; but I am expecting him, and when I heard the key turn in the lock, I firmly believed it was he."

At this answer, which indicated either perfect confidence or deep dissimulation on Madame de Sauve's part, Catharine could not repress a slight shiver. She clinched her short plump hand.

"And yet you knew perfectly well," said she with her evil smile, "you knew perfectly well, Carlotta, that the King of Navarre would not come to-night."

"I, madame? I knew that?" exclaimed Charlotte, with a tone of surprise perfectly well assumed.

"Yes, you knew it!"

"If he does not come, he must be dead!" replied the young woman, shuddering at the mere supposition.

What gave Charlotte the courage to lie so was the certainty that she would suffer from a terrible vengeance if her little treason should be discovered.

"But did you not write to the king, Carlotta mia?" inquired Catharine, with the same cruel and silent laugh.

"No, madame," answered Charlotte, with well-assumed naïveté, "I cannot recollect receiving your majesty's commands to do so."

A short silence followed, during which Catharine continued to gaze on Madame de Sauve as the serpent looks at the bird it wishes to fascinate.

"You think you are pretty," said Catharine, "you think you are clever, do you not?"

"No, madame," answered Charlotte; "I only know that sometimes your majesty has been graciously pleased to commend both my personal attractions and address."

"Well, then," said Catharine, growing eager and animated, "you were mistaken if you think so, and I lied when I told you so; you are a simpleton and hideous compared to my daughter Margot."

"Oh, madame," replied Charlotte, "that is a fact I will not even try to deny—

least of all in your presence."

"So, then, the King of Navarre prefers my daughter to you; a circumstance, I presume, not to your wishes, and certainly not what we agreed should be the case."

"Alas, madame," cried Charlotte, bursting into a torrent of tears which now flowed from no feigned source, "if it be so, I can but say I am very unfortunate!"

"It is so," said Catharine, darting the two-fold keenness of her eyes like a double poniard into Madame de Sauve's heart.

"But who can make you believe that?" asked Charlotte.

"Go down to the Queen of Navarre's *pazza*, and you will find your lover there!"

"Oh!" exclaimed Madame de Sauve.

Catharine shrugged her shoulders.

"Are you jealous, pray?" asked the queen mother.

"I?" exclaimed Madame de Sauve, recalling her fast-failing strength.

"Yes, you! I should like to see a Frenchwoman's jealousy."

"But," said Madame de Sauve, "how should your majesty expect me to be jealous except out of vanity? I love the King of Navarre only as far as your majesty's service requires it."

Catharine gazed at her for a moment with dreamy eyes.

"What you tell me may on the whole be true," she murmured.

"Your majesty reads my heart."

"And your heart is wholly devoted to me?"

"Command me, madame, and you shall judge for yourself."

"Well, then, Carlotta, since you are ready to sacrifice yourself in my service, you must still continue for my sake to be in love with the King of Navarre and, above all, to be very jealous,—jealous as an Italian woman."

"But, madame," asked Charlotte, "how does an Italian woman show her jealousy?"

"I will tell you," replied Catharine, and after nodding her head two or three times she left the room as deliberately and noiselessly as she had come in.

Charlotte, confused by the keen look of those eyes dilated like a cat's or a panther's without thereby losing anything of their inscrutability, allowed her to go without uttering a single word, without even letting her breathing be heard, and she did not even take a respiration until she heard the door close behind her and Dariole came to say that the terrible apparition had departed.

"Dariole," said she, "draw up an armchair close to my bed and spend the night in it. I beg you to do so, for I should not dare to stay alone."

Dariole obeyed; but in spite of the company of her faithful attendant, who stayed near her, in spite of the light from the lamp which she commanded to be left burning for the sake of greater tranquillity, Madame de Sauve also did not fall asleep till daylight, so insistently rang in her ears the metallic accent of Catharine's voice.

Though Marguerite had not fallen asleep till daybreak she awoke at the first blast of the trumpets, at the first barking of the dogs. She instantly arose and began to put on a costume so negligent that it could not fail to attract attention. Then she summoned her women, and had the gentlemen ordinarily in attendance on the King of Navarre shown into her antechamber, and finally opening the door which shut Henry and De la Mole into the same room, she gave the count an affectionate glance and addressing her husband she said:

"Come, sire, it is not sufficient to have made madame my mother believe in what is not; it still remains for you to convince your whole court that a perfect understanding exists between us. But make yourself quite easy," added she, laughing, "and remember my words, rendered almost solemn by the circumstances. To-day will be the last time that I shall put your majesty to such a cruel test."

The King of Navarre smiled and ordered his gentlemen to be admitted.

Just as they were bowing to him he pretended suddenly to recollect having left his mantle on the queen's bed and begged their excuse for receiving them in such a way; then, taking his mantle from the hands of Marguerite, who stood blushing by his side, he clasped it on his shoulder. Next, turning to his gentlemen, he inquired what news there was in the city and at court.

Marguerite was engaged in watching out of the corner of her eye the imperceptible signs of astonishment betrayed by the gentlemen at detecting this newly revealed intimacy between the king and queen of Navarre, when an usher entered, followed by three or four gentlemen, and announced the Duc d'Alençon.

To bring him there Gillonne had only to tell him that the king had spent the night in the queen's room.

François rushed in so precipitately that he almost upset those who preceded him. His first glance was for Henry; his next was for Marguerite.

Henry replied with a courteous bow; Marguerite composed her features so that they expressed the utmost serenity.

Then the duke cast a vague but scrutinizing look around the whole room: he saw the two pillows placed at the head of the bed, the derangement of its tapestried coverings, and the king's hat thrown on a chair.

He turned pale, but quickly recovering himself, he said:

"Does my royal brother Henry join this morning with the King in his game of tennis?"

"Does his Majesty do me the honor to select me as his partner?" inquired Henry, "or is it only a little attention on your part, my brother-in-law?"

"His Majesty has not so said, certainly," replied the duke, somewhat embarrassed; "but don't you generally play with him?"

Henry smiled, for so many and such serious events had occurred since he last played with the King that he would not have been astonished to learn that the King had changed his habitual companions at the game.

"I shall go there," said Henry, with a smile.

"Come," cried the duke.

"Are you going away?" inquired Marguerite.

"Yes, sister!"

"Are you in great haste?"

"In great haste."

"Might I venture to detain you for a few minutes?"

Such a request was so unusual coming from Marguerite that her brother looked at her while her color came and went.

"What can she be going to say to him?" thought Henry, no less surprised than the duke himself.

Marguerite, as if she had guessed her husband's thought, turned toward him.

"Sire," said she, with a charming smile, "you may go back to his majesty if it seem good to you, for the secret which I am going to reveal to my brother is already known to you, for the reason that the request which I made you yesterday in regard to this secret was as good as refused by your majesty. I should not wish, therefore," continued Marguerite, "to weary your majesty a second time by expressing in your presence a wish which seemed to be disagreeable."

"What do you mean?" asked François, looking at both of them with astonishment.

"Aha!" exclaimed Henry, flushing, with indignation, "I know what you mean, madame. In truth, I regret that I am not free. But if I cannot offer Monsieur de la Mole such hospitality as would be equivalent to an assurance, I cannot do less than to recommend to my brother D'Alençon the person *in whom you feel such a lively interest.* Perhaps," he added, in order to give still more emphasis to the words italicized, "perhaps my brother will discover some way whereby you will be permitted to keep Monsieur de la Mole here near you—that would be better than anything else, would it not, madame?"

"Come, come!" said Marguerite to herself, "the two together will do what neither of them would do individually."

And she opened the closet door and invited the wounded young man to come forth, saying to Henry as she did so:

"Your majesty must now explain to my brother why we are interested in Monsieur de la Mole."

Henry, caught in the snare, briefly related to M. d'Alençon, half a Protestant for the sake of opposition, as he himself was partly a Catholic from prudence, the arrival of Monsieur de la Mole at Paris, and how the young man had been severely wounded while bringing to him a letter from M. d'Auriac.

When the duke turned round, La Mole had come out from the closet and was standing before him.

François, at the sight of him, so handsome, so pale, and consequently doubly captivating by reason of his good looks and his pallor, felt a new sense of distrust spring up in the depths of his soul. Marguerite held him both through jealousy and through pride.

"Brother," said Marguerite, "I will engage that this young gentleman will be useful to whoever may employ him. Should you accept his services, he will obtain a powerful protector, and you, a devoted servitor. In such times as the present, brother," continued she, "we cannot be too well surrounded by devoted friends; more especially," added she, lowering her voice so as to be heard by no one but the duke, "when one is ambitious, and has the misfortune to be only third in the succession to the throne."

Then she put her finger on her lip, to intimate to François that in spite of the initiation she still kept secret an important part of her idea.

"Perhaps," she added, "you may differ from Henry, in considering it not befitting that this young gentleman should remain so immediately in the vicinity of my apartments."

"Sister," replied François, eagerly, "if it meet your wishes, Monsieur de la Mole shall, in half an hour, be installed in my quarters, where, I think, he can have no cause to fear any danger. Let him love me and I will love him."

François was untruthful, for already in the very depths of his heart he detested La Mole.

"Well, well! So then I was not mistaken," said Marguerite to herself, seeing the King of Navarre's scowling face. "Ah, I see that to lead you two, one must lead the other."

Then finishing her thought:

"There! 'then you are doing well, Marguerite,' Henriette would say."

In fact, half an hour later La Mole, having been solemnly catechised by Marguerite, kissed the hem of her gown and with an agility remarkable in a wounded man was mounting the stairs that led to the Duc d'Alençon's quarters.

Two or three days passed, during which the excellent understanding between Henry and his wife seemed to grow more and more firmly established.

Henry had obtained permission not to make a public renunciation of his religion; but he had formally recanted in the presence of the king's confessor, and every morning he listened to the mass performed at the Louvre. At night he made a show of going to his wife's rooms, entered by the principal door, talked a few minutes with her, and then took his departure by the small secret door, and went up to Madame de Sauve, who had duly informed him of the queen mother's visit as well as the unquestionable danger which threatened him. Warned on both sides, Henry redoubled his watchfulness against the queen mother and felt all distrust of her because little by little her face began to unbend, and one morning Henry detected a friendly smile on her bloodless lips. That day he had the greatest difficulty to bring himself to eat anything else than eggs cooked by himself or to drink anything else than water which his own eyes had seen dipped up from the Seine.

The massacres were still going on, but nevertheless were diminishing in violence. There had been such a wholesale butchery of the Huguenots that their number was greatly reduced. The larger part were dead; many had fled; a few had remained in concealment. Occasionally a great outcry arose in one district or another; it meant that one of these was discovered. Then the execution was either private or public according as the victim was driven into a corner or could escape. In such circumstances it furnished great amusement for the neighborhood where the affair took place; for instead of growing calmer as their enemies were annihilated, the Catholics grew more and more ferocious; the fewer the remaining victims, the more bloodthirsty they seemed in their persecution of the rest.

Charles IX. had taken great pleasure in hunting the Huguenots, and when he could no longer continue the chase himself he took delight in the noise of others hunting them.

One day, returning from playing at mall, which with tennis and hunting were his favorite amusements, he went to his mother's apartments in high spirits, followed by his usual train of courtiers.

"Mother," he said, embracing the Florentine, who, observing his joy, was already trying to detect its cause; "mother, good news! *Mort de tous les diables!* Do you know that the admiral's illustrious carcass which it was said was lost has been found?"

"Aha!" said Catharine.

"Oh, heavens! yes. You thought as I did, mother, the dogs had eaten a wedding dinner off him, but it was not so. My people, my dear people, my good people, had a clever idea and have hung the admiral up at the gibbet of Montfaucon.

> *"Du haut en bas Gaspard on a jété,*
> *Et puis de bas en haut on l'a monté."*[3]

"Well!" said Catharine.

"Well, good mother," replied Charles IX., "I have a strong desire to see him again, dear old man, now I know he is really dead. It is very fine weather and everything seems to be blooming to-day. The air is full of life and perfume, and I feel better than I ever did. If you like, mother, we will get on horseback and go to Montfaucon."

"Willingly, my son," said Catharine, "if I had not made an appointment which I cannot defer; and beside, to pay a visit to a man of such importance as the admiral, we should invite the whole court. It will be an occasion for observers to make curious observations. We shall see who comes and who stays away."

"Faith, you are right, mother, we will put it off till to-morrow; that will be better, so send out your invitations and I will send mine; or rather let us not invite any one. We will only say we are going, and then every one will be free. Good-by, mother! I am going to play on the horn."

"You will exhaust yourself, Charles, as Ambroise Paré is always telling you, and he is right. It is too severe an exercise for you."

"Bah! bah! bah!" said Charles; "I wish I were sure nothing else would be the cause of my death. I should then bury every one here, including Harry, who will one day succeed us all, as Nostradamus prophesies."

Catharine frowned.

"My son," she said, "mistrust especially all things that appear impossible, and meanwhile take care of yourself."

"Only two or three blasts to rejoice my dogs, poor things; they are wearied to death with doing nothing. I ought to have let them loose on the Huguenots; that would have done them good!"

And Charles IX. left his mother's room, went into his armory, took down a horn, and played on it with a vigor that would have done honor to Roland himself. It was difficult to understand how so weak a frame and such pale lips could blow a blast so powerful.

Catharine, in truth, was awaiting some one as she had told her son. A moment after he had left her, one of her women came and spoke to her in a low voice. The queen smiled, rose, and saluting the persons who formed her court, followed the messenger.

Réné the Florentine, the man to whom on the eve of Saint Bartholomew the King of Navarre had given such a diplomatic reception, had just entered her oratory.

"Ah, here you are, Réné," said Catharine, "I was impatiently waiting for you."

Réné bowed.

"Did you receive the note I wrote you yesterday?"

"I had that honor."

"Did you make another trial, as I asked you to do, of the horoscope cast by Ruggieri, and agreeing so well with the prophecy of Nostradamus, which says that all my three sons shall reign? For several days past, affairs have decidedly changed, Réné, and it has occurred to me that possibly fate has become less threatening."

"Madame," replied Réné, shaking his head, "your majesty knows well that affairs do not change fate; on the contrary, fate controls affairs."

"Still, you have tried the sacrifice again, have you not?"

"Yes, madame," replied Réné; "for it is my duty to obey you in all things."

"Well—and the result?"

"Still the same, madame."

"What, the black lamb uttered its three cries?"

"Just the same as before, madame."

"The sign of three cruel deaths in my family," murmured Catharine.

"Alas!" said Réné.

"What then?"

"Then, madame, there was in its entrails that strange displacement of the liver which we had already observed in the first two—it was wrong side up!"

"A change of dynasty! Still—still—still the same!" muttered Catharine; "yet we must fight against this, Réné," she added.

Réné shook his head.

"I have told your majesty," he said, "that fate rules."

"Is that your opinion?" asked Catharine.

"Yes, madame."

"Do you remember Jeanne d'Albret's horoscope?"

"Yes, madame."

"Repeat it to me, I have quite forgotten it."

"*Vives honorata*," said Réné, "*morieris reformidata, regina amplificabere*."

"That means, I believe," said Catharine, "*Thou shalt live honored*—and she lacked common necessaries, poor thing! *Thou shalt die feared*—and we laughed at her. *Thou shalt be greater than thou hast been as a queen*—and she is dead, and sleeps in a tomb on which we have not even engraved her name."

"Madame, your majesty does not translate the *vives honorata* rightly. The Queen of Navarre lived honored; for all her life she enjoyed the love of her children, the respect of her partisans; respect and love all the more sincere in that she was poor."

"Yes," said Catharine, "I grant you the *vives honorata*; but *morieris reformidata*: how will you explain that?"

"Nothing more easy: *Thou shalt die feared*."

"Well—did she die feared?"

"So much so that she would not have died had not your majesty feared her. Then—*As a queen thou shalt be greater*; or, *Thou shalt be greater than thou hast been as a queen*. This is equally true, madame; for in exchange for a terrestrial crown she has doubtless, as a queen and martyr, a celestial crown; and, besides, who knows what the future may reserve for her posterity?"

Catharine was excessively superstitious; she was even more alarmed at Réné's coolness than at the steadfastness of the auguries, and as in her case any scrape was a chance for her boldly to master the situation, she said suddenly to him, without any other transition than the working of her own thoughts:

"Are any perfumes come from Italy?"

"Yes, madame."

"Send me a boxful."

"Of which?"

"Of the last, of those"—

Catharine stopped.

"Of those the Queen of Navarre was so fond of?" asked Réné.

"Exactly."

"I need not prepare them, for your majesty is now as skilful at them as I am."

"You think so?" said Catharine. "They certainly succeed."

"Has your majesty anything more to say to me?" asked the perfumer.

"Nothing," replied Catharine, thoughtfully; "at least I think not, only if there is any change in the sacrifices, let me know it in time. By the way, let us leave the lambs, and try the hens."

"Alas, madame, I fear that in changing the victim we shall not change the presages."

"Do as I tell you."

The perfumer bowed and left the apartment.

Catharine mused for a short time, then rose and returning to her bedchamber, where her women awaited her, announced the pilgrimage to Montfaucon for the morrow.

The news of this pleasure party caused great excitement in the palace and great confusion in the city: the ladies prepared their most elegant toilets; the gentlemen, their finest arms and steeds; the tradesmen closed their shops, and the populace killed a few straggling Huguenots, in order to furnish company for the dead admiral.

There was a tremendous hubbub all the evening and during a good part of the night.

La Mole had spent a miserable day, and this miserable day had followed three or four others equally miserable. Monsieur d'Alençon, to please his sister, had installed him in his apartments, but had not seen him since. He felt himself like a poor deserted child, deprived of the tender care, the soothing attention of two women, the recollection of one of whom occupied him perpetually. He had heard of her through the surgeon Ambroise Paré, whom she had sent to him, but what he heard from a man of fifty who was ignorant or pretended to be ignorant of the interest felt by La Mole in everything appertaining to Marguerite was very fragmentary and insufficient. Gillonne, indeed, had come once, of her own accord, be it understood, to ask after him, and the visit was to him like a sunbeam darting into a dungeon, and La Mole had remained dazzled by it, and had expected a second visit, and yet two days passed and she had not appeared.

As soon, therefore, as the convalescent heard of this magnificent reunion of the whole court for the following day he sent to ask Monsieur d'Alençon the favor of accompanying it.

The duke did not even inquire whether La Mole was able to bear the fatigue, but merely answered:

"Capital! Let him have one of my horses."

That was all La Mole wanted. Maître Ambroise Paré came as usual to dress his wounds, and La Mole explained to him the necessity he was under of mounting on horseback, and begged him to put on the bandages with double care.

The two wounds, both that on the breast and that on the shoulder, were closed; the one on the shoulder only pained him. Both were rose-red in color, which showed that they were in a fair way of healing. Maître Ambroise Paré covered them with gummed taffetas, a remedy greatly in vogue then, and promised La Mole that if he did not exert himself too much everything would go well.

La Mole was at the height of joy. Save for a certain weakness caused by loss of blood and a slight giddiness attributable to the same cause, he felt as well as could be. Besides, doubtless Marguerite would be in the party; he should see Marguerite again. And when he remembered what benefit he had received from the sight of Gillonne, he had no doubt that her mistress would have a still more efficacious influence upon him.

So La Mole spent a part of the money which he had received when he went away from his family in the purchase of the most beautiful white satin doublet and the finest embroidered mantle that could be furnished by a fashionable tailor. The same tailor procured for him a pair of those perfumed boots such as were worn at that period. The whole outfit was brought to him in the morning only a half hour later than the time at which La Mole had ordered it, so that he had not much fault to find.

He dressed himself quickly, looked in the glass, and found that he was suitably attired, arranged, and perfumed. Then by walking up and down the room several times, he assured himself that though it caused him some sharp pangs, still the happiness which he felt in his heart would render these physical inconveniences of no account. A cherry-colored mantle of his own design, and cut rather longer than they were worn then, proved to be very becoming to him.

While he was thus engaged in the Louvre, another scene, of a similar kind, was going on at the Hôtel de Guise. A tall gentleman, with red hair, was examining, before a glass, a reddish mark which went across his face very disagreeably; he combed and perfumed his mustache, and while he was perfuming it, he kept spreading over that unfortunate mark which, in spite of all the cosmetics then in use, persisted in reappearing, a three-fold layer of white and red; but as the application was insufficient an idea came to him: a hot sun, an August sun, was flashing its rays into the court-yard; he made his way down there, took his hat in his hand, and with his nose in the air and his eyes closed, he walked up and down for ten minutes, fully exposed to the devouring flame which fell from heaven like a torrent. At the end of these ten minutes, owing to the unexampled ardor of the sun, the gentleman's face had acquired such a brilliant color that the red streak was now no more in harmony with the rest than it had been, but in comparison seemed yellow.

Nevertheless, the gentleman did not seem much dissatisfied with this rainbow effect which he did his best to bring into accord with the rest of his face by spreading a layer of vermilion over it, after which he put on a magnificent suit which a tailor had brought to his room without any commands from him. Thus attired, scented, and armed from head to foot, he again went down into the court-yard and began to pat a large black horse whose beauty would have been matchless but for a small cut, like his own, made by a reiter's sabre in one of the last civil conflicts.

Yet, enchanted with the good steed as he was with himself, the gentleman, whom no doubt our readers have easily recognized, was on his back a quarter of an hour before any of the others and making the court-yard of the Hôtel de Guise resound with the whinnying of the charger accompanied by exclamations of *mordi*, pronounced in every variety of accent according as he compelled the horse to submit to this authority. At the end of a moment the horse completely subdued, recognized by his obedience and subjection his master's legitimate control, but the victory had not been obtained without noise, and this noise, which was perhaps the very thing our gentleman reckoned upon, this noise had attracted to the windows a lady whom our queller of horses saluted respectfully, and who smiled at him in the most agreeable manner.

Five minutes later Madame de Nevers summoned her steward.

"Sir," said she, "has Monsieur le Comte Annibal de Coconnas been furnished a suitable breakfast?"

"Yes, madame," replied the steward, "he ate this morning with a better appetite than usual."

"Very well, sir," said the duchess.

Then addressing her first gentleman in waiting:

"Monsieur d'Arguzon," she said, "let us set out for the Louvre, and keep an eye, I beg, on Monsieur le Comte Annibal de Coconnas, for he is wounded, and consequently still weak; and I would not for all the world any accident should happen to him. That would make the Huguenots laugh, for they owe him a spite since the blessed night of Saint Bartholomew."

And Madame de Nevers, mounting her horse, went joyfully towards the Louvre, which was the general rendezvous.

It was two o'clock in the afternoon as a file of cavaliers, overflowing with gold, jewels, and magnificent garments, appeared in the Rue Saint Denis, entering by the corner of the Cemetery of the Innocents and stretching itself out in the sunlight between the two rows of gloomy looking houses like an immense reptile with variegated rings.

CHAPTER XVI.

A DEAD ENEMY'S BODY ALWAYS SMELLS SWEET.

No brilliant company, however, could give any idea of this spectacle. The rich and elegant silk dresses, bequeathed as a magnificent fashion by François I. to his successors, had not yet been changed into those formal and sombre vestments which came into fashion under Henry III.; so that the costume of Charles IX., less rich, but perhaps more elegant than those of preceding reigns, displayed its perfect harmony. In our day no similar cortège could have any standard of comparison, for when we wish magnificence of display we are reduced to mere symmetry and uniform.

Pages, esquires, gentlemen of low degree, dogs and horses, following on the flanks and in the rear, formed of the royal cortège an absolute army. Behind this army came the populace, or rather the populace was everywhere.

It followed, trooped alongside, and rushed ahead; there were shouts of *Noel* and *Haro*, for there were distinguishable in the procession many Calvinists to hoot at, and the populace harbors resentment.

That morning Charles, in presence of Catharine and the Duc de Guise, had, as a perfectly natural thing spoken before Henry of Navarre of going to visit the gibbet of Montfaucon, or, rather, the admiral's mutilated corpse which had been suspended from it. Henry's first impulse had been to refuse to take part in this excursion. Catharine supposed he would. At the first words in which he expressed his repugnance she exchanged a glance and a smile with the Duc de Guise. Henry detected them both, understood what they meant, and suddenly recovering his presence of mind said:

"But why should I not go? I am a Catholic, and am bound to my new religion."

Then addressing the King:

"Your Majesty may reckon on my company," he said; "and I shall be always happy to accompany you wheresoever you may go."

And he threw a sweeping glance around, to see whose brows might be frowning.

Perhaps of all that cortège, the person who was looked at with the greatest curiosity was that motherless son, that kingless king, that Huguenot turned Catholic. His long and marked countenance, his somewhat vulgar figure, his familiarity with his inferiors, which he carried to a degree almost derogatory to a king,—a familiarity acquired by the mountaineer habits of his youth, and which he preserved till his death,—marked him out to the spectators, some of whom cried:

"To mass, Harry, to mass!"

To which Henry replied:

"I attended it yesterday, to-day, and I shall attend it again to-morrow. *Ventre saint gris!* surely that is sufficient."

Marguerite was on horseback—so lovely, so fresh, so elegant that admiration made a regular concert around her, though it must be confessed that a few notes of it were addressed to her companion, the Duchesse de Nevers, who had just joined her on a white horse so proud of his burden that he kept tossing his head.

"Well, duchess!" said the Queen of Navarre, "what is there new?"

"Why, madame," replied the duchess, aloud, "I know of nothing."

Then in a lower tone:

"And what has become of the Huguenot?"

"I have found him a retreat almost safe," replied Marguerite. "And the wholesale assassin, what have you done with him?"

"He wished to take part in the festivity, and so we mounted him on Monsieur de Nevers' war-horse, a creature as big as an elephant. He is a fearful cavalier. I allowed him to be present at the ceremony to-day, as I felt that your Huguenot would be prudent enough to keep his chamber and that there was no fear of their meeting."

"Oh, faith!" replied Marguerite, smiling, "if he were here, and he is not here, I do not think a collision would take place. My Huguenot is remarkably handsome, but nothing more—a dove, and not a hawk; he coos, but does not bite. After all," she added, with a gesture impossible to describe, and shrugging her shoulders slightly, "after all, perhaps our King thought him a Huguenot while he is only a Brahmin, and his religion forbids him to shed blood."

"But where, pray, is the Duc d'Alençon?" inquired Henriette; "I do not see him."

"He will join us later; his eyes troubled him this morning and he was inclined not to come, but as it is known that because he holds a different opinion from Charles and his brother Henry he inclines toward the Huguenots, he became convinced that the King might put a bad interpretation on his absence and he changed his mind. There, hark! people are gazing and shouting yonder; it must be that he is coming by the Porte Montmartre."

"You are right; 'tis he; I recognize him. How elegant he looks to-day," said Henriette. "For some time he has taken particular pains with his appearance; he must be in love. See how nice it is to be a prince of the blood, he gallops over every one, they all draw on one side."

"Yes," said Marguerite, laughing, "he will ride over us. For Heaven's sake draw your attendants to one side, duchess, for there is one of them who will be killed if he does not give way."

"It is my hero!" cried the duchess; "look, only look!"

Coconnas had left his place to approach the Duchesse de Nevers, but just as his horse was crossing the kind of exterior boulevard which separates the street from the Faubourg Saint Denis, a cavalier of the Duc d'Alençon's suite, trying in vain to rein in his excited horse, dashed full against Coconnas. Coconnas, shaken by the collision, reeled on his colossal mount, his hat nearly fell off; he put it on more firmly and turned round furiously.

"Heavens!" said Marguerite, in a low tone, to her friend, "Monsieur de la Mole!"

"That handsome, pale young man?" exclaimed the duchess, unable to repress her first impression.

"Yes, yes; the very one who nearly upset your Piedmontese."

"Oh," said the duchess, "something terrible will happen! they look at each other—recollect each other!"

Coconnas had indeed recognized La Mole, and in his surprise dropped his bridle, for he believed he had killed his old companion, or at least put him *hors de combat* for some time. La Mole had also recognized Coconnas, and he felt a fire mount up into his face. For some seconds, which sufficed for the expression of all the sentiments these two men harbored, they gazed at each other in a way which made the two women shudder.

After which, La Mole, having looked about him, and doubtless seeing that the place was ill chosen for an explanation, spurred his horse and rejoined the Duc d'Alençon. Coconnas remained stationary for a moment, twisting his mustache until the point almost entered his eye; then seeing La Mole dash off without a word, he did the same.

"Ah, ha!" said Marguerite, with pain and contempt, "so I was not mistaken —it is really too much;" and she bit her lips till the blood came.

"He is very handsome," added the Duchesse de Nevers, with commiseration.

Just at this moment the Duc d'Alençon reached his place behind the King and the queen mother, so that his suite, in following him, were obliged to pass before Marguerite and the Duchesse de Nevers. La Mole, as he rode before the two princesses, raised his hat, saluted the queen, and, bowing to his horse's neck, remained uncovered until her majesty should honor him with a look.

But Marguerite turned her head aside disdainfully.

La Mole, no doubt, comprehended the contemptuous expression of the queen's features, and from pale he became livid, and that he might not fall from his horse was compelled to hold on by the mane.

"Oh, oh!" said Henriette to the queen; "look, cruel that you are!—he is going to faint."

169

"Good," said the queen, with a cruel smile; "that is the only thing we need. Where are your salts?"

Madame de Nevers was mistaken. La Mole, with an effort, recovered himself, and sitting erect on his horse took his place in the Duc d'Alençon's suite.

Meantime they kept on their way and at length saw the lugubrious outline of the gibbet, erected and first used by Enguerrand de Marigny. Never before had it been so adorned.

The ushers and guards went forward and made a wide circle around the enclosure. As they drew near, the crows perched on the gibbet flew away with croakings of despair.

The gibbet erected at Montfaucon generally offered behind its posts a shelter for the dogs that gathered there attracted by frequent prey, and for philosophic bandits who came to ponder on the sad chances of fortune.

That day at Montfaucon there were apparently neither dogs nor bandits. The ushers and guards had scared away the dogs together with the crows, and the bandits had mingled with the throng so as to make some of the lucky hits which are the more cheerful vicissitudes of their profession.

The procession moved forward; the King and Catharine arrived first, then came the Duc d'Anjou, Duc d'Alençon, the King of Navarre, Monsieur de Guise, and their followers, then Madame Marguerite, the Duchesse de Nevers, and all the women who composed what was called the queen's flying squadron; then the pages, squires, attendants, and people—in all ten thousand persons.

From the principal gibbet hung a misshapen mass, a black corpse stained with coagulated blood and mud, whitened by layers of dust. The carcass was headless, and it was hung by the legs, and the populace, ingenious as it always is, had replaced the head with a bunch of straw, to which was fastened a mask; and in the mouth of this mask some wag, knowing the admiral's habit, had introduced a toothpick.

At once appalling and singular was the spectacle of all these elegant lords and handsome ladies like a procession painted by Goya, riding along in the midst of those blackened carcasses and gibbets, with their long lean arms.

The noisier the exultation of the spectators, the more strikingly it contrasted with the melancholy silence and cold insensibility of those corpses—objects of ridicule which made even the jesters shudder.

Many could scarcely endure this horrible spectacle, and by his pallor might be distinguished, in the centre of collected Huguenots, Henry, who, great as was his power of self-control and the degree of dissimulation conferred on him by Heaven, could no longer bear it.

He made as his excuse the strong stench which emanated from all those human remains, and going to Charles, who, with Catharine, had stopped in front of the admiral's dead body, he said:

"Sire, does not your Majesty find that this poor carcass smells so strong that it is impossible to remain near it any longer?"

"Do you find it so, Harry?" inquired the King, his eyes sparkling with ferocious joy.

"Yes, sire."

"Well, then, I am not of your opinion; a dead enemy's corpse always smells sweet."

"Faith, sire," said Tavannes, "since your Majesty knew that we were going to make a little call on the admiral, you should have invited Pierre Ronsard, your teacher of poetry; he would have extemporized an epitaph for the old Gaspard."

"There is no need of him for that," said Charles IX., after an instant's thought:

> *"Ci-gît,—mais c'est mal entendu,*
> *Pour lui le mot est trop honnête,—*
> *Ici l'amiral est pendu*
> *Par les pieds, à faute de tête."*[4]

"Bravo! bravo!" cried the Catholic gentlemen in unison, while the collected Huguenots scowled and kept silent, and Henry, as he was talking with Marguerite and Madame de Nevers, pretended not to have heard.

"Come, come, sir!" said Catharine, who, in spite of the perfumes with which she was covered, began to be made ill by the odor. "Come, however agreeable company may be, it must be left at last; let us therefore say good-by to the admiral, and return to Paris."

She nodded ironically as when one takes leave of a friend, and, taking the head of the column, turned to the road, while the cortège defiled before Coligny's corpse.

The sun was sinking in the horizon.

The throng followed fast on their majesties so as to enjoy to the very end all the splendors of the procession and the details of the spectacle; the thieves followed the populace, so that in ten minutes after the King's departure there was no person about the admiral's mutilated carcass on which now blew the first breezes of the evening.

When we say no person, we err. A gentleman mounted on a black horse, and who, doubtless, could not contemplate at his ease the black mutilated trunk when it was honored by the presence of princes, had remained behind, and was examining, in all their details, the bolts, stone pillars, chains, and in fact the gibbet, which no doubt appeared to him (but lately arrived in Paris, and ignorant of the perfection to which things could be brought in the capital) the paragon of all that man could invent in the way of awful ugliness.

We need hardly inform our friends that this man was M. Annibal de Coconnas.

A woman's practised eye had vainly looked for him in the cavalcade and had searched among the ranks without being able to find him.

Monsieur de Coconnas, as we have said, was standing ecstatically contemplating Enguerrand de Marigny's work.

But this woman was not the only person who was trying to find Monsieur de Coconnas. Another gentleman, noticeable for his white satin doublet and gallant plume, after looking toward the front and on all sides, bethought him to look back, and saw Coconnas's tall figure and the silhouette of his gigantic horse standing out strongly against the sky reddened by the last rays of the setting sun.

Then the gentleman in the white satin doublet turned out from the road taken by the majority of the company, struck into a narrow footpath, and describing a curve rode back toward the gibbet.

Almost at the same time the lady whom we have recognized as the Duchesse de Nevers, just as we recognized the tall gentleman on the black horse as Coconnas, rode alongside of Marguerite and said to her:

"We were both mistaken, Marguerite, for the Piedmontese has remained behind and Monsieur de la Mole has gone back to meet him."

"By Heaven!" exclaimed Marguerite, laughing, "then something is going to happen. Faith, I confess I should not be sorry to revise my opinion about him."

Marguerite then turned her horse and witnessed the manœuvre which we have described La Mole as performing.

The two princesses left the procession; the opportunity was most favorable:

they were passing by a hedge-lined footpath which led up the hill, and in doing so passed within thirty yards of the gibbet. Madame de Nevers whispered a word in her captain's ear, Marguerite beckoned to Gillonne, and the four turned into this cross path and went and hid behind the shrubbery nearest to the place where the scene which they evidently expected to witness was to take place. It was about thirty yards, as we have already said, from the spot where Coconnas in a state of ecstasy was gesticulating before the admiral.

Marguerite dismounted, Madame de Nevers and Gillonne did the same; the captain then got down and took the bridles of the four horses. Thick green furnished the three women a seat such as princesses often seek in vain. The glade before them was so open that they would not miss the slightest detail.

La Mole had accomplished his circuit. He rode up slowly and took his stand behind Coconnas; then stretching out his hand tapped him on the shoulder.

The Piedmontese turned round.

"Oh!" said he, "so it was not a dream! You are still alive!"

"Yes, sir," replied La Mole; "yes, I am still alive. It is no fault of yours, but I am still alive."

"By Heaven! I know you again well enough," replied Coconnas, "in spite of your pale face. You were redder than that the last time we met!"

"And I," said La Mole, "I also recognize you, in spite of that yellow line across your face. You were paler than that when I made that mark for you!"

Coconnas bit his lips, but, evidently resolved on continuing the conversation in a tone of irony, he said:

"It is curious, is it not, Monsieur de la Mole, particularly for a Huguenot, to be able to look at the admiral suspended from that iron hook? And yet they say there are people extravagant enough to accuse us of killing even small Huguenots, sucklings."

"Count," said La Mole, bowing, "I am no longer a Huguenot; I have the happiness of being a Catholic!"

"Bah!" exclaimed Coconnas, bursting into loud laughter; "so you are a convert, sir? Oh, that was clever of you!"

"Sir," replied La Mole, with the same seriousness and the same politeness, "I made a vow to become a convert if I escaped the massacre."

"Count," said the Piedmontese, "that was a very prudent vow, and I beg to congratulate you. Perhaps you made still others?"

"Yes, I made a second," answered La Mole, patting his horse with entire coolness.

"And what might that be?" inquired Coconnas.

"To hang you up there, by that small nail which seems to await you beneath Monsieur de Coligny."

"What, as I am now?" asked Coconnas, "alive and merry?"

"No, sir; after I have passed my sword through your body!"

Coconnas became purple, and his eyes darted flames.

"Do you mean," said he in a bantering tone, "to that nail?"

"Yes," replied La Mole, "to that nail."

"You are not tall enough to do it, my little sir!"

"Then I'll get on your horse, my great man-slayer," replied La Mole. "Ah, you believe, my dear Monsieur Annibal de Coconnas, that one may with impunity assassinate people under the loyal and honorable excuse of being a hundred to one, forsooth! But the day comes when a man finds his man; and I believe that day has come now. I should very well like to send a bullet through your ugly head; but, bah! I might miss you, for my hand is still trembling from the traitorous wounds you inflicted upon me."

"My ugly head!" shouted Coconnas, leaping down from his steed. "Down—down from your horse, M. le Comte, and draw!"

And he drew his sword.

"I believe your Huguenot called Monsieur de Coconnas an 'ugly head,'" whispered the Duchesse de Nevers. "Do you think he is bad looking?"

"He is charming," said Marguerite, laughing, "and I am compelled to acknowledge that fury renders Monsieur de La Mole unjust; but hush! let us watch!"

In fact, La Mole had dismounted from his horse with as much deliberation as Coconnas had shown of precipitation; he had taken off his cherry-colored cloak, laid it leisurely on the ground, drawn his sword, and put himself on guard.

"Aïe!" he exclaimed, as he stretched out his arm.

"Ouf!" muttered Coconnas, as he moved his,—for both, as it will be remembered, had been wounded in the shoulder and it hurt them when they made any violent movement.

A burst of laughter, ill repressed, came from the clump of bushes. The princesses could not quite contain themselves at the sight of their two champions rubbing their omoplates and making up faces.

This burst of merriment reached the ears of the two gentlemen, who were ignorant that they had witnesses; turning round, they beheld their ladies.

La Mole resumed his guard as firm as an automaton, and Coconnas crossed his blade with an emphatic "By Heaven!"

"Ah ça! now they will murder each other in real earnest, if we do not interfere. There has been enough of this. Holá, gentlemen!—holá!" cried Marguerite.

"Let them be! let them be!" said Henriette, who having seen Coconnas at work, hoped in her heart that he would have as easy a victory over La Mole as he had over Mercandon's son and two nephews.

"Oh, they are really beautiful so!" exclaimed Marguerite. "Look—they seem to breathe fire!"

Indeed, the combat, begun with sarcasms and mutual insults, became silent as soon as the champions had crossed their swords. Each distrusted his own strength, and each, at every quick pass, was compelled to restrain an expression of pain occasioned by his own wounds. Nevertheless, with eyes fixed and burning, mouth half open, and teeth clenched, La Mole advanced with short and firm steps toward his adversary, who, seeing in him a most skilful swordsman, retreated step by step. They both thus reached the edge of the ditch on the other side of which were the spectators; then, as if his retreat had been only a simple stratagem to draw nearer to his lady, Coconnas took his stand, and as La Mole made his guard a little too wide, he made a thrust with the quickness of lightning and instantly La Mole's white satin doublet was stained with a spot of blood which kept growing larger.

"Courage!" cried the Duchesse de Nevers.

"Ah, poor La Mole!" exclaimed Marguerite, with a cry of distress.

La Mole heard this cry, darted at the queen one of those looks which penetrate the heart even deeper than a sword-point, and taking advantage of a false parade, thrust vigorously at his adversary.

This time the two women uttered two cries which seemed like one. The point of La Mole's rapier had appeared, all covered with blood, behind Coconnas's back.

Yet neither fell. Both remained erect, looking at each other with open mouth, and feeling that on the slightest movement they must lose their balance. At last the Piedmontese, more dangerously wounded than his adversary, and feeling his senses forsaking him with his blood, fell on La Mole, grasping him with one hand, while with the other he endeavored to unsheath his poniard.

La Mole roused all his strength, raised his hand, and let fall the pommel of his sword on Coconnas's forehead. Coconnas, stupefied by the blow, fell, but in his fall drew down his adversary with him, and both rolled into the ditch.

Then Marguerite and the Duchesse de Nevers, seeing that, dying as they were, they were still struggling to destroy each other, hastened to them, followed by the captain of the guards; but before they could reach them the combatants' hands unloosened, their eyes closed, and letting go their grasp of their weapons they stiffened in what seemed like their final agony. A wide stream of blood bubbled round them.

"Oh, brave, brave La Mole!" cried Marguerite, unable any longer to repress her admiration. "Ah! pardon me a thousand times for having a moment doubted your courage."

And her eyes filled with tears.

"Alas! alas!" murmured the duchess, "gallant Annibal. Did you ever see two such intrepid lions, madame?"

And she sobbed aloud.

"Heavens! what ugly thrusts," said the captain, endeavoring to stanch the streams of blood. "Holá! you, there, come here as quickly as you can—here, I say"—

He addressed a man who, seated on a kind of tumbril or cart painted red, appeared in the evening mist singing this old song, which had doubtless been suggested to him by the miracle of the Cemetery of the Innocents:

"*Bel aubespin fleurissant*
        Verdissant,
Le long de ce beau rivage,
Tu es vêtu, jusqu'au bas
        Des longs bras
D'une lambrusche sauvage.

"*Le chantre rossignolet,*
        Nouvelet,
Courtisant sa bien-aimée

Pour ses amours alléger
    Vient loger
Tous les ans sous ta ramée.

"Or, vis, gentil aubespin
    Vis sans fin;
Vis, sans que jamais tonnerre,
Ou la cognée, ou les vents
    Ou le temps
Te puissent ruer par."...[5]

"Holá! hé!" shouted the captain a second time, "come when you are called. Don't you see that these gentlemen need help?"

The carter, whose repulsive exterior and coarse face formed a singular contrast with the sweet and sylvan song we have just quoted, stopped his horse, got out, and bending over the two bodies said:

"These be terrible wounds, sure enough, but I have made worse in my time."

"Who are you, pray?" inquired Marguerite, experiencing, in spite of herself, a certain vague terror which she could not overcome.

"Madame," replied the man, bowing down to the ground, "I am Maître Caboche, headsman to the provostry of Paris, and I have come to hang up at the gibbet some companions for Monsieur the Admiral."

"Well! and I am the Queen of Navarre," replied Marguerite; "cast your corpses down there, spread in your cart the housings of our horses, and bring these two gentlemen softly behind us to the Louvre."

CHAPTER XVII.

MAÎTRE AMBROISE PARÉ'S CONFRÈRE.

The tumbril in which Coconnas and La Mole were laid started back toward Paris, following in the shadow the guiding group. It stopped at the Louvre, and the driver was amply rewarded. The wounded men were carried to the

Duc d'Alençon's quarters, and Maître Ambroise Paré was sent for.

When he arrived, neither of the two men had recovered consciousness.

La Mole was the least hurt of the two. The sword had struck him below the right armpit, but without touching any vital parts. Coconnas was run through the lungs, and the air that escaped from his wound made the flame of a candle waver.

Ambroise Paré would not answer for Coconnas.

Madame de Nevers was in despair. Relying on Coconnas's strength, courage, and skill, she had prevented Marguerite from interfering with the duel. She would have had Coconnas taken to the Hôtel de Guise and gladly bestowed on him a second time the care which she had already lavished on his comfort, but her husband was likely to arrive from Rome at any moment and find fault with the introduction of a strange man in the domestic establishment.

To hide the cause of the wounds, Marguerite had had the two young men brought to her brother's rooms, where one of them, to be sure, had already been installed, by saying that they were two gentlemen who had been thrown from their horses during the excursion, but the truth was divulged by the captain, who, having witnessed the duel, could not help expressing his admiration, and it was soon known at court that two new *raffinés*[6] had burst into sudden fame. Attended by the same surgeon, who divided his attentions between them, the two wounded men passed through the different phases of convalescence arising from the greater or less severity of their wounds. La Mole, who was less severely wounded of the two, was the first to recover consciousness. A terrible fever had taken possession of Coconnas and his return to life was attended by all the symptoms of the most horrible delirium.

Though La Mole was confined in the same room with Coconnas, he had not, when he came to himself, seen his companion, or if he saw him, he betrayed no sign that he saw him. Coconnas, on the contrary, as soon as he opened his eyes, fastened them on La Mole with an expression which proved that the blood he had lost had not modified the passions of his fiery temperament.

Coconnas thought he was dreaming, and that in this dream he saw the enemy he imagined he had twice slain, only the dream was unduly prolonged. After having observed La Mole laid, like himself, on a couch, and his wounds dressed by the surgeon, he saw him rise up in bed, while he himself was still confined to his by his fever, his weakness, and his pain; he saw him get out of bed, then walk, first leaning on the surgeon's arm, and then on a cane, and finally without assistance.

Coconnas, still delirious, viewed these different stages of his companion's recovery with eyes sometimes dull, at others wandering, but always threatening.

All this presented to the Piedmontese's fiery spirit a fearful mixture of the fantastic and the real. For him La Mole was dead, wholly dead, having been actually killed twice and not merely once, and yet he recognized this same La Mole's ghost lying in a bed like his own; then, as we have said, he saw this ghost get up, walk round, and, horrible to relate, come toward his bed. This ghost, whom Coconnas would have wished to avoid, even had it been in the depths of hell, came straight to him and stopped beside his pillow, standing there and looking at him; there was in his features a look of gentleness and compassion which Coconnas took for the expression of hellish derision.

There arose in his mind, possibly more wounded than his body, an insatiable thirst of vengeance. He was wholly occupied with one idea, that of procuring some weapon, and with that weapon piercing the body or the ghost of La Mole which so cruelly persecuted him. His clothes, stained with blood, had been placed on a chair by his bed, but afterwards removed, it being thought imprudent to leave them in his sight; but his poniard still remained on the chair, for it was imagined it would be some time before he would want to use it.

Coconnas saw the poniard; three nights while La Mole was slumbering he strove to reach it; three nights his strength failed him, and he fainted. At length, on the fourth night, he clutched it convulsively, and groaning with the pain of the effort, hid the weapon beneath his pillow.

The next day he saw something he had never deemed possible. La Mole's ghost, which every day seemed to gain strength, while he, occupied with the terrible dream, kept losing his in the eternal weaving of the scheme which was to rid him of it,—La Mole's ghost, growing more and more energetic, walked thoughtfully up and down the room three or four times, then, after having put on his mantle, buckled on his sword, and put on a broad-brimmed felt hat, opened the door and went out.

Coconnas breathed again. He thought that he was freed from his phantom. For two or three hours his blood circulated more calmly and coolly in his veins than it had done since the duel. La Mole's absence for one day would have restored Coconnas to his senses; a week's absence would perhaps have cured him; unfortunately, La Mole returned at the end of two hours.

This reappearance of La Mole was like a poniard-stab for Coconnas; and although La Mole did not return alone, Coconnas did not give a single look at his companion.

And yet his companion was worth looking at.

He was a man of forty, short, thick-set, and vigorous, with black hair which came to his eyebrows, and a black beard, which, contrary to the fashion of the period, thickly covered the chin; but he seemed one who cared little for the fashion.

He wore a leather jerkin, all covered with brown spots; red hose and leggings, thick shoes coming above the ankle, a cap the same color as his stockings, and a girdle, from which hung a large knife in a leather sheaf, completed his attire.

This singular personage, whose presence in the Louvre seemed so anomalous, threw his brown mantle on a chair and unceremoniously approached Coconnas, whose eyes, as if fascinated, remained fixed upon La Mole, who remained at some distance. He looked at the sick man, and shaking his head, said to La Mole:

"You have waited till it was rather late, my dear gentleman."

"I could not get out sooner," said La Mole.

"Eh! Heavens! you should have sent for me."

"Whom had I to send?"

"True, I forgot where we are. I had told those ladies, but they would not listen to me. If my prescriptions had been followed instead of those of that ass, Ambroise Paré, you would by this time have been in a condition to go in pursuit of adventures together, or exchange another sword-thrust if such had been your good pleasure; but we shall see. Does your friend listen to reason?"

"Scarcely."

"Hold out your tongue, my dear gentleman."

Coconnas thrust out his tongue to La Mole, making such a hideous grimace that the practitioner shook his head a second time.

"Oho!" he muttered, "contraction of the muscles. There's no time to be lost. This evening I will send you a potion ready prepared; you must make him take it three times: once at midnight, once at one o'clock, and once at two."

"Very well."

"But who will make him take it?"

"I will."

"You?"

"Yes."

"You give me your word?"

"On my honor."

"And if any physician should attempt to abstract the slightest portion to analyze it and discover what its ingredients are"—

"I will spill it to the last drop."

"This also on your honor?"

"I swear it!"

"Whom shall I send you this potion by?"

"Any one you please."

"But my messenger"—

"Well?"

"How will he get to you?"

"That is easily managed. He will say that he comes from Monsieur Réné, the perfumer."

"That Florentine who lives on the Pont Saint Michel?"

"Exactly. He is allowed to enter the Louvre at any hour, day or night."

The man smiled.

"In fact," said he, "the queen mother at least owes him that much. It is understood, then; he will come from Maître Réné, the perfumer. I may surely use his name for once: he has often enough practised my profession without having taken his degree either."

"Then," said La Mole, "I may rely on you."

"You may."

"And about the payment?"

"Oh, we will arrange about that with the gentleman himself when he is well again."

"You may be quite easy on that score, for I am sure he will pay you generously."

"I believe you. And yet," he added with a strange smile, "as the people with whom I have to do are not wont to be grateful, I should not be surprised if when he is on his legs again he should forget or at least not think to give a single thought to me."

"All right," said La Mole, smiling also, "in that case I should have to jog his memory."

"Very well, we'll leave it so. In two hours you will receive the medicine."

"Au revoir!"

"You said"—

"Au revoir."

The man smiled.

"It is always my custom," he added, "to say adieu! So adieu, Monsieur de la Mole. In two hours you will have the potion. You understand, it must be given at midnight—in three doses—at intervals of an hour."

So saying he took his departure, and La Mole was left alone with Coconnas.

Coconnas had heard the whole conversation, but understood nothing of it; a senseless babble of words, a senseless jangling of phrases, was all that came to him. Of the whole interview he remembered nothing except the word "midnight."

He continued to watch La Mole, who remained in the room, pacing thoughtfully up and down.

The unknown doctor kept his word, and at the appointed time sent the medicine, which La Mole placed on a small silver chafing-dish, and having taken this precaution, went to bed.

This action on the part of La Mole gave Coconnas a little quietude. He tried to shut his eyes, but his feverish slumbers were only a continuation of his waking delirium. The same phantom which haunted him by day came to disturb him by night; across his hot eyelids he still saw La Mole as threatening as ever, and a voice kept repeating in his ear: "Midnight, midnight, midnight!"

Suddenly the echoing note of a clock's bell awoke in the night and struck twelve. Coconnas opened his blood-shot eyes; the fiery breath from his breast scorched his dry lips, an unquenchable thirst devoured his burning throat; the little night lamp was burning as usual, and its dim light made thousands of phantoms dance before his wandering eyes.

And then a horrible vision—he saw La Mole get out of bed, and after walking up and down the room two or three times, as the sparrow-hawk flits before the little bird it is trying to fascinate, come toward him with his fist clinched.

Coconnas seized his poniard and prepared to plunge it into his enemy.

La Mole kept coming nearer.

Coconnas muttered:

"Ah! here you are again! you are always here! Come on! You threaten me, do you! you smile! Come, come, come! ah, you still keep coming nearer, a step at a time! Come, come, and let me kill you."

And suiting the action to the word, just as La Mole bent down to him, Coconnas flashed out the poniard from under the clothes; but the effort he made in rising exhausted him, the weapon dropped from his hand, and he fell back upon his pillow.

"There, there!" said La Mole, gently lifting his head; "drink this, my poor fellow, for you are burning up."

It was really a cup La Mole presented to Coconnas, who in the wild excitement of his delirium took it to be a threatening fist.

But at the nectarous sensation of this beneficent draught, soothing his lips and cooling his throat, Coconnas's reason, or rather his instinct, came back to him, a never before experienced feeling of comfort pervaded his frame; he turned an intelligent look at La Mole, who was supporting him in his arms, and smiling on him; and from those eyes, so lately glowing with fury, a tear rolled down his burning cheek, which drank it with avidity.

"*Mordi!*" whispered Coconnas, as he fell back on his bolster. "If I get over this, Monsieur de la Mole, you shall be my friend."

"And you will get over it," said La Mole, "if you will drink the other two cups, and have no more ugly dreams."

An hour afterward La Mole, assuming the duties of a nurse, and scrupulously carrying out the unknown doctor's orders, rose again, poured a second dose into the cup, and carried it to Coconnas, who instead of waiting for him with his poniard, received him with open arms, eagerly swallowed the potion, and calmly fell asleep.

The third cup had a no less marvellous effect. The sick man's breathing became more regular, his stiff limbs relaxed, a gentle perspiration diffused itself over his burning skin, and when Ambroise Paré visited him the next morning, he smiled complacently, saying:

"I answer for Monsieur de Coconnas now; and this will not be one of the least difficult cures I have effected."

This scene, half-dramatic, half-burlesque, and yet not lacking in a certain poetic touch when Coconnas's fierce ways were taken into consideration, resulted in the friendship which the two gentlemen had begun at the Inn of the *Belle Étoile*, and which had been so violently interrupted by the Saint Bartholomew night's occurrences, from that time forth taking on a new vigor and soon surpassing that of Orestes and Pylades by five sword-thrusts and one pistol-wound exchanged between them.

At all events, wounds old and new, slight or serious, were at last in a fair way of cure. La Mole, faithful to his duties as nurse, would not forsake the sick-room until Coconnas was entirely well. As long as weakness kept the invalid on the bed, he lifted him, and when he began to improve he helped him to walk; in a word, he lavished on him all the attentions suggested by his gentle and affectionate disposition, and this care, together with the Piedmontese's natural vigor, brought about a more rapid convalescence than would have been expected.

However, one and the same thought tormented both the young men. Each had in his delirium apparently seen the woman he loved approach his couch, and yet, certainly since they had recovered their senses, neither Marguerite nor Madame de Nevers had entered the room. However, that was perfectly comprehensible; the one, wife of the King of Navarre, the other, the Duc de Guise's sister-in-law, could not have publicly shown two simple gentlemen such a mark of evident interest, could they? No! La Mole and Coconnas could not make any other reply to this question. But still the absence of the ladies, tantamount perhaps to utter forgetfulness, was not the less painful.

It is true the gentleman who had witnessed the duel had come several times, as if of his own accord, to inquire after them; it is true Gillonne had done the same; but La Mole had not ventured to speak to the one concerning the queen; Coconnas had not ventured to speak to the other of Madame de Nevers.

CHAPTER XVIII.

THE GHOSTS.

For some time each of the young men kept his secret confined to his own heart. At last their reserve burst its barriers, and the thought which had so long occupied them escaped their lips, and both cemented their friendship by this final proof, without which there is no friendship,—namely, perfect confidence.

They were both madly in love—one with a princess and the other with a queen.

For these two poor suitors there was something frightful in the almost insuperable distance separating them from the objects of their desires.

And yet hope is a sentiment so deeply rooted in man's heart that in spite of the madness of their love they hoped!

They both, as they recovered from their illness, took great pains with their personal appearance. Every man, even the most indifferent to physical appearance, has, at certain times, mute interviews with his looking-glass, signs of intelligence, after which he generally leaves his confidant, quite satisfied with the interview. Now our two young men were not persons whose mirrors were compelled to give them harsh advice. La Mole, delicate, pale, and elegant, had the beauty of distinction; Coconnas, powerful, large-framed, and fresh-colored, had the beauty of strength. He had more, for his recent illness had been of advantage to him. He had become thinner, grown paler, and the famous scar which had formerly caused him so much anxiety from its prismatic relationship to the rainbow had disappeared, giving promise, probably like the post-diluvian phenomenon, of a long series of lovely days and calm nights.

Moreover, the most delicate attentions continued to be lavished on the two wounded men, and each of them on the day when he was well enough to rise found a *robe-de-chambre* on the easy-chair nearest his bed; on the day when he was able to dress himself, a complete suit of clothes; moreover, in the pocket of each doublet was a well-filled purse, which they each kept, intending, of course, to return, in the proper time and place, to the unknown protector who watched over them.

This unknown protector could not be the prince in whose quarters the two young men resided, for the prince had not only never once paid them a visit, but he had not even sent to make any inquiry after them.

A vague hope whispered to each heart that this unknown protector was the woman he loved.

So the two wounded men awaited with intense impatience the moment when they could go out. La Mole, stronger and sooner cured than Coconnas, might have done so long before, but a kind of tacit convention bound him to his friend. It was agreed between them that the first time they went out they should make three calls:

The first should be upon the unknown doctor whose suave medicine had brought such a remarkable improvement in the inflammation of Coconnas's lungs.

The second to the dwelling of the defunct Maître La Hurière, where each of them had left his portmanteau and horse.

The third to the Florentine Réné, who, uniting to his title of perfumer that of magician, not only sold cosmetics and poisons, but also concocted philters and delivered oracles.

At length, after two months passed in convalescence and confinement, the long-looked-for day arrived.

We used the word "confinement;" the use of it is accurate because several times in their impatience they had tried to hasten that day; but each time a sentinel posted at the door had stopped their passage and they had learned that they could not step out unless Maître Ambroise Paré gave them their *exeat*.

Now, one day that clever surgeon, having come to the conclusion that the two invalids were, if not completely cured, at least on the road to complete recovery, gave them this *exeat*, and about two o'clock in the afternoon on a fine day in autumn, such as Paris sometimes offers to her astonished population, who have already laid up a store of resignation for the winter, the two friends, arm in arm, set foot outside the Louvre.

La Mole, finding to his great satisfaction, on an armchair, the famous cherry-colored mantle which he had folded so carefully before the duel, undertook to be Coconnas's guide, and Coconnas allowed himself to be guided without resistance or reflection. He knew that his friend was taking him to the unknown doctor's whose potion (not patented) had cured him in a single night, when all of Master Ambroise Paré's drugs were slowly killing him. He had divided the money in his purse into two parts, and intended a hundred rose-nobles for the anonymous Esculapius to whom his recovery was due. Coconnas was not afraid of death, but Coconnas was not the less satisfied to be alive and well, and so, as we see, he was intending to recompense his deliverer generously.

La Mole proceeded along the Rue de l'Astruce, the wide Rue Saint Honoré, the Rue des Prouvelles, and soon found himself on the Place des Halles. Near the ancient fountain, at the place which is at the present time called the Carreau des Halles, was an octagon stone building, surmounted by a vast wooden lantern, which was again surmounted by a pointed roof, on the top of which was a weathercock. This wooden lantern had eight openings, traversed, as that heraldic piece which they call the *fascis* traverses the field of blazonry, by a kind of wooden wheel, which was divided in the middle, in order to admit in the holes cut in it for that purpose the head and hands of such sentenced person or persons as were exposed at one or more of these eight openings.

This singular arrangement, which had nothing like it in the surrounding buildings, was called the pillory.

An ill-constructed, irregular, crooked, one-eyed, limping house, the roof spotted with moss like a leper's skin, had, like a toadstool, sprung up at the foot of this species of tower.

This house was the executioner's.

A man was exposed, and was thrusting out his tongue at the passers-by; he was one of the robbers who had been following his profession near the gibbet of Montfaucon, and had by ill luck been arrested in the exercise of his functions.

Coconnas believed that his friend had brought him to see this singular spectacle, and he joined the crowd of sightseers who were replying to the patient's grimaces by vociferations and gibes.

Coconnas was naturally cruel, and the sight very much amused him, only he would have preferred that instead of gibes and vociferations they had thrown stones at a convict so insolent as to thrust out his tongue at the noble lords that condescended to visit him.

So when the moving lantern was turned on its base, in order to show the culprit to another portion of the square, and the crowd followed, Coconnas would have accompanied them, had not La Mole checked him, saying, in a low tone:

"We did not come here for this."

"Well, what did we come for, then?" asked Coconnas.

"You will see," replied La Mole.

The two friends had got into the habit of addressing each other with the familiar "thee" and "thou" ever since the morning of that famous night when Coconnas had tried to thrust his poniard into La Mole's vitals. And he led Coconnas directly to a small window in the house which abutted on the tower; a man was leaning on the window-sill.

"Aha! here you are, gentlemen," said the man, raising his blood-red cap, and showing his thick black hair, which came down to his eyebrows. "You are welcome."

"Who is this man?" inquired Coconnas, endeavoring to recollect, for it seemed to him he had seen that face during one of the crises of his fever.

"Your preserver, my dear friend," replied La Mole; "he who brought to you at the Louvre that refreshing drink which did you so much good."

"Oho!" said Coconnas; "in that case, my friend"—

And he held out his hand to him.

But the man, instead of returning the gesture, drew himself up and withdrew from the two friends just the distance occupied by the curve of his body.

"Sir!" he said to Coconnas, "thanks for the honor you wish to confer on me, but it is probable that if you knew me you would not do so."

"Faith!" said Coconnas, "I declare that, even if you were the devil himself, I am very greatly obliged to you, for if it had not been for you I should be dead at this time."

"I am not exactly the devil," replied the man in the red cap; "but yet persons are frequently found who would rather see the devil than me."

"Who are you, pray?" asked Coconnas.

"Sir," replied the man, "I am Maître Caboche, the executioner of the provostry of Paris"—

"Ah"—said Coconnas, withdrawing his hand.

"You see!" said Maître Caboche.

"No, no; I will touch your hand, or may the devil fetch me! Hold it out"—

"Really?"

"Wide as you can."

"Here it is."

"Open it—wider—wider!"

And Coconnas took from his pocket the handful of gold he had prepared for his anonymous physician and placed it in the executioner's hand.

"I would rather have had your hand entirely and solely," said Maître Caboche, shaking his head, "for I do not lack money, but I am in need of hands to touch mine. Never mind. God bless you, my dear gentleman."

"So then, my friend," said Coconnas, looking at the executioner with curiosity, "it is you who put men to the rack, who break them on the wheel, quarter them, cut off heads, and break bones. Aha! I am very glad to have made your acquaintance."

"Sir," said Maître Caboche, "I do not do all myself; just as you noble gentlemen have your lackeys to do what you do not choose to do yourself, so have I my assistants, who do the coarser work and despatch clownish fellows. Only when, by chance, I have to do with folks of quality, like you and your companion, for instance, ah! then it is another thing, and I take a pride in doing everything myself, from first to last,—that is to say, from the first putting of the *question*, to the decapitation."

In spite of himself, Coconnas felt a shudder pervade his veins, as if the brutal wedge was pressing his leg—as if the edge of the axe was against his neck.

La Mole, without being able to account for it, felt the same sensation.

But Coconnas overcame the emotion, of which he was ashamed, and desirous of taking leave of Maître Caboche with a jest on his lips, said to him:

"Well, master, I hold you to your word, and when it is my turn to mount Enguerrand de Marigny's gallows or Monsieur de Nemours's scaffold you alone shall lay hands on me."

"I promise you."

"Then, this time here is my hand, as a pledge that I accept your promise," said Coconnas.

And he offered the executioner his hand, which the latter touched timidly with his own, although it was evident that he had a great desire to grasp it warmly.

At this light touch Coconnas turned rather pale; but the same smile lingered on his lips, while La Mole, ill at ease, and seeing the crowd turn as the lantern did and come toward them, touched his cloak.

Coconnas, who in reality had as great a desire as La Mole to put an end to this scene, which by the natural bent of his character he had delayed longer than he would have wished, nodded to the executioner and went his way.

"Faith!" said La Mole, when he and his companion had reached the Croix du Trahoir, "I must confess we breathe more freely here than in the Place des Halles."

"Decidedly," replied Coconnas; "but I am none the less glad at having made Maître Caboche's acquaintance. It is well to have friends everywhere."

"Even at the sign of the *Belle Étoile*," said La Mole, laughing.

"Oh! as for poor Maître La Hurière," said Coconnas, "he is dead and dead again. I saw the arquebuse spitting flame, I heard the thump of the bullet, which sounded as if it had struck against the great bell of Notre-Dame, and I left him stretched out in the gutter with streams of blood flowing from his nose and mouth. Taking it for granted that he is a friend, he is a friend we shall have in the next world."

Thus chatting, the two young men entered the Rue de l'Arbre Sec and proceeded toward the sign of the *Belle Étoile*, which was still creaking in the same place, still presenting to the traveller its astronomic hearth and its appetizing inscription. Coconnas and La Mole expected to find the house in a desperate state, the widow in mourning, and the little ones wearing crêpe on their arms; but to their great astonishment they found the house in full swing of activity, Madame La Hurière mightily resplendent, and the children gayer than ever.

"Oh, the faithless creature!" cried La Mole; "she must have married again."

Then addressing the new Artémise:

"Madame," said he, "we are two gentlemen, acquaintances of poor Monsieur La Hurière. We left here two horses and two portmanteaus which we have come to claim."

"Gentlemen," replied the mistress of the house, after she had tried to bring them to her recollection, "as I have not the honor of knowing you, with your permission I will go and call my husband. Grégoire, ask your master to come."

Grégoire stepped from the first kitchen, which was the general pandemonium, into the second, which was the laboratory where Maître La Hurière in his life-time had been in the habit of concocting the dishes which he felt deserved to be prepared by his clever hands.

"The devil take me," muttered Coconnas, "if it does not make me feel badly to see this house so gay when it ought to be so melancholy. Poor La Hurière!"

"He tried to kill me," said La Mole, "but I pardon him with all my heart."

La Mole had hardly uttered these words when a man appeared holding in his hand a stew-pan, in the bottom of which he was browning some onions, stirring them with a wooden spoon.

La Mole and Coconnas gave vent to a cry of amazement.

As they did so the man lifted his head and, replying by a similar cry, dropped his stew-pan, retaining in his hand only his wooden spoon.

In nomine Patris," said the man, waving his spoon as he would have done with a holy-water sprinkler, "*et Filii, et Spiritus sancti*"—

"Maître La Hurière!" exclaimed the two young men.

"Messieurs de Coconnas and de la Mole!" cried La Hurière.

"So you are not dead?" asked Coconnas.

"Why! can it be that you are alive?" asked the landlord.

"Nevertheless, I saw you fall," said Coconnas, "I heard the crash of the bullet, which broke something in you, I don't know what. I left you lying in the gutter, with blood streaming out of your nose, out of your mouth, and even out of your eyes."

"All that is as true as the gospel, Monsieur de Coconnas. But the noise you heard was the bullet striking against my sallat, on which fortunately it flattened itself; but the blow was none the less severe, and the proof of it," added La Hurière, lifting his cap and displaying a pate as bald as a man's knee, "is that as you see I have not a spear of hair left."

The two young men burst out laughing when they saw his grotesque appearance.

"Aha! you laugh, do you?" said La Hurière, somewhat reassured, "you do not come, then, with any evil intentions."

"Now tell us, Maître La Hurière, are you entirely cured of your bellicose inclinations?"

"Faith, that I am, gentlemen; and now"—

"Well, and now"—

"Now I have vowed not to meddle with any other fire than that in my kitchen."

"Bravo!" cried Coconnas, "see how prudent he is! Now," added the Piedmontese, "we left in your stables two horses, and in your rooms two portmanteaus."

"Oh, the devil!" replied the landlord, scratching his ear.

"Well?"

"Two horses, you say?"

"Yes, in your stable."

"And two portmanteaus?"

"Yes, in the rooms we had."

"The truth is, don't you see—you thought I was dead, didn't you?"

"Certainly we did."

"You will agree that as you were mistaken, I also might be."

"What? In believing that we also were dead? You were perfectly free."

"Now that's it. You see, as you died intestate," continued Maître La Hurière.

"Go on"—

"I believed something, I was mistaken, I see it now"—

"Tell us, what was it you believed?"

"I believed that I might consider myself your heir."

"Oho!" exclaimed the two young men.

"Nevertheless, I could not be more grateful to find that you are alive, gentlemen."

"So you sold our horses, did you?" asked Coconnas.

"Alas!" cried La Hurière.

"And our portmanteaus?" insisted La Mole.

"Oh! your portmanteaus? Oh, no," cried La Hurière, "only what was in them."

"Now look here, La Mole," persisted Coconnas, "it seems to me that this is a bold rascal; suppose we disembowel him!"

This threat seemed to have great effect on Maître La Hurière, who stammered out these words:

"Well, gentlemen, I rather think the affair can be arranged."

"Listen!" said La Mole, "I am the one who has the greatest cause of complaint against you."

"Certainly, Monsieur le Comte, for I recollect that in a moment of madness I had the audacity to threaten you."

"Yes, with a bullet which flew only a couple of inches above my head."

"Do you think so?"

"I am certain of it."

"If you are certain of it, Monsieur de la Mole," said La Hurière, picking up his stew-pan with an innocent air, "I am too thoroughly at your service to give you the lie."

"Well," said La Mole, "as far as I am concerned I make no demand upon you."

"What, my dear gentleman"—

"Except"—

"Aïe! aïe!" groaned La Hurière.

"Except a dinner for myself and my friends every time I find myself in your neighborhood."

"How is this?" exclaimed La Hurière in an ecstasy. "I am at your service, my dear gentleman; I am at your service."

"So it is a bargain, is it?"

"With all my heart—and you, Monsieur de Coconnas," continued the landlord, "do you agree to the bargain?"

"Yes; but, like my friend, I must add one small condition."

"What is that?"

"That you restore to Monsieur de la Mole the fifty crowns which I owe him, and which I put into your keeping."

"To me, sir? When was that?"

"A quarter of an hour before you sold my horse and my portmanteau."

La Hurière showed that he understood.

"Ah! I remember," said he; and he stepped toward a cupboard and took out from it, one after the other, fifty crowns, which he brought to La Mole.

"Very well, sir," said that gentleman; "very well. Serve me an omelet. The fifty crowns are for Grégoire."

"Oh!" cried La Hurière; "in truth, my dear gentlemen, you are genuine princes, and you may count on me for life and for death."

"If that is so," said Coconnas, "make us the omelet we want, and spare neither butter nor lard."

Then looking at the clock,

"Faith, you are right, La Mole," said he, "we still have three hours to wait, and we may as well be here as anywhere else. All the more because, if I am not mistaken, we are already half way to the Pont Saint Michel."

And the two young men went and sat down at table in the very same room and at the very same place which they had occupied during that memorable evening of the twenty-sixth of August, 1572, when Coconnas had proposedto

La Mole to play each against the other the first mistress which they should have!

Let us grant for the honor of the morality of our two young men that neither of them this evening had the least idea of making such a proposition to his companion.

CHAPTER XIX.

THE ABODE OF MAÎTRE RÉNÉ, PERFUMER TO THE QUEEN MOTHER.

At the period of this history there existed in Paris, for passing from one part of the city to another, but five bridges, some of stone and the others of wood, and they all led to the Cité; there were le Pont des Meuniers, le Pont au Change, le Pont Notre-Dame, le Petit Pont, and le Pont Saint Michel.

In other places when there was need of crossing the river there were ferries.

These five bridges were loaded with houses like the Pont Vecchio at Florence at the present time. Of these five bridges, each of which has its history, we shall now speak more particularly of the Pont Saint Michel.

The Pont Saint Michel had been built of stone in 1373; in spite of its apparent solidity, a freshet in the Seine undermined a part of it on the thirty-first of January, 1408; in 1416 it had been rebuilt of wood; but during the night of December 16, 1547, it was again carried away; about 1550, in other words twenty-two years anterior to the epoch which we have reached, it was again built of wood, and though it needed repairs it was regarded as solid enough.

In the midst of the houses which bordered the line of the bridge, facing the small islet on which the Templers had been burnt, and where at the present time the platform of the Pont Neuf rests, stood a wooden panelled house over which a large roof impended like the lid of an immense eye. At the only window, which opened on the first story, over the window and door of the ground floor, hermetically sealed, shone a reddish light, which attracted the attention of the passers-by to the low, wide façade, painted blue, with rich gold mouldings. A kind of frieze separating the ground floor from the first floor represented groups of devils in the most grotesque postures imaginable; and a wide scroll painted blue like the façade ran between the frieze and the window, with this inscription: "RÉNÉ, FLORENTIN, PERFUMER DE SA MAJESTÉ LA REINE MÈRE."

The door of this shop was, as we have said, well bolted; but it was defended from nocturnal attacks better than by bolts by its occupant's reputation, so redoubtable that the passengers over the bridge usually described a curve which took them to the opposite row of houses, as if they feared the very smell of the perfumes that might exhale through the walls.

More than this, the right and left hand neighbors, doubtless fearing that they might be compromised by the proximity, had, since Maître Réné's occupancy of the house, taken their departure one after the other so that the two houses next to Réné's were left empty and closed. Yet, in spite of this solitude and desertedness, belated passers-by had frequently seen, glittering through the crevices of the shutters of these empty habitations, strange rays of light, and had felt certain they heard strange noises like groans, which proved that some beings frequented these abodes, although they did not know if they belonged to this world or the other.

The result was that the tenants of the two buildings contiguous to the two empty houses from time to time queried whether it would not be wise in them to do as their neighbors had done.

It was, doubtless, owing to the privilege which the dread of him, widely circulated, had procured for him, that Maître Réné had ventured to keep up a light after the prescribed hour. No round or guard, moreover, would have dared to molest him, a man doubly dear to her majesty as her fellow-countryman and perfumer.

As we suppose that the reader, panoplied by the philosophical wisdom of this century, no longer believes in magic or magicians, we will invite him to accompany us into this dwelling which, at that epoch of superstitious faith, shed around it such a profound terror.

The shop on the ground floor is dark and deserted after eight o'clock in the evening—the hour at which it closes, not to open again until next morning; there it is that the daily sale of perfumery, unguents, and cosmetics of all kinds, such as a skilful chemist makes, takes place. Two apprentices aid him in the retail business, but do not sleep in the house; they lodge in the Rue de la Colandre.

In the evening they take their departure an instant before the shop closes; in the morning they wait at the door until it opens.

This ground-floor shop is therefore dark and deserted, as we have said.

In this shop, which is large and deep, there are two doors, each leading to a staircase. One of these staircases is in the wall itself and is lateral, and the other is exterior and visible from the quay now called the Quai des Augustins, and from the riverbank, now called the Quai des Orfévres.

Both lead to the principal room on the first floor. This room is of the same size as the ground floor, except that it is divided into two compartments by tapestry suspended in the centre and parallel to the bridge. At the end of the first compartment opens the door leading to the exterior staircase. On the side face of the second opens the door of the secret staircase. This door is invisible, being concealed by a large carved cupboard fastened to it by iron cramps, and moving with it when pushed open. Catharine alone, besides Réné, knows the secret of this door, and by it she comes and departs; and with eye or ear placed against the cupboard, in which are several small holes, she sees and hears all that occurs in the chamber.

Two other doors, visible to all eyes, present themselves at the sides of the second compartment. One opens into a small chamber lighted from the roof, and having nothing in it but a large stove, some alembecs, retorts, and crucibles: it is the alchemist's laboratory; the other opens into a cell more singular than the rest of the apartment, for it is not lighted at all—has neither carpet nor furniture, but only a kind of stone altar.

The floor slopes from the centre to the ends, and from the ends to the base of the wall is a kind of gutter ending in a funnel, through whose orifice may be seen the dark waters of the Seine. On nails driven into the walls are hung singular-shaped instruments, all keen or pointed with points as fine as a needle and edges as sharp as a razor; some shine like mirrors; others, on the contrary, are of a dull gray or murky blue.

In a corner are two black fowls struggling with each other and tied together by the claws. This is the soothsayer's sanctuary.

Let us return to the middle chamber, that with two compartments.

Here the common herd of clients are introduced; here ibises from Egypt; mummies, with gilded bands; the crocodile, yawning from the ceiling; death's-heads, with eyeless sockets and loose teeth; and old musty volumes, torn and rat-eaten, are presented to the visitor's eye in pellmell confusion. Behind the curtain are phials, singularly shaped boxes, and weird-looking vases; all this is lighted up by two small silver lamps exactly alike, perhaps stolen from some altar of Santa Maria Novella or the Church Dei Lervi of Florence; these, supplied with perfumed oil, cast their yellow flames around the sombre vault from which each hangs by three blackened chains.

Réné, alone, his arms crossed, is pacing up and down the second compartment with long strides, and shaking his head. After a lengthened and painful musing he pauses before an hour-glass:

"Ah! ah!" says he, "I forget to turn it; and perhaps the sand has all run through a long time ago."

Then, looking at the moon as it struggled through a heavy black cloud which seemed to hang over Notre-Dame, he said: "It is nine o'clock. If she comes, she will come, as usual, in an hour or an hour and a half; then there will be time for all."

At this moment a noise was heard on the bridge. Réné applied his ear to the orifice of a long tube, the other end of which reached down the street, terminating in a heraldic viper-head.

"No," he said, "it is neither *she* nor *they*; it is men's footsteps, and they stop at my door—they are coming here."

And three sharp knocks were heard at the door.

Réné hurried downstairs and put his ear against the door, without opening it.

The three sharp blows were repeated.

"Who's there?" asked Maître Réné.

"Must we mention our names?" inquired a voice.

"It is indispensable," replied Réné.

"Well, then, I am the Comte Annibal de Coconnas," said the same voice.

"And I am the Comte Lerac de la Mole," said another voice, which had not as yet been heard.

"Wait, wait, gentlemen, I am at your service."

And at the same moment Réné drew the bolts and, lifting the bars, opened the door to the two young men locking it after him. Then, conducting them by the exterior staircase, he introduced them into the second compartment.

La Mole, as he entered, made the sign of the cross under his cloak. He was pale, and his hand trembled without his being able to repress this symptom of weakness.

Coconnas looked at everything, one after the other; and seeing the door of the cell, was about to open it.

"Allow me to observe, my dear young gentleman," said Réné, in his deep voice, and placing his hand on Coconnas's, "those that do me the honor of a visit have access only to this part of the room."

"Oh, very well," replied Coconnas; "besides, I feel like sitting down." And he took a seat.

There was unbroken silence for a moment—Maître Réné was waiting for one or the other of the young men to open the conversation.

"Maître Réné," at length said Coconnas, "you are a skilful man, and I pray you tell me if I shall always remain a sufferer from my wound—that is, always experience this shortness of breath, which prevents me from riding on horseback, using my sword, and eating larded omelettes?"

Réné put his ear to Coconnas's chest and listened attentively to the play of the lungs.

"No, Monsieur le Comte," he replied, "you will get well."

"Really?"

"Yes, I assure you."

"Well, you fill me with delight."

There was silence once more.

"Is there nothing else you would desire to know, M. le Comte?"

"I wish to know," said Coconnas, "if I am really in love?"

"You are," replied Réné.

"How do you know?"

"Because you asked the question."

"By Heaven! you are right. But with whom?"

"With her who now, on every occasion, uses the oath you have just uttered."

"Ah!" said Coconnas, amazed; "Maître Réné, you are a clever man! Now, La Mole, it is your turn."

La Mole reddened, and seemed embarrassed.

"I, Monsieur Réné," he stammered, and speaking more firmly as he proceeded, "do not care to ask you if I am in love, for I know that I am, and I do not hide it from myself; but tell me, shall I be beloved in return? for, in truth, all that at first seemed propitious now turns against me."

"Perchance you have not done all you should do."

"What is there to do, sir, but to testify, by one's respect and devotion to the lady of one's thoughts, that she is really and profoundly beloved?"

"You know," replied Réné, "that these demonstrations are frequently very meaningless."

"Then must I despair?"

"By no means; we must have recourse to science. In human nature there are antipathies to be overcome—sympathies which may be forced. Iron is not the lodestone; but by rubbing it with a lodestone we make it, in its turn, attract iron."

"Yes, yes," muttered La Mole; "but I have an objection to all these sorceries."

"Ah, then, if you have any such objections, you should not come here," answered Réné.

"Come, come, this is child's play!" interposed Coconnas. "Maître Réné, can you show me the devil?"

"No, Monsieur le Comte."

"I'm sorry for that; for I had a word or two to say to him, and it might have encouraged La Mole."

"Well, then, let it be so," said La Mole, "let us go to the point at once. I have been told of figures modelled in wax to look like the beloved object. Is that one way?"

"An infallible one."

"And there is nothing in the experiment likely to affect the life or health of the person beloved?"

"Nothing."

"Let us try, then."

"Shall I make first trial?" said Coconnas.

"No," said La Mole, "since I have begun, I will go through to the end."

"Is your desire mighty, ardent, imperious to know what the obstacle is, Monsieur de la Mole?"

"Oh," exclaimed La Mole, "I am dying with anxiety."

At this moment some one rapped lightly at the street door—so lightly that no one but Maître Réné heard the noise, doubtless because he had been expecting it.

Without any hesitation he went to the speaking-tube and put his ear to the mouthpiece, at the same time asking La Mole several idle questions. Then he added, suddenly:

"Now put all your energy into your wish, and call the person whom you love."

La Mole knelt, as if about to address a divinity; and Réné, going into the other compartment, went out noiselessly by the exterior staircase, and an instant afterward light steps trod the floor of his shop.

When La Mole rose he beheld before him Maître Réné. The Florentine held in his hand a small wax figure, very indifferently modelled; it wore a crown and mantle.

"Do you desire to be always beloved by your royal mistress?" demanded the perfumer.

"Yes, even if it cost me my life—even if my soul should be the sacrifice!" replied La Mole.

"Very good," said the Florentine, taking with the ends of his fingers some drops of water from a ewer and sprinkling them over the figure, at the same time muttering certain Latin words.

La Mole shuddered, believing that some sacrilege was committed.

"What are you doing?" he asked.

"I am christening this figure with the name of Marguerite."

"What for?"

"To establish a sympathy."

La Mole opened his mouth to prevent his going any further, but a mocking look from Coconnas stopped him.

Réné, who had noticed the impulse, waited. "Your absolute and undivided will is necessary," he said.

"Go on," said La Mole.

Réné wrote on a small strip of red paper some cabalistic characters, put it into the eye of a steel needle, and with the needle pierced the small wax model in the heart.

Strange to say, at the orifice of the wound appeared a small drop of blood; then he set fire to the paper.

The heat of the needle melted the wax around it and dried up the spot of blood.

"Thus," said Réné, "by the power of sympathy, your love shall pierce and burn the heart of the woman whom you love."

Coconnas, true to his repute as a bold thinker, laughed in his mustache, and in a low tone jested; but La Mole, desperately in love and full of superstition, felt a cold perspiration start from the roots of his hair.

"And now," continued Réné, "press your lips to the lips of the figure, and say: 'Marguerite, I love thee! Come, Marguerite!'"

La Mole obeyed.

At this moment the door of the second chamber was heard to open, and light steps approached. Coconnas, curious and incredulous, drew his poniard, and fearing that if he raised the tapestry Réné would repeat what he said about the door, he cut a hole in the thick curtain, and applying his eye to the hole, uttered a cry of astonishment, to which two women's voices responded.

"What is it?" exclaimed La Mole, nearly dropping the waxen figure, which Réné caught from his hands.

"Why," replied Coconnas, "the Duchesse de Nevers and Madame Marguerite are there!"

"There, now, you unbelievers!" replied Réné, with an austere smile; "do you still doubt the force of sympathy?"

La Mole was petrified on seeing the queen; Coconnas was amazed at beholding Madame de Nevers. One believed that Réné's sorceries had evoked the phantom Marguerite; the other, seeing the door half open, by which the lovely phantoms had entered, gave at once a worldly and substantial explanation to the mystery.

While La Mole was crossing himself and sighing enough to split a rock, Coconnas, who had taken time to indulge in philosophical questionings and to drive away the foul fiend with the aid of that holy water sprinkler called scepticism, having observed, through the hole in the curtain, the astonishment shown by Madame de Nevers and Marguerite's somewhat caustic smile, judged the moment to be decisive, and understanding that a man may say in behalf of a friend what he cannot say for himself, instead of going to Madame de Nevers, went straight to Marguerite, and bending his knee, after the fashion of the great Artaxerxes as represented in the farces of the day, cried, in a voice to which the whistling of his wound added a peculiar accent not without some power:

"Madame, this very moment, at the demand of my friend the Comte de la Mole, Maître Réné was evoking your spirit; and to my great astonishment, your spirit is accompanied with a body most dear to me, and which I recommend to my friend. Shade of her majesty the Queen of Navarre, will you desire the body of your companion to come to the other side of the curtain?"

Marguerite began to laugh, and made a sign to Henriette, who passed to the other side of the curtain.

"La Mole, my friend," continued Coconnas, "be as eloquent as Demosthenes, as Cicero, as the Chancellor de l'Hôpital! and be assured that my life will be imperilled if you do not persuade the body of Madame de Nevers that I am her most devoted, most obedient, and most faithful servant."

"But"—stammered La Mole.

"Do as I say! And you, Maître Réné, watch that we are not interrupted."

Réné did as Coconnas asked.

"By Heaven, monsieur," said Marguerite, "you are a clever man. I am listening to you. What have you to say?"

"I have to say to you, madame, that the shadow of my friend—for he is a shadow, and he proves it by not uttering a single little word—I say, that this shadow begs me to use the faculty which material bodies possess of speaking so as to be understood, and to say to you: Lovely shadow, the gentleman thus disembodied has lost his whole body and all his breath by the cruelty of your eyes. If this were really you, I should ask Maître Réné to plunge me in some sulphurous pit rather than use such language to the daughter of King Henry II., to the sister of King Charles IX., to the wife of the King of Navarre. But shades are freed from all earthly pride and they are never angry when men love them. Therefore, pray your body, madame, to love the soul of this poor La Mole a little—a soul in trouble, if ever there was one; a soul first persecuted by friendship, which three times thrust into him several inches of cold steel; a soul burnt by the fire of your eyes—fire a thousand times more consuming than all the flames of hell. So have pity on this poor soul! Love a little what was the handsome La Mole; and if you no longer possess speech, ah! bestow a gesture, bestow a smile upon him. My friend's soul is a very intelligent soul, and will comprehend everything. Be kind to him, then; or, by Heaven! I will run my sword through Réné's body in order that, by virtue of the power which he possesses over spirits, he may force yours, which he has already so opportunely evoked, to do all a shade so amiably disposed as yours appears to be should do."

At this burst of eloquence delivered by Coconnas as he stood in front of the queen like Æneas descending into Hades, Marguerite could not refrain from a hearty burst of laughter, yet, preserving the silence which on such an occasion may be the supposed characteristic of a royal shade, she presented her hand to Coconnas. He took it daintily in his, and, calling to La Mole, said:

"Shade of my friend, come hither instantly!"

La Mole, amazed, overcome, silently obeyed.

"'T is well," said Coconnas, taking him by the back of the head; "and now bring the shadow of your handsome brown countenance into contact with the white and vaporous hand before you."

And Coconnas, suiting the action to the word, raised the delicate hand to La Mole's lips, and kept them for a moment respectfully united, without the hand seeking to withdraw itself from the gentle pressure.

Marguerite had not ceased to smile, but Madame de Nevers did not smile at all; she was still trembling at the unexpected appearance of the two gentlemen. She was conscious that her awkwardness was increased by all the fever of a growing jealousy, for it seemed to her that Coconnas ought not thus to forget her affairs for those of others.

La Mole saw her eyebrows contracted, detected the flashing threat of her eyes, and in spite of the intoxicating fever to which his delight was insensibly urging him to succumb he realized the danger which his friend was running and perceived what he should try to do to rescue him.

So rising and leaving Marguerite's hand in Coconnas's, he grasped the Duchesse de Nevers's, and bending his knee he said:

"O loveliest—O most adorable of women—I speak of living women, and not of shades!" and he turned a look and a smile to Marguerite; "allow a soul released from its mortal envelope to repair the absence of a body fully absorbed by material friendship. Monsieur de Coconnas, whom you see, is only a man—a man of bold and hardy frame, of flesh handsome to gaze upon perchance, but perishable, like all flesh. *Omnis caro fenum.* Although this gentleman keeps on from morning to night pouring into my ears the most touching litanies about you, though you have seen him distribute as heavy blows as were ever seen in wide France—this champion, so full of eloquence in presence of a spirit, dares not address a woman. That is why he has addressed the shade of the queen, charging me to speak to your lovely body, and to tell you that he lays at your feet his soul and heart; that he entreats from your divine eyes a look in pity, from your rosy fingers a beckoning sign, and from your musical and heavenly voice those words which men can never forget; if not, he has supplicated another thing, and that is, in case he should not soften you, you will run my sword—which is a real blade, for swords have no shadows except in the sunshine—run my sword right through his body for the second time, for he can live no longer if you do not authorize him to live exclusively for you." All the verve and comical exaggeration which Coconnas had put into his speech found their counterpart in the tenderness, the intoxicating vigor, and the mock humility which La Mole introduced into his supplication.

Henriette's eyes turned from La Mole, to whom she had listened till he ended, and rested on Coconnas, to see if the expression of that gentleman's countenance harmonized with his friend's ardent address. It seemed that she was satisfied, for blushing, breathless, conquered, she said to Coconnas, with a smile which disclosed a double row of pearls enclosed in coral:

"Is this true?"

"By Heaven!" exclaimed Coconnas, fascinated by her look, "it is true, indeed. Oh, yes, madame, it is true—true on your life—true on my death!"

"Come with me, then," said Henriette, extending to him her hand, while her eyes proclaimed the feelings of her heart.

Coconnas flung his velvet cap into the air and with one stride was at the young woman's side, while La Mole, recalled to Marguerite by a gesture, executed at the same time an amorous *chassez* with his friend.

Réné appeared at the door in the background.

"Silence!" he exclaimed, in a voice which at once damped all the ardor of the lovers; "silence!"

And they heard in the solid wall the sound of a key in a lock, and of a door grating on its hinges.

"But," said Marguerite, haughtily, "I should think that no one has the right to enter whilst we are here!"

"Not even the queen mother?" whispered Réné in her ear.

Marguerite instantly rushed out by the exterior staircase, leading La Mole after her; Henriette and Coconnas almost arm-in-arm followed them, all four taking flight, as fly at the first noise the birds seen engaged in loving parley on the boughs of a flowering shrub.

CHAPTER XX.

THE BLACK HENS.

It was time the two couples disappeared! Catharine was putting the key in the lock of the second door just as Coconnas and Madame de Nevers stepped out of the house by the lower entrance, and Catharine as she entered could hear the steps of the fugitives on the stairs.

She cast a searching glance around, and then fixing her suspicious eyes on Réné, who stood motionless, bowing before her, said:

"Who was that?"

"Some lovers, who are satisfied with the assurance I gave them that they are really in love."

"Never mind them," said Catharine, shrugging her shoulders; "is there no one else here?"

"No one but your majesty and myself."

"Have you done what I ordered you?"

"About the two black hens?"

"Yes!"

"They are ready, madame."

"Ah," muttered Catharine, "if you were a Jew!"

"Why a Jew, madame?"

"Because you could then read the precious treatises which the Hebrews have written about sacrifices. I have had one of them translated, and I found that the Hebrews did not look for omens in the heart or liver as the Romans did, but in the configuration of the brain, and in the shape of the letters traced there by the all-powerful hand of destiny."

"Yes, madame; so I have heard from an old rabbi."

"There are," said Catharine, "characters thus marked that reveal all the future. Only the Chaldean seers recommend"—

"Recommend—what?" asked Réné, seeing the queen hesitate.

"That the experiment shall be tried on the human brain, as more developed and more nearly sympathizing with the wishes of the consulter."

"Alas!" said Réné, "your majesty knows it is impossible."

"Difficult, at least," said Catharine; "if we had known this at Saint Bartholomew's, what a rich harvest we might have had—The first convict—but I will think of it. Meantime, let us do what we can. Is the chamber of sacrifice prepared?"

"Yes, madame."

"Let us go there."

Réné lighted a taper made of strange substances, the odor of which, both insidious and penetrating as well as nauseating and stupefying, betokened the introduction of many elements; holding this taper up, he preceded Catharine into the cell.

Catharine selected from amongst the sacrificial instruments a knife of blue steel, while Réné took up one of the two fowls that were huddling in one corner, with anxious, golden eyes.

"How shall we proceed?"

"We will examine the liver of the one and the brain of the other. If these two experiments lead to the same result we must be convinced, especially if these results coincide with those we got before."

"Which shall we begin with?"

"With the liver."

"Very well," said Réné, and he fastened the bird down to two rings attached to the little altar, so that the creature, turned on its back, could only struggle, without stirring from the spot.

Catharine opened its breast with a single stroke of her knife; the fowl uttered three cries, and, after some convulsions, expired.

"Always three cries!" said Catharine; "three signs of death."

She then opened the body.

"And the liver inclining to the left, always to the left,—a triple death, followed by a downfall. 'T is terrible, Réné."

"We must see, madame, whether the presages from the second will correspond with those of the first."

Réné unfastened the body of the fowl from the altar and tossed it into a corner; then he went to the other, which, foreseeing what its fate would be by its companion's, tried to escape by running round the cell, and finding itself pent up in a corner flew over Réné's head, and in its flight extinguished the magic taper Catharine held.

"You see, Réné, thus shall our race be extinguished," said the queen; "death shall breathe upon it, and destroy it from the face of the earth! Yet three sons! three sons!" she murmured, sorrowfully.

Réné took from her the extinguished taper, and went into the adjoining room to relight it.

On his return he saw the hen hiding its head in the tunnel.

"This time," said Catharine, "I will prevent the cries, for I will cut off the head at once."

And accordingly, as soon as the hen was bound, Catharine, as she had said, severed the head at a single blow; but in the last agony the beak opened three times, and then closed forever.

"Do you see," said Catharine, terrified, "instead of three cries, three sighs? Always three!—they will all three die. All these spirits before they depart count and call three. Let us now see the prognostications in the head."

She severed the bloodless comb from the head, carefully opened the skull, and laying bare the lobes of the brain endeavored to trace a letter formed in the bloody sinuosities made by the division of the central pulp.

"Always so!" cried she, clasping her hands; "and this time clearer than ever; see here!"

Réné approached.

"What is the letter?" asked Catharine.

"An H," replied Réné.

"How many times repeated?"

Réné counted.

"Four," said he.

"Ay, ay! I see it! that is to say, HENRY IV. Oh," she cried, flinging the knife from her, "I am accursed in my posterity!"

She was terrible, that woman, pale as a corpse, lighted by the dismal taper, and clasping her bloody hands.

"He will reign!" she exclaimed with a sigh of despair; "he will reign!"

"He will reign!" repeated Réné, plunged in meditation.

Nevertheless, the gloomy expression of Catharine's face soon disappeared under the light of a thought which unfolded in the depths of her mind.

"Réné," said she, stretching out her hand toward the perfumer without lifting her head from her breast, "Réné, is there not a terrible history of a doctor at Perugia, who killed at once, by the aid of a pomade,[7] his daughter and his daughter's lover?"

"Yes, madame."

"And this lover was"—

"Was King Ladislas, madame."

"Ah, yes!" murmured she; "have you any of the details of this story?"

"I have an old book which mentions it," replied Réné.

"Well, let us go into the other room, and you can show it me."

They left the cell, the door of which Réné closed after him.

"Has your majesty any other orders to give me concerning the sacrifices?"

"No, Réné, I am for the present sufficiently convinced. We will wait till we can secure the head of some criminal, and on the day of the execution you must arrange with the hangman."

Réné bowed in token of obedience, then holding his candle up he let the light fall on the shelves where his books stood, climbed on a chair, took one down, and handed it to the queen.

Catharine opened it.

"What is this?" she asked; "'On the Method of Raising and Training Tercels, Falcons, and Gerfalcons to be Courageous, Valiant, and always ready for Flight.'"

"Ah! pardon me, madame, I made a mistake. That is a treatise on venery written by a scientific man of Lucca for the famous Castruccio Castracani. It stood next the other and was bound exactly like it. I took down the wrong one. However, it is a very precious volume; there are only three copies extant —one belongs to the library at Venice, the other was bought by your grandfather Lorenzo and was offered by Pietro de Médicis to King Charles VIII., when he visited Florence, and the third you have in your hands."

"I venerate it," said Catharine, "because of its rarity, but as I do not need it, I return it to you."

And she held out her right hand to Réné to receive the book which she wished, while with her left hand she returned to him the one which she had first taken.

This time Réné was not mistaken; it was the volume she wished. He stepped down, turned the leaves for a moment, and gave it to her open.

Catharine went and sat down at a table. Réné placed the magic taper near her and by the light of its bluish flame she read a few lines in an undertone:

"Good!" said she, shutting the book; "that is all I wanted to know."

She rose from her seat, leaving the book on the table, but bearing away the idea which had germinated in her mind and would ripen there.

Réné waited respectfully, taper in hand, until the queen, who seemed about to retire, should give him fresh orders or ask fresh questions.

Catharine, with her head bent and her finger on her mouth, walked up and down several times without speaking.

Then suddenly stopping before Réné, and fixing on him her eyes, round and piercing like a hawk's:

"Confess you have made for her some love-philter," said she.

"For whom?" asked Réné, starting.

"La Sauve."

"I, madame?" said Réné; "never!"

"Never?"

"I swear it on my soul."

"There must be some magic in it, however, for he is desperately in love with her, though he is not famous for his constancy."

"Who, madame?"

"He, Henry, the accursed,—he who is to succeed my three sons,—he who shall one day be called Henry IV., and is yet the son of Jeanne d'Albret."

And Catharine accompanied these words with a sigh which made Réné shudder, for he thought of the famous gloves he had prepared by Catharine's order for the Queen of Navarre.

"So he still runs after her, does he?" said Réné.

"He does," replied the queen.

"I thought that the King of Navarre was quite in love with his wife now."

"A farce, Réné, a farce! I know not why, but every one is seeking to deceive me. My daughter Marguerite is leagued against me; perhaps she, too, is looking forward to the death of her brothers; perhaps she, too, hopes to be Queen of France."

"Perhaps so," re-echoed Réné, falling back into his own reverie and echoing Catharine's terrible suspicion.

"Ha! we shall see," said Catharine, going to the main door, for she doubtless judged it useless to descend the secret stair, now that she was sure that they were alone.

Réné preceded her, and in a few minutes they stood in the perfumer's shop.

"You promised me some new kind of cosmetic for my hands and lips, Réné; the winter is at hand and you know how sensitive my skin is to the cold."

"I have already provided for this, madame; and I shall bring you some to-morrow."

"You would not find me in before nine o'clock to-morrow evening; I shall be occupied with my devotions during the day."

"I will be at the Louvre at nine o'clock, then, madame."

"Madame de Sauve has beautiful hands and beautiful lips," said Catharine in a careless tone. "What pomade does she use?"

"For her hands?"

"Yes, for her hands first."

"Heliotrope."

"What for her lips?"

"She is going to try a new opiate of my invention. I was going to bring your majesty a box of it at the same time."

Catharine mused an instant.

"She is certainly a very beautiful creature," said she, pursuing her secret thoughts; "and the passion of the Béarnais for her is not strange at all."

"And she is so devoted to your majesty," said Réné. "At least I should think so."

Catharine smiled and shrugged her shoulders.

"When a woman loves, is she faithful to any one but her lover? You must have given her some philter, Réné."

"I swear I have not, madame."

"Well, well; we'll say no more about it. Show me this new opiate you spoke of, that is to make her lips fresher and rosier than ever."

Réné approached a shelf and showed Catharine six small boxes of the same shape, *i.e.*, round silver boxes ranged side by side.

"This is the only philter she ever asked me for," observed Réné; "it is true, as your majesty says, I composed it expressly for her, for her lips are so tender that the sun and wind affect them equally."

Catharine opened one of the boxes; it contained a most fascinating carmine paste.

"Give me some paste for my hands, Réné," said she; "I will take it away with me."

Réné took the taper, and went to seek, in a private compartment, what the queen asked for. As he turned, he fancied that he saw the queen quickly conceal a box under her mantle; he was, however, too familiar with these little thefts of the queen mother to have the rudeness to seem to perceive the movement; so wrapping the cosmetic she demanded in a paper bag, ornamented with fleurs-de-lis:

"Here it is, madame," he said.

"Thanks, Réné," returned the queen; then, after a moment's silence: "Do not give Madame de Sauve that paste for a week or ten days; I wish to make the first trial of it myself."

And she prepared to go.

"Your majesty, do you desire me to accompany you?" asked Réné.

"Only to the end of the bridge," replied Catharine; "my gentlemen and my litter wait for me there."

They left the house, and at the end of the Rue de la Barillerie four gentlemen on horseback and a plain litter were waiting.

On his return Réné's first care was to count his boxes of opiates. One was wanting.

CHAPTER XXI.

MADAME DE SAUVE'S APARTMENT.

Catharine was not deceived in her suspicions. Henry had resumed his former habits and went every evening to Madame de Sauve's. At first he accomplished this with the greatest secrecy; but gradually he grew negligent and ceased to take any precautions, so that Catharine had no trouble in finding out that while Marguerite was still nominally Queen of Navarre, Madame de Sauve was the real queen.

At the beginning of this story we said a word or two about Madame de Sauve's apartment; but the door opened by Dariole to the King of Navarre closed hermetically behind him, so that these rooms, the scene of the Béarnais's mysterious amours, are totally unknown to us. The quarters, like those furnished by princes for their dependents in the palaces occupied by them in order to have them within reach, were smaller and less convenient than what she could have found in the city itself. As the reader already knows, they were situated on the second floor of the palace, almost immediately above those occupied by Henry himself. The door opened into a corridor, the end of which was lighted by an arched window with small leaded panes, so that even in the loveliest days of the year only a dubious light filtered through. During the winter, after three o'clock in the afternoon, it was necessary to light a lamp, but as this contained no more oil than in summer, it went out by ten o'clock, and thus, as soon as the winter days arrived, gave the two lovers the greatest security.

A small antechamber, carpeted with yellow flowered damask; a reception-room with hangings of blue velvet; a sleeping-room, the bed adorned with twisted columns and rose-satin curtains, enshrining a *ruelle* ornamented with a looking-glass set in silver, and two paintings representing the loves of Venus and Adonis,—such was the residence, or as one would say nowadays the nest, of the lovely lady-in-waiting to Queen Catharine de Médicis.

If one had looked sharply one would have found, opposite a toilet-table provided with every accessory, a small door in a dark corner of this room opening into a sort of oratory where, raised on two steps, stood a *priedieu*. In this little chapel on the wall hung three or four paintings, to the highest degree spiritual, as if to serve as a corrective to the two mythological pictures which we mentioned. Among these paintings were hung on gilded nails weapons such as women carried.

That evening, which was the one following the scenes which we have described as taking place at Maître Réné's, Madame de Sauve, seated in her bedroom on a couch, was telling Henry about her fears and her love, and was giving him as a proof of her love the devotion which she had shown on the famous night following Saint Bartholomew's, the night which, it will be remembered, Henry spent in his wife's quarters.

Henry on his side was expressing his gratitude to her. Madame de Sauve was charming that evening in her simple batiste wrapper; and Henry was very grateful.

At the same time, as Henry was really in love, he was dreamy. Madame de Sauve, who had come actually to love instead of pretending to love as Catharine had commanded, kept gazing at Henry to see if his eyes were in accord with his words.

"Come, now, Henry," she was saying, "be honest; that night which you spent in the boudoir of her majesty the Queen of Navarre, with Monsieur de la Mole at your feet, didn't you feel sorry that that worthy gentleman was between you and the queen's bedroom?"

"Certainly I did, sweetheart," said Henry, "for the only way that I could reach this room where I am so comfortable, where at this instant I am so happy, was for me to pass through the queen's room."

Madame de Sauve smiled.

"And you have not been there since?"

"Only as I have told you."

"You will never go to her without informing me?"

"Never."

"Would you swear to it?"

"Certainly I would, if I were still a Huguenot, but"—

"But what?"

"But the Catholic religion, the dogmas of which I am now learning, teach me that one must never take an oath."

"Gascon!" exclaimed Madame de Sauve, shaking her head.

"But now it is my turn, Charlotte," said Henry. "If I ask you some questions, will you answer?"

"Certainly I will," replied the young woman, "I have nothing to hide from you."

"Now look here, Charlotte," said the king, "explain to me just for once how it came about that after the desperate resistance which you made to me before my marriage, you became less cruel to me who am an awkward Béarnais, an absurd provincial, a prince too poverty-stricken, indeed, to keep the jewels of his crown polished."

"Henry," said Charlotte, "you are asking the explanation of the enigma which the philosophers of all countries have been trying to determine for the past three thousand years! Henry, never ask a woman why she loves you; be satisfied with asking, 'Do you love me?'"

"Do you love me, Charlotte?" asked Henry.

"I love you," replied Madame de Sauve, with a fascinating smile, dropping her pretty hand into her lover's.

Henry retained the hand.

"But," he went on to say, following out his thought, "supposing I have guessed the word which the philosophers have been vainly trying to find for three thousand years—at least as far as you are concerned, Charlotte?"

Madame de Sauve blushed.

"You love me," pursued Henry, "consequently I have nothing else to ask you and I consider myself the happiest man in the world. But you know happiness is always accompanied by some lack. Adam, in the midst of Eden, was not perfectly happy, and he bit into that miserable apple which imposed upon us all that love for novelty that makes every one spend his life in the search for something unknown. Tell me, my darling, in order to help me to find mine, didn't Queen Catharine at first bid you love me?"

"Henry," exclaimed Madame de Sauve, "speak lower when you speak of the queen mother!"

"Oh!" exclaimed Henry, with a spontaneity and boldness which deceived Madame de Sauve herself, "it was a good thing formerly to distrust her, kind mother that she is, but then we were not on good terms; but now that I am her daughter's husband"—

"Madame Marguerite's husband!" exclaimed Charlotte, flushing with jealousy.

"Speak low in your turn," said Henry; "now that I am her daughter's husband we are the best friends in the world. What was it they wanted? For me to become a Catholic, so it seems. Well, grace has touched me, and by the intercession of Saint Bartholomew I have become one. We live together like brethren in a happy family—like good Christians."

"And Queen Marguerite?"

"Queen Marguerite?" repeated Henry; "oh, well, she is the link uniting us."

"But, Henry, you said that the Queen of Navarre, as a reward for the devotion I showed her, had been generous to me. If what you say is true, if this generosity, for which I have cherished deep gratitude toward her, is genuine, she is a connecting link easy to break. So you cannot trust to this support, for you have not made your pretended intimacy impose on any one."

"Still I do rest on it, and for three months it has been the bolster on which I have slept."

"Then, Henry!" cried Madame de Sauve, "you have deceived me, and Madame Marguerite is really your wife."

Henry smiled.

"There, Henry," said Madame de Sauve, "you have given me one of those exasperating smiles which make me feel the cruel desire to scratch your eyes out, king though you are."

215

"Then," said Henry, "I seem to be imposing now by means of this pretended friendship, since there are moments when, king though I am, you desire to scratch out my eyes, because you believe that it exists!"

"Henry! Henry!" said Madame de Sauve, "I believe that God himself does not know what your thoughts are."

"My sweetheart," said Henry, "I think that Catharine first told you to love me, next, that your heart told you the same thing, and that when those two voices are speaking to you, you hear only your heart's. Now here I am. I love you and love you with my whole heart, and that is the very reason why if ever I should have secrets I should not confide them to you,—for fear of compromising you, of course,—for the queen's friendship is changeable, it is a mother-in-law's."

This was not what Charlotte expected; it seemed to her that the thickening veil between her and her lover every time she tried to sound the depths of his bottomless heart was assuming the consistency of a wall, and was separating them from each other. So she felt the tears springing to her eyes as he made this answer, and as it struck ten o'clock just at that moment:

"Sire," said Charlotte, "it is my bed-time; my duties call me very early to-morrow morning to the queen mother."

"So you drive me away to-night, do you, sweetheart?"

"Henry, I am sad. As I am sad, you would find me tedious and you would not like me any more. You see that it is better for you to withdraw."

"Very good," said Henry, "I will withdraw if you insist upon it, only, *ventre saint gris*! you must at least grant me the favor of staying for your toilet."

"But Queen Marguerite, sire! won't you keep her waiting if you remain?"

"Charlotte," replied Henry, gravely, "it was agreed between us that we should never mention the Queen of Navarre, but it seems to me that this evening we have talked about nothing but her."

Madame de Sauve sighed; then she went and sat down before her toilet-table. Henry took a chair, pulled it along toward the one that served as his mistress's seat, and setting one knee on it while he leaned on the back of the other, he said:

"Come, my good little Charlotte, let me see you make yourself beautiful, and beautiful for me whatever you said. Heavens! What things! What scent-bottles, what powders, what phials, what perfumery boxes!"

"It seems a good deal," said Charlotte, with a sigh, "and yet it is too little, since with it all I have not as yet found the means of reigning exclusively over your majesty's heart."

"There!" exclaimed Henry; "let us not fall back on politics! What is that little fine delicate brush? Should it not be for painting the eyebrows of my Olympian Jupiter?"

"Yes, sire," replied Madame de Sauve, "and you have guessed at the first shot!"

"And that pretty little ivory rake?"

"'Tis for parting the hair!"

"And that charming little silver box with a chased cover?"

"Oh, that is something Réné sent, sire; 'tis the famous opiate which he has been promising me so long—to make still sweeter the lips which your majesty has been good enough sometimes to find rather sweet."

And Henry, as if to test what the charming woman said, touched his lips to the ones which she was looking at so attentively in the mirror. Now that they were returning to the field of coquetry, the cloud began to lift from the baroness's brow. She took up the box which had thus been explained, and was just going to show Henry how the vermilion salve was used, when a sharp rap at the antechamber door startled the two lovers.

"Some one is knocking, madame," said Dariole, thrusting her head through the opening of the portière.

"Go and find out who it is, and come back," said Madame de Sauve. Henry and Charlotte looked at each other anxiously, and Henry was beginning to think of retiring to the oratory, in which he had already more than once taken refuge, when Dariole reappeared.

"Madame," said she, "it is Maître Réné, the perfumer."

At this name Henry frowned, and involuntarily bit his lips.

"Do you want me to refuse him admission?" asked Charlotte.

"No!" said Henry; "Maître Réné never does anything without having previously thought about it. If he comes to you, it is because he has a reason for coming."

"In that case, do you wish to hide?"

"I shall be careful not to," said Henry, "for Maître Réné knows everything; therefore Maître Réné knows that I am here."

"But has not your majesty some reason for thinking his presence painful to you?"

"I!" said Henry, making an effort, which in spite of his will-power he could not wholly dissimulate. "I! none at all! we are rather cool to each other, it is true; but since the night of Saint Bartholomew we have been reconciled."

"Let him enter!" said Madame de Sauve to Dariole.

A moment later Réné appeared, and took in the whole room at a glance.

Madame de Sauve was still before her toilet-table.

Henry had resumed his place on the couch.

Charlotte was in the light, and Henry in the shadow.

"Madame," said Réné, with respectful familiarity, "I have come to offer my apologies."

"For what, Réné?" asked Madame de Sauve, with that condescension which pretty women always use towards the world of tradespeople who surround them, and whose duty it is to make them more beautiful.

"Because long ago I promised to work for these pretty lips, and because"—

"Because you did not keep your promise until to-day; is that it?" asked Charlotte.

"Until to-day?" repeated Réné.

"Yes; it was only to-day, in fact, this evening, that I received the box you sent me."

"Ah! indeed!" said Réné, looking strangely at the small opiate box on Madame de Sauve's table, which was precisely like those he had in his shop. "I thought so!" he murmured. "And you have used it?"

"No, not yet. I was just about to try it as you entered." Réné's face assumed a dreamy expression which did not escape Henry. Indeed, very few things escaped him.

"Well, Réné, what are you going to do now?" asked the king.

"I? Nothing, sire," said the perfumer, "I am humbly waiting until your majesty speaks to me, before taking leave of Madame la Baronne."

"Come, now!" said Henry, smiling. "Do you need my word to know that it is a pleasure to me to see you?"

Réné glanced around him, made a tour of the room as if to sound the doors and the curtains with his eye and ear, then he stopped and standing so that he could embrace at a glance both Madame de Sauve and Henry:

"I do not know it," said he, thanks to that admirable instinct which like a sixth sense guided him during the first part of his life in the midst of impending dangers. Henry felt that at that moment something strangely resembling a struggle was passing through the mind of the perfumer, and turned towards him, still in the shadow, while the Florentine's face was in the light.

"You here at this hour, Réné?" said he.

"Am I unfortunate enough to be in your majesty's way?" asked the perfumer, stepping back.

"No, but I want to know one thing."

"What, sire?"

"Did you think you would find me here?"

"I was sure of it."

"You wanted me, then?"

"I am glad to have found you, at least."

"Have you something to say to me?" persisted Henry.

"Perhaps, sire!" replied Réné.

Charlotte blushed, for she feared that the revelation which the perfumer seemed anxious to make might have something to do with her conduct towards Henry. Therefore she acted as though, having been wholly engrossed with her toilet, she had heard nothing, and interrupted the conversation.

"Ah! really, Réné," said she, opening the opiate box, "you are a delightful man. This cake is a marvellous color, and since you are here I am going to honor you by experimenting with your new production."

She took the box in one hand, and with the other touched the tip of her finger to the rose paste, which she was about to raise to her lips.

Réné gave a start.

The baroness smilingly lifted the opiate to her mouth.

Réné turned pale.

Still in the shadow, but with fixed and glowing eyes, Henry lost neither the action of the one nor the shudder of the other.

Charlotte's hand had but a short distance to go before it would touch her lips when Réné seized her arm, just as Henry rose to do so.

Henry fell back noiselessly on the couch.

"One moment, madame," said René, with a constrained smile, "you must not use this opiate without special directions."

"Who will give me these directions?"

"I."

"When?"

"As soon as I have finished saying what I have to say to his Majesty the King of Navarre."

Charlotte opened her eyes wide, understanding nothing of the mysterious language about her, and sat with the opiate pot in one hand, gazing at the tip of her finger, red with the rouge.

Henry rose, and moved by a thought which, like all those of the young king, had two sides, one which seemed superficial, the other which was deep, he took Charlotte's hand and red as it was, made as though to raise it to his lips.

"One moment," said René, quickly, "one moment! Be kind enough, madame, to rinse your lovely hands with this soap from Naples which I neglected to send you at the same time as the rouge, and which I have the honor of bringing you now."

Drawing from its silver wrapping a cake of green soap, he put it in a vermilion basin, poured some water over it, and, with one knee on the floor, offered it to Madame de Sauve.

"Why, really, Maître René, I no longer recognize you," said Henry, "you are so gallant that you far outstrip every court fop."

"Oh, what a delicious perfume!" cried Charlotte, rubbing her beautiful hands with the pearly foam made by the scented cake.

René performed his office of courtier to the end. He offered a napkin of fine Frisian linen to Madame de Sauve, who dried her hands on it.

"Now," said the Florentine to Henry. "Let your mind be at rest, monseigneur."

Charlotte gave her hand to Henry, who kissed it, and while she half turned on her chair to listen to what René was about to say, the King of Navarre returned to his couch, more convinced than ever that something unusual was passing through the mind of the perfumer.

"Well?" asked Charlotte. The Florentine apparently made an effort to collect all his strength, and then turned towards Henry.

CHAPTER XXII.

"SIRE, YOU SHALL BE KING."

"Sire," said Réné to Henry, "I have come to speak of something which has been on my mind for some time."

"Perfumery?" said Henry, smiling.

"Well, yes, sire,—perfumery," replied Réné, with a singular nod of acquiescence.

"Speak, I am listening to you. This is a subject which has always interested me deeply."

Réné looked at Henry to try, in spite of his words, to read the impenetrable thought; but seeing that it was perfectly impossible, he continued:

"One of my friends, sire, has just arrived from Florence. This friend is greatly interested in astrology."

"Yes," interrupted Henry, "I know that it is a passion with Florentines."

"In company with the foremost students of the world he has read the horoscopes of the chief gentlemen of Europe."

"Ah! ah!" exclaimed Henry.

"And as the house of Bourbon is at the head of the highest, descended as it is from the Count of Clermont, the fifth son of Saint Louis, your majesty must know that your horoscope has not been overlooked."

Henry listened still more attentively.

"Do you remember this horoscope?" said the King of Navarre, with a smile which he strove to render indifferent.

"Oh!" replied Réné, shaking his head, "your horoscope is not one to be forgotten."

"Indeed!" said Henry, ironically.

"Yes, sire; according to this horoscope your majesty is to have a most brilliant destiny."

The young prince gave a lightning glance which was almost at once lost under cover of indifference.

"Every Italian oracle is apt to flatter," said Henry; "but he who flatters lies. Are there not those who have predicted that I would command armies? I!" He burst out laughing. But an observer less occupied with himself than Réné would have noticed and realized the effort of this laugh.

"Sire," said Réné, coldly, "the horoscope tells better than that."

"Does it foretell that at the head of one of these armies I shall win battles?"

"Better than that, sire."

"Well," said Henry; "you will see that I shall be conqueror!"

"Sire, you shall be king."

"Well! *Ventre saint gris!*" exclaimed Henry, repressing a violent beating of his heart; "am I not that already?"

"Sire, my friend knows what he promises; not only will you be king, but you will reign."

"In that case," said Henry, in the same mocking tone, "your friend must have ten crowns of gold, must he not, Réné? for such a prophecy is very ambitious, especially in times like these. Well, Réné, as I am not rich, I will give your friend five now and five more when the prophecy is fulfilled."

"Sire," said Madame de Sauve, "do not forget that you are already pledged to Dariole, and do not overburden yourself with promises."

"Madame," said Henry, "I hope when this time comes that I shall be treated as a king, and that they will be satisfied if I keep half of my promises."

"Sire," said Réné, "I will continue."

"Oh, that is not all, then?" said Henry. "Well, if I am emperor, I will give twice as much."

"Sire, my friend has returned from Florence with the horoscope, which he renewed in Paris, and which always gives the same result; and he told me a secret."

"A secret of interest to his majesty?" asked Charlotte, quickly.

"I think so," said the Florentine.

"He is searching for words," thought Henry, without in any way coming to Réné's rescue. "Apparently the thing is difficult to tell."

"Speak, then," went on the Baroness de Sauve; "what is it about?"

"It is about all the rumors of poisoning," said the Florentine, weighing each of his words separately, "it is about all the rumors of poisoning which for some time have been circulated around court." A slight movement of the nostrils of the King of Navarre was the only indication of his increased attention at the sudden turn in the conversation.

"And your friend the Florentine," said Henry, "knows something about this poisoning?"

"Yes, sire."

"How can you tell me a secret which is not yours, Réné, especially when the secret is such an important one?" said Henry, in the most natural tone he could assume.

"This friend has some advice to ask of your majesty."

"Of me?"

"What is there surprising in that, sire? Remember the old soldier of Actium who, having a law-suit on hand, asked advice of Augustus."

"Augustus was a lawyer, Réné, and I am not."

"Sire, when my friend confided this secret to me, your majesty still belonged to the Calvinist party, of which you were the chief head, and of which Monsieur de Condé was the second."

"Well?" said Henry.

"This friend hoped that you would use your all-powerful influence over Monsieur de Condé and beg him not to be hostile to him."

"Explain this to me, Réné, if you wish me to understand it," said Henry, without betraying the least change in his face or voice.

"Sire, your majesty will understand at the first word. This friend knows all the particulars of the attempt to poison Monseigneur de Condé."

"There has been an attempt to poison the Prince de Condé?" exclaimed Henry with a well-assumed astonishment. "Ah, indeed, and when was this?"

Réné looked fixedly at the king, and replied merely by these words:

"A week ago, your majesty."

"Some enemy?" asked the king.

"Yes," replied Réné, "an enemy whom your majesty knows and who knows your majesty."

"As a matter of fact," said Henry, "I think I have heard this mentioned, but I am ignorant of the details which your friend has to reveal. Tell them to me."

"Well, a perfumed apple was offered to the Prince of Condé. Fortunately, however, when it was brought to him his physician was with him. He took it from the hands of the messenger and smelled it to test its odor and soundness. Two days later a gangrene swelling of the face, an extravasation of the blood, a running sore which ate away his face, were the price of his devotion or the result of his imprudence."

"Unfortunately," replied Henry, "being half Catholic already, I have lost all influence over Monsieur de Condé. Your friend was wrong, therefore, in addressing himself to me."

"It was not only in regard to the Prince de Condé that your majesty could be of use to my friend, but in regard to the Prince de Porcian also, the brother of the one who was poisoned."

"Ah!" exclaimed Charlotte, "do you know, Réné, that your stories partake of the gruesome? You plead at a poor time. It is late, your conversation is death-like. Really, your perfumes are worth more." Charlotte again extended her hand towards the opiate box.

"Madame," said Réné, "before testing that, as you are about to do, hear what cruel results wicked men can draw from it."

"Really, Réné," said the baroness, "you are funereal this evening."

Henry frowned, but he understood that Réné wished to reach a goal which he did not yet see, and he resolved to push towards this end the conversation which awakened in him such painful memories.

"And," he continued, "you knew the details of the poisoning of the Prince de Porcian?"

"Yes," said he. "It is known that every night he left a lamp burning near his bed; the oil was poisoned and he was asphyxiated."

Henry clinched his fingers, which were damp with perspiration.

"So," he murmured, "he whom you call your friend knows not only the details of the poisoning, but the author of it?"

"Yes, and it is for this reason that he wished to ask you if you would use over the Prince of Porcian the remains of that influence and have the murderer pardoned for the death of his brother."

"Unfortunately," replied Henry, "still being half Huguenot, I have no influence over Monsieur le Prince de Porcian; your friend therefore would have done wrong in speaking to me."

"But what do you think of the intentions of Monsieur le Prince de Condé and of Monsieur de Porcian?"

"How should I know their intentions, Réné? God, whom I may know, has not given me the privilege of reading their hearts."

"Your majesty must ask yourself," said the Florentine calmly. "Is there not in the life of your majesty some event so gloomy that it can serve as a test of clemency, so painful that it is a touchstone for generosity?"

These words were uttered in a tone which made Charlotte herself tremble. It was an allusion so direct, so pointed, that the young woman turned aside to hide her blush, and to avoid meeting Henry's eyes. Henry made a supreme effort over himself; his forehead, which during the words of the Florentine wore threatening lines, unbent, and he changed the dignified, filial grief which tightened his heart into vague meditation.

"In my life," said he, "a gloomy circumstance—no, Réné, no; I remember in my youth only folly and carelessness mingled with more or less cruel necessity imposed on every one by the demands of nature and the proofs of God."

Réné in turn became constrained as he glanced from Henry to Charlotte, as though to rouse the one and hold back the other; for Charlotte had returned to her toilet to hide the anxiety caused by their conversation, and had again extended her hand towards the opiate box.

"But, sire, if you were the brother of the Prince of Porcian or the son of the Prince of Condé, and if they had poisoned your brother or assassinated your father"—Charlotte uttered a slight cry and raised the opiate to her lips. Réné saw the gesture, but this time he stopped her neither by word nor gesture; he merely exclaimed:

"In Heaven's name, sire, answer! Sire, if you were in their place what would you do?"

Henry recovered himself. With trembling hand he wiped his forehead, on which stood drops of cold perspiration, and rising to his full height, replied in the midst of the silence which until then had held Réné and Charlotte:

"If I were in their place, and if I were sure of being king, that is, sure of representing God on earth, I would act like God, I should pardon."

"Madame," cried Réné, snatching the opiate from the hands of Madame de Sauve, "madame, give me back this box; my messenger boy, I see, has made a mistake in it. To-morrow I will send you another."

———

CHAPTER XXIII.

A NEW CONVERT.

The following day there was to be a hunt in the forest of Saint Germain.

Henry had ordered a small Béarnais horse to be made ready for him; that is, to be saddled and bridled at eight o'clock in the morning. He had intended giving this horse to Madame de Sauve, but he wanted to try it first. At a quarter before eight the horse was ready. On the stroke of eight Henry came down to the court-yard. The horse, proud and fiery in spite of its small size, pricked up its ears and pawed the ground. The weather was cold and a light frost covered the pavement. Henry started to cross the court-yard to the stables where the horse and the groom were waiting, when a Swiss soldier whom he passed standing sentinel at the gate presented arms and said:

"God keep his Majesty the King of Navarre."

At this wish and especially at the tone in which it was uttered the Béarnais started.

He turned and stepped back.

"De Mouy!" he murmured.

"Yes, sire, De Mouy."

"What are you doing here?"

"Looking for you."

"Why are you looking for me?"

"I must speak to your majesty."

"Unfortunately," said the king, approaching him, "do you not know you risk your head?"

"I know it."

"Well?"

"Well, I am here."

Henry turned slightly pale, for he knew that he shared the danger run by this rash young man. He looked anxiously about him, and stepped back a second time, no less quickly than he had done at first. He had seen the Duc d'Alençon at a window.

At once changing his manner Henry took the musket from the hands of De Mouy, standing, as we have said, sentinel, and while apparently measuring it:

"De Mouy," said he, "it is certainly not without some very strong motive that you have come to beard the lion in his den in this way?"

"No, sire, I have waited for you a week; only yesterday I heard that your majesty was to try a horse this morning, and I took my position at the gate of the Louvre."

"But how in this uniform?"

"The captain of the company is a Protestant and is one of my friends."

"Here is your musket; return to your duty of sentinel. We are watched. As I come back I will try to say a word to you, but if I do not speak, do not stop me. Adieu."

De Mouy resumed his measured walk, and Henry advanced towards the house.

"What is that pretty little animal?" asked the Duc d'Alençon from his window.

"A horse I am going to try this morning," replied Henry.

"But that is not a horse for a man."

"Therefore it is intended for a beautiful woman."

"Take care, Henry; you are going to be indiscreet, for we shall see this beautiful woman at the hunt; and if I do not know whose knight you are, I shall at least know whose equerry you are."

"No, my lord, you will not know," said Henry, with his feigned good-humor, "for this beautiful woman cannot go out this morning; she is indisposed."

He sprang into the saddle.

"Ah, bah!" cried d'Alençon, laughing; "poor Madame de Sauve."

"François! François! it is you who are indiscreet."

"What is the matter with the beautiful Charlotte?" went on the Duc d'Alençon.

"Why," replied Henry, spurring his horse to a gallop, and making him describe a graceful curve; "why, I have no idea,—a heaviness in the head, according to what Dariole tells me. A torpor of the whole body; in short, general debility."

"And will this prevent you from joining us?" asked the duke.

"I? Why should it?" asked Henry. "You know that I dote on a hunt, and that nothing could make me miss one."

"But you will miss this one, Henry," said the duke, after he had turned and spoken for an instant with some one unnoticed by Henry, who addressed François from the rear of the room, "for his Majesty tells me that the hunt cannot take place."

"Bah!" said Henry, in the most disappointed tone imaginable. "Why not?"

"Very important letters from Monsieur de Nevers, it seems. There is a council among the King, the queen mother, and my brother the Duc d'Anjou."

"Ah! ah!" said Henry to himself, "could any news have come from Poland?"

Then aloud:

"In that case," he continued, "it is useless for me to run any further risk on this frost. Good-by, brother!"

Pulling up his horse in front of De Mouy:

"My friend," said he, "call one of your comrades to finish your sentinel duty for you. Help the groom ungirth my horse. Put the saddle over your head and carry it to the saddler's; there is some embroidery to be done on it, which there was not time to finish for to-day. You will bring an answer to my apartments."

De Mouy hastened to obey, for the Duc d'Alençon had disappeared from his window, and it was evident that he suspected something.

In fact, scarcely had De Mouy disappeared through the gate before the Duc d'Alençon came in sight. A real Swiss was in De Mouy's place. D'Alençon looked carefully at the new sentinel; then turning to Henry:

"This is not the man you were talking with just now, is it, brother?"

"The other is a young man who belongs to my household and whom I had enter the Swiss guards. I have just given him a commission and he has gone to carry it out."

"Ah!" said the duke, as if this reply sufficed. "And how is Marguerite?"

"I am going to ask her, brother."

"Have you not seen her since yesterday?"

"No. I went to her about eleven o'clock last night, but Gillonne told me that she was tired and had gone to sleep."

"You will not find her in her room. She has gone out."

"Oh!" said Henry. "Very likely. She was to go to the *Convent de l'Annonciade.*"

There was no way of carrying the conversation further, as Henry had seemingly made up his mind simply to answer. The two brothers-in-law therefore departed, the Duc d'Alençon to go for news, he said, the King of Navarre to return to his room.

Henry had been there scarcely five minutes when he heard a knock at the door.

"Who is it?" he asked.

"Sire," replied a voice which Henry recognized as that of De Mouy, "it is the answer from the saddler."

Henry, visibly moved, bade the young man enter and closed the door behind him.

"Is it you, De Mouy?" said he; "I hoped that you would reflect."

"Sire," replied De Mouy, "I have reflected for three months; that is long enough. Now it is time to act." Henry made a gesture of impatience.

"Fear nothing, sire, we are alone, and I will make haste, for time is precious. Your majesty can tell in a word all that the events of the year have lost to the cause of religion. Let us be clear, brief, and frank."

"I am listening, my good De Mouy," replied Henry, seeing that it was impossible for him to elude the explanation.

"Is it true that your majesty has abjured the Protestant religion?"

"It is true," said Henry.

"Yes, but is it with your lips or at heart?"

"One is always grateful to God when he saves our life," replied Henry, turning the question as he had a habit of doing in such cases, "and God has evidently saved me from this cruel danger."

"Sire," resumed De Mouy, "let us admit one thing."

"What?"

"That your abjuring is not a matter of conviction, but of calculation. You have abjured so that the King would let you live, and not because God has saved your life."

"Whatever the cause of my conversion, De Mouy," replied Henry, "I am none the less a Catholic."

"Yes, but shall you always be one? The first chance you have for resuming your freedom of life and of conscience, will you not resume it? Well! this opportunity has presented itself. La Rochelle has revolted, Roussillon and Béarn are merely waiting for one word before acting. In Guyenne every one cries for war. Merely tell me if you were forced into taking this step, and I will answer for the future."

"A gentleman of my birth is not forced, my dear De Mouy. That which I have done, I have done voluntarily."

"But, sire," said the young man, his heart oppressed with this resistance which he had not expected, "you do not remember that in acting thus you abandon and betray us."

Henry was unmoved.

"Yes," went on De Mouy, "yes, you betray us, sire, for several of us, at the risk of our lives, have come to save your honor and your liberty; we are prepared to offer you a throne, sire; do you realize this? not only liberty, but power; a throne of your own choice, for in two months you could choose between Navarre and France."

"De Mouy," said Henry, covering his eyes, which in spite of himself had emitted a flash at the above suggestion, "De Mouy, I am safe, I am a Catholic, I am the husband of Marguerite, I am the brother of King Charles, I am the son-in-law of my good mother Catharine. De Mouy, in assuming these various positions, I have calculated their opportunities and also their obligations."

"But, sire," said De Mouy, "what must one believe? I am told that your marriage is not contracted, that at heart you are free, that the hatred of Catharine"—

"Lies, lies," interrupted the Béarnais hastily. "Yes, you have been shamefully deceived, my friend; this dear Marguerite is indeed my wife, Catharine is really my mother, and King Charles IX. is the lord and master of my life and of my heart."

De Mouy shuddered, and an almost scornful smile passed over his lips.

"In that case, sire," said he dropping his arms dejectedly, and trying to fathom that soul filled with shadows, "this is the answer I am to take back to my brothers,—I shall tell them that the King of Navarre extends his hand and opens his heart to those who have cut our throats; I shall tell them that he has become the flatterer of the queen mother and the friend of Maurevel."

"My dear De Mouy," said Henry, "the King is coming out of the council chamber, and I must go and find out from him the reasons for our having had to give up so important a thing as a hunt. Adieu; imitate me, my friend, give up politics, return to the King and attend mass."

Henry led or rather pushed into the antechamber the young man, whose amazement was beginning to change into fury.

Scarcely was the door closed before, unable any longer to resist the longing to avenge himself on something in defence of some one, De Mouy twisted his hat between his hands, threw it upon the floor, and stamping on it as a bull would stamp on the cloak of the matador:

"By Heaven!" he cried, "he is a wretched prince, and I have half a mind to kill myself here in order to stain him forever with my blood."

"Hush, Monsieur de Mouy!" said a voice through a half-open door; "hush! some one besides myself might hear you."

De Mouy turned quickly and perceived the Duc d'Alençon enveloped in a cloak, advancing into the corridor with pale face, to make sure that he and De Mouy were entirely alone.

"Monsieur le Duc d'Alençon," cried De Mouy, "I am lost!"

"On the contrary," murmured the prince, "perhaps you have found what you are looking for, and the proof of this is that I do not want you to kill yourself here as you had an idea of doing just now. Believe me, your blood can in all probability be put to better use than to redden the threshold of the King of Navarre."

At these words the duke threw back the door which he had been holding half open.

"This chamber belongs to two of my gentlemen," said the duke. "No one will interrupt us here. We can, therefore, talk freely. Come in, monsieur."

"I, here, monseigneur!" cried the conspirator in amazement. He entered the room, the door of which the Duc d'Alençon closed behind him no less quickly than the King of Navarre had done.

De Mouy entered, furious, exasperated, cursing. But by degrees the cold and steady glance of the young Duc François had the same effect on the Huguenot captain as does the enchanted lake which dissipates drunkenness.

"Monseigneur," said he, "if I understand correctly, your highness wishes to speak to me."

"Yes, Monsieur de Mouy," replied François. "In spite of your disguise I thought I recognized you, and when you presented arms to my brother Henry, I recognized you perfectly. Well, De Mouy, so you are not pleased with the King of Navarre?"

"Monseigneur!"

"Come, come! tell me frankly, unless you distrust me; perhaps I am one of your friends."

"You, monseigneur?"

"Yes, I; so speak."

"I do not know what to say to your highness, monseigneur. The matter I had to discuss with the King of Navarre concerned interests which your highness would not comprehend. Moreover," added De Mouy with a manner which he strove to render indifferent, "they were mere trifles."

"Trifles?" said the duke.

"Yes, monseigneur."

"Trifles, for which you felt you would risk your life by coming back to the Louvre, where you know your head is worth its weight in gold. We are not ignorant of the fact that you, as well as the King of Navarre and the Prince de Condé, are one of the leaders of the Huguenots."

"If you think that, monseigneur, act towards me as the brother of King Charles and the son of Queen Catharine should act."

"Why should you wish me to act in that way, when I have told you that I am a friend of yours? Tell me the truth."

"Monseigneur," said De Mouy, "I swear to you"—

"Do not swear, monseigneur; the reformed church forbids the taking of oaths, and especially of false oaths."

De Mouy frowned.

"I tell you I know all," continued the duke.

De Mouy was still silent.

"You doubt it?" said the prince with affected persistence. "Well, my dear De Mouy, we shall have to be convinced. Come, now, you shall judge if I am wrong. Did you or did you not propose to my brother-in-law Henry, in his room just now," the duke pointed to the chamber of the Béarnais, "your aid and that of your followers to reinstate him in his kingdom of Navarre?"

De Mouy looked at the duke with a startled gaze.

"A proposition which he refused with terror."

De Mouy was still amazed.

"Did you then invoke your old friendship, the remembrance of a common religion? Did you even hold out to the King of Navarre a very brilliant hope, a hope so brilliant that he was dazzled by it—the hope of winning the crown of France? Come, tell me; am I well informed? Is that what you came to propose to the Béarnais?"

"Monseigneur!" cried De Mouy, "this is so true, that I now wonder if I should not tell your royal highness that you have lied! to arouse in this chamber a combat without mercy, and thus to make sure of the extinction of this terrible secret by the death of both of us."

"Gently, my brave De Mouy, gently!" said the Duc d'Alençon without changing countenance, or without taking the slightest notice of this terrible threat.

"The secret will die better with us if we both live than if one of us were to die. Listen to me, and stop pulling at the handle of your sword. For the third time I say that you are with a friend. Now tell me, did not the King of Navarre refuse everything you offered him?"

"Yes, monseigneur, and I admit it, because my avowal can compromise only myself."

"On leaving his room did you not stamp on your hat, and cry out that he was a cowardly prince, and unworthy of being your leader?"

"That is true, monseigneur, I said that."

"Ah! you did? you admit it at last?"

"Yes."

"And this is still your opinion?"

"More than ever, monseigneur."

"Well, am I, Monsieur de Mouy, I, the third son of Henry II., I, a son of France, am I a good enough gentleman to command your soldiers? Come, now; do you think me loyal enough for you to trust my word?"

"You, monseigneur! you, the leader of the Huguenots!"

"Why not? This is an epoch of conversions, you know. Henry has turned Catholic; I can turn Protestant."

"Yes, no doubt, monseigneur; so I am waiting for you to explain to me"—

"Nothing is easier; and in two words I can tell you the policy of every one. My brother Charles kills the Huguenots in order to reign more freely. My brother of Anjou lets them be killed because he is to succeed my brother Charles, and because, as you know, my brother Charles is often ill. But with me it is entirely different. I shall never reign—at least in France—as long as I have two elder brothers. The hatred of my mother and of my two brothers more than the law of nature keeps me from the throne. I have no claim to any family affection, any glory, or any kingdom. Yet I have a heart as great as my elder brother's. Well, De Mouy, I want to look about and with my sword cut a kingdom out of this France they cover with blood. Now this is what I want, De Mouy, listen: I want to be King of Navarre, not by birth but by election. And note well that you have no objection to this system. I am not a usurper, since my brother refuses your offers, and buries himself in his torpor, and pretends aloud that this kingdom of Navarre is only a myth. With Henry of Béarn you have nothing. With me, you have a sword and a name, François d'Alençon, son of France, protector of all his companions or all his accomplices, as you are pleased to call them. Well, what do you say to this offer, Monsieur de Mouy?"

"I say that it dazzles me, monseigneur."

"De Mouy, De Mouy, we shall have many obstacles to overcome. Do not, therefore, from the first be so exacting and so obstinate towards the son of a king and the brother of a king who comes to you."

"Monseigneur, the matter would be already settled if my opinion were the only one to be considered, but we have a council, and brilliant as the offer may be, perhaps even on that very account the leaders of the party will not consent to the plan unconditionally."

"That is another thing, and your answer comes from an honest heart and a prudent mind. From the way I have just acted, De Mouy, you must have recognized my honesty. Treat me, therefore, on your part as a man who is esteemed, not as a man who is flattered. De Mouy, have I any chance?"

"On my word, monseigneur, since your highness wants me to give my opinion, your highness has every chance, since the King of Navarre has refused the offer I have just made him. But I tell you again, monseigneur, I shall have to confer with our leaders."

"Do so, monsieur," replied d'Alençon. "But when shall I have an answer?"

De Mouy looked at the prince in silence. Then apparently coming to a decision:

"Monseigneur," said he, "give me your hand. I must have the hand of a son of France touch mine to make sure that I shall not be betrayed."

The duke not only extended his hand towards De Mouy, but grasped De Mouy's and pressed it.

"Now, monseigneur, I am satisfied," said the young Huguenot. "If we were betrayed I should say that you had nothing to do with it; otherwise, monseigneur, however slightly you might be concerned in the treason, you would be dishonored."

"Why do you say that to me, De Mouy, before telling me that you will bring me the answer from your leaders?"

"Because, monseigneur, asking me when you would have your answer was the same as asking me where are the leaders, and because if I said to you, 'This evening,' you would know that the chiefs were hiding in Paris." As he uttered these words, with a gesture of mistrust, De Mouy fixed his piercing glance on the false vacillating eyes of the young man.

"Well, well," said the duke, "you still have doubts, Monsieur de Mouy. But I cannot expect entire confidence from you at first. You will understand me better later. We shall be bound by common interests which will rid you of all suspicion. You say this evening, then, Monsieur de Mouy?"

"Yes, monseigneur, for time presses. Until this evening. But where shall I see you, if you please?"

"At the Louvre, here in this room; does that suit you?"

"Is this occupied?" said De Mouy, glancing at the two beds opposite each other.

"By two of my gentlemen, yes."

"Monseigneur, it seems to me imprudent to return to the Louvre."

"Why so?"

"Because if you have recognized me, others also may have as good eyes as your highness, and may recognize me. However, I will return to the Louvre if you will grant me what I am about to ask of you."

"What is that?"

"A passport."

"A passport from me found on you would ruin me and would not save you. I can do nothing for you unless in the eyes of the world we are strangers to each other; the slightest relation between us, noticed by my mother or my brother, would cost me my life. You were therefore protected by my interest for myself from the moment I compromised myself with the others, as I am now compromising myself with you. Free in my sphere of action, strong if I am unknown, so long as I myself remain impenetrable, I will guarantee you everything. Do not forget this. Make a fresh appeal to your courage, therefore. Try on my word of honor what you tried without the word of honor of my brother. Come this evening to the Louvre."

"But how do you wish me to come? I can not venture in these rooms in my present uniform—it is for the vestibules and the courts. My own is still more dangerous, since everyone knows me here, and since it in no way disguises me."

"Therefore I will look—wait—I think that—yes, here it is."

The duke had looked around him, and his eyes stopped at La Mole's clothes, thrown temporarily on the bed; that is, on the magnificent cherry-colored cloak embroidered in gold, of which we have already spoken; on a cap ornamented with a white plume surrounded by a rope of gold and silver marguerites, and finally on a pearl-gray satin and gold doublet.

"Do you see this cloak, this plume, and this doublet?" said the duke; "they belong to Monsieur de la Mole, one of my gentlemen, a fop of the highest type. The cloak was the rage at court, and when he wore it, Monsieur de la Mole was recognized a hundred feet away. I will give you the address of the tailor who made it for him. By paying him double what it is worth, you will have one exactly like it by this evening. You will remember the name of Monsieur de la Mole, will you not?"

Scarcely had the Duc d'Alençon finished making the suggestion, when a step was heard approaching in the corridor, and a key was turned in the lock.

"Who is that?" cried the duke, rushing to the door and drawing the bolt.

"By Heaven!" replied a voice from outside; "I find that a strange question. Who are you yourself? This is pleasant! I return to my own room, and am asked who I am!"

"Is it you, Monsieur de la Mole?"

"Yes, it is I, without a doubt. But who are you?"

While La Mole was expressing his surprise at finding his room occupied, and while he was trying to discover its new occupant, the Duc d'Alençon turned quickly, one hand on the lock, the other on the key.

"Do you know Monsieur de la Mole?" he asked of De Mouy.

"No, monseigneur."

"Does he know you?"

"I think not."

"In that case it will be all right. Appear to be looking out of the window."

De Mouy obeyed in silence, for La Mole was beginning to grow impatient, and was knocking on the door with all his might.

The Duc d'Alençon threw a last glance towards De Mouy, and seeing that his back was turned, he opened the door.

"Monseigneur le Duc!" cried La Mole, stepping back in surprise. "Oh, pardon, pardon, monseigneur!"

"It is nothing, monsieur; I needed your room to receive a visitor."

"Certainly, monseigneur, certainly. But allow me, I beg you, to take my cloak and hat from the bed, for I lost both to-night on the quay of the Grève, where I was attacked by robbers."

"In fact, monsieur," said the prince, smiling, himself handing to La Mole the articles asked for, "you are very poorly accommodated here. You have had an encounter with some very obstinate fellows, apparently!"

The duke handed to La Mole the cloak and the hat. The young man bowed and withdrew to the antechamber to change his clothes, paying no attention to what the duke was doing in his room; for it was an ordinary occurrence at the Louvre for the rooms of the gentlemen to be used as reception-rooms by the prince to whom the latter were attached.

De Mouy then approached the duke, and both listened for La Mole to finish and go out; but when the latter had changed his clothes, he himself saved them all further trouble by drawing near to the door.

"Pardon me, monseigneur," said he, "but did your highness meet the Count de Coconnas on your way?"

"No, count, and yet he was at service this morning."

"In that case they will assassinate me," said La Mole to himself as he went away.

The duke heard the noise of his retreating steps; then opening the door and drawing De Mouy after him:

"Watch him going away," said he, "and try to copy his inimitable walk."

"I will do my best," replied De Mouy. "Unfortunately I am not a lady's man, but a soldier."

"At all events I shall expect you in this corridor before midnight. If the chamber of my gentlemen is free, I will receive you there; if not, we will find another."

"Yes, monseigneur."

"Until this evening then, beforemidnight."

"Until this evening, before midnight."

"Ah! by the way, De Mouy, swing your right arm a good deal as you walk. This is a peculiar trick of Monsieur de la Mole's."

CHAPTER XXIV.

THE RUE TIZON AND THE RUE CLOCHE PERCÉE.

La Mole hurriedly left the Louvre, and set out to search Paris for poor Coconnas.

His first move was to repair to the Rue de l'Arbre Sec and to enter Maître La Hurière's, for La Mole remembered that he had often repeated to the Piedmontese a certain Latin motto which was meant to prove that Love, Bacchus, and Ceres are gods absolutely necessary to us, and he hoped that Coconnas, to follow up the Roman aphorism, had gone to the *Belle Étoile* after a night which must have been as full for his friend as it had been for himself.

La Mole found nothing at La Hurière's except the reminder of the assumed obligation. A breakfast which was offered with good grace was eagerly accepted by our gentleman, in spite of his anxiety. His stomach calmed in default of his mind, La Mole resumed his walk, ascending the bank of the Seine like a husband searching for his drowned wife. On reaching the quay of the Grève, he recognized the place where, as he had said to Monsieur d'Alençon, he had been stopped during his nocturnal tramp three or four hours before. This was no unusual thing in Paris, older by a hundred years than that in which Boileau was awakened at the sound of a ball piercing his window shutter. A bit of the plume from his hat remained on the battle-field. The sentiment of possession is innate in man. La Mole had ten plumes each more beautiful than the last, and yet he stopped to pick up that one, or, rather, the sole fragment of what remained of it, and was contemplating it with a pitiful air when he heard the sound of heavy steps approaching, and rough voices ordering him to stand aside. La Mole raised his head and perceived a litter preceded by two pages and accompanied by an outrider. La Mole thought he recognized the litter, and quickly stepped aside.

The young man was not mistaken.

"Monsieur de la Mole!" exclaimed a sweet voice from the litter, while a hand as white and as smooth as satin drew back the curtains.

"Yes, madame, in person," replied La Mole bowing.

"Monsieur de la Mole with a plume in his hand," continued the lady in the litter. "Are you in love, my dear monsieur, and are you recovering lost traces?"

"Yes, madame," replied La Mole, "I am in love, and very much so. But just now these are my own traces that I have found, although they are not those for which I am searching. But will your majesty permit me to inquire after your health?"

"It is excellent, monsieur; it seems to me that I have never been better. This probably comes from the fact of my having spent the night in retreat."

"Ah! in retreat!" said La Mole, looking at Marguerite strangely.

"Well, yes; what is there surprising in that?"

"May I, without indiscretion, ask you in what convent?"

"Certainly, monsieur, I make no mystery of it; in the convent of the *Annonciade*. But what are you doing here with this startled air?"

"Madame, I too passed the night in retreat, and in the vicinity of the same convent. This morning I am looking for my friend who has disappeared, and in seeking him I came upon this plume."

"Whom does it belong to? Really, you frighten me about him; the place is a bad one."

"Your majesty may be reassured; the plume belongs to me. I lost it here about half-past five, as I was escaping from the hands of four bandits who tried with all their might to murder me, or at least I think they did."

Marguerite repressed a quick gesture of terror.

"Oh! tell me about it!" said she.

"Nothing is easier, madame. It was, as I have had the honor to tell your majesty, about five o'clock in the morning."

"And you were already out at five o'clock in the morning?" interrupted Marguerite.

"Your majesty will excuse me," said La Mole, "I had not yet returned."

"Ah! Monsieur de la Mole! you returned at five o'clock in the morning!" said Marguerite with a smile which was fatal for every one, and which La Mole was unfortunate enough to find adorable; "you returned so late, you merited this punishment!"

"Therefore I do not complain, madame," said La Mole, bowing respectfully, "and I should have been cut to pieces had I not considered myself a hundred times more fortunate than I deserve to be. But I was returning late, or early, as your majesty pleases, from that fortunate house in which I had spent the night in retreat, when four cut-throats rushed from the Rue de la Mortellerie and pursued me with indescribably long knives. It is grotesque, is it not, madame?

240

but it is true—I had to run away, for I had forgotten my sword."

"Oh! I understand," said Marguerite, with an admirably naïve manner, "and you have come back to find your sword?"

La Mole looked at Marguerite as though a suspicion flashed through his mind.

"Madame, I would return to some place and very willingly too, since my sword is an excellent blade, but I do not know where the house is."

"What, monsieur?" exclaimed Marguerite. "You do not know where the house is in which you passed the night?"

"No, madame, and may Satan exterminate me if I have any idea!"

"Well this is strange! your story, then, is a romance?"

"A true romance, as you say, madame."

"Tell it to me."

"It is somewhat long."

"Never mind, I have time."

"And, above all, it is improbable."

"Never mind, no one could be more credulous than I."

"Does your majesty command me?"

"Why, yes; if necessary."

"In that case I obey. Last evening, having left two adorable women with whom we had spent the evening on the Saint Michel bridge, we took supper at Maître La Hurière's."

"In the first place," said Marguerite, perfectly naturally, "who is Maître La Hurière?"

"Maître La Hurière, madame," said La Mole, again glancing at Marguerite with the suspicion he had already felt, "Maître La Hurière is the host of the inn of the *Belle Étoile* in the Rue de l'Arbre Sec."

"Yes, I can see it from here. You were supping, then, at Maître La Hurière's with your friend Coconnas, no doubt?"

"Yes, madame, with my friend Coconnas, when a man entered and handed us each a note."

"Were they alike?" asked Marguerite.

"Exactly alike. They contained only a single line:

"'*You are awaited in the Rue Saint Antoine, opposite the Rue Saint Jouy.*'"

"And had the note no signature?" asked Marguerite.

"No; only three words—three charming words which three times promised the same thing, that is to say, a three-fold happiness."

"And what were these three words?"

"*Eros, Cupido, Amor.*"

"In short, three sweet words; and did they fulfil what they promised?"

"Oh! more, madame, a hundred times more!" cried La Mole with enthusiasm.

"Continue. I am curious to know who was waiting for you in the Rue Saint Antoine, opposite the Rue de Jouy."

"Two duennas, each with a handkerchief in her hand. They said we must let them bandage our eyes. Your majesty may imagine that it was not a difficult thing to have done. We bravely extended our necks. My guide turned me to the left, my friend's guide turned him to the right, and we were separated."

"And then?" continued Marguerite, who seemed determined to carry out the investigation to the end.

"I do not know," said La Mole, "where his guide led my friend. To hell, perhaps. As to myself, all I know is that mine led me to a place I consider paradise."

"And whence, no doubt, your too great curiosity drove you?"

"Exactly, madame; you have the gift of divination. I waited, impatiently, for daylight, that I might see where I was, when at half-past four the same duenna returned, again bandaged my eyes, made me promise not to try to raise my bandage, led me outside, accompanied me for a hundred feet, made me again swear not to remove my bandage until I had counted fifty more. I counted fifty, and found myself in the Rue Saint Antoine, opposite the Rue de Jouy."

"And then"—

"Then, madame, I returned so happy that I paid no attention to the four wretches, from whose clutches I had such difficulty in escaping. Now, madame," continued La Mole, "in finding a piece of my plume here, my heart trembled with joy, and I picked it up, promising myself to keep it as a souvenir of this glad night. But in the midst of my happiness, one thing troubles me; that is, what may have become of my companion."

"Has he not returned to the Louvre?"

"Alas! no, madame! I have searched everywhere, in the *Étoile d'Or*, on the tennis courts, and in many other respectable places; but no Annibal, and no Coconnas"—

As La Mole uttered these words he accompanied them with a gesture of hopelessness, extended his arms and opened his cloak, underneath which at various points his doublet was seen, the lining of which showed through the rents like so many elegant slashes.

"Why, you were riddled through and through!" exclaimed Marguerite.

"Riddled is the word!" said La Mole, who was not sorry to turn to his account the danger he had run. "See, madame, see!"

"Why did you not change your doublet at the Louvre, since you returned there?" asked the queen.

"Ah!" said La Mole, "because some one was in my room."

"Some one in your room?" said Marguerite, whose eyes expressed the greatest astonishment; "who was in your room?"

"His highness."

"Hush!" interrupted Marguerite.

The young man obeyed.

"*Qui ad lecticam meam stant?*" she asked La Mole.

"*Duo pueri et unus eques.*"

"*Optime, barbari!*" said she. "*Dic, Moles, quem inveneris in biculo tuo?*"

"*Franciscum ducem.*"

"*Agentem?*"

"*Nescio quid.*"

"*Quocum?*"

"*Cum ignoto.*"[8]

"That is strange," said Marguerite. "So you were unable to find Coconnas?" she continued, without evidently thinking of what she was saying.

"So, madame, as I have had the honor of telling you, I am really dying of anxiety."

"Well," said Marguerite, sighing, "I do not wish to detain you longer in your search for him; I do not know why I think so, but he will find himself! Never mind, however, go, in spite of this."

The queen laid a finger on her lips. But as beautiful Marguerite had confided no secret, had made no avowal to La Mole, the young man understood that this charming gesture, meaning only to impose silence on him, must have another significance.

The procession resumed its march, and La Mole, intent on following out his investigation, continued to ascend the quay as far as the Rue Long Pont which led him to the Rue Saint Antoine.

Opposite the Rue Jouy he stopped. It was there that the previous evening the two duennas had bandaged his eyes and those of Coconnas. He had turned to the left, then he had counted twenty steps. He repeated this and found himself opposite a house, or rather a wall, behind which rose a house; in this wall was a door with a shed over it ornamented with large nails and loop-holes.

The house was in the Rue Cloche Percée, a small narrow street beginning in the Rue Saint Antoine and ending in the Rue Roi de Sicile.

"By Heaven!" cried La Mole, "it was here—I would swear to it—in extending my hand, as I came out, I felt the nails in the door, then I descended two steps. The man who ran by crying 'Help!' who was killed in the Rue Roi de Sicile, passed just as I reached the first. Let us see, now."

La Mole went to the door and knocked. The door opened and a mustached janitor appeared.

"*Was ist das?*" (Who is that?) asked the janitor.

"Ah! ah!" said La Mole, "we are Swiss, apparently." "My friend," he continued, assuming the most charming manner, "I want my sword which I left in this house in which I spent the night."

"*Ich verstehe nicht,*" (I do not understand,) replied the janitor.

"My sword," went on La Mole.

"*Ich verstehe nicht,*" repeated the janitor.

"—which I left—my sword which I left"—

"*Ich verstehe nicht.*"

"—in this house, in which I spent the night."

"*Gehe zum Teufel!*" (Go to the devil!) And he slammed the door in La Mole's face.

"By Heaven!" cried La Mole, "if I had this sword I have just asked for, I would gladly put it through that fellow's body. But I have not, and this must wait for another day."

Thereupon La Mole continued his way to the Rue Roi de Sicile, took about fifty steps to the right, then to the left again, and came to the Rue Tizon, a little street running parallel with the Rue Cloche Percée, and like it in every way. More than this, scarcely had he gone thirty steps before he came upon the door with the large nails, with its shed and loop-holes, the two steps and the wall. One would have said that the Rue Cloche Percée had returned to see him pass by.

La Mole then reflected that he might have mistaken his right for his left, and he knocked at this door, to make the same demand he had made at the other. But this time he knocked in vain. The door was not opened.

Two or three times La Mole made the same trip, which naturally led him to the idea that the house had two entrances, one on the Rue Cloche Percée, the other on the Rue Tizon.

But this conclusion, logical as it was, did not bring him back his sword, and did not tell him where his friend was. For an instant he conceived the idea of buying another sword and cutting to pieces the wretched janitor who so persistently refused to speak anything but German, but he thought this porter belonged to Marguerite, and that if Marguerite had chosen thus, it was because she had her reasons, and that it might be disagreeable for her to be deprived of him.

Now La Mole would not have done anything disagreeable to Marguerite for anything in the world.

Fearing to yield to this temptation he returned about two o'clock in the afternoon to the Louvre.

As his room was not occupied this time he could enter it. The matter was urgent enough as far as his doublet was concerned, which, as the queen had already remarked to him, was considerably torn.

He therefore at once approached his bed to substitute the beautiful pearl-gray doublet for the one he wore, when to his great surprise the first thing he perceived near the pearl-gray doublet was the famous sword which he had left in the Rue Cloche Percée.

La Mole took it and turned it over and over.

It was really his.

"Ah! ah!" said he, "is there some magic under all this?" Then with a sigh, "Ah! if poor Coconnas could be found like my sword!"

Two or three hours after La Mole had ceased his circular tramp around the small double house, the door on the Rue Tizon had opened. It was about five o'clock in the evening, consequently night had closed in.

A woman wrapped in a long cloak trimmed with fur, accompanied by an attendant, came out of the door which was held open by a duenna of forty, and hurrying rapidly along to the Rue Roi de Sicile, knocked at a small door of the Hôtel Argenson, which opened for her; she then left by the main entrance of the same hôtel which opened on to the Vieille Rue du Temple, went toward a small postern in the Hôtel de Guise, unlocked it with a key which she carried in her pocket, and disappeared.

Half an hour later a young man with bandaged eyes left by the same door of the small house, guided by a woman who led him to the corner of the Rue Geoffroy Lasnier and La Mortellerie. There she asked him to count fifty steps and then remove his bandage.

The young man carefully obeyed the order, and when he had counted fifty, removed the handkerchief from his eyes.

"By Heaven!" cried he, looking around. "I'll be hanged if I know where I am! Six o'clock!" he cried, as the clock of Notre-Dame struck, "and poor La Mole, what can have become of him? Let us run to the Louvre, perhaps they may have news of him there."

Coconnas hurriedly descended the Rue La Mortellerie, and reached the gates of the Louvre in less time than it would have taken an ordinary horse. As he went he jostled and knocked down the moving hedge of brave bourgeois who were walking peacefully about the shops of the Place de Baudoyer, and entered the palace.

There he questioned the Swiss and the sentinel. The former thought they had seen Monsieur de la Mole enter that morning, but had not seen him go out.

The sentinel had been there only an hour and a half and had seen nothing.

He ran to his room and hastily threw open the door; but he found only the torn doublet of La Mole on the bed, which increased his fears still more.

Then he thought of La Hurière and hastened to the worthy inn of the *Belle Étoile*. La Hurière had seen La Mole; La Mole had breakfasted there. Coconnas was thus wholly reassured, and as he was very hungry he ordered supper.

Coconnas was in the two moods necessary for a good supper—his mind was relieved and his stomach was empty; therefore he supped so well that the meal lasted till eight o'clock. Then strengthened by two bottles of light wine from Anjou, of which he was very fond and which he tossed off with a sensual enjoyment shown by winks of his eyes and repeated smacking of his lips, he set out again in his search for La Mole, accompanying it through the crowd by kicks and knocks of his feet in proportion to the increasing friendship inspired in him by the comfort which always follows a good meal.

That lasted one hour, during which time Coconnas searched every street in the vicinity of the Quay of the Grève, the Port au Charbon, the Rue Saint Antoine, and the Rues Tizon and Cloche Percée, to which he thought his friend might have returned. Finally he bethought himself that there was a place through which he had to pass, the gate of the Louvre, and he resolved to wait at this gate until his return.

He was not more than a hundred steps from the Louvre, and had just put on her feet a woman whose husband he had already overturned on the Place Saint Germain l'Auxerrois, when in the distance he perceived before him in the doubtful light of a great lantern near the drawbridge of the Louvre the cherry-colored velvet cloak and the white plume of his friend, who like a shadow was disappearing under the gate and returning the sentinel's greeting.

The famous cherry-colored cloak was so well known to every one that he could not be mistaken in it.

"Well! by Heaven!" cried Coconnas; "it is really he this time, and he is returning. Well! well! La Mole, my friend! Plague it! Yet I have a good voice. How does it happen that he does not hear me? Fortunately I have as good legs as I have voice, so I will join him."

In this hope Coconnas set out as fast as he could, and reached the Louvre in an instant, but, fast as he was, just as he stepped into the court the red cloak, which seemed in haste also, disappeared in the vestibule.

"Hi there! La Mole!" cried Coconnas, still hastening. "Wait for me. It is I, Coconnas. What in the devil are you hurrying so for? Are you running away?"

In fact the red cloak, as though it had wings, scaled the stairs rather than mounted them.

"Ah! you will not hear me!" cried Coconnas. "I am angry with you! Are you sorry? Well, the devil! I can run no further." It was from the foot of the staircase that Coconnas hurled this final apostrophe to the fugitive whom he gave up following with his feet, but whom he still followed with his eyes through the screw of the stairway, and who had reached Marguerite's chamber. Suddenly a woman came out of this room and took the arm of the man Coconnas was following.

"Oh! oh!" said Coconnas, "that looked very much like Queen Marguerite. He was expected. In that case it is different. I understand why he did not

247

answer me."

Crouching down by the banister he looked through the opening of the stairway. Then after a few words in a low voice he saw the red cloak follow the queen to her apartments.

"Good! good!" said Coconnas, "that is it. I was not mistaken. There are moments when the presence of our best friend is necessary to us, and dear La Mole has one of those moments."

And Coconnas ascending the stairs softly sat down on a velvet bench which ornamented the landing place, and said to himself:

"Very well, instead of joining him I will wait—yes; but," he added, "I think as he is with the Queen of Navarre I may have to wait long—it is cold, by Heaven! Well! well! I can wait just as well in my room. He will have to come there sometime."

Scarcely had he finished speaking, and started to carry out his resolution, when a quick light step sounded above him, accompanied by a snatch of song so familiar that Coconnas at once turned his head in the direction of the step and the song. It was La Mole descending from the upper story, where his room was. When he perceived Coconnas, he began to descend the stairs four steps at a time, and this done he threw himself into his arms.

"Oh, Heavens! is it you?" said Coconnas. "How the devil did you get out?"

"By the Rue Cloche Percée, by Heavens!"

"No, I do not mean that house."

"What then?"

"The queen's apartment."

"The queen's apartment?"

"The Queen of Navarre."

"I have not been there."

"Come now!"

"My dear Annibal," said La Mole, "you are out of your head. I have come from my room where I have been waiting for you for two hours."

"You have come from your room?"

"Yes."

"Was it not you I followed from the Place du Louvre?"

"When?"

"Just now."

"No."

"It was not you who disappeared under the gate ten minutes ago?"

"No."

"It was not you who just ascended the stairs as if you were pursued by a legion of devils?"

"No."

"By Heaven!" cried Coconnas, "the wine of the *Belle Étoile* is not poor enough to have so completely turned my head. I tell you that I have just seen your cherry-colored cloak and your white plume under the gate of the Louvre, that I followed both to the foot of the stairway, and that your cloak, your plume, everything, to your swinging arm, was expected here by a lady whom I greatly suspect to be the Queen of Navarre, and who led you through that door, which, unless I am mistaken, is that of the beautiful Marguerite."

"By Heaven!" cried La Mole, growing pale, "could there be treason?"

"Very good!" said Coconnas, "swear as much as you please, but do not tell me I am mistaken."

La Mole hesitated an instant, pressing his head between his hands, deterred by respect and jealousy. His jealousy conquered him, however, and he hastened to the door, at which he knocked with all his might. This caused a somewhat unusual hubbub considering the dignity of the place in which it occurred.

"We shall be arrested," said Coconnas, "but no matter, it is very funny. Tell me, La Mole, are there ghosts in the Louvre?"

"I know nothing about it," said the young man as pale as the plume which shaded his brow; "but I have always wanted to see one, and as the opportunity presents itself I shall do my best to come face to face with this one."

"I shall not prevent you," said Coconnas, "only knock a little less fiercely if you do not wish to frighten it away."

La Mole, exasperated as he was, felt the justice of the remark, and began to knock more gently.

———

CHAPTER XXV.

THE CHERRY-COLORED CLOAK.

Coconnas was not mistaken. The lady who had stopped the cavalier of the cherry-colored cloak was indeed the Queen of Navarre. As to the cavalier, our reader has already guessed, I presume, that he was no other than brave De Mouy. Upon recognizing the Queen of Navarre the young Huguenot realized that there was some mistake; but he dared not speak, fearing a cry from Marguerite would betray him. He preferred to let himself be led to her apartments, and when once there to say to his beautiful guide:

"Silence for silence, madame."

Marguerite had gently pressed the arm of him whom in the semi-darkness she had mistaken for La Mole, and leaning toward him whispered in Latin:

"*Sola sum; introito, carissime.*"[9]

De Mouy without answering let her lead him along; but scarcely was the door closed behind him and he found himself in the antechamber, which was better lighted than the stairway, before Marguerite saw that he was not La Mole.

Thereupon the cry which the cautious Huguenot had feared escaped Marguerite; but fortunately there was no further danger from it.

"Monsieur de Mouy!" cried she, stepping back.

"In person, madame, and I beg your majesty to leave me free to continue my way without mentioning my presence in the Louvre to any one."

"Oh! Monsieur de Mouy!" reiterated Marguerite, "I was mistaken, then!"

"Yes," said De Mouy, "I understand. Your majesty mistook me for the King of Navarre. I am the same height, I wear the same white plume, and many, no doubt in order to flatter me, say I have the same gait."

Marguerite looked closely at De Mouy.

"Do you understand Latin, Monsieur de Mouy?" she asked.

"I used to know it," replied the young man, "but I have forgotten it."

Marguerite smiled.

"Monsieur de Mouy," said she, "you may rely on my discretion. But as I think I know the name of the one you are seeking in the Louvre, I will offer my services to guide you directly to him."

"Excuse me, madame," said De Mouy, "I think you are mistaken, and that you are completely ignorant of"—

"What!" exclaimed Marguerite, "are you not looking for the King of Navarre?"

"Alas, madame," said De Mouy, "I regret to have to beg you especially to conceal my presence in the Louvre from your husband, his majesty the king."

"Listen, Monsieur de Mouy," said Marguerite in surprise, "I have considered you until now one of the strongest leaders of the Huguenot party, and one of the most faithful partisans of the king my husband. Am I mistaken?"

"No, madame, for this very morning I was all that you say."

"And what has changed you since this morning?"

"Madame," said De Mouy, bowing, "kindly excuse me from answering, and do me the favor to accept my homage."

De Mouy, respectful but firm, started towards the door.

Marguerite stopped him.

"But, monsieur," said she, "if I were to ask you for a word of explanation, my word is good, it seems to me?"

"Madame," replied De Mouy, "I am obliged to keep silent, and this duty must be very imperative for me not to have answered your majesty."

"But, monsieur"—

"Your majesty may ruin me, madame, but you cannot ask me to betray my new friends."

"But the old ones, monsieur, have they too not some rights?"

"Those who have remained true, yes; those who not only have abandoned us, but themselves as well, no."

Marguerite, thoughtful and anxious, would no doubt have answered by a new question, had not Gillonne suddenly entered the apartment.

"The King of Navarre!" she cried.

"How is he coming?"

"By the secret corridor."

"Take monsieur out by the other."

"Impossible, madame. Listen."

"Some one is knocking?"

"Yes, at the door to which you wish me to take monsieur."

"Who is knocking?"

"I do not know."

"Go and see, and come back and tell me."

"Madame," said De Mouy, "might I venture to remark to your majesty that if the King of Navarre sees me at this hour and in this costume in the Louvre, I am lost?"

Marguerite seized De Mouy and pushed him towards the famous cabinet.

"Step in here, monsieur," said she; "you will be as safe and as well protected as if you were in your own house; I give you my word of honor."

De Mouy entered hastily. Scarcely was the door closed when Henry appeared.

This time Marguerite had no anxiety to hide—she was merely gloomy, and love was far from her thoughts.

As to Henry, he entered with that mistrust which in the most dangerous moments caused him to notice the smallest details; whatever the circumstances, Henry was an acute observer. Therefore he at once saw the cloud on Marguerite's brow.

"You are busy, madame?" said he.

"I? Why, yes, sire, I was dreaming."

"You do well, madame. Dreaming is becoming to you. I too was dreaming; but contrary to you who seek solitude, I have come on purpose to share my dreams, with you." Marguerite gave the king a gesture of welcome, and indicating an armchair to him, seated herself on a chair of sculptured ebony, as delicate and as strong as steel. There was an instant's silence; then Henry broke it.

"I remembered, madame," said he, "that my dreams as to the future corresponded with yours in so far as although separated as husband and wife, nevertheless we both desire to unite our fortune."

"That is true, sire."

"I think I understood you to say also that in all the plans I might make toward our mutual rising, I would find in you not only a faithful but an active ally."

"Yes, sire, and I ask only one thing, that in beginning the work as soon as possible, you will give me the opportunity to begin also."

"I am glad to find you of this mind, madame, and I trust that you have not for one instant doubted that I would lose sight of the plan I resolved to carry out the very day when, thanks to your brave intervention, I was almost sure of being safe."

"Monsieur, I think that your carelessness is nothing but a mask, and I have faith not only in the predictions by the astrologers, but in your good genius as well."

"What should you say, madame, if someone were to upset our plans and threaten to reduce us to an ordinary position?"

"I should say that I was ready to fight with you, either openly or in secret, against this someone, whoever he might be."

"Madame," continued Henry, "it is possible for you, is it not, to gain immediate admission into the room of your brother, Monsieur d'Alençon? You are in his confidence and he is very friendly to you; might I venture to beg you to find out if he is at present holding a secret conference with someone?"

Marguerite gave a start.

"With whom, monsieur?" she asked.

"With De Mouy."

"Why?" asked Marguerite, repressing her emotion.

"Because if such is the case, madame, farewell to all our projects, or to all mine, at least."

"Sire, speak softly," said Marguerite, making a sign with her eyes and lips, and pointing to the cabinet.

"Oh! oh!" said Henry, "still someone? Indeed, that cabinet is so often occupied that it makes your room uninhabitable."

Marguerite smiled.

"Is it still Monsieur de la Mole?" asked Henry.

"No, sire, it is Monsieur de Mouy."

"He?" cried Henry with surprise mingled with joy. "He is not with the Duc d'Alençon, then? Oh! have him come in, that I may talk to him."

Marguerite stepped to the cabinet, opened it, and taking De Mouy by the hand led him without preamble to the King of Navarre.

"Ah! madame," said the young Huguenot, in a tone of reproach more sad than bitter, "you have betrayed me in spite of your promise; that is wrong. What should you do if I were to avenge myself by saying"—

"You will not avenge yourself, De Mouy," interrupted Henry, pressing the young man's hand, "or at least you will listen to me first. Madame," continued Henry, turning to the queen, "be kind enough, I beg you, to see that no one overhears us."

Scarcely had Henry uttered these words when Gillonne entered, frightened, and whispered a few words to Marguerite, which caused the latter to spring from her seat. While she hastened to the antechamber with Gillonne, Henry, without troubling himself as to why she had left the room, examined the bed, the side of it, as well as the draperies, and sounded the wall with his fingers. As to Monsieur de Mouy, frightened at all these preparations, he first of all made sure that his sword was out of its sheath.

Leaving her sleeping-room, Marguerite hastened to the antechamber and came face to face with La Mole, who in spite of all the protests of Gillonne had forced his way into Marguerite's room.

Coconnas was behind him, ready to urge him forward or sustain a retreat.

"Ah! it is you, Monsieur la Mole!" cried the queen; "but what is the matter, and why are you so pale and trembling?"

"Madame," said Gillonne, "Monsieur de la Mole knocked at the door so that, in spite of your majesty's orders, I was forced to open it."

"What is the meaning of this?" said the queen, severely; "is this true, Monsieur de la Mole?"

"Madame, I wanted to warn your majesty that a stranger, a robber perhaps, had gained admittance to your rooms with my cloak and my hat."

"You are mad, monsieur," said Marguerite, "for I see your cloak on your shoulders, and, God forgive me, I think I see your hat on your head, even though you are speaking to a queen."

"Oh! pardon me, madame, pardon me!" cried La Mole, quickly uncovering; "but God is my witness, it is not my respect which is lacking."

"No, it is your trust, is it not?" said the queen.

"What can you expect?" cried La Mole, "when a man is in your majesty's rooms; when he gains admittance by assuming my clothes, and perhaps my name, who knows"—

"A man!" cried Marguerite, softly pressing her poor lover's arm; "a man! You are modest, Monsieur de la Mole. Look through the opening of the portière and you will see two men."

Marguerite drew back the velvet portière embroidered in gold, and La Mole saw Henry talking with the man in the cherry-colored cloak. Coconnas, as though he himself were concerned, looked also, saw, and recognized De Mouy. Both men stood amazed.

"Now that you are reassured, or at least now that I hope you are," said Marguerite, "take your stand outside my door, and for your life, my dear La Mole, let no one enter. If any one even approaches the stairs, warn me." La Mole, weak and obedient as a child, withdrew, glancing at Coconnas, who looked at him. Both found themselves outside without having thoroughly recovered from their astonishment.

"De Mouy!" cried Coconnas.

"Henry!" murmured La Mole.

"De Mouy with your cherry-colored cloak, your white plume, and your swinging arm."

"Ah!" went on La Mole, "the moment it is not a question of love, it is a question of plot."

"By Heaven! here we are in the midst of politics," said Coconnas grumbling. "Fortunately I do not see Madame de Nevers mixed up in it."

Marguerite returned and sat down by the two speakers. She had been gone only a moment, but had made the most of her time. Gillonne, on guard in the secret passage, and the two gentlemen on duty at the main entrance, assured perfect safety for her.

"Madame," said Henry, "do you think it would be possible for us to be overheard in any way?"

"Monsieur," said Marguerite, "the walls of this room are wadded, and a double wainscoting deadens all sound."

"I depend on you," replied Henry smiling. Then turning to De Mouy:

"Now," said the king, in a low tone, as if in spite of the assurance of Marguerite his fears were not wholly overcome, "what are you here for?"

"Here?" said De Mouy.

"Yes, here, in this room," repeated Henry.

"He had nothing to do here," said Marguerite; "I induced him to come."

"You?"

"I guessed everything."

"You see, De Mouy, we can discover what is going on."

"This morning," continued Marguerite, "Monsieur de Mouy was with Duc François in the apartment of two of his gentlemen."

"You see, De Mouy," repeated Henry, "we know everything."

"That is true," said De Mouy.

"I was sure," said Henry, "that Monsieur d'Alençon had taken possession of you."

"That is your fault, sire. Why did you so persistently refuse what I offered you?"

"You refused!" exclaimed Marguerite. "The refusal I feared, then, was real?"

"Madame," said Henry, shaking his head, "and you, my brave De Mouy, really, you make me laugh with your exclamations. What! a man enters my chamber, speaks to me of a throne, of a revolt, of a revolution, to me, Henry, a prince tolerated provided that I eat humble pie, a Huguenot spared on condition that I play the Catholic; and I am expected to accept, when these propositions are made in a room without padding or double wainscoting! *Ventre saint gris!* You are either children or fools!"

"But, sire, could not your majesty have left me some hope, if not by word, at least by a gesture or sign?"

"What did my brother-in-law say to you, De Mouy?" asked Henry.

"Oh, sire, that is not my secret."

"Well, my God!" continued Henry, with a certain impatience at having to deal with a man who so poorly understood his words. "I do not ask what you proposed to him, I ask you merely if he listened to you, if he heard you."

"He listened, sire, and he heard."

"He listened and he heard! You admit it yourself, De Mouy, tactless conspirator that you are! Had I said one word you would have been lost, for I did not know, I merely suspected that he was there, or if not he, someone else, the Duc d'Anjou, Charles IX., or the queen mother, for instance. You do not know the walls of the Louvre, De Mouy; it was for them that the proverb was made which says that walls have ears; and knowing these walls you expected me to speak! Well, well, De Mouy, you pay a small compliment to the common sense of the King of Navarre, and I am surprised that not esteeming him more highly you should have offered him a crown."

"But, sire," said De Mouy, "could you not even while refusing this crown have given me some sign? In that case I should not have considered everything hopeless and lost."

"Well! *Ventre saint gris!*" exclaimed Henry, "if one can hear cannot one see also? and is not one lost by a sign as much as by a word? See, De Mouy," continued the king, looking around him, "at the present moment, so near to you that my words do not reach beyond the circle of our three chairs, I still fear I may be overheard when I say: De Mouy, repeat your proposal to me."

"But, sire," cried De Mouy in despair, "I am now engaged with Monsieur d'Alençon."

Marguerite angrily clasped and unclasped her beautiful hands.

"Then it is too late?" said she.

"On the contrary," murmured Henry, "know that even in this, God's hand is visible. Continue your arrangement, De Mouy, for in Duc François lies our safety. Do you suppose that the King of Navarre would guarantee your heads? On the contrary, wretched man, I should have you all killed to the last one, and on the least suspicion. But with a son of France it is different. Secure proofs, De Mouy, ask for guarantees; but, stupid that you are, you will be deeply involved, and one word will suffice for you."

"Oh, sire, it was my despair at your having left us, believe me, which threw me into the arms of the duke; it was also the fear of being betrayed, for he kept our secret."

"Keep his, now, De Mouy; it rests with you. What does he wish? To leave court? Furnish him with means to escape. Work for him, De Mouy, as if you were working for me, turn the shield so that he may parry every blow they aim at us. When it is time to flee, we will both flee. When it is time to fight and reign, I will reign alone."

"Do not trust the duke," said Marguerite, "he is gloomy and acute, without hatred as without love; ever ready to treat his friends like enemies and his enemies like friends."

"And he is expecting you now, De Mouy?" said Henry.

"Yes, sire."

"Where?"

"In the apartment belonging to his two gentlemen."

"At what time?"

"Before midnight."

"It is not yet eleven o'clock," said Henry, "so you have lost no time; now you may go, De Mouy."

"We have your word, monsieur?" said Marguerite.

"Come now, madame!" said Henry, with the confidence he knew so well how to use with certain people and on certain occasions, "with Monsieur de Mouy, such things are not even asked for."

"You are right, sire," replied the young man; "but I need your word, for I shall have to tell the leaders that I have it. You are not a Catholic, are you?"

Henry shrugged his shoulders.

"You do not renounce the kingdom of Navarre?"

"I renounce no kingdom, De Mouy, I merely reserve for myself the choice of the best; that is, the one which shall best suit me and you."

"And if in the meantime your majesty should be arrested, you would promise to reveal nothing even should they torture your royal majesty?"

"De Mouy, I swear that, before God."

"One further word, sire. How am I to see you in future?"

"After to-morrow you shall have a key to my room. You will come there, De Mouy, as often as it may be necessary and when you please. It is for the Duc d'Alençon to answer for your presence in the Louvre. In the meantime, use the small stairway. I will show you the way. The queen will have the cherry-colored cloak like yours come here—the one who was in the antechamber just now. No one must notice any difference between you, or know that there are two of you, De Mouy. Do you not agree with me? And you, madame?" Henry looked at Marguerite and uttered the last words with a smile.

"Yes," said she, without moving a feature; "for this Monsieur de la Mole belongs to my brother, the duke."

"Well, madame, try to win him over to our side," said Henry, in perfect seriousness. "Spare neither gold nor promises; I will put all my treasures at his disposal."

"In that case," said Marguerite, with one of the smiles which belong only to the women of Boccaccio, "since this is your wish, I will do my best to second it."

"Very good, madame; and you, De Mouy, return to the duke, and make sure of him."

CHAPTER XXVI.

MARGARITA.

During the conversation which we have just related, La Mole and Coconnas mounted guard. La Mole somewhat chagrined, Coconnas somewhat anxious. La Mole had had time to reflect, and in this he had been greatly aided by Coconnas.

"What do you think of all this, my friend?" La Mole had asked of Coconnas.

"I think," the Piedmontese had replied, "that there is some court intrigue connected with it."

"And such being the case, are you disposed to play a part in it?"

"My dear fellow," replied Coconnas, "listen well to what I am going to say to you and try and profit by it. In all these princely dealings, in all royal affairs, we can and should be nothing but shadows. Where the King of Navarre leaves a bit of his plume and the Duc d'Alençon a piece of his cloak, we leave our lives. The queen has a fancy for you, and you for her. Nothing is better. Lose your head in love, my dear fellow, but not in politics."

That was wise council. Therefore it was heard by La Mole with the melancholy of a man who feels that, placed between reason and madness, it is madness he will follow.

"I have not a fancy for the queen, Annibal, I love her; and fortunately or unfortunately I love her with all my heart. This is madness, you will say. Well, I admit that I am mad. But you are wise, Coconnas, you ought not to suffer for my foolishness and my misfortune. Go back to our master and do not compromise yourself."

Coconnas pondered an instant. Then raising his head:

"My dear fellow," he replied, "all that you tell me is perfectly reasonable; you are in love—act, therefore, like a lover. I am ambitious, and being so, I think life is worth more to me than a woman's kiss. When I risk my life, I make my own conditions. Try, so far as you are concerned, my poor Medor, to make yours."

Whereupon Coconnas extended his hand to La Mole and withdrew, having exchanged a final glance and a final smile with his friend.

About ten minutes after he left his post, the door opened, and Marguerite, peering out cautiously, took La Mole by the hand and, without uttering a word, drew him from the corridor into the furthest corner of her room. She closed the door behind her with a care which indicated the importance of the conversation she was about to have.

Once in her room she stopped, seated herself on her ebony chair, and drawing La Mole to her, she clasped her hands over both of his.

"Now that we are alone," said she, "let us talk seriously, my very dear friend."

"Seriously, madame," said La Mole.

"Or lovingly. Does that please you better? But there can be serious things in love, and especially in the love of a queen."

"Then—let us talk of serious things; but on condition that your majesty will not be vexed at the lighter things I have to say to you."

"I shall be vexed only at one thing, La Mole, and that is if you address me as 'madame' or 'your majesty.' For you, my beloved, I am just Marguerite."

"Yes, Marguerite! Yes, Margarita! Yes, my pearl!" cried the young man, devouring the queen with his eyes.

"Yes, that is right," said Marguerite. "So you are jealous, my fine gentleman?"

"Oh! unreasonably."

"Still?"

"Madly, Marguerite."

"Jealous of whom? Come!"

"Of everyone."

"But really?"

"Of the king first."

"I should think after what you had seen and heard you might be easy on that point."

"Of this Monsieur de Mouy, whom I saw this morning for the first time, and whom this evening I find so far advanced in his intimacy with you."

"Monsieur de Mouy?"

"Yes."

"Who gave you such ideas about Monsieur de Mouy?"

"Listen! I recognized him from his figure, from the color of his hair, from a natural feeling of hatred. He is the one who was with Monsieur d'Alençon this morning."

"Well, what connection has that with me?"

"Monsieur d'Alençon is your brother. It is said that you are very fond of him. You may have confided to him a vague feeling of your heart, and, according to the custom at court, he has aided your wish by admitting Monsieur de Mouy to your apartment. Now, what I do not understand is how I was fortunate enough to find the king here at the same time. But in any case, madame, be frank with me. In default of other sentiment, a love like mine has the right to demand frankness in return. See, I prostrate myself at your feet. If what you have felt for me is but a passing fancy, I will give you back your trust, your promise, your love; I will give back to Monsieur d'Alençon his kind favors and my post of gentleman, and I will go and seek death at the siege of La Rochelle, if love does not kill me before I have gone as far as that."

Marguerite listened smilingly to these charming words, watching La Mole's graceful gestures, then leaning her beautiful dreamy head on her feverish hand:

"You love me?" she asked.

"Oh, madame! more than life, more than safety, more than all; but you, you —you do not love me."

"Poor fool!" she murmured.

"Ah, yes, madame," cried La Mole, still at her feet, "I have told you I was that."

"The chief thought of your life, then, is your love, dear La Mole!"

"It is the only thought, madame, the sole thought."

"Well, be it so; I will make of all the rest only an accessory to this love. You love me; do you wish to remain near me?"

"My one prayer is that God will never take me from you."

"Well, you shall not leave me. I need you, La Mole."

"You need me? Does the sun need the glow-worm?"

"If I will tell you that I love you, would you be wholly devoted to me?"

"Ah! am I not that already, madame, and more than wholly?"

"Yes, but, God forgive me, you still doubt!"

"Oh! I am wrong, I am ungrateful, or, rather, as I have told you and repeated to you, I am a fool. But why was Monsieur de Mouy with you this evening? why did I see him this morning with Monsieur le Duc d'Alençon? Why that cherry-colored cloak, that white plume, that affected imitation of my gait? Ah! madame, it is not you whom I suspect, but your brother."

"Wretched man!" said Marguerite, "wretched man to suppose that Duc François would push complacency so far as to introduce a wooer to his sister's room! Mad enough to be jealous, and yet not to have guessed! Do you know, La Mole, that the Duc d'Alençon would run you through with his own sword if he knew that you were here, this evening, at my feet, and that instead of sending you away I were saying to you: 'Stay here where you are, La Mole; for I love you, my fine gentleman, do you hear? I love you!' Ah, yes! he would certainly kill you."

"Great God!" cried La Mole, starting back and looking at Marguerite in terror, "is it possible?"

"Everything is possible, my friend, in these times and at this court. Now, one word; it was not for me that Monsieur de Mouy, in your cloak, his face hidden under your hat, came to the Louvre. It was for Monsieur d'Alençon. But I, thinking it was you, brought him here. He knows our secret, La Mole, and must be carefully managed."

"I should prefer to kill him," said La Mole; "that is shorter and surer."

"And I, my brave gentleman," said the queen, "I prefer him to live, and for you to know everything, for not only is his life useful to us, but it is necessary. Listen and weigh your words well before you answer. Do you love me enough, La Mole, to be glad if I were really to become a queen; that is, queen of a real kingdom?"

"Alas, madame, I love you enough to wish what you wish, even should this desire ruin my whole life!"

"Well, do you want to aid me to realize this desire, which would make you still happier?"

"Oh! I should lose you, madame," cried La Mole hiding his head in his hands.

"No, on the contrary. Instead of being the first of my servants, you would become the first of my subjects, that is all."

"Oh! no interest—no ambition, madame—do not sully the feeling I have for you—the devotion, nothing but devotion!"

"Noble nature!" said Marguerite; "well, yes, I accept your devotion, and I shall find out how to reward it."

She extended both her hands, and La Mole covered them with kisses.

"Well!" said she.

"Well, yes!" replied La Mole, "yes, Marguerite, I am beginning to comprehend this vague project already talked of by us Huguenots before the massacre of Saint Bartholomew, the scheme for the execution of which I, like many another worthier than myself, was sent to Paris. You covet this actual kingdom of Navarre which is to take the place of an imaginary kingdom. King Henry drives you to it; De Mouy conspires with you, does he not? But the Duc d'Alençon, what is he doing in it all? Where is there a throne for him? I do not see. Now, is the Duc d'Alençon sufficiently your—friend to aid you in all this without asking anything in exchange for the danger he runs?"

"The duke, my friend, is conspiring on his own account. Let us leave him to his illusions. His life answers for ours."

"But I, who belong to him, can I betray him?"

"Betray him! In what are you betraying him? What has he confided to you? Is it not he who has betrayed you by giving your cloak and hat to De Mouy as a means of gaining him admittance to his apartments? You belong to him, you say! Were you not mine, my gentleman, before you were his? Has he given you a greater proof of friendship than the proof of love you have from me?"

La Mole arose, pale and completely overcome.

"Oh!" he murmured, "Coconnas was right, intrigue is enveloping me in its folds. It will suffocate me."

"Well?" asked Marguerite.

"Well," said La Mole, "this is my answer: it is said, and I heard it at the other end of France, where your illustrious name and your universal reputation for beauty touched my heart like a vague desire for the unknown, —it is said that sometimes you love, but that your love is always fatal to those you love, so that death, jealous, no doubt, almost always removes your lovers."

"La Mole!"

"Do not interrupt me, oh, my well-loved Margarita, for they add that you preserve the hearts of these faithful friends in gold boxes[10], and that occasionally you bestow a melancholy thought, a pious glance on the sad remains. You sigh, my queen, your eyes droop; it is true. Well! make me the dearest and the happiest of your favorites. You have pierced the hearts of others, and you keep their hearts. You do more with me, you expose my head. Well, Marguerite, swear to me before the image of the God who has saved my life in this very place, swear to me, that if I die for you, as a sad presentiment tells me I shall do, swear to me that you will keep my head, which the hangman will separate from my body; and that you will sometimes press your lips to it. Swear, Marguerite, and the promise of such reward bestowed by my queen will make me silent, and, if necessary, a traitor and a coward; this is being wholly devoted, as your lover and your accomplice should be."

"Oh! what ghastly foolishness, dear heart!" said Marguerite. "Oh! fatal thought, sweet love."

"Swear"—

"Swear?"

"Yes, on this silver chest with its cross. Swear."

"Well!" said Marguerite, "if—and God forbid!—your gloomy presentiment is realized, my fine gentleman, on this cross I swear to you that you shall be near me, living or dead, so long as I live; and if I am unable to rescue you from the peril which comes to you through me, through me alone, I will at least give to your poor soul the consolation for which you ask, and which you will so well have deserved."

"One word more, Marguerite. I can die now. I shall not mind death; but I can live, too, for we may succeed. The King of Navarre, king, you may be queen, in which case he will take you away. This vow of separation between you will some day be broken, and will do away with ours. Now, Marguerite, my well-beloved Marguerite, with a word you have taken away my every fear of death; now with a word keep up my courage concerning life."

"Oh, fear nothing, I am yours, body and soul!" cried Marguerite, again raising her hand to the cross on the little chest. "If I leave, you follow, and if the king refuses to take you, then I shall not go."

"But you dare not resist!"

"My well-beloved Hyacinthe," said Marguerite, "you do not know Henry. At present he is thinking of only one thing, that is, of being king. For this he would sacrifice everything he owns, and, still more, what he does not own. Now, adieu!"

"Madame," said La Mole, smiling, "are you going to send me away?"

"It is late," said Marguerite.

"No doubt; but where would you have me go? Monsieur de Mouy is in my room with Monsieur le Duc d'Alençon."

"Ah! yes," said Marguerite, with a beautiful smile. "Besides, I have still some things to tell you about this conspiracy."

From that night La Mole was no longer an ordinary favorite. He well might carry his head high, for which, living or dead, so sweet a future was in store.

And yet at times his weary brow was bent, his cheek grew pale, and deep thoughts ploughed their furrows on the forehead of the young man, once so light-hearted, now so happy!

———

CHAPTER XXVII.

THE HAND OF GOD.

On leaving Madame de Sauve Henry had said to her:

"Go to bed, Charlotte. Pretend that you are very ill, and on no account see any one all day to-morrow."

Charlotte obeyed without questioning the reason for this suggestion from the king. She was beginning to be accustomed to his eccentricities, as we should call them to-day, or to his whims as they were then called. Moreover, she knew that deep in his heart Henry hid secrets which he told to no one, in his mind plans which he feared to reveal even in his dreams; so that she carried out all his wishes, knowing that his most peculiar ideas had an object.

Whereupon that evening she complained to Dariole of great heaviness in her head, accompanied by dizziness. These were the symptoms which Henry had suggested to her to feign.

The following day she pretended that she wanted to rise, but scarcely had she put her foot on the floor when she said she felt a general debility, and went back to bed.

This indisposition, which Henry had already announced to the Duc d'Alençon, was the first news brought to Catharine when she calmly asked why La Sauve was not present as usual at her levee.

"She is ill!" replied Madame de Lorraine, who was there.

"Ill!" repeated Catharine, without a muscle of her face betraying the interest she took in the answer. "Some idle fatigue, perhaps."

"No, madame," replied the princess. "She complains of a severe headache and of weakness which prevents her from walking." Catharine did not answer. But, to hide her joy, she turned to the window, and perceiving Henry, who was crossing the court after his conversation with De Mouy, she rose the better to see him. Driven by that conscience which, although invisible, always throbs in the deepest recesses of hearts most hardened to crime:

"Does not my son Henry seem paler than usual this morning?" she asked her captain of the guards.

There was nothing in the question. Henry was greatly troubled mentally; but physically he was very strong.

By degrees those usually present at the queen's levee withdrew. Three or four intimate ones remained longer than the others, but Catharine impatiently dismissed them, saying that she wished to be alone. When the last courtier had gone Catharine closed the door and going to a secret closet hidden in one of the panels of her room she slid back a door in a groove of wood and took out a book, the worn leaves of which showed frequent use. Placing the volume on a table, she opened it to a book-mark, then resting her elbow on the table and her head on one hand:

"That is it," murmured she, reading, "'headache, general weakness, pain in the eyes, swelling of the palate.' As yet they have mentioned only the pains in

266

the head and weakness. But the other symptoms will not be slow in forthcoming."

She continued:

"'Then the inflammation reaches the throat, extends to the stomach, surrounds the heart like a circle of fire, and causes the brain to burst like a thunderclap,'" she read on to herself. Then in a low voice:

"For the fever, six hours; for the general inflammation, twelve hours; for the gangrene, twelve hours; for the suffering, six hours; in all thirty-six hours. Now, suppose that the absorption is slow, and that instead of thirty-six hours we have forty, even forty-eight, yes, forty-eight hours should suffice. But Henry, how is it that he is still up? Because he is a man, because he has a strong constitution, because perhaps he drank after he kissed her, and wiped his lips after drinking."

Catharine awaited the dinner hour with impatience.

Henry dined every day at the king's table. He came, he in turn complained of pain in his head; he ate nothing, and withdrew immediately after the meal, saying that having been awake a part of the previous night, he felt a pressing need of sleep.

Catharine listened as his uncertain steps died away. Then she had him followed. She was told that the King of Navarre had gone to Madame de Sauve's apartments.

"Henry," said she to herself, "will this evening complete the work of death which some unfortunate chance has left half finished."

The King of Navarre had indeed gone to Madame de Sauve's room, but it was to tell her to continue playing her rôle.

The whole of the following morning Henry did not leave his chamber; nor did he appear at dinner. Madame de Sauve, they said, was growing worse and worse, and the report of Henry's illness, spread abroad by Catharine herself, sped like one of those presentiments which hover in the air, but which no one can explain.

Catharine was delighted. The previous morning she had sent Ambroise Paré to help one of her favorite servants, who was ill at Saint Germain, so it had to be one of her own men who was called in to see Madame de Sauve and Henry. This man would say only what she wished him to say. If, contrary to all expectation, some other doctor had been summoned, and if some whisper concerning poison had frightened the court, in which so many such reports had already been circulated, she counted greatly on the rumor to arouse the jealousy of Marguerite regarding the various loves of her husband. We remember she had spoken strongly of this jealousy which had been apparent on various occasions; among others, on the hawthorn walk, where, in the presence of several persons, she had said to her daughter:

"So you are very jealous, Marguerite?" Therefore, with unruffled features she waited for the door to open, when some pale, startled servant would enter, crying:

"Your majesty, the King of Navarre has been hurt, and Madame de Sauve is dead!" Four o'clock in the afternoon struck. Catharine finished her luncheon in the aviary, where she was crumbling some bread for her rare birds which she herself had raised. Although her face was calm and even gloomy, as usual, her heart throbbed violently at the slightest sound. Suddenly the door opened.

"Madame," said the captain of the guards, "the King of Navarre is"—

"Ill?" hastily interrupted Catharine.

"No, madame, thank God! His majesty seems to be wonderfully well."

"What is it, then?"

"The King of Navarre is here."

"What does he want?"

"He is bringing your majesty a rare kind of monkey."

Just then Henry entered holding in his hand a basket, in which was a little monkey he was petting.

He entered smiling and seemed wholly absorbed in the dear little animal he brought; but occupied as he appeared to be, he did not fail to give his usual first glance around. This was sufficient for him under trying circumstances. As to Catharine, she was very pale, of a pallor which deepened as she saw that the cheeks of the young man were flushed with the glow of health.

The queen mother was amazed at this turn of affairs. She accepted Henry's gift mechanically, appeared agitated, complimented him on looking so well, and added:

"I am all the more pleased to see you looking so, because I heard that you were ill, and because, if I remember rightly, you yourself complained of not feeling well, in my presence. But I understand now," she added, trying to smile, "it was an excuse so that you might be free."

"No, I have really been very ill, madame," said Henry, "but a specific used in our mountains, and which comes from my mother, has cured my indisposition."

"Ah! you will give me the recipe, will you not, Henry?" said Catharine, really smiling this time, but with an irony she could not disguise.

"Some counter-poison," she murmured. "We must look into this; but no, seeing Madame de Sauve ill, it will be suspected. Indeed, I believe that the hand of God is over this man."

Catharine waited impatiently for the night. Madame de Sauve did not appear. At play she inquired for her, but was told that she was suffering more and more.

All the evening she was restless, and everyone anxiously wondered what were the thoughts which could move this face usually so calm.

At length everyone retired. Catharine had herself undressed and put to bed by her ladies-in-waiting. Then when everyone had gone to sleep in the Louvre, she rose, slipped on a long black dressing-gown, took a lamp, chose from her keys the one which unlocked the door of Madame de Sauve's apartments, and ascended the stairs to see her maid-of-honor.

Had Henry foreseen this visit? Was he busy in his own rooms? Was he hiding somewhere? However this may have been, the young woman was alone. Catharine opened the door cautiously, crossed the antechamber, entered the reception-room, set her lamp on a table, for a night lamp was burning near the sick woman, and glided like a shadow into the sleeping-room. Dariole in a deep armchair was sleeping near the bed of her mistress.

This bed was entirely shut in by curtains.

The respiration of the young woman was so light that for an instant Catharine thought she was not breathing at all.

At length she heard a slight sigh, and with an evil joy she raised the curtain in order to see for herself the effect of the terrible poison. She trembled in advance at the sight of the livid pallor or the devouring purple of the mortal fever she hoped for. But instead of this, calm, with eyes hidden under their white lids, her mouth rosy and half open, her moist cheek pressed gently against one of her gracefully rounded arms, while the other arm, fresh and pearly, was thrown across the crimson damask which served as counterpane, the beautiful young woman lay sleeping with a smile still on her lips. No doubt some sweet dream brought the smile to her lips, and to her cheek the flush of health which nothing could disturb. Catharine could not refrain from uttering a cry of surprise which roused Dariole for a moment. The queen mother hastily stepped behind the curtains of the bed.

Dariole opened her eyes, but overcome with sleep, without even wondering in her drowsy mind why she had wakened, the young girl dropped her heavy lids and slept again.

Then Catharine came from behind the curtain, and glancing at the other objects in the room, saw on a table a bottle of Spanish wine, some fruit, pastry, and two glasses. Henry must have had supper with the baroness, who apparently was as well as himself. Walking on tiptoe, Catharine took up the small silver box that was partly empty. It was the same or very similar to the one she had sent to Charlotte. She removed from it a piece as large as a pearl on the point of a gold needle, returned to her room, and gave it to the little ape which Henry had brought her that evening. Attracted by the aromatic odor the animal devoured it eagerly, and turning around in his basket, went to sleep. Catharine waited a quarter of an hour.

"With half of what he has just eaten," said she, "my dog Brutus died, swelling up instantly. Some one has played me a trick. Is it Réné? Impossible. Then it is Henry. O fatality! It is very evident that since he is to reign he cannot die. But perhaps the poison was not strong enough. We shall see by trying steel."

And Catharine went to bed revolving in her mind a fresh idea which no doubt was perfected the following day; for she called her captain of the guards to her, gave him a letter, ordered him to take it to its address and to deliver it only into the hands of the one for whom it was intended. It was addressed to the Sire de Louvièrs de Maurevel, Captain of the King's Petard Makers, Rue de la Cerisaie, near the Arsenal.

CHAPTER XXVIII.

THE LETTER FROM ROME.

Several days elapsed after the events we have just described, when one morning a litter escorted by several gentlemen wearing the colors of Monsieur de Guise entered the Louvre, and word was brought to the Queen of Navarre that Madame la Duchesse de Nevers begged the honor of an audience. Marguerite was receiving a call from Madame de Sauve. It was the first time the beautiful baroness had been out since her pretended illness. She knew that the queen had expressed to her husband great anxiety on account of her indisposition, which for almost a week had been court gossip, and she had come to thank her.

Marguerite congratulated her on her convalescence and on her good fortune at having recovered so quickly from the strange malady, the seriousness of which as a daughter of France she could not fail to appreciate.

"I trust you will attend the hunt, already once postponed," said Marguerite. "It is planned positively for to-morrow. For winter, the weather is very mild. The sun has softened the earth, and the hunters all say that the day will be fine."

"But, madame," said the baroness, "I do not know if I shall be strong enough."

"Bah!" exclaimed Marguerite, "make an effort; moreover, since I am one of the hunters, I have told the King to reserve a small Béarnese horse which I was to ride, but which will carry you perfectly. Have you not already heard of it?"

"Yes, madame, but I did not know that it was meant for your majesty. Had I known that I should not have accepted it."

"From a feeling of pride, baroness?"

"No, madame, from a feeling of humility, on the contrary."

"Then you will come?"

"Your majesty overwhelms me with honor. I will come, since you command me."

At that moment Madame la Duchesse de Nevers was announced. At this name Marguerite gave a cry of such delight that the baroness understood that the two women wanted to talk together. She rose to leave.

"Until to-morrow, then," said Marguerite.

"Until to-morrow, madame."

"By the way," continued Marguerite holding the baroness by the hand, "you know that in public I hate you, for I am horribly jealous of you."

"But in private?" asked Madame de Sauve.

"Oh! in private, not only do I forgive you, but more than that, I thank you."

"Then your majesty will permit me"—

Marguerite held out her hand, the baroness kissed it respectfully, made a low courtesy and went out.

While Madame de Sauve ascended her stairway, bounding like a deer whose tether has been broken, Madame de Nevers was exchanging a few formal words with the queen, which gave time to the gentlemen who had accompanied her to retire.

"Gillonne," cried Marguerite when the door was closed behind the last, "Gillonne, see that no one interrupts us."

"Yes," said the duchess, "for we have matters of grave importance to discuss."

Taking a chair she seated herself without ceremony in the best place near the fire and in the sunlight, sure that no one would interrupt the pleasant intimacy between herself and the Queen of Navarre.

"Well," said Marguerite, with a smile, "what about our famous slaughterer?"

"My dear queen," said the duchess, "he is a mythological creature, upon my word. He is incomparable, so far as his mind is concerned, and never dries up. He makes witty remarks that would make a saint in her shrine die of laughing. In other respects he is the maddest heathen who ever walked in the skin of a Catholic! I dote on him! And you, what are you doing with your Apollo?"

"Alas!" said Marguerite with a sigh.

"Oh, how that 'alas!' frightens me, dear queen! Is the gentle La Mole too respectful or too sentimental? In that, I am forced to admit he would be exactly the opposite of his friend Coconnas."

"Oh, no, he has his moments," said Marguerite, "but this 'alas!' concerned only myself."

"What does it mean, then?"

"It means, dear duchess, that I am terribly afraid I am actually in love."

"Really?"

"On my honor!"

"Oh! so much the better! What a merry life we can lead!" cried Henriette. "To love a little is my dream; to love much, is yours. It is so sweet, dear and learned queen, to rest the mind by the heart, is it not? and to have the smile after the delirium. Ah, Marguerite, I have a feeling that we are going to have a glorious year!"

"Do you think so?" said the queen. "I, on the contrary, do not know how that may be; I see things through a veil. All these politics occupy me so much. By the way, do you know if your Annibal is as devoted to my brother as he seems to be? Find out for me. I must know."

"He, devoted to anybody or anything! It is easy to see that you do not know him as I do. If he ever is devoted to anything it will be his ambition, and that is all. If your brother is a man to make great promises to him, well, he will be devoted to your brother; but let your brother, son of France that he is, be careful not to break the promises he makes him. If he does, my faith, look out for your brother!"

"Really?"

"It is just as I say. Truly, Marguerite, there are times when this tiger whom I have tamed frightens me. The other day I said to him, 'Annibal, be careful, do not deceive me, for if you do!'—I said it, however, with my emerald eyes which prompted Ronsard's lines:

> "*La Duchesse de Nevers,*[11]
>> *Aux yeux verts,*
> *Qui, sous leur paupière blonde*
> *Lancent sur nous plus d'éclairs*
> *Que ne font vingt Jupiters*
>> *Dans les airs*
> *Lorsque la tempête gronde.*'"

"Well?"

"Well, I supposed he would answer me: 'I deceive you! I! never! etc., etc.' But do you know what he did answer?"

"No."

"Well, judge of the man! 'And you,' he replied, 'if you deceive me, you take care too, for, princess that you are'—and as he said this he threatened me not only with his eyes, but with his slender pointed finger, with its nail cut like a steel lance, which he held before my nose. At that moment, my poor queen, I confess he looked so fierce that I trembled, and yet you know I am no coward."

"He threatened you, Henriette, he dared?"

"Well, I had threatened him! For that matter he was right. So you see he is devoted up to a certain point, or rather to a very uncertain point."

"In that case we shall see," said Marguerite thoughtfully; "I will speak to La Mole. Have you nothing else to tell me?"

273

"Yes; something most interesting for which I came. But, the idea, you have told me more interesting things still. I have received news."

"From Rome?"

"Yes, through a courier from my husband."

"Ah! the Poland affair?"

"It is progressing beautifully, and probably in a day or two you will be rid of your brother of Anjou."

"So the pope has ratified his election?"

"Yes, my dear."

"And you never told me!" cried Marguerite. "Well, quick, quick, the details."

"Oh, mercy, I have none except those I have given you. But wait, I will give you the letter from Monsieur de Nevers. Here it is. Oh, no, those are some verses from Annibal, atrocious ones too, my poor Marguerite. He can not write any other kind. But wait, here it is. No, it isn't, that is a note of my own which I brought for you to have La Mole give him. Ah! at last, here it is." And Madame de Nevers handed the letter to the queen.

Marguerite opened it hastily and read it; but it told nothing more than she had already learned from her friend.

"How did you receive this?" continued the queen.

"From a courier of my husband, who had orders to stop at the Hôtel de Guise before going to the Louvre, and to deliver this letter to me before delivering that of the King. I knew the importance my queen would attach to this news, and I had written to Monsieur de Nevers to act thus. He obeyed, you see; he is not like that monster of a Coconnas. Now there is no one in the whole of Paris, except the King, you, and I, who knows this news; except the man who followed our courier"—

"What man?"

"Oh! the horrid business! Imagine how tired, worn out, and dusty the wretched messenger was when he arrived! He rode seven days, day and night, without stopping an instant."

"But the man you spoke of just now?"

"Wait a minute. Constantly followed by a wild-looking fellow who had relays like himself and who rode as far as he did for the four hundred leagues, the poor courier constantly expected to be shot in his back. Both reached the

Saint Marcel gate at the same time, both galloped down the Rue Mouffetard, both crossed the city. But at the end of the bridge of Notre-Dame our courier turned to the right, while the other took the road to the left by the Place du Châtelet, and sped along the quays by the side of the Louvre, like an arrow from a bow."

"Thanks, my good Henriette, thanks!" cried Marguerite. "You are right; that is very interesting news. By whom was the other courier sent? I must know. So leave me until this evening. Rue Tizon, is it not? and the hunt to-morrow. Do take a frisky horse, so that he will run away, and we can be by ourselves. I will tell you this evening what is necessary for you to try and find out from your Coconnas."

"You will not forget my letter?" said the duchess of Nevers smiling.

"No, no, do not worry; he shall have it, and at once."

Madame de Nevers left, and Marguerite immediately sent for Henry, who came to her quickly. She gave him the letter from the Duc de Nevers.

"Oh! oh!" he exclaimed.

Then Marguerite told him about the second courier.

"Yes," said Henry; "I saw him enter the Louvre."

"Perhaps he was for the queen mother."

"No, I am sure of that, for I ventured to take my stand in the corridor, and I saw no one pass."

"Then," said Marguerite, looking at her husband, "he must be"—

"For your brother D'Alençon, must he not?" said Henry.

"Yes; but how can we be sure?"

"Could not one of his two gentlemen be sent for?" said Henry, carelessly, "and through him"—

"You are right," said Marguerite, put at her ease at her husband's suggestion. "I will send for Monsieur de la Mole. Gillonne! Gillonne!"

The young girl appeared.

"I must speak at once with Monsieur de la Mole," said the queen. "Try to find him and bring him here."

Gillonne disappeared. Henry seated himself before a table on which was a German book containing engravings by Albert Durer, which he began to examine with such close attention that when La Mole entered he did not seem to hear him, and did not even raise his head.

On his side, the young man, seeing the king with Marguerite, stopped on the threshold, silent from surprise and pale from anxiety.

Marguerite went to him.

"Monsieur de la Mole," said she, "can you tell me who is on guard to-day at Monsieur d'Alençon's?"

"Coconnas, madame," said La Mole.

"Try to find out for me from him if he admitted to his master's room a man covered with mud, who apparently had a long or hasty ride."

"Ah, madame, I fear he will not tell me; for several days he has been very taciturn."

"Indeed! But by giving him this note, it seems to me that he will owe you something in exchange."

"From the duchess! Oh, with this note I will try."

"Add," said Marguerite, lowering her voice, "that this note will serve him as a means of gaining entrance this evening to the house you know about."

"And I, madame," said La Mole, in a low tone, "what shall be mine?"

"Give your name. That will be enough."

"Give me the note, madame," said La Mole, with throbbing heart, "I will bring back the answer."

He withdrew.

"We shall know to-morrow if the duke has been informed of the Poland affair," said Marguerite calmly, turning to her husband.

"That Monsieur de la Mole is really a fine servant," said the Béarnais, with his peculiar smile, "and, by Heaven! I will make his fortune!"

CHAPTER XXIX.

THE DEPARTURE.

When on the following day a beautiful sun, red but rayless, as is apt to be the case on privileged days of winter, rose behind the hills of Paris, everything had already been awake for two hours in the court of the Louvre. A magnificent Barbary horse, nervous and spirited, with limbs like those of a stag, on which the veins crossed one another like network, pawed the ground, pricked up his ears and snorted, while waiting for Charles IX. He was less impatient, however, than his master who, detained by Catharine, had been stopped by her in the hall. She had said she wished to speak to him on a matter of importance. Both were in the corridor with the glass windows. Catharine was cold, pale, and quiet as usual. Charles IX. fretted, bit his nails, and whipped his two favorite dogs. The latter were covered with cuirasses of mail, so that the snout of the wild boar should not harm them, and that they might be able to encounter the terrible animal with impunity. A small scutcheon with the arms of France had been stitched on their breasts similar to those on the breasts of the pages, who, more than once, had envied the privileges of these happy favorites.

"Pay attention, Charles," said Catharine, "no one but you and I knows as yet of the expected arrival of these Polonais. But, God forgive me, the King of Navarre acts as if he knew. In spite of his abjuration, which I always mistrust, he is in communication with the Huguenots. Have you noticed how often he has gone out the past few days? He has money, too, he who has never had any. He buys horses, arms, and on rainy days he practises fencing from morning until night."

"Well, my God, mother!" exclaimed Charles IX., impatiently, "do you think he intends to kill me, or my brother D'Anjou? In that case he will need a few more lessons, for yesterday I counted eleven buttonholes with my foil on his doublet, which, however, had only six. And as to my brother D'Anjou, you know that he fences as well if not better than I do; at least so people say."

"Listen, Charles," continued Catharine, "and do not treat lightly what your mother tells you. The ambassadors will arrive; well, you will see! As soon as they are in Paris, Henry will do all he can to gain their attention. He is insinuating, he is crafty; without mentioning his wife who seconds him, I know not why, and will chat with them, and talk Latin, Greek, Hungarian, and I know not what, to them! Oh, I tell you, Charles,—and you know that I am not mistaken,—I tell you that there is something on foot."

Just then the clock struck and Charles IX. stopped listening to his mother to count the strokes.

"Good heavens! seven o'clock!" he exclaimed, "one hour before we get off, that will make it eight; one hour to reach the meeting-place, and to start again —we shall not be able to begin hunting before nine o'clock. Really, mother, you make me lose a great deal of time! Down, Risquetout! great Heavens! down, I say, you brigand!"

And a vigorous blow of the bloody whip on the mastiff's back brought a howl of real pain from the poor beast, thoroughly astonished at receiving punishment in exchange for a caress.

"Charles!" said Catharine, "listen to me, in God's name, and do not leave to chance your fortune and that of France! The hunt, the hunt, the hunt, you cry; why, you will have time enough to hunt when your work of king is settled."

"Come now, mother!" exclaimed Charles, pale with impatience, "explain quickly, for you bother me to death. Really, there are days when I cannot comprehend you."

He stopped beating his whip against his boot.

Catharine thought that the time had come and that it should not be passed by.

"My son," said she, "we have proof that De Mouy has returned to Paris. Monsieur de Maurevel, whom you are well acquainted with, has seen him. This can be only for the King of Navarre. That is enough, I trust, for us to suspect him more than ever."

"Come, there you go again after my poor Henriot! You want me to have him killed; do you not?"

"Oh, no."

"Exiled? But why can you not see that if he were exiled he would be much more dangerous than he will ever be here, in the Louvre, under our eyes, where he can do nothing without our knowing it at once?"

"Therefore I do not wish him exiled."

"What do you want, then? Tell me quickly!"

"I want him to be held in safe keeping while these Polonais are here; in the Bastille, for instance."

"Ah! my faith, no!" cried Charles IX. "We are going to hunt the boar this morning and Henry is one of my best men. Without him the fun would be spoiled. By Heaven, mother! really, you do nothing but vex me."

"Why, my dear son, I did not say this morning. The ambassadors do not arrive until to-morrow or the day after. Arrest him after your hunt, this evening—to-night"—

"That is a different matter. Well, we will talk about it later and see. After the hunt I will not refuse. Adieu! Come here, Risquetout! Is it your turn to sulk now?"

"Charles," said Catharine, laying a detaining hand on his arm at the risk of a fresh explosion which might result from this new delay, "I think that the best thing to do is to sign the order for arrest at once, even though it is not to be carried out until this evening or to-night."

"Sign, write an order, look up a seal for the parchment when they are waiting for me to go hunting, I, who never keep anyone waiting! The devil take the thought!"

"Why, no, I love you too dearly to delay you. I arranged everything beforehand; step in here and see!"

And Catharine, as agile as if she were only twenty years old, pushed open a door of her cabinet, and pointed to an ink-stand, pen, parchment, the seal, and a lighted candle.

The king took the parchment and read it through hastily.

"Order, etc., etc., to arrest and conduct to the Bastille our brother Henry of Navarre."

"Good, that is done!" he exclaimed, signing hurriedly. "Adieu, mother."

He hastened from the room, followed by his dogs, greatly pleased to have gotten rid of Catharine so easily.

Charles IX. had been waited for with impatience, and as his promptness in hunting matters was well known, every one wondered at the delay. So when he finally appeared, the hunters welcomed him by shouts of "Long live the King!" the outriders by a flourish of trumpets, the horses by neighing, the dogs by barking. All this noise and hubbub brought a flush to his pale cheeks, his heart swelled, and for a moment Charles was young and happy.

The King scarcely took the time to salute the brilliant company gathered in the court-yard. He nodded to the Duc d'Alençon, waved his hand to his sister Marguerite, passed Henry without apparently seeing him, and sprang upon the fiery Barbary horse, which started off at once. But after curvetting around three or four times, he realized what sort of a rider he had to deal with and quieted down. The trumpets again sounded, and the King left the Louvre followed by the Duc d'Alençon, the King of Navarre, Marguerite, Madame de Nevers, Madame de Sauve, Tavannes, and the principal courtiers.

It goes without saying that La Mole and Coconnas were of the number.

As to the Duc d'Anjou, he had been at the siege of La Rochelle for three months.

While waiting for the King, Henry had spoken to his wife, who in returning his greeting had whispered,

"The courier from Rome was admitted by Monsieur de Coconnas himself to the chamber of the Duc d'Alençon a quarter of an hour before the messenger from the Duc de Nevers saw the King."

"Then he knows all," said Henry.

"He must know all," replied Marguerite; "but keep your eyes on him and see how, in spite of his usual dissimulation, his eyes shine."

"*Ventre saint gris!*" murmured the Béarnais. "I should think they would; he hunts triple game to-day: France, Poland, and Navarre, without counting the wild boar."

He bowed to his wife, returned to his place, and calling one of his servants whose ancestors had been in the service of his father for more than a century, and whom he employed as ordinary messenger in his love affairs:

"Orthon," said he, "take this key to the cousin of Madame de Sauve, who you know lives with his mistress at the corner of the Rue des Quatre Fils. Say to him that his cousin desires to speak to him this evening; that he is to enter my room, and, in case I am not there, to wait for me. If I am late, he is to lie down on my bed."

"Is there an answer, sire?"

"No, except to tell me if you find him. The key is for him alone, you understand?"

"Yes, sire."

"Wait; do not start now, plague you! Before leaving Paris I will call you to tighten my saddle-girths; in that way you will naturally have to lag behind, and you can carry out your commission and join us at Bondy."

The servant made a sign of obedience and rode away.

They set out by the Rue Saint Honoré, through the Rue Saint Denis, and the Faubourg. At the Rue Saint Laurent the saddle-girths of the King of Navarre became loose. Orthon rode up to him, and everything happened as had been agreed on between him and his master, who followed the royal procession along the Rue des Récollets, where his faithful servant sought the Rue du Temple.

When Henry overtook the King, Charles was engaged in such an interesting conversation with the Duc d'Alençon, on the subject of the weather, the age of the wild boar which was a recluse, and as to where he had made his lair, that he did not notice, or pretended he did not notice, that Henry had lagged behind a moment.

In the meantime Marguerite had watched each countenance from afar and thought she perceived a certain embarrassment in the eyes of her brother every time she looked at him. Madame de Nevers was abandoning herself to mad gayety, for Coconnas, supremely happy that day, was making numberless jokes near her to make the ladies laugh.

As to La Mole he had already twice found an opportunity to kiss Marguerite's white scarf with gold fringe, without the act, which was carried out with the skill usual to lovers, having been seen by more than three or four.

About a quarter-past eight they reached Bondy. The first thought of Charles IX. was to find out if the wild boar had held out.

The boar was in his lair, and the outrider who had turned him aside answered for him. A breakfast was ready. The King drank a glass of Hungarian wine. Charles IX. invited the ladies to take seats at table, and in his impatience to pass away the time set out to visit the kennels and the roosts, giving orders not to unsaddle his horse, as he said he had never had a better or a stronger mount.

While the King was taking this stroll, the Duc de Guise arrived. He was armed for war rather than for hunting, and was accompanied by twenty or thirty gentlemen equipped in like manner. He asked at once for the King, joined him, and returned talking with him.

At exactly nine o'clock the King himself gave the signal to start, and each one mounted and set out to the meet. During the ride Henry found another opportunity to be near his wife.

"Well," said he, "do you know anything new?"

"No," replied Marguerite, "unless it is that my brother Charles looks at you strangely."

"I have noticed it," said Henry.

"Have you taken precautions?"

"I have on a coat of mail, and at my side a good Spanish hunting knife, as sharp as a razor, and as pointed as a needle. I could pierce pistols with it."

"In that case," said Marguerite, "God protect you!"

The outrider in charge of the hunt made a sign. They had reached the lair.

CHAPTER XXX.

MAUREVEL.

While all this careless, light-hearted youth, apparently so at least, was scattering like a gilded whirlwind along the road to Bondy, Catharine, still rolling up the precious parchment to which King Charles had just affixed his signature, admitted into her room a man to whom, a few days before, her captain of the guards had carried a letter, addressed to Rue de la Cerisaie, near the Arsenal.

A broad silk band like a badge of mourning hid one of the man's eyes, showing only the other eye, two prominent cheek-bones, and the curve of a vulture's nose, while a grayish beard covered the lower part of his face. He wore a long thick cloak, beneath which one might have imagined a whole arsenal. Besides this, although it was not the custom of those called to court, he wore at his side a long campaign sword, broad, and with a double blade. One of his hands was hidden beneath his cloak, and never left the handle of a long dagger.

"Ah! you here, monsieur?" said the queen seating herself; "you know that I promised you after Saint Bartholomew, when you rendered us such signal service, not to let you be idle. The opportunity has arisen, or rather I have made it. Thank me, therefore."

"Madame, I humbly thank your majesty," replied the man with the black bandage, in a reserved voice at once low and insolent.

"A fine opportunity; you will not find another such in your whole life. Make the most of it, therefore."

"I am waiting, madame, only after the preamble, I fear"—

"That the commission may not be much? Are not those who wish to advance fond of such commissions? The one of which I speak would be envied by the Tavannes and even by the De Guises."

"Ah! madame," said the man, "believe me, I am at your majesty's orders, whatever they may be."

"In that case, read," said Catharine.

She handed him the parchment. The man read it and grew pale.

"What!" he exclaimed, "an order to arrest the King of Navarre!"

"Well! what is there strange in that?"

"But a king, madame! Really, I think—I fear I am not of sufficiently high rank."

"My confidence makes you the first gentleman of my court, Monsieur de Maurevel," said Catharine.

"I thank your majesty," said the assassin so moved that he seemed to hesitate.

"You will obey, then?"

"If your majesty orders it, is it not my duty?"

"Yes, I order it."

"Then I will obey."

"How shall you go to work?"

"Why, madame, I do not know, I should greatly like to be guided by your majesty."

"You fear noise?"

"I admit it."

"Take a dozen sure men, if necessary."

"I understand, of course, that your majesty will permit me to do the best I can for myself, and I am grateful to you for this; but where shall I arrest the King of Navarre?"

"Where would it best please you to arrest him?"

"In some place in which I should be warranted in doing so, if possible, even by his Majesty."

"Yes, I understand, in some royal palace; what do you say to the Louvre, for instance?"

"Oh, if your majesty would permit it, that would be a great favor."

"You will arrest him, then, in the Louvre."

"In what part?"

"In his own room."

Maurevel bowed.

"When, madame?"

"This evening, or rather to-night."

"Very well, madame. Now, will your majesty deign to inform me on one point?"

"On what point?"

"About the respect due to his position."

"Respect! position!" said Catharine, "why, then, you do not know, monsieur, that the King of France owes respect to no one in his kingdom, whoever he may be, recognizing no position as equal to his own?"

Maurevel bowed a second time.

"I insist on this point, however, madame, if your majesty will allow me."

"I will, monsieur."

"If the king contests the authenticity of the order, which is not probable, but"—

"On the contrary, monsieur, he is sure to do so."

"He will contest it?"

"Without a doubt."

"And consequently he will refuse to obey it?"

"I fear so."

"And he will resist?"

"Probably."

"Ah! the devil!" said Maurevel; "and in that case"—

"In what case?" said Catharine, not moving her eyes from him.

"Why, in case he resists, what is to be done?"

"What do you do when you are given an order from the King, that is, when you represent the King, and when there is any resistance, Monsieur de Maurevel?"

"Why, madame," said the sbirro, "when I am honored with such an order, and when this order refers to a simple gentleman, I kill him."

"I told you, monsieur," said Catharine, "and I scarcely think that sufficient time has elapsed for you to have forgotten it, that the King of France recognizes no position in his kingdom, and that after him the greatest are simple gentlemen."

Maurevel grew pale, for he was beginning to comprehend.

"Oh! oh!" he cried, "kill the King of Navarre?"

"Why, who is speaking of killing him? Where is the order to kill him? The King wishes him taken to the Bastille, and the order contains nothing more. If he lets himself be arrested, very good; but as he will not let himself be arrested, as he will resist, as he will endeavor to kill you"—

Maurevel grew paler.

"You will defend yourself," continued Catharine. "One cannot ask a brave man like you to let himself be killed without defending himself; and in defending yourself, what can you expect? You must let come what may. You understand me, do you not?"

"Yes, madame; and yet"—

"Come, do you want me to write *dead or alive* after the words *order to arrest*?"

"I confess, madame, that that would do away with my scruples."

"Well, it must be done, of course, since you do not think the order can be carried out without it."

And Catharine shrugged her shoulders, unrolled the parchment with one hand, and wrote with the other: "*dead or alive.*"

"Now," said she, "do you consider the order all right?"

"Yes, madame," replied Maurevel; "but I beg your majesty to leave the carrying out of the entire affair to me."

"What have I said that will interfere with it?"

"Your majesty told me to take a dozen men."

"Yes, to make sure"—

"Well, I ask permission to take only six."

"Why so?"

"Because, madame, if anything happens to the prince, as it probably will, it would be easy to excuse six men for having been afraid of losing the prisoner, but no one would excuse a dozen guards for not having let half of their number be killed before laying hands on royalty."

"Fine royalty, in truth, which has no kingdom."

"Madame," said Maurevel, "it is not the kingdom which makes the king: it is birth."

"Very well," said Catharine; "do as you please. Only I must warn you that I do not wish you to leave the Louvre."

"But, madame, to get my men together?"

"Have you not a sort of sergeant whom you can charge with this duty?"

"I have my lackey, who not only is a faithful fellow, but who has even occasionally aided me in this sort of thing."

"Send for him, and confer with him. You know the chamber hung with the King's arms, do you not? Well, your breakfast shall be served there; and from there you shall give your orders. The place will aid you to collect your wits in case they are scattered. Then when my son returns from the hunt, you are to go into my oratory, and wait until the time comes."

"But how are we to get into the room? Probably the king suspects something, and he will shut himself up in it."

"I have a duplicate key to every door," said Catharine, "and the bolts have been removed from Henry's room. Adieu, Monsieur de Maurevel, for a while. I will have you taken to the King's armory. Ah! by the way! remember that the order of a King must be carried out before anything else. No excuse is admissible; a defeat, even a failure, would compromise the honor of the King. It is a serious matter."

And Catharine, without giving Maurevel time to answer, called Monsieur de Nancey, the captain of the guards, and ordered him to conduct Maurevel to the king's armory.

"My God!" exclaimed Maurevel as he followed his guide, "I have risen to the hierarchy of assassination; from a simple gentleman to a captain, from a captain to an admiral, from an admiral to a king without a crown. Who knows if I shall not some day be a king with a crown!"

CHAPTER XXXI.

THE HUNT.

The outrider who had turned aside the boar and who had told the King that the animal had not left the place was not mistaken. Scarcely were the bloodhounds put on the trail before it plunged into the thickets, and from a cluster of thorn bushes drove out the boar which the outrider had recognized by its track. It was a recluse; that is, the strangest kind of animal.

It started straight ahead and crossed the road fifty feet from the King, followed only by the bloodhound which had driven it back. The first relay of dogs was at once let loose, twenty in number, which sprang after it.

Hunting was Charles' chief passion. Scarcely had the animal crossed the road before he started after it, followed by the Duc d'Alençon and Henry, to whom a sign had indicated that he must not leave Charles.

The rest of the hunters followed the King.

At the time of which we are writing, the royal forests were far from being what they are to-day, great parks intersected by carriage roads. Then traffic was almost wanting. Kings had not yet conceived the idea of being merchants, and of dividing their woods into fellings, copses, and forests. The trees, planted, not by learned foresters, but by the hand of God, who threw the grain to the will of the winds, were not arranged in quincunxes, but grew as they pleased, as they do to-day in any virginal forest of America. In short, a forest in those days was a den of the wild boar, the stag, the wolf, and robbers; and a dozen paths starting from one point starred that of Bondy, surrounded by a circular road as the circle of a wheel surrounds its fellies.

To carry the comparison further, the nave would not be a bad representation of the single point where the parties meet in the centre of the wood, where the wandering hunters rally to start out again towards the point where the lost animal again appears.

At the end of a quarter of an hour there happened what always happens in such cases. Insurmountable obstacles rose in the path of the hunters, the cries of the dogs were lost in the distance, and the King returned to the meeting-place cursing and swearing as was his habit.

"Well, D'Alençon! Well, Henriot!" said he, "there you are, by Heaven, as calm and unruffled as nuns following their abbess. That is not hunting. Why, D'Alençon, you look as though you had just stepped out of a band-box, and you are so saturated with perfumery that if you were to pass between the boar and my dogs, you might put them off the scent. And you, Henry, where is your spear, your musket? Let us see!"

"Sire," said Henry, "of what use is a musket? I know that your Majesty likes to shoot the beast when the dogs have caught it. As to a spear, I am clumsy enough with this weapon, which is not much used among our mountains, where we hunt the bear with a simple dagger."

"By Heavens, Henry, when you return to your Pyrenees you will have to send me a whole cartload of bears. It must be a pretty hunt that is carried on at such close quarters with an animal which might strangle us. Listen, I think I hear the dogs. No, I am mistaken." The King took his horn and blew a blast; several horns answered him. Suddenly an outrider appeared who blew another blast.

"The boar! the boar!" cried the King.

He galloped off, followed by the rest of the hunters who had rallied round him.

The outrider was not mistaken. As the King advanced they began to hear the barking of the pack, which consisted of more than sixty dogs, for one after another they had let loose all the relays placed at the points the boar had already passed. The King saw the boar again, and taking advantage of a clump of high trees, he rushed after him, blowing his horn with all his might.

For some time the princes followed him. But the King had such a strong horse and was so carried away by his ardor, and he rode over such rough roads and through such thick underbrush, that at first the ladies, then the Duc de Guise and his gentlemen, and finally the two princes, were forced to abandon him. Tavannes held out for a time longer, but at length he too gave up.

Except Charles and a few outriders who, excited over a promised reward, would not leave the King, everyone had gathered about the open space in the centre of the wood. The two princes were together on a narrow path, the Duc de Guise and his gentlemen had halted a hundred feet from them. Further on were the ladies.

"Does it not really seem," said the Duc d'Alençon to Henry, indicating by a wink the Duc de Guise, "that that man with his escort sheathed in steel is the real king? Poor princes that we are, he does not even honor us by a glance."

"Why should he treat us better than we treat our own relatives?" replied Henry. "Why, brother, are not you and I prisoners at the court of France, hostages from our party?"

Duc François started at these words, and looked at Henry as if to provoke further explanation; but Henry had said more than he usually did and was silent.

"What do you mean, Henry?" asked the Duc François, visibly annoyed that his brother-in-law by stopping had left him to open the conversation.

"I say, brother," said Henry, "that all these men who are so well armed, whose duty seems to be not to lose sight of us, look exactly like guards preventing two people from running away."

"Running away? why? how?" asked D'Alençon, admirably successful in his pretended surprise and innocence.

"You have a magnificent mount, François," said Henry, following out his thoughts, while apparently changing the conversation. "I am sure he could make seven leagues in an hour, and twenty between now and noon. It is a fine day. And one feels like saying good-by. See the beautiful cross-road. Does it not tempt you, François? As to me, my spurs burn me."

François did not reply. But he first turned red and then white. Then he bent his head, as if listening for sounds from the hunters.

"The news from Poland is having its effect," said Henry, "and my dear brother-in-law has his plans. He would like me to escape, but I shall not do so by myself."

Scarcely had this thought passed through his mind before several new converts, who had come to court during the past two or three months, galloped up and smiled pleasantly on the two princes. The Duc d'Alençon, provoked by Henry's remarks, had but one word to say, one gesture to make, and it was evident that thirty or forty horsemen, who at that moment gathered around them as though to oppose the troop belonging to Monsieur de Guise, favored his flight; but he turned aside his head, and, raising his horn to his lips, he sounded the rally. But the newcomers, as if they thought that the hesitation on the part of the Duc d'Alençon was due to the presence of the followers of the De Guises, had by degrees glided among them and the two princes, and had drawn themselves up in echelons with a strategic skill which showed the usual military disposition. In fact, to reach the Duc d'Alençon and the King of Navarre it would have been necessary to pass through this company, while, as far as eye could reach, a perfectly free road stretched out before the brothers.

Suddenly from among the trees, ten feet from the King of Navarre, another gentleman appeared, as yet unperceived by the two princes. Henry was trying to think who he was, when the gentleman raised his hat and Henry recognized him as the Vicomte de Turenne, one of the leaders of the Protestant party, who was supposed to be in Poitou.

The vicomte even ventured to make a sign which clearly meant,

"Will you come?"

But having consulted the impassable face and dull eye of the Duc d'Alençon, Henry turned his head two or three times over his shoulder as if something was the matter with his neck or doublet.

This was a refusal. The vicomte understood it, put both spurs to his horse and disappeared in the thicket. At that moment the pack was heard approaching, then they saw the boar followed by the dogs cross the end of the path where they were all gathered; then Charles IX., like an infernal hunter, hatless, the horn at his mouth blowing enough to burst his lungs; three or four outriders followed. Tavannes had disappeared.

"The King!" cried the Duc d'Alençon, and he rode after him.

Reassured by the presence of his good friends, Henry signed to them not to leave, and advanced towards the ladies.

"Well!" said Marguerite, taking a few steps towards him.

"Well, madame," said Henry, "we are hunting the wild boar."

"Is that all?"

"Yes, the wind has changed since morning; but I believe you predicted this."

"These changes of the wind are bad for hunting, are they not, monsieur?" asked Marguerite.

"Yes," said Henry; "they sometimes upset all plans, which have to be made over again." Just then the barking of the dogs began to be heard as they rapidly approached, and a sort of noisy dust warned the hunters to be on their guard. Each one raised his head and listened.

Almost immediately the boar appeared again, but instead of returning to the woods, he followed the road that led directly to the open space where were the ladies, the gentlemen paying court to them, and the hunters who had given up the chase.

Behind the animal came thirty or forty great dogs, panting; then, twenty feet behind them, King Charles without hat or cloak, his clothes torn by the thorns, his face and hands covered with blood.

One or two outriders were with him.

The King stopped blowing his horn only to urge on his dogs, and stopped urging on his dogs only to return to his horn. He saw no one. Had his horse stumbled, he might have cried out as did Richard III.: "My kingdom for a horse!" But the horse seemed as eager as his master. His feet did not touch the ground, and his nostrils breathed forth fire. Boar, dogs, and King passed like a dream.

"Halloo! halloo!" cried the King as he went by, raising the horn to his bloody lips.

A few feet behind him came the Duc d'Alençon and two outriders. But the horses of the others had given out or else they were lost.

Everyone started after the King, for it was evident that the boar would soon be taken.

In fact, at the end of about ten minutes the animal left the path it had been following, and sprang into the bushes; but reaching an open space, it ran to a rock and faced the dogs.

At the shouts from Charles, who had followed it, everyone drew near.

They arrived at an interesting point in the chase. The boar seemed determined to make a desperate defence. The dogs, excited by a run of more than three hours, rushed on it with a fury which increased the shouts and the oaths of the King.

All the hunters formed a circle, the King somewhat in advance, behind him the Duc d'Alençon armed with a musket, and Henry, who had nothing but his simple hunting knife.

The Duc d'Alençon unfastened his musket and lighted the match. Henry moved his knife in its sheath.

As to the Duc de Guise, disdainful of all the details of hunting, he stood somewhat apart from the others with his gentlemen. The women, gathered together in a group, formed a counterpart to that of the duke.

Everyone who was anything of a hunter stood with eyes fixed on the animal in anxious expectation.

To one side an outrider was endeavoring to restrain the King's two mastiffs, which, encased in their coats of mail, were waiting to take the boar by the ears, howling and jumping about in such a manner that every instant one might think they would burst their chains.

The boar made a wonderful resistance. Attacked at once by forty or more dogs, which enveloped it like a roaring tide, which covered it by their motley carpet, which on all sides was striving to reach its skin, wrinkled with bristles, at each blow of its snout it hurled a dog ten feet in the air. The dogs fell back, torn to pieces, and, with entrails dragging, at once returned to the fray. Charles, with hair on end, bloodshot eyes, and inflated nostrils, leaned over the neck of his dripping horse shouting furious "halloos!"

In less than ten minutes twenty dogs were out of the fight.

"The mastiffs!" cried Charles; "the mastiffs!"

At this shout the outrider opened the carbine-swivels of the leashes, and the two bloodhounds rushed into the midst of the carnage, overturning everything, scattering everything, making a way with their coats of mail to the animal, which they seized by the ear.

The boar, knowing that it was caught, clinched its teeth both from rage and pain.

"Bravo, Duredent! Bravo, Risquetout!" cried Charles. "Courage, dogs! A spear! a spear!"

"Do you not want my musket?" said the Duc d'Alençon.

"No," cried the King, "no; one cannot feel a bullet when he shoots; there is no fun in it; but one can feel a spear. A spear! a spear!"

They handed the King a hunting spear hardened by fire and armed with a steel point.

"Take care, brother!" cried Marguerite.

"Come! come!" cried the Duchesse de Nevers. "Do not miss, sire. Give the beast a good stab!"

"Be easy, duchess!" said Charles.

Couching his lance, he darted at the boar which, held by the two bloodhounds, could not escape the blow. But at sight of the shining lance it turned to one side, and the weapon, instead of sinking into its breast, glided over its shoulder and blunted itself against the rock to which the animal had run.

"A thousand devils!" cried the King. "I have missed him. A spear! a spear!"

And bending back, as horsemen do when they are going to take a fence, he hurled his useless lance from him.

An outrider advanced and offered him another.

But at that moment, as though it foresaw the fate which awaited it, and which it wished to resist, by a violent effort the boar snatched its torn ears from the teeth of the bloodhounds, and with eyes bloody, protruding, hideous, its breath burning like the heat from a furnace, with chattering teeth and lowered head it sprang at the King's horse. Charles was too good a hunter not to have foreseen this. He turned his horse, which began to rear, but he had miscalculated the pressure, and the horse, too tightly reined in, or perhaps giving way to his fright, fell over backwards. The spectators gave a terrible cry: the horse had fallen, and the King's leg was under him.

"Your hand, sire, give me your hand," said Henry.

The King let go his horse's bridle, seized the saddle with his left hand, and tried to draw out his hunting knife with his right; but the knife, pressed into his belt by the weight of his body, would not come from its sheath.

"The boar! the boar!" cried Charles; "it is on me, D'Alençon! on me!"

The horse, recovering himself as if he understood his master's danger, stretched his muscles, and had already succeeded in getting up on its three legs, when, at the cry from his brother, Henry saw the Duc François grow frightfully pale and raise the musket to his shoulder, but, instead of striking the boar, which was but two feet from the King, the ball broke the knee of the horse, which fell down again, his nose touching the ground. At that instant the boar, with its snout, tore Charles's boot.

"Oh!" murmured D'Alençon with ashy lips, "I suppose that the Duc d'Anjou is King of France, and that I am King of Poland."

The boar was about to attack Charles's leg, when suddenly the latter felt someone raise his arm; then he saw the flash of a sharp-pointed blade which was driven into the shoulder of the boar and disappeared up to its guard, while a hand gloved in steel turned aside the head already poked under his clothes.

As the horse had risen, Charles had succeeded in freeing his leg, and now raising himself heavily, he saw that he was dripping with blood, whereupon he became as pale as a corpse.

"Sire," said Henry, who still knelt holding the boar pierced to the heart, "sire, it is nothing, I turned aside the teeth, and your Majesty is not hurt."

Then he rose, let go the knife, and the boar fell back pouring forth more blood from its mouth than from its wound.

Charles, surrounded by a breathless crowd, assailed by cries of terror which would have dashed the greatest courage, was for a moment ready to fall on the dying animal. But he recovered himself and, turning toward the King of Navarre, he pressed his hand with a look in which shone the first spark of feeling that had been roused in his heart for twenty-four years.

"Thank you, Henriot!" said he.

"My poor brother!" cried D'Alençon, approaching Charles.

"Ah! it is you, D'Alençon, is it?" said the King. "Well, famous marksman that you are, what became of your ball?"

"It must have flattened itself against the boar," said the duke.

"Well! my God!" exclaimed Henry, with admirably assumed surprise; "you see, François, your bullet has broken the leg of his Majesty's horse. That is strange!"

"What!" said the King; "is that true?"

"It is possible," said the duke terrified; "my hand shook so!"

"The fact is that for a clever marksman that was a strange thing to do, François!" said Charles frowning. "A second time, Henriot, I thank you!"

"Gentlemen," continued the King, "let us return to Paris; I have had enough of this."

Marguerite came up to congratulate Henry.

"Yes, indeed, Margot," said Charles, "congratulate him, and sincerely too, for without him the King of France would be Henry III."

"Alas, madame," said the Béarnais, "Monsieur le Duc d'Anjou, who is already my enemy, will be angrier than ever at me. But what can you expect? One does what one can. Ask Monsieur d'Alençon."

And bowing, he drew his knife from the wild boar's body and dug it two or three times into the earth to wipe off the blood.

PART II.

———

CHAPTER XXXII.

FRATERNITY.

In saving the life of Charles, Henry had done more than save the life of a man,—he had prevented three kingdoms from changing sovereigns.

Had Charles IX. been killed, the Duc d'Anjou would have become King of France, and the Duc d'Alençon in all probability would have been King of Poland. As to Navarre, as Monsieur le Duc d'Anjou was the lover of Madame de Condé, its crown would probably have paid to the husband the complacency of his wife. Now in all this no good would have come to Henry. He would have changed masters, that would have been all. Instead of Charles IX. who tolerated him, he would have seen the Duc d'Anjou on the throne of France, and being of one heart and mind with his mother Catharine, the latter had sworn that he should die, and he would not have failed to keep his oath. All these thoughts entered his mind when the wild boar sprang at Charles IX., and we know that the result of his rapid thinking was that his own life was attached to that of Charles IX.

Charles IX. had been saved by an act of devotion, the motive of which the King could not fathom. But Marguerite had understood, and she had admired that strange courage of Henry which, like flashes of lightning, shone only in a storm.

Unfortunately it was not all to have escaped the kingdom of the Duc d'Anjou. Henry had to make himself king. He had to dispute Navarre with the Duc d'Alençon and with the Prince of Condé; above all he had to leave the court where one walked only between two precipices, and go away protected by a son of France.

As he returned from Bondy Henry pondered deeply on the situation. On arriving at the Louvre his plan was formed. Without removing his riding-boots, just as he was, covered with dust and blood, he betook himself to the apartments of the Duc d'Alençon, whom he found striding up and down in great agitation.

On perceiving him the prince gave a start of surprise.

"Yes," said Henry, taking him by both hands; "yes, I understand, my good brother, you are angry because I was the first to call the King's attention to the fact that your ball struck the leg of his horse instead of the boar, as you intended it should. But what can you expect? I could not prevent an exclamation of surprise. Besides, the King would have noticed it, would he not?"

"No doubt, no doubt," murmured D'Alençon. "And yet I can think of it only as an evil intention on your part to denounce me as you did, and which, as you yourself saw, had no result except to make my brother Charles suspect me, and to make hard feeling between us."

"We will return to this in a few moments. As to my good or evil intentions regarding you, I have come to you on purpose that you may judge them."

"Very good!" said D'Alençon with his customary reserve. "Speak, Henry, I am listening."

"When I have spoken, François, you will readily see what my intentions are, for the confidence I am going to place in you does away with all reserve and prudence. And when I have told you, you will be able to ruin me by a single word!"

"What is it?" said François, beginning to be anxious.

"And yet," continued Henry, "I have hesitated a long time to speak to you of the thing which brings me here, especially after the way in which you turned a deaf ear to-day."

"Really," said François, growing pale, "I do not know what you mean, Henry."

"Brother, your interests are too dear to me not to tell you that the Huguenots have made advances to me."

"Advances!" said D'Alençon. "What advances?"

"One of them, Monsieur de Mouy of Saint Phal, the son of the brave De Mouy, assassinated by Maurevel, you know"—

"Yes."

"Well, he came at the risk of his life to show me that I was in captivity."

"Ah! indeed! and what did you say to him?"

"Brother, you know that I love Charles dearly. He has saved my life, and the queen mother has been like a real mother to me. So I refused all the offers he made me."

"What were these offers?"

"The Huguenots want to reconstruct the throne of Navarre, and as in reality this throne belongs to me by inheritance, they offered it to me."

"Yes; and Monsieur de Mouy, instead of the consent he expected to ask for, has received your relinquishment?"

"My formal relinquishment—even in writing. But since," continued Henry.

"You have repented, brother?" interrupted D'Alençon.

"No, I merely thought I noticed that Monsieur de Mouy had become discontented with me, and was paying his visits elsewhere."

"Where?" asked François quickly.

"I do not know. At the Prince of Condé's perhaps."

"Yes, that might be," said the duke.

"Besides," went on Henry, "I have positive knowledge as to the leader he has chosen."

François grew pale.

"But," continued Henry, "the Huguenots are divided among themselves, and De Mouy, brave and loyal as he is, represents only one-half of the party. Now this other half, which is not to be scorned, has not given up the hope of having Henry of Navarre on the throne, who having hesitated at first may have reflected since."

"You think this?"

"Oh, every day I receive proofs of it. The troops which joined us at the hunt, did you notice of what men it was composed?"

"Yes, of converted gentlemen."

"Did you recognize the leader of the troop who signed to me?"

"Yes, it was the Vicomte de Turenne."

"Did you know what they wanted ofme?"

"Yes, they proposed to you to escape."

"Then," said Henry to François, who was growing restless, "there is evidently a second party which wants something else besides what Monsieur de Mouy wants."

"A second party?"

"Yes, and a very powerful one, I tell you, so that in order to succeed it is necessary to unite the two—Turenne and De Mouy. The conspiracy progresses, the troops are ready, the signal alone is waited for. Now in this supreme situation, which demands prompt solution on my part, I have come to two decisions between which I am wavering. I have come to submit these decisions to you as to a friend."

"Say rather as to a brother."

"Yes, as to a brother," went on Henry.

"Speak, then, I am listening."

"In the first place I ought to explain to you the condition of my mind, my dear François. No desire, no ambition, no ability. I am an honest country gentleman, poor, sensual, and timid. The career of conspirator offers me indignities poorly compensated for even by the certain prospect of a crown."

"Ah, brother," said François, "you do wrong. Sad indeed is the position of a prince whose fortune is limited by the boundary of the paternal estate or by a man in a career for honors! I do not believe, therefore, in what you tell me."

"And yet what I tell you is so true, brother, that if I thought I had a true friend, I would resign in his favor the power which this party wishes to give me; but," he added with a sigh, "I have none."

"Perhaps you have. You probably are mistaken."

"No, *ventre saint gris*!" said Henry, "except yourself, brother, I see no one who is attached to me; so that rather than let fail an attempt which might bring to light some unworthy man, I truly prefer to inform my brother the King of what is taking place. I will mention no names, I will designate neither country nor date, but I will foretell the catastrophe."

"Great God!" exclaimed D'Alençon unable to repress his terror, "what do you mean? What! you, you, the sole hope of the party since the death of the admiral; you, a converted Huguenot, a poor convert, or at least such you were thought to be, you would raise the knife against your brothers! Henry, Henry, by doing this, do you know that you would be delivering to a second Saint Bartholomew all the Calvinists in the kingdom? Do you know that Catharine is waiting for just such a chance to exterminate all who have survived?"

And the duke trembling, his face spotted with red and white blotches, pressed Henry's hand to beg him to give up this idea which would ruin him.

"What!" said Henry, with an expression of perfect good-humor, "do you think there would be so much trouble, François? With the King's word, however, it seems to me that I should avoid it."

"The word of King Charles IX., Henry! Did not the admiral have it? Did not Téligny have it? Did not you yourself have it? Oh, Henry, I tell you if you do this, you will ruin us all. Not only them, but all who have had direct or indirect relations with them."

Henry seemed to ponder an instant.

"If I were an important prince at court," said he, "I should act differently. In your place, for instance, in your place, François, a son of France, and probable heir to the crown"—

François shook his head ironically.

"In my place," said he, "what would you do?"

"In your place, brother," replied Henry, "I should place myself at the head of the movement and direct it. My name and my credit should answer to my conscience for the life of the rebellious, and I should derive some benefit first for myself, then for the King, perhaps, from an enterprise which otherwise might do the greatest injury to France."

D'Alençon listened to these words with a joy which caused every muscle of his face to expand.

"Do you think," said he, "that this method is practicable and that it would save us all the disasters you foresee?"

"I think so," said Henry. "The Huguenots love you. Your bearing is modest, your position both high and interesting, and the kindness you have always shown to those of the faith will incline them to serve you."

"But," said D'Alençon, "there is a division in the party. Will those who want you want me?"

"I will undertake to bring them together by two means."

"What means?"

"First, by the confidence the leaders have in me; then by the fear that your highness, knowing their names"—

"But who will tell me these names?"

"I, *ventre saint gris!*"

"You will do that?"

"Listen, François; as I told you, you are the only one I love at court," said Henry. "This, no doubt, is because you are persecuted like myself; and then

300

my wife, too, loves you with an affection which is unequalled"—

François flushed with pleasure.

"Believe me, brother," continued Henry; "take this thing in hand, reign in Navarre; and provided you keep a place at your table for me, and a fine forest in which to hunt, I shall consider myself fortunate."

"Reign in Navarre!" said the duke; "but if"—

"If the Duc d'Anjou is chosen King of Poland; is that it? I will finish your thought for you."

François looked at Henry with something like terror.

"Well, listen, François," continued Henry, "since nothing escapes you. This is how I reason: If the Duc d'Anjou is chosen King of Poland, and our brother Charles, God keep him! should happen to die, it is but two hundred leagues from Pau to Paris, while it is four hundred from Paris to Cracovie. So you would be here to receive the inheritance by the time the King of Poland learned it was vacant. Then, if you are satisfied with me, you could give me the kingdom of Navarre, which would thenceforth be merely one of the jewels in your crown. In that way I would accept it. The worst that could happen to you would be that you would remain king there and bring up a race of kings by living with me and my family, while here, what are you? a poor persecuted prince, a poor third son of a king, the slave of two elder brothers, and one whom a whim may send to the Bastille."

"Yes, yes," said François; "I know that very well, so well that I do not see why you should give up this plan you propose to me. Is there no throb there?"

And the Duc d'Alençon put his hand on his brother's heart.

"There are," said Henry, smiling, "burdens too heavy for some hands; therefore I shall not try to raise this one; fear of fatigue is greater than the desire of possession."

"So, Henry, you really renounce it?"

"I said so to De Mouy and I repeat it to you."

"But in such cases, my dear brother," said D'Alençon, "one does not say, one proves."

Henry breathed like a pugilist who feels his enemy's back bending.

"I will prove it this evening," said he. "At nine o'clock we shall have the names of the leaders and the plan of the undertaking. I have already sent my renunciation to De Mouy."

François took Henry's hand and pressed it effusively between his own.

At that moment Catharine entered the Duc d'Alençon's rooms, unannounced, as was her habit.

"Together!" said she, smiling; "two good brothers, truly!"

"I trust so, madame," said Henry, with great coolness, while the Duc d'Alençon turned white from distress.

Henry stepped back to leave Catharine free to speak with her son.

The queen mother drew a magnificent jewel from her bag.

"This clasp comes from Florence," said she. "I will give it to you for the belt of your sword."

Then in a low tone:

"If to-night you hear any noise in your good brother Henry's room, do not stir."

François pressed his mother's hand, and said:

"Will you allow me to show Henry the beautiful gift you have just given me?"

"You may do more. Give it to him in your name and in mine, for I have ordered a second one just like it."

"You hear, Henry," said François, "my good mother brings me this jewel and doubles its value by allowing me to give it to you."

Henry went into ecstasies over the beauty of the clasp, and was enthusiastic in his thanks. When his delight had grown calmer:

"My son," said Catharine, "I feel somewhat indisposed and I am going to bed; your brother Charles is greatly wearied from his fall and is going to do the same. So we shall not have supper together this evening, but each will be served in his own room. Oh, Henry, I forgot to congratulate you on your bravery and quickness. You saved your king and your brother, and you shall be rewarded for it."

"I am already rewarded, madame," replied Henry, bowing.

"By the feeling that you have done your duty?" replied Catharine. "That is not enough, and Charles and I will do something to pay the debt we owe you."

"Everything that comes to me from you and my good brother will be welcome, madame."

Then he bowed and withdrew.

"Ah! brother François!" thought Henry as he left, "I am sure now of not leaving alone, and the conspiracy which had a body has found a head and a heart. Only let us look out for ourselves. Catharine gives me a present, Catharine promises me a reward. There is some deviltry beneath it all. I must confer this evening with Marguerite."

CHAPTER XXXIII.

THE GRATITUDE OF KING CHARLES IX.

Maurevel had spent a part of the day in the King's armory; but when it was time for the hunters to return from the chase Catharine sent him into her oratory with the guards who had joined him.

Charles IX., informed by his nurse on his arrival that a man had spent part of the day in his room, was at first very angry that a stranger had been admitted into his apartments. But his nurse described the man, saying that he was the same one she herself had been ordered to admit one evening, and the King realized that it was Maurevel. Then remembering the order his mother had wrung from him that morning, he understood everything.

"Oh, ho!" murmured Charles, "the same day on which he has saved my life. The time is badly chosen."

He started to go to his mother, but one thought deterred him.

"By Heaven! If I mention this to her it will result in a never-ending discussion. Better for us to act by ourselves.

"Nurse," said he, "lock every door, and say to Queen Elizabeth[12] that I am suffering somewhat from the fall I have had, and that I shall sleep alone to-night."

The nurse obeyed, and as it was not yet time for the execution of his plan, Charles sat himself down to compose poetry. It was this occupation which made the time pass most quickly for the King. Nine o'clock struck before he thought it was more than seven. He counted the strokes of the clock one by one, and at the last he rose.

"The devil!" said he, "it is just time." Taking his hat and cloak, he left his room by a secret door he had had made in the wall, the existence of which even Catharine herself was ignorant.

Charles went directly to Henry's apartments. On leaving the Duc d'Alençon, the latter had gone to his room to change his clothes and had left again at once.

"He probably has decided to take supper with Margot," said the King. "He was very pleasant with her to-day, at least so it seemed to me."

He went to the queen's apartments. Marguerite had brought back with her the Duchesse de Nevers, Coconnas, and La Mole, and was having a supper of preserves and pastry with them.

Charles knocked at the hall door, which was opened by Gillonne. But at sight of the King she was so frightened that she scarcely had sufficient presence of mind to courtesy, and instead of running to inform her mistress of the august visit she was to have, she let Charles enter without other warning than the cry that had escaped her. The King crossed the antechamber, and guided by the bursts of laughter advanced towards the dining-room.

"Poor Henriot!" said he, "he is enjoying himself without a thought of evil."

"It is I," said he, raising the portière and showing a smiling face.

Marguerite gave a terrible cry. Smiling as he was, his face appeared to her like the face of Medusa. Seated opposite the door, she had recognized him at once. The two men turned their backs to the King.

"Your Majesty!" cried the queen, rising in terror.

The three other guests felt their heads begin to swim; Coconnas alone retained his self-possession. He rose also, but with such tactful clumsiness that in doing so he upset the table, and with it the glass, plate, and candles. Instantly there was complete darkness and the silence of death.

"Run," said Coconnas to La Mole; "quick! quick!"

La Mole did not wait to be told twice. Springing to the side of the wall, he began groping with his hands for the sleeping-room, that he might hide in the cabinet that opened out of it and which he knew so well. But as he stepped across the threshold he ran against a man who had just entered by the secret corridor.

"What does all this mean?" asked Charles, in the darkness, in a tone which was beginning to betray a formidable accent of impatience. "Am I such a mar-joy that the sight of me causes all this confusion? Come, Henriot! Henriot! where are you? Answer me."

"We are saved!" murmured Marguerite, seizing a hand which she took for that of La Mole. "The King thinks my husband is one of our guests."

"And I shall let him think so, madame, you may be sure," said Henry, answering the queen in the same tone.

"Great God!" cried Marguerite, hastily dropping the hand she held, which was that of the King of Navarre.

"Silence!" said Henry.

"In the name of a thousand devils! why are you whispering in this way?" cried Charles. "Henry, answer me; where are you?"

"Here, sire," said the King of Navarre.

"The devil!" said Coconnas, who was holding the Duchesse de Nevers in a corner, "the plot thickens."

"In that case we are doubly lost," said Henriette.

Coconnas, brave to the point of rashness, had reflected that the candles would have to be lighted sooner or later, and thinking the sooner the better, he dropped the hand of Madame de Nevers, picked up a taper from the midst of the débris, and going to a brazier blew on a piece of coal, with which he at once made a light. The chamber was again illuminated. Charles IX. glanced around inquiringly.

Henry was by the side of his wife, the Duchesse de Nevers was alone in a corner, while Coconnas stood in the centre of the room, candle-stick in hand, lighting up the whole scene.

"Excuse me, brother," said Marguerite, "we were not expecting you."

"So, as you may have perceived, your Majesty filled us with strange terror," said Henriette.

"For my part," said Henry, who had surmised everything, "I think the fear was so real that in rising I overturned the table."

Coconnas glanced at the King of Navarre as much as to say:

"Good! Here is a man who understands at once."

"What a frightful hubbub!" repeated Charles IX. "Your supper is ruined, Henriot; come with me and you shall finish it elsewhere; I will carry you off this evening."

"What, sire!" said Henry, "your Majesty will do me the honor?"

"Yes, my Majesty will do you the honor of taking you away from the

Louvre. Lend him to me, Margot, I will bring him back to you to-morrow morning."

"Ah, brother," said Marguerite, "you do not need my permission for that; you are master."

"Sire," said Henry, "I will get another cloak from my room, and will return immediately."

"You do not need it, Henriot; the cloak you have is all right."

"But, sire," began the Béarnais.

"In the name of a thousand devils, I tell you not to go to your rooms! Do you not hear what I say? Come along!"

"Yes, yes, go!" said Marguerite, suddenly pressing her husband's arm; for a singular look from Charles had convinced her that something unusual was going on.

"Here I am, sire," said Henry.

Charles looked at Coconnas, who was still carrying out his office of torch-bearer by lighting the other candles.

"Who is this gentleman?" asked the King of Henry, eyeing the Piedmontese from head to foot. "Is he Monsieur de la Mole?"

"Who has told him of La Mole?" asked Marguerite in a low tone.

"No, sire," replied Henry, "Monsieur de la Mole is not here, I regret to say. Otherwise I should have the honor of presenting him to your Majesty at the same time as Monsieur de Coconnas, his friend. They are perfectly inseparable, and both are in the suite of Monsieur d'Alençon."

"Ah! ah! our famous marksman!" said Charles. "Good!" Then frowning:

"Is not this Monsieur de la Mole a Huguenot?" he asked.

"He is converted, sire, and I will answer for him as for myself."

"When you answer for any one, Henriot, after what you did to-day, I have no further right to doubt him. But I should have liked to see this Monsieur de la Mole. However, I can meet him another time."

Giving a last glance about the room, Charles embraced Marguerite, took hold of the arm of the King of Navarre, and led him off.

At the gate of the Louvre Henry wanted to speak to some one.

"Come, come! pass out quickly, Henriot," said Charles. "When I tell you that the air of the Louvre is not good for you this evening, the devil! you must believe me!"

"*Ventre saint gris!*" murmured Henry; "and what will De Mouy do all alone in my room? I trust the air which is not good for me may be no worse for him!"

"Ah!" exclaimed the King, when Henry and he had crossed the drawbridge, "does it suit you, Henry, to have the gentlemen of Monsieur d'Alençon courting your wife?"

"How so, sire?"

"Truly, is not this Monsieur de Coconnas making eyes at Margot?"

"Who told you that?"

"Well," said the King, "I heard it."

"A mere joke, sire; Monsieur de Coconnas does make eyes at some one, but it is at Madame de Nevers."

"Ah, bah."

"I can answer to your Majesty for what I tell you."

Charles burst into laughter.

"Well," said he, "let the Duc de Guise come to me again with his gossip, and I will gently pull his mustache by telling him of the exploits of his sister-in-law. But after all," said the King, thinking better of it, "I do not know whether it was Monsieur de Coconnas or Monsieur de la Mole he referred to."

"Neither the one more than the other, sire, and I can answer to you for the feelings of my wife."

"Good, Henriot, good!" said the King. "I like you better now than the way you were before. On my honor, you are such a good fellow that I shall end by being unable to get along without you."

As he spoke the King gave a peculiar whistle, whereupon four gentlemen who were waiting for him at the end of the Rue de Beauvais joined him. The whole party set out towards the middle of the city.

Ten o'clock struck.

"Well!" said Marguerite, after the King and Henry had left, "shall we go back to table?"

"Mercy, no!" cried the duchess, "I have been too badly frightened. Long live the little house in the Rue Cloche Percée! No one can enter that without regularly besieging it, and our good men have the right to use their swords there. But what are you looking for under the furniture and in the closets, Monsieur de Coconnas?"

"I am trying to find my friend La Mole," said the Piedmontese.

"Look in my room, monsieur," said Marguerite, "there is a certain closet"—

"Very well," said Coconnas, "I will go there."

He entered the room.

"Well!" said a voice from the darkness; "where are we?"

"Oh! by Heaven! we have reached the dessert."

"And the King of Navarre?"

"He has seen nothing. He is a perfect husband, and I wish my wife had one like him. But I fear she never will, even if she marries again."

"And King Charles?"

"Ah! the King. That is another thing. He has taken off the husband."

"Really?"

"It is as I tell you. Furthermore, he honored me by looking askance at me when he discovered that I belonged to Monsieur d'Alençon, and cross when he found out that I was your friend."

"You think, then, that he has heard me spoken of?"

"I fear that he has heard nothing very good of you. But that is not the point. I believe these ladies have a pilgrimage to make to the Rue de Roi de Sicile, and that we are to take them there."

"Why, that is impossible! You know that very well."

"How impossible?"

"We are on duty at his royal highness's."

"By Heavens, that is so; I always forget that we are ranked, and that from the gentlemen we once were we have had the honor to pass into valets."

Thereupon the two friends went and told the queen and the duchess the necessity of their being present at least when Monsieur le Duc retired.

"Very well," said Madame de Nevers, "we will go by ourselves."

"Might we know where you are going?" asked Coconnas.

"Oh! you are too curious!" said the duchess. "*Quære et invenies.*"

The young men bowed and went at once to Monsieur d'Alençon.

The duke seemed to be waiting for them in his cabinet.

"Ah! ah!" said he, "you are very late, gentlemen."

"It is scarcely ten o'clock, monseigneur," said Coconnas.

The duke drew out his watch.

"That is true," said he. "And yet every one has gone to sleep in the Louvre."

"Yes, monsieur, but we are here at your orders. Must we admit into the chamber of your highness the gentlemen who are with the King until he retires?"

"On the contrary, go into the small reception-room and dismiss every one."

The young men obeyed, carried out the order, which surprised no one, because of the well-known character of the duke, and returned to him.

"Monseigneur," said Coconnas, "your highness will probably either go to bed or work, will you not?"

"No, gentlemen; you may have leave of absence until to-morrow."

"Well, well," whispered Coconnas into La Mole's ear, "the court is going to stay up all night, apparently. It will be devilishly pleasant. Let us have our share of it."

And both young men descended the stairs four steps at a time, took their cloaks and their night swords, and hastily left the Louvre after the two ladies, whom they overtook at the corner of the Rue du Coq Saint Honoré.

Meanwhile the Duc d'Alençon, with open eyes and ears, locked himself in his room to await the unexpected events he had been promised.

———

CHAPTER XXXIV.

MAN PROPOSES BUT GOD DISPOSES.

As the duke had said to the young men, the most profound silence reigned in the Louvre.

Marguerite and Madame de Nevers had departed for the Rue Tizon. Coconnas and La Mole had followed them. The King and Henry were knocking about the city. The Duc d'Alençon was in his room vaguely and anxiously waiting for the events which the queen mother had predicted. Catharine had gone to bed, and Madame de Sauve, seated by her, was reading some Italian stories which greatly amused the good queen. Catharine had not been in such good humor for a long time. Having done justice to a collation with her ladies in waiting, having consulted her physician and arranged the daily accounts of her household, she had ordered prayers for the success of a certain enterprise, which she said was of great importance to the happiness of her children. Under certain circumstances it was Catharine's habit—a habit, for that matter, wholly Florentine—to have prayers and masses read the object of which was known only to God and herself.

Finally she had seen Réné, and had chosen several novelties from among her rich collection of perfumed bags.

"Let me know," said Catharine, "if my daughter the Queen of Navarre is in her rooms; and if she is there, beg her to come to me."

The page to whom this order was given withdrew, and an instant later he returned, accompanied by Gillonne.

"Well!" said the queen mother, "I asked for the mistress, not the servant."

"Madame," said Gillonne, "I thought I ought to come myself and tell your majesty that the Queen of Navarre has gone out with her friend the Duchesse de Nevers"—

"Gone out at this hour!" exclaimed Catharine, frowning; "where can she have gone?"

"To a lecture on chemistry," replied Gillonne, "which is to be held in the Hôtel de Guise, in the pavilion occupied by Madame de Nevers."

"When will she return?" asked the queen mother.

"The lecture will last until late into the night," replied Gillonne, "so that probably her majesty will stay with her friend until to-morrow morning."

"The Queen of Navarre is happy," murmured Catharine; "she has friends and she is queen; she wears a crown, is called your majesty, yet has no subjects. She is happy indeed."

After this remark, which made her listeners smile inwardly:

"Well," murmured Catharine, "since she has gone out—for she has gone, you say?"

"Half an hour ago, madame."

"Everything is for the best; you may go."

Gillonne bowed and left.

"Go on with your reading, Charlotte," said the queen.

Madame de Sauve continued. At the end of ten minutes Catharine interrupted the story.

"Ah, by the way," said she, "have the guards dismissed from the corridor."

This was the signal for which Maurevel was waiting. The order of the queen mother was carried out, and Madame de Sauve went on with her story. She had read for about a quarter of an hour without any interruption, when a prolonged and terrible scream reached the royal chamber and made the hair of those present stand on end.

The scream was followed by the sound of a pistol-shot.

"What is it?" said Catharine; "why do you stop reading, Carlotta?"

"Madame," said the young woman, turning pale, "did you not hear?"

"What?" asked Catharine.

"That cry."

"And that pistol-shot?" added the captain of the guards.

"A cry, a pistol-shot?" asked Catharine; "I heard nothing. Besides, is a shout or a pistol-shot such a very unusual thing at the Louvre? Read, read, Carlotta."

"But listen, madame," said the latter, while Monsieur de Nancey stood up, his hand on his sword, but not daring to leave without permission from the queen, "listen, I hear steps, curses."

"Shall I go and find out about it, madame?" said De Nancey.

"Not at all, monsieur, stay where you are," said Catharine, raising herself on one hand to give more emphasis to her order. "Who, then, would protect me in case of an alarm? It is only some drunken Swiss fighting."

The calmness of the queen, contrasted with the terror on the faces of all present, was so remarkable that, timid as she was, Madame de Sauve fixed a questioning glance on the queen.

"Why, madame, I should think they were killing some one."

"Whom do you think they are killing?"

"The King of Navarre, madame; the noise comes from the direction of his apartments."

"The fool!" murmured the queen, whose lips in spite of her self-control were beginning to move strangely, for she was muttering a prayer; "the fool sees her King of Navarre everywhere."

"My God! my God!" cried Madame de Sauve, falling back in her chair.

"It is over, it is over," said Catharine. "Captain," she continued, turning to Monsieur de Nancey, "I hope if there is any scandal in the palace you will have the guilty ones severely punished to-morrow. Go on with your reading, Carlotta." And Catharine sank back on her pillow with a calmness that greatly resembled weakness, for those present noticed great drops of perspiration rolling down her face.

Madame de Sauve obeyed this formal order, but her eyes and her voice were mere machines. Her thoughts wandered to other things which represented a terrible danger hanging over a loved head. Finally, after struggling on for several minutes, she became so oppressed between her feelings and etiquette that her words became unintelligible, the book fell from her hands, and she fainted.

Suddenly a louder noise was heard; a quick, heavy step fell on the corridor, two pistol-shots shook the windows; and Catharine, astonished at the interminable struggle, rose in terror, erect, pale, with dilating eyes. As the captain of the guard was about to hurry out, she stopped him, saying:

"Let every one remain here. I myself will go and see what is the matter."

This is what was taking place, or rather what had taken place. That morning De Mouy had received the key of Henry's room from the hands of Orthon. In this key, which was piped, he had noticed a roll of paper. He drew it out with a pin. It was the password of the Louvre for that night.

Besides, Orthon had verbally transmitted to him the words of Henry, asking De Mouy to come to the king at ten o'clock in the Louvre.

At half-past nine De Mouy put on a suit of armor, the strength of which he had already more than once had occasion to test; over this he buttoned a silk doublet, fastened on his sword, put his pistols in his belt, and over everything threw the red cloak of La Mole.

We have seen how, before going back to his rooms, Henry had thought best to pay a visit to Marguerite, and how he arrived by the secret stairway just in time to run against La Mole in Marguerite's sleeping-room, and to appear in the dining-room before the King. It was at that very moment when, thanks to the password sent by Henry, and above all to the famous red cloak, that De Mouy passed under the gate of the Louvre.

The young man went directly to the apartments of the King of Navarre, imitating as well as he could, as was his habit, the gait of La Mole. He found Orthon waiting for him in the antechamber.

"Sire de Mouy," said the mountaineer, "the king has gone out, but he told me to admit you, and to tell you to wait for him. If he should be late in returning, he wants you, you know, to lie down on his bed."

De Mouy entered without asking for further explanation, for what Orthon had just told him was only the repetition of what he had already heard that morning. In order to pass away the time he took a pen and ink and, approaching a fine map of France which hung on the wall, he set to work to count and determine the stopping-places between Paris and Pau. But this was only the work of a quarter of an hour, and then De Mouy did not know what to do.

He made two or three rounds of the room, rubbed his eyes, yawned, sat down, got up, and sat down again. Finally, taking advantage of Henry's invitation, and the familiarity which existed between princes and their gentlemen, he placed his pistols and the lamp on a table, stretched himself out on the great bed with the sombre hangings which furnished the rear of the room, laid his sword by his side, and, sure of not being surprised since a servant was in the adjoining room, he fell into a pleasant sleep, the noise of which soon made the vast canopy ring with its echoes. De Mouy snored like a regular old soldier, and in this he could have vied with the King of Navarre himself.

It was then that six men, their swords in their hands and their knives at their belts, glided silently into the corridor which communicated by a small door with the apartments of Catharine and by a large one with those of Henry.

One of the six men walked ahead of the others. Besides his bare sword and his dagger, which was as strong as a hunting-knife, he carried his faithful pistols fastened to his belt by silver hooks.

This man was Maurevel. Having reached Henry's door, he stopped.

"Are you perfectly sure that the sentinels are not in the corridor?" he asked of the one who apparently commanded the little band.

"Not a single one is at his post," replied the lieutenant.

"Very good," said Maurevel. "Now there is nothing further except to find out one thing—that is, if the man we are looking for is in his room."

"But," said the lieutenant, arresting the hand which Maurevel had laid on the handle of the door, "but, captain, these apartments are those of the King of

Navarre."

"Who said they were not?" asked Maurevel.

The guards looked at one another in amazement, and the lieutenant stepped back.

"What!" exclaimed he, "arrest some one at this hour, in the Louvre, and in the apartments of the King of Navarre?"

"What should you say," said Maurevel, "were I to tell you that the one you are about to arrest is the King of Navarre himself?"

"I should say, captain, that it is serious business and that without an order signed by King Charles IX."—

"Read this," said Maurevel.

And drawing from his doublet the order which Catharine had given him he handed it to the lieutenant.

"Very well," replied the latter after he had read it. "I have nothing further to say."

"And you are ready?"

"I am ready."

"And you?" continued Maurevel, turning to the other five sbirros.

They all saluted respectfully.

"Listen to me, then, gentlemen," said Maurevel; "this is my plan: two of you will remain at this door, two at the door of the sleeping-room, and two will go with me."

"Afterwards?" said the lieutenant.

"Pay close attention to this: we are ordered to prevent the prisoner from calling out, shouting, or resisting. Any infraction of this order is to be punished by death."

"Well, well, he has full permission," said the lieutenant to the man chosen by him to follow Maurevel into the king's room.

"Full," said Maurevel.

"Poor devil of the King of Navarre!" said one of the men. "It was written above that he should not escape this."

"And here too," said Maurevel, taking Catharine's order from the hands of the lieutenant and returning it to his breast.

Maurevel inserted the key Catharine had given him into the lock, and leaving two men at the outer door, as had been agreed on, he entered the antechamber with the four others.

"Ah! ah!" said Maurevel, hearing the noisy breathing of the sleeper, the sound of which reached even as far as that, "it seems that we shall find what we are looking for."

Orthon, thinking it was his master returning, at once started up and found himself face to face with five armed men in the first chamber.

At sight of the sinister face of Maurevel, who was called the King's Slayer, the faithful servant sprang back, and placing himself before the second door:

"Who are you?" said he, "and what do you want?"

"In the King's name," replied Maurevel, "where is your master?"

"My master?"

"Yes, the King of Navarre."

"The King of Navarre is not in his room," said Orthon, barring the door more than ever, "so you cannot enter."

"Excuses, lies!" said Maurevel. "Come, stand back!"

The Béarnais people are stubborn; this one growled like one of his own mountain dogs, and far from being intimidated:

"You shall not enter," said he; "the king is out."

And he clung to the door.

Maurevel made a sign. The four men seized the stubborn servant, snatched him from the door-sill to which he was clinging, and as he started to open his mouth and cry out, Maurevel clapped a hand to his lips.

Orthon bit furiously at the assassin, who dropped his hand with a dull cry, and brought down the handle of his sword on the head of the servant. Orthon staggered and fell back, shouting, "Help! help! help!"

Then his voice died away. He had fainted.

The assassins stepped over his body, two stopped at the second door, and two entered the sleeping-room with Maurevel.

In the glow of the lamp burning on the night table they saw the bed.

The curtains were drawn.

"Oh! oh!" said the lieutenant, "he has stopped snoring, apparently."

"Be quick!" cried Maurevel.

At this, a sharp cry, resembling the roar of a lion rather than a human voice, came from behind the curtains, which were violently thrown back, and a man appeared sitting there armed with a cuirass, his head covered with a helmet which reached to his eyes. Two pistols were in his hand, and his sword lay across his knees.

No sooner did Maurevel perceive this figure and recognize De Mouy than he felt his hair rise on end; he became frightfully pale, foam sprang to his lips, and he stepped back as if he had come face to face with a ghost. Suddenly the armed figure rose and stepped forward as Maurevel drew back, so that from the position of threatener, the latter now became the one threatened, and *vice versa*.

"Ah, scoundrel!" cried De Mouy, in a dull voice, "so you have come to murder me as you murdered my father!"

The two guards who had entered the room with Maurevel alone heard these terrible words. As they were uttered a pistol was placed to Maurevel's forehead. The latter sank to his knees just as De Mouy put his hand on the trigger; the shot was fired and one of the guards who stood behind him and whom he had unmasked by this movement dropped to the floor, struck to the heart. At the same instant Maurevel fired back, but the ball glanced off De Mouy's cuirass.

Then, measuring the distance, De Mouy sprang forward and with the edge of his broadsword split open the head of the second guard, and turning towards Maurevel crossed swords with him.

The struggle was brief but terrible. At the fourth pass Maurevel felt the cold steel in his throat. He uttered a stifled cry and fell backwards, upsetting the lamp, which went out in the fall.

At once De Mouy, strong and agile as one of Homer's heroes, took advantage of the darkness and sprang, with head lowered, into the antechamber, knocked down one guard, pushed aside the other, and shot like an arrow between those at the outer door. He escaped two pistol-shots, the balls of which grazed the wall of the corridor, and from that moment was safe, for one loaded pistol still was left him, besides the sword which had dealt such terrible blows.

For an instant he hesitated, undecided whether to go to Monsieur d'Alençon's, the door of whose room he thought had just opened, or to try and escape from the Louvre. He determined on the latter course, continued on his way, slow at first, jumped ten steps at a time, and reaching the gate uttered the two passwords and rushed on, shouting out:

"Go upstairs; there is murder going on by order of the King."

Taking advantage of the amazement produced on the sentinel by his words and the sound of the pistol-shots, he ran on and disappeared in the Rue du Coq without having received a scratch.

It was at this moment that Catharine stopped the captain of the guards, saying:

"Stay here; I myself will go and see what is the matter."

"But, madame," replied the captain, "the danger your majesty runs compels me to follow you."

"Stay here, monsieur," said Catharine, in a still more imperious tone, "stay here. There is a more powerful protection around kings than the human sword."

The captain remained where he was.

Taking a lamp, Catharine slipped her bare feet into a pair of velvet slippers, left her room, and reaching the corridor, still full of smoke, advanced as impassible and as cold as a shadow towards the apartments of the King of Navarre.

Silence reigned supreme.

Catharine reached the door, crossed the threshold, and first saw Orthon, who had fainted in the antechamber.

"Ah! ah!" said she, "here is the servant; further on we shall probably find the master." She entered the second door.

Then her foot ran against a corpse; she lowered her lamp; it was the guard who had had his head split open. He was quite dead.

A few feet further on the lieutenant, who had been struck by a bullet, was drawing his last breath.

Finally, before the bed lay a man whose face was as pale as death and who was bleeding from a double wound in his throat. He was clinching his hands convulsively in his efforts to rise.

It was Maurevel.

Catharine shuddered. She saw the empty bed, she looked around the room seeking in vain for the body she hoped to find among the three corpses.

Maurevel recognized Catharine. His eyes were horribly dilated and he made a despairing gesture towards her.

"Well," said she in a whisper, "where is he? what has happened? Unfortunate man! have you let him escape?"

Maurevel strove to speak, but an unintelligible sound came from his throat, a bloody foam covered his lips, and he shook his head in sign of inability and pain.

"Speak!" cried Catharine, "speak! if only one word!"

Maurevel pointed to his wound, again made several inarticulate gasps, which ended in a hoarse rattle, and fainted.

Catharine looked around her. She was surrounded by the bodies of dead and dying; blood flowed in every direction, and the silence of death hovered over everything.

Once again she spoke to Maurevel, but failed to rouse him; he was not only silent but motionless; a paper was in his doublet. It was the order of arrest signed by the King. Catharine seized it and hid it in her breast. Just then she heard a light step behind her, and turning, she saw the Duc d'Alençon at the door. In spite of himself he had been drawn thither by the noise, and the sight before him fascinated him.

"You here?" said she.

"Yes, madame. For God's sake what has happened?"

"Go back to your room, François; you will know soon enough."

D'Alençon was not as ignorant of the affair as Catharine supposed.

At the sound of the first steps in the corridor he had listened. Seeing some men enter the apartments of the King of Navarre, and by connecting this with some words Catharine had uttered, he had guessed what was about to take place, and was rejoiced at having so dangerous an enemy destroyed by a hand stronger than his own. Before long the noises of pistol-shots and the rapid steps of a man running had attracted his attention, and he had seen disappearing in the light space caused by the opening of the door leading to the stairway the red cloak too well known not to be recognized.

"De Mouy!" he cried, "De Mouy in the apartments of the King of Navarre! Why, that is impossible! Can it be Monsieur de la Mole?"

He grew alarmed. Remembering that the young man had been recommended to him by Marguerite herself, and wishing to make sure that it was he whom he had just seen, he ascended hurriedly to the chamber of the two young men. It was vacant. But in a corner he found the famous red cloak hanging against the wall. His suspicions were confirmed. It was not La Mole, but De Mouy. Pale and trembling lest the Huguenot should be discovered, and would betray the secrets of the conspiracy, he rushed to the gate of the Louvre. There he was told that the red cloak had escaped safe and sound, shouting out as he passed that some one was being murdered in the Louvre by order of the King.

"He is mistaken," murmured D'Alençon; "it is by order of the queen mother."

Returning to the scene of combat, he found Catharine wandering like a hyena among the dead.

At the order from his mother the young man returned to his rooms, affecting calmness and obedience, in spite of the tumultuous thoughts which were passing through his mind.

In despair at the failure of this new attempt, Catharine called the captain of the guards, had the bodies removed, gave orders that Maurevel, who was only wounded, be carried to his home, and told them not to waken the King.

"Oh!" she murmured, as she returned to her rooms, her head sunk on her bosom, "he has again escaped. The hand of God is over this man. He will reign! he will reign!"

Entering her room, she passed her hand across her brow, and assumed an ordinary smile.

"What was the matter, madame?" asked every one except Madame de Sauve, who was too frightened to ask any questions.

"Nothing," replied Catharine; "a noise, that was all."

"Oh!" cried Madame de Sauve, suddenly pointing to the floor, "your majesty says there is nothing the matter, and every one of your majesty's steps leaves a trace of blood on the carpet!"

CHAPTER XXXV.

A NIGHT OF KINGS.

Charles IX. walked along with Henry leaning on his arm, followed by his four gentlemen and preceded by two torch-bearers.

"When I leave the Louvre," said the poor King, "I feel a pleasure similar to that which comes to me when I enter a beautiful forest. I breathe, I live, I am free."

Henry smiled.

"In that case," said he, "your Majesty would be in your element among the mountains of the Béarn."

"Yes, and I understand that you want to go back to them; but if you are very anxious to do so, Henriot," added Charles, laughing, "my advice is to be careful, for my mother Catharine loves you so dearly that it is absolutely impossible for her to get along without you."

"What does your Majesty plan to do this evening?" asked Henry, changing this dangerous conversation.

"I want to have you meet some one, Henriot, and you shall give me your opinion."

"I am at your Majesty's orders."

"To the right! to the right! We will take the Rue des Barres."

The two kings, followed by their escort, had passed the Rue de la Savonnerie, when in front of the Hôtel de Condé they saw two men, wrapped in large cloaks, coming out of a secret door which one of them noiselessly closed behind him.

"Oh! oh!" said the King to Henry, who as usual had seen everything, but had not spoken, "this deserves attention."

"Why do you say that, sire?" asked the King of Navarre.

"It is not on your account, Henriot. You are sure of your wife," added Charles with a smile; "but your cousin De Condé is not sure of his, or if so, he is making a mistake, the devil!"

"But how do you know, sire, that it is Madame de Condé whom these gentlemen have been visiting?"

"Instinct tells me. The fact that the men stood in the doorway without moving until they saw us; then the cut of the shorter one's cloak—by Heaven! that would be strange!"

"What?"

"Nothing. An idea I had, that is all; let us go on."

He walked up to the two men, who, seeing him, started to walk away.

"Hello, gentlemen!" cried the King; "stop!"

"Are you speaking to us?" asked a voice which made Charles and his companion tremble.

"Well, Henriot," said Charles, "do you recognize the voice now?"

"Sire," said Henry, "if your brother the Duc d'Anjou was not at La Rochelle, I would swear it was he speaking."

"Well," said Charles, "he is not at La Rochelle, that is all."

"But who is with him?"

"Do you not recognize his companion?"

"No, sire."

"Yet his figure is unmistakable. Wait, you shall see who he is—hello, there! I tell you," cried the King, "do you not hear, by Heaven?"

"Are you the watch, that you order us to stop?" said the taller of the two men, freeing his arm from the folds of his cloak.

"Pretend that we are the watch," said the King, "and stop when we tell you to do so."

Leaning over to Henry's ear, he added:

"Now you will see the volcano send forth its fire."

"There are eight of you," said the taller of the two men, this time showing not only his arm but his face, "but were you a hundred, pass on!"

"Ah! ah! the Duc de Guise!" said Henry.

"Ah! our cousin from Lorraine," said the King; "at last you will meet! How fortunate!"

"The King!" cried the duke.

At these words the other man covered himself with his cloak and stood motionless, having first uncovered out of respect.

"Sire," said the Duc de Guise, "I have just been paying a visit to my sister-in-law, Madame de Condé."

"Yes—and you brought one of your gentlemen with you? Which one?"

"Sire," replied the duke, "your Majesty does not know him."

"We will meet him, however," said the King.

Walking up to the other figure, he signed to one of the lackeys to bring a torch.

"Pardon me, brother!" said the Duc d'Anjou, opening his cloak and bowing with poorly disguised anger.

"Ah! ah! Henry, is it you? But no, it is not possible, I am mistaken—my brother of Anjou would not have gone to see any one else before first calling on me. He knows that for royal princes, returning to the capital, Paris has but one entrance, the gate of the Louvre."

"Pardon me, sire," said the Duc d'Anjou; "I beg your Majesty to excuse my thoughtlessness."

"Ah, yes!" replied the King, mockingly; "and what were you doing, brother, at the Hôtel de Condé?"

"Why," said the King of Navarre in his sly way, "what your Majesty intimated just now."

And leaning over to the King he ended his sentence in a burst of laughter.

"What is it?" asked the Duc de Guise, haughtily; for like every one else at court, he had a way of treating the poor King of Navarre very rudely, "why should I not go and see my sister-in-law. Does not Monsieur le Duc d'Alençon visit his?"

Henry flushed slightly.

"What sister-in-law?" asked Charles. "I know none except Queen Elizabeth."

"Pardon, sire! it was your sister I should have said—Madame Marguerite, whom we saw pass in her litter as we came by here half an hour ago. She was accompanied by two courtiers who rode on either side of her."

"Indeed!" said Charles. "What do you say to that, Henry?"

"That the Queen of Navarre is perfectly free to go where she pleases, but I doubt if she has left the Louvre."

"Well, I am sure she did," said the Duc de Guise.

"And I too," said the Duc d'Anjou, "from the fact that the litter stopped in the Rue Cloche Percée."

"Your sister-in-law, not this one," said Henry, pointing to the Hôtel de Condé, "but that one," turning in the direction of the Hôtel de Guise, "must also be of the party, for we left them together, and, as you know, they are inseparable."

"I do not know what your majesty means," replied the Duc de Guise.

"On the contrary," said the king, "nothing is simpler. That is why a courtier was riding at either side of the litter."

"Well!" said the duke, "if there is any scandal concerning my sisters-in-law, let us beg the King to withhold justice."

"Well, by Heaven," said Henry, "let us leave Madame de Condé and Madame de Nevers; the King is not anxious about his sister—and I have confidence in my wife."

"No, no," said Charles, "I want to make sure of it; but let us attend to the matter ourselves. The litter stopped in the Rue Cloche Percée, you say, cousin?"

"Yes, sire."

"Do you know the house?"

"Yes, sire."

"Well, let us go to it. And if in order to find out who is in it, it is necessary to burn it down, we will burn it."

It was with this end in view, which was rather discouraging for the tranquillity of those concerned, that the four chief lords of the Christian world set out to the Rue Saint Antoine.

They reached the Rue Cloche Percée. Charles, who wished to work privately, dismissed the gentlemen of his suite, saying that they might have the rest of the night to themselves, but for them to be at the Bastille with two horses at six o'clock in the morning.

There were only three houses in the Rue Cloche Percée. The search was much less difficult as two of the buildings were perfectly willing to open their doors. One of the houses faced the Rue Saint Antoine and the other the Rue du Roi de Sicile.

As to the third house, that was a different matter. It was the one which was guarded by the German janitor, and this janitor was not easily managed. That night Paris seemed destined to offer memorable examples of conjugal fidelity. In vain did Monsieur de Guise threaten in his purest Saxon; in vain did Henry of Anjou offer a purse filled with gold; in vain Charles went so far as to say that he was lieutenant of the watch; the brave German paid attention neither to the statement, the offer, nor the threats. Seeing that they insisted, and in a way that was becoming importunate, he slipped the nose of a gun under the iron bars, a move which brought forth bursts of laughter from three of the four visitors. Henry of Navarre stood apart, as if the affair had no interest for him. But as the weapon could not be turned between the bars, it was scarcely dangerous for any except a blind man, who might stand directly in front of it.

Seeing that the porter was neither to be intimidated, bribed, nor persuaded, the Duc de Guise pretended to leave with his companions; but the retreat did not last long. At the corner of the Rue Saint Antoine the duke found what he sought. This was a rock similar in size to those which three thousand years before had been moved by Ajax, son of Telamon, and Diomed. The duke raised it to his shoulder and came back, signing to his companions to follow. Just then the janitor, who had seen those he took for malefactors depart, closed the door. But he had not time to draw the bolts before the Duc de Guise took advantage of the moment, and hurled his veritable living catapult against the door. The lock broke, carrying away a portion of the wall to which it had been fastened. The door sprang open, knocking down the German, who, in falling, gave a terrible cry. This cry awakened the garrison, which otherwise

324

would have run great risk of being surprised.

At that moment La Mole and Marguerite were translating an idyl of Theocritus, and Coconnas, pretending that he too was a Greek, was drinking some strong wine from Syracuse with Henriette. The scientific and bacchanalian conversation was violently interrupted.

La Mole and Coconnas at once extinguished the candles, and opening the windows, sprang out on the balcony. Then perceiving four men in the darkness, they set to work to hurl at them everything they had at hand, in the meantime making a frightful noise with blows from the flat of their swords, which, however, struck nothing but the wall. Charles, the most infuriated of the besiegers, received a sharp blow on the shoulder, the Duc d'Anjou a bowl full of orange and lemon marmalade, and the Duc de Guise a leg of venison. Henry received nothing. He was downstairs questioning the porter, whom Monsieur de Guise had strapped to the door, and who continued to answer by his eternal *"Ich verstehe nicht."* The women encouraged the besieged by handing them projectiles, which succeeded one another like hailstones.

"The devil!" exclaimed Charles IX., as a table struck his head, driving his hat over his eyes, "if they don't open the door pretty soon I will have them all hanged."

"My brother!" whispered Marguerite to La Mole.

"The King!" cried the latter to Henriette.

"The King! the King!" repeated Henriette to Coconnas, who was dragging a chest to the window, and who was trying to exterminate the Duc de Guise. Without knowing who the latter was he was having a private struggle with him.

"The King, I tell you," repeated Henriette.

Coconnas let go of the chest and looked up in amazement.

"The King?" said he.

"Yes, the King."

"Then let us hide."

"Yes. La Mole and Marguerite have already fled. Come!"

"Where?"

"Come, I tell you."

And seizing him by the hand, Henriette pushed Coconnas through the secret door which connected with the adjoining house, and all four, having locked this door behind them, escaped into the Rue Tizon.

"Oh! oh!" said Charles, "I think that the garrison has surrendered."

They waited a few minutes. No sound reached the besiegers.

"They are preparing some ruse," said the Duc de Guise.

"It is more likely that they have recognized my brother's voice and have fled," said the Duc d'Anjou.

"They would have to pass by here," said Charles.

"Yes," said the Duc d'Anjou, "unless the house has two exits."

"Cousin," said the King, "take up your stone again and hurl it against the other door as you did at this."

The duke thought it unnecessary to resort to such means, and as he had noticed that the second door was not as solid as the first he broke it down by a simple kick.

"The torches! the torches!" cried the King.

The lackeys approached. The torches were out, but the men had everything necessary for relighting them. This was done. Charles IX. took one and handed the other to the Duc d'Anjou.

The Duc de Guise entered first, sword in hand.

Henry brought up the rear.

They reached the first floor.

In the dining-room the table was set or rather upset, for it was the supper which had furnished the projectiles. The candlesticks were overturned, the furniture topsy-turvy, and everything which was not silver plate lay in fragments.

They entered the reception-room, but found no more clue there than in the other room as to the identity of the revellers. Some Greek and Latin books and several musical instruments were all they saw.

The sleeping-room was more silent still. A night lamp burned in an alabaster globe suspended from the ceiling; but it was evident that the room had not been occupied.

"There is a second door," said the King.

"Very likely," said the Duc d'Anjou.

"But where is it?" asked the Duc de Guise.

They looked everywhere, but could not find it.

"Where is the janitor?" asked the King.

"I bound him to the gate," said the Duc de Guise.

"Ask him, cousin."

"He will not answer."

"Bah! we will have a dry fire built around his legs," said the King, laughing, "then he will speak."

Henry glanced hurriedly out of the window.

"He is not there," said he.

"Who untied him?" asked the Duc de Guise, quickly.

"The devil!" exclaimed the King, "and we know nothing as yet."

"Well!" said Henry, "you see very clearly, sire, that there is nothing to prove that my wife and Monsieur de Guise's sister-in-law have been in this house."

"That is so," said Charles. "The Scriptures tell us that there are three things which leave no trace—the bird in the air, the fish in the sea, and the woman— no, I am wrong, the man, in"—

"So," interrupted Henry, "what we had better do is"—

"Yes," said Charles, "what we had better do is for me to look after my bruise, for you, D'Anjou, to wipe off your orange marmalade, and for you, De Guise, to get rid of the grease." Thereupon they left without even troubling to close the door. Reaching the Rue Saint Antoine:

"Where are you bound for, gentlemen?" asked the King of the Duc d'Anjou and the Duc de Guise.

"Sire, we are going to the house of Nantouillet, who is expecting my Lorraine cousin and myself to supper. Will your Majesty come with us?"

"No, thanks, we are going in a different direction. Will you take one of my torch-bearers?"

"Thank you, no, sire," said the Duc d'Anjou, hastily.

"Good; he is afraid I will spy on him," whispered Charles to the King of Navarre.

Then taking the latter by the arm:

"Come, Henriot," said he, "I will take you to supper to-night."

"Are we not going back to the Louvre?" asked Henry.

"No, I tell you, you stupid! Come with me, since I tell you to come. Come!"

And he dragged Henry down the Rue Geoffroy Lasnier.

———

CHAPTER XXXVI.

THE ANAGRAM.

The Rue Garnier sur l'Eau runs into the Rue Geoffroy Lasnier, and the Rue des Barres lies at right angles to the former.

On the right, a short distance down the Rue de la Mortellerie, stands a small house in the centre of a garden surrounded by a high wall, which has but one entrance. Charles drew a key from his pocket and inserted it into the lock. The gate was unbolted and immediately opened. Telling Henry and the lackey bearing the torch to enter, the King closed and locked the gate behind him.

Light came from one small window which Charles smilingly pointed out to Henry.

"Sire, I do not understand," said the latter.

"But you will, Henriot."

The King of Navarre looked at Charles in amazement. His voice and his face had assumed an expression of gentleness so different from usual that Henry scarcely recognized him.

"Henriot," said the King, "I told you that when I left the Louvre I came out of hell. When I enter here I am in paradise."

"Sire," said Henry, "I am happy that your Majesty has thought me worthy of taking this trip to Heaven with you."

"The road thither is a narrow one," said the King, turning to a small stairway, "but nothing can be compared to it."

"Who is the angel who guards the entrance to your Eden, sire?"

"You shall see," replied Charles IX.

Signing to Henry to follow him noiselessly, he opened first one door, then another, and finally paused on a threshold.

"Look!" said he.

Henry approached and gazed on one of the most beautiful pictures he had ever seen.

A young woman of eighteen or nineteen lay sleeping, her head resting on the foot of a little bed in which a child was asleep. The woman held its little feet close to her lips, while her long hair fell over her shoulders like a flood of gold. It was like one of Albane's pictures of the Virgin and the Child Jesus.

"Oh, sire," said the King of Navarre, "who is this lovely creature?"

"The angel of my paradise, Henriot, the only one who loves me."

Henry smiled.

"Yes," said Charles, "for she loved me before she knew I was King."

"And since she has known it?"

"Well, since she has known it," said Charles, with a smile which showed that royalty sometimes weighed heavily on him, "since she has known it she loves me still; so you may judge."

The King approached the woman softly and pressed a kiss as light as that which a bee gives to a lily on her rosy cheek.

Yet, light as it was, she awakened at once.

"Charles!" she murmured, opening her eyes.

"You see," said the King, "she calls me Charles. The queen says 'sire'!"

"Oh!" cried the young woman, "you are not alone, my King."

"No, my sweet Marie, I wanted to bring you another king, happier than myself because he has no crown; more unhappy than I because he has no Marie Touchet. God makes compensation for everything."

"Sire, is it the King of Navarre?" asked Marie.

"Yes, my child; come here, Henriot." The King of Navarre drew near; Charles took him by the hand.

"See this hand, Marie," said he, "it is the hand of a good brother and a loyal friend. Were it not for this hand"—

"Well, sire?"

"Well, had it not been for this hand to-day, Marie, our child would have no father."

Marie uttered a cry, fell on her knees, and seizing Henry's hand covered it with kisses.

"Very good, Marie, very good," said Charles.

"What have you done to thank him, sire?"

"I have done for him what he did for me."

Henry looked at Charles in astonishment.

"Some day you will know what I mean, Henriot; meanwhile come here and see." He approached the bed, on which the child still slept.

"Ah!" said he, "if this little fellow were in the Louvre instead of here in this little house in the Rue des Barres, many things would be changed for the present as well as for the future perhaps."[13]

"Sire," said Marie, "if your Majesty is willing, I prefer him to stay here; he sleeps better."

"Let us not disturb his slumber, then," said the King; "it is so sweet to sleep when one does not dream!"

"Well, sire," said Marie, pointing to a door opening out of the room.

"Yes, you are right, Marie," said Charles IX., "let us have supper."

"My well-beloved Charles," said Marie, "you will ask the king your brother to excuse me, will you not?"

"Why?"

"For having dismissed our servants, sire," continued Marie, turning to the King of Navarre; "you must know that Charles wants to be served by me alone."

"*Ventre saint gris!*" said Henry, "I should think so!"

Both men entered the dining-room. The mother, anxious and careful, laid a warm blanket over the little Charles, who, thanks to the sound sleep of childhood, so envied by his father, had not wakened.

Marie rejoined them.

"There are only two covers!" said the King.

"Permit me," said Marie, "to serve your majesties."

"Now," said Charles, "this is where you cause me trouble, Henriot."

"How so, sire?"

"Did you not hear?"

"Forgive me, Charles, forgive me."

"Yes, I will forgive you. But sit here, near me, between us."

"I will obey," said Marie.

She brought a plate, sat down between the two kings, and served them.

"Is it not good, Henriot," said Charles, "to have one place in the world in which one can eat and drink without needing any one to taste the meats and wines beforehand?"

"Sire," said Henry, smiling, and by the smile replying to the constant fear in his own mind, "believe me, I appreciate your happiness more than any one."

"And tell her, Henriot, that in order for us to live happily, she must not mingle in politics. Above all, she must not become acquainted with my mother."

"Queen Catharine loves your Majesty so passionately that she would be jealous of any other love," replied Henry, finding by a subterfuge the means of avoiding the dangerous confidence of the King.

"Marie," said the latter, "I have brought you one of the finest and the wittiest men I know. At court, you see, and this is saying a great deal, he puts every one in the shade. I alone have clearly understood, not his heart, perhaps, but his mind."

"Sire," said Henry, "I am sorry that in exaggerating the one as you do, you mistrust the other."

"I exaggerate nothing, Henriot," said the King; "besides, you will be known some day."

Then turning to the young woman:

"He makes delightful anagrams. Ask him to make one of your name. I will answer that he will do it."

"Oh, what could you expect to find in the name of a poor girl like me? What gentle thought could there be in the letters with which chance spelled Marie Touchet?"

"Oh! the anagram from this name, sire," said Henry, "is so easy that there is no great merit in finding it."

"Ah! ah! it is already found," said Charles. "You see—Marie."

Henry drew his tablets from the pocket of his doublet, tore out a paper, and below the name *Marie Touchet* wrote *Je charme tout.* Then he handed the paper to the young woman.

"Truly," she cried, "it is impossible!"

"What has he found?" asked Charles.

"Sire, I dare not repeat it."

"Sire," said Henry, "in the name Marie Touchet there is, letter for letter, by changing the 'i' into a 'j,' as is often done, *Je charme tout*." (I charm all.)

"Yes," exclaimed Charles, "letter for letter. I want this to be your motto, Marie, do you hear? Never was one better deserved. Thanks, Henriot. Marie, I will give it to you written in diamonds."

The supper over, two o'clock struck from Notre-Dame.

"Now," said Charles, "in return for this compliment, Marie, you will give the king an armchair, in which he can sleep until daybreak; but let it be some distance from us, because he snores frightfully. Then if you waken before I do, you will rouse me, for at six o'clock we have to be at the Bastille. Good-night, Henriot. Make yourself as comfortable as possible. But," he added, approaching the King of Navarre and laying his hand on his shoulder, "for your life, Henry,—do you hear? for your life,—do not leave here without me, especially to return to the Louvre."

Henry had suspected too many things in what still remained unexplained to him to disobey such advice. Charles IX. entered his room, and Henry, the sturdy mountaineer, settled himself in an armchair, in which he soon justified the precaution taken by his brother-in-law in keeping at a distance.

At dawn he was awakened by Charles. As he had not undressed, it did not take him long to finish his toilet. The King was more happy and smiling than he ever was at the Louvre. The hours spent by him in that little house in the Rue des Barres were his hours of sunshine.

Both men went out through the sleeping-room. The young woman was still in bed. The child was asleep in its cradle. Both were smiling.

Charles looked at them for a moment with infinite tenderness.

Then turning to the King of Navarre:

"Henriot," said he, "if you ever hear what I did for you last night, or if misfortune come to me, remember this child asleep in its cradle."

Then kissing both mother and child on the forehead, without giving Henry time to question him:

"Good-by, my angels," said he, and went out.

Henry followed, deep in thought. The horses were waiting for them at the

Bastille, held by the gentlemen to whom Charles IX. had given the order.

Charles signed to Henry to mount, sprang into his own saddle, and riding through the garden of the Arbalite, followed the outside highways.

"Where are we going?" asked Henry.

"We are going to see if the Duc d'Anjou returned for Madame de Condé alone," replied Charles, "and if there is as much ambition as love in his heart, which I greatly doubt."

Henry did not understand the answer, but followed Charles in silence.

They reached the Marais, and as from the shadow of the palisades they could see all which at that time was called the Faubourg Saint Laurent, Charles pointed out to Henry through the grayish mist of the morning some men wrapped in great cloaks and wearing fur caps. They were on horseback, and rode ahead of a wagon which was heavily laden. As they drew near they became outlined more clearly, and one could see another man in a long brown cloak, his face hidden by a French hat, riding and talking with them.

"Ah! ah!" said Charles, smiling, "I thought so."

"Well, sire," said Henry, "if I am not mistaken, that rider in the brown cloak is the Duc d'Anjou."

"Yes," said Charles IX. "Turn out a little, Henriot, I do not want him to see us."

"But," asked Henry, "who are the men in gray cloaks with fur caps?"

"Those men," said Charles, "are Polish ambassadors, and in that wagon is a crown. And now," said he, urging his horse to a gallop, and turning into the road of the Porte du Temple, "come, Henriot, I have seen all that I wanted to see."

―――――――

CHAPTER XXXVII.

THE RETURN TO THE LOUVRE.

When Catharine thought that everything was over in the King of Navarre's rooms, when the dead guards had been removed, when Maurevel had been carried to her apartments, and the carpet had been cleaned, she dismissed her women, for it was almost midnight, and strove to sleep. But the shock had been too violent, and the disappointment too keen.

That detested Henry, constantly escaping her snares, which were usually fatal, seemed protected by some invincible power which Catharine persisted in calling chance, although in her heart of hearts a voice told her that its true name was destiny. The thought that the report of the new attempt in spreading throughout the Louvre and beyond the Louvre would give a greater confidence than ever in the future to Henry and the Huguenots exasperated her, and at that moment had chance, against which she was so unfortunately struggling, delivered her enemy into her hands, surely with the little Florentine dagger she wore at her belt she could have thwarted that destiny so favorable to the King of Navarre.

The hours of the night, hours so long for one waiting and watching struck one after another without Catharine's being able to close her eyes. A whole world of new plans unrolled in her visionary mind during those nocturnal hours. Finally at daybreak she rose, dressed herself, and went to the apartments of Charles IX.

The guards, who were accustomed to see her go to the King at all hours of the day and night, let her pass. She crossed the antechamber, therefore, and reached the armory. But there she found the nurse of Charles, who was awake.

"My son?" said the queen.

"Madame, he gave orders that no one was to be admitted to his room before eight o'clock."

"This order was not for me, nurse."

"It was for every one, madame."

Catharine smiled.

"Yes, I know very well," said the nurse, "that no one has any right to oppose your majesty; I therefore beg you to listen to the prayer of a poor woman and to refrain from entering."

"Nurse, I must speak to my son."

"Madame, I will not open the door except on a formal order from your majesty."

"Open, nurse," said Catharine, "I order you to open!"

At this voice, more respected and much more feared in the Louvre than that of Charles himself, the nurse handed the key to Catharine, but the queen had no need of it. She drew from her pocket her own key of the room, and under its heavy pressure the door yielded.

The room was vacant, Charles's bed was untouched, and his greyhound Actéon, asleep on the bear-skin that covered the step of the bed, rose and came forward to lick the ivory hands of Catharine.

"Ah!" said the queen, frowning, "he is out! I will wait for him."

She seated herself, pensive and gloomy, at the window which overlooked the court of the Louvre, and from which the chief entrance was visible.

For two hours she sat there, as motionless and pale as a marble statue, when at length she perceived a troop of horsemen returning to the Louvre, at whose head she recognized Charles and Henry of Navarre.

Then she understood all. Instead of arguing with her in regard to the arrest of his brother-in-law, Charles had taken him away and so had saved him.

"Blind, blind, blind!" she murmured. Then she waited. An instant later footsteps were heard in the adjoining room, which was the armory.

"But, sire," Henry was saying, "now that we have returned to the Louvre, tell me why you took me away and what is the service you have rendered me."

"No, no, Henriot," replied Charles, laughing, "some day, perhaps, you will find out; but for the present it must remain a mystery. Know only that for the time being you have in all probability brought about a fierce quarrel between my mother and me."

As he uttered these words, Charles raised the curtain and found himself face to face with Catharine.

Behind him and above his shoulder rose the pale, anxious countenance of the Béarnais.

"Ah! you here, madame?" said Charles IX., frowning.

"Yes, my son," said Catharine, "I want to speak to you."

"To me?"

"To you alone."

"Well, well," said Charles, turning to his brother-in-law, "since there is no escape, the sooner the better."

"I will leave you, sire," said Henry.

"Yes, yes, leave us," replied Charles; "and as you are a Catholic, Henriot, go and hear a mass for me while I stay for the sermon."

Henry bowed and withdrew.

Charles IX. went directly to the point.

"Well, madame," said he, trying to make a joke of the affair. "By Heaven! you are waiting to scold me, are you not? I wickedly upset your little plan. Well, the devil! I could not let the man who had just saved my life be arrested and taken to the Bastille. Nor did I want to quarrel with my mother. I am a good son. Moreover," he added in a low tone, "the Lord punishes children who quarrel with their mothers. Witness my brother François II. Forgive me, therefore, frankly, and confess that the joke was a good one."

"Sire," said Catharine, "your Majesty is mistaken; it is not a joke."

"Yes, yes! and you will end by looking at it in that way, or the devil take me!"

"Sire, by your blunder you have baffled a project which would have led to an important discovery."

"Bah! a project. Are you embarrassed because of a baffled project, mother? You can make twenty others, and in those,—well, I promise I will second you."

"Now that you will second me it is too late, for he is warned and will be on his guard."

"Well," said the King, "let us come to the point. What have you against Henriot?"

"The fact that he conspires."

"Yes, I know that this is your constant accusation; but does not every one conspire more or less in this charming royal household called the Louvre?"

"But he conspires more than any one, and he is much more dangerous than one imagines."

"A regular Lorenzino!" said Charles.

"Listen," said Catharine, becoming gloomy at mention of this name, which reminded her of one of the bloodiest catastrophes in the history of Florence. "Listen; there is a way of proving to me that I am wrong."

"What way, mother?"

"Ask Henry who was in his room last night."

"In his room last night?"

"Yes; and if he tells you"—

"Well?"

"Well, I shall be ready to admit that I have been mistaken."

"But in case it was a woman, we cannot ask."

"A woman?"

"Yes."

"A woman who killed two of your guards and perhaps mortally wounded Monsieur de Maurevel!"

"Oh! oh!" said the King, "this is serious. Was there any bloodshed?"

"Three men were stretched on the floor."

"And the one who reduced them to this state?"

"Escaped safe and sound."

"By Gog and Magog!" exclaimed Charles, "he was a brave fellow, and you are right, mother, I must know him."

"Well, I tell you in advance that you will not know him, at least not through Henry."

"But through you, mother? The man did not escape without leaving some trace, without your noticing some part of his clothing."

"Nothing was noticed except the very elegant red cloak which he wore."

"Ah! ah! a red cloak!" cried Charles. "I know only one at court remarkable enough to attract attention."

"Exactly," said Catharine.

"Well?" demanded Charles.

"Well," said Catharine, "wait for me in your rooms, my son, and I will go and see if my orders have been carried out."

Catharine left, and Charles, alone, began walking up and down distractedly, whistling a hunting-song, one hand in his doublet, the other hanging down, which his dog licked every time he paused.

As to Henry he had left his brother-in-law greatly disturbed, and instead of going along the main corridor he had taken the small private stairway, to which we have already referred more than once, and which led to the second story. Scarcely had he ascended four steps before he perceived a figure at the

337

first landing. He stopped, raising his hand to his dagger. But he soon saw it was a woman, who took hold of his hand and said in a charming voice which he well knew:

"Thank God, sire, you are safe and sound. I was so afraid for you, but no doubt God heard my prayer."

"What has happened?" said Henry.

"You will know when you reach your rooms. You need not worry over Orthon. I have seen to him."

The young woman descended the stairs hastily, making Henry believe that she had met him by chance.

"That is strange," said Henry to himself. "What is the matter? What has happened to Orthon?"

Unfortunately, the question was not heard by Madame de Sauve, for the latter had already disappeared.

Suddenly at the top of the stairs Henry perceived another figure, but this time it was that of a man.

"Hush!" said the man.

"Ah! is it you, François?"

"Do not call me by my name."

"What has happened?"

"Return to your rooms and you will see, then slip into the corridor, look carefully around to make sure that no one is spying on you, and come to my apartments. The door will be ajar."

He, too, disappeared down the stairs, like the phantoms in a theatre who glide through a trap door.

"*Ventre saint gris!*" murmured the Béarnais, "the puzzle continues; but since the answer is in my rooms, let us go thither and find it."

However, it was not without emotion that Henry went on his way. He had the sensitiveness and the superstition of youth. Everything was clearly reflected on his mind, the surface of which was as smooth as a mirror, and what he had just heard foretold trouble.

He reached the door of his rooms and listened. Not a sound. Besides, since Charlotte had said to return to his apartments, it was evident that there was nothing for him to fear by doing so. He glanced hurriedly around the first room—it was vacant. Nothing showed that anything had occurred.

"Orthon is not here," said he.

He passed on to the next room. There everything was explained.

In spite of the water which had been thrown on in bucketsful, great red spots covered the floor. A piece of furniture was broken, the bed curtains had been slashed by the sword, a Venetian mirror had been shattered by a bullet; and a bloody hand which had left its terrible imprint on the wall showed that this silent chamber had been the scene of a frightful struggle. Henry embraced all these details at a glance, and passing his hand across his forehead, now damp with perspiration, murmured:

"Ah, I know now the service the King has rendered me. They came here to assassinate me—and—ah! De Mouy! what have they done to De Mouy? The wretches! They may have killed him!"

And as anxious to learn the news as the Duc d'Alençon was to tell it, Henry threw a last mournful glance on the surrounding objects, hurried from the room, reached the corridor, made sure that it was vacant, and pushing open the half-closed door, which he carefully shut behind him, he hurried to the Duc d'Alençon's.

The duke was waiting for him in the first room. Laying his finger on his lips, he hastily took Henry's hand and drew him into a small round tower which was completely isolated, and which consequently was out of range of spies.

"Ah, brother," said he, "what a horrible night!"

"What happened?" asked Henry.

"They tried to arrest you."

"Me?"

"Yes, you."

"For what reason?"

"I do not know. Where were you?"

"The King took me into the city with him last night."

"Then he knew about it," said D'Alençon. "But since you were not in your rooms, who was?"

"Was some one there?" asked Henry as if he were ignorant of the fact.

"Yes, a man. When I had heard the noise, I ran to help you; but it was too late."

"Was the man arrested?" asked Henry, anxiously.

"No, he escaped, after he had wounded Maurevel dangerously and killed two guards."

"Ah! brave De Mouy!" cried Henry.

"It was De Mouy, then?" said D'Alençon, quickly.

Henry saw that he had made a mistake.

"I presume so," said he, "for I had an appointment with him to discuss your escape, and to tell him that I had yielded all my rights to the throne of Navarre to you."

"If that is known," said D'Alençon, growing pale, "we are lost."

"Yes, for Maurevel will speak."

"Maurevel received a sword-thrust in his throat, and I found out from the surgeon who dressed the wound that it would be a week before he would utter a single word."

"A week! That is more than enough for De Mouy to escape."

"For that matter," said D'Alençon, "it might have been some one besides Monsieur de Mouy."

"You think so?" said Henry.

"Yes, the man disappeared very quickly, and nothing but his red cloak was seen."

"And a red cloak," said Henry, "is more apt to be worn by a courtier than by a soldier. I should never suspect De Mouy in a red cloak."

"No, if any one were suspected," said D'Alençon, "it would be more apt to be"—

He stopped.

"It would be more likely to be Monsieur de la Mole," said Henry.

"Certainly, since I myself, who saw the man running away, thought so for an instant."

"You thought so? Why, it must have been Monsieur de la Mole, then."

"Does he know anything?" asked D'Alençon.

"Absolutely nothing; at least, nothing of importance."

"Brother," said the duke; "I really think now that it was he."

"The devil!" said Henry; "if it was, that will trouble the queen greatly, for she is interested in him."

"Interested, you say?" said D'Alençon in amazement.

"Yes. Do you not remember, François, that it was your sister who recommended him to you?"

"Yes," said the duke, in a dull voice; "so I tried to be agreeable to him. The proof of this is that, fearing his red cloak might compromise him, I went up to his rooms and took the cloak away."

"Oh! oh!" exclaimed Henry, "that was doubly prudent. And now I would not bet, but I would swear, that it was he."

"Even in court?" asked François.

"Faith, yes," replied Henry. "He probably came to bring me some message from Marguerite."

"If I were sure of being upheld by your testimony," said D'Alençon, "I would almost accuse him."

"If you were to accuse him," replied Henry, "you understand, brother, that I would not contradict you."

"But the queen?" said D'Alençon.

"Ah, yes, the queen."

"We must know what she would do."

"I will undertake to find out."

"Plague it, brother! she will do wrong to lie to us, for this affair will make a glorious reputation of bravery for the young man, and which, cannot have cost him dear either, for he probably bought it on credit. Furthermore, it is true that he is well able to pay back both interest and capital."

"Well, what can you expect?" said Henry; "in this base world one has nothing for nothing!"

And bowing and smiling to D'Alençon, he cautiously thrust his head into the corridor, and making sure that no one had been listening, he hurried rapidly away, and disappeared down the private stairway which led to the apartments of Marguerite.

As far as she was concerned, the Queen of Navarre was no less anxious than her husband. The night's expedition sent against her and the Duchesse de Nevers by the King, the Duc d'Anjou, the Duc de Guise, and Henry, whom she had recognized, troubled her greatly. In all probability there was nothing which could compromise her. The janitor unfastened from the gate by La Mole and Coconnas had promised to be silent. But four lords like those with whom two simple gentlemen, such as La Mole and Coconnas, had coped, would not have gone out of their way by chance, or without having had some reason for thus inconveniencing themselves. Marguerite had returned at daybreak, having passed the rest of the night with the Duchesse de Nevers. She had retired at once, but had been unable to sleep, and had started at the slightest sound.

In the midst of this anxiety she heard some one knocking at the secret door, and being informed that the visitor was Gillonne, she gave orders to have her admitted.

Henry waited at the outer door. Nothing in his appearance showed the wounded husband. His usual smile lay on his delicate lips, and not a muscle of his face betrayed the terrible anxiety through which he had just passed. He seemed to glance inquiringly at Marguerite to discover if she would allow him to talk with her alone. Marguerite understood her husband's look, and signed to Gillonne to withdraw.

"Madame," said Henry, "I know how deeply you are attached to your friends, and I fear I bring you bad news."

"What is it, monsieur?" asked Marguerite.

"One of your dearest servants is at present greatly compromised."

"Which one?"

"The dear Count de la Mole."

"Monsieur le Comte de la Mole compromised! And why?"

"Because of the affair of last night."

In spite of her self-control Marguerite could not keep from blushing.

But she made an effort over herself.

"What affair?" she asked.

"What," said Henry, "did you not hear all the noise which was made in the Louvre?"

"No, monsieur."

"I congratulate you, madame," said Henry, with charming simplicity. "This proves that you are a sound sleeper."

"But what happened?"

"It seems that our good mother gave an order to Monsieur de Maurevel and six of his men to arrest me."

"You, monsieur, you?"

"Yes, me."

"For what reason?"

"Ah, who can tell the reasons of a mind as subtle as that of your mother? I suspect the reasons, but I do not know them positively."

"And you were not in your rooms?"

"No; I happened not to be. You have guessed rightly, madame, I was not. Last evening the King asked me to go out with him. But, although I was not in my rooms, some one else was."

"Who?"

"It seems that it was the Count de la Mole."

"The Count de la Mole!" exclaimed Marguerite, astonished.

"By Heavens! what a lively little fellow this man from the provinces is!" continued Henry. "Do you know that he wounded Maurevel and killed two guards?"

"Wounded Monsieur de Maurevel and killed two guards!—impossible!"

"What! You doubt his courage, madame?"

"No, but I say that Monsieur de la Mole could not have been in your rooms."

"Why not?"

"Why, because—because"—said Marguerite, embarrassed, "because he was elsewhere."

"Ah! If he can prove an alibi," said Henry, "that is different; he will tell where he was, and the matter will be settled."

"Where was he?" said Marguerite, quickly.

"In all probability the day will not pass without his being arrested and questioned. But unfortunately as there are proofs"—

"Proofs! what proofs?"

"The man who made this desperate defence wore a red cloak."

"But Monsieur de la Mole is not the only one who has a red cloak—I know another man who has one."

"No doubt, and I too know one. But this is what will happen: if it was not Monsieur de la Mole who was in my rooms, it must have been the other man who wears a red cloak, like La Mole. Now, do you know who this other man is?"

"Heavens!"

"There lies the danger. You, as well as myself, madame, have seen it. Your emotion proves this. Let us now talk like two people who are discussing the most desirable thing in the world—a throne; a most precious gift—life. De Mouy arrested, we are ruined."

"Yes, I understand that."

"While Monsieur de la Mole compromises no one; at least you would not suppose him capable of inventing a story such as, for instance, that he was with some ladies—whom I know?"

"Monsieur," said Marguerite, "if you fear only that, you may be easy. He will not say it."

"What!" said Henry, "would he remain silent if death were to be the price of his silence?"

"He would remain silent, monsieur."

"You are sure of this?"

"I am sure."

"Then everything is for the best," said Henry, rising.

"You are going, monsieur?" asked Marguerite, quickly.

"Oh, my God, yes. This is all I had to say to you."

"And you are going"—

"To try and get out of the trouble we have been put to by this devil of a man in the red cloak."

"Oh, my God! my God! the poor young man!" cried Marguerite, pitifully, wringing her hands.

"Really," said Henry, as he went out, "this dear Monsieur de la Mole is a faithful servant."

———

CHAPTER XXXVIII.

THE GIRDLE OF THE QUEEN MOTHER.

Charles entered his room, smiling and joking. But after a conversation of ten minutes with his mother, one would have said that the latter had given him her pallor and anger in exchange for the light-heartedness of her son.

"Monsieur de la Mole," said Charles, "Monsieur de la Mole! Henry and the Duc d'Alençon must be sent for. Henry, because this young man was a Huguenot; the Duc d'Alençon, because he is in his service."

"Send for them if you wish, my son, but you will learn nothing. Henry and François, I fear, are much more closely bound together than one would suppose from appearances. To question them is to suspect them. I think it would be better to wait for the slow but sure proof of time. If you give the guilty ones time to breathe again, my son, if you let them think they have escaped your vigilance, they will become bold and triumphant, and will give you a better opportunity to punish them. Then we shall know everything."

Charles walked up and down, undecided, gnawing his anger, as a horse gnaws his bit, and pressing his clinched hand to his heart, which was consumed by his one idea.

"No, no," said he, at length; "I will not wait. You do not know what it is to wait, beset with suspicions as I am. Besides, every day these courtiers become more insolent. Even last night did not two of them dare to cope with us? If Monsieur de la Mole is innocent, very good; but I should not be sorry to know where Monsieur de la Mole was last night, while they were attacking my guards in the Louvre, and me in the Rue Cloche Percée. So let the Duc d'Alençon be sent for, and afterwards Henry. I will question them separately. You may remain, mother."

Catharine sat down. For a determined spirit such as hers was, every incident turned by her powerful hand would lead her to her goal, although it might seem to be leading away from it. From every blow there would result noise and a spark. The noise would guide, the spark give light.

The Duc d'Alençon entered. His previous conversation with Henry had prepared him for this interview; therefore he was quite calm.

His replies were very exact. Warned by his mother to remain in his own rooms, he was completely ignorant of the events of the night. But as his apartments opened upon the same corridor as did those of the King of Navarre, he had at first thought he heard a sound like that of a door being broken in, then curses, then pistol-shots. Thereupon he had ventured to push his door partly open, and had seen a man in a red cloak running away.

Charles and his mother exchanged glances.

"In a red cloak?" said the King.

"In a red cloak," replied D'Alençon.

"And did you have any suspicions regarding this red cloak?"

D'Alençon rallied all his strength that he might lie as naturally as possible.

"At first sight," said he, "I must confess to your Majesty that I thought I recognized the red cloak of one of my gentlemen."

"What is the name of this gentleman?"

"Monsieur de la Mole."

"Why was not Monsieur de la Mole with you as his duty required him to be?"

"I had given him leave of absence," said the duke.

"That is well; now you may go," said Charles.

The Duc d'Alençon started towards the door by which he had entered.

"Not that way," said Charles; "this way."

And he indicated the door opening into his nurse's room. Charles did not want François and Henry to meet.

He did not know that they had already seen each other for an instant, and that this instant had sufficed for the two brothers-in-law to agree on their plans.

At a sign from Charles, Henry entered.

He did not wait for Charles to question him, however.

"Sire," said he, "your Majesty has done well to send for me, for I was just coming to demand justice of you."

Charles frowned.

"Yes, justice," said Henry. "I will begin by thanking your Majesty for having taken me with you last night; for, by doing this, I now know that you saved my life. But what had I done that an attempt should be made to assassinate me?"

"Not to assassinate," said Catharine, quickly, "but to arrest you."

"Well," said Henry, "even so. What crime have I committed to merit arrest? If I am guilty I am as much so this morning as I was last evening. Tell me my offence, sire."

Embarrassed as to what reply to make, Charles looked at his mother.

"My son," said Catharine, "you receive suspicious characters."

"Very good," said Henry, "and these suspicious characters compromise me; is that it, madame?"

"Yes, Henry."

"Give me their names! Give me their names! Who are they? Let me see them!"

"Really," said Charles, "Henriot has the right to demand an explanation."

"And I do demand it!" said Henry, realizing the superiority of his position and anxious to make the most of it. "I ask it from my good brother Charles, and from my good mother Catharine. Since my marriage with Marguerite have I not been a kind husband? ask Marguerite. A good Catholic? ask my confessor. A good relative? ask those who were at the hunt yesterday."

"Yes, that is true, Henriot," said the King; "but what can you do? They claim that you conspire."

"Against whom?"

"Against me."

"Sire, if I had been conspiring against you, I had merely to let events take their course, when your horse broke his knee and could not rise, or when the furious boar turned on your Majesty."

"Well, the devil! mother, do you know that he is right?"

"But who was in your rooms last night?"

"Madame," said Henry, "in times when so few dare to answer for themselves, I should never attempt to answer for others. I left my rooms at seven o'clock in the evening, at ten o'clock my brother Charles took me away, and I spent the night with him. I could not be with your Majesty and know what was going on in my rooms at the same time."

"But," said Catharine, "it is none the less true that one of your men killed two of his Majesty's guards and wounded Monsieur de Maurevel."

"One of my men?" said Henry. "What man, madame? Name him."

"Every one accuses Monsieur de la Mole."

"Monsieur de la Mole is not in my suite, madame; Monsieur de la Mole belongs to Monsieur d'Alençon, to whom he was recommended by your daughter."

"But," said Charles, "was it Monsieur de la Mole who was in your rooms, Henriot?"

"How can you expect me to know, sire? I can say neither yes nor no. Monsieur de la Mole is an exceptional servant, thoroughly devoted to the Queen of Navarre. He often brings me messages, either from Marguerite, to whom he is grateful for having recommended him to Monsieur le Duc d'Alençon, or from Monsieur le Duc himself. I cannot say that it was not Monsieur de la Mole"—

"It was he," said Catharine. "His red cloak was recognized."

"Has Monsieur de la Mole a red cloak, then?"

"Yes."

"And the man who so cleverly disposed of two of my guards and Monsieur de Maurevel"—

"Had a red cloak?" asked Henry.

"Exactly," said Charles.

"I have nothing to say," said the Béarnais. "But in any case it seems to me that instead of summoning me here, since I was not in my rooms, it is Monsieur de la Mole, who, having been there, as you say, should be questioned. But," said Henry, "I must observe one thing to your Majesty."

"What is that?"

"This, that if I had seen an order signed by my King and had defended myself instead of obeying this order, I should be guilty and should deserve all sorts of punishment; but it was not I but some stranger whom this order in no way concerned. There was an attempt made to arrest him unjustly, he defended himself too well, perhaps, but he was in the right."

"And yet"—murmured Catharine.

"Madame," said Henry, "was the order to arrest me?"

"Yes," said Catharine, "and his Majesty himself signed it."

"Was it an order to arrest any one found in my place in case I was not there?"

"No," said Catharine.

"Well!" said Henry, "unless you prove that I was conspiring and that the man who was in my rooms was conspiring with me, this man is innocent."

Then turning to Charles IX.:

"Sire," continued Henry, "I shall not leave the Louvre. At a simple word from your Majesty I shall even be ready to enter any state prison you may be pleased to suggest. But while waiting for the proof to the contrary I have the right to call myself and I do call myself the very faithful servant, subject, and brother of your Majesty."

And with a dignity hitherto unknown in him, Henry bowed to Charles and withdrew.

"Bravo, Henriot!" said Charles, when the King of Navarre had left.

"Bravo! because he has defeated us?" said Catharine.

"Why should I not applaud? When we fence together and he touches me do I not say 'bravo'? Mother, you are wrong to hate this boy as you do."

"My son," said Catharine, pressing the hand of Charles IX., "I do not hate him, I fear him."

"Well, you are wrong, mother. Henriot is my friend, and as he said, had he been conspiring against me he had only to let the wild boar alone."

"Yes," said Catharine, "so that Monsieur le Duc d'Anjou, his personal enemy, might be King of France."

"Mother, whatever Henriot's motive in saving my life, the fact is that he saved it, and, the devil! I do not want any harm to come to him. As to Monsieur de la Mole, well, I will talk about him with my brother D'Alençon, to whom he belongs."

This was Charles IX.'s way of dismissing his mother, who withdrew endeavoring to fix her suspicions. On account of his unimportance, Monsieur de la Mole did not answer to her needs.

Returning to her rooms, Catharine found Marguerite waiting for her.

"Ah! ah!" said she, "is it you, my daughter? I sent for you last evening."

"I know it, madame, but I had gone out."

"And this morning?"

"This morning, madame, I have come to tell your majesty that you are about to do a great wrong."

"What is that?"

"You are going to have Monsieur le Comte de la Mole arrested."

"You are mistaken, my daughter, I am going to have no one arrested. It is the King, not I, who gives orders for arrests."

"Let us not quibble over the words, madame, when the circumstances are serious. Monsieur de la Mole is going to be arrested, is he not?"

"Very likely."

"Accused of having been found in the chamber of the King of Navarre last night, and of having killed two guards and wounded Monsieur de Maurevel?"

"Such indeed is the crime they impute to him."

"They impute it to him wrongly, madame," said Marguerite; "Monsieur de la Mole is not guilty."

"Monsieur de la Mole not guilty!" said Catharine, giving a start of joy, and thinking that what Marguerite was about to tell her would throw light on the subject.

"No," went on Marguerite, "he is not guilty, he cannot be so, for he was not in the king's room."

"Where was he, then?"

"In my room, madame."

"In your room?"

"Yes, in my room."

At this avowal from a daughter of France, Catharine felt like hurling a withering glance at Marguerite, but she merely crossed her arms on her lap.

"And," said she after a moment's silence, "if Monsieur de la Mole is arrested and questioned"—

"He will say where he was and with whom he was, mother," replied Marguerite, although she felt sure of the contrary.

"Since this is so, you are right, my daughter; Monsieur de la Mole must not be arrested."

Marguerite shivered. It seemed to her that there was something strange and terrible in the way her mother uttered these words; but she had nothing to say, for what she had come to ask for had been granted her.

"But," said Catharine, "if it was not Monsieur de la Mole who was in the king's room, it was some one else!"

Marguerite was silent.

"Do you know who it was, my daughter?" said Catharine.

"No, mother," said Marguerite, in an unsteady voice.

"Come, do not be half confidential."

"I repeat, madame, that I do not know," replied Marguerite again, growing pale in spite of herself.

"Well, well," said Catharine, carelessly, "we shall find out. Go now, my daughter. You may rest assured that your mother will watch over your honor."

Marguerite went out.

"Ah!" murmured Catharine, "they are in league. Henry and Marguerite are working together. While the wife is silent, the husband is blind. Ah, you are very clever, my children, and you think yourselves very strong. But your strength is in your union and I will break you, one after the other. Besides, the day will come when Maurevel can speak or write, utter a name, or spell six letters, and then we shall know everything. Yes, but in the meantime the guilty shall be in safe-keeping. The best thing to do would be to separate them at once."

Thereupon Catharine set out for the apartments of her son, whom she found holding a conference with D'Alençon.

"Ah! ah!" exclaimed Charles IX., frowning, "is it you, mother?"

"Why did you not say 'again'? The word was in your mind, Charles."

"What is in my mind belongs to me, madame," said the King, in the rough tone he sometimes used even when speaking to Catharine. "What do you want of me? Tell me quickly."

"Well, you were right, my son," said Catharine to Charles, "and you, D'Alençon, were wrong."

"In what respect, madame?" asked both princes.

"It was not Monsieur de la Mole who was in the apartments of the King of Navarre."

"Ah! ah!" cried François, growing pale.

"Who was it, then?" asked Charles.

"We do not know yet, but we shall know when Maurevel is able to speak. So let us drop the subject, which will soon be explained, and return to Monsieur de la Mole."

"Well, what do you want of Monsieur de la Mole, mother, since he was not in the rooms of the King of Navarre?"

"No," said Catharine, "he was not there, but he was with—the queen."

"With the queen!" cried Charles, bursting into a nervous laugh.

"With the queen," murmured D'Alençon, turning as pale as death.

"No, no," said Charles, "De Guise told me he had met Marguerite's litter."

"Yes," said Catharine, "she has a house in town."

"In the Rue Cloche Percée!" cried the King.

"Oh! oh! this is too much," said D'Alençon, driving his nails into his breast. "And to have had him recommended to me!"

"Ah! now that I think of it!" said the King, stopping suddenly, "it was he who defended himself against us last night, and who hurled the silver bowl at my head, the wretch!"

"Oh, yes!" repeated François, "the wretch!"

"You are right, my children," said Catharine, without appearing to understand the feelings which incited both of her sons to speak. "You are right, for a single indiscreet act of this gentleman might cause a horrible scandal, and ruin a daughter of France. One moment of madness would be enough for that."

"Or of vanity," said François.

"No doubt, no doubt," said Charles. "And yet we cannot bring the case into court unless Henriot consents to appear as plaintiff."

"My son," said Catharine, placing her hand on Charles's shoulder in such a way as to call the King's attention to what she was about to propose, "listen to what I say. A crime has been committed, and there may be scandal. But this sort of offence to royalty is not punished by judges and hangmen. If you were simple gentlemen, I should have nothing to say to you, for you are both brave, but you are princes, you cannot cross swords with mere country squires. Think how you can avenge yourselves as princes."

"The devil!" cried Charles, "you are right, mother, and I will consider it."

"I will help you, brother," cried François.

"And I," said Catharine, unfastening the black silk girdle which was wound three times about her waist, and the two tassels of which fell to her knees. "I will retire, but I leave you this to represent me."

And she threw the girdle at the feet of the two princes.

"Ah! ah!" said Charles, "I understand."

"This girdle"—said D'Alençon, picking it up.

"Is punishment and silence," said Catharine, victorious; "but," she added, "there would be no harm in mentioning this to Henry."

She withdrew.

"By Heaven!" said D'Alençon; "a good idea, and when Henry knows that his wife has betrayed him—So," he added, turning to the King, "you will adopt our mother's suggestion?"

"In every detail," said Charles, not doubting but that he would drive a thousand daggers into D'Alençon's heart. "This will annoy Marguerite, but it will delight Henriot."

Then, calling one of his guards, he ordered Henry summoned, but thinking better of it:

"No, no," said he, "I will go for him myself. Do you, D'Alençon, inform D'Anjou and De Guise."

Leaving his apartments, he ascended the private stairway to the second floor, which led to Henry's chamber.

CHAPTER XXXIX.

PROJECTS OF REVENGE.

Henry took advantage of the respite afforded him by his well-sustained examination to go to Madame de Sauve's. He found Orthon completely recovered from his fainting-fit. But Orthon could tell him nothing, except that some men had broken into the king's rooms, that the leader had struck him with the handle of his sword, and that the blow had stunned him. No one had troubled about Orthon. Catharine had seen that he had fainted and had believed him to be dead.

As he had come to himself between the departure of the queen mother and the arrival of the captain of the guards charged with clearing up the room, he had taken refuge in Madame de Sauve's apartments.

Henry begged Charlotte to keep the young man until news came from De Mouy, who would not fail to write him from his hiding-place. Then he would send Orthon to carry his answer to De Mouy, and instead of one devoted man he could count on two. This decided on, he returned to his rooms and began further to consider matters, walking up and down the while. Suddenly the door opened and the King appeared.

"Your Majesty!" cried Henry, rising to meet him.

"In person. Really, Henriot, you are a good fellow, and I love you more and more."

"Sire," said Henry, "your Majesty overwhelms me."

"You have but one fault, Henriot."

"What is that? The one for which your Majesty has already reproached me several times?" said Henry. "My preferring to hunt animals rather than birds?"

"No, no, I am not referring to that, Henriot, I mean something else."

"If your Majesty will explain," said Henry, who saw from the smile on Charles's lips that the King was in a good humor, "I will try and correct it."

"It is this, that having such good eyes, you see no better than you do."

"Bah!" said Henry, "can I be short-sighted, then, sire, without knowing it?"

"Worse than that, Henry, worse than that, you are blind."

"Ah, indeed," said the Béarnais, "but is it not when I shut my eyes that this happens?"

"Well, yes!" said Charles, "you are perfectly capable of that. At all events, I am going to open your eyes."

"God said, 'Let there be light,' and there was light. Your Majesty is the

354

representative of God on earth. Therefore you can do here what God does in heaven. Proceed; I am all attention."

"When De Guise said last night that your wife had just passed escorted by a gallant you would not believe it."

"Sire," said Henry, "how could I believe that the sister of your Majesty could commit an act of such imprudence?"

"When he told you that your wife had gone to the Rue Cloche Percée, you would not believe that either!"

"How was I to suppose, sire, that a daughter of France would thus publicly risk her reputation?"

"When we besieged the house in the Rue Cloche Percée, and when I had a silver bowl hurled at my shoulder, D'Anjou some orange marmalade on his head, and De Guise a haunch of venison in the face, you saw two women and two men, did you not?"

"I saw nothing, sire. Does not your Majesty remember that I was questioning the janitor?"

"Yes, but, by Heaven, I saw"—

"Ah, if your Majesty saw anything, that is a different thing."

"I saw two men and two women. Well, I know now beyond a doubt that one of the women was Margot, and that one of the men was Monsieur de la Mole."

"Well," said Henry, "if Monsieur de la Mole was in the Rue Cloche Percée, he was not here."

"No," said Charles, "he was not here. But never mind who was here; we shall know this as soon as that imbecile of a Maurevel is able to speak or write. The point is that Margot is deceiving you."

"Bah!" said Henry; "do not believe such nonsense."

"When I tell you that you are more than near-sighted, that you are blind, the devil! will you believe me just once, stupid? I tell you that Margot is deceiving you, and that this evening we are going to strangle her lover."

Henry gave a start of surprise, and looked at his brother-in-law in amazement.

"Confess, Henry, that at heart you are not sorry. Margot will cry out like a thousand Niobes; but, faith! so much the worse. I do not want you to be made a fool of. If Condé is deceived by the Duc d'Anjou, I will wink; Condé is my enemy. But you are my brother; more than this, you are my friend."

"But, sire"—

"And I do not want you to be annoyed, and made a fool of. You have been a quintain long enough for all these popinjays who come from the provinces to gather our crumbs, and court our women. Let them come, or rather let them come again. By Heaven! you have been deceived, Henriot,—that might happen to any one,—but I swear, you shall have shining satisfaction, and tomorrow they shall say: In the name of a thousand devils! it seems that King Charles loves his brother Henriot, for last night he had Monsieur de la Mole's tongue pulled out in a most amusing manner."

"Is this really decided on, sire?" asked Henry.

"Decided on, determined on, arranged. The coxcomb will have no time to plead his cause. The expedition will consist of myself, D'Anjou, D'Alençon, and De Guise—a king, two sons of France, and a sovereign prince, without counting you."

"How without counting me?"

"Why, you are to be one of us."

"I!"

"Yes, you! you shall stab the fellow in a royal manner, while the rest of us strangle him."

"Sire," said Henry, "your kindness overpowers me; but how do you know"—

"Why, the devil! it seems that the fellow boasts of it. He goes sometimes to your wife's apartments in the Louvre, sometimes to the Rue Cloche Percée. They compose verses together. I should like to see the stanzas that fop writes. Pastorales they are. They discuss Bion and Moschus, and read first Daphne and then Corydon. Ah! take a good dagger with you!"

"Sire," said Henry, "upon reflection"—

"What?"

"Your Majesty will see that I cannot join such an expedition. It seems to me it would be inconvenient to be there in person. I am too much interested in the affair to take any calm part in it. Your Majesty will avenge the honor of your sister on a coxcomb who boasts of having calumniated my wife; nothing is simpler, and Marguerite, whom I hold to be innocent, sire, is in no way dishonored. But were I of the party, it would be a different thing. My co-operation would convert an act of justice into an act of revenge. It would no longer be an execution, but an assassination. My wife would no longer be calumniated, but guilty."

"By Heaven, Henry, as I said just now to my mother, you speak words of wisdom. You have a devilishly quick mind."

And Charles gazed complacently at his brother-in-law, who bowed in return for the compliment.

"Nevertheless," added Charles, "you are willing to be rid of this coxcomb, are you not?"

"Everything your Majesty does is well done," replied the King of Navarre.

"Well, well, let me do your work for you. You may be sure it shall not be the worse for it."

"I leave it to you, sire," said Henry.

"At what time does he usually go to your wife's room?"

"About nine o'clock."

"And he leaves?"

"Before I reach there, for I never see him."

"About"—

"About eleven."

"Very well. Come this evening at midnight. The deed will be done."

Charles pressed Henry's hand cordially, and renewing his vows of friendship, left the apartment, whistling his favorite hunting-song.

"*Ventre saint gris!*" said the Béarnais, watching Charles, "either I am greatly mistaken, or the queen mother is responsible for all this deviltry. Truly, she does nothing but invent plots to make trouble between my wife and myself. Such a pleasant household!"

And Henry began to laugh as he was in the habit of laughing when no one could see or hear him.

About seven o'clock that evening a handsome young man, who had just taken a bath, was finishing his toilet as he calmly moved about his room, humming a little air, before a mirror in one of the rooms of the Louvre. Near him another young man was sleeping, or rather lying on a bed.

The one was our friend La Mole who, unconsciously, had been the object of so much discussion all day; the other was his companion Coconnas.

The great storm had passed over him without his having heard the rumble of the thunder or seen the lightning. He had returned at three o'clock in the morning, had stayed in bed until three in the afternoon, half asleep, half awake, building castles on that uncertain sand called the future. Then he had risen, had spent an hour at a fashionable bath, had dined at Maître La Hurière's, and returning to the Louvre had set himself to finish his toilet before making his usual call on the queen.

"And you say you have dined?" asked Coconnas, yawning.

"Faith, yes, and I was hungry too."

"Why did you not take me with you, selfish man?"

"Faith, you were sleeping so soundly that I did not like to waken you. But you shall sup with me instead. Be sure not to forget to ask Maître La Hurière for some of that light wine from Anjou, which arrived a few days ago."

"Is it good?"

"I merely tell you to ask for it."

"Where are you going?"

"Where am I going?" said La Mole, surprised that his friend should ask him such a question; "I am going to pay my respects to the queen."

"Well," said Coconnas, "if I were going to dine in our little house in the Rue Cloche Percée, I should have what was left over from yesterday. There is a certain wine of Alicante which is most refreshing."

"It would be imprudent to go there, Annibal, my friend, after what occurred last night. Besides, did we not promise that we would not go back there alone? Hand me my cloak."

"That is so," said Coconnas, "I had forgotten. But where the devil is your cloak? Ah! here it is."

"No, you have given me the black one, and it is the red one I want. The queen likes me better in that."

"Ah, faith," said Coconnas, searching everywhere, "look for yourself, I cannot find it."

"What!" said La Mole, "you cannot find it? Why, where can it be?"

"You probably sold it."

"Why, I have six crowns left."

"Well, take mine."

"Ah, yes,—a yellow cloak with a green doublet! I should look like a popinjay!"

"Faith, you are over-particular, so wear what you please."

Having tossed everything topsy-turvy in his search, La Mole was beginning to abuse the thieves who managed to enter even the Louvre, when a page from the Duc d'Alençon appeared bringing the precious cloak in question.

"Ah!" cried La Mole, "here it is at last!"

"Is this your cloak, monsieur?" said the page. "Yes; monseigneur sent for it to decide a wager he made regarding its color."

"Oh!" said La Mole, "I asked for it only because I was going out, but if his highness desires to keep it longer"—

"No, Monsieur le Comte, he is through with it."

The page left. La Mole fastened his cloak.

"Well," he went on, "what have you decided to do?"

"I do not know."

"Shall I find you here this evening?"

"How can I tell?"

"Do you not know what you are going to do for two hours?"

"I know well enough what I shall do, but I do not know what I may be ordered to do."

"By the Duchesse de Nevers?"

"No, by the Duc d'Alençon."

"As a matter of fact," said La Mole, "I have noticed for some time that he has been friendly to you."

"Yes," said Coconnas.

"Then your fortune is made," said La Mole, laughing.

"Poof!" said Coconnas. "He is only a younger brother!"

"Oh!" said La Mole, "he is so anxious to become the elder one that perhaps Heaven will work some miracle in his favor."

"So you do not know where you will be this evening?"

"No."

"Go to the devil, then,—I mean good-by!"

"That La Mole is a terrible fellow," thought Coconnas, "always wanting me to tell him where I am going to be! as if I knew. Besides, I believe I am sleepy." And he threw himself on the bed again.

La Mole betook himself to the apartments of the queen. In the corridor he met the Duc d'Alençon.

"Ah! you here, Monsieur la Mole?" said the prince.

"Yes, my lord," replied La Mole, bowing respectfully.

"Are you going away from the Louvre?"

"No, your highness. I am on my way to pay my respects to her Majesty the Queen of Navarre."

"About what time shall you leave, Monsieur de la Mole?"

"Has monseigneur any orders for me?"

"No, not at present, but I shall want to speak to you this evening."

"About what time?"

"Between nine and ten."

"I shall do myself the honor of waiting on your highness at that time."

"Very good. I shall depend on you."

La Mole bowed and went on.

"There are times," said he, "when the duke is as pale as death. It is very strange."

He knocked at the door of the queen's apartments. Gillonne, who apparently was expecting him, led him to Marguerite.

The latter was occupied with some work which seemed to be wearying her greatly. A paper covered with notes and a volume of Isocrates lay before her. She signed to La Mole to let her finish a paragraph. Then, in a few moments, she threw down her pen and invited the young man to sit beside her. La Mole was radiant. Never had he been so handsome or so light-hearted.

"Greek!" said he, glancing at the book. "A speech of Isocrates! What are you doing with that? Ah! and Latin on this sheet of paper! *Ad Sarmatiæ legatos reginæ Margaritæ concio!* So you are going to harangue these barbarians in Latin?"

"I must," said Marguerite, "since they do not speak French."

"But how can you write the answer before you have the speech?"

"A greater coquette than I would make you believe that this was impromptu; but I cannot deceive you, my Hyacinthe: I was told the speech in advance, and I am answering it."

"Are these ambassadors about to arrive?"

"Better still, they arrived this morning."

"Does any one know it?"

"They came incognito. Their formal arrival is planned for to-morrow afternoon, I believe, and you will see," said Marguerite, with a little satisfied air not wholly free from pedantry, "that what I have done this evening is quite Ciceronian. But let us drop these important matters and speak of what has happened to you."

"To me?"

"Yes."

"What has happened to me?"

"Ah! it is in vain you pretend to be brave, you look pale."

"Then it is from having slept too much. I am humbly sorry for it."

"Come, come, let us not play the braggart; I know everything."

"Have the kindness to inform me, then, my pearl, for I know nothing."

"Well, answer me frankly. What did the queen mother ask you?"

"Had she something to say to me?"

"What! Have you not seen her?"

"No."

"Nor King Charles?"

"No."

"Nor the King of Navarre?"

"No."

"But you have seen the Duc d'Alençon?"

"Yes, I met him just now in the corridor."

"What did he say to you?"

"That he had some orders to give me between nine and ten o'clock this evening."

"Nothing else?"

"Nothing else."

"That is strange."

"But what is strange? Tell me."

"That nothing has been said to you."

"What has happened?"

"All day, unfortunately, you have been hanging over an abyss."

"I?"

"Yes, you."

"Why?"

"Well, listen. It seems that last night De Mouy was surprised in the apartments of the King of Navarre, who was to have been arrested. De Mouy killed three men, and escaped without anything about him having been recognized except the famous red cloak."

"Well?"

"Well, this red cloak, which once deceived me, has thrown others besides myself off the track. You have been suspected and even accused of this triple murder. This morning they wanted to arrest, judge, and perhaps convict you. Who knows? For in order to save yourself you would not have told where you were, would you?"

"Tell where I was?" cried La Mole; "compromise you, my beautiful queen? Oh! you are right. I should have died singing, to spare your sweet eyes one tear."

"Alas!" said Marguerite, "my sweet eyes would have been filled with many, many tears."

"But what caused the great storm to subside?"

"Guess."

"How can I tell?"

"There was only one way to prove that you were not in the king's room."

"And that was"—

"To tell where you were."

"Well?"

362

"Well, I told."

"Whom did you tell?"

"My mother."

"And Queen Catharine"—

"Queen Catharine knows that I love you."

"Oh, madame! after having done so much for me, you can demand anything from your servant. Ah, Marguerite, truly, what you did was noble and beautiful. My life is yours, Marguerite."

"I hope so, for I have snatched it from those who wanted to take it from me. But now you are saved."

"And by you!" cried the young man; "by my adored queen!"

At that instant a sharp noise made them start. La Mole sprang back, filled with a vague terror. Marguerite uttered a cry, and stood with her eyes riveted on the broken glass of one of the window-panes.

Through this window a stone the size of an egg had entered and lay on the floor.

La Mole saw the broken pane, and realized the cause of the noise.

"Who dared to do this?" he cried, springing to the window.

"One moment," said Marguerite. "It seems to me that something is tied around the stone."

"Yes," said La Mole, "it looks like a piece of paper."

Marguerite went to the strange projectile and removed the thin sheet which, folded like a narrow band, encircled the middle of the stone.

The paper was attached to a cord, which came through the broken window.

Marguerite unfolded the letter and read.

"Unfortunate man!" she cried, holding out the paper to La Mole, who stood as pale and motionless as a statue of Terror.

With a heart filled with gloomy forebodings he read these words:

"They are waiting for Monsieur de la Mole, with long swords, in the corridor leading to the apartments of Monsieur d'Alençon. Perhaps he would prefer to escape by this window and join Monsieur de Mouy at Mantes"—

"Well!" asked La Mole, after reading it, "are these swords longer than mine?"

363

"No, but there may be ten against one."

"Who is the friend who has sent us this note?" asked La Mole.

Marguerite took it from the young man's hand and looked at it attentively.

"The King of Navarre's handwriting!" she cried. "If he warns us, the danger is great. Flee, La Mole, flee, I beg you."

"How?" asked La Mole.

"By this window. Does not the note refer to it?"

"Command, my queen, and I will leap from the window to obey you, if I broke my head twenty times by the fall."

"Wait, wait," said Marguerite. "It seems to me that there is a weight attached to this cord."

"Let us see," said La Mole.

Both drew up the cord, and with indescribable joy saw a ladder of hair and silk at the end of it.

"Ah! you are saved," cried Marguerite.

"It is a miracle of heaven!"

"No, it is a gift from the King of Navarre."

"But suppose it were a snare?" said La Mole. "If this ladder were to break under me? Madame, did you not acknowledge your love for me to-day?"

Marguerite, whose joy had dissipated her grief, became ashy pale.

"You are right," said she, "that is possible."

She started to the door.

"What are you going to do?" cried La Mole.

"To find out if they are really waiting for you in the corridor."

"Never! never! For their anger to fall on you?"

"What can they do to a daughter of France? As a woman and a royal princess I am doubly inviolable."

The queen uttered these words with so much dignity that La Mole understood she ran no risk, and that he must let her do as she wished.

Marguerite put La Mole under the protection of Gillonne, leaving to him to decide, according to circumstances, whether to run or await her return, and started down the corridor. A side hall led to the library as well as to several reception-rooms, and at the end led to the apartments of the King, the queen mother, and to the small private stairway by which one reached the apartments of the Duc d'Alençon and Henry. Although it was scarcely nine o'clock, all the lights were extinguished, and the corridor, except for the dim glimmer which came from the side hall, was quite dark. The Queen of Navarre advanced boldly. When she had gone about a third of the distance she heard whispering which sounded mysterious and startling from an evident effort made to suppress it. It ceased almost instantly, as if by order from some superior, and silence was restored. The light, dim as it was, seemed to grow less. Marguerite walked on directly into the face of the danger if danger there was. To all appearances she was calm, although her clinched hands indicated a violent nervous tension. As she approached, the intense silence increased, while a shadow like that of a hand obscured the wavering and uncertain light.

At the point where the transverse hall crossed the main corridor a man sprang in front of the queen, uncovered a red candlestick, and cried out:

"Here he is!"

Marguerite stood face to face with her brother Charles. Behind him, a silken cord in hand, was the Duc d'Alençon. At the rear, in the darkness, stood two figures side by side, reflecting no light other than that of the drawn swords which they held in their hands. Marguerite saw everything at a glance. Making a supreme effort, she said smilingly to Charles:

"You mean, here *she* is, sire!"

Charles recoiled. The others stood motionless.

"You, Margot!" said he. "Where are you going at this hour?"

"At this hour!" said Marguerite. "Is it so late?"

"I ask where you are going?"

"To find a book of Cicero's speeches, which I think I left at our mother's."

"Without a light?"

"I supposed the corridor was lighted."

"Do you come from your own apartments?"

"Yes."

"What are you doing this evening?"

"Preparing my address for the Polish ambassadors. Is there not a council to-morrow? and does not each one have to submit his address to your Majesty?"

"Have you not some one helping you with this work?"

Marguerite summoned all her strength.

"Yes, brother," said she, "Monsieur de la Mole. He is very learned."

"So much so," said the Duc d'Alençon, "that I asked him when he had finished with you, sister, to come and help me, for I am not as clever as you are."

"And were you waiting for him?" asked Marguerite as naturally as possible.

"Yes," said D'Alençon, impatiently.

"Then," said Marguerite, "I will send him to you, brother, for we have finished my work."

"But your book?" said Charles.

"I will have Gillonne get it."

The two brothers exchanged a sign.

"Go," said Charles, "and we will continue our round."

"Your round!" said Marguerite; "whom are you looking for?"

"The little red man," said Charles. "Do you not know that there is a little red man who is said to haunt the old Louvre? My brother D'Alençon claims to have seen him, and we are looking for him."

"Good luck to you," said Marguerite, and she turned round. Glancing behind her, she saw the four figures gather close to the wall as if in conference. In an instant she had reached her own door.

"Open, Gillonne," said she, "open."

Gillonne obeyed.

Marguerite sprang into the room and found La Mole waiting for her, calm and quiet, but with drawn sword.

"Flee," said she, "flee. Do not lose a second. They are waiting for you in the corridor to kill you."

"You command me to do this?" said La Mole.

"I command it. We must part in order to see each other again."

While Marguerite had been away La Mole had made sure of the ladder at the window. He now stepped out, but before placing his foot on the first round he tenderly kissed the queen's hand.

"If the ladder is a trap and I should perish, Marguerite, remember your promise."

"It was not a promise, La Mole, but an oath. Fear nothing. Adieu!"

And La Mole, thus encouraged, let himself slip down the ladder. At the same instant there was a knock at the door.

Marguerite watched La Mole's perilous descent and did not turn away from the window until she was sure he had reached the ground in safety.

"Madame," said Gillonne, "madame!"

"Well?" asked Marguerite.

"The King is knocking at the door."

"Open it."

Gillonne did so.

The four princes, impatient at waiting, no doubt, stood on the threshold.

Charles entered.

Marguerite came forward, a smile on her lips.

The King cast a rapid glance around.

"Whom are you looking for, brother?" asked Marguerite.

"Why," said Charles, "I am looking—I am looking—why, the devil! I am looking for Monsieur de la Mole."

"Monsieur de la Mole!"

"Yes; where is he?"

Marguerite took her brother by the hand and led him to the window.

Just then two horsemen were seen galloping away, around the wooden tower. One of them unfastened his white satin scarf and waved it in the darkness, as a sign of adieu. The two men were La Mole and Orthon.

Marguerite pointed them out to Charles.

"Well!" said the King, "what does this mean?"

"It means," replied Marguerite, "that Monsieur le Duc d'Alençon may put his cord back into his pocket, and that Messieurs d'Anjou and de Guise may sheathe their swords, for Monsieur de la Mole will not pass through the corridor again to-night."

CHAPTER XL.

THE ATRIDES.

Since his return to Paris, Henry of Anjou had not seen his mother Catharine alone, and, as every one knows, he was her favorite son.

This visit was not merely for the sake of etiquette, nor the carrying out of a painful ceremony, but the accomplishment of a very sweet duty for this son who, if he did not love his mother, was at least sure of being tenderly loved by her.

Catharine loved this son best either because of his bravery, his beauty,—for besides the mother, there was the woman in Catharine,—or because, according to some scandalous chronicles, Henry of Anjou reminded the Florentine of a certain happy epoch of secret love.

Catharine alone knew of the return of the Duc d'Anjou to Paris. Charles IX. would have been ignorant of it had not chance led him to the Hôtel de Condé just as his brother was leaving it. Charles had not expected him until the following day, and Henry of Anjou had hoped to conceal from him the two motives which had hastened his arrival by a day, namely, his visit to the beautiful Marie of Clèves, princess of Condé, and his conference with the Polish ambassadors.

It was this last reason, of the object of which Charles was uncertain, which the Duc d'Anjou had to explain to his mother. And the reader, ignorant on this point as was Henry of Navarre, will profit by the explanation.

When the Duc d'Anjou, so long expected, entered his mother's rooms, Catharine, usually so cold and formal, and who since the departure of her favorite son had embraced with effusion no one but Coligny, who was to be assassinated the following day, opened her arms to the child of her love, and pressed him to her heart with a burst of maternal affection most surprising in a heart already long grown cold.

Then pushing him from her she gazed at him and again drew him into her arms.

"Ah, madame," said he, "since Heaven grants me the privilege of embracing my mother in private, console me, for I am the most wretched man alive."

"Oh, my God! my beloved child," cried Catharine, "what has happened to you?"

"Nothing which you do not know, mother. I am in love. I am loved; but it is this very love which is the cause of my unhappiness."

"Tell me about it, my son," said Catharine.

"Well, mother,—these ambassadors,—this departure"—

"Yes," said Catharine, "the ambassadors have arrived; the departure is near at hand."

"It need not be near at hand, mother, but my brother hastens it. He detests me. I am in his way, and he wants to rid himself of me."

Catharine smiled.

"By giving you a throne, poor, unhappy crowned head!"

"Oh, no, mother," said Henry in agony, "I do not wish to go away. I, a son of France, brought up in the refinement of polite society, near the best of mothers, loved by one of the dearest women in the world, must I go among snows, to the ends of the earth, to die by inches among those rough people who are intoxicated from morning until night, and who gauge the capacity of their king by that of a cask, according to what he can hold? No, mother, I do not want to go; I should die!"

"Come, Henry," said Catharine, pressing her son's hands, "come, is that the real reason?"

Henry's eyes fell, as though even to his mother he did not dare to confess what was in his heart.

"Is there no other reason?" asked Catharine; "less romantic, but more rational, more political?"

"Mother, it is not my fault if this thought comes to me, and takes stronger hold of me, perhaps, than it should; but did not you yourself tell me that the horoscope of my brother Charles prophesied that he would die young?"

"Yes," said Catharine, "but a horoscope may lie, my son. Indeed, I myself hope that all horoscopes are not true."

"But his horoscope said this, did it not?"

"His horoscope spoke of a quarter of a century; but it did not say whether it referred to his life or his reign."

"Well, mother, bring it about so that I can stay. My brother is almost twenty-four. In one year the question will be settled."

Catharine pondered deeply.

"Yes," said she; "it would certainly be better if it could be so arranged."

"Oh, imagine my despair, mother," cried Henry, "if I were to exchange the crown of France for that of Poland! My being tormented there with the idea that I might be reigning in the Louvre in the midst of this elegant and lettered court, near the best mother in the world, whose advice would spare me half my work and fatigue, who, accustomed to bearing, with my father, a portion of the burden of the State, would like to bear it with me too! Ah, mother, I should have been a great king!"

"There! there! dear child," said Catharine, to whom this outlook had always been a very sweet hope, "there! do not despair. Have you thought of any way of arranging the matter?"

"Oh, yes, certainly, and that is why I came back two or three days before I was expected, letting my brother Charles suppose that it was on account of Madame de Condé. Then I have been with De Lasco, the chief ambassador. I became acquainted with him, and did all I could in that first interview to make him hate me. I hope I have succeeded."

"Ah, my dear child," said Catharine, "that is wrong. You must place the interest of France above your petty dislikes."

"Mother, in case any accident happened to my brother, would it be to the interest of France for the Duc d'Alençon or the King of Navarre to reign?"

"Oh! the King of Navarre, never, never!" murmured Catharine, letting anxiety cover her face with that veil of care which spread over it every time this question arose.

"Faith," continued Henry, "my brother D'Alençon is not worth much more, and is no fonder of you."

"Well," said Catharine, "what did Lasco say?"

"Even Lasco hesitated when I urged him to seek an audience. Oh, if he could write to Poland and annul this election!"

"Folly, my son, madness! What a Diet has consecrated is sacred."

"But, mother, could not these Poles be prevailed on to accept my brother in my stead?"

"It would be difficult, if not impossible," said Catharine.

"Never mind, try, make the attempt, speak to the King, mother. Ascribe everything to my love for Madame de Condé; say that I am mad over her, that I am losing my mind. He saw me coming out of the prince's hôtel with De Guise, who did everything for me a friend could do."

"Yes, in order to help the League. You do not see this, but I do."

"Yes, mother, yes; but meanwhile I am making use of him. Should we not be glad when a man serves us while serving himself?"

"And what did the King say when he met you?"

"He apparently believed what I told him, that love alone had brought me back to Paris."

"But did he ask you what you did the rest of the night?"

"Yes, mother; but I had supper at Nantouillet's, where I made a frightful riot, so that the report of it might get abroad and deceive the King as to where I was."

"Then he is ignorant of your visit to Lasco?"

"Absolutely."

"Good, so much the better. I will try to influence him in your favor, dear child. But you know no influence makes any impression on his coarse nature."

"Oh, mother, mother, what happiness if I could stay! I would love you even more than I do now if that were possible!"

"If you stay you will be sent to war."

"Oh, never mind! if only I do not have to leave France."

"You will be killed."

"Mother, one does not die from blows; one dies from grief, from meanness. But Charles will not let me remain; he hates me."

"He is jealous of you, my beautiful conqueror, that is well known. Why are you so brave and so fortunate? Why, at scarcely twenty years of age, have you won battles like Alexander or Cæsar? But, in the meantime, do not let your wishes be known to any one; pretend to be resigned, pay your court to the King. To-day there is a private council to read and discuss the speeches which are to be made at the ceremony. Act like the King of Poland, and leave the rest to me. By the way, how about your expedition of last night?"

"It failed, mother. The gallant was warned and escaped by the window."

"Well," said Catharine, "some day I shall know who this evil genius is who upsets all my plans in this way. Meanwhile I suspect and—let him beware!"

"So, mother"—said the Duc d'Anjou.

"Let me manage this affair."

She kissed Henry tenderly on his eyes and pushed him from the room.

Before long the princes of her household arrived at the rooms of the queen. Charles was in a good humor, for the cleverness of his sister Margot had pleased rather than vexed him. Moreover, he had nothing against La Mole, and he had waited for him somewhat eagerly in the corridor merely because it was a kind of hunt.

D'Alençon, on the contrary, was greatly preoccupied. The repulsion he had always felt for La Mole had turned into hate the instant he knew that La Mole was loved by his sister.

Marguerite possessed both a dreamy mind and a quick eye. She had to remember as well as to watch.

The Polish deputies had sent a copy of the speeches which they were to make.

Marguerite, to whom no more mention had been made of the affair of the previous evening than as if it had never occurred, read the speeches, and, except Charles, every one discussed what he would answer. Charles let Marguerite reply as she pleased. As far as D'Alençon was concerned he was very particular as to the choice of terms; but as to the discourse of Henry of Anjou he seemed determined to attack it, and made numerous corrections.

This council, without being in any way decisive, had greatly embittered the feelings of those present.

Henry of Anjou, who had to rewrite nearly all his discourse, withdrew to begin the task.

Marguerite, who had not heard of the King of Navarre since the injury he had given to her window-pane, returned to her rooms, hoping to find him there.

D'Alençon, who had read hesitation in the eyes of his brother of Anjou, and who had surprised a meaning glance between him and his mother, retired to ponder on what he regarded as a fresh plot. Charles was about to go to his workshop to finish a boar-spear he was making for himself when Catharine stopped him.

The King, who suspected that he was to meet some opposition to his will, paused and looked at his mother closely.

"Well," he said, "what now?"

"A final word, sire, which we forgot, and yet it is of much importance: what day shall we decide on for the public reception?"

"Ah, that is true," said the King, seating himself again. "Well, what day would suit you?"

"I thought," replied Catharine, "from your Majesty's silence and apparent forgetfulness, that there was some deep-laid plan."

"No," said Charles; "why so, mother?"

"Because," added Catharine, very gently, "it seems to me, my son, that these Poles should not see us so eager after their crown."

"On the contrary, mother," said Charles, "it is they who are in haste. They have come from Varsovia by forced marches. Honor for honor, courtesy for courtesy."

"Your Majesty may be right in one sense; I am not curious. So your idea is that the public reception should be held soon?"

"Faith, yes, mother; is this not your idea too?"

"You know that my ideas are only such as can further your glory. I will tell you, therefore, that by this haste I fear you will be accused of profiting very quickly by this opportunity to relieve the house of France of the burdens your brother imposes on it, but which he certainly returns in glory and devotion."

"Mother," said Charles, "on his departure from France I will endow my brother so richly that no one will ever dare to think what you fear may be said."

"Well," said Catharine, "I surrender, since you have such a ready reply to each of my objections. But to receive this warlike people, who judge of the power of the states by exterior signs, you must have a considerable array of troops, and I do not think there are enough yet assembled in the Isle de France."

"Pardon me, mother. I have foreseen this event, and am prepared for it. I have recalled two battalions from Normandy and one from Guyenne; my company of archers arrived yesterday from Brittany; the light horse, scattered throughout Lorraine, will be in Paris in the course of the day; and while it is supposed that I have scarcely four regiments at my disposition, I have twenty thousand men ready to appear."

"Ah, ah!" said Catharine, surprised. "In that case only one thing is lacking, but that can be procured."

"What is that?"

"Money. I believe that you are not furnished with an over-supply."

"On the contrary, madame, on the contrary," said Charles IX., "I have fourteen hundred thousand crowns in the Bastille; my private estates have yielded me during the last few days eight hundred thousand crowns, which I have put in my cellar in the Louvre, and in case of need Nantouillet holds three hundred thousand crowns at my disposal."

Catharine shivered. Until then she had known Charles to be violent and passionate, but never provident.

"Well," said she, "your Majesty thinks of everything. That is fine; and provided the tailors, the embroiderers, and the jewellers make haste, your Majesty will be in a position to hold this audience within six weeks."

"Six weeks!" exclaimed Charles. "Mother, the tailors, the embroiderers, and the jewellers have been at work ever since we heard of my brother's nomination. As a matter of fact, everything could be ready to-day, but, at the latest, it will take only three or four days."

"Oh!" murmured Catharine; "you are in greater haste than I supposed, my son."

"Honor for honor, I told you."

"Well, is it this honor done to the house of France which flatters you?"

"Certainly."

"And is your chief desire to see a son of France on the throne of Poland?"

"Exactly."

"Then it is the event, the fact, and not the man, which is of interest to you, and whoever reigns there"—

"No, no, mother, by Heaven! Let us keep to the point! The Poles have made a good choice. They are a skilful and strong people! A military people, a nation of soldiers, they choose a captain for their ruler. That is logical, plague it! D'Anjou is just the man for them. The hero of Jarnac and Montcontour fits them like a glove. Whom would you have me send them? D'Alençon? a coward! He would give them a fine idea of the Valois!—D'Alençon! He would run at the first bullet that whistled by his ears, while Henry of Anjou is a fighter. Yes! his sword always in his hand, he is ever pushing forward, on foot or horseback!—forward! thrust! overpower! kill! Ah! my brother of Anjou is a man, a valiant soldier, who will lead them to battle from morning until night, from one year's end to the next. He is not a hard drinker, it is true; but he will kill in cold blood. That is all. This dear Henry will be in his element; there! quick! quick! to battle! Sound the trumpet and the drum! Long live the king! Long live the conqueror! Long live the general! He will be proclaimed *imperator* three times a year. That will be fine for the house of France, and for the honor of the Valois; he may be killed, but, by Heaven, it will be a glorious death!"

374

Catharine shuddered. Her eyes flashed fire.

"Say that you wish to send Henry of Anjou away from you," she cried, "say that you do not love your brother!"

"Ah! ah! ah!" cried Charles, bursting into a nervous laugh, "you have guessed, have you, that I want to send him away? You have guessed that I do not love him? And when did you reach this conclusion? Come! Love my brother! Why should I love him? Ah! ah! ah! Do you want to make me laugh?"

As he spoke, his pale cheeks grew flushed with a feverish glow.

"Does he love me? Do you love me? Has any one, except my dogs, and Marie Touchet, and my nurse, ever loved me? No! I do not love my brother, I love only myself. Do you hear? And I shall not prevent my brother from doing as I do."

"Sire," said Catharine, growing excited on her part, "since you have opened your heart to me I must open mine to you. You are acting like a weak king, like an ill-advised monarch; you are sending away your second brother, the natural support of the throne, who is in every way worthy to succeed you if any accident happened, in which case your crown would be left in jeopardy. As you said, D'Alençon is young, incapable, weak, more than weak, cowardly! And the Béarnais rises up in the background, you understand?"

"Well, the devil!" exclaimed Charles, "what does it matter to me what happens when I am dead? The Béarnais rises behind my brother, you say! By Heaven! so much the better! I said that I loved no one—I was mistaken, I love Henriot. Yes, I love this good Henriot. He has a frank manner, a warm handshake, while I see nothing but false looks around me, and touch, only icy hands. He is incapable of treason towards me, I swear. Besides, I owe him amends, poor boy! His mother was poisoned by some members of my family, I am told. Moreover, I am well. But if I were to be taken ill, I would call him, I should want him to stay with me, I would take nothing except from him, and when I died I would make him King of France and of Navarre. And by Heaven! instead of laughing at my death as my brothers would do, he would weep, or at least he would pretend to weep."

Had a thunderbolt fallen at Catharine's feet she would have been less startled than at these words. She stood speechless, gazing at Charles with haggard eyes. Then at the end of a few moments:

"Henry of Navarre!" she cried, "Henry of Navarre King of France to the detriment of my children! Ah! Holy Virgin! we shall see! So this is why you wish to send away my son?"

"Your son—and what am I, then? the son of a wolf, like Romulus?" cried Charles, trembling with anger, his eyes shining as though they were on fire. "Your son, you are right; the King of France is not your son, the King of France has no brothers, the King of France has no mother, the King of France has only subjects. The King of France has no need of feelings, he has wishes. He can get on without being loved, but he shall be obeyed."

"Sire, you have misunderstood my words. I called my son the one who was going to leave me. I love him better just now because just now he is the one I am most afraid I shall lose. Is it a crime for a mother to wish that her child should not leave her?"

"And I, I tell you that he shall leave you. I tell you that he shall leave France, that he shall go to Poland, and within two days, too, and if you add one word he shall go to-morrow. Moreover, if you do not smooth your brow, if you do not take that threatening look from your eyes, I will strangle him this evening, as yesterday you yourself would have strangled your daughter's lover. Only I shall not fail, as we failed in regard to La Mole."

At the first threat Catharine's head fell; but she raised it again almost immediately.

"Ah, poor child!" said she, "your brother would kill you. But do not fear, your mother will protect you."

"Ah, you defy me!" cried Charles. "Well! by the blood of Christ, he shall die, not this evening, not soon, but this very instant. Ah, a weapon! a dagger! a knife! Ah!"

Having looked around in vain for what he wanted, Charles perceived the little dagger his mother always wore at her belt, sprang toward it, snatched it from its shagreen case encrusted with silver, and rushed from the room to strike down Henry of Anjou wherever he might meet him. But on reaching the hall, his strength, excited beyond human endurance, suddenly left him. He put out his arm, dropped the sharp weapon, which stuck point downwards into the wood, uttered a piercing cry, sank down, and rolled over on the floor.

At the same instant a quantity of blood spurted forth from his mouth and nose.

"Jesus!" said he. "They kill me! Help! help!"

Catharine, who had followed, saw him fall. For one instant she stood motionless, watching him. Then recollecting herself, not because of any maternal affection, but because of the awkwardness of the situation, she called out:

"The King is ill! Help! help!"

At the cry a crowd of servants, officers, and courtiers gathered around the young King. But ahead of them all a woman rushed out, pushed aside the others, and raised Charles, who had grown as pale as death.

"They kill me, nurse, they kill me," murmured the King, covered with perspiration and blood.

"They kill you, my Charles?" cried the good woman, glancing at the group of faces with a look which reached even Catharine. "Who kills you?"

Charles heaved a feeble sigh, and fainted.

"Ah!" said the physician, Ambroise Paré, who was summoned at once, "ah! the King is very ill!"

"Now, from necessity or compulsion," said the implacable Catharine to herself, "he will have to grant a delay."

Whereupon she left the King to join her second son, who was in the oratory, anxiously waiting to hear the result of an interview which was of such importance to him.

———

CHAPTER XLI.

THE HOROSCOPE.

On leaving the oratory, in which she had just informed Henry all that had occurred, Catharine found Réné in her chamber. It was the first time that the queen and the astrologer had seen each other since the visit the queen had made to his shop at the Pont Saint Michel. But the previous evening she had written him, and Réné had brought the answer to her note in person.

"Well," said the queen, "have you seen him?"

"Yes."

"How is he?"

"Somewhat better."

"Can he speak?"

"No, the sword traversed his larynx."

"I told you in that case to have him write."

"I tried. He collected all his strength, but his hand could trace only two letters. They are almost illegible. Then he fainted. The jugular vein was cut and the blood he lost has taken away all his strength."

"Have you seen the letters?"

"Here they are."

Réné drew a paper from his pocket and handed it to Catharine, who hastily unfolded it.

"An *m* and an *o*," said she. "Could it have been La Mole, and was all that acting of Marguerite done to throw me off the track?"

"Madame," said Réné, "if I dared to express my opinion in a matter about which your majesty hesitates to give yours I should say that I believe Monsieur de la Mole is too much in love to be seriously interested in politics."

"You think so?"

"Yes, and above all too much in love with the Queen of Navarre to serve the King very devotedly; for there is no real love without jealousy."

"You think that he is very much in love, then?"

"I am sure of it."

"Has he been to you?"

"Yes."

"Did he ask you for some potion or philter?"

"No, we kept to the wax figure."

"Pierced to the heart?"

"To the heart."

"And this figure still exists?"

"Yes."

"Have you it?"

"It is in my rooms."

"It would be strange," said Catharine, "if these cabalistic preparations really had the power attributed to them."

"Your majesty is a better judge of that than I."

"Is the Queen of Navarre in love with Monsieur de la Mole?"

"She loves him enough to ruin herself for him. Yesterday she saved him from death at the risk of her honor and her life. You see, madame, and yet you still doubt."

"Doubt what?"

"Science."

"Science also deceives me," said Catharine, looking steadily at Réné, who bore her gaze without flinching.

"About what?"

"Oh! you know what I mean; unless, of course, it was the scholar and not science."

"I do not know what you mean, madame," replied the Florentine.

"Réné, have your perfumes lost their odor?"

"No, madame, not when I use them; but it is possible that in passing through the hands of others"—

Catharine smiled and shook her head.

"Your opiate has done wonders, Réné," said she; "Madame de Sauve's lips are fresher and rosier than ever."

"It is not my opiate that is responsible for that, madame. The Baroness de Sauve, using the privilege of every pretty woman to be capricious, has said nothing more to me about this opiate, and after the suggestion from your majesty I thought it best to send her no more of it. So that all the boxes are still in my house just as you left them, with the exception of one which disappeared, I know not how or why."

"That is well, Réné," said Catharine; "perhaps later we may return to this. In the meantime, let us speak of the other matter."

"I am all attention, madame."

"What is necessary to gain an idea of the length of any one's life?"

"In the first place to know the day of his birth, his age, and under what condition he first saw light."

"And then?"

"To have some of his blood and a lock of his hair."

"If I bring you some of his blood and a lock of his hair, if I tell you the circumstance connected with his birth, the time, and his present age, will you tell me the probable date of his death?"

"Yes, to within a few days."

"Very well; I have a lock of his hair and will get some of his blood."

"Was he born during the day or night?"

"At twenty-three minutes past five in the afternoon."

"Be at my room at five o'clock to-morrow. The experiment must be made at the hour of his birth."

"Very well," said Catharine, "*we* will be there."

Réné bowed, and withdrew without apparently noticing the "*we* will be there," which, however, contrary to her usual habit, indicated that Catharine would not go alone.

The following morning at dawn Catharine went to her son's apartments. At midnight she had sent to inquire after him, and had been told that Maître Ambroise Paré was with him, ready to bleed him if the nervous troubles continued.

Still starting up from his sleep, and still pale from loss of blood, Charles dozed on the shoulder of his faithful nurse, who leaning against the bed had not moved for three hours for fear of waking her dear child.

A slight foam appeared from time to time on the lips of the sick man, and the nurse wiped it off with a fine embroidered linen handkerchief. On the bed lay another handkerchief covered with great spots of blood.

For an instant Catharine thought she would take possession of the handkerchief; but she feared that this blood mixed with the saliva would be weak, and would not be efficacious. She asked the nurse if the doctor had bled her son as he had said he would do. The nurse answered "Yes" and that the flow of blood had been so great that Charles had fainted twice. The queen mother, who, like all princesses in those days, had some knowledge of medicine, asked to see the blood. Nothing was easier to do, as the physician had ordered that the blood be kept in order that he might examine it. It was in a basin in an adjoining closet. Catharine went in to look at it, poured some into a small bottle which she had brought for this purpose; and then came back, hiding in her pocket her fingers, the tips of which otherwise would have betrayed her.

Just as she came back from the closet Charles opened his eyes and saw his mother. Then remembering as in a dream all his bitter thoughts:

"Ah! is it you, madame?" said he. "Well, say to your well loved son, to your Henry of Anjou, that it shall be to-morrow."

"My dear Charles," said Catharine, "it shall be just when you please. Be quiet now and go to sleep."

As if yielding to this advice Charles closed his eyes; and Catharine, who had spoken to him as one does to calm a sick person or a child, left the room. But when he heard the door close Charles suddenly sat up, and in a voice still weak from suffering, said:

"My chancellor! The seals! the court!—send for them all."

The nurse, with gentle insistence, laid the head of the King back on her shoulder, and in order to put him to sleep strove to rock him as she would have done a child.

"No, no, nurse, I cannot sleep any more. Call my attendants. I must work this morning."

When Charles spoke in that way he was obeyed; and even the nurse, in spite of the privileges allowed her by her foster-child, dared not disobey. She sent for those whom the King wanted, and the council was planned, not for the next day, which was out of the question, but for five days from then.

At the hour agreed on, that is, at five o'clock, the queen mother and the Duc d'Anjou repaired to the rooms of Réné, who, expecting their visit, had everything ready for the mysterious seance. In the room to the right, that is, in the chamber of sacrifices, a steel blade was heating over a glowing brazier. From its fanciful arabesques this blade was intended to represent the events of the destiny about which the oracle was to be consulted. On the altar lay the Book of Fate, and during the night, which had been very clear, Réné had studied the course and the position of the stars.

Henry of Anjou entered first. He wore a wig, a mask concealed his face, and a long cloak hid his figure. His mother followed. Had she not known beforehand that the man who had preceded her was her son she never would have recognized him. Catharine removed her mask; the Duc d'Anjou kept his on.

"Did you make any observations last night?" asked Catharine.

"Yes, madame," said Réné; "and the answer of the stars has already told me the past. The one you wish to know about, like every one born under the sign of the Cancer, has a warm heart and great pride. He is powerful. He has lived nearly a quarter of a century. He has until now had glory and wealth. Is this so, madame?"

"Possibly," said Catharine.

"Have you a lock of his hair, and some of his blood?"

"Yes."

Catharine handed to the necromancer a lock of fair hair and a small bottle filled with blood.

Réné took the flask, shook it thoroughly, so that the fibrine and water would mix, and poured a large drop of it on the glowing steel. The living liquid boiled for an instant, and then spread out into fantastic figures.

"Oh, madame," cried Réné, "I see him twisting in awful agony. Hear how he groans, how he calls for help! Do you see how everything around him becomes blood? Do you see how about his death-bed great combats are taking place? See, here are the lances; and look, there are the swords!"

"Will it be long before this happens?" asked Catharine, trembling from an indescribable emotion and laying her hand on that of Henry of Anjou, who in his eager curiosity was leaning over the brazier.

Réné approached the altar and repeated a cabalistic prayer, putting such energy and conviction into the act that the veins of his temples swelled, and caused the prophetic convulsions and nervous twinges from which the ancient priestesses suffered before their tripods, and even on their death-beds.

At length he rose and announced that everything was ready, took the flask, still three-quarters full, in one hand, and in the other the lock of hair. Then telling Catharine to open the book at random, and to read the first words she looked at, he poured the rest of the blood on the steel blade, and threw the hair into the brazier, pronouncing a cabalistic sentence composed of Hebrew words which he himself did not understand.

Instantly the Duc d'Anjou and Catharine saw a white figure appear on the sword like that of a corpse wrapped in his shroud. Another figure, which seemed that of a woman, was leaning over the first.

At the same time the hair caught fire and threw out a single flame, clear, swift, and barbed like a fiery tongue.

"One year," cried Réné, "scarcely one year, and this man shall die. A woman alone shall weep for him. But no, there at the end of the sword is another woman, with a child in her arms."

Catharine looked at her son, and, mother though she was, seemed to ask him who these two women were.

But Réné had scarcely finished speaking before the steel became white and everything gradually disappeared from its surface. Then Catharine opened the book and read the following lines in a voice which, in spite of her effort at control, she could not keep from shaking:

"'*Ains a peri cil que l'on redoutoit,*
Plus tôt, trop tôt, si prudence n'etoit.'"[14]

A deep silence reigned for some moments.

"For the one whom you know," asked Catharine, "what are the signs for this month?"

"As favorable as ever, madame; unless Providence interferes with his destiny he will be fortunate. And yet"—

"And yet what?"

"One of the stars in his pleiad was covered with a black cloud while I made my observations."

"Ah!" exclaimed Catharine, "a black cloud—there is some hope, then?"

"Of whom are you speaking, madame?" asked the Duc d'Anjou.

Catharine drew her son away from the light of the brazier and spoke to him in a low tone.

Meanwhile Réné knelt down, and in the glow of the flame poured into his hand the last drop of blood which had remained in the bottom of the flask.

"Strange contradiction," said he, "which proves how little to be depended on is the evidence of simple science practised by ordinary men! To any one but myself, a physician, a scholar, even for Maître Ambroise Paré, this blood would seem so pure, so healthy, so full of life and animal spirits, that it would promise long years of life; and yet all this vigor will soon disappear, all this life will be extinct within a year!"

Catharine and Henry of Anjou had turned round and were listening.

The eyes of the prince glowed through his mask.

"Ah!" continued Réné, "the present alone is known to ordinary mortals; while to us the past and the future are known."

"So," continued Catharine, "you still think he will die within the year?"

"As surely as we are three living persons who some day will rest in our coffins."

"Yet you said that the blood was pure and healthy, and that it indicated a long life."

"Yes, if things followed their natural course. But might not an accident"—

"Ah, yes, do you hear?" said Catharine to Henry, "an accident"—

"Alas!" said the latter, "all the more reason for my staying."

"Oh, think no more about that: it is not possible."

Then turning to Réné:

"Thanks," said the young man, disguising his voice, "thanks; take this purse."

"Come, *count*," said Catharine, intentionally giving her son this title to throw Réné off the track.

They left.

"Oh, mother, you see," said Henry, "an accident—and if an accident should happen, I shall not be on hand; I shall be four hundred leagues from you"—

"Four hundred leagues are accomplished in eight days, my son."

"Yes; but how do I know whether those Poles will let me come back? If I could only wait, mother!"

"Who knows?" said Catharine; "might not this accident of which Réné speaks be the one which since yesterday has laid the King on a bed of pain?

Listen, return by yourself, my child. I shall go back by the private door of the monastery of the Augustines. My suite is waiting for me in this convent. Go, now, Henry, go, and keep from irritating your brother in case you see him."

<hr />

CHAPTER XLII.

CONFIDENCES.

The first thing the Duc d'Anjou heard on arriving at the Louvre was that the formal reception of the ambassadors was arranged for the fifth day from that. The tailors and the jewellers were waiting for the prince with magnificent clothes and superb jewels which the King had ordered for him.

While the duke tried them on with an anger which brought the tears to his eyes, Henry of Navarre was very gay in a magnificent collar of emeralds, a sword with a gold handle, and a precious ring which Charles had sent him that morning.

D'Alençon had just received a letter and had shut himself up in his own room to read it.

As to Coconnas, he was searching every corner of the Louvre for his friend.

In fact, as may easily be imagined, he had been somewhat surprised at not seeing La Mole return that night, and by morning had begun to feel some anxiety.

Consequently he had started out to find his friend. He began his search at the Hôtel de la Belle Étoile, went from there to the Rue Cloche Percée, from the Rue Cloche Percée to the Rue Tizon, from there to the Pont Saint Michel, and finally from the Pont Saint Michel to the Louvre. This search, so far as those who had been questioned were concerned, had been carried on in a way so original and exacting (which may easily be believed when one realizes the eccentric character of Coconnas) that it had caused some explanations between him and three courtiers. These explanations had ended, as was the fashion of the times, on the ground. In these encounters Coconnas had been as conscientious as he usually was in affairs of that kind, and had killed the first man and wounded the two others, saying:

"Poor La Mole, he knew Latin so well!"

The last victim, who was the Baron de Boissey, said as he fell:

"Oh, for the love of Heaven, Coconnas, do vary a little and at least say that he knew Greek!"

At last the report of the adventure in the corridor leaked out. Coconnas was heartbroken over it; for an instant he thought that all these kings and princes had killed his friend and thrown him into some dungeon.

He learned that D'Alençon had been of the party; and overlooking the majesty which surrounded a prince of the blood, he went to him and demanded an explanation as he would have done of a simple gentleman.

At first D'Alençon was inclined to thrust out of the door the impertinent fellow who came and asked for an account of his actions. But Coconnas spoke so curtly, his eyes flashed with such brightness, and the affair of the three duels in less than twenty-four hours had raised the Piedmontese so high, that D'Alençon reflected, and instead of yielding to his first inclination, he answered the gentleman with a charming smile:

"My dear Coconnas, it is true that the King was furious at receiving a silver bowl on his shoulder, that the Duc d'Anjou was vexed at being hit on the head by some orange marmalade, and the Duc de Guise humiliated at having the breath knocked out of him by a haunch of venison, and so they were all determined to kill Monsieur de la Mole. But a friend of your friend's turned aside the blow. The party therefore failed in their attempt. I give you my word as prince."

"Ah!" said Coconnas, breathing as hard as a pair of bellows. "By Heaven, monseigneur, this is good news, and I should like to know this friend to show him my gratitude."

Monsieur d'Alençon made no reply, but smiled more pleasantly than he had yet done, implying to Coconnas that this friend was none other than the prince himself.

"Well, monseigneur!" said Coconnas, "since you have gone so far as to tell me the beginning of the story, crown your kindness by finishing it. They tried to kill him, but failed, you say. Well, what happened then? I am brave and can bear the news. Have they thrown him into some dungeon? So much the better. It will make him more careful in future. He never would listen to my advice; besides, we can get him out, by Heaven! Stone does not baffle every one."

D'Alençon shook his head.

"The worst of all this, my brave Coconnas," said he, "is that your friend disappeared after the affair, and no one knows where he went."

"By Heaven!" cried the Piedmontese, again growing pale, "had he gone to hell I should at least have known where he is."

"Listen," said D'Alençon, who, although for different reasons, was as anxious as Coconnas to know La Mole's whereabouts, "I will give you the advice of a friend."

"Give it, my lord," said Coconnas, eagerly.

"Go to Queen Marguerite. She must know what has become of the friend you mourn."

"I will confess to your highness," said Coconnas, "that I had thought of going to her, but I scarcely dared. Madame Marguerite has a way of making me feel somewhat uncomfortable at times, and besides this, I feared that I might find her in tears. But since your highness assures me that La Mole is not dead and that her majesty knows where he is I will take heart and go to her."

"Do so, my friend," said François. "And when you find out where La Mole is, let me know, for really I am as anxious as you are. But remember one thing, Coconnas"—

"What?"

"Do not say you have come at my suggestion, for if you do you will learn nothing."

"Monseigneur," said Coconnas, "since your highness recommends secrecy on this point, I shall be as silent as a tench or as the queen mother."

"What a kind, good, generous prince he is!" murmured Coconnas as he set out to find the Queen of Navarre.

Marguerite was expecting Coconnas, for the report of his despair had reached her, and on hearing by what exploits his grief had showed itself she almost forgave him for his somewhat rude treatment of her friend Madame la Duchesse de Nevers, to whom he had not spoken for two or three days, owing to some misunderstanding between them. Therefore as soon as he was announced to the queen he was admitted.

Coconnas entered the room, unable to overcome the constraint which he had mentioned to D'Alençon, and which he had always felt in the presence of the queen. It was caused more by her superior intellect than by her rank. But Marguerite received him with a smile which at once put him at his ease.

"Ah, madame," said he, "give me back my friend, I beg you, or at least tell me what has become of him, for without him I cannot live. Imagine Euryalus without Nisus, Damon without Pythias, or Orestes without Pylades, and pity my grief for the sake of one of the heroes I have just mentioned, whose heart, I swear, was no more tender than mine."

Marguerite smiled, and having made Coconnas promise not to reveal the secret, she told him of La Mole's escape from the window. As to his hiding-place, insistent as were the prayers of the Piedmontese, she preserved the strictest silence. This only half satisfied Coconnas, so he resorted to diplomatic speeches of the highest order.

The result was that Marguerite saw clearly that the Duc d'Alençon was partly the cause of the courtier's great desire to know what had become of La Mole.

"Well," said the queen, "if you must know something definite about your friend, ask King Henry of Navarre. He alone has the right to speak. As to me, all I can tell you is that the friend for whom you are searching is alive, and you may believe what I say."

"I believe one thing still more, madame," replied Coconnas; "that is, that your beautiful eyes have not wept."

Thereupon, thinking that there was nothing to add to a remark which had the double advantage of expressing his thought as well as the high opinion he had of La Mole, Coconnas withdrew, pondering on a reconciliation with Madame de Nevers, not on her account, but in order that he might find out from her what he had been unable to learn from Marguerite.

Deep griefs are abnormal conditions in which the mind shakes off the yoke as soon as possible. The thought of leaving Marguerite had at first broken La Mole's heart, and it was in order to save the reputation of the queen rather than to preserve his own life that he had consented to run away.

Therefore, the following evening he returned to Paris to see Marguerite from her balcony. As if instinct told her of the young man's plan, the queen spent the whole evening at her window. The result was that the lovers met again with the indescribable delight which accompanies forbidden pleasures. More than this, the melancholy and romantic temperament of La Mole found a certain charm in the situation. But a man really in love is happy only for the time being, while he sees or is with the woman he loves. After he has left her he suffers. Anxious to see Marguerite again, La Mole set himself busily to work to bring about the event which would make it possible for him to be with her; namely, the flight of the King of Navarre.

Marguerite on her part willingly gave herself up to the happiness of being loved with so pure a devotion. Often she was angry with herself for what she regarded as a weakness. Her strong mind despised the poverty of ordinary love, insensible to the details which for tender souls make it the sweetest, the most delicate, and the most desirable of all pleasures. So she felt that the days, if not happily filled, were at least happily ended. When, at about nine o'clock every evening, she stepped out on her balcony in a white dressing-gown, she perceived in the darkness of the quay a horseman whose hand was raised first to his lips, then to his heart. Then a significant cough reminded the lover of a cherished voice. Sometimes a note was thrown by a little hand, and in the note was hidden some costly jewel, precious not on account of its value, but because it had belonged to her who threw it; and this would fall on the pavement a few feet from the young man. Then La Mole would swoop down on it like a kite, press it to his heart, answer in the same voice, while Marguerite stood at her balcony until the sound of the horse's hoofs had died away in the darkness. The steed, ridden at full speed when coming, on leaving seemed as if made of material as lifeless as that of the famous horse which lost Troy.

This was why the queen was not anxious as to the fate of La Mole. But fearing that he might be watched and followed she persistently refused all interviews except these clandestine ones, which began immediately after La Mole's flight and continued every evening until the time set for the formal reception of the ambassadors, a reception which by the express orders of Ambroise Paré, as we have seen, was postponed for several days.

The evening before this reception, at about nine o'clock, when every one in the Louvre was engaged in preparations for the following day, Marguerite opened her window and stepped out upon her balcony. As she did so, without waiting for her note, La Mole, in greater haste than usual, threw his note which with his usual skill fell at the feet of his royal mistress.

Marguerite realized that the missive contained something special, and retired from the balcony to read it. The note consisted of two separate sheets.

On the first page were these words:

"Madame, I must speak to the King of Navarre. The matter is urgent. I will wait."

On the second page were these words:

"My lady and my queen, arrange so that I may give you one of the kisses I now send you. I will wait."

Marguerite had scarcely finished the second part of the letter when she heard the voice of Henry of Navarre, who with his usual caution had knocked on the outer door, and was asking Gillonne if he might enter.

The queen at once separated the letter, put one of the sheets in her robe, the other in her pocket, hurriedly closed the window, and stepped to the door.

"Enter, sire," said she.

Notwithstanding the fact that Marguerite had been careful to close the window quickly and gently, the sound had reached Henry, whose acute senses, in the midst of people he greatly mistrusted, had almost acquired the exquisite delicacy they attain in the savage. But the King of Navarre was not one of those tyrants who forbid their wives from taking the air and watching the stars.

Henry was as gracious and smiling as ever.

"Madame," said he, "while every one is rehearsing the coming ceremonial, I thought I would come and have a little talk with you about my affairs, which you still regard as yours, do you not?"

"Certainly, monsieur," replied Marguerite; "are not our interests one and the same?"

"Yes, madame, and that is why I wanted to ask what you thought about Monsieur le Duc d'Alençon's avoiding me so for the last few days. The day before yesterday he even went to Saint Germain. Does it not mean either that he is planning to leave by himself, for he is watched very little, or that he is not going to leave at all? Give me your opinion, madame, if you please. I confess it will be a great relief to me to tell you mine."

"Your majesty is right in being anxious at my brother's silence. I have been thinking about it all day, and my idea is that as circumstances have changed he has changed with them."

"You mean, do you not, that seeing King Charles ill and the Duc d'Anjou King of Poland he would not be averse to staying in Paris to keep watch over the crown of France?"

"Exactly."

"Be it so. I ask nothing better than for him to remain," said Henry; "only that will change our entire plan. To leave without him I shall need three times the guarantees I should have asked for had I gone with your brother, whose name and presence in the enterprise would have been my safeguard. But what surprises me is that I have not heard from Monsieur de Mouy. It is not like him to stay away so long. Have you had any news of him, madame?"

"I, sire!" exclaimed Marguerite, in astonishment; "why, how could you expect"—

"Why, by Heaven, my dear, nothing would be more natural. In order to please me, you were kind enough to save the life of young La Mole,—he must have reached Nantes,—and if one can get to a place he can easily get away from it."

"Ah! this explains an enigma, the answer to which I could not make out," said Marguerite. "I had left my window open, and found, on coming back to my room, a note on my floor."

"There now," said Henry.

"A note which at first I could not understand, and to which I attached no importance whatsoever," continued Marguerite. "Perhaps I was wrong, and that it comes from that quarter."

"That is possible," said Henry; "I might even say probable. Might I see this note?"

"Certainly, sire," replied Marguerite, handing to the king the missive she had put into her pocket. The king glanced at it.

"Is it not Monsieur de la Mole's handwriting?" said he.

"I do not know," replied Marguerite. "It looks to me like a counterfeit."

"No matter, let us read it." And he read:

"Madame, I must speak to the King of Navarre. The matter is urgent. I will wait."

"So!" said Henry—"you see, he says he will wait."

"Certainly I see that," said Marguerite. "But what would you expect?"

"Why! *ventre saint gris!* I expect that he is waiting!"

"That he is waiting!" cried Marguerite, looking at her husband in astonishment. "How can you say such a thing, sire? A man whom the King tried to kill—a man who is watched, threatened—waiting, you say! Would that be possible?—are the doors made for those who have been"—

"Obliged to escape by the window—you were going to say?"

"Yes, you have finished my sentence."

"Well, but if they know the way by the window, let them take it, since it is perfectly impossible for them to enter by the door. It is very simple."

"Do you think so?" said Marguerite, flushing with pleasure at the thought of again being near La Mole.

"I am sure of it."

"But how could one reach the window?" asked the queen.

"Did you not keep the rope ladder I sent you? Where is your usual foresight?"

"Yes, sire, I kept it," said Marguerite.

"In that case there will be no difficulty," said Henry.

"What does your majesty wish?"

"Why, it is very simple," said Henry. "Fasten it to your balcony and let it hang down. If it is De Mouy who is waiting and he wants to mount it, he will do so."

Without losing his gravity Henry took the candle to aid Marguerite in her search for the ladder. They did not have to look long; it was in a wardrobe in the famous closet.

"There it is," said Henry; "now, madame, if I am not asking too much, fasten it to the balcony, I beg you."

"Why should I fasten it and not you, sire?" said Marguerite.

"Because the best conspirators are the most careful. Seeing a man might perhaps frighten away our friend, you see." Marguerite smiled and tied the ladder.

"There," said Henry, concealing himself in a corner of the room, "stand so he can see you; now drop the ladder; good! I am sure that De Mouy will climb up."

In fact, about ten minutes later a man, mad with joy, stepped over the balcony, but seeing that the queen did not come to him, he hesitated a moment. Instead of Marguerite it was Henry who stepped forward.

"Ah!" said he, graciously, "it is not De Mouy, but Monsieur de la Mole. Good evening, Monsieur de la Mole. Come in, I beg you."

La Mole paused a moment, overwhelmed. Had he still been on the ladder instead of on the balcony he might possibly have fallen backward.

"You wanted to speak to the King of Navarre on matters of importance," said Marguerite. "I have told him so and here he is."

Henry closed the window.

"I love you," said Marguerite, hastily pressing the young man's hand.

"Well, monsieur," said Henry, placing a chair for La Mole, "what is it?"

"This, sire," replied La Mole. "I have left Monsieur de Mouy at the city gates. He desires to know if Maurevel has spoken, and if his presence in your majesty's room is known."

"Not yet, but it will be before long; so we must make haste."

"That is my opinion, sire, and if to-morrow evening Monsieur d'Alençon is ready to start, De Mouy will be at the Porte Saint Marcel with five hundred men. These will take you to Fontainebleau. Then you can easily reach Blois, Angoulême, and Bordeaux."

"Madame," said Henry, turning to his wife, "I can be ready by to-morrow; can you?"

La Mole's eyes were anxiously fixed on those of Marguerite.

"You have my promise," said the queen. "Wherever you go, I will follow. But you know Monsieur d'Alençon must leave at the same time. No half way with him; either he serves us or he betrays us. If he hesitates we do not stir."

"Does he know anything of this plan, Monsieur de la Mole?" asked Henry.

"He should have received a letter from Monsieur de Mouy several days ago."

"Why," said Henry, "he said nothing to me about it!"

"Be careful, monsieur," said Marguerite, "be careful."

"I shall be on my guard, you may be sure. How can we get an answer to De Mouy?"

"Do not worry, sire. On the right, on the left, of your majesty, visible or invisible, he will be on hand to-morrow during the reception of the ambassadors. One word in the address of the queen will suffice for him to understand whether you consent or not, whether he must leave or wait for you. If the Duc d'Alençon refuses, he asks but a fortnight to reorganize everything in your name."

"Really," said Henry, "De Mouy is invaluable. Can you insert the necessary words in your address, madame?"

"Nothing will be easier," replied Marguerite.

"Then I will see Monsieur d'Alençon to-morrow," said Henry. "Let de Mouy be at his post ready to understand at a word."

"He will be there, sire."

"And, Monsieur de la Mole," said Henry, "take my answer to him. You probably have a horse or a servant near by?"

"Orthon is waiting for me at the quay."

"Go back to him, monsieur. Oh, no, not by the window, which is good only for an emergency. You might be seen, and as it would not be known that you had taken this risk for me, it might compromise the queen."

"How shall I leave, sire?"

"Although you may not be able to enter the Louvre by yourself, you can at least leave it with me, for I have the password. You have your cloak, I have mine; we will put them on and can pass the gate without difficulty. Besides, I shall be glad to give some special orders to Orthon. Wait here while I go and see if there is any one in the corridor."

With the most natural air possible Henry went out to investigate. La Mole was left alone with the queen.

"Ah! when shall I see you again?" said he.

"To-morrow evening, if we leave. Otherwise some evening soon in the Rue Cloche Percée."

"Monsieur de la Mole," said Henry, returning, "you can come; there is no one here."

La Mole bowed respectfully to the queen.

"Give him your hand to kiss, madame," said Henry; "Monsieur de la Mole is no ordinary servitor."

Marguerite obeyed.

"By the way," said Henry, "be sure and keep the rope ladder. It is a valuable instrument for conspirators; and when we least expect it we may need it. Come, Monsieur de la Mole."

CHAPTER XLIII.

THE AMBASSADORS.

The following day the entire population of Paris rushed towards the Faubourg Saint Antoine, by which it had been decided that the Polish ambassadors were to enter. A line of Swiss restrained the crowd, and a regiment of horse protected the lords and the ladies of the court who rode ahead of the procession.

Soon, near the Abbey Saint Antoine, a troop of cavaliers appeared, dressed in red and yellow, with caps and furred mantles, and carrying long curved sabres like Turkish cimeters.

The officers rode at the side of the lines.

Behind this troop came a second, clothed with Oriental magnificence. They preceded the ambassadors, who, four in number, represented in a gorgeous manner the most mythological of the chivalrous kingdoms of the sixteenth century.

One of the ambassadors was the Bishop of Cracow. His costume was half ecclesiastical, half military, resplendent with gold and precious stones.

His white horse, with long mane and tail, walked with proud step and seemed to breathe out fire from his nostrils. No one would have supposed that for a month the noble animal had made fifteen leagues daily over roads which the weather had rendered almost impassable.

Beside the bishop rode the Palatine Lasco, a powerful noble, closely related to the royal family, as rich as a king and as proud.

Behind these two chief ambassadors, who were accompanied by two other palatines of high rank, came a number of Polish lords, whose horses in their harness of silk, studded with gold and precious stones, excited the applause of the people. The French horsemen, in spite of their rich apparel, were completely eclipsed by the newcomers, whom they scornfully called barbarians.

Up to the last moment Catharine had hoped the reception would be postponed on account of the King's illness. But when the day came, and she saw Charles, as pale as a corpse, put on the gorgeous royal mantle, she realized that apparently at least she must yield to his iron will, and began to believe that after all the safest plan for Henry of Anjou was to accept the magnificent exile to which he was condemned. With the exception of the few words he had uttered when he opened his eyes as his mother came out of the closet, Charles had not spoken to Catharine since the scene which had brought about the illness to which he had succumbed. Every one in the Louvre knew that there had been a dreadful altercation between mother and son, but no one knew the cause of it, and the boldest trembled before that coldness and silence, as birds tremble before the calm which precedes a storm.

Everything had been prepared in the Louvre, not as though there were to be a reception, but as if some funeral ceremony were to occur. Every one had obeyed orders in a gloomy or passive manner. It was known that Catharine had almost trembled, and consequently every one else trembled.

The large reception-hall of the palace had been prepared, and as such ceremonies were usually public, the guards and the sentinels had received orders to admit with the ambassadors as many people as the apartments and the courts would hold. As for Paris, it presented the same aspect that every large city presents under similar circumstances; that is, confusion and curiosity. But had any one looked closely at the population that day, he would have noticed, among the groups of honest bourgeois with smiling faces, a considerable number of men in long cloaks, who exchanged glances and signs when at a distance, and when they met, a few rapid words in a low tone. These men seemed greatly occupied with the procession, followed it closely, and appeared to receive their orders from an old man, whose sharp black eyes, in spite of his white beard and grayish eyebrows, showed a vigorous activity. This old man, either by his own efforts or by those of his companions, was among the first to gain admission to the Louvre, and, thanks to the kindness of the Swiss guard, succeeded in finding a place behind the ambassadors, opposite Marguerite and Henry of Navarre.

Henry, informed by La Mole that De Mouy would be present in some disguise or other, looked round on all sides. At last his eyes encountered those of the old man and held them.

A sign from De Mouy had dispelled all doubt. He was so changed that Henry himself was doubtful whether this old man with the white beard could be the intrepid Huguenot chief who five or six days before had made so desperate a defence.

A word from Henry whispered into Marguerite's ear called the attention of the queen to De Mouy. Then her beautiful eyes wandered around the great hall in search of La Mole; but in vain—La Mole was not there.

The speeches began. The first was to the King. Lasco, in the name of the Diet, asked him to consent that the crown of Poland be offered to a prince of the house of France.

Charles's reply was short and to the point. He presented his brother, the Duc d'Anjou, whose courage he praised highly to the Polish ambassadors. He spoke in French, and an interpreter translated his reply at the end of each sentence. While the interpreter was speaking, the King was seen applying a handkerchief to his lips, and each time he removed it, it was covered with blood. When Charles's reply was finished, Lasco turned to the Duc d'Anjou, bowed, and began a Latin address, in which he offered him the throne in the name of the Polish nation.

The duke replied in the same language, and in a voice he strove in vain to render firm, that he accepted with gratitude the honor which was offered to him. While he spoke, Charles remained standing, with lips compressed, and fixed on him eyes as calm and threatening as those of an eagle.

When the duke had finished, Lasco took the crown of the Jagellos from the red velvet cushion on which it rested, and while two Polish nobles placed the royal mantle on the duke, he laid the crown in Charles's hands.

Charles signed to his brother, the Duc d'Anjou knelt down before him, and with his own hand the King placed the crown on his brother's head. Then the two kings exchanged one of the most bitter kisses ever exchanged between two brothers.

At once a herald cried:

"Alexander Edward Henry of France, Duc d'Anjou, is crowned King of Poland. Long live the King of Poland!"

The entire assembly repeated the cry: "Long live the King of Poland!" Then Lasco turned to Marguerite. The discourse of the beautiful queen had been reserved for the last. Now, as it was a compliment accorded her in order to display her brilliant talents, as they were called, every one paid great attention to the reply, which was in Latin, and which, as we have said, Marguerite had composed herself. Lascos's address was more of a eulogy than an address. He had yielded, Sarmatian that he was, to the admiration which the beautiful queen of Navarre inspired in every one. He had borrowed his language from Ovid; his style was that of Ronsard. He said that having left Varsovia in the middle of a very dark night, neither he nor his companions would have been able to find their way, had they not, like the Magi, been guided by two stars which became more and more brilliant as they drew nearer to France, and which now they recognized as the two beautiful eyes of the Queen of Navarre. Finally, passing from the Gospel to the Koran, from Syria to Arabia, from Nazareth to Mecca, he concluded by saying that he was quite prepared to do what the ardent votaries of the prophet did. When they were fortunate enough to see his tomb, they put out their eyes, feeling that after they had looked at such a sight, nothing in the world was worth being admired.

This address was loudly applauded by those who understood Latin because they were of the same opinion as the orator, and by those who did not understand it because they wished to appear as though they did.

Marguerite made a gracious courtesy to the gallant Sarmatian; then fixing her eyes on De Mouy, began her reply in these words:

"Quod nunc hac in aulâ insperati adestis exultaremus, ego et conjux, nisi ideo immineret calamitas, scilicet non solum fratris sed etiam amici orbitas."[15]

These words had a double meaning, and, while intended for De Mouy, were apparently addressed to Henry of Anjou. The latter, therefore, bowed in token of gratitude.

Charles did not remember having read this sentence in the address which had been submitted to him some days before; but he attached no importance to Marguerite's words, which he knew were merely conventional. Besides, he understood Latin very imperfectly.

Marguerite continued:

"Adeo dolemur a te dividi ut tecum proficisci maluissemus. Sed idem fatum quo nunc sine ullâ morâ Lutetiâ cedere juberis, hac in urbe detinet. Proficiscere ergo, frater; proficiscere, amice; proficiscere sine nobis; proficiscentem sequuntur spes et desideria nostra."[16]

It may easily be imagined that De Mouy listened with the closest attention to these words which, although addressed to the ambassadors, were intended for him alone. Two or three times Henry had glanced indifferently over his shoulder to intimate to the young Huguenot that D'Alençon had refused; but the act, which appeared involuntary, would have been insufficient for De Mouy, had not Marguerite's words confirmed it.

While looking at Marguerite and listening with his whole soul, his piercing black eyes beneath their gray brows struck Catharine, who started as if she had had a shock of electricity, and who did not remove her eyes from him.

"What a strange face!" thought she, continuing to change her expression according as the ceremony required it. "Who is this man who watches Marguerite so attentively and whom Marguerite and Henry on their part look at so earnestly?"

The Queen of Navarre went on with her address, which from that point was a reply to the courtesies of the Polish ambassador. While Catharine was racking her brain to discover the name of this fine old man the master of ceremonies came up behind her and handed her a perfumed satin bag containing a folded paper. She opened the bag, drew out the paper, and read these words:

"By the aid of a cordial which I have just administered to him Maurevel has somewhat recovered his strength, and has succeeded in writing the name of the man who was in the apartment of the King of Navarre. This man was

Monsieur de Mouy."

"De Mouy!" thought the queen; "well, I felt it was he. But this old man—ah! *cospetto!*—this old man is"—

She leaned toward the captain of the guard.

"Look, Monsieur de Nancey," said she, "but without attracting attention; look at Lasco who is speaking. Behind him—do you see the old man with the white beard, in the black velvet suit?"

"Yes, madame," replied the captain.

"Well, do not lose sight of him."

"The one to whom the King of Navarre made a sign just now?"

"Exactly. Station yourself at the door of the Louvre with ten men, and when he comes out invite him in the King's name to dinner. If he accepts, take him into some room in which you must keep him a prisoner. If he resists, seize him, dead or alive."

Fortunately Henry, who had been paying but little attention to Marguerite's address, was looking at Catharine, and had not lost a single expression of her face. Seeing the eyes of the queen mother fixed so earnestly on De Mouy, he grew uneasy; when he saw her give an order to the captain of the guard he comprehended everything.

It was at this moment that he made the sign which had surprised Monsieur de Nancey, and which meant, "You are discovered, save yourself!"

De Mouy understood this gesture, which was a fitting climax to the portion of Marguerite's address intended for him. He did not delay an instant, but mingled with the crowd and disappeared.

Henry, however, was not easy until Monsieur de Nancey had returned to Catharine, and he saw from the frown on the queen mother's face that the captain had not been in time.

The audience was over. Marguerite exchanged a few unofficial words with Lasco.

The King staggered to his feet, bowed, and went out, leaning on the arm of Ambroise Paré, who had not left him since his illness.

Catharine, pale with anger, and Henry, silent from disappointment, followed.

As to the Duc d'Alençon, he had scarcely been noticed during the ceremony, and not once had Charles, whose eyes had not left the Duc d'Anjou, glanced at him.

The new King of Poland felt himself lost. Far from his mother, carried away by those barbarians of the north, he was like Antæus, the son of Terra, who lost his strength when lifted in the arms of Hercules. Once beyond the frontier the Duc d'Anjou felt that he was forever excluded from the throne of France.

Instead of following the King he retired to his mother's apartments.

He found her no less gloomy and preoccupied than himself, for she was thinking of that fine mocking face she had not lost sight of during the ceremony, of the Béarnais for whom destiny had seemed to make way, sweeping aside kings, royal assassins, enemies, and obstacles.

Seeing her beloved son pale beneath his crown, and bent under his royal mantle, clasping his beautiful hands in silence, and holding them out to her piteously, Catharine rose and went to him.

"Oh, mother," cried the King of Poland, "I am condemned to die in exile!"

"My son," said Catharine, "have you so soon forgotten Réné's prediction? Do not worry, you will not have to stay there long."

"Mother, I entreat you," said the Duc d'Anjou, "if there is the slightest hint, or the least suspicion, that the throne of France is to be vacant, send me word."

"Do not worry, my son," said Catharine. "Until the day for which both of us are waiting, there shall always be a horse saddled in my stable, and in my antechamber a courier ready to set out for Poland."

CHAPTER XLIV.

ORESTES AND PYLADES.

Henry of Anjou having departed, peace and happiness seemed to have returned to the Louvre, among this family of the Atrides.

Charles, forgetting his melancholy, recovered his vigorous health, hunting with Henry, and on days when this was not possible discussing hunting affairs with him, and reproaching him for only one thing, his indifference to hawking, declaring that he would be faultless if he knew how to snare falcons, gerfalcons, and hawks as well as he knew how to hunt brocks and hounds.

Catharine had become a good mother again. Gentle to Charles and D'Alençon, affectionate to Henry and Marguerite, gracious to Madame de Nevers and Madame de Sauve; and under the pretext that it was in obedience to an order from her that he had been wounded, she carried her amiabilities so far as to visit Maurevel twice during his convalescence, in his house in the Rue de la Cerisaie.

Marguerite continued to carry on her love affair after the Spanish fashion.

Every evening she opened her window and by gestures and notes kept up her correspondence with La Mole, while in each of his letters the young man reminded his lovely queen of her promise of a few moments in the Rue Cloche Percée as a reward for his exile.

Only one person was lonely and unhappy in the now calm and peaceful Louvre.

This was our friend Count Annibal de Coconnas.

It was certainly something to know that La Mole was alive; it was much to be the favorite of Madame de Nevers, the most charming and the most whimsical of women. But all the pleasure of a meeting granted him by the beautiful duchess, all the consolation offered by Marguerite as to the fate of their common friend, did not compensate in the eyes of the Piedmontese for one hour spent with La Mole at their friend La Hurière's before a bottle of light wine, or for one of those midnight rambles through that part of Paris in which an honest man ran the risk of receiving rents in his flesh, his purse, or his clothes.

To the shame of humanity it must be said that Madame de Nevers bore with impatience her rivalry with La Mole.

It was not that she hated the Provincial; on the contrary, carried away by the irresistible instinct which, in spite of herself, makes every woman a coquette with another woman's lover, especially when that woman is her friend, she had not spared La Mole the flashes of her emerald eyes, and Coconnas might have envied the frank handclasps and the amiable acts done by the duchess in favor of his friend during those days in which the star of the Piedmontese seemed growing dim in the sky of his beautiful mistress; but Coconnas, who would have strangled fifteen persons for a single glance from his lady, was so little jealous of La Mole that he had often after some indiscretions of the duchess whispered certain offers which had made the man from the Provinces blush.

At this stage of affairs it happened that Henriette, who by the absence of La Mole was deprived of all the enjoyment she had had from the company of

Coconnas, that is, his never-ending flow of spirits and fun, came to Marguerite one day to beg her to do her this three-fold favor without which the heart and the mind of Coconnas seemed to be slipping away day by day.

Marguerite, always sympathetic and, besides, influenced by the prayers of La Mole and the wishes of her own heart, arranged a meeting with Henriette for the next day in the house with the double entrance, in order to discuss these matters thoroughly and uninterruptedly.

Coconnas received with rather bad grace the note from Henriette, asking him to be in the Rue Tizon at half-past nine.

Nevertheless he went to the place appointed, where he found Henriette, who was provoked at having arrived first.

"Fie, Monsieur!" she cried, "it is very bad to make—I will not say a princess —but a lady—wait in this way."

"Wait?" said Coconnas, "what an idea! I'll wager, on the contrary, that we are ahead of time."

"I was."

"Well! and I too; it cannot be more than ten o'clock at the latest."

"Well! my note said half-past nine."

"Therefore I left the Louvre at nine o'clock. I am in the service of Monsieur le Duc d'Alençon, be it said in passing, and for this reason I shall be obliged to leave you in an hour."

"Which pleases you, no doubt?"

"No, indeed! considering the fact that Monsieur d'Alençon is an ill-tempered and capricious master; moreover, if I am to be found fault with, I prefer to have it done by pretty lips like yours rather than by such sullen ones as his."

"Ah!" said the duchess, "that is a little better. You say, then, that you left the Louvre at nine o'clock."

"Yes, and with every idea of coming directly here, when at the corner of the Rue de Grenelle I saw a man who looked like La Mole."

"Good! La Mole again."

"Always, with or without permission."

"Brutal man!"

"Ah!" said Coconnas, "we are going to begin our complimentary speeches again."

"Not at all; but finish your story."

"I was not the one who wanted to tell it. It was you who asked me why I was late."

"Yes; was it my place to arrive first?"

"Well, you are not looking for any one."

"You are growing tiresome, my dear friend; but go on. At the corner of the Rue de Grenelle you saw a man who looked like La Mole—But what is that on your doublet—blood?"

"Yes, and here is more which was probably sprinkled over me as he fell."

"You had a fight?"

"I should think so."

"On account of your La Mole?"

"On whose account do you think I would fight? For a woman?"

"I thank you!"

"So I followed this man who had the impudence to look like my friend. I joined him in the Rue Coquillière, I overtook him, and stared into his face under the light from a shop. But it was not La Mole."

"Good! that was well done."

"Yes, but he did not think so. 'Monsieur,' said I to him, 'you are an ass to take it upon yourself to resemble from afar my friend Monsieur de la Mole, who is an accomplished cavalier; while on nearer view one can easily perceive that you are nothing but a vagrant.' Whereupon he drew his sword, and I mine. At the third pass he fell down, sprinkling me with his blood."

"But you assisted him at least?"

"I was about to do so when a horseman rode by. Ah! this time, duchess, I was sure that it was La Mole. Unfortunately he was galloping. I ran after him as hard as I could, and those who collected around to see the fight ran behind me. Now as I might easily have been mistaken for a thief, followed as I was by all that rabble shouting at my heels, I was obliged to turn back to scatter them, which made me lose a little time. In the meanwhile the rider disappeared; I followed, inquired of every one, gave the color of the horse; but it was useless; no one had noticed him. At last, tired out from the chase, I came here."

"Tired of the chase!" said the duchess. "How flattering you are!"

"Listen, dear friend," said Coconnas, turning nonchalantly in his chair. "You are going to bother me again on account of poor La Mole. Now, you are wrong, for friendship, you see,—I wish I had his wit or knowledge, I would then find some comparison which would make you understand how I feel— friendship, you see, is a star, while love—love—wait! I have it!—love is only a candle. You will tell me there are several varieties"—

"Of love?"

"No! of candles, and that some are better than others. The rose, for instance, is the best; but rose as it is, the candle burns out, while the star shines forever. You will answer this by saying that when the candle is burned out, another is put in its place."

"Monsieur de Coconnas, you are a goose."

"Indeed!"

"Monsieur de Coconnas, you are impertinent."

"Ah?"

"Monsieur de Coconnas, you are a scoundrel."

"Madame, I warn you that you will make me trebly regret La Mole."

"You no longer love me."

"On the contrary, duchess, you do not know it, but I idolize you. But I can love and cherish and idolize you, and yet in my spare moments praise my friend."

"So you call the time spent with me spare moments, do you?"

"What can you expect? Poor La Mole is constantly in my thoughts."

"You prefer him to me; that is shameful! and I detest you, Annibal! Why not be frank, and tell me you prefer him to me? Annibal, I warn you of one thing: if you prefer anything in the world to me"—

"Henriette, the loveliest of duchesses! For your own peace of mind, believe me, do not ask such unwise questions. I love you more than any woman, and I love La Mole more than any man."

"Well answered!" said a strange voice suddenly. A damask curtain was raised in front of a great panel, which, sliding back into the wall, opened a passage between the two rooms, and showed La Mole in the doorway, like one of Titian's fine portraits in its gilded frame.

"La Mole!" exclaimed Coconnas, without paying any attention to Marguerite or taking the time to thank her for the surprise she had arranged for him; "La Mole, my friend, my dear La Mole!" and he rushed into the arms of his friend, upsetting the armchair in which he had been sitting and the table that stood in his way.

La Mole returned his embrace with effusion; then, turning to the Duchesse de Nevers:

"Pardon me, madame, if the mention of my name has sometimes disturbed your happiness." "Certainly," he added, glancing at Marguerite with a look of ineffable tenderness, "it has not been my fault that I have not seen you sooner."

"You see, Henriette," said Marguerite, "I have kept my word; here he is!"

"Is it, then, to the prayers of Madame la Duchesse that I owe this happiness?" asked La Mole.

"To her prayers alone," replied Marguerite.

Then, turning to La Mole, she continued:

"La Mole, I will allow you not to believe one word of what I say."

Meanwhile Coconnas pressed his friend to his heart over and over again, walked round him a dozen times, and even held a candelabrum to his face the better to see him; then suddenly turning, he knelt down before Marguerite and kissed the hem of her robe.

"Ah! that is pleasant!" said the Duchesse de Nevers. "I suppose now you will find me bearable."

"By Heaven!" cried Coconnas, "I shall find you as adorable as ever; only now I can tell you so with a lighter heart, and were there any number of Poles, Sarmatians, and other hyperborean barbarians present I should make them all admit that you were the queen of beauties."

"Gently, gently, Coconnas," said La Mole, "Madame Marguerite is here!"

"Oh! I cannot help that," cried Coconnas, with the half-comic air which belonged to him alone, "I still assert that Madame Henriette is the queen of beauties and Madame Marguerite is the beauty of queens."

But whatever he might say or do, the Piedmontese, completely carried away by the joy of having found his dear La Mole, had neither eyes nor ears for any one but him.

"Come, my beautiful queen," said Madame de Nevers, "come, let us leave these dear friends to chat awhile alone. They have a thousand things to say to each other which would be interrupted by our conversation. It is hard for us, but it is the only way, I am sure, to make Monsieur Annibal perfectly sane. Do this for me, my queen! since I am foolish enough to love this worthless fellow, as his friend La Mole calls him."

Marguerite whispered a few words to La Mole, who, anxious as he had been to see his friend, would have been glad had the affection of Coconnas for him been less exacting. Meanwhile Coconnas was endeavoring to bring back a smile and a gentle word to Henriette's lips, a result which was easily attained. Then the two women passed into the next room, where supper was awaiting them.

The young men were alone. The first questions Coconnas asked his friend were about that fatal evening which had almost cost him his life. As La Mole proceeded in his story the Piedmontese, who, however, was not easily moved, trembled in every limb.

"But why," said he, "instead of running about the country as you have done, and causing me such uneasiness, did you not seek refuge with our master? The duke who had defended you would have hidden you. I should have been near you and my grief, although feigned, would nevertheless have disturbed every simpleton at court."

"Our master!" said La Mole, in a low voice, "the Duc d'Alençon?"

"Yes. According to what he told me, I supposed it was to him you owed your life."

"I owe my life to the King of Navarre," replied La Mole.

"Oh!" exclaimed Coconnas, "are you sure?"

"Beyond a doubt."

"Oh! what a good, kind king! But what part did the Duc d'Alençon play in it all?"

"He held the rope to strangle me."

"By Heaven!" cried Coconnas, "are you sure of what you say, La Mole? What! this pale-faced, pitiful-looking cur strangle my friend! Ah! by Heaven, by to-morrow I will let him know what I think of him."

"Are you mad?"

"That is true, he would begin again. But what does it matter? Things cannot go on like this."

"Come, come, Coconnas, calm yourself and try and remember that it is half-past eleven o'clock and that you are on duty to-night."

"What do I care about my duty to him! Bah! Let him wait! My attendance! I serve a man who has held a rope? You are joking! No! This is providential; it is said that I should find you to leave you no more. I shall stay here."

"Why, man alive, think what you are saying. You are not drunk, I hope."

"No, fortunately; if I were I would set fire to the Louvre."

"Come, Annibal," said La Mole, "be reasonable. Return to your duties. Service is a sacred thing."

"Will you return with me?"

"Impossible."

"Are they still thinking of killing you?"

"I think not. I am of too little importance for them to have any plot on hand about me. For an instant they wanted to kill me, but that was all. The princes were on a frolic that night."

"What are you going to do, then?"

"Nothing; wander about or take a walk."

"Well, I will walk, too, and wander with you. That will be charming. Then, if you are attacked, there will be two of us, and we will give them no end of trouble. Let him come, your duke! I will pin him to the wall like a butterfly!"

"But, at least, say that you are going to leave his service!"

"Yes, I am."

"In that case, tell him so."

"Well, that seems only right. I will do so. I will write to him."

"Write to him! That would be discourteous, Coconnas, to a prince of the blood."

"Yes, of the blood! of the blood of my friend. Take care," cried Coconnas, rolling his large, tragic eyes, "lest I trifle with points of etiquette!"

"Probably," said La Mole to himself, "in a few days he will need neither the prince nor any one else, for if he wants to come with us, we will take him."

Thereupon Coconnas took the pen without further opposition from his friend and hastily composed the following specimen of eloquence:

"*Monseigneur: There can be no doubt but that your highness, versed as you are in the writings of all authors of antiquity, must know the touching story of Orestes and Pylades, who were two heroes celebrated for their misfortunes and their friendship. My friend La Mole is no less unfortunate than was Orestes, while I am no less tender than Pylades. At present he has affairs of importance which demand my aid. It is therefore impossible for me to leave him. So with the consent of your highness I will take a short vacation, determined as I am to attach myself to my friend's fortune, whithersoever it may lead me. It is with the deepest grief that I tear myself away from the service of your highness, but for this I trust I may obtain your pardon. I venture to subscribe myself with respect, my lord,*

> *"Your highness's very humble and very obedient servant,*
> *"ANNIBAL, COMTE DE COCONNAS,*
> *"The inseparable friend of Monsieur de la Mole."*

This masterpiece finished, Coconnas read it aloud to La Mole, who merely shrugged his shoulders.

"Well! what do you say to it?" asked Coconnas, who had not seen the shrug, or who had pretended not to see it.

"I say," replied La Mole, "that Monsieur d'Alençon will laugh at us."

"At us?"

"Both of us."

"That will be better, it seems to me, than to strangle each of us separately."

"Bah!" said La Mole, laughing, "the one will not necessarily prevent the other."

"Well! so much the worse. Come what may, I will send the letter to-morrow morning. Where shall we sleep when we leave here?"

"At Maître la Hurière's, in that little room in which you tried to stab me before we were Orestes and Pylades!"

"Very well, I will send my letter to the Louvre by our host."

Just then the panel moved.

"Well!" asked both princesses at once, "where are Orestes and Pylades?"

"By Heaven! madame," replied Coconnas, "Pylades and Orestes are dying of hunger and love."

It was Maître la Hurière himself who, at nine o'clock the following morning, carried to the Louvre the respectful missive of Count Annibal de Coconnas.

———

CHAPTER XLV.

ORTHON.

After the refusal of the Duc d'Alençon, which left everything in peril, even his life, Henry became more intimate with the prince than ever, if that were possible. Catharine concluded from the intimacy that the two princes not only understood each other perfectly, but also that they were planning some mutual conspiracy. She questioned Marguerite on the subject, but Marguerite was worthy of her mother, and the Queen of Navarre, whose chief talent lay in avoiding explanations, parried her mother's questions so cleverly that although replying to all she left Catharine more mystified than ever.

The Florentine, therefore, had nothing to guide her except the spirit of intrigue she had brought with her from Tuscany, the most interesting of the small states of that period, and the feeling of hatred she had imbibed from the court of France, which was more divided in its interests and opinions than any court at that time.

She realized that a part of the strength of the Béarnais came from his alliance with the Duc d'Alençon, and she determined to separate them.

From the moment she formed this resolution she beset her son with the patience and the wiles of an angler, who, when he has dropped his bait near the fish, unconsciously draws it in until his prey is caught.

François perceived this increase of affection on the part of his mother and made advances to her. As for Henry, he pretended to see nothing, but kept a closer watch on his ally than he had yet done.

Every one was waiting for some event.

During this state of things, one morning when the sun rose clear, giving out that gentle warmth and sweet odor which announce a beautiful day, a pale man, leaning on a cane, and walking with difficulty, came out of a small house situated behind the arsenal, and walked slowly along the Rue du Petit Muse.

At the Porte Saint Antoine he turned into the street which encircles the moat of the Bastille like a marsh, left the boulevard on his left and entered the Archery Garden, where the gatekeeper received him with every mark of respect.

There was no one in the garden, which, as its name implies, belonged to a particular society called the Taxopholites. Had there been any strollers there the pale man would have merited their sympathy, for his long mustache, his military step and bearing, though weakened by suffering, sufficiently indicated that he was an officer who had been recently wounded, and who was endeavoring to regain his strength by moderate exercise in the open air.

Yet, strange to say, when the cloak opened in which, in spite of the increasing heat, this apparently harmless man was wrapped, it displayed a pair of long pistols suspended from the silver clasps of his belt. This belt also sustained a dagger and a sword so enormously long that it seemed almost impossible to be handled, and which, completing this living arsenal, clattered against his shrunken and trembling legs.

As an additional precaution the lonely soldier glanced around at every step as though to question each turn of the path, each bush and ditch.

Having entered the garden without being molested, the man reached a sort of small arbor, facing the boulevard, from which it was separated by a thick hedge and a small ditch which formed a double inclosure. He threw himself upon a grassy bank within reach of a table on which the host of the establishment, who combined with his duties as gatekeeper the vocation of cook, at once placed a bottle of cordial.

The invalid had been there about ten minutes and had several times raised the china cup to his lips, taking little sips of its contents, when suddenly his countenance, in spite of its interesting pallor, assumed a startled expression. From the Croix Faubin, along a path which to-day is the Rue de Naples, he had perceived a cavalier, wrapped in a great cloak, stop near the moat.

Not more than five minutes had elapsed, during which the man of the pale face, whom the reader has perhaps already recognized as Maurevel, had scarcely had time to recover from the emotion caused by his unexpected presence, when the horseman was joined by a man in a close-fitting coat, like that of a page, who came by the road which is since known as the Rue des Fossés Saint Nicholas.

Hidden in his leafy arbor, Maurevel could easily see and hear everything, and when it is known that the cavalier was De Mouy and the young man in the tight-fitting cloak Orthon, one may imagine whether Maurevel's eyes and ears were not on the alert.

Both men looked very carefully around. Maurevel held his breath.

"You may speak, monsieur," said Orthon, who being the younger was the more confident; "no one can either see or hear us."

"That is well," said De Mouy, "you are to go to Madame de Sauve, and if you find her in her rooms give her this note. If she is not there, you will place it behind the mirror where the king is in the habit of putting his letters. Then you will wait in the Louvre. If you receive an answer, you will bring it you know where; if no reply is sent, you will meet me this evening with a petronel at the spot I showed you, and from which I have just come."

"Very well," said Orthon, "I understand."

"I will now leave you. I have much to do to-day. You need make no haste—there is no use in it, for you do not need to reach the Louvre until he is there, and I think he is taking a lesson in hawking this morning. Now go, and show me what you can do. You have recovered, and you apparently are going to thank Madame de Sauve for her kindness to you during your illness. Now go, my boy."

Maurevel listened, his eyes fixed, his hair on end, his forehead covered with perspiration. His first impulse had been to detach one of his pistols from his belt and aim at De Mouy; but a movement of the latter had opened his cloak and displayed a firm and solid cuirass. Therefore in all probability the ball would flatten itself against this cuirass or strike some part of the body wherein the wound would not be fatal. Besides, he reflected that De Mouy, strong and well armed, would have an advantage over him, wounded as he was. So with a sigh he drew back the weapon which he had pointed at the Huguenot.

"How unfortunate," he murmured, "that I am unable to stretch him dead on the spot, without other witness than that young varlet who would have been such a good mark for my second ball!"

But Maurevel thought that the note given to Orthon and which he was to deliver to Madame de Sauve might perhaps be of more importance than the life of the Huguenot chief.

"Well!" said he, "you have escaped me again this morning; be it so. To-morrow I will have my turn at you if I have to follow you into that hell from which you have come to ruin me, unless I destroy you."

De Mouy raised his cloak over his face, and set out rapidly in the direction of the Temple. Orthon took the road along the moat which led to the banks of the river.

Then Maurevel, rising with more energy and vigor than he had dared to hope for, regained the Rue de la Cerisaie, reached his home, ordered a horse to be saddled, and weak as he was and at the risk of opening his wounds again, set off at a gallop to the Rue Saint Antoine, reached the quays, and entered the Louvre.

Five minutes after he had passed under the gate Catharine knew all that had just taken place, and Maurevel had received the thousand golden crowns promised him for the arrest of the King of Navarre.

"Oh!" said Catharine, "either I am mistaken or this De Mouy is the black spot that was discovered by Réné in the horoscope of the accursed Béarnais."

A quarter of an hour after Maurevel Orthon entered the Louvre, showed himself as De Mouy had directed, and went to the apartments of Madame de Sauve, after having spoken to several attendants of the palace.

Dariole was the only one in her mistress's rooms. Catharine had asked the latter to write certain important letters, and she had been with the queen for the last five minutes.

"No matter," said Orthon, "I will wait."

Taking advantage of his intimacy in the house, the young man went into the sleeping-room of the baroness, and, having assured himself that he was alone, he laid the note behind the mirror. Just as he was removing his hand Catharine entered.

Orthon turned pale, for it seemed to him that the quick, searching glance of the queen mother was first directed to the mirror.

"What are you doing here, my little man?" asked Catharine; "looking for Madame de Sauve?"

"Yes, madame; it is a long time since I saw her, and if I delay any longer in thanking her I fear she will think me ungrateful."

"You love this dear Charlotte very much, do you not?"

"With all my heart, madame!"

"And you are faithful, from what I hear."

"Your majesty will understand that this is very natural when you know that Madame de Sauve took more care of me than I, being only an humble servant, deserved."

"And upon what occasion did she bestow all this care on you?" asked Catharine, pretending to be ignorant of what had happened to the youth.

"When I was wounded, madame."

"Ah, poor boy!" said Catharine, "you were wounded?"

"Yes, madame."

"When was that?"

"The night they tried to arrest the King of Navarre. I was so terrified at sight of the soldiers that I called and shouted; and one of the men gave me a blow on the head which knocked me senseless."

"Poor boy! And are you quite recovered now?"

"Yes, madame."

"So that you are trying to get back into the service of the King of Navarre?"

"No, madame. When the King of Navarre learned that I had dared to resist your majesty's order he dismissed me at once."

"Indeed!" said Catharine, in a tone full of interest; "well, I will see to that affair. But if you are waiting for Madame de Sauve you will wait in vain, for she is occupied in my apartments."

Whereupon, thinking that Orthon perhaps had not had time to hide his note behind the mirror, Catharine stepped into the adjoining room in order to give him the necessary opportunity.

But just as Orthon, anxious at the unexpected arrival of the queen mother, was wondering whether her coming did not forebode some plot against his master, he heard three gentle taps against the ceiling. This was the signal which he himself was in the habit of giving his master in case of danger when the latter was with Madame de Sauve and Orthon was keeping guard.

He started at the sound; a light broke upon his mind; he fancied that this time the warning had been given to him. Springing to the mirror, he removed the note he had just placed there.

Through an opening in the tapestry Catharine had followed every movement of the boy. She saw him dart to the mirror, but she did not know whether it was to hide the note or take it away.

"Well!" murmured the impatient Florentine; "why does he not leave now?"

And she returned to the room smiling.

"Still here, my boy?" said she; "why, what do you want? Did I not tell you that I would look after your fortune? When I say a thing you do not doubt it, do you?"

"Oh, madame, God forbid!" replied Orthon.

And approaching the queen, he bent his knee, kissed the hem of her robe, and at once withdrew.

As he went through the antechamber he saw the captain of the guards, who was waiting for Catharine. The sight of this man, instead of allaying his suspicions, augmented them.

On her part, no sooner had she seen the curtains fall behind Orthon than Catharine sprang to the mirror. But in vain she sought behind it with hands trembling with impatience. She found no note.

And yet she was sure that she had seen the boy approach the mirror. It was to remove the note, therefore, and not to leave it. Fate had given to her enemies a strength equal to her own.

A child had become a man the moment he fought with her.

She moved the mirror, looked behind it, tapped it; nothing was there!

"Oh! unhappy boy!" cried she, "I wished him no ill and now by removing the note he hastens his destiny. Ho, there, Monsieur de Nancey!"

The vibrating tones of the queen mother rang through the salon and penetrated into the anteroom, where, as we have said, Monsieur de Nancey was waiting.

The captain of the guards hastened to the queen.

"Here I am, madame," said he, "what is your majesty's will?"

"Have you been in the antechamber?"

"Yes, madame."

"Did you see a young man, a child, pass through?"

"Just now."

"He cannot have gone far, can he?"

"Scarcely to the stairway."

"Call him back."

"What is his name?"

"Orthon. If he refuses to come bring him back by force; but do not frighten him unless he resists. I must speak to him at once."

The captain of the guards hurriedly withdrew.

As he had said, Orthon was scarcely half way down the stairs, for he was descending slowly, hoping to meet or see the King of Navarre or Madame de Sauve somewhere.

He heard his name and gave a start.

His first impulse was to run, but with forethought beyond his years he realized that by doing so all would be lost.

He stopped therefore.

"Who calls me?"

"I, Monsieur de Nancey," replied the captain of the guards, hurrying down the stairs.

"But I am in haste," said Orthon.

"By order of her majesty the queen mother," said Monsieur de Nancey, as he came up to him.

The youth wiped the perspiration from his brow and turned back.

The captain followed.

Catharine's first idea had been to stop the young man, have him searched, and take possession of the note which she knew he had. She had planned to accuse him of theft, and with this end in view she had removed from the toilet table a diamond clasp which she was going to say he had taken.

But on reflection she concluded that this would be dangerous, in that it would arouse the boy's suspicions and he would inform his master, who would then begin to mistrust something, and so her enemy would gain an advantage over her.

She could, no doubt, have the young man taken to some dungeon, but the rumor of the arrest, however secretly it might be done, would spread through the Louvre, and the slightest inkling of it would put Henry on his guard. However, she must have the note, for a note from Monsieur de Mouy to the King of Navarre, a note sent with such precautions, surely meant conspiracy.

She put back the clasp from where she had taken it.

"No, no," said she, "that would be the method of a guard; it is poor. But for a note—which perhaps after all is not worth the trouble," she continued, frowning, and speaking so low that she herself could scarcely hear the sound of her words. "Well, it is not my fault, but his. Why did not the little scoundrel put the note where he should have put it? I must have this letter."

Just then Orthon entered.

Catharine's face wore such a terrible expression that the youth stopped on the threshold pale as death. He was still too young to be perfect master of himself.

"Madame," said he, "you have done me the honor of calling me back. In what can I serve your majesty?"

Catharine's face lighted up as if a ray of sunlight had touched it.

"I called you back, my child," said she, "because your face pleases me, and having promised to help you I am anxious to do so without delay. We queens are sometimes accused of being forgetful. But this is not on account of our hearts, but because our minds are filled with business. Now I remembered that kings hold men's fortunes in their hands, and so I called you back. Follow me, my child."

Monsieur de Nancey, who was taking the affair seriously, was greatly surprised at Catharine's affectionate manner.

"Can you ride, my child?" asked Catharine.

"Yes, madame."

"Then come into my room. I want to give you a message to carry to Saint Germain."

"I am at your majesty's command."

"Order a horse to be saddled, De Nancey."

Monsieur de Nancey disappeared.

"Come, boy," said Catharine, leading the way.

Orthon followed. The queen mother descended to the next floor, entered the corridor in which were the apartments of the king and the Duc d'Alençon, reached the winding staircase, again descended a flight of stairs, and opened a door leading to a circular gallery to which none but the king and herself possessed the key. Bidding Orthon pass in first, she entered after him and locked the door. This gallery formed a sort of rampart to a certain portion of the apartments of the king and the queen mother, and, like the corridor of the castle of Saint Angelo at Rome, or that of the Pitti Palace at Florence, was a safe place in case of danger. The door locked, Catharine was alone with the young man in the dark corridor. Each advanced a few steps, the queen leading the way, Orthon following.

Suddenly Catharine turned and Orthon again saw on her face the same sinister expression which he had seen on it a few minutes before. Her eyes were as round as those of a cat or a panther and seemed to dart forth fire in the darkness.

"Stop!" she cried.

Orthon felt a shiver run through him; a deathly cold like an icy cloak seemed to fall from the ceiling. The floor felt like the covering of a tomb. Catharine's glance was so sharp that it seemed to penetrate to the very soul of the page. He recoiled and leaned against the wall, trembling from head to foot.

"Where is the note you were charged to give to the King of Navarre?"

"The note?" stammered Orthon.

"Yes; which, if you did not find him, you were to place behind the mirror?"

"I, madame," said Orthon, "I do not know what you mean."

"The note which De Mouy gave you an hour ago, behind the Archery Garden."

"I have no note," said Orthon; "your majesty must be mistaken."

"You lie," said Catharine; "give me the note, and I will keep the promise I made you."

"What promise, madame?"

"I will make your fortune."

"I have no note, madame," repeated the child.

Catharine ground her teeth; then assuming a smile:

"Give it to me," said she, "and you shall have a thousand golden crowns."

"I have no note, madame."

"Two thousand crowns."

"Impossible; since I have no note, how can I give it to you?"

"Ten thousand crowns, Orthon."

Orthon, who saw the anger of the queen rising, felt that there was only one way of saving his master, and that was to swallow the note. He put his hand to his pocket, but Catharine guessed his intention and stopped him.

"There, my child," said she, laughing, "you are certainly faithful. When kings wish to attach a follower to them there is no harm in their making sure of his trustworthiness. Here, take this purse as a first reward. Go and carry your note to your master, and tell him that from to-day you are in my service. You can get out without me by the door we entered. It opens from within."

And giving the purse to the astonished youth Catharine walked on a few steps and placed her hand against the wall.

But the young man stood still, hesitating. He could not believe that the danger he had felt hovering over him was gone.

"Come, do not tremble so," said Catharine. "Have I not told you that you were free to go, and that if you wish to come back your fortune is made?"

"Thank you, madame," said Orthon. "Then you pardon me?"

"I do more, I reward you; you are a faithful bearer of notes, a gentle messenger of love. But you forget your master is waiting for you."

"Ah! that is true," said the young man, springing towards the door.

But scarcely had he advanced three steps before the floor gave way beneath his feet. He stumbled, extended both hands, gave a fearful cry, and disappeared in the dungeon of the Louvre, the spring of which Catharine had just touched.

"So," murmured the queen, "thanks to the fellow's obstinacy I shall have to descend a hundred and fifty steps."

The queen mother returned to her apartments, lighted a dark lantern, came back to the corridor, closed the spring, and opened the door of a spiral staircase which seemed to lead to the bowels of the earth. Urged on by the insatiable thirst of a curiosity which was but the minister of her hatred, she reached an iron door which turned on its hinges and admitted her to the depths of the dungeon. Bleeding, crushed, and mutilated by a fall of a hundred feet or more, but still breathing, lay poor Orthon.

Beyond the thick wall the waters of the Seine were heard roaring, brought to the foot of the stairs by a subterranean channel.

Catharine entered the damp and unwholesome place, which during her reign had witnessed many a fall similar to the one it had just seen, searched the body, seized the letter, made sure that it was the one she desired, then pushing aside the body with her foot she pressed a spring, the bottom of the dungeon sank, and the corpse, carried down by its own weight, disappeared in the direction of the river.

Closing the door again, Catharine ascended, shut herself in her closet, and read the note, which contained these words:

"This evening at ten o'clock, Rue de l'Arbre Sec, Hôtel de la Belle Étoile. If you come send no reply; otherwise send back NO by the bearer.

"DE MOUY DE SAINT PHALE."

As Catharine read this note a smile came to her lips. She was thinking of the victory she was to gain, forgetting the price at which she had bought it. But after all what was Orthon? A faithful, devoted follower, a handsome young boy; that was all.

That, one may well imagine, would not for an instant have turned the scales on which the fate of empires had been weighed.

The note read, Catharine at once went to Madame de Sauve's and placed it behind the mirror.

As she came down she found the captain of the guards at the entrance of the corridor.

"Madame," said Monsieur de Nancey, "according to your majesty's orders the horse is ready."

"My dear baron," said Catharine, "we shall not need it. I have made the boy speak, and he is really too stupid to be charged with the errand I wanted to entrust to him. I thought he was a lackey, but he is nothing but a groom at best. I gave him some money and dismissed him by the private gate."

"But," said Monsieur de Nancey, "the errand?"

"The errand?" asked Catharine.

"The one on which he was to go to Saint Germain. Does your majesty wish me to undertake it, or shall I have one of my men attend to it?"

"No, no," said Catharine, "this evening you and your men will have something else to do."

Whereupon the queen mother returned to her room, hoping that evening to hold in her hands the fate of the accursed King of Navarre.

CHAPTER XLVI.

THE INN OF LA BELLE ÉTOILE.

Two hours after the event we have described, no trace of which remained on Catharine's face, Madame de Sauve, having finished her work for the queen, returned to her own rooms. Henry followed her, and learning from Dariole that Orthon had been there he went directly to the mirror and found the note.

It was, as we have said, couched in these terms:

"This evening at ten o'clock, Rue de l'Arbre Sec, Hôtel de la Belle Étoile. If you come send no reply; otherwise send back NO by the bearer."

There was no address.

"Henry will not fail to keep the appointment," said Catharine, "for even had he not wished to do so there is no longer a messenger to take back his answer."

Catharine was not mistaken.

Henry inquired for Orthon. Dariole said that he had gone out with the queen mother; but as the note had been found in its place, and as the poor boy was known to be incapable of treason, Henry felt no anxiety.

He dined as usual at the table of the King, who joked him greatly on the mistakes he had made while hawking that morning.

Henry made excuses for himself, saying that he came from the mountains and not the plain, but he promised Charles to study the art. Catharine was charming, and on leaving the table begged Marguerite to pass the evening with her.

At eight o'clock Henry took two attendants, left by the Porte Saint Honoré, made a long circuit, returned by the Tour de Bois, and crossing the Seine at the ferry of Nesle, rode up the Rue Saint Jacques, where he dismissed his gentlemen, as if he were going to keep some love appointment. At the corner of the Rue des Mathurins he found a man on horseback, wrapped in a cloak. He approached him.

"Mantes!" said the man.

"Pau!" replied the king.

The man at once dismounted. Henry put on his splashed mantle, mounted the horse, which was covered with foam, returned by the Rue de la Harpe, crossed the Pont Saint Michel, passed down the Rue Barthélemy, again crossed the river at the Pont aux Meuniers, descended the quays, took the Rue de l'Arbre Sec, and knocked at the door of Maître la Hurière's.

La Mole was in a room writing a long love-letter—to whom may easily be imagined.

Coconnas was in the kitchen with La Hurière, watching half a dozen partridges roasting, and disputing with his friend the host as to when they should be removed from the spit. At this moment Henry knocked. Grégoire opened the door and led the horse to the stable, while the traveller entered, stamping on the floor as if to warm his benumbed feet.

"Maître La Hurière," said La Mole, as he continued to write, "here is a gentleman asking for you."

La Hurière advanced, looked at Henry from head to foot, and as his thick cloth mantle did not inspire the innkeeper with very great veneration:

"Who are you?" he asked.

"Well, by Heaven!" said Henry, pointing to La Mole, "monsieur has just told you; I am a gentleman from Gascony come to court."

"What do you want?"

"A room and supper."

"Humph!" said La Hurière, "have you a lackey?"

This was the question usually asked, as is well known.

"No," replied Henry, "but I hope to have one when I make my fortune."

"I do not let rooms to any one unless he has a lackey," said La Hurière.

"Even if I offered to pay you double for your supper?"

"Oh! you are very generous, worthy sir!" said La Hurière, looking suspiciously at Henry.

"Not at all, but, hoping to pass the night in your hotel, which has been highly recommended by a nobleman from my county who has been here, I invited a friend to sup with me. Have you any good wine of Arbois?"

"I have some which is better than the King of Navarre drinks."

"Good! I will pay well for it. Ah! here is my friend."

Just then the door opened and a gentleman entered older by a few years than the first, and dragging a long rapier at his side.

"Ah!" said he, "you are prompt, my young friend. For a man who has just made two hundred leagues it is something to be so punctual."

"Is this your guest?" asked La Hurière.

"Yes," said the first, going up to the young man with the rapier and shaking him by the hand, "we will have our supper now."

"Here or in your room?"

"Wherever you please."

"Maître," said La Mole to La Hurière, "rid us of these Huguenot fellows. Coconnas and I cannot say a word before them."

"Carry the supper to room No. 2, on the third floor. Upstairs, gentlemen."

The two travellers followed Grégoire, who preceded them with lights.

La Mole watched them until they had disappeared. Then turning round he saw Coconnas, whose head was thrust out of the kitchen door. Two great eyes and an open mouth gave to the latter's face a remarkable expression of astonishment.

La Mole stepped up to him.

"By Heaven!" said Coconnas, "did you see?"

"What?"

"Those two gentlemen."

"Well?"

"I would swear that it was"—

"Who?"

"Why—the King of Navarre and the man in the red cloak."

"Swear if you will, but not too loud."

"Did you recognize them too?"

"Certainly."

"What are they here for?"

"Some love affair."

"You think so?"

"I am sure of it."

"La Mole, I prefer sword-thrusts to these love affairs. I would have sworn a moment ago, now I will bet."

"What will you bet?"

"That there is some plot on hand."

"You are mad."

"I tell you"—

"I tell you that even if they are plotting it is their own affair."

"That is true. However," said Coconnas, "I no longer belong to Monsieur d'Alençon. So let them do as they see fit."

As the partridges had apparently reached the state in which Coconnas liked them, the Piedmontese, who counted on making the most of his dinner of them, called Maître la Hurière to remove them from the spit.

Meantime Henry and De Mouy were installed in their chamber.

"Well, sire," said De Mouy, when Grégoire had set the table, "have you seen Orthon?"

"No; but I found the note he left behind the mirror. The boy must have become frightened, I suppose, for Queen Catharine came in while he was there, so he went away without waiting for my answer."

"For a moment I felt somewhat anxious about him, as Dariole told me that the queen mother had had a long talk with him."

"Oh! there is no danger. The boy is clever, and although the queen mother knows his profession he will not let her find out much from him, I am sure."

"But have you seen him, De Mouy?" asked Henry.

"No, but I expect to this evening. At midnight he is to come here for me with a good petronel. He will tell me what happened as we walk along."

"And the man at the corner of the Rue des Mathurins?"

"What man?"

"The man who gave me his horse and cloak. Are you sure of him?"

"He is one of our most devoted followers. Besides, he neither knows your majesty nor why he himself was there."

"Can we discuss our affairs without fear, then?"

"Certainly. Besides, La Mole is on the watch."

"Well, sire, what says Monsieur d'Alençon?"

"Monsieur d'Alençon will not go, De Mouy. He said so positively. The election of D'Anjou to the throne of Poland and the king's illness have changed his mind."

"So he is the one who spoiled our plan?"

"Yes."

"Has he betrayed us?"

"Not yet; but he will do so at the first opportunity."

"Coward! traitor! Why did he not answer my letters?"

"In order to have proofs against you, and none against himself. Meantime, all is lost, is it not, De Mouy?"

"On the contrary, sire, all is won. You know that the whole party, except the faction of the Prince de Condé, was for you, and used the duke, with whom it seemed to have relations, only as a safeguard. Well, since the day of the ceremony I have arranged so that everything is for you. One hundred men were enough to escape with the Duc d'Alençon; I have raised fifteen hundred. In one week they will be ready and drawn up on the road to Pau. It will not be a flight but a retreat. Fifteen hundred men will suffice, sire, will they not? Shall you feel safe with such an army?"

Henry smiled and touched him on the shoulder.

"You know, De Mouy," said he, "and you alone know it, that Henry of Navarre is not naturally such a coward as is supposed."

"Yes, I know that, sire; and I trust before long that all France will know it too."

"But where one plots one must succeed. The first condition of success is decision; and for decision to be rapid, frank, and to the point, one must be sure of success."

"Well, sire, what days do you hunt?"

"Every week or ten days we either hunt or hawk."

"When did you hunt last?"

"To-day."

"Then a week or ten days from now you will hunt again?"

"No doubt; possibly before then."

"Listen, sire; everything seems perfectly quiet. The Duc d'Anjou has left; no one thinks of him. The King is getting better every day. The persecution against us has almost ceased. Play the amiable with the queen mother and Monsieur d'Alençon; keep telling him that you cannot go without him, and try to make him believe you, which is more difficult."

"Do not worry, he will believe me."

"Do you think he has such confidence in you?"

"No, God forbid, but he believes everything the queen says."

"And is the queen true to us?"

"Oh! I have proof of it. Besides, she is ambitious and is dying for this far-off crown of Navarre."

"Well! three days before the hunt send me word where it will take place—whether it is to be at Bondy, at Saint Germain, or at Rambouillet. Monsieur de la Mole will ride ahead of you; follow him, and ride fast. Once out of the forest if the queen mother wants you she will have to run after you; and I trust that her Norman horses will not see even the hoofs of our Barbary steeds and our Spanish ponies."

"Agreed, De Mouy."

"Have you any money, sire?"

Henry made the same grimace he made all his life at this question.

"Not much," said he; "but I think Margot has some."

"Well! whether it is yours or hers, bring as much as you can."

"And in the meantime what are you going to do?"

"Having paid some attention to your majesty's affairs, as you see, will your majesty permit me to devote a little time to my own?"

"Certainly, De Mouy, certainly, but what are yours?"

"Yesterday Orthon told me (he is a very intelligent boy, whom I recommend to your majesty) that he met that scoundrel of a Maurevel near the arsenal, that thanks to Réné he has recovered, and that he was warming himself in the sun like the snake that he is."

"Ah, yes, I understand," said Henry.

"Very good, then. You will be king some day, sire, and if you have anything such as I have to avenge you can do so in a kingly way. I am a soldier and must avenge myself like a soldier. So while all our little affairs are being arranged, which will give that scoundrel five or six days in which to recover more fully, I too shall take a stroll around the arsenal, and I will pin him to the grass with four blows of my rapier, after which I shall leave Paris with a lighter heart."

"Attend to your affairs, my friend, by all means," said the Béarnais. "By the way, you are pleased with La Mole, are you not?"

"Yes; he is a charming fellow, devoted to you body and soul, sire, and on whom you can depend as you can on me—brave"—

"And above all, discreet. So he must follow us to Navarre, De Mouy; once there we will look about and see what we can do to recompense him."

As Henry concluded these words with a sly smile, the door opened or rather was broken in, and the man they had just been praising appeared, pale and agitated.

"Quick, sire," cried he; "quick, the house is surrounded."

"Surrounded!" cried Henry, rising; "by whom?"

"By the King's guards."

"Oh!" said De Mouy, drawing his pistols from his belt, "we are to have a battle, apparently."

"Well," said La Mole, "you may well talk of pistols and battle, but what can you do against fifty men?"

"He is right," said the king; "and if there were any means of escape"—

"There is one which has already been of use to me, and if your majesty will follow me"—

"And De Mouy?"

"And De Mouy too if he wishes, but you must be quick."

Steps were heard on the stairs.

"It is too late," said Henry.

"Ah! if any one would only engage them for five minutes," cried La Mole, "I would save the king."

"Save him, then, monsieur," said De Mouy; "I will look after them. Go, sire, go."

"But what shall you do?"

"Do not fear, sire, but go."

And De Mouy began by hiding the king's plate, napkin, and goblet, so that it might seem as though he had been alone at table.

"Come, sire, come," cried La Mole, seizing the king by the arm and dragging him towards the stairway.

"De Mouy, my brave De Mouy!" exclaimed Henry, holding out his hand to the young man.

De Mouy kissed the hand, pushed Henry from the room, and closed and bolted the door after him.

"Yes, I understand," said Henry, "he will be caught, while we escape; but

426

who the devil can have betrayed us?"

"Come, sire, come. They are on the stairs."

In fact, the light of the torches was beginning to be seen on the wall, while at the foot of the stairs sounds like the clanking of swords were heard.

"Quick, quick, sire!" cried La Mole.

And, guiding the king in the darkness, he ascended two flights, pushed open a door, which he locked behind him, and, opening the window of a closet:

"Sire," said he, "is your majesty very much afraid of a walk across the roofs?"

"I?" said Henry, "come, now; am I not a chamois hunter?"

"Well, your majesty must follow me. I know the way and will guide you."

"Go on," said Henry, "I will follow."

La Mole stepped out, went along the ledge, which formed a sort of gutter, at the end of which they came to a depression between two roofs. In this way they reached an open window leading to an empty garret.

"Sire," said La Mole, "here we are at the opening."

"Ah! so much the better," said Henry, wiping the perspiration from his pale face.

"Now," said La Mole, "it will be easier: this garret opens on to a stairway, the stairway leads to an alley, and the alley to the street. I travelled the same road, sire, on a much more terrible night than this."

"Go on, go on," said Henry.

La Mole sprang through the open window, reached the unlocked door, opened it, came to a winding stairway, and placing in the king's hand the cord that served as a baluster:

"Come, sire," said he.

Half way down the stairs Henry stopped. He was before a window which overlooked the courtyard of the *Belle Étoile*. On the opposite stairway soldiers were seen running, some carrying swords, others torches.

Suddenly in the midst of a group the King of Navarre perceived De Mouy. He had surrendered his sword and was quietly descending the stairs.

"Poor fellow," said Henry, "so brave and devoted!"

"Faith, sire," said La Mole, "your majesty is right. He certainly does seem calm; and see, he even laughs! It must be that he is planning some scheme, for you know he seldom laughs."

"And the young man who was with you?"

"Monsieur de Coconnas?" asked La Mole.

"Yes; what has become of him?"

"Oh! sire, I am not anxious about him. On seeing the soldiers he said only one word to me: 'Do we risk anything?'

"'Our heads,' I answered.

"'Can you escape?'

"'I hope so.'

"'Well, I can too,' he replied. And I promise you he will! Sire, when Coconnas is caught it will be because he wishes to be caught."

"Then," said Henry, "all is well. Let us try to get back to the Louvre."

"That will be easy enough, sire," said La Mole. "Let us wrap ourselves in our cloaks and start. The street is full of people running to see the commotion, and we shall be taken for spectators."

The gate was open and Henry and La Mole encountered no obstacle beyond the crowds in the street.

They reached the Rue d'Avernon; but in passing by the Rue Poulies they saw De Mouy and his escort cross the Place Saint Germain l'Auxerrois, led by the captain of the guards, Monsieur de Nancey.

"Ah!" said Henry, "they are taking him to the Louvre, apparently. The devil! the gates will be closed. They will take the names of all those who enter, and if I am seen returning after him they will think I have been with him."

"Well! but, sire," said La Mole, "enter some other way than by the gate."

"How the devil do you mean?"

"Well, sire, there is the Queen of Navarre's window."

"*Ventre saint gris*, Monsieur de la Mole," said Henry, "you are right. I never thought of that! But how can I attract the attention of the queen?"

"Oh," said La Mole, bowing with an air of respectful gratitude, "your majesty throws stones so well!"

CHAPTER XLVII.

DE MOUY DE SAINT PHALE.

This time Catharine had taken such precautions that she felt sure of her object.

Consequently, about ten o'clock she sent away Marguerite, thoroughly convinced, as was the case, that the Queen of Navarre was ignorant of the plot against her husband, and went to the King, begging him not to retire so early.

Mystified by the air of triumph which, in spite of her usual dissimulation, appeared on his mother's face, Charles questioned Catharine, who merely answered:

"I can say only one thing to your Majesty: that this evening you will be freed from two of your bitterest enemies."

Charles raised his eyebrows like a man who says to himself:

"That is well; we shall see;" and whistling to his great boar-hound, who came to him dragging his belly along the ground like a serpent to lay his fine and intelligent head on his master's knee, he waited. At the end of a few minutes, during which Catharine sat with eyes and ears alert, a pistol-shot was heard in the courtyard of the Louvre.

"What is that noise?" asked Charles, frowning, while the hound sprang up and pricked his ears.

"Nothing except a signal," said Catharine; "that is all."

"And what is the meaning of the signal?"

"It means that from this moment, sire, your one real enemy can no longer injure you."

"Have they killed a man?" asked Charles, looking at his mother with that look of command which signifies that assassination and mercy are two inherent attributes of royal power.

"No, sire, they have only arrested two."

"Oh!" murmured Charles, "always hidden plots, always conspiracies around the King. And yet, the devil! mother, I am grown up, and big enough to look out for myself. I need neither leading-strings nor padded caps. Go to Poland with your son Henry if you wish to reign; I tell you you are wrong to play this kind of game here."

"My son," said Catharine, "this is the last time I shall meddle with your affairs. But the enterprise in which you have always thwarted me was begun long ago, and I have earnestly endeavored to prove to your Majesty that I am right."

At that moment several men stopped in the outer hall and the butt-ends of muskets were heard on the pavement. Almost at the same instant Monsieur de Nancey begged an audience of the King.

"Let him enter," said Charles, hastily.

Monsieur de Nancey appeared, saluted the King, and turning to Catharine said:

"Madame, your majesty's orders are executed; he is captured."

"What *he*?" cried Catharine, greatly troubled. "Have you arrested only one?"

"He was alone, madame."

"Did he defend himself?"

"No, he was supping quietly in a room, and gave up his sword the moment it was demanded."

"Who?" asked the King.

"You shall see," said Catharine. "Bring in the prisoner, Monsieur de Nancey."

Five minutes later De Mouy was there.

"De Mouy!" cried the King; "what is the matter now, monsieur?"

"Well, sire," said De Mouy, with perfect composure, "if your Majesty will allow me the liberty, I will ask the same of you."

"Instead of asking this question of the King," said Catharine, "have the kindness, Monsieur de Mouy, to tell my son who was the man found in the chamber of the King of Navarre a certain night, and who on that night resisted the orders of his Majesty like the rebel that he is, killed two guards, and wounded Monsieur de Maurevel?"

"Yes," said Charles, frowning, "do you know the name of that man, Monsieur de Mouy?"

"Yes, sire; does your Majesty wish to hear it?"

"That will please me, I admit."

"Well, sire, he is called De Mouy de Saint Phale."

"It was you?"

"It was I."

Catharine, astonished at this audacity, recoiled a step.

"How did you dare resist the orders of the King?" asked Charles.

"In the first place, sire, I did not know that there was an order from your Majesty; then I saw only one thing, or rather one man, Monsieur de Maurevel, the assassin of my father and of the admiral. I remembered that a year and a half ago, in the very room in which we now are, on the evening of the 24th of August, your Majesty promised me to avenge us on the murderer, and as since that time very grave events have occurred I thought that in spite of himself the King had changed his mind. Seeing Maurevel within reach, I believed Heaven had sent him to me. Your Majesty knows the rest. Sire, I sprang upon him as upon an assassin and fired at his men as I would have fired at bandits."

Charles made no reply. His friendship for Henry had for some time made him look at many things in a different light from which he had at first seen them, and more than once with terror.

In regard to Saint Bartholomew the queen mother had registered in her memory remarks which had fallen from her son's lips and which resembled remorse.

"But," observed Catharine, "what were you doing at that hour in the apartments of the King of Navarre?"

"Oh!" replied De Mouy, "it is a long story, but if his Majesty has the patience to listen"—

"Yes," said Charles; "speak, I wish to hear it."

"I will obey, sire," said De Mouy, bowing.

Catharine sat down, fixing an anxious look on the young chief.

"We are listening," said Charles. "Here, Actéon!"

The dog resumed the place he had occupied before the prisoner had been admitted.

"Sire," said De Mouy, "I came to his majesty the King of Navarre as the deputy of our brethren, your faithful subjects of the reformed religion."

Catharine signed to Charles IX.

"Be quiet, mother," said the latter. "I do not lose a word. Go on, Monsieur de Mouy, go on; why did you come?"

"To inform the King of Navarre," continued Monsieur de Mouy, "that his abjuration had lost for him the confidence of the Huguenot party; but that, nevertheless, in remembrance of his father, Antoine de Bourbon, and especially on account of his mother, the courageous Jeanne d'Albret, whose name is dear among us, the followers of the reformed religion owed him this mark of deference, to beg him to desist from his claims to the crown of Navarre."

"What did he say?" asked Catharine, unable in spite of her self-control to receive this unexpected blow calmly.

"Ah! ah!" said Charles, "and yet this crown of Navarre, which without my permission has been made to jump from head to head, seems to belong a little to me."

"The Huguenots, sire, recognize better than any one the principle of sovereignty to which your Majesty has just referred. Therefore they hope to induce your Majesty to place the crown on a head that is dear to you."

"To me!" said Charles; "on a head that is dear to me! The devil! what head do you mean, monsieur? I do not understand."

"On the head of Monsieur le Duc d'Alençon."

Catharine became as pale as death, and gave De Mouy a flashing glance.

"Did my brother D'Alençon know this?"

"Yes, sire."

"And did he accept the crown?"

"Subject to the consent of your Majesty, to whom he referred us."

"Ah!" said Charles, "it is a crown which would suit our brother D'Alençon wonderfully well. And I never thought of it! Thanks, De Mouy, thanks! When you have such ideas you will always be welcome at the Louvre."

"Sire, you would long since have been informed of this project had it not been for that unfortunate affair of Maurevel's, which made me afraid I had fallen into disgrace with your Majesty."

"Yes, but what did Henry say to this plan?" asked Catharine.

"The King of Navarre, madame, yielded to the desire of his brethren, and his renunciation was ready."

"In that case," said Catharine, "you must have the renunciation."

"It happens that I have it with me, madame, signed by him and dated."

"Dated previous to the affair in the Louvre?" said Catharine.

"Yes, the evening before, I think."

De Mouy drew from his pocket an abdication in favor of the Duc d'Alençon, written and signed in Henry's hand, and bearing the date indicated.

"Faith, yes," said Charles, "and all is in due form."

"What did Henry demand in return for this renunciation?"

"Nothing, madame; the friendship of King Charles, he told us, would amply repay him for the loss of a crown."

Catharine bit her lips in anger and wrung her beautiful hands.

"All this is perfectly correct, De Mouy," said the King.

"Then," said the queen mother, "if everything was settled between you and the King of Navarre, what was the object of your interview with him this evening?"

"I, madame! with the King of Navarre?" said De Mouy. "Monsieur de Nancey, who arrested me, will bear witness that I was alone. Your majesty can ask him."

"Monsieur de Nancey!" called the King.

The captain of the guards entered.

"Monsieur de Nancey," said Catharine, quickly, "was Monsieur de Mouy entirely alone at the inn of the *Belle Étoile*?"

"In the room, yes, madame; in the hostelry, no."

"Ah!" said Catharine, "who was his companion?"

"I do not know if he was the companion of Monsieur de Mouy, madame, but I know that a man escaped by a back door after having stretched two of my men on the floor."

"And you recognized this gentleman, no doubt?"

"No, I did not, but my guards did."

"Who was he?" asked Charles IX.

"Monsieur le Comte Annibal de Coconnas."

"Annibal de Coconnas!" exclaimed the King, gloomy and thoughtful; "the one who made such a terrible slaughter of the Huguenots during the massacre of Saint Bartholomew?"

433

"Monsieur de Coconnas, a gentleman in the suite of Monsieur d'Alençon," said Monsieur de Nancey.

"Very good," said Charles IX. "You may go, Monsieur de Nancey, and another time, remember one thing."

"What is it, sire?"

"That you are in my service, and that you are to obey no one but me."

Monsieur de Nancey withdrew backwards, bowing respectfully.

De Mouy smiled ironically at Catharine.

There was an instant's silence. The queen twisted the tassels of her girdle; Charles caressed his dog.

"But what was your intention, monsieur?" continued Charles; "were you acting violently?"

"Against whom, sire?"

"Why, against Henry, or François, or myself."

"Sire, we have the renunciation of your brother-in-law, the consent of your brother; and, as I have had the honor of telling you, we were on the point of soliciting your Majesty's sanction when that unfortunate affair occurred at the Louvre."

"Well, mother," said Charles, "I see nothing wrong in all this. You were right, Monsieur de Mouy, in asking for a king. Yes, Navarre may and ought to be a separate kingdom. Moreover, it seems made expressly to give to my brother D'Alençon, who has always had so great a desire for a crown that when we wear ours he cannot keep his eyes off of it. The only thing which stood in the way of this coronation was Henriot's rights; but since Henriot voluntarily abdicates"—

"Voluntarily, sire."

"It seems that it is the will of God! Monsieur de Mouy, you are free to return to your brethren, whom I have chastised somewhat roughly, perhaps, but that is between God and myself. Tell them that since they desire to have my brother d'Alençon for King of Navarre the King of France accedes to their wishes. From this moment Navarre is a kingdom, and its sovereign is called François. I ask only eight days for my brother to leave Paris with the brilliancy and pomp befitting a king. Now go, Monsieur de Mouy, go! Monsieur de Nancey, allow Monsieur de Mouy to pass; he is free."

"Sire," said De Mouy, advancing a step, "will your Majesty permit me?"

"Yes," said the King, and he extended his hand to the young Huguenot.

De Mouy knelt and kissed the King's hand.

"By the way," said Charles, detaining him as he was about to rise, "did you not demand from me justice on that scoundrel of a Maurevel?"

"Yes, sire."

"I do not know where he is, as he is hiding; but if you meet him, take justice into your own hands. I authorize you to do this and gladly."

"Ah! sire," cried De Mouy, "your Majesty overwhelms me. Your Majesty may rely on me. I have no idea where he is, but I will find him, you may rest assured."

De Mouy respectfully saluted King Charles and Queen Catharine, and withdrew without hindrance from the guards who had brought him thither. He passed rapidly through the corridors, reached the gate, and once outside hurried to Place Saint Germain l'Auxerrois, to the inn of the *Belle Étoile*. Here he found his horse, thanks to which, three hours after the scene we have just described, the young man breathed in safety behind the walls of Mantes.

Catharine, consumed with rage, returned to her apartments, whence she passed into those of Marguerite.

She found Henry there in his dressing-gown, apparently ready for bed.

"Satan!" she murmured, "aid a poor queen for whom God will do nothing more!"

CHAPTER XLVIII.

TWO HEADS FOR ONE CROWN.

"Ask Monsieur d'Alençon to come to me," said Charles as he dismissed his mother.

Monsieur de Nancey, in accordance with the remark of the King that henceforth he was to obey him alone, hastened to the duke's apartments and delivered word for word the order he had just received.

The Duc d'Alençon gave a start. He had always feared Charles, and now more than ever since by conspiring he had reason to be afraid.

Nevertheless, he went to his brother in all haste.

Charles was standing up, whistling a hunting-song.

As he entered, the Duc d'Alençon caught from the glassy eye of the King one of those bitter looks of hatred which he knew so well.

"Your Majesty has sent for me," said he. "Here I am; what does your Majesty desire?"

"I desire to tell you, my good brother, that as a reward for the great friendship you bear me I have decided to-day to do for you the thing you most want."

"For me?"

"Yes, for you. Think what for some time you have been dreaming of, without daring to ask it of me, and I will give it to you."

"Sire," said François, "I swear to you that I desire nothing but the continued good health of the King."

"In that case you will be glad to know, D'Alençon, that the indisposition I experienced at the time the Poles arrived has passed by. Thanks to Henriot, I escaped a furious wild boar, which would have ripped me open, and I am so well that I do not envy the most healthy man in my kingdom. Without being an unkind brother you can, therefore, ask for something besides the continuation of my health, which is excellent."

"I want nothing, sire."

"Yes, yes, François," said Charles, impatiently, "you desire the crown of Navarre, since you have had an understanding with Henriot and De Mouy,— with the first, that he would abdicate; with the second, that he would give it to you. Well! Henriot renounces it! De Mouy has told me of your wish, and this crown for which you are ambitious"—

"Well?" asked D'Alençon in a trembling voice.

"Well, the devil! it is yours."

D'Alençon turned frightfully pale; then suddenly the blood rushed from his heart, which almost burst, flowed to his face, and his cheeks became suffused with a burning flush. The favor the King granted him at that moment threw him into despair.

"But, sire," said he, trembling with emotion and trying in vain to recover his self-possession, "I never desired and certainly never asked for such a thing."

"That is possible," said the King, "for you are very discreet, brother; but it has been desired and asked for you."

"Sire, I swear to you that never"—

"Do not swear."

"But, sire, are you going to exile me, then?"

"Do you call this exile, François? Plague it, you are hard to please! What better do you hope for?"

D'Alençon bit his lips in despair.

"Faith!" continued Charles, affecting kindness, "I did not think you were so popular, François, especially with the Huguenots. But they have sought you, and I have to confess to myself that I was mistaken. Besides, I could ask nothing better than to have one of my family—my brother who loves me and who is incapable of betraying me—at the head of a party which for thirty years has made war against us. This will quell everything as if by enchantment, to say nothing of the fact that we shall all be kings in the family. There will be no one except poor Henriot who will be nothing but my friend. But he is not ambitious and he shall take this title which no one else claims."

"Oh, sire! you are mistaken. I claim this title, and who has a better right to it than I? Henry is only your brother by marriage. I am your brother by blood, and more than this, my love—Sire, I beg you, keep me near you."

"No, no, François," replied Charles; "that would be to your unhappiness."

"How so?"

"For many reasons."

"But, sire, shall you ever find as faithful a companion as I am? From my childhood I have never left your Majesty."

"I know that very well; and sometimes I have wished you farther away."

"What does your Majesty mean?"

"Nothing, nothing; I understand myself. Oh, what fine hunts you will have there, François! How I envy you! Do you know that in those devilish mountains they hunt the bear as here we do the wild boar? You will send us all such magnificent skins! They hunt there with a dagger, you know; they wait for the animal, excite him, irritate him; he advances towards the hunter, and when within four feet of him he rises on his hind legs. It is then that they plunge the steel into his heart as Henry did to the boar at our last hunt. It is dangerous sport, but you are brave, François, and the danger will be a real pleasure for you."

"Ah! your Majesty increases my grief, for I shall hunt with you no more."

"By Heaven! so much the better!" said the King. "It helps neither of us to hunt together."

"What does your Majesty mean?"

"That hunting with me causes you such pleasure and rouses in you such emotion that you who are the personification of skill, you who with any musket can bring down a magpie a hundred feet away, the last time we hunted together failed at twenty paces to hit a wild boar; but with your weapon, a weapon, too, with which you are familiar, you broke the leg of my best horse. The devil, François, that makes one reflect, you know!"

"Oh! sire, pardon me, it was from emotion," said D'Alençon, who had become livid.

"Yes," replied Charles, "I can well imagine what the emotion was; and it is on account of this emotion that I realize all that it means when I say to you: 'Believe me, François, when one has such emotions it is best for us to hunt at a distance from each other. Think about it, brother, not while you are with me, because I can see my presence troubles you, but when you are alone, and you will see that I have every reason to fear that in another hunt you might be seized with another emotion. There is nothing like emotion for causing the hand to rise, and you might kill the rider instead of the horse, the king instead of the beast. Plague it, a bullet aimed too high or too low changes an entire government. We have an example of this in our own family. When Montgommery killed our father, Henry II., by accident—emotion, perhaps— the blow placed our brother, François II., on the throne and sent our father Henry to Saint Denis. So little is necessary for Providence to effect much!"

The duke felt the perspiration running down his face at this attack, as formidable as it was unforeseen.

It would have been impossible for the King to show more clearly that he had surmised all. Veiling his anger under a jesting manner, Charles was perhaps more terrible than as if he had let himself pour forth the lava of hate which was consuming his heart; his vengeance seemed in proportion to his rancor. As the one grew sharper, the other increased, and for the first time D'Alençon felt remorse, or rather regret for having meditated a crime which had not succeeded. He had sustained the struggle as long as he could, but at this final blow he bent his head, and Charles saw dawning in his eyes that devouring fire which in beings of a tender nature ploughs the furrow from which spring tears.

But D'Alençon was one of those who weep only from anger. Charles fixed on him his vulture gaze, watching the feelings which succeeded one another across the face of the young man, and all those sensations appeared to him as accurately, thanks to the deep study he had made of his family as if the heart of the duke had been an open book.

He left him a moment, crushed, motionless, and mute; then in a voice stamped with the firmness of hatred:

"Brother," said he, "we have declared to you our resolution; it is immutable. You will go."

D'Alençon gave a start, but Charles did not appear to notice it, and continued:

"I wish Navarre to be proud of having for king a brother of the King of France. Gold, power, honor, all that belongs to your birth you shall have, as your brother Henry had, and like him," he added, smiling, "you will bless me from afar. But no matter, blessings know no distance."

"Sire"—

"Accept my decision, or rather, resign yourself. Once king, we shall find a wife for you worthy of a son of France, and she, perhaps, may bring you another throne."

"But," said the Duc d'Alençon, "your Majesty forgets your good friend Henry."

"Henry! but I told you that he did not want the throne of Navarre! I told you he had abdicated in favor of you! Henry is a jovial fellow, and not a pale-face like you. He likes to laugh and amuse himself at his ease, and not mope, as we who wear crowns are condemned to do."

D'Alençon heaved a sigh.

"Your Majesty orders me then to occupy myself"—

"No, not at all. Do not disturb yourself at all; I will arrange everything; rely on me, as on a good brother. And now that everything is settled, go. However, not a word of our conversation to your friends. I will take measures to give publicity to the affair very soon. Go now, François."

There was nothing further to be said, so the duke bowed and withdrew, rage in his heart.

He was very anxious to find Henry and talk with him about all that had just taken place; but he found only Catharine. As a matter of fact, Henry wished to avoid the interview, whereas the latter sought for it.

On seeing Catharine the duke swallowed his anger and strove to smile. Less fortunate than Henry of Anjou, it was not a mother he sought in Catharine, but merely an ally. He began therefore by dissimulation, for in order to make good alliances it is necessary for each party to be somewhat deceived.

He met Catharine with a face on which there remained only a slight trace of anxiety.

"Well, madame," said he, "here is great news; have you heard it?"

"I know that there is a plan on hand to make a king of you, monsieur."

"It is a great kindness on the part of my brother, madame."

"Is it not?"

"And I am almost tempted to believe that I owe a part of my gratitude to you; for it was really you who advised Charles to make me the present of a throne; it is to you I owe it. However, I will confess that, at heart, it gives me pain thus to rob the King of Navarre."

"You love Henriot very much, apparently."

"Why, yes; we have been intimate for some time."

"Do you think he loves you as much as you love him?"

"I hope so, madame."

"Such a friendship is very edifying; do you know it? especially between princes. Court friendships mean very little, François."

"Mother, you must remember we are not only friends, but almost brothers."

Catharine smiled a strange smile.

"Ah," said she, "are there brothers among kings?"

"Oh! as to that, neither of us was a king, mother, when our intimacy began. Moreover, we never expected to be kings; that is why we loved each other."

"Yes, but things are changed."

"How changed?"

"Why, who can say now whether both of you will not be kings?"

From the nervous start of the duke and the flush which rose to his brow Catharine saw that the arrow aimed by her had hit the mark.

"He?" said he, "Henriot king? And of what kingdom, mother?"

"One of the most magnificent kingdoms in Christendom, my son."

"Oh! mother," said D'Alençon, growing pale, "what are you saying?"

"What a good mother ought to say to her son, and what you have thought of more than once, François."

"I?" said the duke; "I have thought of nothing, madame, I swear to you."

"I can well believe you, for your friend, your brother Henry, as you call him, is, under his apparent frankness, a very clever and wily person, who keeps his secrets better than you keep yours, François. For instance, did he ever tell you that De Mouy was his man of business?"

As she spoke, Catharine turned a glance upon François as though it were a dagger aimed at his very soul.

But the latter had but one virtue, or rather vice,—the art of dissimulation; and he bore her look unflinchingly.

"De Mouy!" said he in surprise, as if it were the first time he had heard the name mentioned in that connection.

"Yes, the Huguenot De Mouy de Saint Phale; the one who nearly killed Monsieur de Maurevel, and who, secretly and in various disguises, is running all over France and the capital, intriguing and raising an army to support your brother Henry against your family."

Catharine, ignorant that on this point her son François knew as much if not more than she, rose at these words and started majestically to leave the room, but François detained her.

"Mother," said he, "another word, if you please. Since you deign to initiate me into your politics, tell me how, with his feeble resources, and being so slightly known, Henry could succeed in carrying on a war serious enough to disturb my family?"

"Child," said the queen, smiling, "he is supported by perhaps more than thirty thousand men; he has but to say the word and these thirty thousand men will appear as suddenly as if they sprang from the ground; and these thirty thousand men are Huguenots, remember, that is, the bravest soldiers in the world, and then he has a protector whom you neither could nor would conciliate."

"Who is that?"

"He has the King, the King, who loves him and who urges him on; the King, who from jealousy of your brother of Poland, and from spite against you, is looking about for a successor. But, blind man that you are if you do not see it, he seeks somewhere else besides in his own family."

"The King!—you think so, mother?"

"Have you not noticed how he loves Henriot, his Henriot?"

"Yes, mother, yes."

"And how he is repaid, for this same Henriot, forgetting that his brother-in-law would have shot him at the massacre of Saint Bartholomew, grovels to the earth like a dog which licks the hand that has beaten him."

"Yes, yes," murmured François, "I have already noticed that Henry is very humble with my brother Charles."

"Clever in trying to please him in everything."

"So much so that because of being always rallied by the King as to his ignorance of hawking he has begun to study it; and yesterday, yes, it was only yesterday, he asked me if I had not some books on that sport."

"Well," said Catharine, whose eyes sparkled as if an idea had suddenly come to her, "what did you answer him?"

"That I would look in my library."

"Good," said Catharine, "he must have this book."

"But I looked, madame, and found nothing."

"I will find one—and you shall give it to him as though it came from you."

"And what will come of this?"

"Have you confidence in me, D'Alençon?"

"Yes, mother."

"Will you obey me blindly so far as Henry is concerned? For whatever you may have said you do not love him."

D'Alençon smiled.

"And I detest him," continued Catharine.

"Yes, I will obey you."

"Well, the day after to-morrow come here for the book; I will give it to you, you shall take it to Henry, and"—

"And?"

"Leave the rest to Providence or to chance."

François knew his mother well enough to realize that she was not in the habit of leaving to Providence or to chance the care of friendships or hatreds. But he said nothing, and bowing like a man who accepts the commission with which he is charged, he returned to his own apartments.

"What does she mean?" thought the young man as he mounted the stairs. "I cannot see. But what I do understand in all this is that she acts like our common enemy. Well, let her go ahead."

Meantime Marguerite, through La Mole, had received a letter from De Mouy to the King of Navarre. As in politics the two illustrious allies had no secrets, she opened the letter and read it.

The letter must have interested her, for, taking advantage of the darkness which was beginning to overshadow the walls of the Louvre, Marguerite at once hurried along the secret corridor, ascended the winding stairway, and, having looked carefully about on all sides, glided on like a shadow and disappeared within the antechamber of the King of Navarre.

This room had been unguarded since the disappearance of Orthon.

This circumstance, of which we have not spoken since the reader learned of the tragic fate of poor Orthon, had greatly troubled Henry. He had spoken of it to Madame de Sauve and to his wife, but neither of them knew any more about it than he did. Madame de Sauve had given him some information from which it was perfectly clear to Henry's mind that the poor boy had been a victim of some machination of the queen mother, and that this was why he himself had been interrupted with De Mouy in the inn of the *Belle Étoile*. Any other than Henry would have kept silence, fearing to speak, but Henry calculated everything. He realized that his silence would betray him. One does not as a rule lose one's servitor and confidant thus, without making inquiries about him and looking for him. So Henry asked and searched even in the presence of the King and the queen mother, and of every one, from the sentinel who walked before the gate of the Louvre to the captain of the guards, keeping watch in the antechamber of the King; but all inquiry and search was in vain, and Henry seemed so affected by the circumstance and so attached to the poor absent servitor that he said he would not put another in his place until he was perfectly sure that Orthon had disappeared forever.

So the antechamber, as we have said, was empty when Marguerite reached it.

Light as were the steps of the queen, Henry heard them and turned round.

"You, madame!" he exclaimed.

"Yes," said Marguerite. "Quick! Read this!" and she handed him the open letter.

It contained these lines:

"Sire: The moment has come for putting our plan of flight into execution. The day after to-morrow there will be hunting along the Seine, from Saint Germain to Maisons, that is, all along the forest.

"Go to the hunt, although it is hawking; wear a good coat of mail under your suit; take your best sword and ride the best horse in your stable. About noon, when the chase is at its height, and the King is galloping after the falcon, escape alone if you come alone; with the Queen of Navarre if the queen will follow you.

"Fifty of our men will be hidden in the Pavilion of François I., of which we have the key; no one will know that they will be there, for they will have come at night, and the shutters will be closed.

"You will pass by the Alley of the Violettes, at the end of which I shall be watching; at the right of this alley in an open space will be Messieurs de la Mole and Coconnas, with two horses. These horses are intended to replace yours and that of her majesty the Queen of Navarre, if necessary.

"Adieu, sire; be ready, as we shall be."

"You will be," said Marguerite, uttering after sixteen hundred years the same words that Cæsar spoke on the banks of the Rubicon.

"Be it so, madame," replied Henry; "I will not fail you."

"Now, sire, be a hero; it is not difficult. You have but to follow the path that is indicated, and make a beautiful throne for me," said the daughter of Henry II.

An imperceptible smile rose to the thin lips of the Béarnais. He kissed Marguerite's hand, and went out to explore the corridor, whistling the refrain of an old song:

> *"Cil qui mieux battit la muraille*
> *N'entra pas dedans le chasteau."*[17]

The precaution was wise, for just as he opened the door of his sleeping-room the Duc d'Alençon opened that of his antechamber. Henry motioned to Marguerite, and then, aloud, said:

"Ah! is it you, brother? Welcome."

At the sign from her husband the queen had understood everything, and stepped hurriedly into a dressing-closet, in front of the door of which hung a thick tapestry. The Duc d'Alençon entered with a timorous step and looked around him.

"Are we alone, brother?" asked he in a whisper.

"Entirely. But what is the matter? You seem disturbed."

"We are discovered, Henry."

"How?—discovered?"

"Yes, De Mouy has been arrested."

"I know it."

"Well, De Mouy has told the King all."

"What has he told him?"

"He has told him that I desire the throne of Navarre, and that I have conspired to obtain it."

"Ah, the stupid!" cried Henry, "so that now you are compromised, my poor brother! How is it, then, that you have not been arrested?"

"I do not know. The King joked with me by pretending to offer me the throne of Navarre. He hoped, no doubt, to draw some confession from me, but I said nothing."

"And you did well, *ventre saint gris*!" said the Béarnais. "Stand firm, for our lives depend on that."

"Yes," said François, "the position is unsafe, I know. That is why I came to ask your advice, brother; what do you think I ought to do—run or stay?"

"You must have seen the King, since he spoke to you?"

"Yes, of course."

"Well! you must have read his thoughts. So follow your inspiration."

"I prefer to remain," replied François.

Notwithstanding the fact that he was almost thorough master of himself, Henry could not prevent a movement of joy from escaping him, and slight as it was, François saw it.

"Remain, then," said Henry.

"But you?"

"Why!" replied Henry, "if you remain, I have no motive for leaving. I was going only to follow you from devotion, in order not to be separated from my brother."

"So," said D'Alençon, "there is an end to all our plans; you give up without a struggle at the first stroke of ill luck?"

"I do not look upon it as a stroke of ill luck to remain here," said Henry. "Thanks to my careless disposition, I am contented everywhere."

"Well, then," said D'Alençon, "we need say no more about it, only in case you decide anything different let me know."

"By Heaven! I shall not fail to do that, you may be sure," replied Henry. "Was it not agreed that we were to have no secrets from each other?"

D'Alençon said no more, but withdrew, pondering, however; for at one time he thought he had seen the tapestry in front of the closet move.

Scarcely was the duke gone when the curtain was raised and Marguerite reappeared.

"What do you think of this visit?" asked Henry.

"That there is something new and important on hand."

"What do you think it is?"

"I do not know yet; but I will find out."

"In the meanwhile?"

"In the meanwhile do not fail to come to my room to-morrow evening."

"Indeed I will not fail, madame!" said Henry, gallantly kissing the hand of his wife.

With the same caution she had used in coming Marguerite returned to her own apartments.

CHAPTER XLIX.

THE TREATISE ON HUNTING.

Three days had elapsed since the events we have just related. Day was beginning to dawn, but every one was already up and awake at the Louvre as usual on hunting days, when the Duc d'Alençon entered the apartments of the queen mother in answer to the invitation he had received. Catharine was not in her bedroom; but she had left orders that if her son came he was to wait for her.

At the end of a few minutes she came out of a private closet, to which no one but herself had admission, and in which she carried on her experiments in chemistry. As Catharine entered the room there came either from the closet or from her clothes the penetrating odor of some acrid perfume, and through the open door D'Alençon perceived a thick vapor, as of some burnt aromatic substance, floating in the laboratory like a white cloud.

The duke could not repress a glance of curiosity.

"Yes," said Catharine de Médicis, "I have been burning several old parchments which gave out such an offensive smell that I put some juniper into the brazier, hence this odor."

D'Alençon bowed.

"Well," said the queen, concealing under the wide sleeves of her dressing-gown her hands, which here and there were stained with reddish spots, "is there anything new since yesterday?"

"Nothing, mother."

"Have you seen Henry?"

"Yes."

"Does he still refuse to leave?"

"Absolutely."

"The knave!"

"What do you say, madame?"

"I say that he will go."

"You think so?"

"I am sure of it."

"Then he will escape us?"

"Yes," said Catharine.

"And shall you let him go?"

"Not only that, but I tell you he must go."

"I do not understand, mother."

"Listen well to what I am about to tell you, François. A very skilful physician, the one who let me take the book on hunting which you are to give him, has told me that the King of Navarre is on the point of being attacked with consumption, one of those incurable diseases for which science has no remedy. Now, you understand that if he has to die from such a cruel malady it would be better for him to die away from us than among us here at court."

"In fact," said the duke, "that would cause us too much pain."

"Especially your brother Charles," said Catharine; "whereas, if he dies after having betrayed him the King will regard his death as a punishment from Heaven."

"You are right, mother," said François in admiration, "he must leave. But are you sure that he will?"

"All his plans are made. The meeting-place is in the forest of Saint Germain. Fifty Huguenots are to escort him as far as Fontainebleau, where five hundred others will await him."

"And," said D'Alençon, with a slight hesitation and visible pallor, "will my sister Margot accompany him?"

"Yes," replied Catharine, "that is agreed on. But at Henry's death Margot is to return to court a widow and free."

"And Henry will die, madame? Are you sure of this?"

"The physician who gave me the book assured me of it."

"Where is this book, madame?"

Catharine went slowly towards the mysterious closet, opened the door, entered, and a moment later appeared with the book in her hand.

"Here it is," said she.

D'Alençon looked at the volume with a certain feeling of terror.

"What is this book, madame?" he asked, shuddering.

"I have already told you, my son. It is a treatise on the art of raising and training falcons, gerfalcons, and hawks, written by a very learned scholar for Lord Castruccio Castracani, tyrant of Lucca."

"What must I do with it?"

"Take it to your good friend Henriot, who you told me had asked you for a treatise on the art of hunting. As he is going hawking to-day with the King he will not fail to read some of it, in order to prove to Charles that he has followed his advice and taken a lesson or two. The main thing is to give it into Henry's own hands."

"Oh! I do not dare!" said D'Alençon, shuddering.

"Why not?" asked Catharine; "it is a book like any other except that it has been packed away for so long that the leaves stick together. Do not attempt to read it, François, for it can be read only by wetting the finger and turning over each leaf, and this takes time and trouble."

"So that only a man who is very anxious to be instructed in the sport of hawking would waste his time and go to this trouble?" asked D'Alençon.

"Exactly, my son; you understand."

"Oh!" said D'Alençon; "there is Henriot in the court-yard. Give me the book, madame. I will take advantage of his absence and go to his room with it. On his return he will find it."

"I should prefer you to give it to him yourself, François, that would be surer."

"I have already said that I do not dare, madame," replied the duke.

"Very well; but at least put it where he can see it."

"Open? Is there any reason why it should not be open?"

"None."

"Then give it to me."

D'Alençon tremblingly took the book, which Catharine with a firm hand held out to him.

"Take it," said the queen, "there is no danger—I touch it; besides, you have gloves on."

This precaution was not enough for D'Alençon, who wrapped the volume in his cloak.

"Make haste," said Catharine; "Henry may return at any moment."

"You are right, madame. I will go at once."

The duke went out, trembling with fright.

We have often introduced the reader into the apartments of the King of Navarre, and he has been present at the events which have taken place in them, events bright or gloomy, according to the smile or frown of the protecting genius of the future king of France.

But perhaps never had these walls, stained with the blood of murders, sprinkled with the wine of orgies, scented with the perfumes of love,— perhaps never had this corner of the Louvre seen a paler face than that of the Duc d'Alençon, as with book in hand he opened the door of the bedchamber of the King of Navarre. And no one, as the duke had expected, was in the room to question with curious or anxious glances what he was about to do. The first rays of the morning sun alone were lighting up the vacant chamber.

On the wall in readiness hung the sword which Monsieur de Mouy had advised Henry to take with him. Some links of a coat of mail were scattered on the floor. A well-filled purse and a small dagger lay on a table, and some light ashes in the fireplace, joined to the other evidence, clearly showed D'Alençon that the King of Navarre had put on the shirt of mail, collected some money from his treasurer, and burned all papers that might compromise him.

"My mother was not mistaken," said D'Alençon "the knave would have betrayed me."

Doubtless this conviction gave added strength to the young man. He sounded the corners of the room at a glance, raised the portieres, and realizing from the loud noise in the court-yard below and the dense silence in the apartments that no one was there to spy on him, he drew the book from under his cloak, hastily laid it on the table, near the purse, propping it up against a desk of sculptured oak; then drawing back, he reached out his arm, and, with a hesitation which betrayed his fears, with his gloved hand he opened the volume to an engraving of a hunt. This done, D'Alençon again stepped back, and drawing off his glove threw it into the still warm fire, which had just consumed the papers. The supple leather crackled over the coals, twisted and flattened itself out like the body of a great reptile, leaving nothing but a burned and blackened lump.

D'Alençon waited until the flame had consumed the glove, then rolling up the cloak which had been wrapped around the book, he put it under his arm, and hastily returned to his own apartments. As he entered with beating heart, he heard steps on the winding stairs, and not doubting but that it was Henry he quickly closed his door. Then he stepped to the window, but he could see only a part of the court-yard of the Louvre. Henry was not there, however, and he felt convinced that it was the King of Navarre who had just returned.

The duke sat down, opened a book, and tried to read. It was a history of France from Pharamond to Henry II., for which, a few days after his accession to the throne, Henry had given a license.

But the duke's thoughts were not on what he was reading; the fever of expectation burned in his veins. His temples throbbed clear to his brain, and as in a dream or some magnetic trance, it seemed to François that he could see through the walls. His eyes appeared to probe into Henry's chamber, in spite of the obstacles between.

In order to drive away the terrible object before his mind's eye the duke strove to fix his attention on something besides the terrible book opened on the oak desk; but in vain he looked at his weapons, his ornaments; in vain he gazed a hundred times at the same spot on the floor; every detail of the picture at which he had merely glanced remained graven on his memory. It consisted of a gentleman on horseback fulfilling the duties of a beater of hawking, throwing the bait, calling to the falcon, and galloping through the deep grass of a swamp. Strong as was the duke's will, his memory triumphed over it.

Then it was not only the book he saw, but the King of Navarre approaching it, looking at the picture, trying to turn the pages, finally wetting his thumb and forcing the leaves apart. At this sight, fictitious and imaginary as it was, D'Alençon staggered and was forced to lean one hand against a table, while with the other he covered his eyes, as if by so doing he did not see more clearly than before the vision he wished to escape. This vision was in his own thoughts.

Suddenly D'Alençon saw Henry cross the court; he stopped a few moments before the men who were loading two mules with the provisions for the chase —none other than the money and other things he wished to take with him; then, having given his orders, he crossed the court diagonally and advanced towards the door.

D'Alençon stood motionless. It was not Henry, then, who had mounted the secret staircase. All the agony he had undergone during the last quarter of an hour had been useless. What he thought was over or almost over was only beginning.

François opened the door of his chamber, then holding it so he listened. This time he could not be mistaken, it was Henry himself; he recognized his step and the peculiar jingle of his spurs.

Henry's door opened and closed.

D'Alençon returned to his room and sank into an armchair.

"Good!" said he, "this is what is now taking place: he has passed through the antechamber, the first room, the sleeping-room; then he glances to see if his sword, his purse, his dagger are there; at last he finds the book open on his table.

"'What book is this?' he asks himself. 'Who has brought it?'

"Then he draws nearer, sees the picture of the horseman calling his falcon, wants to read, tries to turn the leaves."

A cold perspiration started to the brow of François.

"Will he call? Is the effect of the poison sudden? No, no, for my mother said he would die of slow consumption."

This thought somewhat reassured him.

Ten minutes passed thus, a century of agony, dragging by second after second, each supplying all that the imagination could invent in the way of maddening terror, a world of visions.

D'Alençon could stand it no longer. He rose and crossed the antechamber, which was beginning to fill with gentlemen.

"Good morning, gentlemen," said he, "I am going to the King."

And to distract his consuming anxiety, and perhaps to prepare an *alibi*, D'Alençon descended to his brother's apartments. Why did he go there? He did not know. What had he to say? Nothing! It was not Charles he sought—it was Henry he fled.

He took the winding staircase and found the door of the King's apartments half opened. The guards let the duke enter without opposition. On hunting days there was neither etiquette nor orders.

François traversed successively the antechamber, the salon, and the bedroom without meeting any one. He thought Charles must be in the armory and opened the door leading thither.

The King was seated before a table, in a deep carved armchair. He had his back to the door, and appeared to be absorbed in what he was doing.

The duke approached on tiptoe; Charles was reading.

"By Heaven!" cried he, suddenly, "this is a fine book. I had heard of it, but I did not know it could be had in France."

D'Alençon listened and advanced a step.

"Cursed leaves!" said the King, wetting his thumb and applying it to the pages; "it looks as though they had been stuck together on purpose to conceal the wonders they contain from the eyes of man."

D'Alençon bounded forward. The book over which Charles was bending was the one he had left in Henry's room. A dull cry broke from him.

"Ah, is it you, François?" said Charles, "you are welcome; come and see the finest book on hunting which ever came from the pen of man."

D'Alençon's first impulse was to snatch the volume from the hands of his brother; but an infernal thought restrained him; a frightful smile passed over his pallid lips, and he rubbed his hand across his eyes like a man dazed. Then recovering himself by degrees, but without moving:

452

"Sire," he asked, "how did this book come into your Majesty's possession?"

"I went into Henriot's room this morning to see if he was ready; he was not there, he was probably strolling about the kennels or the stables; at any rate, instead of him I found this treasure, which I brought here to read at my leisure."

And the King again moistened his thumb, and again turned over an obstinate page.

"Sire," stammered D'Alençon, whose hair stood on end, and whose whole body was seized with a terrible agony. "Sire, I came to tell you"—

"Let me finish this chapter, François," said Charles, "and then you shall tell me anything you wish. I have read or rather devoured fifty pages."

"He has tasted the poison twenty-five times," murmured François; "my brother is a dead man!"

Then the thought came to him that there was a God in heaven who perhaps after all was not chance.

With trembling hand the duke wiped away the cold perspiration which stood in drops on his brow, and waited in silence, as his brother had bade him do, until the chapter was finished.

CHAPTER L.

HAWKING.

Charles still read. In his curiosity he seemed to devour the pages, and each page, as we have said, either because of the dampness to which it had been exposed for so long or from some other cause, adhered to the next.

With haggard eyes D'Alençon gazed at this terrible spectacle, the end of which he alone could see.

"Oh!" he murmured, "what will happen? I shall go away, into exile, and seek an imaginary throne, while at the first news of Charles's illness Henry will return to some fortified town near the capital, and watch this prey sent us by chance, able at a single stride to reach Paris; so that before the King of

Poland even hears the news of my brother's death the dynasty will be changed. This cannot be!"

Such were the thoughts which dominated the first involuntary feeling of horror that had urged François to warn Charles. It was the never-failing fatality which seemed to preserve Henry and follow the Valois which the duke was again going to try to thwart. In an instant his whole plan with regard to Henry was altered. It was Charles and not Henry who had read the poisoned book. Henry was to have gone, and gone condemned to die. The moment fate had again saved him, Henry must remain; for Henry was less to be feared in the Bastille or as prisoner at Vincennes than as the King of Navarre at the head of thirty thousand men.

The Duc d'Alençon let Charles finish his chapter, and when the King had raised his head:

"Brother," said the duke, "I have waited because your Majesty ordered me to do so, but I regret it, because I have something of the greatest importance to say to you."

"Go to the devil!" said Charles, whose cheeks were slowly turning a dull red, either because he had been too much engrossed in his reading or because the poison had begun to act. "Go to the devil! If you have come to discuss that same subject again, you shall leave as did the King of Poland. I rid myself of him, and I will do the same to you without further talk about it."

"It is not about my leaving, brother, that I want to speak to you, but about some one else who is going away. Your Majesty has touched me in my most sensitive point, my love for you as a brother, my devotion to you as a subject; and I hope to prove to you that I am no traitor."

"Well," said Charles, as he leaned his elbow on the book, crossed his legs, and looked at D'Alençon like a man who is trying to be patient. "Some fresh report, some accusation?"

"No, sire, a certainty, a plot, which my foolish scruples alone prevented my revealing to you before."

"A plot?" said Charles, "well, let us hear about it."

"Sire," said François, "while your Majesty hawks near the river in the plain of Vesinet the King of Navarre will escape to the forest of Saint Germain, where a troop of friends will be waiting to flee with him."

"Ah, I knew it," said Charles, "another calumny against my poor Henry! When will you be through with him?"

"Your Majesty need not wait long at least to find out whether or not what I have just had the honor of telling you is a calumny."

"How so?"

"Because this evening our brother-in-law will be gone."

Charles rose.

"Listen," said he, "I will try for the last time to believe you; but I warn you, both you and your mother, that it will be the last time."

Then raising his voice:

"Summon the King of Navarre!" he cried.

A guard started to obey, but François stopped him with a gesture.

"This is a poor way, brother, to learn anything," said he. "Henry will deny, will give a signal, his accomplices will be warned and will disappear. Then my mother and myself will be accused not only of being visionary but of being calumniators."

"What do you want, then?"

"In the name of our brotherly love I ask your Majesty to listen to me, in the name of my devotion, which you will realize, I want you to do nothing hastily. Act so that the real culprit, who for two years has been betraying your Majesty in will as well as in deed, may at last be recognized as guilty by an infallible proof, and punished as he deserves."

Charles did not answer, but going to a window raised it. The blood was rushing to his head.

Then turning round quickly:

"Well!" said he, "what would you do? Speak, François."

"Sire," said D'Alençon, "I would surround the forest of Saint Germain with three detachments of light horse, who at a given hour, eleven o'clock, for instance, should start out and drive every one in the forest to the Pavilion of Francis I., which I would, as if by chance, have indicated as the meeting-place. Then I would spur on, as if following my falcon, to the meeting-place, where Henry should be captured with his companions."

"The idea is good," said the King; "summon the captain of the guards."

D'Alençon drew from his doublet a silver whistle, suspended from a gold chain, and raised it to his lips.

De Nancey appeared.

Charles gave him some orders in a low tone.

Meanwhile Actéon, the great greyhound, had dragged a book from the table, and was tossing it about the room, making great bounds after it.

Charles turned round and uttered a terrible oath. The book was the precious treatise on hunting, of which there existed only three copies in the world.

The punishment was proportionate to the offence.

Charles seized a whip and gave the dog three whistling blows.

Actéon uttered a howl, and fled under a table covered with a large cloth which served him as a hiding-place.

Charles picked up the book and saw with joy that only one leaf was gone, and that was not a page of the text, but an engraving. He placed the volume carefully away on a shelf where Actéon could not reach it. D'Alençon looked anxiously at him. Now that the book had fulfilled its dread mission he would have liked to see it out of Charles's hands.

Six o'clock struck. It was time for the King to descend to the court-yard, already filled with horses richly caparisoned, and elegantly dressed ladies and gentlemen. The hunters held on their wrists their hooded falcons; some outriders carried horns wound with scarfs, in case the King, as sometimes happened, grew weary of hawking, and wished to hunt a deer or a chamois.

Charles closed the door of his armory and descended. D'Alençon watched each movement closely, and saw him put the key in his pocket.

As he went down the stairs Charles stopped and raised his hand to his head.

The limbs of the Duc d'Alençon trembled no less than did those of the King.

"It seems to me," said the duke, "that there is going to be a storm."

"A storm in January!" said Charles; "you are mad. No, I am dizzy, my skin is dry, I am weak, that is all."

Then in a low tone:

"They will kill me," he murmured, "with their hatred and their plots."

But on reaching the court the fresh morning air, the shouts of the hunters, the loud greetings of the hundred people gathered there, produced their usual effect on Charles.

He breathed freely and happily. His first thought was for Henry, who was beside Marguerite.

This excellent couple seemed to care so much for each other that they were unable to be apart.

On perceiving Charles, Henry spurred his horse, and in three bounds was beside him.

"Ah, ah!" said Charles, "you are mounted as if you were going to hunt the stag, Henriot; but you know we are going hawking to-day."

Then without waiting for a reply:

"Forward, gentlemen, forward! we must be hunting by nine o'clock!" and Charles frowned and spoke in an almost threatening tone.

Catharine was watching everything from a window, behind which a curtain was drawn back, showing her pale face. She herself was dressed in black and was hidden from view.

At the order from Charles all this gilded, embroidered, perfumed crowd, with the King at its head, lengthened out to pass through the gate of the Louvre, and swept like an avalanche along the road to Saint Germain, amid the shouts of the people, who saluted the young King as he rode by, thoughtful and pensive, on his white horse.

"What did he say to you?" asked Marguerite of Henry.

"He congratulated me on the speed of my horse."

"Was that all?"

"Yes."

"Then he suspects something."

"I fear so."

"Let us be cautious."

Henry's face lighted up with one of his beautiful smiles, which meant especially to Marguerite, "Be easy, my love." As to Catharine, scarcely had the cortège left the court of the Louvre before she dropped the curtain.

But she had not failed to see one thing, namely, Henry's pallor, his nervousness, and his low-toned conversation with Marguerite.

Henry was pale because, not having physical courage, his blood, under all circumstances in which his life was at stake, instead of rushing to his head, as is usually the case, flowed to his heart. He was nervous because the manner in which he had been received by Charles, so different from usual, had made a deep impression on him. Finally, he had conferred with Marguerite because, as we know, the husband and wife had formed, so far as politics were concerned, an alliance offensive and defensive.

But Catharine had interpreted these facts differently.

"This time," she murmured, with her Florentine smile, "I think I may rely on my dear Henriot."

Then to satisfy herself, having waited a quarter of an hour to give the party time to leave Paris, she went out of her room, mounted the winding staircase, and with the help of her pass-key opened the door of the apartments of the King of Navarre. She searched, but in vain, for the book. In vain she looked on every table, shelf, and in every closet; nowhere could she find it.

"D'Alençon must have taken it away," said she, "that was wise."

And she descended to her own chamber, quite sure this time that her plan would succeed.

The King went on towards Saint Germain, which he reached after a rapid ride of an hour and a half. They did not ascend to the old castle, which rose dark and majestic in the midst of the houses scattered over the mountain. They crossed the wooden bridge, which at that time was opposite the tree to-day called the "Sully Oak." Then they signed for the boats adorned with flags which followed the hunting-party to aid the King and his suite in crossing the river. This was done. Instantly all the joyous procession, animated by such varied interests, again began to move, led by the King, over the magnificent plain which stretched from the wooded summit of Saint Germain, and which suddenly assumed the appearance of a great carpet covered with people, dotted with a thousand colors, and of which the river foaming along its banks seemed a silver fringe.

Ahead of the King, still on his white horse and holding his favorite falcon, rode the beaters, in their long green close-fitting coats and high boots, calling now and then to the half dozen great dogs, and beating, with their whips, the reeds which grew along the river banks.

At that moment the sun, until then hidden behind a cloud, suddenly burst forth and lighted with one of its rays all that procession of gold, all the ornaments, all the glowing eyes, and turned everything into a torrent of flame. Then, as if it had waited for that moment so that the sun might shine on its defeat, a heron rose from the midst of the reeds with a prolonged and plaintiff cry.

"Haw! Haw!" cried Charles, unhooding his falcon and sending it after the fugitive.

"Haw! Haw!" cried every voice to encourage the bird.

The falcon, dazzled for an instant by the light, turned, described a circle, then suddenly perceiving the heron, dashed after it.

458

But the heron, like a prudent bird, had risen a hundred yards before the beaters, and while the King had been unhooding his falcon, and while the latter had been growing accustomed to the light, it had gained a considerable height, so that by the time its enemy saw it, it had risen more than five hundred feet, and finding in the higher zones the air necessary for its powerful wings, continued to mount rapidly.

"Haw! Haw! Iron Beak!" cried Charles, cheering his falcon. "Show us that you are a thoroughbred! Haw! Haw!"

As if it understood the words the noble bird rose like an arrow, described a diagonal line, then a vertical one, as the heron had done, and mounted higher as though it would soon disappear in the upper air.

"Ah! coward!" cried Charles, as if the fugitive could hear him, and, spurring his horse, he followed the flight of the birds as far as he could, his head thrown back so as not to lose sight of them for an instant. "Ah! double coward! You run! My Iron Beak is a thoroughbred; on! on! Haw, Iron Beak! Haw!"

The contest was growing exciting. The birds were beginning to approach each other, or rather the falcon was nearing the heron. The only question was which could rise the higher.

Fear had stronger wings than courage. The falcon passed under the heron, and the latter, profiting by its advantage, dealt a blow with its long beak.

The falcon, as though hit by a dagger, described three circles, apparently overcome, and for an instant it looked as if the bird would fall. But like a warrior, who when wounded rises more terrible than before, it uttered a sharp and threatening cry, and went after the heron. The latter, making the most of its advantage, had changed the direction of its flight and turned toward the forest, trying this time to gain in distance instead of in height, and so escape. But the falcon was indeed a thoroughbred, with the eye of a gerfalcon.

It repeated the same manœuvre, rose diagonally after the heron, which gave two or three cries of distress and strove to rise perpendicularly as at first.

At the end of a few seconds the two birds seemed again about to disappear. The heron looked no larger than a lark, and the falcon was a black speck which every moment grew smaller.

Neither Charles nor his suite any longer followed the flight of the birds. Each one stopped, his eyes fixed on the clouds.

"Bravo! Bravo! Iron-beak!" cried Charles, suddenly. "See, see, gentlemen, he is uppermost! Haw! haw!"

"Faith, I can see neither of them," said Henry.

"Nor I," said Marguerite.

"Well, but if you cannot see them, Henry, you can hear them," said Charles, "at least the heron. Listen! listen! he asks quarter!"

Two or three plaintive cries were heard which a practised ear alone could detect.

"Listen!" cried Charles, "and you will see them come down more quickly than they went up."

As the King spoke, the two birds reappeared. They were still only two black dots, but from the size of the dots the falcon seemed to be uppermost.

"See! see!" cried Charles, "Iron Beak has him!"

The heron, outwitted by the bird of prey, no longer strove to defend itself. It descended rapidly, constantly struck at by the falcon, and answered only by its cries. Suddenly it folded its wings and dropped like a stone; but its adversary did the same, and when the fugitive again strove to resume its flight a last blow of the beak finished it; it continued to fall, turning over and over, and as it touched the earth the falcon swooped down and uttered a cry of victory which drowned the cry of defeat of the vanquished.

"To the falcon! the falcon!" shouted Charles, spurring his horse to the place where the birds had fallen. But suddenly he reined in his steed, uttered a cry, dropped his bridle, and grasping his horse's mane with one hand pressed the other to his stomach as though he would tear out his very vitals.

All the courtiers hastened to him.

"It is nothing, nothing," said Charles, with inflamed face and haggard eye; "it seemed as if a red-hot iron were passing through me just now; but forward! it is nothing."

And Charles galloped on.

D'Alençon turned pale.

"What now?" asked Henry of Marguerite.

"I do not know," replied she; "but did you see? My brother was purple in the face."

"He is not usually so," said Henry.

The courtiers glanced at one another in surprise and followed the King.

They arrived at the scene of combat. The falcon had already begun to peck at the head of the heron.

Charles sprang from his horse to obtain a nearer view; but on alighting he was obliged to seize hold of the saddle. The ground seemed to spin under him. He felt very sleepy.

"Brother! Brother!" cried Marguerite; "what is the matter?"

"I feel," said Charles, "as Portia must have felt when she swallowed her burning coals. I am burning up and my breath seems on fire."

Charles exhaled his breath and seemed surprised not to see fire issue from his lips.

The falcon had been caught and hooded again, and every one had gathered around the King.

"Why, what does it mean? Great Heavens! It cannot be anything, or if it is it must be the sun which is affecting my head and blinding my eyes. So on, on, to the hunt, gentlemen! There is a whole flight of herons. Unhood the falcons, all of them, by Heaven! now for some sport!"

Instantly five or six falcons were unhooded and let loose. They rose in the direction of the prey, while the entire party, the King at their head, reached the bank of the river.

"Well! what do you say, madame?" asked Henry of Marguerite.

"That the moment is favorable, and that if the King does not look back we can easily reach the forest from here."

Henry called the attendant who was carrying the heron, and while the noisy, gilded avalanche swept along the road which to-day is a terrace he remained behind as if to examine the dead bird.

CHAPTER LI.

THE PAVILION OF FRANÇOIS I.

Hawking was a beautiful sport as carried on by kings, when kings were almost demi-gods, and when the chase was not only a pastime but an art.

Nevertheless we must leave the royal spectacle to enter a part of the forest where the actors in the scene we have just described will soon join us.

The Allée des Violettes was a long, leafy arcade and mossy retreat in which, among lavender and heather, a startled hare now and then pricked up its ears, and a wandering stag raised its head heavy with horns, opened its nostrils, and listened. To the right of this alley was an open space far enough from the road to be invisible, but not so far but that the road could be seen from it.

In the middle of the clearing two men were lying on the grass. Under them were travellers' cloaks, at their sides long swords, and near each of them a musketoon (then called a petronel) with the muzzle turned from them. In the richness of their costume they resembled the joyous characters of the "Decameron;" on closer view, by the threatening aspect of their weapons, they seemed like those forest robbers whom a hundred years later Salvator Rosa painted from nature in his landscapes. One of them was leaning on his hand and on one knee, listening as attentively as the hare or deer we mentioned above.

"It seems to me," said this one, "that the hunt was very near us just now. I heard the cries of the hunters cheering the falcon."

"And now," said the other, who seemed to await events with much more philosophy than his companion, "now I hear nothing more; they must have gone away. I told you this was a poor place from which to see anything. We cannot be seen, it is true; but we cannot see, either."

"The devil! my dear Annibal," said the first speaker, "we had to put our horses somewhere, as well as the mules, which, by the way, are so heavily laden that I do not see how they can follow us. Now I know that these old beeches and oaks are perfectly suited to this difficult task. I should venture to say that far from blaming Monsieur de Mouy as you are doing, I recognize in every detail of the enterprise he is directing the common sense of a true conspirator."

"Good!" said the second gentleman, whom no doubt our reader has already recognized as Coconnas; "good! that is the word! I expected it! I relied on you for it! So we are conspiring?"

"We are not conspiring; we are serving the king and the queen."

"Who are conspiring and which amounts to the same for us."

"Coconnas, I have told you," said La Mole, "that I do not in the least force you to follow me in this affair. I have undertaken it only because of a particular sentiment, which you can neither feel nor share."

"Well, by Heaven! Who said that you were forcing me? In the first place, I know of no one who could compel Coconnas, to do what he did not wish to do; but do you suppose that I would let you go without following you, especially when I see that you are going to the devil?"

"Annibal! Annibal!" said La Mole, "I think that I see her white palfrey in the distance. Oh! it is strange how my heart throbs at the mere thought of her coming!"

"Yes, it is strange," said Coconnas, yawning; "my heart does not throb in the least."

"It is not she," said La Mole. "What can have happened? They were to be here at noon, I thought."

"It happens that it is not noon," said Coconnas, "that is all, and, apparently, we still have time to take a nap."

So saying, Coconnas stretched himself on his cloak like a man who is about to add practice to precept; but as his ear touched the ground he raised his finger and motioned La Mole to be silent.

"What is it?" asked the latter.

"Hush! this time I am sure I hear something."

"That is singular; I have listened, but I hear nothing."

"Nothing?"

"No."

"Well!" said Coconnas, rising and laying his hand on La Mole's arm, "look at that deer."

"Where?"

"Yonder."

Coconnas pointed to the animal.

"Well?"

"Well, you will see."

La Mole watched the deer. With head bent forward as though about to browse it listened without stirring. Soon it turned its head, covered with magnificent branching horns, in the direction from which no doubt the sound came. Then suddenly, without apparent cause, it disappeared like a flash of lightning.

"Oh!" said La Mole, "I believe you are right, for the deer has fled."

"Because of that," said Coconnas, "it must have heard what you have not heard."

In short, a faint, scarcely perceptible sound quivered vaguely through the passes; to less practised ears it would have seemed like the breeze; for the two men it was the far-off galloping of horses. In an instant La Mole was on his feet.

"Here they are!" said he; "quick."

Coconnas rose, but more calmly. The energy of the Piedmontese seemed to have passed into the heart of La Mole, while on the other hand the indolence of the latter seemed to have taken possession of his friend. One acted with enthusiasm; the other with reluctance. Soon a regular and measured sound struck the ear of the two friends. The neighing of a horse made the coursers they had tied ten paces away prick up their ears, as through the alley there passed like a white shadow a woman who, turning towards them, made a strange sign and disappeared.

"The queen!" they exclaimed together.

"What can it mean?" asked Coconnas.

"She made a sign," said La Mole, "which meant 'presently.'"

"She made a sign," said Coconnas, "which meant 'flee!'"

"The signal meant 'wait for me.'"

"The signal meant 'save yourself.'"

"Well," said La Mole, "let each act on his own conviction; you leave and I will remain."

Coconnas shrugged his shoulders and lay down again.

At that moment in the opposite direction from that in which the queen was going, but in the same alley, there passed at full speed a troop of horsemen whom the two friends recognized as ardent, almost rabid Protestants. Their steeds bounded like the locusts of which Job said, 'They came and went.'"

"The deuce! the affair is growing serious," said Coconnas, rising. "Let us go to the pavilion of François I."

"No," said La Mole; "if we are discovered it will be towards the pavilion that the attention of the King will be at first directed, since that is the general meeting-place."

"You may be right, this time," grumbled Coconnas.

Scarcely had Coconnas uttered these words before a horseman passed

464

among the trees like a flash of lightning, and leaping ditches, bushes, and all barriers reached the two gentlemen.

He held a pistol in each hand and with his knees alone guided his horse in its furious chase.

"Monsieur de Mouy!" exclaimed Coconnas, uneasy and now more on the alert than La Mole; "Monsieur de Mouy running away! Every one for himself, then!"

"Quick! quick!" cried the Huguenot; "away! all is lost! I have come around to tell you so. Away!"

As if he had not stopped to utter these words, he was gone almost before they were spoken, and before La Mole and Coconnas realized their meaning.

"And the queen?" cried La Mole.

But the young man's voice was lost in the distance; De Mouy was too far away either to hear or to answer him.

Coconnas had speedily made up his mind. While La Mole stood motionless, gazing after De Mouy, who had disappeared among the trees, he ran to the horses, led them out, sprang on his own, and, throwing the bridle of the other to La Mole, prepared to gallop off.

"Come! come!" cried he; "I repeat what De Mouy said: Let us be off! De Mouy knows what he is doing. Come, La Mole, quick!"

"One moment," said La Mole; "we came here for something."

"Unless it is to be hanged," replied Coconnas, "I advise you to lose no more time. I know you are going to parse some rhetoric, paraphrase the word 'flee,' speak of Horace, who hurled his buckler, and Epaminondas, who was brought back on his. But I tell you one thing, when Monsieur de Mouy de Saint Phale flees all the world may run too."

"Monsieur de Mouy de Saint Phale," said La Mole, "was not charged to carry off Queen Marguerite! Nor does Monsieur de Mouy de Saint Phale love Queen Marguerite!"

"By Heaven! he is right if this love would make him do such foolish things as you plan doing. May five hundred thousand devils from hell take away the love which may cost two brave gentlemen their heads! By Heaven! as King Charles says, we are conspiring, my dear fellow; and when plans fail one must run. Mount! mount, La Mole!"

"Mount yourself, my dear fellow, I will not prevent you. I even urge you to do so. Your life is more precious than mine. Defend it, therefore."

"You must say to me: 'Coconnas, let us be hanged together,' and not 'Coconnas, save yourself.'"

"Bah! my friend," replied La Mole, "the rope is made for clowns, not for gentlemen like ourselves."

"I am beginning to think," said Coconnas, "that the precaution I took is not bad."

"What precaution?"

"To have made friends with the hangman."

"You are sinister, my dear Coconnas."

"Well, what are we going to do?" cried the latter, impatiently.

"Set out and find the queen."

"Where?"

"I do not know—seek the king."

"Where?"

"I have not the least idea; but we must find him, and we two by ourselves can do what fifty others neither could nor would dare to do."

"You appeal to my pride, Hyacinthe; that is a bad sign."

"Well! come; to horse and away!"

"A good suggestion!"

La Mole turned to seize the pommel of his saddle, but just as he put his foot in the stirrup an imperious voice was heard:

"Halt there! surrender!"

At the same moment the figure of a man appeared behind an oak, then another, then thirty. They were the light-horse, who, dismounted, had glided on all fours in and out among the bushes, searching the forest.

"What did I tell you?" murmured Coconnas, in a low tone.

A dull groan was La Mole's only answer.

The light-horse were still thirty paces away from the two friends.

"Well!" continued the Piedmontese, in a loud tone, to the lieutenant of the dragoons. "What is it, gentlemen?"

The lieutenant ordered his men to aim.

Coconnas continued under breath:

"Mount, La Mole, there is still time. Spring into your saddle as I have seen you do hundreds of times, and let us be off."

Then turning to the light-horse:

"The devil, gentlemen, do not fire; you would kill friends."

Then to La Mole:

"Between the trees they cannot aim well; they will fire and miss us."

"Impossible," said La Mole, "we cannot take Marguerite's horse with us or the two mules. They would compromise us, whereas by my replies I can avert all suspicion. Go, my friend, go!"

"Gentlemen," said Coconnas, drawing his sword and raising it, "gentlemen, we surrender."

The light-horse dropped their muskets.

"But first tell us why we must do so?"

"You must ask that of the King of Navarre."

"What crime have we committed?"

"Monsieur d'Alençon will inform you."

Coconnas and La Mole looked at each other. The name of their enemy at such a moment did not greatly reassure them.

Yet neither of them made any resistance. Coconnas was asked to dismount, a manœuvre which he executed without a word. Then both were placed in the centre of the light-horse and took the road to the pavilion.

"You always wanted to see the pavilion of François I.," said Coconnas to La Mole, perceiving through the trees the walls of a beautiful Gothic structure; "now it seems you will."

La Mole made no reply, but merely extended his hand to Coconnas.

By the side of this lovely pavilion, built in the time of Louis XII., and named after François I., because the latter always chose it as a meeting-place when he hunted, was a kind of hut built for prickers, partly hidden behind the muskets, halberds, and shining swords like an ant-hill under a whitening harvest.

The prisoners were conducted to this hut.

We will now relate what had happened and so throw some light on the situation, which looked very dark, especially for the two friends.

The Protestant gentlemen had assembled, as had been agreed on, in the pavilion of François I., of which, as we know, De Mouy had the key.

Masters of the forest, or at least so they had believed, they had placed sentinels here and there whom the light-horse, having exchanged their white scarfs for red ones (a precaution due to the ingenious zeal of Monsieur de Nancey), had surprised and carried away without a blow.

The light-horse had continued their search surrounding the pavilion; but De Mouy, who, as we know, was waiting for the king at the end of the Allée des Violettes, had perceived the red scarfs stealing along and had instantly suspected them. He sprang to one side so as not to be seen, and noticed that the vast circle was narrowing in such a way as to beat the forest and surround the meeting-place. At the same time, at the end of the principal alley, he had caught a glimpse of the white aigrettes and the shining arquebuses of the King's bodyguard.

Finally he saw the King himself, while in the opposite direction he perceived the King of Navarre.

Then with his hat he had made a sign of the cross, which was the signal agreed on to indicate that all was lost.

At this signal the king had turned back and disappeared. De Mouy at once dug the two wide rowels of his spurs into the sides of his horse and galloped away, shouting as he went the words of warning which we have mentioned, to La Mole and Coconnas.

Now the King, who had noticed the absence of Henry and Marguerite, arrived, escorted by Monsieur d'Alençon, just as the two men came out of the hut to which he had said that all those found, not only in the pavilion but in the forest, were to be conducted.

D'Alençon, full of confidence, galloped close by the King, whose sharp pains were augmenting his ill humor. Two or three times he had nearly fainted and once he had vomited blood.

"Come," said he on arriving, "let us make haste; I want to return to the Louvre. Bring out all these rascals from their hole. This is Saint Blaise's day; he was cousin to Saint Bartholomew."

At these words of the King the entire mass of pikes and muskets began to move, and one by one the Huguenots were forced out not only from the forest and the pavilion but from the hut.

But the King of Navarre, Marguerite, and De Mouy were not there.

"Well," said the King, "where is Henry? Where is Margot? You promised them to me, D'Alençon, and, by Heaven, they will have to be found!"

"Sire, we have not even seen the King and the Queen of Navarre."

"But here they are," said Madame de Nevers.

At that moment, at the end of an alley leading to the river, Henry and Margot came in sight, both as calm as if nothing had happened; both with their falcons on their wrists, riding lovingly side by side, so that as they galloped along their horses, like themselves, seemed to be caressing each other.

It was then that D'Alençon, furious, commanded the forest to be searched, and that La Mole and Coconnas were found within their ivy bower. They, too, in brotherly proximity entered the circle formed by the guards; only, as they were not sovereigns, they could not assume so calm a manner as Henry and Marguerite. La Mole was too pale and Coconnas too red.

CHAPTER LII.

THE EXAMINATION.

The spectacle which struck the young men as they entered the circle, although seen but for a few moments, was one never to be forgotten.

As we have said, Charles IX. had watched the gentlemen as the guards led them one by one from the pricker's hut.

Both he and D'Alençon anxiously followed every movement, waiting to see the King of Navarre come out. Both, however, were doomed to disappointment. But it was not enough to know that the king was not there, it was necessary to find out what had become of him.

Therefore when the young couple were seen approaching from the end of the alley, D'Alençon turned pale, while Charles felt his heart grow glad; he instinctively desired that everything his brother had forced him to do should fall back on the duke.

"He will outwit us again," murmured François, growing still paler.

At that moment the King was seized with such violent pains that he dropped his bridle, pressed both hands to his sides, and shrieked like a madman.

Henry hastily approached him, but by the time he had traversed the few hundred feet which separated them, Charles had recovered.

"Whence do you come, monsieur?" said the King, with a sternness that frightened Marguerite.

"Why, from the hunt, brother," replied she.

"The hunt was along the river bank, and not in the forest."

"My falcon swooped down on a pheasant just as we stopped behind every one to look at the heron."

"Where is the pheasant?"

"Here; a beautiful bird, is it not?"

And Henry, in perfect innocence, held up his bird of purple, blue, and gold plumage.

"Ah!" said Charles, "and this pheasant caught, why did you not rejoin me?"

"Because the bird had directed its flight towards the park, sire, and when we returned to the river bank we saw you half a mile ahead of us, riding towards the forest. We set out to gallop after you, therefore, for being in your Majesty's hunting-party we did not wish to lose you."

"And were all these gentlemen invited also?" said Charles.

"What gentlemen?" asked Henry, casting an inquiring look about.

"Why, your Huguenots, by Heaven!" said Charles; "at all events if they were invited it was not by me."

"No, sire," replied Henry, "but possibly Monsieur d'Alençon asked them."

"Monsieur d'Alençon? How so?"

"I?" said the duke.

"Why, yes, brother," said Henry; "did you not announce yesterday that you were King of Navarre? The Huguenots who demanded you for their king have come to thank you for having accepted the crown, and the King for having given it. Is it not so, gentlemen?"

"Yes! yes!" cried twenty voices. "Long live the Duc d'Alençon! Long live King Charles!"

"I am not king of the Huguenots," said François, white with anger; then, glancing stealthily at Charles, "and I sincerely trust I never shall be!"

"No matter!" said Charles, "but you must know, Henry, that I consider all this very strange."

"Sire," said the King of Navarre, firmly, "God forgive me, but one would say that I were undergoing an examination."

"And if I should tell you that you were, what would you answer?"

"That I am a king like yourself, sire," replied Henry, proudly, "for it is not the crown but birth that makes royalty, and that I would gladly answer any questions from my brother and my friend, but never from my judge."

"And yet," murmured Charles, "I should really like to know for once in my life how to act."

"Let Monsieur de Mouy be brought out," said D'Alençon, "and then you will know. Monsieur de Mouy must be among the prisoners."

"Is Monsieur de Mouy here?" asked the King.

Henry felt a moment's anxiety and exchanged glances with Marguerite; but his uneasiness was of short duration.

No voice replied.

"Monsieur de Mouy is not among the prisoners," said Monsieur de Nancey; "some of our men think they saw him, but no one is sure of it."

D'Alençon uttered an oath.

"Well!" said Marguerite, pointing to La Mole and Coconnas, who had heard all that had passed, and on whose intelligence she felt she could depend, "there are two gentlemen in the service of Monsieur d'Alençon; question them; they will answer."

The duke felt the blow.

"I had them arrested on purpose to prove that they do not belong to me," said he.

The King looked at the two friends and started on seeing La Mole again.

"Ah! that Provençal here?" said he.

Coconnas bowed graciously.

"What were you doing when you were arrested?" asked the King.

"Sire, we were planning deeds of war and of love."

"On horseback, armed to the teeth, ready for flight!"

"No, sire," said Coconnas; "your Majesty is misinformed. We were lying under the shade of a beech tree—*sub tegmine fagi.*"

"Ah! so you were lying under the shade of a beech tree?"

"And we might easily have escaped had we thought that in any way we had roused your Majesty's anger. Now, gentlemen, on your honor as soldiers," continued Coconnas, turning to the light-horse, "do you not think that had we so wished we could have escaped?"

"The fact is," said the lieutenant, "that these gentlemen did not even attempt to run."

"Because their horses were too far away," said the Duc d'Alençon.

"I humbly beg monseigneur's pardon," said Coconnas; "but I was on mine, and my friend the Comte Lerac de la Mole was holding his by the bridle."

"Is this true, gentlemen?" said the King.

"Yes, sire," replied the lieutenant; "on seeing us Monsieur de Coconnas even dismounted."

Coconnas smiled in a way which signified, "You see, sire!"

"But the other horses, the mules, and the boxes with which they were laden?" asked François.

"Well," said Coconnas, "are we stable boys? Send for the groom who had charge of them."

"He is not here," exclaimed the duke, furious.

"Then he must have become frightened and run away," said Coconnas; "one cannot expect a clown to have the manners of a gentleman."

"Always the same system," said D'Alençon, gnashing his teeth. "Fortunately, sire, I told you that for some time these gentlemen have not been in my service."

"I!" exclaimed Coconnas, "am I unfortunate enough no longer to belong to your highness?"

"By Heaven! monsieur, you ought to know that better than any one, since you yourself gave me your dismissal, in a letter so impertinent that, thank God, I kept it, and fortunately have it with me."

"Oh!" exclaimed Coconnas, "I had hoped that your highness would forgive me for a letter written under the first impulse of anger. I had been told that your highness had tried to strangle my friend La Mole in one of the corridors of the Louvre."

472

"What is he saying?" interrupted the King.

"At first I thought your highness was alone," continued Coconnas, ingenuously, "but afterwards I learned that three others"—

"Silence!" exclaimed Charles; "we have heard enough. Henry," said he to the King of Navarre, "your word not to try to escape."

"I give it to your Majesty, sire."

"Return to Paris with Monsieur de Nancey, and remain in your chamber under arrest. You, gentlemen," continued he, addressing the two friends, "give up your swords."

La Mole looked at Marguerite. She smiled. La Mole at once handed his sword to the nearest officer. Coconnas did the same.

"Has Monsieur de Mouy been found?" asked the King.

"No, sire," said Monsieur de Nancey; "either he was not in the forest or he escaped."

"So much the worse," said the King; "but let us return. I am cold and dizzy."

"Sire, it is from anger, probably," said François.

"Possibly; but my eyes trouble me. Where are the prisoners? I cannot see them. Is it night already? Oh! mercy! I am burning up! Help! Help!"

The unfortunate King dropped the bridle of his horse, stretched out his arms, and fell backward. The courtiers, frightened at this second attack, caught him as he fell.

François, standing apart, wiped the perspiration from his brow, for he alone knew the cause of the trouble from which his brother was suffering.

On the other side the King of Navarre, already under the guard of Monsieur de Nancey, looked upon the scene with growing astonishment.

"Well! well!" murmured he, with that wonderful intuition which at times made him seem inspired, "was I perhaps fortunate in having been stopped in my flight?"

He glanced at Margot, whose great eyes, wide open with surprise, were looking first at him and then at the King.

This time Charles was unconscious. A litter was brought and he was laid on it. They covered him with a cloak, taken from the shoulders of one of the courtiers. The procession silently set out in the direction of Paris, whence that morning light-hearted conspirators and a happy King had started forth, and to which now a dying King was returning, surrounded by rebel prisoners.

Marguerite, who throughout all this had lost neither the control of her mind nor body, gave her husband a look of intelligence; then, passing so close to La Mole that the latter was able to catch the following two Greek words, she said:

"*Me deide*," which meant, "Fear nothing."

"What did she say?" asked Coconnas.

"She told me to fear nothing," replied La Mole.

"So much the worse," murmured the Piedmontese, "so much the worse; that means that it is not good for us to be here. Every time that word has been said to me in an encouraging tone I have either received a bullet or a sword-thrust in my body, or a flower pot on my head. 'Fear nothing,' whether in Hebrew, Greek, Latin, or French, has always meant for me: 'Take care!'"

"Forward, gentlemen!" said the lieutenant of the light-horse.

"Without being indiscreet, monsieur," said Coconnas, "may we know where we are going?"

"To Vincennes, I think," said the lieutenant.

"I would rather go elsewhere," said Coconnas; "but one does not always go just where one wishes."

On the way the King recovered consciousness and some strength.

At Nanterre he even wanted to ride, but this was not allowed.

"Summon Maître Ambroise Paré," said Charles, on reaching the Louvre.

He descended from his litter, ascended the stairs, leaning on the arm of Tavannes, and entered his apartment, giving orders that no one be allowed to follow him.

Every one had noticed that he seemed very grave. During the journey he had been in a deep study, not addressing a word to any one, concerned neither with conspiracy nor conspirators. It was evident that he was occupied with his illness; a malady so sudden, so strange, so severe, some of the symptoms of which had been noticed in his brother François II. a short time before his death.

So the order to admit no one whomsoever to his rooms, except Maître Paré, caused no surprise. It was well known that the prince was a misanthrope. Charles entered his sleeping-room, seated himself in a folding-chair, and leaned his head against the cushions. Then reflecting that Maître Ambroise Paré might not be at home, and that there might be some delay before he saw him, he decided to employ the intervening time.

He clapped his hands, thus summoning a guard.

"Say to the King of Navarre that I wish to speak with him," said Charles.

The man bowed and withdrew.

Just then Charles's head fell back, a great weight seemed to oppress him; his ideas grew confused; it was as if a sort of bloody vapor were floating before his eyes; his mouth was dry, although he had already swallowed a whole carafe of water.

While he was in this drowsy state the door opened and Henry appeared. Monsieur de Nancey had followed him, but stopped in the antechamber.

The King of Navarre waited until the door was closed. Then he advanced.

"Sire," said he, "you sent for me; I am here."

The King started at the voice and mechanically extended his hand.

"Sire," said Henry, letting his arms hang at his side, "your Majesty forgets that I am no longer your brother but your prisoner."

"Ah! that is true," said Charles. "Thank you for having reminded me of it. Moreover, it seems to me that when we last spoke together you promised to answer frankly what I might ask you."

"I am ready to keep my word, sire. Ask your questions."

The King poured some cold water into his hand and applied it to his forehead.

"Tell me, Henry, how much truth is there in the accusation brought against you by the Duc d'Alençon?"

"Only a little. It was Monsieur d'Alençon who was to have fled, and I who was to have accompanied him."

"And why should you have gone with him? Are you dissatisfied with me, Henry?"

"No, sire; on the contrary, I have only praise for your majesty; and God, who reads our hearts, knows how deeply I love my brother and my King."

"It seems to me," said Charles, "that it is not natural to flee from those we love and who love us."

"I was not fleeing from those who love me; I was fleeing from those who hate me. Will your Majesty permit me to speak openly?"

"Speak, monsieur."

"Those who hate me, sire, are Monsieur d'Alençon and the queen mother."

"As for Monsieur d'Alençon I will not answer; but the queen mother overwhelms you with attentions."

"That is just why I mistrust her, sire. And I do well to do so."

"Mistrust her?"

"Her, or those about her. You know, sire, that the misfortune of kings is not always that they are too little but that they are too well served."

"Explain yourself; you promised to tell me everything."

"Your Majesty will see that I will do so."

"Continue."

"Your Majesty loves me, you have said."

"I loved you before your treason, Henry."

"Pretend that you still love me, sire."

"Very well."

"If you love me you must want me to live, do you not?"

"I should be wretched were any harm to befall you."

"Well, sire, twice your Majesty has just escaped being wretched."

"How so?"

"Twice Providence has saved my life. It is true that the second time Providence assumed the features of your Majesty?"

"What form did it assume the first time?"

"That of a man who would be greatly surprised to see himself mistaken for Providence; I mean Réné. You, sire, saved me from steel."

Charles frowned, for he remembered the night when he had taken Henry to the Rue des Barres.

"And Réné?" said he.

"Réné saved me from poison."

"The deuce, Henriot, you have luck," said the King, trying to smile. But a quick spasm of pain changed the effort into a nervous contraction of the lips. "That is not his profession."

"Two miracles saved me, sire. A miracle of repentance on the part of the Florentine, and a miracle of goodness on your part. Well! I will confess to your Majesty that I am afraid Heaven will grow weary of working miracles, and I tried to run away, because of the proverb: 'Heaven helps those who help themselves.'"

"Why did you not tell me this sooner, Henriot?"

"Had I uttered these words yesterday I should have been a denunciator."

"And to-day?"

"To-day is different—I am accused and I am defending myself."

"Are you sure of the first attempt, Henriot?"

"As sure as I am of the second."

"And they tried to poison you?"

"Yes."

"With what?"

"With an opiate."

"How could they poison you with an opiate?"

"Why, sire, ask René; poisoning is done with gloves"—

Charles frowned; then by degrees his brow cleared.

"Yes," said he, as if speaking to himself. "It is the nature of wild creatures to flee from death. Why, then, should not knowledge do what instinct does?"

"Well, sire!" said Henry, "is your Majesty satisfied with my frankness, and do you believe that I have told you everything?"

"Yes, Henriot, and you are a good fellow. Do you think that those who hate you have grown weary, or will new attempts be made on your life?"

"Sire, every evening I am surprised to find myself still living."

"It is because they know I love you, Henriot, that they wish to kill you. But do not worry. They shall be punished for their evil intentions. Meanwhile you are free."

"Free to leave Paris, sire?" asked Henry.

"No; you well know that I cannot possibly do without you. In the name of a thousand devils! I must have some one here who loves me."

"Then, sire, if your Majesty keep me with you, will you grant me a favor"—

"What is it?"

"Not to keep me as a friend, but as a prisoner. Yes; does not your Majesty see that it is your friendship for me that is my ruin?"

"Would you prefer my hatred?"

"Your apparent hatred, sire. It will save me. As soon as they think I am in disgrace they will be less anxious for my death."

"Henriot," said Charles, "I know neither what you desire, nor what object you seek; but if your wishes do not succeed, and if your object is not accomplished, I shall be greatly surprised."

"I may, then, count on the severity of the King?"

"Yes."

"In that case I shall be less uneasy. Now what are your Majesty's commands?"

"Return to your apartments, Henriot, I am in pain. I will see my dogs and then go to bed."

"Sire," said Henry, "your Majesty ought to send for a physician. Your trouble is perhaps more serious than you imagine."

"I have sent for Maître Ambroise Paré, Henriot."

"Then I shall retire more satisfied."

"Upon my soul," said the King, "I believe that of all my family you are the only one who really loves me."

"Is this indeed your opinion, sire?"

"On the word of a gentleman."

"Then commend me to Monsieur de Nancey as a man your deep anger may not allow to live a month. By this means you will have me many years to love you."

"Monsieur de Nancey!" cried Charles.

The captain of the guards entered.

"I commit into your hands the most guilty man of my kingdom. You will answer for him with your life."

Henry assumed an air of consternation, and followed Monsieur de Nancey.

478

CHAPTER LIII.

ACTÉON.

Charles, left alone, wondered greatly at not having seen either of his favorites, his nurse Madeleine or his greyhound Actéon.

"Nurse must have gone to chant psalms with some Huguenot of her acquaintance," said he to himself; "and Actéon is probably still angry with me for the whipping I gave him this morning."

Charles took a candle and went into his nurse's room. The good woman was not there. From her chamber a door opened into the armory, it may be remembered. The King started towards this door, but as he did so he was seized with one of those spasms he had already felt, and which seemed to attack him suddenly. He felt as if his entrails were being run through with a red-hot iron, and an unquenchable thirst consumed him. Seeing a cup of milk on the table, he swallowed it at a gulp, and felt somewhat relieved.

Taking the candle he had set down, he entered the armory.

To his great astonishment Actéon did not come to meet him. Had he been shut up? If so, he would have known that his master had returned from hunting, and would have barked.

Charles called and whistled, but no animal appeared. He advanced a few steps, and as the light from the candle fell upon a corner of the room, he perceived an inert something lying there on the floor.

"Why! hello, Actéon!" cried Charles. He whistled again, but the dog did not stir. Charles hastened forward and touched him; the poor beast was stiff and cold. From his throat, contracted by pain, several drops of gall had fallen, mixed with foamy and bloody saliva. The dog had found an old cap of his master's in the armory, and had died with his head resting on this object, which represented a friend.

At the sight, which made him forget his own pain and restored all his energy, rage boiled in Charles's veins. He would have cried out; but, restrained as they are in their greatness, kings are not free to yield to that first impulse which every man turns to the profit of his passion or to his defence. Charles reflected that there had been some treason, and was silent.

Then he knelt down before his dog and with experienced eye examined the body. The eyes were glassy, the tongue red and covered with pustules. It was a strange disease, and one which made Charles shudder. The King put on his gloves, which he had taken off and slipped into his belt, opened the livid lips of the dog to examine his teeth, and perceived in the interstices some white-looking fragments clinging to the sharp points of the molars. He took out these pieces, and saw that they were paper. Near where the paper had been the swelling was greater, the gums were swollen, and the skin looked as if it had been eaten by vitriol.

Charles gazed carefully around him. On the carpet lay two or three bits of the paper similar to that which he had already recognized in the dog's mouth. One of the pieces, larger than the others, showed the marks of a woodcut. Charles's hair stood on end, for he recognized a fragment of the picture which represented a gentleman hawking, and which Actéon had torn from the treatise on hunting.

"Ah!" said he, turning pale; "the book was poisoned!"

Then, suddenly remembering:

"A thousand devils!" he exclaimed, "I touched every page with my finger, and at every page I raised my finger to my lips. These fainting-spells, these attacks of pain and vomiting! I am a dead man!"

For an instant Charles remained motionless under the weight of this terrible thought. Then, rising with a dull groan, he hastened to the door of the armory.

"Maître Réné!" he cried, "I want Maître Réné, the Florentine; send some one as quickly as possible to the Pont Saint Michel and bring him to me! He must be here within ten minutes. Let some one mount a horse and lead another that he may come more quickly. If Maître Ambroise Paré arrives have him wait."

A guard went instantly to carry out the King's commands.

"Oh!" murmured Charles, "if I have to put everybody to the torture, I will know who gave this book to Henriot;" and with perspiration on his brow, clenched hands, and heaving breast, he stood with his eyes fixed on the body of his dead dog.

Ten minutes later the Florentine knocked timidly and not without some anxiety at the door of the King's apartments. There are some consciences to which the sky is never clear.

"Enter!" said Charles.

The perfumer appeared. Charles went towards him with imperious air and compressed lip.

"Your Majesty sent for me," said Réné, trembling.

"You are a skilful chemist, are you not?"

"Sire"—

"And you know all that the cleverest doctors know?"

"Your Majesty exaggerates."

"No; my mother has told me so. Besides, I have confidence in you, and I prefer to consult you rather than any one else. See," he continued, pointing to the dog, "look at what this animal has between his teeth, I beg you, and tell me of what he died."

While Réné, candle in hand, bent over the floor as much to hide his emotion as to obey the King, Charles stood up, his eyes fixed on the man, waiting with an impatience easy to understand for the reply which was to be his sentence of death or his assurance of safety.

Réné drew a kind of scalpel from his pocket, opened it, and with the point detached from the mouth of the greyhound the particles of paper which adhered to the gums; then he looked long and attentively at the humor and the blood which oozed from each wound.

"Sire," said he, trembling, "the symptoms are very bad."

Charles felt an icy shudder run through his veins to his very heart.

"Yes," said he, "the dog has been poisoned, has he not?"

"I fear so, sire."

"With what sort of poison?"

"With mineral poison, I think."

"Can you ascertain positively that he has been poisoned?"

"Yes, certainly, by opening and examining the stomach."

"Open it. I wish there to be no doubt."

"I must call some one to assist me."

"I will help you," said Charles.

"You, sire!"

"Yes. If he has been poisoned, what symptoms shall we find?"

"Red blotches and herborizations in the stomach."

"Come, then," said Charles, "begin."

With a stroke of the scalpel Réné opened the hound's body and with his two hands removed the stomach, while Charles, one knee on the floor, held the light with clenched and trembling hand.

481

"See, sire," said Réné; "here are evident marks. These are the red spots I spoke of; as to these bloody veins, which seem like the roots of a plant, they are what I meant by herborizations. I find here everything I looked for."

"So the dog was poisoned?"

"Yes, sire."

"With mineral poison?"

"In all probability."

"And what symptoms would a man have who had inadvertently swallowed some of the same poison?"

"Great pain in the head, internal burning as if he had swallowed hot coals, pains in the bowels, and vomiting."

"Would he be thirsty?" asked Charles.

"Intensely thirsty."

"That is it! that is it!" murmured the King.

"Sire, I seek in vain for the motive for all these questions."

"Of what use to seek it? You need not know it. Answer my questions, that is all."

"Yes, sire."

"What is the antidote to give a man who may have swallowed the same substance as my dog?"

Réné reflected an instant.

"There are several mineral poisons," said he; "and before answering I should like to know what you mean. Has your Majesty any idea of the way in which your dog was poisoned?"

"Yes," said Charles; "he chewed the leaf of a book."

"The leaf of a book?"

"Yes."

"Has your Majesty this book?"

"Here it is," said Charles, and, taking the volume from the shelf where he had placed it, he handed it to Réné.

The latter gave a start of surprise which did not escape the King.

"He ate a leaf of this book?" stammered Réné.

"Yes, this one," and Charles pointed to the torn page.

"Will you allow me to tear out another, sire?"

"Do so."

Réné tore out a leaf and held it over the candle. The paper caught fire, filling the room with a strong smell of garlic.

"He has been poisoned with a preparation of arsenic," said he.

"You are sure?"

"As sure as if I had prepared it myself."

"And the antidote?"

Réné shook his head.

"What!" said Charles in a hoarse voice, "you know no remedy?"

"The best and most efficacious is the white of eggs beaten in milk; but"—

"But what?"

"It must be administered at once; otherwise"—

"Otherwise?"

"Sire, it is a terrible poison," said Réné, again.

"Yet it does not kill immediately," said Charles.

"No, but it kills surely, no matter how long the time, though even this may sometimes be calculated."

Charles leaned against the marble table.

"Now," said he, putting his hand on Réné's shoulder, "you know this book?"

"I, sire?" said Réné, turning pale.

"Yes, you; on seeing it you betrayed yourself."

"Sire, I swear to you"—

"Réné," said Charles, "listen to me. You poisoned the Queen of Navarre with gloves; you poisoned the Prince of Porcion with the smoke from a lamp; you tried to poison Monsieur de Condé with a scented apple. Réné, I will have your skin removed with red-hot pincers, bit by bit, if you do not tell me to whom this book belongs."

The Florentine saw that he could not dally with the anger of Charles IX., and resolved to be bold.

"If I tell the truth, sire, who will guarantee that I shall not be more cruelly punished than if I keep silent?"

"I will."

"Will you give me your royal word?"

"On my honor as a gentleman your life shall be spared," said the King.

"The book belongs to me, then," said Réné.

"To you!" cried Charles, starting back and looking at the poisoner with haggard eyes.

"Yes, to me."

"How did it leave your possession?"

"Her majesty the queen mother took it from my house."

"The queen mother!" exclaimed Charles.

"Yes."

"With what object?"

"With the intention, I think, of having it sent to the King of Navarre, who had asked the Duc d'Alençon for a book of the kind in order to study the art of hawking."

"Ah!" cried Charles, "that is it. I see it all. The book indeed was in Henriot's room. There is a destiny about this and I submit to it."

At that moment Charles was seized with a violent fit of coughing, followed by fresh pain in the bowels. He gave two or three stifled cries, and fell back in his chair.

"What is the matter, sire?" asked Réné in a frightened voice.

"Nothing," said Charles, "except that I am thirsty. Give me something to drink."

Réné filled a glass with water and with trembling hand gave it to Charles, who swallowed it at a draught.

"Now," said he, taking a pen and dipping it into the ink, "write in this book."

"What must I write?"

"What I am going to dictate to you:

"'*This book on hawking was given by me to the queen mother, Catharine de Médicis.*'"

Réné took the pen and wrote.

"Now sign your name."

The Florentine obeyed.

"You promised to save my life."

"I will keep my promise."

"But," said Réné, "the queen mother?"

"Oh!" said Charles, "I have nothing to do with her; if you are attacked defend yourself."

"Sire, may I leave France, where I feel that my life is in danger?"

"I will reply to that in a fortnight."

"But, in the meantime"—

Charles frowned and placed his finger on his livid lips.

"You need not be afraid of me, sire."

And happy to have escaped so easily the Florentine bowed and withdrew.

Behind him the nurse appeared at the door of her room.

"What is the matter, my Charlot?" said she.

"Nurse, I have been walking in the dew, and have taken cold."

"You are very pale, Charlot."

"It is because I am so weak. Give me your arm, nurse, as far as my bed."

The nurse hastily came forward.

Charles leaned on her and reached his room.

"Now," said Charles, "I will put myself to bed."

"If Maître Ambroise Paré comes?"

"Tell him that I am better and that I do not need him."

"But, meanwhile, what will you take?"

"Oh! a very simple medicine," said Charles, "the whites of eggs beaten in milk. By the way, nurse," he continued, "my poor Actéon is dead. To-morrow morning he must be buried in a corner of the garden of the Louvre. He was one of my best friends. I will have a tomb made for him—if I have time."

CHAPTER LIV.

THE FOREST OF VINCENNES.

According to the order given by Charles IX., Henry was conducted that same evening to Vincennes. Such was the name given at that time to the famous castle of which to-day only a fragment remains, colossal enough, however, to give an idea of its past grandeur.

The trip was made in a litter, on either side of which walked four guards.

Monsieur de Nancey, bearing the order which was to open to Henry the door of the protecting abode, walked first.

At the postern of the prison they stopped. Monsieur de Nancey dismounted from his horse, opened the gate, which was closed with a padlock, and respectfully asked the king to follow.

Henry obeyed without uttering a word. Any dwelling seemed to him safer than the Louvre, and ten doors closed on him were at the same time ten doors shut between him and Catharine de Médicis.

The royal prisoner crossed the drawbridge between two soldiers, passed through the three doors on the ground floor and the three at the foot of the staircase; then, still preceded by Monsieur de Nancey, he ascended one flight. Arrived there, the captain of the guards, seeing that the king was about to mount another flight, said to him:

"My lord, you are to stop here."

"Ah!" said Henry, pausing, "it seems that I am given the honors of the first floor."

"Sire," replied Monsieur de Nancey, "you are treated like a crowned head."

"The devil! the devil!" said Henry to himself, "two or three floors more would in no way have humiliated me. I shall be too comfortable here; I suspect something."

"Will your majesty follow me?" asked Monsieur de Nancey.

"*Ventre saint gris!*" said the King of Navarre, "you know very well, monsieur, that it is not a question of what I will or will not do, but of what my brother Charles orders. Did he command that I should follow you?"

"Yes, sire."

"Then I will do so, monsieur."

They reached a sort of corridor at the end of which they came to a good-sized room, with dark and gloomy looking walls. Henry gazed around him with a glance not wholly free from anxiety.

"Where are we?" he asked.

"In the chamber of torture, my lord."

"Ah!" replied the king, looking at it more closely.

There was something of everything in this chamber—pitchers and wooden horses for the torture by water; wedges and mallets for the torture of the boot; besides stone benches nearly all around the room for the wretches who awaited the torture. Above these benches, at the seats themselves, and at their feet, were iron rings fastened into the walls, without other symmetry than that of the torturing art. But their proximity to the seats sufficiently indicated that they were there in order to await the limbs of those who were to occupy them.

Henry walked on without a word, but not a single detail of all the hideous apparatus which, so to speak, had stamped the history of suffering on the walls escaped him.

The king was so taken up with the objects about him that he forgot to look where he was going, and came to a sudden standstill.

"Ah!" said he, "what is that?"

And he pointed to a kind of ditch dug in the damp pavement which formed the floor.

"That is the gutter, sire."

"Does it rain here, then?"

"Yes, sire, blood."

"Ah!" said Henry, "very good. Shall we not soon reach my apartment?"

"Yes, my lord, here it is," said a figure in the dark, which, as it drew nearer, became clearer and more distinguishable.

Henry thought he recognized the voice, and advanced towards the figure.

"So it is you, Beaulieu," said he. "What the devil are you doing here?"

"Sire, I have just received my appointment as governor of the fortress of Vincennes."

"Well, my dear friend, your initiation does you honor. A king for a prisoner is not bad."

"Pardon me, sire," said Beaulieu, "but I have already had two gentlemen."

"Who are they? But, pardon me, perhaps I am indiscreet. If so, assume that I have said nothing."

"My lord, I have not been ordered to keep it secret. They are Monsieur de la Mole and Monsieur de Coconnas."

"Ah! that is true. I saw them arrested. Poor gentlemen, and how do they bear this misfortune?"

"Differently. One is gay, the other sad; one sings, the other groans."

"Which one groans?"

"Monsieur de la Mole, sire."

"Faith," said Henry, "I can understand more easily the one who groans than the one who sings. After what I have seen the prison is not a very lively place. On what floor are they?"

"High up; on the fourth."

Henry heaved a sigh. It was there that he wished to be.

"Come, Monsieur de Beaulieu," said he, "be good enough to show me my room. I am in haste to see it, as I am greatly fatigued from the journey we have just made."

"This is it, my lord," said Beaulieu, pointing to an open door.

"Number two," said Henry; "why not number one?"

"Because that is reserved, my lord."

"Ah! it seems, then, that you expect a prisoner of higher rank than I."

"I did not say, my lord, that it was a prisoner."

"Who is it, then?"

"I beg my lord not to insist, for by refusing to answer I should fail in the obedience due him."

"Ah! that is another thing," said Henry.

And he became more pensive than before. Number one perplexed him, apparently. The governor was assiduous in his attentions. With a thousand apologies he installed Henry in his apartment, made every excuse for the comforts he might lack, stationed two soldiers at the door, and withdrew.

"Now," said the governor, addressing the turnkey, "let us go to the others."

The turnkey walked ahead. They took the same road by which they had come, passed through the chamber of torture, crossed the corridor, and reached the stairway. Then, still following his guide, Monsieur de Beaulieu ascended three flights. On reaching the fourth floor the turnkey opened successively three doors, each ornamented with two locks and three enormous bolts. He had scarcely touched the third door before they heard a joyous voice exclaiming:

"By Heaven! open; if only to give us some air. Your stove is so warm that I am stifled here."

And Coconnas, whom the reader has no doubt already recognized from his favorite exclamation, bounded from where he stood to the door.

"One instant, my gentleman," said the turnkey, "I have not come to let you out, but to let myself in, and the governor is with me."

"The governor!" said Coconnas, "what does he want?"

"To pay you a visit."

"He does me great honor," said Coconnas; "and he is welcome."

Monsieur de Beaulieu entered and at once dispelled the cordial smile of Coconnas by one of those icy looks which belong to governors of fortresses, to jailers, and to hangmen.

"Have you any money, monsieur?" he asked of the prisoner.

"I?" said Coconnas; "not a crown."

"Jewels?"

"I have a ring."

"Will you allow me to search you?"

"By Heaven!" cried Coconnas, reddening with anger, "you take much on yourself, being in prison, and having me there also."

"We must suffer everything for the service of the King."

"So," said the Piedmontese, "those good fellows who rob on the Pont Neuf are like you, then, in the service of the King. By Heavens! I was very unjust, monsieur, for until now I have taken them for thieves."

"Good evening, monsieur," said Beaulieu. "Jailer, lock the door."

The governor went away, taking with him the ring, which was a beautiful sapphire, given him by Madame de Nevers to remind him of the color of her eyes.

"Now for the other," he said as he went out.

They crossed an empty chamber, and the game of three doors, six locks, and nine bolts began anew.

The last door open, a sigh was the first sound that greeted the visitors.

The apartment was more gloomy looking than the one Monsieur de Beaulieu had just left. Four long narrow windows admitted a feeble light into this mournful abode. Before these, iron bars were crossed in such a way that the eye of the prisoner was arrested by a dark line and prevented from catching even a glimpse of the sky. From each corner of the room pointed arches met in the middle of the ceiling, where they spread out in Gothic fashion.

La Mole was seated in a corner, and, in spite of the entrance of the visitors, appeared to have heard nothing.

The governor paused on the threshold and looked for an instant at the prisoner, who sat motionless, his head in his hands.

"Good evening, Monsieur de la Mole," said Beaulieu.

The young man slowly raised his head.

"Good evening, monsieur," said he.

"Monsieur," continued the governor, "I have come to search you."

"That is useless," said La Mole. "I will give you all I have."

"What have you?"

"About three hundred crowns, these jewels, and rings."

"Give them to me, monsieur," said the governor.

"Here they are."

La Mole turned out his pockets, took the rings from his finger, and the clasp from his hat.

"Have you nothing more?"

"Not that I know of."

"And that silk cord around your neck, what may that be?" asked the governor.

"Monsieur, that is not a jewel, but a relic."

"Give it to me."

"What! you demand it?"

"I am ordered to leave you only your clothes, and a relic is not an article of clothing."

La Mole made a gesture of anger, which, in the midst of the dignified and pained calm which distinguished him, seemed to impress the men accustomed to stormy emotions.

But he immediately recovered his self-possession.

"Very well, monsieur," said he, "you shall see what you ask for."

Then, turning as if to approach the light, he unfastened the pretended relic, which was none other than a medallion containing a portrait, which he drew out and raised to his lips. Having kissed it several times, he suddenly pretended to drop it as by accident, and placing the heel of his boot on it he crushed it into a thousand pieces.

"Monsieur!" said the governor.

And he stooped down to see if he could not save the unknown object which La Mole wished to hide from him; but the miniature was literally ground to powder.

"The King wished for this jewel," said La Mole, "but he had no right to the portrait it contained. Now, here is the medallion; you may take it."

"Monsieur," said Beaulieu, "I shall complain of you to the King."

And without taking leave of his prisoner by a single word he went out, so angry that without waiting to preside over the task, he left to the turnkey the care of closing the doors.

The jailer turned to leave, but seeing that Monsieur de Beaulieu had already started down the stairs:

"Faith! monsieur," said he, turning back, "I did well to ask you to give me the hundred crowns at once for which I am to allow you to speak to your companion; for had you not done so the governor would have taken them from you with the three hundred others, and my conscience would not have allowed me to do anything for you; but as I was paid in advance, I promised that you should see your friend. So come. An honest man keeps his word. Only, if it is possible, for your sake as much as for mine, do not talk politics."

La Mole left his apartment and found himself face to face with Coconnas, who was walking up and down the flags of the intermediate room.

The two friends rushed into each other's arms.

The jailer pretended to wipe the corner of his eye, and then withdrew to watch that the prisoners were not surprised, or rather that he himself was not caught.

"Ah! here you are!" said Coconnas. "Well, has that dreadful governor paid his visit to you?"

"Yes, as he did to you, I presume?"

"Did he remove everything?"

"And from you, too?"

"Ah! I had not much; only a ring from Henrietta, that was all."

"And money?"

"I gave all I had to the good jailer, so that he would arrange this interview for us."

"Ah!" said La Mole, "it seems that he had something from both of us."

"Did you pay him too?"

"I gave him a hundred crowns."

"So much the better."

"One can do everything with money, and I trust that we shall not lack for it."

"Do you know what has happened to us?"

"Perfectly; we have been betrayed."

"By that scoundrelly Duc d'Alençon. I should have been right to twist his neck."

"Do you think our position serious?"

"I fear so."

"Then there is likelihood of the torture?"

"I will not hide from you the fact that I have already thought of it."

"What should you do in that case?"

"And you?"

"I should be silent," replied La Mole, with a feverish flush.

"Silent?" cried Coconnas.

"Yes, if I had the strength."

"Well," said Coconnas, "if they insult me in any such way I promise you I will tell them a few things."

"What things?" asked La Mole, quickly.

"Oh, be easy—things which will prevent Monsieur d'Alençon from sleeping for some time."

La Mole was about to reply when the jailer, who no doubt had heard some noise, appeared, and pushing each prisoner into his respective cell, locked the doors again.

CHAPTER LV.

THE FIGURE OF WAX.

For a week Charles was confined to his bed by a slow fever, interrupted by violent attacks which resembled epileptic fits. During these attacks he uttered shrieks which the guards, watching in his chamber, heard with terror, and the echoes of which reached to the farthest corner of the old Louvre, aroused so often by many a dreadful sound. Then, when these attacks passed, Charles, completely exhausted, sank back with closed eyes into the arms of his nurse.

To say that, each in his way, without communicating the feeling to the other, for mother and son sought to avoid rather than to see each other, to say that Catharine de Médicis and the Duc d'Alençon revolved sinister thoughts in the depths of their hearts would be to say that in that nest of vipers moved a hideous swarm.

Henry was shut up in his chamber in the prison; and at his own request no one had been allowed to see him, not even Marguerite. In the eyes of every one his imprisonment was an open disgrace. Catharine and D'Alençon, thinking him lost, breathed once more, and Henry ate and drank more calmly, hoping that he was forgotten.

At court no one suspected the cause of the King's illness. Maître Ambroise Paré and Mazille, his colleague, thought it was inflammation of the bowels, and had prescribed a regimen which aided the special drink given by Réné. Charles received this, his only nourishment, three times a day from the hands of his nurse.

La Mole and Coconnas were at Vincennes in closest confinement. Marguerite and Madame de Nevers had made a dozen attempts to reach them, or at least to send them a note, but without success. One morning Charles felt somewhat better, and wished the court to assemble. This was the usual custom in the morning, although for some time no levee had taken place. The doors were accordingly thrown open, and it was easy to see, from his pale cheeks, yellow forehead, and the feverish light in his deep-sunken eyes, which were surrounded by dark circles, what frightful ravages the unknown disease had made on the young monarch.

The royal chamber was soon filled with curious and interested courtiers. Catharine, D'Alençon, and Marguerite had been informed that the King was to hold an audience. Therefore all three entered, at short intervals, one by one; Catharine calm, D'Alençon smiling, Marguerite dejected. Catharine seated herself by the side of the bed without noticing the look that Charles gave her as he saw her approach.

Monsieur d'Alençon stood at the foot.

Marguerite leaned against a table, and seeing the pale brow, the worn features, and deep-sunken eyes of her brother, could not repress a sigh and a tear.

Charles, whom nothing escaped, saw the tear and heard the sigh, and with his head made a slight motion to Marguerite.

This sign, slight as it was, lighted the face of the poor Queen of Navarre, to whom Henry had not had time or perhaps had not wished to say anything.

She feared for her husband, she trembled for her lover. For herself she had no fear; she knew La Mole well, and felt she could rely on him.

"Well, my dear son," said Catharine, "how do you feel?"

"Better, mother, better."

"What do your physicians say?"

"My physicians? They are clever doctors, mother," said Charles, bursting into a laugh. "I take great pleasure, I admit, in hearing them discuss my malady. Nurse, give me something to drink."

The nurse brought Charles a cup of his usual beverage.

"What do they order you to take, my son?"

"Oh! madame, who knows anything about their preparations?" said the King, hastily swallowing the drink.

"What my brother needs," said François, "is to rise and get out into the open air; hunting, of which he is so fond, would do him a great deal of good."

"Yes," said Charles, with a smile, the meaning of which it was impossible for the duke to understand, "and yet the last hunt did me great harm."

Charles uttered these words in such a strange way that the conversation, in which the others present had not taken part, stopped. Then the King gave a slight nod of his head. The courtiers understood that the audience was over, and withdrew one after another.

D'Alençon started to approach his brother, but some secret feeling stopped him. He bowed and went out.

Marguerite seized the wasted hand her brother held out to her, pressed it, and kissed it. Then she, in turn, withdrew.

"Dear Margot!" murmured Charles.

Catharine alone remained, keeping her place at the side of the bed. Finding himself alone with her, Charles recoiled as if from a serpent.

Instructed by the words of Réné, perhaps still better by silence and meditation, Charles no longer had even the happiness of doubt.

He knew perfectly to whom and to what to attribute his approaching death.

So, when Catharine drew near to the bed and extended to him a hand as cold as his glance, the King shuddered in fear.

"You have remained, madame?" said he.

"Yes, my son," replied Catharine, "I must speak to you on important matters."

"Speak, madame," said Charles, again recoiling.

"Sire!" said the queen, "you said just now that your physicians were great doctors!"

"And I say so again, madame."

"Yet what have they done during your illness?"

"Nothing, it is true—but if you had heard what they said—really, madame, one might afford to be ill if only to listen to their learned discussions."

"Well, my son, do you want me to tell you something?"

"What is it, mother?"

"I suspect that all these clever doctors know nothing whatever about your malady."

"Indeed, madame!"

"They may, perhaps, see a result, but they are ignorant of the cause."

"That is possible," said Charles, not understanding what his mother was aiming at.

"So that they treat the symptoms and not the ill itself."

"On my soul!" said Charles, astonished, "I believe you are right, mother."

"Well, my son," said Catharine, "as it is good neither for my happiness nor the welfare of the kingdom for you to be ill so long, and as your mind might end by becoming affected, I assembled the most skilful doctors."

"In the science of medicine, madame?"

"No, in a more profound science: that which helps not only the body but the mind as well."

"Ah! a beautiful science, madame," said Charles, "and one which the doctors are right in not teaching to crowned heads! Have your researches had any result?" he continued.

"Yes."

"What was it?"

"That which I hoped for; I bring to your Majesty that which will cure not only your body but your mind."

Charles shuddered. He thought that finding that he was still living his mother had resolved to finish knowingly that which she had begun unconsciously.

"Where is this remedy?" said he, rising on his elbow and looking at his mother.

"In the disease itself," replied Catharine.

"Then where is that?"

"Listen to me, my son," said Catharine, "have you not sometimes heard it said that there are secret enemies who in their revenge assassinate their victim from a distance?"

"By steel or poison?" asked Charles, without once turning his eyes from the impassible face of his mother.

"No, by a surer and much more terrible means," said Catharine.

"Explain yourself."

"My son," asked the Florentine, "do you believe in charms and magic?"

Charles repressed a smile of scorn and incredulity.

"Fully," said he.

"Well," said Catharine, quickly, "from magic comes all your suffering. An enemy of your Majesty who would not have dared to attack you openly has conspired in secret. He has directed against your Majesty a conspiracy much more terrible in that he has no accomplices, and the mysterious threads of which cannot be traced."

"Faith, no!" said Charles, aghast at such cunning.

"Think well, my son," said Catharine, "and recall to mind certain plans for flight which would have assured impunity to the murderer."

"To the murderer!" cried Charles. "To the murderer, you say? Has there been an attempt to kill me, mother?"

Catharine's changing eye rolled hypocritically under its wrinkled lid.

"Yes, my son; you doubt it, perhaps, but I know it for a certainty."

"I never doubt what you tell me, mother," replied the King, bitterly. "How was the attempt made? I am anxious to know."

"By magic."

"Explain yourself, madame," said Charles, recalled by his loathing to his rôle of observer.

"If the conspirator I mean, and one whom at heart your Majesty already suspects, had succeeded in his plans, no one would have fathomed the cause of your Majesty's sufferings. Fortunately, however, sire, your brother watched over you."

"Which brother?"

"D'Alençon."

"Ah! yes, that is true; I always forget that I have a brother," murmured Charles, laughing bitterly; "so you say, madame"—

"That fortunately he revealed the conspiracy. But while he, inexperienced child that he is, sought only the traces of an ordinary plot, the proofs of a young man's escapade, I sought for proofs of a much more important deed; for I understand the reach of the guilty one's mind."

"Ah! mother, one would say you were speaking of the King of Navarre," said Charles, anxious to see how far this Florentine dissimulation would go.

Catharine hypocritically dropped her eyes.

"I have had him arrested and taken to Vincennes for his escapade," continued the King; "is he more guilty than I suspected, then?"

"Do you feel the fever that consumes you?" asked Catharine.

"Yes, certainly, madame," said Charles, frowning.

"Do you feel the fire that burns you internally?"

"Yes, madame," replied Charles, his brow darkening more and more.

"And the sharp pains in your head, which shoot from your eyes to your brain like so many arrows?"

"Yes, madame. I feel all that. You describe my trouble perfectly!"

"Well! the explanation is very simple," said the Florentine. "See."

And she drew from under her cloak an object which she gave to the King.

It was a figure of yellow wax, about six inches high, clothed in a robe covered with golden stars also of wax, like the figure; and over this a royal mantle of the same material.

"Well," asked Charles, "what is this little statue?"

"See what it has on its head," said Catharine.

"A crown," replied Charles.

"And in the heart?"

"A needle."

"Well, sire, do you recognize yourself?"

"Myself?"

"Yes, you, with your crown and mantle?"

"Who made this figure?" asked Charles, whom this farce was beginning to weary; "the King of Navarre, no doubt?"

"No, sire."

"No? then I do not understand you."

"I say *no*," replied Catharine, "because you asked the question literally. I should have said *yes* had you put it differently."

Charles made no answer. He was striving to penetrate all the thoughts of that shadowy mind, which constantly closed before him just as he thought himself ready to read it.

"Sire," continued Catharine, "this statue was found by the Attorney-General Laguesle, in the apartment of the man who on the day you last went hawking led a horse for the King of Navarre."

"Monsieur de la Mole?"

"Yes, and, if you please, look again at the needle in the heart, and see what letter is written on the label attached to it."

"I see an 'M,'" said Charles.

"That means *mort*, death; it is the magic formula, sire. The maker thus wrote his vow on the very wound he gave. Had he wished to make a pretence at killing, as did the Duc de Bretagne for King Charles VI., he would have driven the needle into the head and put an 'F' instead of an 'M.'"

"So," said Charles IX., "according to your idea, the person who seeks to end my days is Monsieur de la Mole?"

"Yes, he is the dagger; but behind the dagger is the hand that directs it."

"This then is the sole cause of my illness? the day the charm is destroyed the malady will cease? But how go to work?" asked Charles, "you must know, mother; but I, unlike you, who have spent your whole life studying them, know nothing about charms and spells."

"The death of the conspirator destroys the charm, that is all. The day the charm is destroyed your illness will cease," said Catharine.

"Indeed!" said Charles, with an air of surprise.

"Did you not know that?"

"Why! I am no sorcerer," said the King.

"Well, now," said Catharine, "your Majesty is convinced, are you not?"

"Certainly."

"Conviction has dispelled anxiety?"

"Completely."

"You do not say so out of complaisance?"

"No, mother! I say it from the bottom of my heart."

Catharine's face broke into smiles.

"Thank God!" she exclaimed, as if she believed in God.

"Yes, thank God!" repeated Charles, ironically; "I know now, as you do, to whom to attribute my present condition, and consequently whom to punish."

"And you will punish"—

"Monsieur de la Mole; did you not say that he was the guilty party?"

"I said that he was the instrument."

"Well," said Charles, "Monsieur de la Mole first; he is the most important. All these attacks on me might arouse dangerous suspicions. It is imperative that there be some light thrown on the matter and from this light the truth may be discovered."

"So Monsieur de la Mole"—

"Suits me admirably as the guilty one; therefore I accept him. We will begin with him; and if he has an accomplice, he shall speak."

"Yes," murmured Catharine, "and if he does not, we will make him. We have infallible means for that."

Then rising:

"Will you permit the trial to begin, sire?"

"I desire it, madame," replied Charles, "and the sooner the better."

Catharine pressed the hand of her son without comprehending the nervous grasp with which he returned it, and left the apartment without hearing the sardonic laugh of the King, or the terrible oath which followed the laugh.

Charles wondered if it were not dangerous to let this woman go thus, for in a few hours she would have done so much that there would be no way of stopping it.

As he watched the curtain fall after Catharine, he heard a light rustle behind him, and turning he perceived Marguerite, who raised the drapery before the corridor leading to his nurse's rooms.

Marguerite's pallor, her haggard eyes and oppressed breathing betrayed the most violent emotion.

"Oh, sire! sire!" she exclaimed, rushing to her brother's bedside; "youknow that she lies."

"She? Who?" asked Charles.

"Listen, Charles, it is a terrible thing to accuse one's mother; but I suspected that she remained with you to persecute them again. But, on my life, on yours, on our souls, I tell you what she says is false!"

"To persecute them! Whom is she persecuting?"

Both had instinctively lowered their voices; it seemed as if they themselves feared even to hear them.

"Henry, in the first place; your Henriot, who loves you, who is more devoted to you than any one else."

"You think so, Margot?" said Charles.

"Oh! sire, I am sure of it."

"Well, so am I," said Charles.

"Then if you are sure of it, brother," said Marguerite, surprised, "why did you have him arrested and taken to Vincennes?"

"Because he asked me to do so."

"He asked you, sire?"

"Yes, Henriot has singular ideas. Perhaps he is wrong, perhaps right; at any rate, one of his ideas was that he would be safer in disgrace than in favor, away from me at Vincennes instead of near me in the Louvre."

"Ah! I see," said Marguerite, "and is he safe there?"

"As safe as a man can be whose head Beaulieu answers for with his own."

"Oh! thank you, brother! so much for Henry. But"—

"But what?"

"There is another, sire, in whom perhaps I am wrong to be interested, but"—

"Who is it?"

"Sire, spare me. I would scarcely dare name him to my brother, much less to my King."

"Monsieur de la Mole, is it not?" said Charles.

"Alas!" said Marguerite, "you tried to kill him once, sire, and he escaped from your royal vengeance only by a miracle."

"He was guilty of only one crime then, Marguerite; now he has committed two."

"Sire, he is not guilty of the second."

"But," said Charles, "did you not hear what our good mother said, my poor Margot?"

"Oh, I have already told you, Charles," said Marguerite, lowering her voice, "that what she said was false."

"You do not know perhaps that a waxen figure has been found in Monsieur de la Mole's rooms?"

"Yes, yes, brother, I know it."

"That this figure is pierced to the heart by a needle, and that it bears a tag with an 'M' on it?"

"I know that, too."

"And that over the shoulders of the figure is a royal mantle, and that on its head is a royal crown?"

"I know all that."

"Well! what have you to say to it?"

"This: that the figure with a royal cloak and a crown on its head is that of a woman, and not that of a man."

"Bah!" said Charles, "and the needle in its heart?"

"Was a charm to make himself beloved by this woman, and not a charm to kill a man."

"But the letter 'M'?"

"It does not mean *mort*, as the queen mother said."

"What does it mean, then?" asked Charles.

"It means—it means the name of the woman whom Monsieur de la Mole loves."

"And what is the name of this woman?"

"*Marguerite*, brother!" cried the Queen of Navarre, falling on her knees before the King's bed, taking his hand between both of hers, and pressing her face to it, bathed in tears.

"Hush, sister!" said Charles, casting a sharp glance about him beneath his frowning brow. "For just as you overheard a moment ago, we may now be overheard again."

"What does it matter?" exclaimed Marguerite, raising her head, "if the whole world were present to hear me, I would declare before it that it is infamous to abuse the love of a gentleman by staining his reputation with a suspicion of murder."

"Margot, suppose I were to tell you that I know as well as you do who it is and who it is not?"

"Brother!"

"Suppose I were to tell you that Monsieur de la Mole is innocent?"

"You know this?"

"If I were to tell you that I know the real author of the crime?"

"The real author!" cried Marguerite; "has there been a crime committed, then?"

"Yes; intentionally or unintentionally there has been a crime committed."

"On you?"

"Yes."

"Impossible!"

"Impossible? Look at me, Margot."

The young woman looked at her brother and trembled, seeing him so pale.

"Margot, I have not three months to live!" said Charles.

"You, brother! you, Charles!" she cried.

"Margot, I am poisoned."

Marguerite screamed.

"Hush," said Charles. "It must be thought that I am dying by magic."

"Do you know who is guilty?"

"Yes."

"You said it was not La Mole?"

"No, it is not he."

"Nor Henry either, surely—great God! could it be"—

"Who?"

"My brother—D'Alençon?" murmured Marguerite.

"Perhaps."

"Or—or"—Marguerite lowered her voice as if frightened at what she was going to say, "or—our mother?"

Charles was silent.

Marguerite looked at him, and read all that she asked in his eyes. Then still on her knees she half fell over against a chair.

"Oh! my God! my God!" she whispered, "that is impossible."

"Impossible?" said Charles, with a strident laugh, "it is a pity Réné is not here to tell you the story."

"Réné?"

"Yes; he would tell you that a woman to whom he dares refuse nothing asked him for a book on hunting which was in his library; that a subtle poison was poured on every page of this book; that the poison intended for some one, I know not for whom, fell by a turn of chance, or by a punishment of Heaven, on another. But in the absence of Réné if you wish to see the book it is there in my closet, and written in the Florentine's handwriting you will see that this volume, which still contains the death of many among its pages, was given by him to his fellow countrywoman."

"Hush, Charles, hush!" said Marguerite.

"Now you see that it must be supposed that I die of magic."

"But it is monstrous, monstrous! Pity! Pity! you know he is innocent."

"Yes, I know it, but he must be thought guilty. Let your lover die; it is very little to do in order to save the honor of the house of France; I myself shall die that the secret may die with me."

Marguerite bent her head, realizing that nothing could be obtained from the King towards saving La Mole, and withdrew weeping, having no hope except in her own resources.

Meantime Catharine, as Charles had divined, had lost not a minute, but had written to the Attorney-General Laguesle a letter, every word of which has been preserved by history and which throws a lurid light upon the drama:

"Monsieur le Procureur: I have this evening been informed beyond a doubt that La Mole has committed sacrilege. Many evil things such as books and papers have been found in his apartments in Paris. I beg you to summon the chief president, and to inform him as early as possible of the affair of the waxen figure meant for the King, and which was pierced to the heart.

"CATHARINE."[18]

CHAPTER LVI.

THE INVISIBLE BUCKLERS.

The day after that on which Catharine had written this letter the governor entered Coconnas's cell with an imposing retinue consisting of two halberdiers and four men in black gowns.

Coconnas was asked to descend to a room in which the Attorney Laguesle and two judges waited to question him according to Catharine's instructions.

During the week he had spent in prison Coconnas had reflected a great deal. Besides that, he and La Mole were together for a few minutes each day, through the kindness of their jailer, who, without saying anything to them, had arranged this surprise, which in all probability they did not owe to his philosophy alone,—besides, we say, La Mole and he had agreed on the course they were to pursue, which was to persist in absolute denial; and they were persuaded that with a little skill the affair would take a more favorable turn; the charges were no greater against them than against the others. Henry and Marguerite had made no attempt at flight; they could not therefore be compromised in an affair in which the chief ring-leaders were free. Coconnas did not know that Henry was in the prison, and the complaisance of the jailer told him that above his head hovered a certain protection which he called the *invisible bucklers.*

Up to then the examination had been confined to the intentions of the King of Navarre, his plans of flight, and the part the two friends had played in them. To all these questions Coconnas had constantly replied in a way more than vague and much more than adroit; he was ready still to reply in the same way, and had prepared in advance all his little repartees, when he suddenly found the object of the examination was altered. It turned upon one or more visits to Réné, one or more waxen figures made at the instigation of La Mole.

Prepared as he was, Coconnas believed that the accusation lost much of its intensity, since it was no longer a question of having betrayed a king but of having made a figure of a queen; and this figure not more than ten inches high at the most. He, therefore, replied brightly that neither he nor his friend had played with a doll for some time, and noticed with pleasure that several times his answers made the judges smile.

It had not yet been said in verse: "I have laughed, therefore am I disarmed," but it had been said a great deal in prose. And Coconnas thought that he had partly disarmed his judges because they had smiled.

His examination over, he went back to his cell, singing so merrily that La Mole, for whom he was making all the noise, drew from it the happiest auguries.

La Mole was brought down, and like Coconnas saw with astonishment that the accusation had abandoned its first ground and had entered a new field. He was questioned as to his visits to Réné. He replied that he had gone to the Florentine only once. Then, if he had not ordered a waxen figure. He replied that Réné had showed him such a figure ready made. He was then asked if this figure did not represent a man. He replied that it represented a woman. Then, if the object of the charm was not to cause the death of the man. He replied that the purpose of the charm was to cause himself to be beloved by the woman.

These questions were put in a hundred different forms, but La Mole always replied in the same way. The judges looked at one another with a certain indecision, not knowing what to say or do before such simplicity, when a note brought to the Attorney-General solved the difficulty.

"*If the accused denies resort to the torture.*

"*C.*"

The attorney put the note into his pocket, smiled at La Mole, and politely dismissed him.

La Mole returned to his cell almost as reassured, if not as joyous, as Coconnas.

"I think everything is going well," said he.

An hour later he heard footsteps and saw a note slipped under his door, without seeing the hand that did it. He took it up, thinking that in all probability it came from the jailer?

Seeing it, a hope almost as acute as a disappointment sprang into his heart; he hoped it was from Marguerite, from whom he had had no news since he had been a prisoner.

He took it up with trembling hand, and almost died of joy as he looked at the handwriting.

"*Courage!*" said the note. "*I am watching over you.*"

"Ah! if she is watching," cried La Mole, covering with kisses the paper which had touched a hand so dear, "if she is watching, I am saved."

In order for La Mole to comprehend the note and rely with Coconnas on what the Piedmontese called his *invisible bucklers* it is necessary for us to conduct the reader to that small house, to that chamber in which the reminders of so many scenes of intoxicating happiness, so many half-evaporated perfumes, so many tender recollections, since become agonizing, were breaking the heart of a woman half reclining on velvet cushions.

"To be a queen, to be strong, young, rich, beautiful, and suffer what I suffer!" cried this woman; "oh! it is impossible!"

Then in her agitation she rose, paced up and down, stopped suddenly, pressed her burning forehead against the ice-cold marble, rose pale, her face covered with tears, wrung her hands, and crying aloud fell back again hopeless into a chair.

Suddenly the tapestry which separated the apartment of the Rue Cloche Percée from that in the Rue Tizon was raised, and the Duchesse de Nevers entered.

"Ah!" exclaimed Marguerite, "is it you? With what impatience I have waited for you! Well! What news?"

"Bad news, my poor friend. Catharine herself is hurrying on the trial, and at present is at Vincennes."

"And Réné?"

"Is arrested."

"Before you were able to speak to him?"

"Yes."

"And our prisoners?"

"I have news of them."

"From the jailer?"

"Yes."

"Well?"

"Well! They see each other every day. The day before yesterday they were searched. La Mole broke your picture to atoms rather than give it up."

"Dear La Mole!"

"Annibal laughed in the face of the inquisitors."

"Worthy Annibal! What then?"

"This morning they were questioned as to the flight of the king, his projects of rebellion in Navarre, and they said nothing."

"Oh! I knew they would keep silence; but silence will kill them as much as if they spoke."

"Yes, but we must save them."

"Have you thought over our plan?"

"Since yesterday I have thought of nothing else."

"Well?"

"I have just come to terms with Beaulieu. Ah! my dear queen, what a hard and greedy man! It will cost a man's life, and three hundred thousand crowns."

"You say he is hard and greedy—and yet he asks only the life of a man and three hundred thousand crowns. Why, that is nothing!"

"Nothing! Three hundred thousand crowns! Why, all your jewels and all mine would not be enough."

"Oh! that is nothing. The King of Navarre will pay something, the Duc d'Alençon will pay part, and my brother Charles will pay part, or if not"—

"See! what nonsense you talk. I have the money."

"You?"

"Yes, I."

"How did you get it?"

"Ah! that is telling!"

"Is it a secret?"

"For every one except you."

"Oh, my God!" said Marguerite, smiling through her tears, "did you steal it?"

"You shall judge."

"Well, let me."

"Do you remember that horrible Nantouillet?"

"The rich man, the usurer?"

"If you please."

"Well?"

"Well! One day seeing a certain blonde lady, with greenish eyes, pass by, wearing three rubies, one over her forehead, the other two over her temples, an arrangement which was very becoming to her, this rich man, this usurer, cried out:

"'For three kisses in the place of those three rubies I will give you three diamonds worth one hundred thousand crowns apiece!'"

"Well, Henriette?"

"Well, my dear, the diamonds appeared and are sold."

"Oh, Henriette! Henriette!" cried Marguerite.

"Well!" exclaimed the duchess in a bold tone at once innocent and sublime, which sums up the age and the woman, "well, I love Annibal!"

"That is true," said Marguerite, smiling and blushing at the same time, "you love him a very great deal, too much, perhaps."

And yet she pressed her friend's hand.

"So," continued Henriette, "thanks to our three diamonds, the three hundred thousand crowns and the man are ready."

"The man? What man?"

"The man to be killed; you forget a man must be killed."

"Have you found the necessary man?"

"Yes."

"At the same price?" asked Marguerite, smiling.

"At the same price I could have found a thousand," replied Henriette, "no, no, for five hundred crowns."

"For five hundred crowns you have found a man who has consented to be killed?"

"What can you expect? It is necessary for us to live."

"My dear friend, I do not understand you. Come, explain. Enigmas require too much time to guess at such a moment as this."

"Well, listen; the jailer to whom the keeping of La Mole and Coconnas is entrusted is an old soldier who knows what a wound is. He would like to help save our friends, but he does not want to lose his place. A blow of a dagger skilfully aimed will end the affair. We will give him a reward and the kingdom, indemnification. In this way the brave man will receive money from both parties and will renew the fable of the pelican."

"But," said Marguerite, "a thrust of a dagger"—

"Do not worry; Annibal will give it."

"Well," said Marguerite, "he has given as many as three blows of his sword to La Mole, and La Mole is not dead; there is therefore every reason to hope."

"Wicked woman! You deserve to have me stop."

"Oh! no, no; on the contrary, tell me the rest, I beg you. How are we to save them; come!"

"Well, this is the plan. The chapel is the only place in the castle where women can enter who are not prisoners. We are to be hidden behind the altar. Under the altar cloth they will find two daggers. The door of the vestry-room will be opened beforehand. Coconnas will strike the jailer, who will fall and pretend to be dead; we appear; each of us throws a cloak over the shoulders of her friend; we run with them through the small doors of the vestry-room, and as we have the password we can leave without hindrance."

"And once out?"

"Two horses will be waiting at the door; the men will spring on them, leave France, and reach Lorraine, whence now and then they will return incognito."

"Oh! you restore me to life," said Marguerite. "So we shall save them?"

"I am almost sure of it."

"Soon?"

"In three or four days. Beaulieu is to let us know."

"But if you were recognized in the vicinity of Vincennes that might upset our plan."

"How could any one recognize me? I go there as a nun, with a hood, thanks to which not even the tip of my nose is visible."

"We cannot take too many precautions."

"I know that well enough, by Heaven! as poor Annibal would say."

"Did you hear anything about the King of Navarre?"

"I was careful to ask."

"Well?"

"Well, he has never been so happy, apparently; he laughs, sings, eats, drinks, and sleeps well, and asks only one thing, and that is to be well guarded."

"He is right. And my mother?"

"I told you she is hurrying on the trial as fast as she can."

"Yes, but does she suspect anything about us?"

"How could she? Every one who has a secret is anxious to keep it. Ah! I know that she told the judges in Paris to be in readiness."

"Let us act quickly, Henriette. If our poor prisoners change their abode, everything will have to be done over again."

"Do not worry. I am as anxious as you to see them free."

"Oh, yes, I know that, and thank you, thank you a hundred times for all you have done."

"Adieu, Marguerite. I am going into the country again."

"Are you sure of Beaulieu?"

"I think so."

"Of the jailer?"

"He has promised."

"Of the horses?"

"They will be the best in the stables of the Duc de Nevers."

"I adore you, Henriette."

And Marguerite threw her arms about her friend's neck, after which the two women separated, promising to see each other again the next day, and every day, at the same place and hour.

These were the two charming and devoted creatures whom Coconnas, with so much reason, called his *invisible bucklers*.

CHAPTER LVII.

THE JUDGES.

"Well, my brave friend," said Coconnas to La Mole, when the two were together after the examination, at which, for the first time, the subject of the waxen image had been discussed, "it seems to me that everything is going on finely, and that it will not be long before the judges will dismiss us. And this diagnosis is entirely different from that of a dismissal by physicians. When the doctor gives up the patient it is because he cannot cure him, but when the judge gives up the accused it is because he has no further hope of having him beheaded."

"Yes," said La Mole; "and moreover, it seems to me, from the politeness and gentleness of the jailer and the looseness of the doors, that I recognize our kind friends; but I do not recognize Monsieur de Beaulieu, at least from what I had been told of him."

"I recognize him," said Coconnas; "only it will cost dearly. But one is a princess, the other a queen; both are rich, and they will never have so good an opportunity to use their money. Now let us go over our lesson. We are to be taken to the chapel, and left there in charge of our turnkey; we shall each find a dagger in the spot indicated. I am to make a hole in the body of our guide."

"Yes, but a slight one in the arm; otherwise you will rob him of his five hundred crowns."

"Ah, no; not in the arm, for in that case he would have to lose it, and it would be easy to see that it was given intentionally. No, it must be in his right side, gliding skilfully along his ribs; that would look natural, but in reality would be harmless."

"Well, aim for that, and then"—

"Then you will barricade the front door with benches while our two princesses rush from behind the altar, where they are to be hidden, and Henriette opens the vestry door. Ah, faith, how I love Henriette to-day! She must have been faithless to me in some way for me to feel as I do."

"And then," said La Mole, with the trembling voice which falls from lips like music, "then we shall reach the forest. A kiss given to each of us will make us strong and happy. Can you not picture us, Annibal, bending over our swift horses, our hearts gently oppressed? Oh, what a good thing is fear! Fear in the open air when one has one's naked sword at one's side, when one cries 'hurra' to the courser pricked by the spur, and which at each shout speeds the faster."

"Yes," said Coconnas, "but fear within four walls—what do you say to that, La Mole? I can speak of it, for I have felt something of it. When Beaulieu, with his pale face, entered my cell for the first time, behind him in the darkness shone halberds, and I heard a sinister sound of iron striking against iron. I swear to you I immediately thought of the Duc d'Alençon, and I expected to see his ugly face between the two hateful heads of the halberdiers. I was mistaken, however, and this was my sole consolation. But that was not all; night came, and I dreamed."

"So," said La Mole, who had been following his happy train of thought without paying attention to his friend, "so they have foreseen everything, even the place in which we are to hide. We shall go to Lorraine, dear friend. In reality I should rather have had it Navarre, for there I should have been with her, but Navarre is too far; Nancey would be better; besides, once there, we should be only eighty leagues from Paris. Have you any feeling of regret, Annibal, at leaving this place?"

"Ah, no! the idea! Although I confess I am leaving everything that belongs to me."

"Well, could we manage to take the worthy jailer with us instead of"—

"He would not go," said Coconnas, "he would lose too much. Think of it! five hundred crowns from us, a reward from the government; promotion, perhaps; how happy will be that fellow's life when I shall have killed him! But what is the matter?"

"Nothing! An idea came to me."

"It is not a funny one, apparently, for you are frightfully pale."

"I was wondering why they should take us to the chapel."

"Why," said Coconnas, "to receive the sacrament. This is the time for it, I think."

"But," said La Mole, "they take only those condemned to death or the torture to the chapel."

"Oh!" said Coconnas, becoming somewhat pale in turn, "this deserves our attention. Let us question the good man whom I am to split open. Here, turnkey!"

"Did monsieur call?" asked the jailer, who had been keeping watch at the top of the stairs.

"Yes; come here."

"Well?"

"It has been arranged that we are to escape from the chapel, has it not?"

"Hush!" said the turnkey, looking round him in terror.

"Do not worry; no one can hear us."

"Yes, monsieur; it is from the chapel."

"They are to take us to the chapel, then?"

"Yes; that is the custom."

"The custom?"

"Yes; it is customary to allow every one condemned to death to pass the night in the chapel."

Coconnas and La Mole shuddered and glanced at each other.

"You think we are condemned to death, then?"

"Certainly. You, too, must think so."

"Why should we think so?" asked La Mole.

"Certainly; otherwise you would not have arranged everything for your escape."

"Do you know, there is reason in what he says!" said Coconnas to La Mole.

"Yes; and what I know besides is that we are playing a close game, apparently."

"But do you think I am risking nothing?" said the turnkey. "If in a moment of excitement monsieur should make a mistake"—

"Well! by Heaven! I wish I were in your place," said Coconnas, slowly, "and had to deal with no hand but this; with no sword except the one which is to graze you."

"Condemned to death!" murmured La Mole, "why, that is impossible!"

"Impossible!" said the turnkey, naïvely, "and why?"

"Hush!" said Coconnas, "I think some one is opening the lower door."

"To your cells, gentlemen, to your cells!" cried the jailer, hurriedly.

"When do you think the trial will take place?" asked La Mole.

"To-morrow, or later. But be easy; those who must be informed shall be."

"Then let us embrace each other and bid farewell to these walls."

514

The two friends rushed into each other's arms and then returned to their cells, La Mole sighing, Coconnas singing.

Nothing new happened until seven o'clock. Night fell dark and rainy over the prison of Vincennes, a perfect night for flight. The evening meal was brought to Coconnas, who ate with his usual appetite, thinking of the pleasure he would feel in being soaked in the rain, which was pattering against the walls, and already preparing himself to fall asleep to the dull, monotonous murmur of the wind, when suddenly it seemed to him that this wind, to which he occasionally listened with a feeling of melancholy never before experienced by him until he came to prison, whistled more strangely than usual under the doors, and that the stove roared with a louder noise than common. This had happened every time one of the cells above or opposite him was opened. It was by this noise that Annibal always knew the jailer was coming from La Mole's cell.

But this time it was in vain that Coconnas remained with eye and ear alert.

The moments passed; no one came.

"This is strange," said Coconnas, "La Mole's door has been opened and not mine. Could La Mole have called? Can he be ill? What does it mean?"

With a prisoner everything is a cause for suspicion and anxiety, as everything is a cause for joy and hope.

Half an hour passed, then an hour, then an hour and a half.

Coconnas was beginning to grow sleepy from anger when the grating of the lock made him spring to his feet.

"Oh!" said he, "has the time come for us to leave and are they going to take us to the chapel without condemning us? By Heaven, what joy it would be to escape on such a night! It is as dark as an oven! I hope the horses are not blind."

He was about to ask some jocular question of the turnkey when he saw the latter put his finger to his lips and roll his eyes significantly. Behind the jailer Coconnas heard sounds and perceived shadows.

Suddenly in the midst of the darkness he distinguished two helmets, on which the smoking candle threw a yellow light.

"Oh!" said he in a low voice, "what is this sinister procession? What is going to happen?"

The jailer replied by a sigh which greatly resembled a groan.

"By Heaven!" murmured Coconnas; "what a wretched existence! always on the ragged edge; never on firm land; either we paddle in a hundred feet of water or we hover above the clouds; never a happy medium. Well, where are we going?"

"Follow the halberdiers, monsieur," repeated the same voice.

He had to obey. Coconnas left his room, and perceived the dark man whose voice had been so disagreeable. He was a clerk, small and hunchbacked, who no doubt had put on the gown in order to hide his bandy legs, as well as his back. He slowly descended the winding stairs. At the first landing the guards paused.

"That is a good deal to go down," murmured Coconnas, "but not enough."

The door opened. The prisoner had the eye of a lynx and the scent of a bloodhound. He scented the judges and saw in the shadow the silhouette of a man with bare arms; the latter sight made the perspiration mount to his brow. Nevertheless, he assumed his most smiling manner, and entered the room with his head tipped to one side, and his hand on his hip, after the most approved manner of the times.

A curtain was raised, and Coconnas perceived the judges and the clerks.

A few feet away La Mole was seated on a bench.

Coconnas was led to the front of the tribunal. Arrived there, he stopped, nodded and smiled to La Mole, and then waited.

"What is your name, monsieur?" inquired the president.

"Marcus Annibal de Coconnas," replied the gentleman with perfect ease. "Count de Montpantier, Chenaux, and other places; but they are known, I presume."

"Where were you born?"

"At Saint Colomban, near Suza."

"How old are you?"

"Twenty-seven years and three months."

"Good!" said the president.

"This pleases him, apparently," said Coconnas.

"Now," said the president after a moment's silence which gave the clerk time to write down the answers of the accused; "what was your reason for leaving the service of Monsieur d'Alençon?"

"To rejoin my friend Monsieur de la Mole, who had already left the duke three days before."

"What were you doing the day of the hunt, when you were arrested?"

"Why," said Coconnas, "I was hunting."

"The King was also present at that hunt, and was there seized with the first attack of the malady from which he is at present suffering."

"I was not near the King, and I can say nothing about this. I was even ignorant of the fact that he had been ill."

The judges looked at one another with a smile of incredulity.

"Ah! you were ignorant of his Majesty's illness, were you?" said the president.

"Yes, monsieur, and I am sorry to hear of it. Although the King of France is not my king, I have a great deal of sympathy for him."

"Indeed!"

"On my honor! It is different so far as his brother the Duc d'Alençon is concerned. The latter I confess"—

"We have nothing to do with the Duc d'Alençon, monsieur; this concerns his Majesty."

"Well, I have already told you that I am his very humble servant," said Coconnas, turning about in an adorably impudent fashion.

"If as you pretend, monsieur, you are really his servant, will you tell us what you know of a certain waxen figure?"

"Ah, good! we have come back to the figure, have we?"

"Yes, monsieur; does this displease you?"

"On the contrary, I prefer it; go ahead."

"Why was this statue found in Monsieur de la Mole's apartments?"

"At Monsieur de la Mole's? At Réné's, you mean?"

"You acknowledge that it exists, then, do you?"

"Why, if you will show it to me."

"Here it is. Is this the one you know?"

"It is."

"Clerk," said the president, "write down that the accused recognizes the image as the one seen at Monsieur de la Mole's."

"No, no!" said Coconnas, "do not let us misunderstand each other—as the one seen at Réné's."

"At Réné's; very good! On what day?"

"The only day La Mole and myself were at Réné's."

"You admit, then, that you were at Réné's with Monsieur de la Mole?"

"Why, did I ever deny it?"

"Clerk, write down that the accused admits having gone to Réné's to work conjurations."

"Stop there, Monsieur le Président. Moderate your enthusiasm, I beg you. I did not say that at all."

"You deny having been at Réné's to work conjurations?"

"I deny it. The magic took place by accident. It was unpremeditated."

"But it took place?"

"I cannot deny that something resembling a charm did take place."

"Clerk, write down that the accused admits that he obtained at Réné's a charm against the life of the King."

"What! against the King's life? That is an infamous lie! There was no charm obtained against the life of the King."

"You see, gentlemen!" said La Mole.

"Silence!" said the president; then turning to the clerk: "Against the life of the King," he continued. "Have you that?"

"Why, no, no!" cried Coconnas. "Besides, the figure is not that of a man, but of a woman."

"What did I tell you, gentlemen?" said La Mole.

"Monsieur de la Mole," said the president, "answer when you are questioned, but do not interrupt the examination of others."

"So you say that it is a woman?"

"Certainly I say so."

"In that case, why did it have a crown and a cloak?"

"By Heaven!" said Coconnas, "that is simple enough, because it was"—

La Mole rose and put his finger on his lips.

"That is so," said Coconnas, "what was I going to say that could possibly concern these gentlemen?"

"You persist in stating that the figure is that of a woman?"

"Yes; certainly I persist."

"And you refuse to say what woman?"

"A woman of my country," said La Mole, "whom I loved and by whom I wished to be loved in return."

"We are not asking you, Monsieur de la Mole," said the president; "keep silent, therefore, or you shall be gagged."

"Gagged!" exclaimed Coconnas; "what do you mean, monsieur of the black robe? My friend gagged? A gentleman! the idea!"

"Bring in Réné," said the Attorney-General Laguesle.

"Yes; bring in Réné," said Coconnas; "we shall see who is right here, we two or you three."

Réné entered, pale, aged, and almost unrecognizable to the two friends, bowed under the weight of the crime he was about to commit much more than because of those he had already committed.

"Maître Réné," said the judge, "do you recognize the two accused persons here present?"

"Yes, monsieur," replied Réné, in a voice which betrayed his emotion.

"From having seen them where?"

"In several places; and especially at my house."

"How many times did they go to your house?"

"Once only."

As Réné spoke the face of Coconnas expanded; La Mole's, on the contrary, looked as though he had a presentiment of evil.

"For what purpose were they at your house?"

Réné seemed to hesitate a moment.

"To order me to make a waxen figure," said he.

"Pardon me, Maître Réné," said Coconnas, "you are making a slight mistake."

"Silence!" said the president; then turning to Réné, "was this figure to be that of a man or a woman?"

"A man," replied Réné.

Coconnas sprang up as if he had received an electric shock.

"A man!" he exclaimed.

"A man," repeated Réné, but in so low a tone that the president scarcely heard him.

"Why did this figure of a man have on a mantle and a crown?"

"Because it represented a king."

"Infamous liar!" cried Coconnas, infuriated.

"Keep still, Coconnas, keep still," interrupted La Mole, "let the man speak; every one has a right to sell his own soul."

"But not the bodies of others, by Heaven!"

"And what was the meaning of the needle in the heart of the figure, with the letter 'M' on a small banner?"

"The needle was emblematical of the sword or the dagger; the letter 'M' stands for *mort*."

Coconnas sprang forward as though to strangle Réné, but four guards restrained him.

"That will do," said the Attorney Laguesle, "the court is sufficiently informed. Take the prisoners to the waiting-room."

"But," exclaimed Coconnas, "it is impossible to hear one's self accused of such things without protesting."

"Protest, monsieur, no one will hinder you. Guards, did you hear?"

The guards seized the two prisoners and led them out, La Mole by one door, Coconnas by another.

Then the attorney signed to the man whom Coconnas had perceived in the shadow, and said to him:

"Do not go away, my good fellow, you shall have work this evening."

"Which shall I begin with, monsieur?" asked the man, respectfully holding his cap in his hand.

"With that one," said the president, pointing to La Mole, who could still be seen disappearing in the distance between the two guards. Then approaching Réné, who stood trembling, expecting to be led back to the cell in which he had been confined:

"You have spoken well, monsieur," said he to him, "you need not worry. Both the King and the queen shall know that it is to you they are indebted for the truth of this affair."

But instead of giving him strength, this promise seemed to terrify Réné, whose only answer was a deep sigh.

CHAPTER LVIII.

THE TORTURE OF THE BOOT.

It was only when he had been led away to his new cell and the door was locked on him that Coconnas, left alone, and no longer sustained by the discussion with the judges and his anger at Réné, fell into a train of mournful reflections.

"It seems to me," thought he, "that matters are turning against us, and that it is about time to go to the chapel. I suspect we are to be condemned to death. It looks so. I especially fear being condemned to death by sentences pronounced behind closed doors, in a fortified castle, before faces as ugly as those about me. They really wish to cut off our heads. Well! well! I repeat what I said just now, it is time to go to chapel."

These words, uttered in a low tone, were followed by a silence, which in turn was broken by a cry, shrill, piercing, lugubrious, unlike anything human. It seemed to penetrate the thick walls, and vibrate against the iron bars.

In spite of himself Coconnas shivered; and yet he was so brave that his courage was like that of wild beasts. He stood still, doubting that the cry was human, and taking it for the sound of the wind in the trees or for one of the many night noises which seem to rise or descend from the two unknown worlds between which floats our globe. Then he heard it again, shriller, more prolonged, more piercing than before, and this time not only did Coconnas distinguish the agony of the human tone in it, but he thought it sounded like La Mole's.

As he realized this the Piedmontese forgot that he was confined behind two doors, three gates, and a wall twelve feet thick. He hurled his entire weight against the sides of the cell as though to push them out and rush to the aid of the victim, crying, "Are they killing some one here?" But he unexpectedly encountered the wall and the shock hurled him back against a stone bench on which he sank down.

Then there was silence.

"Oh, they have killed him!" he murmured; "it is abominable! And one is without arms, here, and cannot defend one's self!"

He groped about.

"Ah! this iron chain!" he cried, "I will take it and woe to him who comes near me!"

Coconnas rose, seized the iron chain, and with a pull shook it so violently that it was clear that with two such efforts he would wrench it away.

But suddenly the door opened and the light from a couple of torches fell into the cell.

"Come, monsieur," said the same voice which had sounded so disagreeable to him, and which this time, in making itself heard three floors below, did not seem to him to have acquired any new charm.

"Come, monsieur, the court is awaiting you."

"Good," said Coconnas, dropping his ring, "I am to hear my sentence, am I not?"

"Yes, monsieur."

"Oh! I breathe again; let us go," said he.

He followed the usher, who preceded him with measured tread, holding his black rod.

In spite of the satisfaction he had felt at first, as he walked along Coconnas glanced anxiously about him.

"Oh!" he murmured, "I do not perceive my good jailer. I confess I miss him."

They entered the hall the judges had just left, in which a man was standing alone, whom Coconnas recognized as the Attorney-General. In the course of the examination the latter had spoken several times, always with an animosity easy to understand.

He was the one whom Catharine, both by letter and in person, had specially charged with the trial.

At the farther end of this room, the corners of which were lost in darkness behind a partly raised curtain, Coconnas saw such dreadful sights that he felt his limbs give away, and cried out: "Oh, my God!"

It was not without cause that the cry had been uttered. The sight was indeed terrible. The portion of the room hidden during the trial by the curtain, which was now drawn back, looked like the entrance to hell.

A wooden horse was there, to which were attached ropes, pulleys, and other accessories of torture. Further on glowed a brazier, which threw its lurid glare on the surrounding objects, and which added to the terror of the spectacle. Against one of the pillars which supported the ceiling stood a man motionless as a statue, holding a rope in his hand. He looked as though made of the stone of the column against which he leaned. To the walls above the stone benches, between iron links, chains were suspended and blades glittered.

"Oh!" murmured Coconnas, "the chamber of horrors is all ready, apparently waiting only for the patient! What can it mean?"

"On your knees, Marc Annibal Coconnas," said a voice which caused that gentleman to raise his head. "On your knees to hear the sentence just pronounced on you!"

This was an invitation against which the whole soul of Annibal instinctively rebelled.

But as he was about to refuse two men placed their hands on his shoulders so unexpectedly and so suddenly that his knees bent under him on the pavement. The voice continued.

"Sentence of the court sitting in the prison of Vincennes on Marc Annibal de Coconnas, accused and convicted of high treason, of an attempt to poison, of sacrilege and magic against the person of the King, of a conspiracy against the kingdom, and of having by his pernicious counsels driven a prince of the blood to rebellion."

At each charge Coconnas had shaken his head, keeping time like a fractious child. The judge continued:

"In consequence of which, the aforesaid Marc Annibal de Coconnas shall be taken from prison to the Place Saint Jean en Grève to be there beheaded; his property shall be confiscated; his woods cut down to the height of six feet; his castles destroyed, and a post planted there with a copper plate bearing an inscription of his crime and punishment."

"As for my head," said Coconnas, "I know you will cut that off, for it is in France, and in great jeopardy; but as for my woods and castles, I defy all the saws and axes of this most Christian kingdom to harm them."

"Silence!" said the judge; and he continued:

"Furthermore, the aforesaid Coconnas"—

"What!" interrupted Coconnas, "is something more to be done to me after my head is cut off? Oh! that seems to me very hard!"

"No, monsieur," said the judge, "*before*."

And he resumed:

"Furthermore, the aforesaid Coconnas before the execution of his sentence shall undergo the severest torture, consisting of ten wedges"—

Coconnas sprang up, flashing a burning glance at the judge.

"And for what?" he cried, finding no other words but these simple ones to express the thousand thoughts that surged through his mind.

In reality this was complete ruin to Coconnas' hopes. He would not be taken to the chapel until after the torture, from which many frequently died. The braver and stronger the victim, the more likely he was to die, for it was considered an act of cowardice to confess; and so long as the prisoner refused to confess the torture was continued, and not only continued, but increased.

The judge did not reply to Coconnas; the rest of the sentence answered for him. He continued:

"In order to compel the aforesaid Coconnas to confess in regard to his accomplices, and the details of the plan and conspiracy."

"By Heaven!" cried Coconnas; "this is what I call infamous; more than infamous—cowardly!"

Accustomed to the anger of his victims, which suffering always changed to tears, the impassible judge merely made a sign.

Coconnas was seized by the feet and the shoulders, overpowered, laid on his back, and bound to the rack before he was able even to see those who did the act.

"Wretches!" shouted he, in a paroxysm of fury, straining the bed and the cords so that the tormentors themselves drew back. "Wretches! torture me, twist me, break me to pieces, but you shall know nothing, I swear! Ah! you think, do you, that it is with pieces of wood and steel that a gentleman of my name is made to speak? Go ahead! I defy you!"

"Prepare to write, clerk," said the judge.

"Yes, prepare," shouted Coconnas; "and if you write everything I am going to tell you you infamous hangmen, you will be kept busy. Write! write!"

"Have you anything you wish to confess?" asked the judge in his calm voice.

"Nothing; not a word! Go to the devil!"

"You had better reflect, monsieur. Come, executioner, adjust the boot."

At these words the man, who until then had stood motionless, the ropes in his hand, stepped forward from the pillar and slowly approached Coconnas, who turned and made a grimace at him.

It was Maître Caboche, the executioner of the provostship of Paris.

A look of sad surprise showed itself on the face of Coconnas, who, instead of crying out and growing agitated, lay without moving, unable to take his eyes from the face of the forgotten friend who appeared at that moment.

Without moving a muscle of his face, without showing that he had ever seen Coconnas anywhere except on the rack, Caboche placed two planks between the limbs of the victim, two others outside of his limbs, and bound them securely together by means of the rope he held in his hand.

This was the arrangement called the "boot."

For ordinary torture six wedges were inserted between the two planks, which, on being forced apart, crushed the flesh.

For severe torture ten wedges were inserted, and then the planks not only broke the flesh but the bones.

The preliminaries over, Maître Caboche slipped the end of the wedge between the two planks, then, mallet in hand, bent on one knee and looked at the judge.

"Do you wish to speak?" said the latter.

"No," resolutely answered Coconnas, although he felt the perspiration rise to his brow and his hair begin to stand on end.

"Proceed, then," said the judge. "Insert the first wedge."

Caboche raised his arm, with its heavy mallet, and struck the wedge a tremendous blow, which gave forth a dull sound. The rack shook.

Coconnas did not utter a single word at the first wedge, which usually caused the most resolute to groan. Moreover, the only expression on his face was that of indescribable astonishment. He watched Caboche in amazement, who, with arm raised, half turned towards the judge, stood ready to repeat the blow.

"What was your idea in hiding in the forest?" asked the judge.

"To sit down in the shade," replied Coconnas.

"Proceed," said the judge.

Caboche gave a second blow which resounded like the first.

Coconnas did not move a muscle; he continued to watch the executioner with the same expression.

The judge frowned.

"He is a hard Christian," he murmured; "has the wedge entered?"

Caboche bent down to look, and in doing so said to Coconnas:

"Cry out, you poor fellow!"

Then rising:

"Up to the head, monsieur," said he.

"Second wedge," said the judge, coldly.

The words of Caboche explained all to Coconnas. The worthy executioner had rendered his friend the greatest service in his power: he was sparing him not only pain, but more, the shame of confession, by driving in wedges of leather, the upper part of which was covered with wood, instead of oak wedges. In this way he was leaving him all his strength to face the scaffold.

"Ah! kind, kind Caboche," murmured Coconnas, "fear nothing; I will cry out since you ask me to, and if you are not satisfied it will be because you are hard to please."

Meanwhile Caboche had introduced between the planks the end of a wedge larger than the first.

"Strike," cried the judge.

At this word Caboche struck as if with a single blow he would demolish the entire prison of Vincennes.

"Ah! ah! Stop! stop!" cried Coconnas; "a thousand devils! you are breaking my bones! Take care!"

"Ah!" said the judge, smiling, "the second seems to take effect; that surprises me."

Coconnas panted like a pair of bellows.

"What were you doing in the forest?" asked the judge.

"By Heaven! I have already told you. I was enjoying the fresh air."

"Proceed," said the judge.

"Confess," whispered Caboche.

"What?"

"Anything you wish, but something."

And he dealt a second blow no less light than the former.

Coconnas thought he would strangle himself in his efforts to cry out.

"Oh! oh!" said he; "what is it you want to know, monsieur? By whose order I was in the forest?"

"Yes."

"I was there by order of Monsieur d'Alençon."

"Write," said the judge.

"If I committed a crime in setting a trap for the King of Navarre," continued Coconnas, "I was only an instrument, monsieur, and I was obeying my master."

The clerk began to write.

"Oh! you denounced me, pale-face!" murmured the victim; "but just wait!"

And he related the visit of François to the King of Navarre, the interviews between De Mouy and Monsieur d'Alençon, the story of the red cloak, all as though he were just remembering them between the blows of the hammer.

At length he had given such precise, terrible, uncontestable evidence against D'Alençon, making it seem as though it was extorted from him only by the pain,—he grimaced, roared, and yelled so naturally, and in so many different tones of voice,—that the judge himself became terrified at having to record details so compromising to a son of France.

"Well!" said Caboche to himself, "here is a gentleman who does not need to say things twice, and who gives full measure of work to the clerk. Great God! what if, instead of leather, the wedges had been of wood!"

Coconnas was excused from the last wedge; but he had had nine others, which were enough to have crushed his limbs completely.

The judge reminded the victim of the mercy allowed him on account of his confession, and withdrew.

The prisoner was alone with Caboche.

"Well," asked the latter, "how are you?"

"Ah! my friend! my kind friend, my dear Caboche!" exclaimed Coconnas.

"You may be sure I shall be grateful all my life for what you have done for me."

"The deuce! but you are right, monsieur, for if they knew what I have done it would be I who would have to take your place on the rack, and they would not treat me as I have treated you."

"But how did the idea come to you?"

"Well," said Caboche, wrapping the limbs of Coconnas in bloody bands of linen; "I knew you had been arrested, and that your trial was going on. I knew that Queen Catharine was anxious for your death. I guessed that they would put you to the torture and consequently took my precautions."

"At the risk of what might have happened?"

"Monsieur," said Caboche, "you are the only gentleman who ever gave me his hand, and we all have memories and hearts, even though we are hangmen, and perhaps for that very reason. You will see to-morrow how well I will do my work."

"To-morrow?" said Coconnas.

"Yes."

"What work?"

Caboche looked at Coconnas in amazement.

"What work? Have you forgotten the sentence?"

"Ah! yes, of course! the sentence!" said Coconnas; "I had forgotten it."

The fact is that Coconnas had not really forgotten it, but he had not been thinking of it.

What he was thinking of was the chapel, the knife hidden under the altar cloth, of Henriette and the queen, of the vestry door, and the two horses waiting on the edge of the forest; he was thinking of liberty, of the ride in the open air, of safety beyond the boundaries of France.

"Now," said Caboche, "you must be taken skilfully from the rack to the litter. Do not forget that for every one, even the guards, your limbs are broken, and that at every jar you must give a cry."

"Ah! ah!" cried Coconnas, as the two assistants advanced.

"Come! come! Courage," said Caboche, "if you cry out already, what will you do in a little while?"

"My dear Caboche," said Coconnas, "do not have me touched, I beg, by your estimable acolytes; perhaps their hands are not as light as yours."

"Place the litter near the racks," said Caboche.

The attendants obeyed. Maître Caboche raised Coconnas in his arms as if he were a child and laid him in the litter, but in spite of every care Coconnas uttered loud shrieks.

The jailer appeared with a lantern.

"To the chapel," said he.

The bearers started after Coconnas had given Caboche a second grasp of the hand. The first had been of too much use to the Piedmontese for him not to repeat it.

———

CHAPTER LIX.

THE CHAPEL.

In profound silence the mournful procession crossed the two drawbridges of the fortress and the courtyard which leads to the chapel, through the windows of which a pale light colored the white faces of the red-robed priests.

Coconnas eagerly breathed the night air, although it was heavy with rain. He looked at the profound darkness and rejoiced that everything seemed propitious for the flight of himself and his companion. It required all his will-power, all his prudence, all his self-control to keep from springing from the litter when on entering the chapel he perceived near the choir, three feet from the altar, a figure wrapped in a great white cloak.

It was La Mole.

The two soldiers who accompanied the litter stopped outside of the door.

"Since they have done us the final favor of once more leaving us together," said Coconnas in a drawling voice, "take me to my friend."

The bearers had had no different order, and made no objection to assenting to Coconnas's demand.

La Mole was gloomy and pale; his head rested against the marble wall; his black hair, bathed with profuse perspiration, gave to his face the dull pallor of ivory, and seemed still to stand on end.

At a sign from the turnkey the two attendants went to find the priest for whom Coconnas had asked.

This was the signal agreed on.

Coconnas followed them with anxious eyes; but he was not the only one whose glance was riveted on them.

Scarcely had they disappeared when two women rushed from behind the altar and hurried to the choir with cries of joy, rousing the air like a warm and restless breeze which precedes a storm.

Marguerite rushed towards La Mole, and caught him in her arms.

La Mole uttered a piercing shriek, like one of the cries Coconnas had heard in his dungeon and which had so terrified him.

"My God! What is the matter, La Mole?" cried Marguerite, springing back in fright.

La Mole uttered a deep moan and raised his hands to his eyes as though to hide Marguerite from his sight.

The queen was more terrified at the silence and this gesture than she had been at the shriek.

"Oh!" she exclaimed, "what is the matter? You are covered with blood."

Coconnas, who had rushed to the altar for the dagger, and who was already holding Henriette in his arms, now came back.

"Rise," said Marguerite, "rise, I beg you! You see the time has come."

A hopelessly sad smile passed over the white lips of La Mole, who seemed almost unequal to the effort.

"Beloved queen!" said the young man, "you counted without Catharine, and consequently without a crime. I underwent the torture, my bones are broken, my whole body is nothing but a wound, and the effort I make now to press my lips to your forehead causes me pain worse than death."

Pale and trembling, La Mole touched his lips to the queen's brow.

"The rack!" cried Coconnas, "I, too, suffered it, but did not the executioner do for you what he did for me?"

Coconnas related everything.

"Ah!" said La Mole, "I see; you gave him your hand the day of our visit; I forgot that all men are brothers, and was proud. God has punished me for it!"

La Mole clasped his hands.

Coconnas and the women exchanged a glance of indescribable terror.

"Come," said the jailer, who until then had stood at the door to keep watch, and had now returned, "do not waste time, dear Monsieur de Coconnas; give me my thrust of the dagger, and do it in a way worthy of a gentleman, for they are coming."

Marguerite knelt down before La Mole, as if she were one of the marble figures on a tomb, near the image of the one buried in it.

"Come, my friend," said Coconnas, "I am strong, I will carry you, I will put you on your horse, or even hold you in front of me, if you cannot sit in the saddle; but let us start. You hear what this good man says; it is a question of life and death."

La Mole made a superhuman struggle, a final effort.

"Yes," said he, "it is a question of life or death."

And he strove to rise.

Annibal took him by the arm and raised him. During the process La Mole uttered dull moans, but when Coconnas let go of him to attend to the turnkey, and when he was supported only by the two women his legs gave way, and in spite of the effort of Marguerite, who was wildly sobbing, he fell back in a heap, and a piercing shriek which he could not restrain echoed pitifully throughout the vaults of the chapel, which vibrated long after.

"You see," said La Mole, painfully, "you see, my queen! Leave me; give me one last kiss and go. I did not confess, Marguerite, and our secret is hidden in our love and will die with me. Good-by, my queen, my queen."

Marguerite, herself almost lifeless, clasped the dear head in her arms, and pressed on it a kiss which was almost holy.

"You Annibal," said La Mole, "who have been spared these agonies, who are still young and able to live, flee, flee; give me the supreme consolation, my dear friend, of knowing you have escaped."

"Time flies," said the jailer; "make haste."

Henriette gently strove to lead Annibal to the door. Marguerite on her knees before La Mole, sobbing, and with dishevelled hair, looked like a Magdalene.

"Flee, Annibal," said La Mole, "flee; do not give our enemies the joyful spectacle of the death of two innocent men."

Coconnas quietly disengaged himself from Henriette, who was leading him to the door, and with a gesture so solemn that it seemed majestic said:

"Madame, first give the five hundred crowns we promised to this man."

"Here they are," said Henriette.

Then turning to La Mole, and shaking his head sadly:

"As for you, La Mole, you do me wrong to think for an instant that I could leave you. Have I not sworn to live and die with you? But you are suffering so, my poor friend, that I forgive you."

And seating himself resolutely beside his friend Coconnas leaned forward and kissed his forehead.

Then gently, as gently as a mother would do to her child, he drew the dear head towards him, until it rested on his breast.

Marguerite was numb. She had picked up the dagger which Coconnas had just let fall.

"Oh, my queen," said La Mole, extending his arms to her, and understanding her thought, "my beloved queen, do not forget that I die in order to destroy the slightest suspicion of our love!"

"But what can I do for you, then," cried Marguerite, in despair, "if I cannot die with you?"

"You can make death sweet to me," replied La Mole; "you can come to me with smiling lips."

Marguerite advanced and clasped her hands as if asking him to speak.

"Do you remember that evening, Marguerite, when in exchange for the life I then offered you, and which to-day I lay down for you, you made me a sacred promise."

Marguerite gave a start.

"Ah! you do remember," said La Mole, "for you shudder."

"Yes, yes, I remember, and on my soul, Hyacinthe, I will keep that promise."

Marguerite raised her hand towards the altar, as if calling God a second time to witness her oath.

La Mole's face lighted up as if the vaulted roof of the chapel had opened and a heavenly ray had fallen on him.

"They are coming!" said the jailer.

Marguerite uttered a cry, and rushed to La Mole, but the fear of increasing his agony made her pause trembling before him.

Henriette pressed her lips to Coconnas's brow, and said to him:

"My Annibal, I understand, and I am proud of you. I well know that your heroism makes you die, and for that heroism I love you. Before God I will always love you more than all else, and what Marguerite has sworn to do for La Mole, although I know not what it is, I swear I will do for you also."

And she held out her hand to Marguerite.

"Ah! thank you," said Coconnas; "that is the way to speak."

"Before you leave me, my queen," said La Mole, "one last favor. Give me some last souvenir, that I may kiss it as I mount the scaffold."

"Ah! yes, yes," cried Marguerite; "here!"

And she unfastened from her neck a small gold reliquary suspended from a chain of the same metal.

"Here," said she, "is a holy relic which I have worn from childhood. My mother put it around my neck when I was very little and she still loved me. It was given me by my uncle, Pope Clement and has never left me. Take it! take it!"

La Mole took it, and kissed it passionately.

"They are at the door," said the jailer; "flee, ladies, flee!"

The two women rushed behind the altar and disappeared.

At the same moment the priest entered.

———

CHAPTER LX.

THE PLACE SAINT JEAN EN GRÈVE.

It was seven o'clock in the morning, and a noisy crowd was waiting in the squares, the streets, and on the quays. At six o'clock a tumbril, the same in which after their duel the two friends had been conveyed half dead to the Louvre, had started from Vincennes and slowly crossed the Rue Saint Antoine. Along its route the spectators, so huddled together that they crushed one another, seemed like statues with fixed eyes and open mouths.

This day there was to be a heartrending spectacle offered by the queen mother to the people of Paris.

On some straw in the tumbril, we have mentioned, which was making its way through the streets, were two young men, bareheaded, and entirely clothed in black, leaning against each other. Coconnas supported on his knees La Mole, whose head hung over the sides of the tumbril, and whose eyes wandered vaguely here and there.

The crowd, eager to see even the bottom of the vehicle, crowded forward, lifted itself up, stood on tiptoe, mounted posts, clung to the angles of the walls, and appeared satisfied only when it had succeeded in seeing every detail of the two bodies which were going from the torture to death.

It had been rumored that La Mole was dying without having confessed one of the charges imputed to him; while, on the contrary, Coconnas, it was asserted, could not endure the torture, and had revealed everything.

So there were cries on all sides:

"See the red-haired one! It was he who confessed! It was he who told everything! He is a coward, and is the cause of the other's death! The other is a brave fellow, and confessed nothing."

The two young men heard perfectly, the one the praises, the other the reproaches, which accompanied their funeral march; and while La Mole pressed the hands of his friend a sublime expression of scorn lighted up the face of the Piedmontese, who from the foul tumbril gazed upon the stupid mob as if he were looking down from a triumphal car.

Misfortune had done its heavenly work, and had ennobled the face of Coconnas, as death was about to render divine his soul.

"Are we nearly there?" asked La Mole. "I can stand no more, my friend. I feel as if I were going to faint."

"Wait! wait! La Mole, we are passing by the Rue Tizon and the Rue Cloche Percée; look! look!"

"Oh! raise me, raise me, that I may once more gaze on that happy abode."

Coconnas raised his hand and touched the shoulder of the executioner, who sat at the front of the tumbril driving.

"Maître," said he, "do us the kindness to stop a moment opposite the Rue Tizon."

Caboche nodded in assent, and drew rein at the place indicated.

Aided by Coconnas, La Mole raised himself with an effort, and with eyes blinded by tears gazed at the small house, silent and mute, deserted as a tomb. A groan burst from him, and in a low voice he murmured:

"Adieu, adieu, youth, love, life!"

And his head fell forward on his breast.

"Courage," said Coconnas; "we may perhaps find all this above."

"Do you think so?" murmured La Mole.

"I think so, because the priest said so; and above all, because I hope so. But do not faint, my friend, or these staring wretches will laugh at us."

Caboche heard the last words and whipping his horse with one hand he extended the other, unseen by any one, to Coconnas. It contained a small sponge saturated with a powerful stimulant, and La Mole, after smelling it and rubbing his forehead with it, felt himself revived and reanimated.

"Ah!" said La Mole, "I am better," and he kissed the reliquary, which he wore around his neck.

As they turned a corner of the quay and reached the small edifice built by Henry II. they saw the scaffold rising bare and bloody on its platform above the heads of the crowd.

"Dear friend," said La Mole, "I wish I might be the first to die."

Coconnas again touched the hangman's shoulder.

"What is it, my gentleman?" said the latter, turning around.

"My good fellow," said Coconnas, "you will do what you can for me, will you not? You said you would."

"Yes, and I repeat it."

"My friend has suffered more than I and consequently has less strength"—

"Well?"

"Well, he says that it would cause him too much pain to see me die first. Besides, if I were to die before him he would have no one to support him on the scaffold."

"Very well," said Caboche, wiping away a tear with the back of his hand; "be easy, it shall be as you wish."

"And with one blow, eh?" said the Piedmontese in a low tone.

"With one blow."

"That is well. If you have to make up for it, make up on me."

The tumbril stopped. They had arrived. Coconnas put on his hat.

A murmur like that of the waves at sea reached the ears of La Mole. He strove to rise, but strength failed him. Caboche and Coconnas supported him under the arms.

The place was paved with heads; the steps of the Hôtel de Ville seemed an amphitheatre peopled with spectators. Each window was filled with animated faces, the eyes of which seemed on fire.

When they saw the handsome young man, no longer able to support himself on his bruised legs, make a last effort to reach the scaffold, a great shout rose like a cry of universal desolation. Men groaned and women uttered plaintive shrieks.

"He was one of the greatest courtiers!" said the men; "and he should not have to die at Saint Jean en Grève, but at the Pré aux Clercs."

"How handsome he is! How pale!" said the women; "he is the one who would not confess."

"Dearest friend," said La Mole, "I cannot stand. Carry me!"

"Wait," said Coconnas.

He signed to the executioner, who stepped aside; then, stooping, he lifted La Mole in his arms as if he were a child, and without faltering carried his burden up the steps of the scaffold, where he put him down, amid the frantic shouting and applause of the multitude. Coconnas raised his hat and bowed. Then he threw the hat on the scaffold beside him.

"Look round," said La Mole, "do you not see them somewhere?"

Coconnas slowly glanced around the place, and, having reached a certain point, without removing his eyes from it he laid his hand on his friend's shoulder.

"Look," said he, "look at the window of that small tower!"

With his other hand he pointed out to La Mole the little building which still stands at the corner of the Rue de la Vannerie and the Rue Mouton,—a reminder of past ages.

Somewhat back from the window two women dressed in black were leaning against each other.

"Ah!" said La Mole, "I feared only one thing, and that was to die without seeing her again. I have seen her; now I can go."

And with his eyes riveted on the small window he raised the reliquary to his lips and covered it with kisses.

Coconnas saluted the two women with as much grace as if he were in a drawing-room. In response to this they waved their handkerchiefs bathed in tears.

Caboche now touched Coconnas on the shoulder, and looked at him significantly.

"Yes, yes," said the Piedmontese. Then turning to La Mole:

"Embrace me," said he, "and die like a man. This will not be hard for you, my friend; you are so brave!"

"Ah!" said La Mole, "there will be no merit in my dying bravely, suffering as I do."

The priest approached and held the crucifix before La Mole, who smiled and pointed to the reliquary in his hand.

"Never mind," said the priest, "ask strength from Him who suffered what you are about to suffer."

La Mole kissed the feet of the Christ.

"Commend me to the prayers of the nuns of the Avens Sainte Vierge."

"Make haste, La Mole," said Coconnas, "you cause me such suffering that I feel myself growing weak."

"I am ready," said La Mole.

"Can you keep your head steady?" inquired Caboche, holding his sword behind La Mole, who was on his knees.

"I hope so," said the latter.

"Then all will go well."

"But," said La Mole, "you will not forget what I asked of you? This reliquary will open the doors to you."

"Be easy. Now try to keep your head straight."

La Mole raised his head and turned his eyes towards the little tower.

"Adieu, Marguerite," said he; "bless"—

He never finished. With one blow of his sword, as swift as a stroke of lightning, Caboche severed the head, which rolled to the feet of Coconnas.

The body fell back gently as if going to rest.

A great cry rose from thousands of voices, and, among them, it seemed to Coconnas that he heard a shriek more piercing than all the rest.

"Thank you, my good friend," said Coconnas, and a third time he extended his hand to the hangman.

"My son," said the priest, "have you nothing to confess to God?"

"Faith no, father," said the Piedmontese; "all that I had to say I said to you yesterday."

Then turning to Caboche:

"Now, executioner, my last friend, one more favor!"

Before kneeling down he turned on the crowd a glance so calm and serene that a murmur of admiration rose, which soothed his ear and flattered his pride. Then, raising the head of his friend and pressing a kiss on the purple lips, he gave a last look toward the little tower, and kneeling down, still holding the well-loved head in his hand, he said:

"Now!"

Scarcely had he uttered the word before Caboche had cut off his head.

This done, the poor hangman began to tremble.

"It was time it was over," said he. "Poor fellow!"

And with difficulty he drew from the clinched fingers of La Mole the reliquary of gold. Then he threw his cloak over the sad remains which the tumbril was to convey to his own abode.

The spectacle over, the crowd dispersed.

CHAPTER LXI.

THE HEADSMAN'S TOWER.

Night descended over the city, which still trembled at the remembrance of the execution, the details of which passed from mouth to mouth, saddening the happy supper hour in every home. In contrast to the city, which was silent and mournful, the Louvre was noisy, joyous, and illuminated. There was a grand fête at the palace, a fête ordered by Charles IX., a fête he had planned for that evening at the very time that he had ordered the execution for the morning.

The previous evening the Queen of Navarre had received word to be present, and, in the hope that La Mole and Coconnas would have escaped during the night, since every measure had been taken for their safety, she had promised her brother to comply with his wishes.

But when she had lost all hope, after the scene in the chapel, after, out of a last feeling of piety for that love, the greatest and the deepest she had ever known, she had been present at the execution, she resolved that neither prayers nor threats should force her to attend a joyous festival at the Louvre the same day on which she had witnessed so terrible a scene at the Grève.

That day King Charles had given another proof of the will power which no one perhaps carried as far as he. In bed for a fortnight, weak as a dying man, pale as a corpse, yet he rose about five o'clock and donned his most beautiful clothes, although during his toilet he fainted three times.

At eight o'clock he asked what had become of his sister, and inquired if any one had seen her and what she was doing. No one could tell him, for the queen had gone to her apartments about eleven o'clock and had absolutely refused admittance to every one.

But there was no refusal for Charles. Leaning on the arm of Monsieur de Nancey, he went to the queen's rooms and entered unannounced by the secret corridor.

Although he had expected a melancholy sight, and had prepared himself for it in advance, that which he saw was even more distressing than he had anticipated.

Marguerite, half dead, was lying on a divan, her head buried in the cushions, neither weeping nor praying, but moaning like one in great agony; and this she had been doing ever since her return from the Grève. At the other end of the chamber Henriette de Nevers, that daring woman, lay stretched on the carpet unconscious. On coming back from the Grève her strength, like Marguerite's, had given out, and poor Gillonne was going from one to the other, not daring to offer a word of consolation.

In the crises which follow great catastrophes one hugs one's grief like a treasure, and any one who attempts to divert us, ever so slightly, is looked on as an enemy. Charles IX. closed the door, and leaving Nancey in the corridor entered, pale and trembling.

Neither of the women had seen him. Gillonne alone, who was trying to revive Henriette, rose on one knee, and looked in a startled way at the King.

The latter made a sign with his hand, whereupon the girl rose, courtesied, and withdrew.

Charles then approached Marguerite, looked at her a moment in silence, and in a tone of which his harsh voice was supposed to be incapable, said:

"Margot! my sister!"

The young woman started and sat up.

"Your Majesty!" said she.

"Come, sister, courage."

Marguerite raised her eyes to Heaven.

"Yes," said Charles, "but listen to me."

The Queen of Navarre made a sign of assent.

"You promised me to come to the ball," said Charles.

"I!" exclaimed Marguerite.

"Yes, and after your promise you are expected; so that if you do not come every one will wonder why."

"Excuse me, brother," said Marguerite, "you see that I am suffering greatly."

"Exert yourself."

For an instant Marguerite seemed to try to summon her courage, then suddenly she gave way and fell back among the cushions.

"No, no, I cannot go," said she.

Charles took her hand and seating himself on the divan said:

"You have just lost a friend, I know, Margot; but look at me. Have I not lost all my friends, even my mother? You can always weep when you wish to; but I, at the moment of my greatest sorrows, am always forced to smile. You suffer; but look at me! I am dying. Come, Margot, courage! I ask it of you, sister, in the name of our honor! We bear like a cross of agony the reputation of our house; let us bear it, sister, as the Saviour bore his cross to Calvary; and if on the way we stagger, as he did, let us like him rise brave and resigned."

"Oh, my God! my God!" cried Marguerite.

"Yes," said Charles, answering her thought; "the sacrifice is severe, sister, but each one has his own burden, some of honor, others of life. Do you suppose that with my twenty-five years, and the most beautiful throne in the world, I do not regret dying? Look at me! My eyes, my complexion, my lips are those of a dying man, it is true; but my smile, does not my smile imply that I still hope? and in a week, a month at the most, you will be weeping for me, sister, as you now weep for him who died to-day."

"Brother!" exclaimed Marguerite, throwing her arms about Charles's neck.

"So dress yourself, dear Marguerite," said the King, "hide your pallor and come to the ball. I have given orders for new jewels to be brought to you, and ornaments worthy of your beauty."

"Oh! what are diamonds and dresses to me now?" said Marguerite.

"Life is long, Marguerite," said Charles, smiling, "at least for you."

The pages withdrew; Gillonne alone remained.

"Prepare everything that is necessary for me, Gillonne," said Marguerite.

"Sister, remember one thing: sometimes it is by stifling or rather by dissimulating our suffering that we show most honor to the dead."

"Well, sire," said Marguerite, shuddering, "I will go to the ball."

A tear, which soon dried on his parched eyelid, moistened Charles's eye.

He leaned over his sister, kissed her forehead, paused an instant before Henriette, who had neither seen nor heard him, and murmured:

"Poor woman!"

Then he went out silently.

Soon after several pages entered, bringing boxes and jewel-caskets.

Marguerite made a sign for them to set everything down.

Gillonne looked at her mistress in astonishment.

"Yes," said Marguerite, in a tone the bitterness of which it is impossible to describe; yes, I will dress and go to the ball; I am expected. Make haste; the day will then be complete. A fête on the Grève in the morning, a fête in the

Louvre in the evening."

"And the duchess?" said Gillonne.

"She is quite happy. She may remain here; she can weep; she can suffer at her ease. She is not the daughter of a king, the wife of a king, the sister of a king. She is not a queen. Help me to dress, Gillonne."

The young girl obeyed. The jewels were magnificent, the dress gorgeous. Marguerite had never been so beautiful.

She looked at herself in a mirror.

"My brother is right," said she; "a human being is indeed a miserable creature."

At that moment Gillonne returned.

"Madame," said she, "a man is asking for you."

"For me?"

"Yes."

"Who is he?"

"I do not know, but he is terrible to look at; the very sight of him makes me shudder."

"Go and ask him his name," said Marguerite, turning pale.

Gillonne withdrew, and returned in a few moments.

"He will not give his name, madame, but he begged me to give you this."

Gillonne handed to Marguerite the reliquary she had given to La Mole the previous evening.

"Oh! bring him in, bring him in!" said the queen quickly, growing paler and more numb than before.

A heavy step shook the floor. The echo, indignant, no doubt, at having to repeat such a sound, moaned along the wainscoting. A man stood on the threshold.

"You are"—said the queen.

"He whom you met one day near Montfaucon, madame, and who in his tumbril brought back two wounded gentlemen to the Louvre."

"Yes, yes, I know you. You are Maître Caboche."

"Executioner of the provostship of Paris, madame."

These were the only words Henriette had heard for an hour. She raised her pale face from her hands and looked at the man with her sapphire eyes, from which a double flame seemed to dart.

"And you come"—said Marguerite, trembling.

"To remind you of your promise to the younger of the two gentlemen, who charged me to give you this reliquary. You remember the promise, madame?"

"Yes, yes," exclaimed the queen, "and never has a noble soul had more satisfaction than his shall have; but where is"—

"At my house with the body."

"At your house? Why did you not bring it?"

"I might have been stopped at the gate of the Louvre, and compelled to raise my cloak. What would they have said if they had seen a head under it?"

"That is right; keep it. I will come for it to-morrow."

"To-morrow, madame," said Caboche, "may perhaps be too late."

"How so?"

"Because the queen mother wanted the heads of the first victims executed by me to be kept for her magical experiments."

"Oh! What profanation! The heads of our well-beloved! Henriette," cried Marguerite, turning to her friend, who had risen as if a spring had placed her on her feet, "Henriette, my angel, do you hear what this man says?"

"Yes; what must we do?"

"Go with him."

Then uttering a cry of pain by which great sufferers return to life:

"Ah! I was so happy," said Henriette; "I was almost dead."

Meanwhile Marguerite had thrown a velvet cloak over her bare shoulders.

"Come," said she, "we will go and see them once more."

Telling Gillonne to have all the doors closed, the queen gave orders for a litter to be brought to the private entrance, and taking Henriette by the arm, she descended by the secret corridor, signing to Caboche to follow.

At the lower door was the litter; at the gate Caboche's attendant waited with a lantern. Marguerite's porters were trusty men, deaf and dumb, more to be depended on than if they had been beasts of burden.

They walked for about ten minutes, preceded by Caboche and his servant, carrying the lantern. Then they stopped. The hangman opened the door, while his man went ahead.

Marguerite stepped from the litter and helped out the Duchesse de Nevers. In the deep grief which bound them together it was the nervous organism which was the stronger.

The headsman's tower rose before them like a dark, vague giant, giving out a lurid gleam from two narrow upper windows.

The attendant reappeared at the door.

"You can enter, ladies," said Caboche; "every one is asleep in the tower."

At the same moment the light from above was extinguished.

The two women, holding to each other, passed through the small gothic door, and reached a dark hall with damp and uneven pavement. At the end of a winding corridor they perceived a light and guided by the gruesome master of the place they set out towards it. The door closed behind them.

Caboche, a wax torch in hand, admitted them into a lower room filled with smoke. In the centre was a table containing the remains of a supper for three. These three were probably the hangman, his wife, and his chief assistant. In a conspicuous place on the wall a parchment was nailed, sealed with the seal of the King. It was the hangman's license. In a corner was a long-handled sword. This was the flaming sword of justice.

Here and there were various rough drawings representing martyrs undergoing the torture.

At the door Caboche made a low bow.

"Your majesty will excuse me," said he, "if I ventured to enter the Louvre and bring you here. But it was the last wish of the gentleman, so that I felt I"—

"You did well, Maître," said Marguerite, "and here is a reward for you."

Caboche looked sadly at the large purse which Marguerite laid on the table.

"Gold!" said he; "always gold! Alas! madame, if I only could buy back for gold the blood I was forced to spill to-day!"

"Maître," said Marguerite, looking around with a sad hesitation, "Maître, do we have to go to some other room? I do not see"—

"No, madame, they are here; but it is a sad sight, and one which I could have spared you by wrapping up in my cloak that for which you have come."

Marguerite and Henriette looked at each other.

"No," said the queen, who had read in her friend's eye the same thought as in her own; "no, show us the way and we will follow."

Caboche took the torch and opened an oaken door at the top of a short stairway, which led to an underground chamber. At that instant a current of air blew some sparks from the torch and brought to the princesses an ill-smelling odor of dampness and blood. Henriette, white as an alabaster statue, leaned on the arm of her less agitated friend; but at the first step she swayed.

"I can never do it," said she.

"When one loves truly, Henriette," replied the queen, "one loves beyond death."

It was a sight both horrible and touching presented by the two women, glowing with youth, beauty, and jewels, as they bent their heads beneath the foul, chalky ceiling, the weaker leaning on the stronger, the stronger clinging to the arm of the hangman.

They reached the final step. On the floor of the cellar lay two human forms covered with a wide cloth of black serge.

Caboche raised a corner of it, and, lowering the torch:

"See, madame," said he.

In their black clothes lay the two young men, side by side, in the strange symmetry of death. Their heads had been placed close to their bodies, from which they seemed to be separated only by a bright red circle about the neck. Death had not disunited their hands, for either from chance or the kind care of the hangman the right hand of La Mole rested in Coconnas's left hand.

There was a look of love under the lids of La Mole, and a smile of scorn under those of Coconnas.

Marguerite knelt down by the side of her lover, and with hands that sparkled with gems gently raised the head she had so greatly loved.

The Duchesse de Nevers leaned against the wall, unable to remove her eyes from that pale face on which so often she had gazed for pleasure and for love.

"La Mole! Dear La Mole!" murmured Marguerite.

"Annibal! Annibal!" cried the duchess, "so beautiful! so proud! so brave! Never again will you answer me!"

And her eyes filled with tears.

This woman, so scornful, so intrepid, so insolent in happiness; this woman who carried scepticism as far as absolute doubt, passion to the point of cruelty; this woman had never thought of death.

Marguerite was the first to move.

She put into a bag, embroidered with pearls and perfumed with finest essences, the head of La Mole, more beautiful than ever as it rested against the velvet and the gold, and the beauty of which was to be preserved by a special preparation, used at that time in the embalming of royal personages.

Henriette then drew near and wrapped the head of Coconnas in a fold of her cloak.

And both women, bending beneath their grief more than beneath their burdens, ascended the stairs with a last look at the remains which they left to the mercy of the hangman in that sombre abode of ordinary criminals.

"Do not fear, madame," said Caboche, who understood their look, "the gentlemen, I promise you, shall be buried in holy ground."

"And you will have masses said for them with this," said Henriette, taking from her neck a magnificent necklace of rubies, and handing it to the hangman.

They returned to the Louvre by the same road by which they had gone. At the gate the queen gave her name; at the foot of her private stairway she descended and, returning to her rooms, laid her sad burden in the closet adjoining her sleeping-room, destined from that moment to become an oratory. Then, leaving Henriette in her room, paler and more beautiful than ever, she entered the great ballroom, the same room in which, two years and a half ago, the first chapter of our history opened.

All eyes were turned on her, but she bore the general gaze with a proud and almost joyous air.

She had religiously carried out the last wish of her friend.

Seeing her, Charles pushed tremblingly through the gilded crowd around her.

"Sister," said he, aloud, "I thank you."

Then in a low tone:

"Take care!" said he, "you have a spot of blood on your arm."

"Ah! what difference does that make, sire," said Marguerite, "since I have a smile on my lips?"

CHAPTER LXII.

THE SWEAT OF BLOOD.

A few days after the terrible scene we have just described, that is, on the 30th of May, 1574, while the court was at Vincennes, suddenly a great commotion was heard in the chamber of the King. The latter had been taken ill in the midst of the ball he had given the day of the execution of the two young men, and had been ordered by his physicians into the pure air of the country.

It was eight o'clock in the morning. A small group of courtiers were talking excitedly in the antechamber, when suddenly a cry was heard, and Charles's nurse appeared at the door, her eyes filled with tears, calling frantically:

"Help! Help!"

"Is his Majesty worse?" asked the Captain de Nancey, whom, as we know, the King had relieved from all duty to Queen Catharine in order to attach him to himself.

"Oh! Blood! Blood!" cried the nurse. "The doctors! call the doctors!"

Mozille and Ambroise Paré in turn attended the august patient, and the latter, seeing the King fall asleep, had taken advantage of the fact to withdraw for a few moments. Meanwhile a great perspiration had broken out all over the King; and as Charles suffered from a relaxation of the capillary vessels, which caused a hæmorrhage of the skin, the bloody sweat had alarmed the nurse, unaccustomed to this strange phenomenon, who, being a Protestant, kept repeating that it was a judgment for the blood of the Huguenots shed in the massacre of Saint Bartholomew.

The courtiers went in all directions in search of the doctor, who could not be far away, and whom they could not fail to meet. The antechamber, therefore, became deserted, every one being anxious to show his zeal in bringing the much-needed physician.

Just then a door opened and Catharine appeared. She passed hurriedly through the antechamber and hastily entered the apartment of her son.

Charles was stretched on his bed, his eyes closed, his breast heaving; from his body oozed a crimson sweat. His hand hung over the bed, and from the end of each finger dropped a ruby liquid. It was a horrible sight.

At the sound of his mother's steps, as if he knew she was there, Charles sat up.

"Pardon, madame," said he, looking at her, "but I desire to die in peace."

"To die, my son?" said Catharine. "This is only a passing attack of your wretched trouble. Would you have us despair in this way?"

"I tell you, madame, I feel that my soul is about to pass away. I tell you, madame, that death is near me, by Heaven! I feel what I feel, and I know what I am talking about!"

"Sire," said the queen, "your imagination is your most serious trouble. Since the well-merited punishment of those two sorcerers, those assassins, La Mole and Coconnas, your physical suffering should have diminished. The mental trouble alone continues, and if I could talk with you for just ten minutes I could prove to you"—

"Nurse," said Charles, "watch at the door that no one may enter. Queen Catharine de Médicis wishes to speak with her well-loved son Charles IX."

The nurse withdrew.

"Well," continued Charles, "this interview will have to take place some day or other, and better to-day than to-morrow. Besides, to-morrow may be too late. But a third person must be present."

"Why?"

"Because I tell you I am dying," repeated Charles with frightful seriousness; "because at any moment death may enter this chamber, as you have done, pale, silent, and unannounced. It is, therefore, time. Last night I settled my personal affairs; this morning I will arrange those of the kingdom."

"What person do you desire to see?" asked Catharine.

"My brother, madame. Have him summoned."

"Sire," said the queen, "I see with pleasure that the prejudices dictated by hatred rather than pain are leaving your mind, as they soon will fade from your heart. Nurse!" cried Catharine, "nurse!"

The woman, who was keeping watch outside, opened the door.

"Nurse," said Catharine, "by order of my son, when Monsieur de Nancey returns say to him to summon the Duc d'Alençon."

Charles made a sign which detained the woman.

"I said my brother, madame," said Charles.

Catharine's eyes dilated like those of a tigress about to show her anger. But Charles raised his hand imperatively.

"I wish to speak to my brother Henry," said he. "Henry alone is my brother; not he who is king yonder, but he who is a prisoner here. Henry shall know my last wishes."

"And do you think," exclaimed the Florentine, with unusual boldness in the face of the dread will of her son, her hatred for the Béarnais being strong enough to make her forget her customary dissimulation,—"do you think that if, as you say, you are near the tomb, I will yield to any one, especially a stranger, my right to be present at your last hour; my right as queen and mother?"

"Madame," said Charles, "I am still King; and I still command. I tell you that I desire to speak to my brother Henry and yet you do not summon my captain of the guard. A thousand devils! I warn you, madame, I still have strength enough to go for him myself."

The King made a movement as if to rise from the bed, which brought to light his body, bloody like Christ's after the flogging.

"Sire," cried Catharine, holding him back, "you wrong us all. You forget the insults given to our family, you repudiate our blood. A son of France alone should kneel before the death-bed of a King of France. As to me, my place is marked out; it is here by the laws of nature as well as the laws of royalty. Therefore I shall remain."

"And by what right do you remain, madame?" demanded Charles IX.

"Because I am your mother."

"You are no more my mother, madame, than is the Duc d'Alençon my brother."

"You are mad, monsieur," said Catharine; "since when is she who gives birth to a child no longer his mother?"

"From the moment, madame, when the unnatural mother takes away that which she gives," replied Charles, wiping away a bloody sweat from his lips.

"What do you mean, Charles? I do not understand you," murmured Catharine, gazing at her son, her eyes dilated with astonishment.

"But you will, madame."

Charles searched under his pillow and drew out a small silver key.

"Take this, madame, and open my travelling-box. It contains certain papers which will speak for me."

Charles pointed to a magnificent carved box, closed with a silver lock, like the key, which occupied the most conspicuous place in the room.

Catharine, dominated by the look and manner of Charles, obeyed, advanced slowly to the box, and opened it. But no sooner had she looked into it than she suddenly sprang back as if she had seen some sleeping reptile inside it.

"Well," said Charles, who had not taken his eyes from his mother, "what is there in the box to startle you, madame?"

"Nothing," said Catharine.

"Then put in your hand, madame, and take out a book that is there; there is one, is there not?" added Charles, with a pale smile, more terrible in him than a threat in another.

"Yes," faltered Catharine.

"A book on hunting?"

"Yes."

"Take it out and bring it to me."

In spite of her assurance Catharine turned pale, and trembled in every limb, as she extended her hand towards the box.

"Fatality!" she murmured, raising the book.

"Very good," said Charles, "now listen; this book on hunting—I loved the chase madly, above everything else—I read this book too eagerly, do you understand, madame?"

Catharine gave a dull moan.

"It was a weakness," continued Charles; "burn it, madame. The weakness of kings and queens must not be known!"

Catharine stepped to the glowing hearth, and dropped the book into the flames.

Then, standing motionless and silent, she watched with haggard eye the bluish light which rose from the poisoned leaves.

As the book burned a strong odor of arsenic spread through the room. Soon the volume was entirely destroyed.

"And now, madame," said Charles, with irresistible majesty, "call my brother."

Catharine, overcome, crushed under a multiple emotion which her profound wisdom could not analyze, and which her almost superhuman strength could not combat, took a step forward as if to speak.

The mother grew remorseful; the queen was afraid; the poisoner felt a return

550

of hatred.

The latter sentiment dominated.

"Curse him!" she cried, rushing from the room, "he triumphs, he gains his end; curse him! curse him!"

"You understand, my brother, my brother Henry," cried Charles, calling after his mother; "my brother Henry, with whom I wish to speak instantly regarding the regency of the kingdom!"

Almost at the same instant Maître Ambroise Paré entered through the door opposite the one by which the queen had just left, and, pausing on the threshold, noticed the peculiar odor in the room.

"Who has been burning arsenic here?" said he.

"I," replied Charles.

CHAPTER LXIII.

THE DONJON OF THE PRISON OF VINCENNES.

Henry of Navarre was strolling dreamily along the terrace of the prison. He knew the court was at the château, not a hundred feet away, and through the walls it seemed as if his piercing eye could picture Charles as he lay dying.

The weather was perfect. A broad band of sunlight lay on the distant fields, bathing in liquid gold the tops of the forest trees, proud of the richness of their first foliage. The very stones of the prison itself, gray as they were, seemed impregnated with the gentle light of heaven, and some flowers, lured by the breath of the east wind, had pushed through the crevices of the wall, and were raising their disks of red and yellow velvet to the kisses of the warm air.

But Henry's eyes were fixed neither on the verdant plains nor on the gilded tree tops. His glance went beyond, and was fixed, full of ambition, on the capital of France, destined one day to become the capital of the world.

"Paris," murmured the King of Navarre, "there is Paris; that is, joy, triumph, glory, power, and happiness. Paris, in which is the Louvre, and the Louvre, in which is the throne; and only one thing separates me from this Paris, for which I so long, and that something the stones at my feet, which shut me in with my enemy!"

As he glanced from Paris to Vincennes, he perceived on his left, in a valley, partly hidden by flowering almond-trees, a man, whose cuirass sparkled in the sunlight at its owner's slightest movement.

This man rode a fiery steed and led another which seemed no less impatient.

The King of Navarre fixed his eyes on this cavalier and saw him draw his sword from his sheath, place his handkerchief on the point, and wave it like a signal.

At the same instant the signal was repeated from the opposite hill, then all around the château a belt of handkerchiefs seemed to flutter.

It was De Mouy and his Huguenots, who, knowing the King was dying, and fearing that some attempt might be made on Henry's life, had gathered together, ready to defend or attack.

Henry, with his eyes still on the horseman he had seen first, bent over the balustrade, and shading his eyes with his hand to keep out the dazzling rays of the sun, recognized the young Huguenot.

"De Mouy!" he exclaimed, as though the latter could hear him.

And in his joy at seeing himself surrounded by friends, the king raised his hat and waved his scarf.

All the white banners were again set in motion with an energy which proved the joy of their owners.

"Alas! they are waiting for me," said Henry, "and I cannot join them. Why did I not do so when I could? Now it is too late!"

He made a despairing gesture, to which De Mouy returned a sign which meant, "I will wait."

Just then Henry heard steps on the stone stairs. He hastily withdrew. The Huguenots understood the cause of his sudden disappearance, and their swords were returned to their sheaths and their handkerchiefs disappeared.

Henry saw on the stairs a woman whose quick breathing showed that she had come in haste.

He recognized, not without the secret dread he always felt on seeing her, Catharine de Médicis.

Behind her were two guards who stopped at the head of the stairs.

"Oh!" thought Henry, "it must be something new and important that makes the queen mother come to seek me on the balcony of the prison of Vincennes."

Catharine seated herself on a stone bench against the battlement to recover her breath.

Henry approached her, and with his most gracious smile:

"Are you seeking me, my good mother?"

"Yes, monsieur," replied Catharine, "I wish to give you a final proof of my attachment. The King is dying and wishes to see you."

"Me!" said Henry, with a start of joy.

"Yes. He has been told, I am sure, that not only do you covet the throne of Navarre but that of France as well."

"Oh!" exclaimed Henry.

"It is not true, I know, but he believes it, and no doubt the object of the interview he wishes with you is to lay a snare for you."

"For me?"

"Yes. Before dying Charles wants to know what there is to hope or fear from you. And on your answer to his offer, mark you, will depend his final commands, that is, your life or death."

"But what will he offer me?"

"How do I know? Impossibilities, probably."

"But have you no idea?"

"No; but suppose for instance"—

Catharine paused.

"What."

"Suppose he credited you with these ambitious aims of yours he has heard about; suppose he should wish to hear these aims from your own lips; suppose he should tempt you as once they used to tempt the guilty in order to provoke a confession without torture; suppose," continued Catharine, looking fixedly at Henry, "he were to offer you a kingdom, the regency!"

A thrill of indescribable joy pervaded Henry's weary heart, but he guessed the snare and his strong and supple soul rebounded.

"Me?" said he; "the snare would be too palpable; offer me the regency when there is you yourself and my brother D'Alençon?"

Catharine compressed her lips to conceal her satisfaction.

"Then," said she, quickly, "you would refuse it?"

"The King is dead," thought Henry, "and she is laying a trap for me."

Aloud, he said:

"I must first hear what the King of France has to say; for from your own words, madame, all this is mere supposition."

"Doubtless," said Catharine; "but you can tell me your intentions."

"Why!" said Henry, innocently, "having no pretensions, I have no intentions."

"That is no answer," said Catharine, feeling that time was flying, and giving way to her anger; "you can give some answer."

"I cannot answer suppositions, madame; a positive resolution is so difficult and so grave a thing to assume that I must wait for facts."

"Listen, monsieur," said Catharine; "there is no time to lose, and we are wasting it in vain discussion, in toying with words. Let us play our rôle of king and queen. If you accept the regency you are a dead man."

"The King lives," thought Henry.

Then aloud:

"Madame," said he, firmly, "God holds the lives of men and of kings in his hands. He will inspire me. Let his Majesty be informed that I am ready to see him."

"Reflect, monsieur."

"During the two years in which I have been persecuted, during the month I have been a prisoner," replied Henry, bravely, "I have had time to reflect, madame, and I have reflected. Have the goodness, therefore, to go to the King before me, and to tell him that I am following you. These two guards," added Henry, pointing to the soldiers, "will see that I do not escape. Moreover, that is not my intention."

There was such firmness in Henry's tone that Catharine saw that all her attempts, under whatever disguise, would not succeed. Therefore she hastily descended.

As soon as she had disappeared Henry went to the parapet and made a sign to De Mouy, which meant: "Draw near and be ready in case of necessity."

De Mouy, who had dismounted, sprang into the saddle, and still leading the second horse galloped to within musket-shot of the prison.

Henry thanked him by a gesture, and descended.

On the first landing he found the two soldiers who were waiting for him.

A double troop of Swiss and light-horse guarded the entrance to the court, and to enter or leave the château it was necessary to traverse a double line of halberds.

Catharine had stopped and was waiting for him.

She signed to the two soldiers to go on, and laying her hand on Henry's arm, said:

"This court has two gates. At one, behind the apartments of the King, if you refuse the regency, a good horse and freedom await you. At the other, through which you have just passed, if you listen to the voice of ambition—What do you say?"

"I say that if the King makes me regent, madame, I, and not you, shall give orders to the soldiers. I say that if I leave the castle at night, all these pikes, halberds, and muskets shall be lowered before me."

"Madman!" murmured Catharine, exasperated, "believe me, and do not play this terrible game of life and death with me."

"Why not?" said Henry, looking closely at Catharine; "why not with you as well as with another, since up to this time I have won?"

"Go to the King's apartments, monsieur, since you are unwilling to believe or listen to anything," said Catharine, pointing to the stairway with one hand, and with the other toying with one of the two poisoned daggers she always wore in the black shagreen case, which has become historical.

"Pass before me, madame," said Henry; "so long as I am not regent, the honor of precedence belongs to you."

Catharine, thwarted in all her plans, did not attempt to struggle, but ascended the stairs ahead of the King of Navarre.

———

CHAPTER LXIV.

THE REGENCY.

The King, beginning to grow impatient, had summoned Monsieur de Nancey to his room, and had just given him orders to go in search of Henry, when the latter appeared.

On seeing his brother-in-law at the door Charles uttered a cry of joy, but Henry stood motionless, as startled as if he had come face to face with a corpse.

The two physicians who were at the bedside and the priest who had been with Charles withdrew.

Charles was not loved, and yet many were weeping in the antechambers. At the death of kings, good or bad, there are always persons who lose something and who fear they will not find it again under the successor.

The mourning, the sobbing, the words of Catharine, the sinister and majestic surroundings of the last moments of a king, the sight of the King himself, suffering from a malady common enough afterwards, but which, at that time, was new to science, produced on Henry's mind, which was still youthful and consequently still susceptible, such a terrible impression that in spite of his determination not to cause Charles fresh anxiety as to his condition, he could not as we have said repress the feeling of terror which came to his face on perceiving the dying man dripping with blood.

Charles smiled sadly. Nothing of those around them escapes the dying.

"Come, Henriot," said he, extending his hand with a gentleness of voice Henry had never before noticed in him. "Come in; I have been very unhappy at not seeing you for so long. I have tormented you greatly during my life, my poor friend, and sometimes, believe me, I have reproached myself for it. Sometimes I have taken the hands of those who tormented you, it is true, but a king cannot control circumstances, and besides my mother Catharine, my brothers D'Anjou and D'Alençon, I had to consider during my lifetime something else which was troublesome and which ceases the moment I draw near to death—state policy."

"Sire," murmured Henry, "I remember only the love I have always had for my brother, the respect I have always felt for my King."

"Yes, yes, you are right," said Charles, "and I am grateful to you for saying this, Henriot, for truly you have suffered a great deal under my reign without counting the fact that it was during my reign that your poor mother died. But you must have seen that I was often driven? Sometimes I have resisted, but oftener I have yielded from very fatigue. But, as you said, let us not talk of the past. Now it is the present which concerns me; it is the future which frightens me."

And the poor King hid his livid face in his emaciated hands.

After a moment's silence he shook his head as if to drive away all gloomy thoughts, thus causing a shower of blood to fall about him.

"We must save the state," he continued in a low tone, leaning towards Henry. "We must prevent its falling into the hands of fanatics or women."

As we have just said, Charles uttered these words in a low tone, yet Henry thought he heard behind the headboard something like a dull exclamation of anger. Perhaps some opening made in the wall at the instigation of Charles himself permitted Catharine to hear this final conversation.

"Of women?" said the King of Navarre to provoke an explanation.

"Yes, Henry," said Charles, "my mother wishes the regency until my brother returns from Poland. But mind what I tell you, he will not come back."

"Why not?" cried Henry, whose heart gave a joyful leap.

"No, he cannot return," continued Charles, "because his subjects will not let him leave."

"But," said Henry, "do you not suppose, brother, that the queen mother has already written to him?"

"Yes, but Nancey stopped the courier at Château Thierry, and brought me the letter, in which she said I was to die. I wrote to Varsovia myself, my letter reached there, I am sure, and my brother will be watched. So, in all probability, Henry, the throne will be vacant."

A second sound louder than the first was heard in the alcove.

"She is surely there," thought Henry, "and is listening."

Charles heard nothing.

"Now," he continued, "I am dying without male heir." Then he stopped. A sweet thought seemed to light up his face, and, laying his hand on the King of Navarre's shoulder:

"Alas!" said he, "do you remember, Henriot, the poor little boy I showed you one evening sleeping in his silken cradle, watched over by an angel? Alas! Henriot, they will kill him!"

"Oh, sire!" cried Henry, whose eyes filled with tears, "I swear to you that I will watch over him all the days and nights of my life. Command me, my King."

"Thanks, Henriot, thanks!" said Charles, with a show of feeling unusual in him, but which the situation had roused, "I accept your promise. Do not make him a king,—fortunately he was not born for a throne,—but make him happy. I have left him an independent fortune. Let him inherit his mother's nobility, that of the heart. Perhaps it would be better for him if he were to enter the church. He would inspire less fear. Oh! it seems to me that I should die, if not happy, at least calm, if I had the kisses of the child and the sweet face of its mother to console me."

"Sire, could you not send for them?"

"Ah, poor wretches! They would never be allowed to leave the Louvre! Such is the condition of kings, Henriot. They can neither live nor die as they please. But since you promise I am more resigned."

Henry reflected.

"Yes, no doubt, my King. I have promised, but can I keep my word?"

"What do you mean?"

"Shall I not be persecuted, and threatened like him, even more than him? For I am a man, and he is only a child."

"You are mistaken," said Charles; "after my death you shall be great and powerful. Here is what will make you so."

And the King drew a parchment from under the pillow.

"See!" said he.

Henry glanced over the document sealed with the royal seal.

"The regency for me, sire!" said he, growing pale with joy.

"Yes, for you, until the return of the Duc d'Anjou, and as in all probability the duke will never return it is not the regency only but the throne that this gives you."

"The throne!" murmured Henry.

"Yes," said Charles, "you alone are worthy of it; you alone are capable of governing these debauched gallants, and these bold women who live by blood and tears. My brother D'Alençon is a traitor, and would deceive every one. Leave him in the prison in which I have placed him. My mother will try to kill you, therefore banish her. My brother D'Anjou in three or four months, perhaps in a year, will leave Varsovia and will come to dispute the throne with you. Answer him by a bull from the pope. I have already arranged that matter through my ambassador, the Duc de Nevers, and you will receive the document before long."

"Oh, my King!"

"You have but one thing to fear, Henry,—civil war; but by remaining converted you will avoid this, for the Huguenots are strong only when you put yourself at their head, and Monsieur de Condé is nothing when opposed to you. France is a country of plains, Henry, and consequently a Catholic country. The King of France ought to be the king of the Catholics and not the king of the Huguenots, for the King of France ought to be the king of the majority. It is said I feel remorse for the massacre of Saint Bartholomew; doubts, yes; remorse, no. It is said I am bleeding the blood of those Huguenots from every pore. I know what is flowing from me. It is arsenic and not blood."

"What do you mean, sire?"

"Nothing. If my death must be avenged, Henriot, it must be avenged by God alone. Let us speak now of the future. I leave you a faithful parliament and a trusty army. Lean on them and they will protect you against your only enemies—my mother and the Duc d'Alençon."

Just then the sound of arms and military commands were heard in the vestibule.

"I am dead!" murmured Henry.

"You fear? You hesitate?" said Charles, anxiously.

"I! sire," replied Henry; "no, I do not fear, nor do I hesitate. I accept."

Charles pressed Henry's hand. At that moment the nurse approached with a drink she had been preparing in the adjoining room, not knowing that the fate of France was being decided three feet from her.

"Call my mother, nurse, and have Monsieur d'Alençon also summoned."

————

CHAPTER LXV.

THE KING IS DEAD! LONG LIVE THE KING!

A few moments later Catharine and the Duc d'Alençon, pale with fright and trembling with rage, entered Charles's room. As Henry had conjectured,

Catharine had overheard everything and in a few words had told all to François.

Henry was standing at the head of Charles's bed.

The King spoke his wishes:

"Madame," said he to his mother, "had I a son, you would be regent, or in default of you it would be the King of Poland; or in default of him it would be my brother François; but I have no son, and after me the throne belongs to my brother the Duc d'Anjou, who is absent. As some day he will claim this throne I do not wish him to find in his place a man who by almost equal rights might dispute it with him, and who consequently might expose the kingdom to civil war. This is why I do not appoint you regent, madame, for you would have to choose between your two sons, which would be painful for a mother. This is why I do not choose my brother François, for he might say to his elder brother, 'You had a throne, why did you leave it?' No, I have chosen as regent one who can take the crown on trust, and who will keep it in his hand and not on his head. Salute this regent, madame; salute him, brother; it is the King of Navarre!"

And with a gesture of supreme authority the King himself saluted Henry.

Catharine and D'Alençon made a gesture between a nervous shudder and a salute.

"Here, my Lord Regent," said Charles to the King of Navarre, "here is the parchment which, until the return of the King of Poland, gives you the command of the armies, the keys of the treasury, and the royal power and authority."

Catharine devoured Henry with her eyes; François swayed so that he could scarcely stand; but this weakness of the one and strength of the other, instead of encouraging Henry, showed him the danger which threatened him.

Nevertheless he made a violent effort and overcoming his fears took the parchment from the hands of the king, raised himself to his full height, and gave Catharine and François a look which meant:

"Take care! I am your master."

"No," said she, "never; never shall my race bow to a foreign one; never shall a Bourbon reign in France while a Valois remains!"

"Mother," cried Charles IX., sitting up among the crimson sheets of his bed, more frightful looking than ever, "take care, I am still King. Not for long, I well know; but it does not take long to give an order; it does not take long to punish murderers and poisoners."

"Well! give the order, if you dare, and I will give mine! Come, François, come!"

And the queen left the room rapidly, followed by the Duc d'Alençon.

"Nancey!" cried Charles; "Nancey! come here! I order you, Nancey, to arrest my mother, and my brother, arrest"—

A stream of blood choked his utterance, just as the captain of the guards opened the door, and, almost suffocated, the King fell back on his bed. Nancey had heard only his name; the orders which followed, and which had been uttered in a less audible tone, were lost in space.

"Guard the door," said Henry, "and let no one enter."

Nancey bowed and withdrew.

Henry looked at the almost lifeless body, which already would have seemed like that of a corpse had not a light breath stirred the fringe of foam on the lips.

Henry looked for several moments, then, speaking to himself:

"The final moment has come!" said he; "shall I reign? shall I live?"

Just then the tapestry of the alcove was raised, a pale face appeared behind it, and a voice vibrated through the silence of death which reigned throughout the royal chamber.

"Live!" said this voice.

"Réné!" cried Henry.

"Yes, sire."

"Your prediction was false, then; I shall not be king?"

"You shall be, sire; but the time has not yet come."

"How do you know? Speak, that I may know if I may believe you."

"Listen."

"Well?"

"Stoop down."

Henry leaned over Charles. Réné did the same. They were separated by the width of the bed alone, and even this distance was lessened by their positions. Between them, silent and motionless, lay the dying King.

"Listen," said Réné; "placed here by the queen mother to ruin you, I prefer to serve you, for I have faith in your horoscope. By serving you I shall profit both in body and soul."

"Did the queen mother command you to say this also?" asked Henry, full of doubt and pain.

"No," said Réné; "but I will tell you a secret."

He leaned still further over.

Henry did likewise, so that their heads almost touched.

This interview between two men bending over the body of a dying king was so sombre that the hair of the superstitious Florentine rose on end, and Henry's face became covered with perspiration.

"Listen," continued Réné, "I will tell you a secret known only to me. I will reveal it to you if you will swear over this dying man to forgive me for the death of your mother."

"I have already promised you this," said Henry, with darkening brow.

"You promised, but you did not swear," said Réné, drawing back.

"I swear it," said Henry, raising his right hand over the head of the King.

"Well, sire," said the Florentine, hastily, "the King of Poland will soon arrive!"

"No," said Henry, "the messenger was stopped by King Charles."

"King Charles intercepted only the one on the road to Château Thierry. But the queen mother wisely sent couriers by three different routes."

"Oh! I am lost!" exclaimed Henry.

"A messenger arrived this morning from Varsovia. The king left after him without any one's thinking of opposing him, for at Varsovia the illness of the King of France was not yet known. This courier only preceded Henry of Anjou by a few hours."

"Oh! had I but eight days!" cried Henry.

"Yes, but you have not eight hours. Did you hear the noise of arms?"

"Yes."

"They are making ready to kill you. They will seek you even here in the apartment of the King."

"The King is not yet dead."

Réné looked closely at Charles.

"He will be in ten minutes; you have ten minutes to live, therefore; perhaps less."

"What shall I do?"

"Flee instantly, without delaying a minute, a second."

"But how? If they are waiting in the antechamber they will kill me as I go out."

"Listen! I will risk everything for you. Never forget this."

"Fear not."

"Follow me by the secret corridor. I will lead you to the postern. Then, to gain time, I will tell the queen mother that you are coming down; you will be seen to have discovered this secret passage, and to have profited by it to escape. Flee! Flee!"

"Nurse!" murmured Charles, "nurse!"

Henry took from the bed Charles's sword, of no further use to the dying King, put the parchment which made him regent in his breast, kissed Charles's brow for the last time, and turning away hurried through the door, which closed behind him.

"Nurse!" cried the King, in a stronger voice, "nurse!"

The woman ran to him.

"What is it, Charlot?" she asked.

"Nurse," said the King, his eye dilated by the terrible fixity of death, "something must have happened while I slept. I see a great light. I see God, our Master, I see Jesus, and the Blessed Virgin Mary. They are praying and interceding for me. The all-powerful Lord pardons me—calls to me—My God! my God! In thy mercy, receive me! My God! forget that I have been King, for I come to you without sceptre or crown. My God! forget the crimes of the King, and remember only the suffering of the man. My God, I come!"

And Charles, who as he spoke had risen more and more as if to go to the One who was calling him, after uttering these words heaved a sigh and fell back still and cold in the arms of his nurse.

Meantime, while the soldiers, commanded by Catharine, were beginning to fill the main corridor in which they expected Henry to appear, the latter, guided by Réné, passed along the secret passage and reached the postern, sprang on the horse which was waiting for him, and galloped to the place where he knew he would find De Mouy.

Hearing the sound of the horse's hoofs, the galloping of which fell on the hard pavement, some sentinels turned and cried:

"He flees! He flees!"

"Who?" cried the queen mother, stepping to a window.

"The King of Navarre!" cried the sentinels.

"Fire on him! Fire!" cried Catharine.

The sentinels levelled their muskets, but Henry was already too far away.

"He flees!" cried the queen mother; "then he is vanquished!"

"He flees!" murmured the Duc d'Alençon; "then I am king!"

At that instant, while François and his mother were still before the window, the drawbridge thundered under horses' hoofs and preceded by a clanking of arms and great noise a young man galloped up, his hat in his hand, shouting as he entered the court: "France!" He was followed by four gentlemen, covered like himself with perspiration, dust, and foam.

"My son!" exclaimed Catharine, extending both arms out of the window.

"Mother!" replied the young man, springing from his steed.

"My brother D'Anjou!" cried François, stepping back in amazement.

"Am I too late?" asked Henry d'Anjou.

"No, just in time, and God must have guided you, for you could not have arrived at a better moment. Look and listen!"

Monsieur de Nancey, captain of the guards, had come out upon the balcony from the chamber of the King.

All eyes were turned towards him.

Breaking a wand in two, with arms extended, he took a piece in either hand and cried three times:

"King Charles IX. is dead! King Charles IX. is dead! King Charles IX. is dead!"

Then he dropped the pieces of the wand.

"Long live King Henry III.!" shouted Catharine, making the sign of the cross. "Long live King Henry III.!"

All took up the cry except Duc François.

"Ah, she has betrayed me!" murmured he, digging his nails into his breast.

"I have won," cried Catharine, "and that hateful Béarnais will not reign!"

CHAPTER LXVI.

EPILOGUE.

One year had elapsed since the death of Charles IX. and the accession of his successor to the throne.

King Henry III., happily reigning by the grace of God and his mother Catharine, was attending a fine procession given in honor of Notre Dame de Cléry.

He had gone on foot with the queen, his wife, and all the court.

King Henry III. could well afford this little pastime, for no serious business occupied him for the moment. The King of Navarre was in Navarre, where he had so long desired to be, and where he was said to be very much taken up with a beautiful girl of the blood of the Montmorencies whom he called La Fosseuse. Marguerite was with him, sad and gloomy, finding in the beautiful mountains not distraction but a softening of the two greatest griefs of life,—absence and death.

Paris was very quiet and the queen mother, really regent since her dear son Henry had been King, resided sometimes at the Louvre, sometimes at the Hôtel de Soissons, which occupied the site to-day covered by the Halle au Blé, of which nothing remains beyond the beautiful column which is still standing.

One evening when she was deeply engaged in studying the stars with Réné, of whose little act of treason she was still ignorant, and who had been reinstated in her favor after the false testimony he had so opportunely given at the trial of Coconnas and La Mole, she was informed that a man waited for her in her oratory with something to tell her of the greatest importance.

Hastily descending, the queen found the Sire de Maurevel.

"*He* is here!" cried the ancient captain of the guards, not giving Catharine time to address him, according to royal etiquette.

"What *he*?" demanded Catharine.

"Who but the King of Navarre, madame!"

"Here!" said Catharine, "here! He—Henry—And what has he come for, the madman?"

"If appearances are to be believed, he comes to see Madame de Sauve. That is all. If probabilities are to be considered, he comes to conspire against the

King."

"How do you know he is here?"

"Yesterday I saw him enter a house, and an instant later Madame de Sauve joined him there."

"Are you sure it was he?"

"I waited until he came out, that is, part of the night. At three o'clock the two lovers appeared. The king led Madame de Sauve as far as the gate of the Louvre, where, thanks to the porter, who no doubt is in her pay, she was admitted without opposition, and the king returned, humming a tune, and with a step as free as if he were among his own mountains."

"Where did he go then?"

"To the Rue de l'Arbre Sec, Hôtel de la Belle Étoile, the same inn in which the two sorcerers used to lodge whom your majesty had executed a year ago."

"Why did you not come and tell me this at once?"

"Because I was not yet sure of my man."

"And now?"

"Now I am certain."

"Did you see him?"

"Yes. I hid in a wine merchant's opposite. I saw him enter the same building as on the previous night. Then as Madame de Sauve was late he imprudently put his face against the window pane on the first floor, and I had no further doubt. Besides, a few minutes later Madame de Sauve came and again joined him."

"Do you think that like last night they will remain until three o'clock in the morning?"

"It is probable."

"Where is the house?"

"Near the Croix des Petits Champs, close to Saint Honoré."

"Very good," said Catharine. "Does Monsieur de Sauve know your handwriting?"

"No."

"Sit down, then, and write."

Maurevel took a pen and obeyed.

"I am ready, madame," said he.

Catharine dictated:

"While the Baron de Sauve is on service at the Louvre the baroness is with one of her friends, in a house near the Croix des Petits Champs, close to Saint Honoré. The Baron de Sauve will know the house by a red cross on the wall."

"Well?" said Maurevel.

"Make a copy of the letter," said Catharine.

Maurevel obeyed in silence.

"Now," said the queen, "have one of these letters taken by a clever man to the Baron de Sauve, and drop the other in the corridors of the Louvre."

"I do not understand," said Maurevel.

Catharine shrugged her shoulders.

"You do not understand that a husband who receives such a note will be angry?"

"But the King of Navarre never used to be angry, madame."

"It is not always with a king as with a simple courtier. Besides, if De Sauve is not angry you can be so for him."

"I!"

"Yes. You can take four men or six, if necessary, put on a mask, break down the door, as if you had been sent by the baron, surprise the lovers in the midst of their tête à tête, and strike your blow in the name of the King. The next day the note dropped in the corridor of the Louvre, and picked up by some kind friend who already will have circulated the news, will prove that it was the husband who had avenged himself. Only by chance, the gallant happened to be King of Navarre; but who would have imagined that, when every one thought him at Pau."

Maurevel looked at Catharine in admiration, bowed, and withdrew.

As Maurevel left the Hôtel de Soissons Madame de Sauve entered the small house near the Croix des Petits Champs.

Henry was waiting for her at the half-open door.

As soon as he saw her on the stairs, he said:

"You have not been followed, have you?"

"Why, no," said Charlotte, "at least, not so far as I know."

"I think I have been," said Henry, "not only to-night but last evening as well."

"Oh! my God!" said Charlotte, "you frighten me, sire! If this meeting between you and one of your old friends should bring any harm to you I should be inconsolable."

"Do not worry, my love," said the Béarnais, "we have three swordsmen watching in the darkness."

"Three are very few, sire."

"Three are enough when they are De Mouy, Saucourt, and Barthélemy."

"Is De Mouy in Paris with you?"

"Certainly."

"He dared to return to the capital? Has he, then, like you, some poor woman who is in love with him?"

"No, but he has an enemy whose death he has sworn to have. Nothing but hate, my dear, commits as many follies as love."

"Thank you, sire."

"Oh," said Henry, "I do not refer to our present follies. I mean those of the past and the future. But do not let us discuss this; we have no time to lose."

"You still plan to leave Paris?"

"To-night."

"Are your affairs which brought you back to Paris finished?"

"I came back only to see you."

"Gascon!"

"*Ventre saint gris!* My love, that is true; but let us put aside such thoughts. I have still two or three hours in which to be happy; then farewell forever."

"Ah! sire," said Madame de Sauve, "nothing is forever except my love."

Henry had just said that he had no time for discussion; therefore he did not discuss this point. He believed, or sceptic that he was, he pretended to believe.

As the King of Navarre had said, De Mouy and his two companions were hidden near by.

It was arranged that Henry should leave the small house at midnight instead of at three o'clock; that, as on the previous night, they would escort Madame de Sauve back to the Louvre, and from there they would go to the Rue de la

Cerisaie, where Maurevel lived.

It was only during that day that De Mouy had been sure of his enemy's whereabouts. The men had been on guard about an hour when they perceived a man, followed at a few feet by five others, who drew near to the door of the small house and tried several keys successively. De Mouy, concealed within the shelter of a neighboring door, made one bound from his hiding-place, and seized the man by the arm.

"One moment," said he; "you cannot enter there."

The man sprang back, and in doing so his hat fell off.

"De Mouy de Saint Phale!" he cried.

"Maurevel!" thundered the Huguenot, raising his sword. "I sought you, and you have come to me. Thanks!"

But his anger did not make him forget Henry, and turning to the window he whistled in the manner of the Béarnais shepherds.

"That will be enough," said he to Saucourt. "Now, then, murderer!"

And he sprang towards Maurevel.

The latter had had time to draw a pistol from his belt.

"Ah! now," said the King's Slayer, aiming at the young man, "I think you are a dead man!"

He fired. De Mouy jumped to one side and the ball passed by without touching him.

"It is my turn now!" cried the young man.

And he dealt Maurevel such a violent thrust with his sword that, although the blade had to encounter his buff belt, the sharp point pierced this obstacle and sank into the flesh.

The assassin gave a terrible cry of pain; whereupon the soldiers with him, thinking he was killed, fled in alarm down the Rue Saint Honoré.

Maurevel was not brave. Seeing himself abandoned by his followers, and having to face an adversary like De Mouy, he strove to escape, and ran after the guard, shouting, "help! help!"

De Mouy, Saucourt, and Barthélemy, carried away by their ardor, pursued him. As they entered the Rue de Grenelle, which they had taken as a short cut, a window opened and a man sprang out from the first floor, landing on the ground lately wet by the rain.

It was Henry.

De Mouy's whistle had warned him of some danger and the pistol-shot had showed him that the danger was great, and had drawn him to the aid of his friends.

Energetic and vigorous, he dashed after them, sword in hand.

A cry guided him; it came from the Barrier des Sergents. It was Maurevel, who being hard pressed by De Mouy was calling a second time for help from his men who had run away.

Maurevel had to turn or be run through the back; he turned, therefore, and, meeting his enemy's steel, gave him back so skilful a thrust that the scarf of the latter was cut through. But De Mouy at once lunged. The sword again sank into the flesh it had already broken, and a second jet of blood spurted from a second wound.

"At him!" cried Henry, coming up. "Quick, quick, De Mouy!"

De Mouy needed no encouragement.

Again he charged at Maurevel; but the latter had not waited.

Pressing his left hand over his wound, he again took to flight.

"Kill him! Quick! Kill him!" cried the king, "here are the soldiers, and the despair of cowards is of no moment to the brave."

Maurevel, who was well nigh exhausted, whose every breath caused a bloody perspiration, fell down; but almost immediately he rose again, and turning on one knee presented the point of his sword to De Mouy.

"Friends! Friends!" cried Maurevel. "There are only two. Fire at them! Fire!"

Saucourt and Barthélemy had gone in pursuit of the other soldiers, down the Rue des Poulies, and the king and De Mouy were alone with the four men.

"Fire!" cried Maurevel again, while one of the soldiers levelled his gun.

"Yes, but first," said De Mouy, "die, traitor, murderer, assassin!" and seizing Maurevel's sword with one hand, with the other he plunged his own up to its hilt into the breast of his enemy, with such force that he nailed him to the earth.

"Take care! Take care!" cried Henry.

De Mouy sprang back, leaving his sword in Maurevel's body, just as a soldier was in the act of firing at him.

Henry at once passed his sword through the body of the soldier, who gave a cry and fell by the side of Maurevel.

The two others took to flight.

"Come, De Mouy, come!" cried Henry, "let us not lose an instant; if we are recognized it will be all over with us."

"Wait, sire. Do you suppose I want to leave my sword in the body of this wretch?" and De Mouy approached Maurevel, who lay apparently without sign of life.

But just as he took hold of his sword, which was run through Maurevel's body, the latter raised himself, and with the gun the soldier had dropped fired directly at De Mouy's breast.

The young man fell without a cry. He was killed outright.

Henry rushed at Maurevel, but the latter had fallen again, and the king's sword pierced only a dead body.

It was necessary to flee. The noise had attracted a large number of persons; the night watch might arrive at any moment. Henry looked around to see if there was any face he knew, and gave a cry of delight on recognizing La Hurière.

As the scene had occurred at the foot of the Croix du Trahoir, that is, opposite the Rue de l'Arbre Sec, our old friend, whose naturally gloomy disposition had been still further saddened since the death of La Mole and Coconnas, his two favorite lodgers, had left his furnaces and his pans in the midst of his preparations for the King of Navarre's supper, and had run to the fight.

"My dear La Hurière, I commend De Mouy to your care, although I greatly fear nothing can be done for him. Take him to your inn, and if he still live, spare nothing. Here is my purse. As to the other, leave him in the gutter, that he may die like a dog."

"And yourself?" said La Hurière.

"I have a farewell to make. I must hasten, but in ten minutes I shall be with you. Have my horses ready."

Henry immediately set out towards the Croix des Petits Champs; but as he turned from the Rue de Grenelle he stopped in terror.

A large crowd was before the door.

"What is the matter?" asked Henry. "What is going on in the house?"

"Oh!" answered the man addressed, "a terrible affair, monsieur. A beautiful young woman has just been stabbed by her husband, to whom a note had been given informing him that his wife was here with her lover."

"And the husband?" cried Henry.

"Has escaped."

"And the wife?"

"She is in the house."

"Dead?"

"Not yet, but, thank God, there is scarcely any hope."

"Oh!" exclaimed Henry, "I am accursed indeed!" and he rushed into the house.

The room was full of people standing around a bed on which lay poor Charlotte, who had been stabbed twice.

Her husband, who had hidden his jealousy for two years, had seized this opportunity to avenge himself on her.

"Charlotte! Charlotte!" cried Henry, pushing through the crowd and falling on his knees before the bed.

Charlotte opened her beautiful eyes, already veiled by death, and uttered a cry which caused the blood to flow afresh from her two wounds. Making an effort to rise, she said:

"Oh! I well knew I could not die without seeing you again!"

And as if she had waited only for that moment to return to Henry the soul he had so loved, she pressed her lips to the King's forehead, again whispered for a last time, "I love you!" and fell back dead.

Henry could not remain longer without risking his own life. He drew his dagger, cut a lock of the beautiful blonde hair which he had so often loosened that he might admire its length, and went out sobbing, in the midst of the tears of all present, who did not doubt but that they were weeping for persons of high degree.

"Friend! mistress!" cried Henry in despair—"all forsake me, all leave me, all fail me at once!"

"Yes, sire," said a man in a low tone, who had left the group in front of the house, and who had followed Henry; "but you still have the throne!"

"Réné!" exclaimed Henry.

"Yes, sire, Réné, who is watching over you. That scoundrel Maurevel uttered your name as he died. It is known you are in Paris; the archers are hunting for you. Flee! Flee!"

"And you say that I shall be King, Réné? I, a fugitive?"

"Look, sire," said the Florentine, pointing to a brilliant star, which appeared from behind the folds of a black cloud, "it is not I who say so, but the star!"

Henry heaved a sigh, and disappeared in the darkness.

END.

Lightning Source UK Ltd.
Milton Keynes UK
UKHW041530100820
367994UK00007B/185